The Hybrid City Entrepreneur

The
Hybrid City
Entrepreneur

a novel

Jeremy Bursey

For the writers, directors, actors, and film crews who made 1980s teen movies worth watching.

You've inspired the game that inspired this book.

Author's Note

Thank you for reading *The Hybrid City Entrepreneur*.

You may notice that this book does not have traditional "chapters" but rather "episodes." Perhaps that seems weird. Well, yeah, it probably is. But this convention is a holdover from the book's original format as episodic fiction for a now-defunct serial fiction site.

The purpose of that site was to host fiction that told stories in self-contained episodes that could go on indefinitely, like television. But I wrote my episodes like chapters because I wanted to get to the end.

For this new version, I'd considered changing those episodes to "chapters" and chopping the story up into a more traditionally sized novel, but I realized doing so would've ruined the soul of the story, so I left it as-is, episodic and epic.

None of this should change your reading experience, but I wanted to mention it in case the mystery of having "episodes" instead of "chapters" occupied your attention so much that you stopped paying attention to the story.

I'd rather you pay attention to the story.

It's also worth noting that this story is based on an 8-bit business adventure computer game I started making in May 2009 called *Entrepreneur: The Beginning*. I'm still working on it…very slowly…but I thought I'd mention it in case you wanted to check it out sometime. If you are interested, well, it's in rough shape as of this writing and not yet ready to share, as it still has unlicensed placeholder assets I need to replace. But the best way to keep up to date on its progress, as well as news about my other books and projects, is to subscribe to my newsletter, which you can do by visiting my website (jeremybursey.com). It's also the only way to get exclusive books and bonuses, which I'll talk more about at the end of this book.

Lastly, I've written a brief retrospective and recorded a video about 1980s teen movies that you can read about and watch on my website on *The Hybrid City Entrepreneur*'s official book page if you want to know more about its influences. The page also contains the official book trailer, which features a full 1980s TV-inspired music video of the characters, places, and events featured in the book, as well as clips from the game, all to the score of the Cherry Chicklet* song "Ice Cream Paranoia." It's a fun complement to the reading experience if you want to see parts of the book in action.

But for now, don't worry about that. For now, just enjoy the novel. It's my love letter to my favorite teen movies of the 1980s, especially *The Karate Kid* and *Better Off Dead*, but really to all of them. So, enjoy the trip back to the eighties, and enjoy the trip "Back to the Fut—"

Eh, let's not milk it.

*Cherry Chicklet is a "rock goddess" character from my *A Modern-day Fantasy* series (which I plan to break apart and rewrite in smaller pieces in the near future). I'd written seven songs for her scenes in the series (so far), but I never got to hear them until A.I. made it possible to bring them to life. Ever since April 2024, I've created fifteen albums-worth of her songs, including the seven I'd written between 2008 and 2011, with any of them ready to appear in the rewritten and future novels. "Ice Cream Paranoia" comes from her twelfth album, *Colorized*.

Episode 1

Birthday Boy

THE DAY BUCK STAR turned eighteen, he expected his friends and family to throw him a party. Instead, his bully of four years threw him into a locker. Or, rather, one of his henchmen did, grabbing him by the shirt and forcing him into that tight, metal box, as the bully himself couldn't be bothered to do his own dirty work. Either way, it was an easy misjudgment to make. Eighteen-year-olds weren't typically targets of high school abuse, so when Buck awoke that morning, nervous about getting his eighteenth birthday right but excited about the possibilities for love and respect that lay ahead, he figured today was the day he was finally free from torment.

But old traditions didn't always end with age. Sometimes the tradition lived until the venue died. In Buck's case, if eighteen didn't change his circumstances, then graduating high school would have to. Fortunately, that moment was just three weeks away, and he was ready. High school had taught him nothing but what bad pizza tasted like and what a foot to the butt felt like. Instead of keeping consistent with attending his classes, he'd spent his home away from home in his locker. Garrett Nedmeyer was his next-locker-door neighbor, and Buck was no fan of Garrett's. Garrett was the kid who made the cast of *Revenge of the Nerds* look cool. Every time Buck tried forging his mom's name on his written excuse for missing class, again, Garrett distracted him by talking about the weather. Buck was ready for a new second home.

When the final bell rang, Buck opened his locker door, checked the halls for any sign of Chet or his henchmen, then made a run for the exit. Like most afternoons, today the other students failed to notice his sudden appearance, and they didn't pay attention when he zipped by. Like him, they just wanted to get home. They fixed their eyes on the doors leading out to the sidewalk and the thirty-foot cliff that fell away from it. As long as he didn't bump them, he wouldn't attract their attention. And if he didn't attract *their* attention, odds were he wouldn't attract Chet's, either. Assuming Chet was still on campus. Given his reign over the place, it was reasonable to believe that he'd already used his privilege to leave school early. But Buck kept a careful eye on anyone he passed just in case. Hardly any eyes looked back.

He emerged into the sunlight without an elbow to the face, but someone *had* noticed him. That someone was dressed in a checkered pink, knee-length skirt and kept her arms folded over her chest as she leaned against the railing that separated the sidewalk from the perilous drop to the woods below. When she made eye contact with Buck, she ran her hand over her blonde hair and nudged the pink clip that pulled it back. Her hair wasn't in her eyes, but she liked how she looked running her fingers through it, and she thought Buck liked it, too. He preferred her hair longer. Running her fingers through her locks when they hardly reached her shoulders made no sense to him. But he smiled anyway. After spending the last two hours confined to a smelly, metal box, listening to a whiny kid complain about the highs and lows of the stock market, the sight of her warm eyes and soft lips was more welcome than sunshine. She smiled back as she leaned in his direction and hopped off the railing.

"Happy birthday," she said, as she approached. "I bought you a cake."

"Really?"

"Thought we could eat it on the beach tonight."

Once they were in range, Jennifer Mills, Buck's "squeeze" for the last six months, squeezed him just below the shoulders. She had skinny arms that felt like pool noodles wrapping around his back, but he enjoyed the feel of her holding him. After years of rejection by every one of his crushes, he appreciated the luck he had in getting

Jennifer Mills and her pool noodle arms to call him "boyfriend." The idea of finishing high school without a graduation date had terrified him since his freshman year. With three weeks to go and a genuine smile crossing her lips as she pressed them to his cheek, he had no more reason to fear it. Even if he couldn't shake his bully problem, his girlfriend problem was no longer an issue. All thanks to Jennifer and her willingness to take a chance on him the day he did her ethics homework for her.

"Sounds great," Buck said. "Thanks for thinking of it."

Her smile brightened. If that was even possible. "Also thought we could visit the Liquid Shack afterward. For dessert."

Buck released her. The soft smile on her face drew him to her searching eyes. She was being serious.

"Seriously?" He did not ask this with a smile.

She nodded. "Heard a lot of great things about it. Always wanted to check it out."

Buck felt thumping in his chest, and it wasn't Jennifer's heartbeat, though he wondered if hers was beating right now.

"Isn't that where Chet works?"

She had a glazed look in her eyes as she moved her focus to the puffy clouds floating overhead.

"Chet?"

"Chet Armstrong. Hybrid High's Student Body President. Captain of the Football Team. Captain of the Cheerleading Squad. The guy who thinks it's funny to dunk my head in a toilet on Tuesdays. Calls it 'Toilet Tuesdays.' Chet."

"Oh, sure. Yeah. But Chet doesn't just work there. He *owns* the place. Isn't that amazing?"

Her smile fluttered as she spoke. Her eyes darted from cloud to cloud. The strange thump in Buck's chest moved down into his stomach. He didn't want to see Chet after school or give him money voluntarily. Buck had already given him plenty involuntarily.

"Can't we just stay at the beach? Maybe throw a Frisbee around? I think I have one under my bed."

Jennifer placed one hand on his shoulder and the other on his chest. Her eyes were once again locked with his.

"Please? He makes the best juice in town." Her lips quivered. "So I hear. All my classmates rave about it. Always wanted to taste it. And his chest is so hairy, and he's *so* rich, and…"

Buck shook his head, backed away slightly. Tonight was his night. It was his birthday. *His* birthday. His *birthday*. Why would he want to spend it with Chet? Or his juice?

"I don't know. I'm not sure I'm feeling it, Jenn."

"Aw, come on, Buck. Live a little. It's juice. Apple juice. Pear juice. Lemonade juice. Kiwi juice." She stroked his shoulders, causing that usual electricity to surge into his neck and down through his body. "We're only eighteen once."

Buck couldn't reject the pleas of such a lovely face staring back at him, even if her hair was too short to brush back competently.

"All right. Fine. I guess there's no harm in getting some juice."

Now that his birthday date was finalized, he'd have to figure out how to reach the end of it without the night going horribly wrong. After all, Chet wasn't the type of person who would limit his torment to lockers and toilet bowls. If Buck stepped foot on Chet's business ground, he would essentially be spraying on his turf, and Chet might take it as a threat. As he swayed his sights over the tree line and the gorge below where only one kid had fallen in the four years since he started attending this school, Buck considered the consequences of a misstep. He would have to be careful tonight.

* * *

Buck's beach birthday date started at seven, and he couldn't be late. Jennifer had planned to bring the picnic blanket and the cake. Buck's job was to bring himself and a nice tie. After searching his closet from one end to the other, the best he could find was the tape measure he used every Saturday to measure his biceps and disappoint himself with the results. She wouldn't like it, and neither would he, but going with no neck ornaments was worse, so unless he could find a leftover gift bow lying around in the garage that he could paste on his neck, the tape measure would have to play the formal role tonight. Because keytar neckties were a thing now, he thought he could get away with it.

4

He tucked his blue long-sleeved shirt into his blue slacks, pulled the cyan belt through his loops and buckled it, buttoned the top button on his shirt, and wrapped the tape measure around his collar. A brief memory from that one dark night he considered hanging himself flashed in his mind, then faded again. No need to return to that event. Total misunderstanding. Then he found his blue suede shoes and looked himself over in the mirror. His hair was combed. His zipper was up. Perfect.

As he headed for the bedroom door, he stopped by his dresser to dab on some cologne. Jennifer had given him a bottle for Valentine's Day as a reminder that she cared about how he smelled. She didn't like it when he reminded her too much of his lunch that day, usually a bologna sandwich and a pickle. The cologne, from some place French, helped the bologna smell like French bologna, or "cowboy," as Jennifer described it. Cowboy and pickle.

It was now 6:15, and the beach was on the other side of town. His mom worked late, so she couldn't drive him, and his dad was, well, not home, for other reasons, so Buck had to find another way to get there.

Fortunately, his best friend, Ronnie Michaels, owned a bicycle, and Ronnie had given him an open invitation to use it whenever he wanted, for whatever reason he wanted, as long as he had five bucks. Remembering the rental fee, Buck checked his wallet for the money. He had just over a hundred dollars in there. Mostly twenties.

By 6:18, he was ready to leave, so he checked his answering machine for any missed messages, saw there were none, and headed out the door. At the mailbox, he went left, toward the eastern edge of town. Ronnie lived along the main highway, almost into the woods and farmlands beyond Hybrid City. The beach was in the opposite direction. Fortunately, Ronnie was home.

"She at least gonna kiss you?" Ronnie asked when Buck told him the plan.

Buck shrugged. "Maybe. It *is* my birthday, after all."

"I mean, if she's gonna drag you to Chet's juice stand afterward, you should get something nice for it."

Buck nodded. He had no reason to dispute Ronnie's logic. Ronnie, who often wore a top hat to display his "old wisdom," as he called it, was rarely wrong. As Ronnie touched the rim of his hat, he nodded back. He knew he was right this time, too.

"I can only hope," Buck said. "She's been averse to kissing me anywhere but on the cheek."

"Yeah, and that means nothing. You ever met a European girl? They do that, too. Go to the barber's, kiss on the cheek. Visit the butcher or baker, kiss on the cheek. You sure Jennifer's not a European girl?"

"She's from around here."

Ronnie stroked his chin as he considered Buck's words.

"And you're sure she wants to get juice after your beach date?"

"Part of the gift, I guess."

"Does she not know your history with Chet?"

"Just what I tell her. She knows about Locker Hide and Seek and Toilet Tuesdays."

"You told her about Toilet Tuesday? Are you nuts?"

Buck leaned against Ronnie's front door, careful not to fall into the shrubbery. Ronnie usually let Buck inside, but because Buck was in a hurry to leave, and because Ronnie's dad was fresh at home from lawyer work and sitting in the living room in his underwear, he'd asked Buck to talk outside. With the night temperatures climbing into the seventies, Buck worried he'd start sweating under his armpits if they didn't speed up this conversation.

"We can discuss my wisdom later. I need your bike."

"You didn't tell her about Wedgie Wednesday, did you?"

"No. Bike?"

"Thumper Thursday?"

"Ronnie."

"Please don't tell me she knows about Fat Ass Friday."

Buck shook his head.

"I don't even know about that one."

"Fat Ass Friday? You know, when Chet tells his fat friend to tackle you and sit on your shoulders until you cry 'uncle.'"

Buck shrugged. Never heard of it.

Ronnie stared off into the hedges. "Oh. Doesn't matter. You can't tell her about the ways he tortures you. It runs your man cred down."

"Man cred?"

Ronnie put his hand on Buck's shoulder.

"If I have to explain man cred…"

Buck gave Ronnie a sympathetic smile.

"As much as I want to learn about man cred and Fat Ass Friday, I really need to get going." Buck handed him a twenty-dollar bill. "Can I get the bike?"

Ronnie studied the bill in the dying sunlight. He nodded at its authenticity. Buck often wondered if he should slip him a counterfeit to see if he'd notice.

"Do I have to make change?" Ronnie asked. "Or can I just owe you four rides?"

"Make it five and you can keep the whole thing."

Ronnie thought about the offer. Buck already knew what was going through his mind. Five dollars off or a free ride, whatever perspective he wanted, for the convenience of not breaking the bill. Once the rationale had sunk in, he patted Buck on the shoulder.

"Deal."

Before Buck could ride off, Ronnie stopped him with one final but important question.

"How are you going to prevent him from ruining your birthday?"

Buck set his gaze on the road as he put his foot on the pedal. Even though the question had been lingering in his mind since Jennifer had brought it up, he still didn't have an answer. He had spent the afternoon hoping the visit to the juice stand wouldn't ruin anything.

"I don't know. I guess I'm hoping he'll treat me more like a customer than an enemy."

Ronnie raised his eyebrow at the comment.

"Hmm. I hadn't thought of that. Interesting idea."

Buck thanked Ronnie for the bike and rode off. He had less than twenty-five minutes to ride through the Alley of Pines, the district where shops and homes collided, Downtown Hybrid, the city proper where most of Hybrid's convenience stores, apartment buildings, and police station lived, Hybrid West, where the specialty shops took up rental space, and finally Hybrid Beach, where the rest of Hybrid's food and alcohol needs could be met. The actual beach was just across the street from the district known as Hybrid Beach, and Buck sighed at the sight of the sun dropping toward the Pacific Ocean's waterline just beyond the shore.

As he tugged at his shirt to separate it from his sticky back, he rode his bike down the wooden ramp over the shallow rock wall and dismounted onto the sand strip as soon as his front tire hit the change in surface.

It was 6:57 p.m. Jennifer was still setting up the blanket down by the water. The cake box sat undisturbed beside her feet. When she turned and saw him walking the bike toward her, she smiled at him.

"Nice tie," she said.

Buck smiled back. She didn't even notice the sweat coming out of his armpits or soaking the rest of his shirt.

"Thanks."

She winked at him. Tonight was going to be a great night.

* * *

Tonight was going to be an awful night. Even though the twenty minutes they'd spent sitting on the beach, enjoying a slice of vanilla cake while staring at the ocean and saying nothing was magical, the magic faded the moment Jennifer got up and asked him to fold up the blanket. Buck still hadn't licked the icing off his fingers when she ordered him to stand.

"We gotta get to the Liquid Shack before it closes," she said. "Come on, hurry."

Buck didn't like the stickiness of saliva and sugar on his fingers, so he jogged down to the water to rinse them.

"You can do that later," she said. "We're gonna miss out if we don't leave now. Come on, help me pack."

Buck felt his calves burning as he hiked up the dune toward Jennifer, who was now packing the cake in the box. They'd eaten less than an eighth.

"Why do we need to go there again?" Buck asked.

"We need to wash down the cake with grape juice or apple juice or cranberry juice or whatever you want."

"And for what reason can't we do that here?"

"Because the Liquid Shack isn't here." Now that the cake was packed, she started up the dune. "Can you please get the blanket?"

Buck pulled up the blanket, shook off the sand, and wadded it over his handlebars. He followed about thirty feet behind her, dragging his bike along an unstable surface until he reached the security of the wooden ramp that climbed the ten-foot rock wall to the street where residents could park their cars for a few hours. Jennifer was opening her trunk just beyond the ramp when Buck emerged at the top.

"Put the blanket in there," she said.

He did as he was told. "What about the bike? Will it fit?"

"No, you'll have to ride it over." She got into the driver's seat and leaned out of the cabin to face him. "I'll meet you there."

She closed the door and drove off, leaving him there to watch her taillights wink at him. Even though she'd told him "happy birthday" on the beach, she'd neglected to set the candles on the cake. He was hoping to blow them out while enjoying a beach sunset with his favorite girl. Instead, he was watching her car blowing out its brake lights as the traffic light turned green.

What a memorable eighteenth birthday.

To get to the Liquid Shack, Buck had to return to Hybrid West and ride north, toward the Tri-Park area. Because Chet was a high school student, not a millionaire business owner, he didn't have the luxury of setting up shop in a building downtown. Instead, he had to erect a canvas-top gazebo on a section of field along Park Center Park's parking lot's edge. So, to get to the Liquid Shack, Buck first had to enter Park Center Park, and that meant getting past the guard shack.

"Rules are rules," the guard told him as he rode up to the gate. "Doesn't matter that you're on a bike."

"Even if I'm just here for juice?"

"Still two dollars to enter the park."

Buck reached for his wallet. Handed him a twenty-dollar bill.

"Hybrid Park and North Park don't charge me anything," he said, as he waited for the guard to make change.

"They aren't upscale, either. You want green grass, you pay for green grass."

"And juice?"

"Pay for that, too. The world revolves around money, kid. Better you learn that lesson now than when you're digging around in a trashcan for food or supplies."

Buck smirked.

"I'd never let that happen."

The guard handed him his change. "We'll see."

As the gate rose, Buck pedaled under it and headed up the narrow and winding driveway through the woods. At the end of the road, which was flanked by rows of balloons and signs promoting the Liquid Shack, Buck reached the parking lot. There were a few cars in the lot, possibly belonging to customers or recreationists. But the most noticeable car was the silver Toyota belonging to Jennifer. It was parked directly in front of the canvas-top gazebo that formed the juice stand.

Buck parked his bike beside her car and trekked the rest of the way up the field on foot. When he got to the stand, he found Tommy Slick, a slender kid with a ratty face who always wore a cowboy hat and purple pants, tending the folding table where the Liquid Shack's juice dispensers and paper cups were laid out. Tommy was counting the money in the cash box when Buck approached.

"Hey, Tommy."

Tommy looked up and twitched a smile when he saw him.

"Hey, Buck. Sorry about the locker again."

Buck shrugged.

"Just taking orders, right?"

Tommy waved him off.

"Yeah, what you gonna do? I didn't rough you up too bad, did I?"

"Nothing lasting."

Tommy nodded. Went back to counting the cash box.

"Cool tie."

"Hope so. Have you seen Jennifer? She's supposed to meet me here."

Tommy glanced up at him, then went back to counting the money.

"Yeah, about that. Happy birthday."

"Appreciate it. So, have you seen her?"

Tommy tilted his head toward the concrete restrooms just past his shoulder. She must've gone in.

"Mind if I wait?" Buck asked.

"Up to you, but I don't know when she'll be back."

Buck glanced toward the restroom block. Surely, she'd be just a minute.

"How's the lemonade?"

Tommy reached for a paper cup and filled it with pink lemonade. He handed the cup to Buck.

"Happy birthday, man."

Buck took a sip. It was lip-puckeringly sweet. Between that and the cake, Buck's tongue would stick to the roof of his mouth for the next hour.

"How much I owe you?"

Tommy raised his eyebrow at him.

"I said, happy birthday."

Buck nodded. He understood. Took another sip. And another. And another. And that was all he could do. He'd emptied the cup of liquid on the fourth sip, leaving just ice behind.

"Not much to drink, is it?" he asked.

"Yeah, I keep telling Chet he needs bigger cups for the price he's asking. But as long as the people keep coming, he's gonna keep the same pricing and distribution model. What can you do?"

Buck didn't know, so he sucked on a piece of ice. Nothing fixed a sugar mouth quite like crushed ice.

As the ice soothed him, he glanced around the gazebo. He noticed all four juice containers had the same color liquid in them.

"Is it all pink lemonade?"

"Yeah, Chet got sick of the adults complaining."

"About what?"

"Our old lemonade was pretty bland. Chet thought pink lemonade would appease them more. Sweeter powder for the same price."

Buck raised his eyebrows at the implication.

"Does he not use sugar?"

"No. Doesn't want to spend the extra money."

Buck nodded. He understood the value of savings. But Jennifer had mentioned all types of juice varieties. He saw none of that here.

"I thought Chet sold apple juice, kiwi juice, and other juice types."

Tommy snorted at the comment.

"Who gave you that information? Nah, we're just lemonade here. Classic establishment."

Buck frowned. He didn't necessarily want apple juice, pear juice, or any other type of juice, but he was sold on the idea that there would be other juices. He was here because Jennifer wanted those juices.

Pretty ironic that neither she nor the juices were here right now.

"I guess that's something."

After several minutes passed, he once again looked toward the restroom block for signs of her.

"Sure is taking her sweet time, isn't she?"

Tommy shrugged.

"Happens."

Buck set the paper cup on the table. He'd had enough ice.

"Got a trashcan back there?"

Tommy set the cup in the same place he'd taken it from.

"Not part of Chet's distribution policy," he said.

Buck cringed at Tommy's message. The implication was clear.

"I think I'm gonna be sick."

Tommy laughed.

"Nah, just messing with you." He took the cup and stuffed it in a black plastic trash bag. "He's not that cruel to his customers. Not even to you. Well, *maybe* not even to you." He thought about it more. "Well, I won't be that cruel."

"I appreciate it." Buck looked past Tommy's shoulder. "I think I'll go check on her. Make sure she's okay."

Tommy shook his head.

"I wouldn't, but it's up to you."

Buck stared at Tommy. Tommy continued to count the money. He didn't look up or clarify his meaning.

"All the same, I think I should check up on her. That's what a boyfriend does, right?"

"Not according to my dad."

"Thanks for the lemonade." Buck slapped the table, then moved around the canvas-top gazebo and up the walkway leading toward the restrooms. As he reached the door of the women's restroom, he knocked. There was no answer, so he dared to peek his head inside.

"Jennifer?"

No answer.

Buck looked toward the Liquid Shack. Tommy jerked his attention back toward his cash box. It looked as if he'd been watching Buck. Very strange.

To make sure she hadn't gotten confused, Buck checked inside the men's restroom. That too was empty. Very, very strange.

At that point, it occurred to him that Tommy wasn't saying that she'd gone into the bathroom, but that she'd headed in that direction. So, he moved around the building toward the water fountains. And that's when he found her.

She was leaning against a pine tree across a small stretch of field. Chet, and his six feet of blond hair and muscle, was standing beside her, nodding as she talked, staring at his watch.

Buck's chest pounded. He didn't want to approach Jennifer because he didn't want to approach Chet. But he needed some way to let her know he was here. If he called out to her, he'd alert them both, not just her. And even if Tommy could be nice to him away from school, he wasn't so sure Chet had the same sense of disparity between venues, and he wasn't sure he wanted to risk finding out, especially not in front of Jennifer. Ronnie might've been eccentric in his presentation, but he was down-to-earth in his real-world wisdom. The last thing Buck wanted was for Chet to humiliate him in front of Jennifer.

Make that second-to-last.

When Chet glanced away from his watch and toward the Liquid Shack, he saw Buck standing there by the restrooms watching them. Without a word or a tip of the head, Chet smiled, then leaned into Jennifer and kissed her full on the mouth.

Buck balled his fists out of reflex and took a step forward, as if to challenge the six-foot bully, but stopped himself from coming any closer.

Jennifer didn't slap him, nor did she resist him. Instead, she reached up to his shoulders and embraced him. Fully. He embraced her back. Equally fully.

Buck stood there, frozen, as if all the ice in his cup had assimilated into his bloodstream. Chet and Jennifer fell against the tree, attacking each other's faces without abandon. And like watching a car running a red light as he rides Ronnie's bike through an intersection, wishing the problem away wasn't good enough now. The horror was already in motion.

This qualified as a form of Chet humiliating him in front of Jennifer. Where was Ronnie's wisdom now?

He felt a hand on his shoulder and watched a paper cup emerge from behind.

"Thought you could use another drink," Tommy said some distance away, maybe a foot but maybe a mile. "This one's got a bit more bite. But don't tell Chet."

Buck stared at the cup. *Chet.* Where had he heard that name before? Shook his head. Couldn't think of it. Must've been a figment of his imagination. Where was he even right now? What was this place? And why was it getting darker?

Episode 2

Graduation Night

B UCK FOUND HIS WAY home by ten o'clock, though he wasn't sure how he'd gotten there. Ronnie's bike was involved somehow. Tommy may or may not have followed him to make sure he didn't end up in a ditch somewhere. The events between watching his girlfriend betray him and walking through his front door were hazy. If they even happened.

Buck stumbled into his bedroom, looked at his bed, and wondered if he'd even had a birthday today. Behind him, the bedroom door was open. He spun around. Now his bed was behind him. Now his dresser. His closet. The door. The bed. The floor.

When he awoke the next morning with a splitting headache, he was still dressed in his birthday clothes (the blue ones, not the "suit" kind), but now he'd somehow gotten his tape measure necktie caught between the door and the frame. In the middle of the night, it was possible he'd intentionally closed the door on it to strangle himself, but losing air was so uncomfortable that he cracked the door open to set himself free, and he was potentially too stuck in that dark moment to pick himself off the floor and get into bed, or to ask his mom to make him cookies, or crawl to the television and indulge in a cycle of shallow infomercials, or maybe he believed that sleeping on the floor the rest of the night would've generated sympathy from the girl who had betrayed him, feeling sorry over the fact that she'd told him happy birthday but given his bully the birthday gift. As a result, there was a chance that he'd kicked the door closed, just to catch the tape measure in it once again, even if now he had more room to breathe thanks to the six feet of slack. All hypothetically, of course.

But now that he was awake and clear-headed, or at least thinking clearly—he still had a splitting headache—he could process what had actually happened the night before.

In short, what he saw was an illusion, a figment of his overactive and dark imagination. Jennifer would *never* surrender to the seductions of the Student Body president, or the captain of the football team, or the owner of the Liquid Shack, the most successful student-run business in Hybrid City. Not when she had Buck all to herself. That she'd choose Chet Armstrong, captain of the *cheerleading squad*, over Buck Star, chief maintenance officer of his locker's interior, was completely absurd. She could've had any boy at that high school, and she'd chosen Buck, not the guy who ran to the locker room to change into his cheerleading outfit just to cheer the play he'd made as quarterback. That was recorded history. It was fact. It happened. It was real. She hadn't chosen Chet last November when she'd come asking for help with her homework. She'd chosen Buck.

She'd chosen *Buck*.

So, this whole thing was a misunderstanding. A fluke. His birthday was so amazing that he'd forgotten all of it and replaced it with an imposter, a dream. Yes, he had dreamt the whole thing. They had cake. They kissed. There were candles on the cake. The Liquid Shack was not part of the conversation. It was the perfect evening. Had to be. It was the only thing that made any sense.

Then again, he was wearing the same clothes he'd been wearing in his dream. The tape measure was still wrapped around his neck. And the taste of pink lemonade washing down what was left of vanilla icing was still fresh on his mind, even if the actual flavor had long since dulled. And there was the headache. He'd gotten it from sleeping on the floor all night. His bed was inches behind his head. Would've been simple to crawl right into it.

The pressure behind his eyes increased, and the tears he was fighting to conceal were pushing up toward his ducts. His lips quivered.

Right now was real, and he knew the difference between the four dimensions of reality versus the three dimensions of dreams. In dreams, he might see objects in space, but in reality, he could also feel them, as well as the effects they caused him, and he was feeling something fierce right now. The memory of Jennifer wrapping her arms around Chet, of seeing her suck on his face and vice versa—

Buck's stomach knotted at the thought.

It was no dream.

Now he'd have to punch Chet.

He looked at his fists. They were small compared to the bricks Chet carried around on his wrists. Maybe he'd have to rethink this.

Maybe he'd have to justify Chet's decision to kiss her.

If Buck had been any taller or meatier, he might've cocked and released that fist, anyway. But if he were honest with himself, he couldn't really blame Chet for his impulsive move. Jennifer was irresistible, after all. With her upturned nose and the conservative way she held her arms to her chest as she walked, what wasn't to crave? Chet was obviously weak to her charms.

Buck wasn't about to forgive him, though. For the last four years, Chet had ordered his henchmen to stuff him in lockers and subject him to many other traditional bully-to-bullied activities, like noogies, wedgies, wet willies, and spitting on his food. To give him a pass now, after pulling the most heinous of all malicious attacks, would not only justify his action against him last night, but every humiliation prior, and Buck could not allow for any such thing.

No, he'd have to forgive Jennifer instead. Forgive her for being irresistible? That wasn't her fault. Forgive her for leaning into the kiss? Where was she supposed to go when that jock douchebag was smothering her? No, he'd forgive her for going to the Liquid Shack in the first place. She knew Chet was his nemesis. Her lapse in judgment and lust for juice caused her to forget that. Her oversight required understanding.

As he got ready for school that Friday morning, he repeated to himself that none of this was Jennifer's fault, and as soon as he saw her, he'd tell her. He was also determined to apologize to her, since his dad used to say the best way to get an apology was to give one.

But when school came and went and he didn't see her in the halls or outside by the railing, he called her: "Hey, Jenn, it's Buck. Didn't see you at school today." *Click*. Dial tone. "Hello?" Called again. No answer. Tried again. Still no answer.

Maybe she wasn't ready to face him. She was probably too ashamed of what she'd done with Chet to face anyone. He'd give her another night to process and heal from the personal wound she had inflicted on herself.

Saturday night: "Jennifer, it's Buck." *Click*. Dial tone. Called again. No answer. Something must've been wrong with her phone tonight.

Sunday night: "Hey, it's me. Not sure if there's a problem with your phone, but…hello?"

Monday at school: No sign of her in the halls.

Monday night: "Hey, Jenn, didn't see you today, just wanted to say that everything's okay, and no hard feelings." No answer. "Jenn?" Her dad responded, told him she wasn't home and that he should call back another night.

Tuesday at school: Tommy Slick said he didn't have to perform a Toilet Tuesday routine on Buck today. Buck thanked him. Tommy also said he was sorry about Jennifer. Buck said it was no big deal. Buck went home that afternoon wondering why Tommy was suddenly allowed to be nice to him.

Tuesday night: No answer.

Wednesday at school: No wedgies. No Jennifer in the halls. No Chet.

Wednesday night: Her dad said she wasn't home.

Thursday at school: Buck stood along the cliffside railing, waiting for Jennifer to come through the school's exit. Ronnie found him standing there and joined him. When she finally emerged, Jennifer was walking with a group of girlfriends and barely made eye contact when she passed. Buck stepped out to get her attention, but she ignored him. "Must've been a hell of a birthday," Ronnie said.

Thursday night: Buck held the phone in his hand, but he didn't dial her number. Whatever happened on the night of his birthday, it had changed their relationship. It was clear now. The kiss happened, and she'd felt no shame over it happening.

He hung up instead.

* * *

Turning eighteen was a milestone that adults had spent years convincing him would be unforgettable. Graduating high school was the other "forever memory." For Buck Star, that statement was true on both accounts, for the same reasons.

When graduation happened two weekends later, Buck wasn't surprised to find Jennifer entering the auditorium on Chet's arm. She'd spent the last six months assuring him she'd enter that last night of high school with him and no one else. Yet, here she was, breaking her promise, laughing in Chet's ear and kissing Chet's cheek and rubbing Chet's back and avoiding eye contact with Buck any moment her gaze swept in his direction.

His dad had once told him to expect a girl to betray him, but Buck never dreamed it would happen during the most important window of his young adult life. If he could tell his dad what this girl had done, his dad would likely shrug and tell him, "Welcome to the club." Didn't make the reality any easier.

Buck gave up trying to make eye contact with her and took his place in line. He just sat in his chair between Sam Stack (and his lack of deodorant) and Gregory Stick (and his crab dip dinner afterglow), waiting for his name to be called. The misery would soon be over. Then he could go home, climb into bed, and stay there until college.

"Back Stare, come on down."

It would all be over soon.

After the ceremony, Ronnie slapped Buck on the shoulder and showed him his certificate displaying his name and graduation date. Buck had been sitting on the third step of the stairwell to Hybrid High's science wing. It was the only place Buck could find that was as barren as his heart. Yet, Ronnie still found him, and now he insisted on ignoring Buck's wounded psyche.

"Can you believe it? After four years? Can't believe it's over already."

Buck nodded. He was holding his certificate, too. The moderator calling the names had instructed the students to take their parchments, return to their seats, and go to the cafeteria after the ceremony to pick up their diploma covers. Because he wanted to be around as few people as possible, Buck figured he'd wait until the crowds thinned before heading to the cafeteria. What he really wanted was to be alone. And Ronnie was ruining his plans.

"What's the saying? No more teachers' dirty looks?" Ronnie was stroking his chin, as if this question deserved scrutiny. "Does it become 'Yes, more bosses' dirty looks'?"

"Don't know," Buck said. "And I'm not in the mood to think about it."

Ronnie slapped his back. Buck pitched sideways from the impact.

"Aw, buck up, little camper. Stop worrying. Jennifer's just going through a phase right now. The high school quarterback and head cheerleader took notice of her. It's like the head cheerleader taking notice of you." Ronnie thought about his statement further. "Well, if we were at any other school, of course. You know what I mean."

Buck shrugged. Yes, he knew what Ronnie meant. Didn't make the situation any easier. Graduating with Jennifer beside him was the dream he'd carried since November, and having any girl beside him for his last day of school tickled his mind since the day he started this nightmare called public education. To lose both to "a phase" was an injustice.

"I hate Chet Armstrong," Buck said, just loud enough for Ronnie to hear.

"Yeah, I hear ya, pal. But this is Jennifer's deal, not his. Somehow, I doubt she means anything to him."

Buck glanced at Ronnie, who was staring across the hall at the science posters promoting Einstein. Even though he still had on his cap, Buck could imagine him swapping it out for the top hat. Ronnie "The Wise" Michaels was making his next appearance on the steps of the science wing.

"So, you're saying he'll ditch her?"

"Chet's a bully, not a lover. He'll take what he wants to punish you, then throw away his tools of oppression when the job is complete."

Buck balled his fists.

"So, you're saying I fight him?"

Ronnie shook his head.

"Just the opposite. You roll up to him, unbuckle your pants, drop 'em and bend over, then take the foot until you turn blue. You thank him, ask him for another, and another, and another until he's either bored or disturbed. Then he'll know he can no longer torment you. That's when he dumps her."

Ronnie looked at Buck hard, waiting for a response. His cap was tilting sideways. Buck narrowed his eyebrows at the "wisdom" coming out of his best friend's mouth.

"That's the dumbest thing I've ever heard." Buck shook his head. "No, I'm getting her back my way." He glanced at the science posters across the hall. Einstein's raised eyebrows and outstretched tongue convinced him of everything he needed at that moment. Courage to perform an action that would gain an equal and opposite reaction.

Action = Punch Chet in the face.

Equal and Opposite Reaction = Jennifer says, "Oh, Buck!" and throws her arms around him and kisses him until his face melts off.

After the disappointing graduation ceremony, he had to think of something that could salvage the evening and his final minutes of high school.

He got off the stairs. Marched down the hall. Headed for the cafeteria. One way or another, he was getting his girlfriend back.

* * *

BUCK IGNORED THE ANGUISHED pleas to rethink his plan hitting him from behind. If Ronnie really understood what he was dealing with right now, then he'd offer to help, not just stand behind and shout, "No, don't do it!" Ronnie was great for a lot of things, like bicycles and good advice, but tonight he was a barrier to his happiness, a voice without a soul. If Buck wanted to fix his heart, he'd have to face the bully head-on, or talk his girlfriend back into his life, whichever was easier. He stuck out his chest, raised his chin, and marched outside the science wing doors, determined to get his equal and opposite reaction.

In the next building, Language Arts, the crowds swelled from nothing to congested, like an adjective-stuffed simile, puffy, and obnoxious, bloating a simple turn of phrase into something excessive, more excessive than it deserved to be, just like a simple sentence getting stuffed with needless commas and repetitive repetitions, just as the people in the hall repeated, and repeated, and continued to repeat, and with no end in sight but for the double-door exit that served as the period of mercy. Or maybe the doors were a colon that led to a connected thought: in this case, the building beyond that, Mathematics.

The math building, by comparison, was so packed that Buck couldn't move any further. His odds of getting through were a hundred to one. Its volume was greater than the last building, which was denser than average by a power of two. So, he backtracked and headed for the Physics building, which also led to the cafeteria. Like the math building, it was so packed that he would've had to combine both speed and force to break through, though the friction each graduate and his family member would create as he punched through risked grating his skin. Because he wasn't stuck in the Chemistry building, however, he saw no reason to cause a chain reaction of trouble.

He lost Ronnie back at the Language Arts building, so he no longer listened to the cries of reason assaulting him from behind. But neither Chet nor Jennifer was in sight, and he worried they had already gotten to the cafeteria and collected their books. If that were the case, then all that was left for him was to leave campus and head to whatever graduation party they attended.

Buck couldn't take that chance. He had to catch them, here and now. Of course, he still didn't know what he'd do once he confronted them. Even though he'd balled his fists at the thought of exacting revenge, he didn't believe he was powerful enough to cause Chet any damage. Plus, attacking Chet on school property was a bad idea. The last thing he needed was to earn a detention *after* graduation.

No, he'd have to take a more subdued approach. Something more cultured. Something more akin to an adult response.

But first he'd have to find another way into the cafeteria since the main entrance was clogged. He thought sneaking into the back entrance through the kitchen would've been the best idea, except that no one would've been working tonight, as the cafeteria was dishing out diploma covers only, not food. So, his other option was to circle the building and approach it from the exit. Because the crowds were thinner at that side of the building, it was the better plan.

Graduate after graduate slipped by him as he took his position, each one smiling at a parent or guardian, flexing his muscles at a fellow graduate or pirouetting for a camera as she thrust the diploma at the lens. Buck peeked inside the cafeteria every moment the tide of people thinned, but in every instance, he could not catch sight of Chet or Jennifer.

Then, to his surprise, Ronnie Michaels came spilling out with his diploma cover clutched tightly to his armpit and his missing top hat once again adorning his head.

"How did you—"

Ronnie slapped him on the shoulder.

"Line's quick," he said. "No one really wants to hang out here any longer than necessary."

Buck pinched the bridge of his nose.

"Okay, so did you see Jennifer in there? I have to talk to her."

"Sorry, little camper. Chet and Jennifer are already on their way to Grumpy Balser's party. That's the rumor, anyway."

Buck shuffled where he stood. Grumpy Balser was the twenty-year-old tenth grader whose parents went on vacation every weekend, leaving him alone to watch the house and make sure it stayed peaceful and orderly. His "quiet weekends" were by invitation only.

"Okay. Any chance we can sneak in?"

"I mean, we're graduates now. I'm sure we could just put ourselves on the list."

Buck patted Ronnie's top hat.

"All right, let me just get my cover, and we'll head over."

* * *

TWENTY MINUTES LATER, BUCK and Ronnie climbed out of the back of a pickup truck that was headed in Grumpy's direction. The old man at the wheel leaned his head out of the window when they marched by.

"If you hear sirens," the old man said, "run."

Ronnie tipped his hat to the man.

"Good advice, Mr. Weatherly. Thank you for the ride."

"Hope you got a way home, 'cause I ain't coming back through here. Not for you, and not for anyone."

"I'm sure we can hitchhike."

"Better hope so."

Mr. Weatherly honked as he set the truck in motion. He rounded the next corner and darted out of sight. The squeals coming from his tires as he sped off sounded like a bottle rocket. Buck smiled. He'd miss Mr. Weatherly. He was the greatest history teacher he'd ever had.

"And there goes what's left of our umbilical cord," Ronnie said. "Okay, well, party time?"

Buck said nothing. The time for chat was over.

They headed up the long driveway and its endless span of hot rods, past the naked cherub statue and the fountain it peed in, and up to the front door. The house bouncer, a three-hundred-pound man with sunglasses and a resistance to smiling, stopped them before they could set foot past the threshold.

"No nerds," he said without hesitation.

"Yeah, good," Ronnie said as he puffed up his chest. "We hate nerds. Screw all of 'em."

Buck said nothing.

The bouncer raised his eyebrow as he looked down at Ronnie. The doorman easily had a foot on Ronnie and at least three inches on his top hat.

"Look, we deserve to be here," Ronnie said. He showed the bouncer his diploma, which was still wedged under his armpit. "See? We're graduates."

"But you're still nerds."

Ronnie snorted at him.

"Please. Nerds are so high school. We're *gentlemen.*"

The bouncer glanced inside the doorway and sized up the dozens of beautiful occupants dancing in the living room. Then he cast his gaze back down at Ronnie, then at Buck, then back at Ronnie.

"Lose the top hat, and I'll consider letting you in."

Ronnie pressed his palm against the flat side of his hat.

"Never!"

The bouncer nodded at Buck.

"Then only he goes in."

Ronnie smacked Buck on the spine.

"Fair enough. Go get her, Buck."

Buck slipped past the bouncer before Ronnie could get him kicked out and possibly arrested.

Inside, many of the kids he'd shared classes with danced around, chugged drinks, and held conversations about things he knew nothing about. As he scanned each room for any sign of Chet or Jennifer, he overheard talking points about summer jobs, new cars, trips to Aspen, and other things that required steep price tags. Coming from a simple middle-class home, Buck's experience with money and luxury was limited to single pieces of furniture or appliances every couple of years. Last Christmas, his mom had brought home a microwave. It was a celebration of advancement. She'd set it next to their ten-year-old coffeemaker.

When he got to the kitchen, the conversations quickly transformed from summer plans to drinking challenges. Bobby Mitch was already on the floor, singing about pigeons in a purple sky. The kids around him were spilling their drinks in his mouth every time he said something that rhymed with "ah." Neither Chet nor Jennifer was on this side of the house. Buck moved back toward the living room and headed for the study.

As he passed the front door, he saw Ronnie showing the bouncer a deck of cards. He must've been carrying it around in his top hat. The bouncer picked a card from the middle.

Past the vestibule, Buck entered the study. In this room, the boys and girls were making out, but Chet and Jennifer were not among them, so he headed down the hall toward the family room. They weren't there either, so he stepped out through the sliding glass door and onto the back porch. More conversations, more food and drinks, and more making out, but no Chet, and no Jennifer. In the backyard, another couple dozen teenagers hung out by the pool. A few of them had jumped in fully clothed. Buck started thinking he'd come here for nothing.

Back inside, he returned to the kitchen and peeked through the garage door. Just laundry machines, exercise equipment, and jocks cheering on another kid who was lifting a barbell off the bench press. Nothing else worth noting.

Buck groaned under his breath as he returned to the main hall. There was just one place left to check. Upstairs.

Even though the stairwell was roped off and had a very clear NO ADMITTANCE sign draped across it, Buck defied the message and stepped over the rope. He climbed the stairs to the first landing, then moved left up to the second landing, then crossed the balcony into the house's personal spaces.

The first room he encountered was a guest bathroom that hadn't been cleaned in a while. No one was in there. Next was a bedroom. He cracked the door open to find Grumpy lying on his bed, reading a comic. He was alone, and Buck decided not to bother him, so he squeezed the door shut before Grumpy could figure out he was being watched. The next two bedrooms were empty. One of them looked like it belonged to an older sibling who had moved out, judging by the posters of bands from the early 1970s. The other had bookshelf after bookshelf stuffed to the edges with hardcovers dating back to the days of F. Scott Fitzgerald. Clearly a guest room.

He stepped into the hallway and glanced to his left. One room remaining. The master bedroom.

Buck tiptoed to the door and edged it open. The room inside was black. When he pushed it open wide enough to slip through, allowing more light into the room, most of the furniture materialized in the dimness.

Buck's jaw dropped and his heart raced when his eyes adjusted to the sight before him.

Grumpy's parents had their own private palace in this room! Never mind the English-looking king-sized four-poster bed or its silk canopy draped overhead. Never mind the raised platform it sat on or the many pillows that dotted its ornate headboard. Surrounding it was a hundred square feet of floor space, covered in Middle Eastern rugs, and flanked by French windows, which were concealed behind European window drapes, which looked inward at a Japanese television sitting on a Greek or Roman marble stand, and sat angled to entertain any occupants of the king-sized bed, the walk-in closet, or the private bathroom of unknown origin but probably American.

Buck shuffled across the floor, feeling its hardwood against the soles of his shoes. This was a luxury he had no familiarity with. At home, he had to walk on shag carpets and linoleum floors to get anywhere. But here at Grumpy's, he could walk on polished wood like royalty.

He smiled. So, this was what it felt like to be rich.

It suited him well.

Curious about how the fancy lived, Buck crossed the floor to the walk-in closet and found the light switch. Careful not to attract any attention from the hallway, he drew the closet door shut behind him, then flicked it on. Once the light flared up, he found himself surrounded by banks of shoes, shelves of belts, and racks of variant clothing from slacks to dresses, to jackets and coats, and not a single pair of jeans in sight. He also found a few neckties. Proper ties. Silk ties. The kinds of ties that made him professional, not pathetic. He picked one up and tried it on. Fortunately, there was a full-length mirror on the door he could use to check himself.

As he fumbled with the tie, it became obvious he didn't know how to tie a knot. It was disheveled. Didn't matter. It was still nicer than wearing a tape measure or anything else he had around the house.

Buck wondered if Grumpy's dad would miss it if he'd walked out with it. He counted the other neckties. Each one was patterned, silk, and as fancy as the one in his hand. He counted twenty-four. Two dozen even. He stared at the tie hanging from his shoulders. Someone would have to teach him how to tie it.

Buck nodded. It was a pleasant fantasy. But it was still just a fantasy. Grumpy's dad didn't get rich by miscounting his assets, and Buck was no thief. The tie would have to stay. But at least now he had something to strive for. If anyone were to give him graduation money, he'd use it to buy a tie. Probably a silk tie. Had to be done. It was the first step in looking rich.

He put the tie where he'd found it and shut off the closet light. Then he opened the door, headed for the bathroom, and followed the same procedure. With the door closed, he turned on the light, marveled at the walk-in shower that filled up half the room and the

Jacuzzi jets that lined its walls, then turned off the light and reopened the door.

This was a place he could get used to. He headed over to the bed and sat on it, bounced up and down, then fell backward with his arms outstretched.

That's when he heard the slurping noises coming from under the bed.

His heart thumped. He hadn't believed in monsters lurking under beds since childhood, but now that he sat in the lair of a rich person, he wondered if the tales were true. Grumpy's parents were eccentric enough to keep their own pet monster under the bed, or maybe a dog, which was more likely. But what kind of dog? A big one? A vicious one? Probably no dog he'd want to meet without an invitation.

Except a vicious one would've attacked him the moment he'd walked into the room. This one didn't acknowledge him. Instead, this one bumped the mattress from underneath, likely attacking a particularly aggressive flea, if fleas even existed in this house. Given the thickness of the bed, Buck felt hardly more than a tremor. But it wasn't unnoticeable.

He dared to peek under the bed. Get a good look at that dog.

A minute later, he found himself hitting Chet Armstrong over the head with his diploma cover while Jennifer Mills demanded that he stop.

A minute after that, he was alone again, on the bed, bruised and bleeding, with his pants getting passed among the kids downstairs and Jennifer standing outside the door, crying about whatever had just happened here.

Episode 3

A Bet with Chet

THE HOUSE BOUNCER WAS shining a flashlight in Buck's eyes when he awoke after a short stint in Blackout City.

"Hey, Mr. Stamps," Ronnie said from the doorway. In the juxtaposition of hall light shining into the bedroom, Ronnie and his top hat resembled the silhouette of a tilted Abe Lincoln, but shorter. "He awake?"

"Looks like it," the bouncer said. "Grab his feet and we'll get him out of here."

Ronnie and Mr. Stamps, the bouncer, carried Buck out of the house and loaded him in a jeep. Once Buck was safely buckled in, they looked for his pants. Ronnie came back empty-handed. When Mr. Stamps returned with a wet plastic bag, he told Ronnie he'd found them sinking in the pool and retrieved them with a net, stuffed the dripping blob into a kitchen trash bag, and tied it up. Now he'd dumped the bag onto Buck's lap. Now that Buck was gaining coherence, the bouncer asked him not to get the seat wet. Buck told him not to expect much. His success rate at good fortune had been at the low end these last few weeks.

After the bouncer parked in Buck's driveway, he unbuckled Buck's seat and pulled him onto the lawn, telling him good luck. He reached into his glove compartment and flung a small card through the passenger window. It landed on Buck's chest. In the hazy glow of the streetlight, Buck could just make out the contents. It was Mr. Stamps's business card.

"My rates are affordable, just in case," he said. "But I don't do student discounts."

Mr. Stamps pulled onto the street and drove off. Buck didn't know where Ronnie was, but he imagined the bouncer was off to pick him up and take him home. Or maybe he was off to his next job. Buck had no idea.

It took him another ten minutes to recover his senses. Now that the blood had dried and his head was clear, he took the pants out of the bag and put them on. Then he entered the house, where he could take them off, jump in the shower, and rethink his life.

* * *

BUCK SPENT THE NEXT morning with his phone in hand, contemplating whether to call Jennifer or let things go. From the moment she'd popped out from under the bed, his memory of everything about the night before mashed together and drifted down a whirlpool of painful snapshots. All he remembered was the embarrassed look on her face, the feeling of his diploma making a hard impact with the back of Chet's skull, Chet's fist rounding on him and smashing him in the jaw, the jarring crack of his teeth colliding with each other, the jolt he felt to his ears and into his forehead, and the feeling of the senior Balsers' bed mattress flying up and at him, pressing into his back like a marshmallow against his shoulders. Even as the lace canopy covering the bed faded in the growing darkness, he recalled watching Chet rubbing the back of his head as he wandered off, conjuring up a salty vocabulary the likes of which Buck hadn't learned from his English teacher until his senior year. His punch had leveled Buck. Buck's assault with a weapon had barely caused Chet discomfort. And now Chet had left the party with Jennifer while Buck left it with the bouncer. Nothing about last night had measured up to his hopes.

Buck shook his head. What more could he do? If Jennifer ever respected him, she would've lost it with last night's failure.

He hung up and went back to bed. His headache was still pounding, and his teeth still hurt. He was in no mood to talk, anyway.

As afternoon approached and his health began to recover, Buck wondered how the night might've played out if he were stronger or knew better moves. The only reason he'd gone looking for Chet was to fight him. But whether he'd found him under the bed or in the middle of the dance floor, he'd let Chet have it in the most pathetic way imaginable. Nothing he dished would've made any difference.

If Buck wanted Jennifer back, he'd have to enlist help.

Maybe Mr. Stamps meant what he'd said.

Buck retrieved the phone and dialed the bouncer's number. Instead of the gruff tones of a three-hundred-pound man, however, a woman with a sexy voice answered.

"Hey, baby," she said, with the breath of a Valley girl.

Buck stammered. "Er, do I have the right number?"

"You need a protector, sweetie?"

Buck nodded. The woman on the other end obviously couldn't see him. "Yes," he said.

"Then you called the right place." She coughed. Her sexy voice took on a little gravel and a little phlegm. "Pardon me. What type of business are you protecting?"

Buck shrugged.

"No business. Just me."

The woman was silent.

"Er, my name is Buck, if that's important."

"It's not. You say you need personal protection?"

"Yes, ma'am."

The dull tapping of background keys stopped.

"The Bouncer Depot has two services," she said. "Businesses and events. If you want personal protection, I can give you the number to our sister service, but I gotta warn you, their prices are much higher, and judging by your scratchy voice, I can't imagine you make more than whatever your parents give you for allowance."

"I mean…"

"That's not a rebuttal. So, if I were you, I'd learn self-defense instead. Ever take karate?"

Buck shook his head. The woman still couldn't see him. "No."

"Where do you live?"

"East Hybrid, near the highway out of town."

"Ah, good. Then you're close to the Whipping Shed. I'd suggest you stop over there and speak to the proprietor, Ken Kabuki. We call him Mr. Kabuki. He can teach you a lot. But be ready to wax his car and paint his fence."

"What?"

"Don't ask. He's a strange old man. But he's really good at karate. And his prices are cheap. If you need a good defense, give him a look. But if you need your business or event defended, then we're your solution."

The woman coughed again. She might've been smoking. Either way, she'd given up on sounding sexy.

"Will he teach me how to fight a bully?"

"Probably. It *is* karate, after all."

Buck twanged the phone cord. He'd have to give this some thought. His dad had once tried enrolling him in karate as a child but pulled him out before he finished his white belt because the instructor had spent too much time teaching how to block and not enough time teaching how to dominate. Twelve years later, Buck also wished his old instructor was more offensive than defensive. Perhaps this Mr. Kabuki would be more empathetic to the current situation.

"Okay," he said. "Thanks for the info."

"No problem, sweetie. Just tell me where I can send the consultation bill, and we'll be on our way."

"Consultation bill?"

"Well, sure. Giving advice is one of our side solutions. Twenty dollars an hour. Because we spoke for, er, three minutes, that comes out to a dollar fifty."

Buck thought back to the park attendant who'd charged him two dollars to enter Park Center Park and rubbed his forehead.

"Is nothing free anymore?"

"Sometimes love is, depending on where you get it."

"Never mind. If you got a pen, I'll send you my address. You can mail me an invoice there."

"Oops, we've just hit a fourth minute. Now it's two dollars."

Buck spat out his address before the bill climbed to two fifty.

* * *

Before Buck disconnected with the nice lady who exploited him for her time, he dared to ask where to find the Whipping Shed. After a lengthy explanation, using his location as a point of reference and an extra dollar's worth of consultation, Buck had everything he needed to find this elusive Mr. Kabuki, who apparently wasn't so elusive at all. In fact, the Whipping Shed was on Main Street, just past the bend coming out of the Alley of Pines, a mile from his house and in plain view. The way the Vixen of Bouncer Depot had explained it (that was the name she'd used when she thanked Buck for calling), it seemed he'd seen the building every time he went downtown but never paid attention to the sign.

So, when he got on Ronnie's bike and rode down his street, up through the Alley of Pines, and turned left at the newsstand, he found the building he was looking for just beyond the trees. And as he reached his destination, he realized he'd already been there once upon a time, back in the days when he was trying to sell chocolate to local businesses for a fundraiser. He'd just forgotten the name. He'd always remembered it as "That Karate Place."

Instead of the tinkling of wind chimes he'd expected, a traditional shop bell rang the moment he opened the door. And the front room had a waiting area, complete with a sign-in desk and watercooler. Two potted ferns sat in either corner of the room closest to the front window, and a poster of a traditional Japanese house hung from the wall just over a magazine rack. Another bell sat on the counter. It was quite commercial. Buck tapped it.

A moment later, a stooped, middle-aged Japanese man came waddling in from the hallway beyond the reception desk. He was dressed like a plumber and carried a plunger in his hand. A spot of blood was dripping off his palm down the handle. The man didn't seem to notice.

"What you want?" he asked.

"I was told to come here if I wanted to learn how to fight."

The man's left eyebrow rose as he studied Buck up and down.

"Too skinny," he said and turned back toward the hallway.

"I'll pay you whatever you want!"

Buck regretted the words the moment they left his mouth. He didn't have any financial leverage to offer the man. That was the whole point of his coming here. Otherwise, he would've paid for assistance from the Bouncer Depot's sister site.

But it still stopped the man and forced him to face Buck again.

"Anything?"

Buck shuffled where he stood.

"Er, within reason."

The man walked around the counter and spotted the bicycle leaning against his reception counter.

"Nice bike," he said. "Kabuki could use nice set of wheels."

Buck pulled the handlebars closer.

"Um, this is my friend's bike. Not for sale."

"Boy say anything. Kabuki want bike."

Buck started for the door.

"Never mind."

As Buck reached the door handle, the man cleared his throat.

"Lesson one in winning fight, never give in to enemy. Boy passed first test."

Buck stopped and glanced over his shoulder.

"What now?"

Mr. Kabuki pointed at the chairs by the front window.

"Sit down. Kabuki interview boy, see what boy made of."

Buck wasn't so sure about this anymore.

"Okay, what's this gonna cost me?"

"Figure that out later. Sit down. Training depend on goal."

Buck dropped the kickstand and parked the bike by the counter. He took a seat by the magazine rack. Kabuki pulled up a chair and faced him head-on. He set the plunger on the floor and leaned in close for a better look at Buck.

"What boy want self-defense for?"

"I have a bully problem."

Kabuki made a strange guttural noise with his throat as he nodded, then hummed a sound that resembled agreement. "Hrmm mmm, hrmm mmm."

"So, I need to learn how to punch him, so he'll go down and stay down."

"How old boy?"

"Just turned eighteen."

"Not mind assault charges filed against you?"

Buck hadn't considered that. He was an adult now.

"Well, I have to stop my bully problem somehow."

"Lesson two. Buy guard dog."

Buck got up from his chair.

"If you're not gonna help."

Kabuki signaled Buck to sit.

"Why bully bother boy?"

Buck shrugged.

"I don't know. He's been doing it since freshman year. But lately he's been attacking me personally. Night of my birthday, he stole my girlfriend. Made out with her right in front of me."

Kabuki nodded.

"Yes, yes. Can see that happening to skinny boy."

"I mean, I don't *want* that to happen. I like Jennifer. She's cool and blonde and a girl. You know?"

"Kabuki remember first lady friend. Married her moment he defeated girl's boyfriend in battle."

Buck leaned against his armrest.

"So, you understand?"

Kabuki nodded.

"*Hai.* Boy want defeat enemy in battle to win back lady friend."

"Yes. That's what I want."

Kabuki smashed his palms together and rubbed them together. Flecks of blood flew out and splattered onto the floor. Buck resisted the urge to ask whether it hurt.

"Kabuki can help boy. Come."

He got out of his chair and shuffled toward the hallway. Buck followed him. Down the hall, they passed a few offices and the karate dojo's training floor. One office had a dental chair sitting in the middle. The previous owners must not have cleared out their inventory completely.

Kabuki led Buck to the break room and pointed at a coffeemaker.

"Make Kabuki cup of coffee."

"Huh?"

"Coffee." Kabuki nodded at the coffeemaker.

Buck stared at the complex machine and its glass jar sitting in its cradle. It had a single button on its base, but Buck wasn't sure what would happen if he pressed it. His mom made coffee every weekday morning, but only after Buck left for school, so he never saw how she did it. He'd see the results only when he got home each afternoon to find the jar—she called it a "carafe"—and some cups in the sink.

He glanced at Kabuki and shrugged.

"Don't know how."

Kabuki's eyebrow rose.

"Then how boy expect to defeat bully in battle?"

"Um, I'd still like to punch him and watch him hit the ground, teach him never to mess with me or steal my girlfriend ever again. If that's possible."

Kabuki shook his head.

"What year now?"

Buck didn't understand the question, but he answered it anyway. "Nineteen eighty-five."

"Not eighty-four?"

Buck shrugged.

"No. Hasn't been eighty-four in five months."

Kabuki pointed at the coffeemaker.

"Then karate out, coffee in."

"I don't understand."

Kabuki opened a cupboard and pulled down two ceramic cups. He placed them on either side of the coffeemaker.

"Kabuki see future in dream, and karate not 'in' thing anymore. If boy want defeat enemy, then boy learn way of business. Boy learn how to be entrepr—entraper—entree paper ner."

"An entrepreneur? Heard of it, but I don't know what it is. What is it?"

"In future, there be great movement in coffee beans. Boy lead way and stomp enemies through harsh business practice. Much more effective than karate."

Buck stared at the coffeemaker. Had no idea what Kabuki was talking about. Last he heard, the receptionists were the ones making coffee, not the businessmen.

"Seems impossible. I don't know how to become one such entrepreneur."

Kabuki patted the top of the coffeemaker.

"Lesson three. Make Kabuki coffee."

Buck shook his head.

"I don't get it. I just want to punch Chet and take back my girlfriend."

"Violence not necessary. Rich boy can buy out less rich boy. Make Kabuki coffee."

Buck appreciated what Kabuki was trying to tell him, but he couldn't see the benefit. Chet responded to violence. Whatever Kabuki was trying to tell Buck, it made no sense.

"Sorry for wasting your time, Mr. Kabuki," he said. "But whatever you're talking about, it's not for me."

Kabuki straightened his back and glanced down at Buck. It made him look taller. He was at least six feet at full height now.

"If boy want win battle, boy must adapt. But Kabuki understand. Sometime enemy must coax boy out of shadow and into light. Not boy's time. One day he understand."

Buck left Kabuki a five-dollar tip and walked out of the Whipping Shed. While standing on the sidewalk, glancing down Main Street, he wondered if he was making a mistake giving up on Kabuki's advice. After all, he was a middle-aged Japanese man who'd seen some stuff. And he took his wife from his enemy.

But he'd won by "defeating" him, and that had to require violence. Whatever he was teaching now would not fly in 1985. That anyone could win back a girl through "harsh business practice" seemed ridiculous.

He got on his bike and rode toward the town's restaurant quarter, toward Hybrid Beach. He was getting hungry.

* * *

On his way home, Buck pedaled through the back roads of Hybrid West, hoping to grab a cookie or two from Pound Cake, the neighborhood bakery. Irina Swift, the proprietor, was as friendly as ever, tossing in that extra chocolate chip cookie to incentivize him to return for more. While she was fetching the cookies from behind the counter, Buck felt compelled to tell her about his "training" with Mr. Kabuki. Because she was so chatty with him, he thought it made sense to return the favor.

But when she handed him the bag and rang him up, she offered him a warning.

"I know Kabuki and like him, but you should be mindful of what he teaches you." Irina's face betrayed no smiles, but her expression was stern. Under that blonde head and beneath those sweet, blue eyes was a guardian angel, and this guardian angel kept no reservation of bad feelings. "He's grown tired of his art, but his instincts never change."

Buck handed her a five-dollar bill for the cookies.

"I'm not saying I want to go back," he said. "Just thought it was weird that he wouldn't teach me karate. I just assumed that was his gig, you know?"

Irina's lips pulled back to show off her varnished teeth.

"He's still wise. Just a tad dangerous is all."

"I don't want to fight *him*."

Irina nodded as she passed along the bag of cookies and his change.

"Make sure it stays that way. As far as your friend Jennifer goes, I wouldn't fight so hard to win her back. Sounds like she's chasing trouble, and I don't suppose you really want that."

"I still want *her*. She's my girlfriend. Or was, I guess. I'm not really interested in breaking it off."

"Maybe you should be. Something to think about, at any rate. But if you ignore my advice and decide to keep your broken heart, you can always come back for more cookies. I'll be here with a fresh batch. And Kabuki's right about business. You should get a job. Girls like boys who work."

Buck thanked her and continued on his way home.

Fifteen minutes later, when he rounded onto Main Street, he nearly tipped his bike. Three familiar faces were standing on the sidewalk beside the entrance to Hybrid Silver Screens, a two-screen theater that showed second-run movies. Each boy was slurping a fountain drink. He slammed on his brakes just shy of hitting them.

"Well, if it isn't little Buck Star," Chet said, laughing, as he pointed his straw at his face. "Your face looks awful. Is the little man lost?"

Buck cursed under his breath when he realized he could've solved all his problems if he'd just ridden right into him.

"Hi, Chet. Glad to see you clogging Main Street's arteries again."

"Ooh, big talk from such a little loser."

Chet exchanged glances with Tommy Slick and his other henchman, Pigeon Polluck. Tommy pulled down the front tip of his cowboy hat, apparently embarrassed to be there. Pigeon, on the other hand, puffed up his chest as he laughed along with Chet. Pigeon was a smaller kid, but bullish in his attitude. Rumor had it his back teeth were fangs. Anyone he bit wound up with a gash in their skin. Whenever Chet sicked his henchmen on a nerd, Pigeon was the one who enjoyed it a little too much. Pigeon was clearly enjoying this moment of ridicule, too.

"Yeah, loser," Pigeon said. Cola dribbled down his chin.

Buck was in the middle of Main Street, baking in the afternoon summer sun, and he was no longer a high school student. At eighteen years old, in a season when college was his next big decision, he realized he didn't have to put up with this anymore. Even if Kabuki didn't want to teach him how to fight, allowing Chet to harass him was no longer practical. He could just go home and forget this douche ever existed.

And then the movie theater entrance swung open and out came a blonde girl in a pink checkered skirt and matching blouse.

"Oh, hi, Jennifer," Buck said, suddenly forgetting what he was doing here or where he was going. Jennifer flinched at the sight of him. "You're looking nice today."

Jennifer said nothing.

"Hey, who said you could talk to her?" Chet poked his straw at Buck's chest.

Buck struggled to return his attention to Chet. He wanted to gaze at Jennifer for the rest of the day. She was so beautiful with that blue ribbon in her hair and the box of candy in her hand.

"I was just being nice," he said, "seeing as how we dated for six months and all—"

Chet stabbed him in the chest with his plastic straw again. Buck winced from the discomfort.

"Let me get something straight, loser. She's my girl now. I stole her from you fair and square, and I will not let you talk to her. Got it?"

As much as he wanted to punch Chet right now—so much that it bubbled in his gut—Buck knew he couldn't win a physical battle against Chet, especially if Mr. Kabuki declined to teach him karate. Even if he were to attempt moves like the "Praying Mantis" or the "Crane-kick to the Marbles," he wasn't skilled enough to pull them off. He'd likely get his butt kicked, again, if he tried. No, he'd have to let this one go.

"Yeah, I was just—"

Buck couldn't help it. First, his eyes moved in Jennifer's direction. Then, his entire head turned her way. Her lips were drenched in pink lipstick. And her blouse was tight on her skin. Her neckline dropped in a V, pointing to a place where Buck had never been invited to explore, as much as he'd wanted to—

No, he couldn't surrender to his thoughts. He forced his eyes on Pigeon, on Tommy, on—

"Hey," Chet said. "Were you just looking at her?"

"No, psh. I mean, my eyes might've glanced at her in the split second it took me to see what movies are playing, but—"

"You better not. I don't want you getting any ideas about taking her back. Not gonna happen." Chet poked him in the chest with his entire cup. "And don't look at her again. I don't want to have to embarrass you in front of all these people." He gestured at the pedestrians walking up and down Main Street. "And you know I will."

Buck shook his head. He was eighteen now. No time for this childish jealousy. Giving in to Chet's bullying behavior didn't make sense anymore. He'd have to win Jennifer back another time, when Chet wasn't around.

"Whatever. I have errands to run anyway, so I'm gonna keep riding. Continue to gloat over your cocky victory if you want, but I won't be here to listen."

Seemed like the right call, even though he wanted to put the girl on his bike and ride off with her. If life weren't so cruel.

"What's a loser like you need to run errands for?" Chet said, undulating his shoulders in some kind of taunt. "Your mommy too drunk to do them herself?"

His mom didn't drink. Chet was taking this too far. Pigeon snickered under his breath as he mimed a drunk person. Tommy was looking off toward the neighboring shop, and Jennifer was stepping closer to the movie theater's entrance, with one hand edging closer to the handle.

"Chet, is this really necessary?" Buck asked. "I mean, school's out."

Chet stepped forward and leaned in close to Buck's face.

"It's always necessary, dork. I will always be better than you."

Buck nudged his front tire to the side. It was time for him to go.

"Look, I'm not doing this anymore. Fine, you got Jennifer. You win. Let me go, okay? Besides, I need to find a summer job now. Nothing you'd know about, being rich and spoiled and all."

"Rich and spoiled?" Chet shoved him backward hard enough to knock him off his seat. "You little twerp. I'll have you know I run the most successful juice stand in town. Or have you forgotten?"

Flashes of his birthday "dessert" pummeled his memory.

The cake without the candles.

The lonely ride to the park.

Watching his girlfriend make out with his enemy by a tree.

He hadn't forgotten a thing.

It was all too much.

Buck recovered his balance and lunged for Chet's drink, yanking out the straw. He crushed it between his thumb and index finger. One way or another, Chet would pay for bringing that back up.

"Hey, that's my straw!" Chet said.

Nerd or not, there were still ways for Buck to kick Chet's ass.

"You know what, Chet? I'm sick of you and your bullying. I don't think you're all that hot. You can't even give Hybrid High a football winning streak. How did we finish? Two and fourteen? And you can't cheer for crap. When you wear those tight pants, everyone can see that you're not packing much. No one wants to spend six hours waiting for you to come out of the damn locker room for every play just to watch you cheer for yourself. Your teammates always look cold whenever you're back on the field. And as far as your 'success' goes. You're only successful because your dad is successful. Probably bought off the coach for letting you make games last *six hours*. Your juice sucks. Like piss in a cup."

He glanced at Tommy and shook his head. He actually liked the lemonade, but Chet didn't need to know that.

"Furthermore…" Buck poked Chet in the neck with the straw. Angered by the move, Chet cocked his hand back to punch him, but Tommy blocked him and shook his head, telling him not in front of witnesses.

"I'll kill you," Chet said to Buck.

But Buck wasn't finished. "Your juice sucks, and I bet I can start a business and outsell you in a heartbeat."

Chet's anger hit a sudden reversal, so fast that Buck wondered if he was psychotic. Now he was laughing.

"Ha, is the little man challenging me to a business-off?"

Buck didn't even know what that meant, but he nodded anyway.

"Yeah. I am. You ain't nothing, and I'll prove it."

Chet retreated a step and swatted Pigeon in the chest with the back of his hand.

"Can you believe this loser? Challenging me?" He swept his preppy hair back. His eyes were like those of a lion ready to pounce on a gazelle. "You are *so* on. And while we're at it, let's make this interesting. Loser gives his business and all his earnings to the other."

"Fine."

What was he doing? Buck knew nothing about owning a business. And he didn't want to give Chet any money. He'd already given him a girlfriend.

"Oh, this is gonna be fun," Chet said. "We'll see what you're made of. But to be fair, loser, and I'm a nice guy, I'll give you sixty days to prove yourself. The whole summer. You prove you got a fatter wallet by the end, I'll give you *my* business."

Buck saw the ideal opportunity now.

"And you stop harassing me."

Chet exchanged glances with his henchmen. Thought about it. Nodded.

"Yeah, you know what? If you beat me, you deserve my respect." Chet extended his hand for a shake. "Deal."

"And I want Jennifer back."

Chet glanced at her. Her eyes were bugged out at him.

"Negotiable, but unlikely," Chet said. "But since we're upping the ante, if I win, you also become my employee. And then I'll really own you."

Things were escalating too quickly. Buck needed to stop this. Now. What was he doing?

But he couldn't. He was so pissed.

"Fine."

What was he *doing*? Volunteering to become Chet's slave if he lost? What *the hell* was he doing?

He glanced at Jennifer. She couldn't look at any of them. Her face had gone ashen.

Maybe the look of horror on her face meant she still cared.

Maybe it meant he could still win her back.

For now, though, the terms were not ideal, but Buck would have to take what he could get. The words had already been spoken, so he accepted the risks and shook Chet's hand. It was the only hope of freedom he had.

"Deal."

Chet nodded, then swiped Buck's cookies. "Good luck losing, loser."

He backed off and signaled his henchmen to follow.

"Come on, guys."

Chet headed down the street, and Pigeon and Tommy followed. Jennifer, meanwhile, hung by the door, staring at Buck, shaking her head.

"Jennifer, let's go," Chet demanded.

She hesitated.

"Jennifer!"

Her back straightened as she glanced at Chet, then back at Buck. Her face was solemn.

"Sorry, Buck. I hope he doesn't make too big of a fool out of you."

And with that, she followed Chet and his posse down the street toward Hybrid West and the beach.

"Thanks for the support," Buck mumbled under his breath.

What had he done?

As he watched them blur out of sight, he couldn't help but wonder how he was supposed to win this ridiculous bet. The thought of becoming Chet's employee sent a shiver down his spine.

* * *

A FEW MINUTES LATER, Buck found himself back inside the Whipping Shed, once again ringing the desk bell.

"Okay," he said, when Kabuki came lumbering up the hallway. "I'll learn whatever you teach me. Please show me how to make coffee. I have sixty days."

The middle-aged man nodded.

"Kabuki need just one. Come!"

BET STATISTICS FOR CHET:

DAY 1: MONDAY, JUNE 10, 1985

Chet's Savings Account: $1,196
Chet's Wallet: $52
Chet's Business Funds: $100
Chet's Expenses: $20/week for park space; 50% net earnings or $15-30/day for employee wages, whichever is less; $22/week for inventory; $0 for marketing
Hours of Operation: M-F, 5:00-8:00; Sat 12:00-6:00; Sun 10:00-4:00

CHET ARMSTRONG MUST'VE BEEN the most impressive guy ever to walk the streets of Hybrid City, if not all the Western Hemisphere. Who else could boast such a record of impressiveness by the end of high school? He'd carried his football team to victory every year since ninth grade, even when the seniors ahead of him had mistakenly said they were responsible for the school's excellent win-loss records of 16-0, 15-1, and 12-4 respectively. With his final year's awesome performance of 16-0, he'd proven he was on fire and always would be. And if the losers calling each game had the balls to put Hybrid High in the playoffs, they would've easily taken home the gold, or the belt, or whatever district winners brought to their schools at season's end—Chet wasn't sure because Hybrid High had been cheated out of the opportunity to win anything since its inception because school activity leaders claimed "touchdowns" won the game, not "yardage," which was Hybrid High's superpower and the statistic they dominated. In terms of yardage, Chet had the best passing record in the league. It was that stupid requirement that the kid with the ball entered the end zone that kept them from winning more games and having a record more in line with their stellar passing performance, according to the "rules." The "touchdowns" rule changed their actual win-loss records to 4-12, 7-9, 6-10, and 2-14 respectively. It was enough to burn his stomach.

But then, the rules always got in his way, and he never had the patience for them. It was for that reason that he'd rushed off from the movie theater when he had. If he had stuck around long enough, that dork Buck Star might've talked him into making rules and conditions for the bet.

As far as Chet was concerned, there was no need for rules. He would win, no matter what, mainly because he was the most impressive guy in Hybrid City, but also because he refused to lose his business to some dweeb that Tommy Slick dunked headfirst into the toilet every Tuesday. It just wasn't going to happen. And he certainly wasn't about to let some technicality throw the game for him.

But if there had to be any rules, there would be just one. The guy with the bigger bank account at the end of sixty days was the winner. Of course, Chet never said the score would measure a tare of zero. As far as he was concerned, the money in his savings counted toward the final score. And though that dork had tried to insult him by calling him "rich and spoiled," he was only half right. Chet wasn't spoiled.

Chet laughed under his breath. As he glanced around the Liquid Shack, watching Tommy and Pigeon set up the table and put out the pitchers, he wondered where he'd station Buck once the bet concluded. Probably at the ice station. He'd certainly require him to wear a uniform. Probably a tutu. He laughed again.

"Are you even listening to me?" a shrill voice said from behind.

He took another bite of chocolate chip cookie, now aware that he wasn't alone.

"What?"

"I said you should be marketing right now."

He turned around to see Jennifer staring at him with her hands on her hips. She pecked forward as she spoke, like a chicken. It made his stomach growl just thinking about chicken. He finished off the cookie in his hand. Wherever Buck had bought them, Chet would have to pay the place a visit. Melted in his mouth. Sweetness.

"Don't be ridiculous. Marketing costs money. I'm not about to *spend* money. Just make it."

Jennifer pointed toward the park entrance.

"If you want to beat Buck, you gotta bring in the customers. For the last two weeks, all I've seen in here is me, Tommy, that weird kid—"

"Pigeon."

"I don't care. And a few of your old football pals. You couldn't possibly be earning more than twenty bucks a day. And that's before paying your employees."

Chet snickered as he reached in the bag for another cookie.

"I don't pay them. What are you talking about?"

Jennifer sized him up.

"Aren't they your employees?"

Chet shrugged. He didn't have to explain his reasons to her. Tommy earned half the night's take, based on net earnings, as part of his requirement to stay on the job. Chet didn't like paying him, but he was too good an enforcer to lose, so he pinched his nose every time he passed along half the cash purse. Nobody gave wedgies quite as well as Tommy, but Tommy refused to give wedgies if he couldn't also earn an honest living—in this case, selling juice. It was a tough trade-off. But Pigeon—Chet had his balls in a vice grip. If Pigeon didn't want his dirty little secret spilled, then he'd work for Chet indefinitely, no matter the request. Fortunately, the craziest orders gave Pigeon the highest morale. If Chet didn't have a contingency in place, he might've feared the kid. But he sure as hell didn't have to pay him.

"You ask too many questions," he said. "I know what I'm doing. Besides, what are you even worried about? Buck's a dork. He can't beat me. You ever been to his house? Loserville."

"I have, and he may not be as well off as you, but he's not in poverty, either." She narrowed her eyes at him. "And he's not stupid."

"Has he ever run a business? No?" Chet turned away from her and watched his two employees lay out the tablecloth for the cups. "Then I'm not worried."

"If that's your attitude, then you should be. He may not know the first thing about business, but you give him a good teacher, and he'll learn fast."

"Whatever."

Chet glanced at her, then back at his employees. There was nothing more to add here.

Out of the corner of his eye, however, he noticed she'd moved her arms across her chest. He looked at her again. There was no smile on her face, nor was there an element of softness. Maybe she was serious. And if she'd suffered six months as that dork's girlfriend, then maybe she knew something about him that Chet didn't.

The most impressive guy in Hybrid City didn't get that way by having things handed to him. Jennifer was probably wrong, but he couldn't take that chance if his business was on the line. Buck may have been a dork, but the smart play was to pretend he could win.

"Fine," Chet said. "You want to hold a sign by the road for me? Maybe shake that nice little cupcake of yours for some attention?"

Jennifer smiled. Looked like he'd be investing in a little marketing today.

* * *

BET STATISTICS FOR BUCK:

DAY 1: (CONTINUED)

Buck's Savings Account: $11

Buck's Wallet: $85

Buck's Business Funds: undetermined

Buck's Expenses: not established

Hours of Operation: not established

MR. KABUKI LED BUCK to the dojo's break room and ordered him to sit at the table. As Buck got comfortable, Kabuki unplugged the coffeemaker and placed it before him.

"Study while Kabuki get uniform."

Many questions raced through Buck's mind, but he wasn't sure which ones deserved his focus, so he failed to ask anything. Kabuki left him alone at the table with the coffee machine and no clarity on what to do with it. Buck compensated with curiosity.

While Kabuki was gone, Buck searched the machine with his eyes, then with his fingers. It was made of hard plastic, with a flip-top for loading coffee contents. He didn't know what belonged where, but he was confident that by day's end, he'd figure it out.

At the base of the coffeemaker was a single switch. There was nothing fancy about it. Buck flicked it. Nothing happened. The plug was dangling off the side of the table and snaking down its leg and coiling along the floor toward the wall. Buck considered plugging it in, but he wasn't sure what would happen. Would it come alive? Would it start brewing the moment electricity raced up its prongs? As curious as he was for the answers, Buck didn't want to break it on his first lesson. With the bet in full swing, he didn't want to have to pay for it, either.

Kabuki returned a few minutes later with a crumpled gi in hand. He tossed it onto the table.

"Boy's training uniform," Kabuki said.

Buck drew the gi closer and unfurled it. The fabric was thinning, with a few places wearing out completely. It was a traditional white gi, like what he'd worn for karate as a six-year-old. But this one was mottled with ketchup stains along the lapels and sleeves. Buck sniffed it for freshness. Must've been in a closet for decades, judging how stale it smelled.

"How old is this thing?" he asked.

"Old enough. Get dressed. Come back and help Kabuki set floor."

Even with Kabuki giving him instructions as clearly as only Kabuki could understand, Buck didn't know what he was supposed to do. Set the floor? Make coffee instead of karate? It was all so strange. But he was training now. He'd listen to the master.

In the hallway, he spotted a bathroom near the fire exit and figured that was the best place to change. As he moved toward it, however, Kabuki shouted at him from behind.

"Not that way! Use dojo washroom."

Buck was about to take another step, but the power in Kabuki's voice grabbed him by the shoulders and froze him. The distance between the break room and restroom was just a few strides, whereas the distance to the dojo was more than triple that. Going farther out of his way to accomplish the same goal made no sense.

"You sure? I mean, I could just change in there." Buck pointed at the closer room.

"That Kabuki private washroom. No visitors. Boy use dojo washroom. Everyone use dojo washroom."

In other words, Buck thought, Kabuki's restroom was cleaner than the dojo's restroom, and the middle-aged man didn't want him upsetting the trend. Buck could hardly take offense. He didn't like it when outsiders used his bathroom, either.

Buck gave him a respectful nod and headed for the dojo. He found the public restroom at the back of the room beside a wall-mounted shield and a pair of swords—maybe katanas, though he didn't know swords, so he couldn't be sure. As he approached the bathroom door, he reached out to touch one of the sword points to see if they were replicas. It drew a drop of blood.

"For security," Kabuki said from the dojo entrance. Buck turned to face him. Kabuki nodded at the swords. "Gift from father after last business robbed."

"You ever have to use them?" Buck asked as he sucked on his finger.

Kabuki said nothing. Just folded his arms over his chest.

Buck thought it was best not to ask any more questions. The less he knew, the better. Again, he offered Kabuki a respectful nod, then ducked into the restroom to change his clothes. At least that felt familiar, like changing into a swimsuit at the pool.

He set his street clothes on the counter and checked himself out in the mirror. The gi barely fit. Although Kabuki hadn't given him a belt, he noticed the drawstrings did a sufficient job keeping them snug around his waist. But because they were built for a smaller guy, he wondered if the drawstrings were even necessary. The top was secure, and Buck hadn't worn a tight shirt since his last growth spurt almost three years ago. He worried he might tear it if he moved too fast.

The ketchup stains occupied most of his attention, however. He couldn't help but wonder how anyone taking a skilled and graceful art like karate could be such a slob. Daring to check its freshness, he sniffed a stain on his right sleeve, just below the elbow. Musty, but no evidence of tomatoes. The flavor had worn out long ago. Or maybe the uniform had gone into a washing machine sometime between getting stained and onto Buck's body. The staleness of the sleeve's odor and the stain's faded pink coloring even led Buck to wonder how long it had been since Kabuki had taught karate. Maybe it was no surprise that he was teaching a new art nowadays.

Kabuki clapped when Buck stepped out of the restroom in his new uniform.

"Gi fits," Kabuki said. "Good, good, good. Come! Now boy help Kabuki set floor. Part of training."

Buck followed him back to the break room.

He helped Mr. Kabuki gather various coffee products into a box and brought them to a table on the dojo floor. Among the key items were two coffeemakers, a box of filters, two canisters of grounds, a jug of milk, and a few ceramic mugs. Kabuki ordered Buck to set the coffeemakers on either side of the table and the supplies in between. Then he instructed him to plug in both machines.

"To make good coffee, boy must first learn how power coffeemaker."

Buck had plenty of electronics at home and understood how plugs and outlets worked. He wasn't an idiot. But still, he didn't want to challenge the master. If he'd had the skill to defeat Chet in a "busi-ness-off," then he wouldn't have come here. Buck plugged in both coffeemakers.

"Good. Now peel back canister and smell coffee powder. To be successful at coffee business, boy must know what coffee smell like."

Buck pulled off the canister's lid and sniffed the coffee grounds. It smelled exactly like his kitchen first thing in the morning.

"Boy off to great start. What smell like?"

Buck looked up at Kabuki from over the canister's rim.

"Coffee?" He didn't know how to describe it. It was earthy. That much he knew.

"*Hai*. Smell like anything other than coffee, boy don't use in coffee machine."

Every successful businessman who'd made a name for himself started at an entry level, Buck reminded himself as he put the canister on the table. The basics were just part of the process.

"Now Kabuki teach boy how fill jug with water."

Yes, all part of the process, he thought. Just an important cog in the ridiculous wheel of progress. Now he was going to learn how to fill a jug with water. Perfect follow-up to his high school graduation. He couldn't wait to use this knowledge to defeat Chet Armstrong in a "business-off," whatever the hell that was.

Buck sighed under his breath as he wondered if he was making a big mistake.

M R. KABUKI HAD SPENT the better part of an hour showing Buck how to use a coffee machine effectively. After Buck filled the carafe with water—the thing he'd referred to as a "jug," even though his mom had been calling it the right name all along—he dumped it into the coffeemaker's reservoir. Kabuki explained that using the carafe to measure the water ensured that the machine never overfilled. Next, he showed him how to install a coffee filter.

"Never fill without filter," Kabuki said. "Coffee without filter like pouring sand into engine. Good way to damage machine."

Buck opened the top of the coffeemaker and inserted the corrugated paper cup into a basket. Kabuki told him to remove it.

"Before boy make coffee, make sure machine clean."

Buck removed the filter as he was told, but he didn't know how to check for cleanliness. He ran his finger along the basket's inner walls. Black water and some old coffee grounds came up when he withdrew it.

"Wise man say, when boy make coffee for self, clean when he want. But when boy make coffee for other, clean every morning."

Buck found a paper towel in the inventory box he'd brought from the kitchen and ran it along the basket's walls. Kabuki held out his palm.

"Waste no time," he said. "Remove filter holder. Bring to sink."

Buck noticed a plastic ring sitting along the rim of the basket. He pulled on it, and the whole thing lifted out of the machine. This must've been what Kabuki wanted because he nodded at him.

"Good. Come."

Buck followed Kabuki to the break room, where he ordered him to fill the sink with water and soap.

"Let soak. Practice coffee on other machine."

The lesson continued in the dojo, this time with the spare coffeemaker. Kabuki showed him how to measure the coffee grounds and to load the filter without ruining the basket. Once he showed him how to start the brew, he ordered Buck to watch the carafe get filled with black liquid. Kabuki emphasized the beauty of the process and wanted Buck to admire it.

"As caterpillar become butterfly, coffee bean become breakfast water." Kabuki was now standing behind Buck, watching the brew with him.

Buck scratched at the glass. Then he retracted his forefinger as it made alignment with the coffee. The coffeemaker made "breakfast water" that could burn his skin. Dangerous butterfly.

"Do I have to admire it every time?" Buck asked.

"No talk. Just watch."

Buck sat there and stared at the carafe until the percolated drip stopped. And he watched it for another minute because Kabuki said nothing. If he were still supposed to admire it, he wasn't sure how. Even the undulation of the coffee's surface had reached its end. Now it was stagnant bean water. Stagnant bean water that gave off an earthy aroma that perked Buck right up. It sure smelled lively.

"If brew stop, now time to pour in cup."

Buck peeked over his shoulder to find Kabuki looking off toward the hallway as if expecting a visitor. If Kabuki admired the process too, he must've done so tangentially. But Buck remembered that the karate man was running a business here, and visitors were still invited. Buck picked up on the lesson: Kabuki couldn't admire the coffee if it meant ignoring the potential for incoming customers. Perhaps his business sense grew despite Kabuki's alternative training methods.

Buck removed the carafe by the handle and reached for a nearby ceramic mug.

"Quality matter," Kabuki said. "So, cup matter. Better cup, better quality, better quality, better feeling, better feeling, better money. Business lesson four."

Buck tipped the carafe toward the cup. The liquid reached the spout before Kabuki put out his hand to stop him.

"Always wait for brew to finish before pouring," he said. "Early pour mean early disappointment."

"What do you mean?"

"Pour too early, brew become bad mix. Quality suffer. Wait for brew, coffee become good."

"Brew's done, though, right?"

Kabuki nodded. "*Hai*. Now okay to pour. But not before!"

Buck nodded as if he understood, but he really didn't get Kabuki's point. It was just coffee. No matter how much liquid fell into the carafe, it all came from the same source. Likewise, it was the same coffee whether he'd poured into the cup sooner, later, or now.

But Kabuki was the master. This was another case of experience and not worth second-guessing. Maybe Buck would see his meaning in time. His dad had once tried to teach him about the intricacies of wine. This might've been the same situation. Of course, when his dad had taught him about wine, Buck was just twelve years old and didn't understand the differences between types or brands. Now that he was a man, an *adult*, maybe he could appreciate the art of beverage-making better.

He tilted the liquid into the cup and watched it rise as it neared the rim. He didn't wait for Kabuki's further instruction, though. Just like pouring water or soda into a glass, there was a point when the liquid had to stop filling the cup. That point was now. He tilted the carafe away. He'd left millimeters of space between the liquid and the rim. Kabuki clapped once.

"Good," he said. "Wanted to see if boy smart action-taker. Stopped at right time. So far, so good."

Buck curled his lips as he considered the implication. It seemed the master was waiting for him to pour coffee all over his hand. It seemed as if he wanted to gauge whether Buck would hinge on his every word or act for himself. Or maybe he just wanted to check whether Buck was an idiot.

As Buck stared at the cup, he wondered if there was any other part of the lesson that depended on his foresight. And that, too, had implications.

Buck now stared at his hands, wondering how far Kabuki's testing might go. So far, the lesson had been a cakewalk, but now he wondered how much of it would become an on-the-fly exam. Suddenly, the knot in his stomach became real. There was still room for him to fail this lesson, and if that happened, then what would he do? Would Kabuki still train him? Would he be forced to learn on his own? Would he burn himself trying to figure it out?

"Now taste," Kabuki said.

"What?" Buck was thinking about the future and not about the drink.

"Taste. Time to test. And appreciate."

Buck looked at the cup. Yes, he was still training. The coffee before him was still part of it. The realization that everything was a test couldn't deter him from completing his training.

There was no grade.

Just victory or defeat.

He'd choose victory.

He would taste.

"Okay."

He studied his adversary. A cup of coffee. Simple but potentially dangerous, like a butterfly. The liquid was so close to the cup's rim that he didn't know how to lift it without spilling it. But that wasn't his biggest concern. He remembered the sharp pain he'd felt against his fingertip when he scratched at the carafe. And the steam floating up from the top reminded him of the sauna his physical education teacher had once taken the class to on a field trip. If Kabuki expected him to put that amount of heat into his mouth…

"What boy waiting for? Drink."

"I think it might still be—"

Kabuki slapped the table, causing everything on it, including the cup, to bounce. "Drink!"

Buck snatched the mug's handle and brought the whole thing to his chin. The coffee dripping down the side because of Kabuki's impact burned Buck's knuckles, but he squeezed his eyes shut hoping to bear it.

The steam billowing from the coffee raised the air's temperature by double-digits. His instinct was to pull it away. But Kabuki was watching, so he brought the rim to his lips.

"Stop," Kabuki said.

Buck lowered the cup and muttered a silent thanks to whoever was listening.

"What boy learn about making coffee?" Kabuki asked.

"I learned how to do it," Buck said.

"Boy learn to appreciate coffee?"

"Yes, Master."

"*Sensei*."

"What?"

"Kabuki called *Sensei*."

Buck didn't get it.

"I thought you were called Kabuki."

"*Hai*, but not today. Today, Kabuki called *Sensei*. Boy say 'Yes, *Sensei*.' Not 'Yes, Master.'"

He still didn't get it, but he'd take Kabuki's word for it.

"Yes, *Sensei*," Buck said.

"And boy called Donald-*san*."

Buck shook his head. "What?"

Kabuki pointed at his chest. "*Sensei*." Then he pointed at Buck. "Donald-*san*."

Buck didn't understand what Kabuki was saying. But he took a shot in the dark, anyway. Hopefully, he wouldn't sound like an idiot.

"Is that what you call a trainee? A Donald-*san*?"

"*Hai*. Name, Donald. Title, *San*. Donald-*san*. Like 'Mister.' For respect."

Buck chuckled under his breath. He understood now.

"Okay." Then reality hit him. "Oh, no, but my name is Buck. Buck Star."

"What boy say?"

"Buck."

Kabuki contemplated Buck's words.

"That why boy have bully?"

"Um…"

It had never occurred to him that his name could be the source of his harassment, but he didn't think that was the case.

"Don't think so."

"Either way, not your fault, Donald-*san*. Now wait until coffee cool. Then drink."

Buck frowned. Even his *sensei* didn't respect him enough to get his name right. Whatever perception people had of him—that he didn't earn their respect—he'd have to fix it.

"Okay. And just to be sure, my name is Buck. Not Donald. Buck Star."

"Not your fault, Donald-*san*. Boy can still defeat bully."

Buck rolled his eyes. "Awesome."

This *sensei*-Donald-*san* relationship would need some work.

A few minutes later, the coffee was cool enough for Buck to drink, so he dared to take a sip. He nearly gagged.

"Ugh, bitter." He nearly spat the coffee into the mug. "The hell?"

"That mean coffee good."

Buck set the cup on the table. "People drink this?"

"Not just drink, people like."

"Why?"

Kabuki shrugged. "Secret."

"And I'm supposed to sell this? To people? Who have taste buds?"

"Boy need learn market. Coffee bitter, but boy can make sweet."

"How?"

"Come!"

Buck followed Kabuki to the break room, where the karate master opened a cupboard and searched through a spice rack for an item of interest.

"Hmm, may be out."

"Out of what?"

Kabuki recovered a small empty shaker and set it on the counter.

"Lesson five. When out of supplies, must buy more. We go shop down street. Buy sugar."

"The Shop Down the Street?"

"*Hai.*"

"We're going shopping? At the Shop Down the Street?"

"*Hai.*"

"For sugar? For just sugar?"

"Do boy want more?"

Buck wasn't challenging the master. He wanted clarity. His mom would always tell him never to go to the store for just one thing if there was something else he'd later need. Prevented wasting time.

"Just think we could get a couple of things if we're to get anything. You know?"

"Ah." Kabuki jabbed at his shoulder and winked. "Shopkeeper have cute daughter. You like."

Buck shook his head. He wasn't expecting that remark. He was thinking more about cups or cream.

"I wasn't talking about—"

"Girl sweet."

Buck choked back the rest of his words. A flash of Jennifer crossed his mind. Once upon a time, she had been sweet.

"You mean like sugar plus 'sugar'?"

Kabuki clapped his hands together and grinned.

"That sound like metaphor. Kabuki like metaphor. But no, boy just need sugar sugar. For coffee. But maybe boy talk to shopkeeper about daughter. For sugar sugar." The old man winked again.

Buck smirked at the thought. He wasn't looking for a new girl. He just wanted to win back his original love.

"Thanks, *Sensei*, but there's already this girl I'm into."

"Two girls trouble, Donald-*san*. One plenty. No bite more you can chew."

"Yeah, that's not what I meant—"

"Enough talk, Donald-*san*. We see shopkeeper now."

Buck nodded. Advice about girls. Just another lesson from the old karate master at the Whipping Shed.

* * *

They didn't have far to walk. Buck, of course, felt ridiculous trailing behind the older Japanese man in the plumber's uniform when he himself was wearing a tight-fitting gi with ketchup stains all over it. But the lesson wasn't one in humiliation, as he might've assumed otherwise. Rather, the lesson was in obedience, and Buck wasn't about to challenge the master's authority, not so early in the training.

When they reached the shop down the street, which was actually called "Shop Down the Street," Kabuki instructed Buck to enter first.

"Lesson six, always show leadership, even when subordinate."

Buck pushed on the glass door and immediately breathed in stale air-conditioning. The rumblings of an ancient wall a/c unit mixed with the canned soundtrack of the shop's Muzak. Yet, the air was moist and warm, as if the air-conditioning was a prop. It was cooler and drier outside. Buck wondered if the shop's inventory suffered as a result.

"Hi, Mr. Kabuki," the shopkeeper said when the karate man followed Buck inside. "New trainee, I see?"

"*Hai*. First day."

The shopkeeper was a semi-portly individual, probably in his forties or fifties, with a swirly mop of dark hair and a tight, sketchy mustache. His uniform comprised a dark blue vest over his regular clothes. He nodded at Buck.

"What's your name, kid?"

"Buck. Buck Star."

The shopkeeper saluted him. "Mack Green. I run this place. You need a job?"

Buck glanced at Kabuki for advice. Kabuki looked down at him and nodded.

"Lesson six."

Buck puffed out his chest and saluted the shopkeeper in return.

"I'm starting my own business," he said. "Gonna sell coffee. To people who actually drink it."

"But boy happy to work part-time," Kabuki said over his shoulder.

Buck felt something stab his chest from inside. It sounded like Kabuki had volunteered him for a job. He glanced back at him.

"What now?"

"Great, how's Saturdays work for you?" Mack asked.

Buck wasn't sure how to answer the question. He stammered as he tried to come up with words. He'd never had a job before. And he was no fan of the air-conditioning situation.

"Boy free Saturdays. And Sundays."

Mack smiled.

"Excellent. I'll get the paperwork ready."

"But—"

"Come. We find sugar." Kabuki grabbed Buck by the lapel and pulled him toward the center aisle.

Near the back of the store, they found various coffee products, from beans to powders, from filters to paper cups. Apparently, the Shop Down the Street even sold brewers. The cheapest one was nothing more than a cotton sock, but there was a better one that resembled the coffeemaker that Kabuki had at the Whipping Shed. Cost just seventy-five dollars. The bags of sugar sat along the bottom row beneath the coffeemaker. Kabuki pointed at one.

"That what we want."

Buck assumed Kabuki wanted him to do the shopping here, so he took the sugar off the shelf. Kabuki, meanwhile, admired the bags of coffee available.

"When boy run out of coffee, this good place to resupply. Kabuki fan of Hawaii coffee."

Buck didn't know the difference between Hawaiian coffee and the store's cheaper signature blend, "Store Powder," according to its label, but given its two-dollar price difference, he assumed the Hawaiian blend was of better quality.

"You gonna buy some?" Buck asked.

Kabuki shook his head. "Left money at dojo."

Buck shrugged. That was a no. Nevertheless, they were here for the sugar, so he banked the information for future reference rather than need-to-know-now. If he got to a point where he could discriminate between coffee blends, he'd remember Kabuki's thoughts about Hawaiian coffee and use it for his business. But clearly not today.

Buck brought the sugar to the counter and reached for his wallet. Kabuki followed.

"Tell boy about daughter," Kabuki said to Mack.

Mack nodded and smiled.

"Ah, yes. She's about his age. Well, she's not actually my daughter. I should probably clarify in case there's confusion."

"All the same."

"Well, there's somewhat of a difference, but—"

"Keep talking," Kabuki said. "Boy need girlfriend. But Kabuki need use washroom. Be right back."

"Okay. Bathroom's that way." Mack pointed at a door between a cereal shelf and a magazine rack.

As Kabuki lumbered off, Mack returned his attention to Buck.

"What was I saying?"

"Your daughter," Buck said. "Or stepdaughter, maybe? You were saying she's not actually your daughter."

The shopkeeper nodded. "Right. She's an exchange student I'm hosting. From France. You like French girls?"

Buck shrugged. He'd never given it much thought. Ever since Jennifer entered his life, he was enamored with her and never gave other girls much attention, at least not significantly enough to matter.

"Well, you'd like this one. She speaks very little English, so she doesn't talk much. And I don't think she has a boyfriend, not one she yammers on about at dinner, at least. Well, not that she ever eats dinner with us." He stared off toward a surfing poster he had pinned on the wall behind his station. "Actually, I don't really know anything about her, now that I think about it." He shrugged. "Eh, but I'm sure you'd like her."

Buck was tired of explaining his girl situation, so he let the discussion die. Or he would've if he could.

"If you're interested, she works as a waitress at the tea shop by the beach. You know it?"

"Tealeaf Central?"

Mack snapped his fingers and pointed at him.

"That's the one. You ever been there?"

"I've seen it, but I don't drink tea, so…"

"Well, you should start. And if you do, you should look for her. She's cute."

Buck handed him a five-dollar bill for the sugar. "If you say so."

The shopkeeper handed back the change. Then he leaned forward and rubbed Buck's head.

"You're a promising kid." He looked up and nodded. "And you got a good teacher."

Buck checked behind him to see Kabuki standing there. He'd swept in from behind.

"I'll put in a good word for you with the girl," Mack said. "Maybe she'll like you back. In the meantime, see you at noon, Saturday." He lowered his gaze, now serious. "Don't be late."

Buck frowned. He didn't want a part-time job.

"Okay," he said. What else could he say?

* * *

WHEN BUCK AND MR. Kabuki returned to the Whipping Shed's break room, Kabuki set the bag of sugar on the counter and reached for the empty dispenser along the back wall. He gestured for Buck to unscrew the top.

"If boy want become good at service, he must learn all parts of industry. Must know tools. Feel mechanics. Know difference between glass and plastic shaker."

Buck took the shaker and unscrewed the top. It felt like any other shaker coming apart in his hand. He set both the bottle and the top on the counter.

"Now boy fill bottle. Try not spill. More sugar on table mean less sugar in coffee."

Buck stared at the glass shaker. Its mouth was small, and his coordination was questionable. He wondered if it was better to pour some in a cup first and use it as a funnel. If he were home, then starting with a mediating container would've been his play.

In the open cabinet above his eye line, many of the cups were the right size. Most cups were, of course, depending on how he poured, but he wasn't sure if this test was about ingenuity or coordination, so he erred on the side of coordination, as karate itself lived or died by it, but also, probably, by ingenuity.

He shook his head. He was overthinking this.

Buck opened the bag of sugar and measured with his eyes the position and angle necessary to ensure a clean pour. He could do this.

As he performed geometry in his head, however, he noticed Kabuki's hand moving toward the large pocket on the front of his overalls. Slowly, it went under the denim flap. Then, as Buck lifted the bag in preparation to pour, Kabuki's hand slipped out of the pocket.

A bag of Hawaiian coffee beans appeared between his fingers. He set the bag beside the sugar shaker.

Buck's eyes bugged at the sight of it.

"Wait, isn't that—"

"*Hai.*"

Buck dropped the bag of sugar. It tipped on its side, causing a few teaspoons' worth to spill onto the counter. He couldn't believe what he was looking at.

"When did you pay for it? And how?"

Kabuki drilled his sights onto him. His face was like stone.

"Lesson seven. When boy need supply, money hurdle, not wall."

Buck stared at the man. He didn't know how to respond, what to say, anything.

So, he said nothing.

Kabuki took a spatula from a utensil holder along the back of the counter and shoveled the spilled sugar into the bag. Then he took the bag and bottle in either hand, as if to finish the job Buck couldn't do himself.

As Kabuki poured the sugar into the dispenser, he said nothing, either.

Then Kabuki sang an unfamiliar jingle, a tune that sounded like happiness and sunshine.

Buck just watched him pour the sugar.

Down it went into the shaker.

Like sands of the hourglass.

Down, down, down.

Episode 6

Buck's First Dollar

S SOON AS MR. Kabuki refilled the sugar shaker, he screwed the metal top on and directed Buck to follow him to the dojo. With his head down, Buck did as he was told, but he considered grabbing his bike and running for the exit. How did Mack Green not notice the bulge in Kabuki's overalls pouch? How did Buck not notice it?

And why didn't Kabuki just have Buck pay for the bag of coffee? Buck wasn't rich, but he wasn't broke, either. He could've paid for it. He'd been training for less than two hours, and already he was an accessory to shoplifting. What was this business, anyway?

Kabuki pulled an empty mug from the inventory box and told Buck to fill it.

"Other cup cold now. Not taste good."

Buck noticed the coffeemaker was still on, which meant the carafe was still heated. So, a fresh cup would be as hot as the first cup. Hopefully, Kabuki didn't expect him to put that to his lips.

"Now pour sugar into cup."

He'd filled the cup almost as high as before but left a little room for jostling. In the event Kabuki slammed the table again, it wouldn't spill all over the place or on his fingers.

He dashed a little in. The coffee didn't rise.

Sugar was absorbent, so he poured in a little more. And a little more. The coffee sloshed under its weight, but the coffee level hardly rose. He poured in a little more. Then it occurred to him he didn't know when a little more became too much. He stopped.

"How many teaspoons that?" Kabuki asked.

Buck dared to look at his *sensei*. Ever since that bag of Hawaiian beans came out of his overalls, he was afraid to make eye contact with him, afraid of understanding why he might've done such a thing, afraid that he might expect Buck to do the same.

"I don't know."

"Why boy not measure first?" Kabuki nodded at the inventory box. "Did Donald-*san* not bring spoon?"

"Was I supposed to?"

Kabuki leaned against the table and folded his arms. He was neither angry nor pleased with Buck's question. Just neutral.

"When serving coffee, boy must consider customer need. Some people like lot sugar. Some want just a little. How much boy like?"

"I don't drink coffee, so I don't—"

"Not right answer. If boy sell coffee, then boy drink coffee. Lesson eight, always know product selling."

"Yes, *Sensei*."

"Drink coffee."

Buck frowned. The cup was still scalding hot.

"May I wait for it to cool first?"

Kabuki's face softened.

"*Hai*. Lesson nine, burnt mouth is bad mouth." Kabuki looked Buck in the eyes. Buck shied away. Kabuki grunted. "Boy have problem with Kabuki?"

Buck shook his head. "No, no problem."

"Boy don't like how Kabuki get Hawaii coffee?"

Buck shrugged.

"It's a strategy, I guess."

Kabuki grabbed Buck by the shoulder.

"Come, boy train hard. Must be hungry."

"I'm fine."

"Take break. First eat, then Kabuki take boy to see Sapphire."

"What?"

"Not what. Who. Sapphire. Very important lady to business practice."

Once again, Kabuki's world made no sense to him. And now he wasn't certain he wanted to be any part of it. He wondered whether it was too late to cancel his bet with Chet.

But Buck knew the answer before he completed the thought. This was Chet. If Chet thought he was winning, then he would never cancel the bet. If Buck wanted to stop, then he'd have to win first. And that required training. From the master. From the *sensei*.

He sighed under his breath. All his paths and solutions sucked right about now.

"What am I eating?" Buck asked.

"Whatever boy want. Kabuki have more in fridge than he can eat."

"Okay."

* * *

Mr. Kabuki wasn't kidding about the fridge. For a man in his solitary situation, he sure had a lot of food. Mostly vegetables and rice, but there were half-open packages of ground beef and chicken along the bottom rack, and even some lunch meat for sandwiches. Buck made himself a turkey sandwich with mayonnaise, mustard, Swiss cheese, and a dill pickle on the side.

He spread the mayonnaise thinly across the bread. Then he squeezed a little mustard in the center and wiped that around until it turned the mayonnaise golden.

It wasn't as if he couldn't afford it. A bag of Hawaiian coffee was a little under four bucks. Pricey, sure, but not enough to wound the wallet.

The turkey smelled fresh, but its texture was greasy. He laid two slices on a single piece of dressed bread, then licked his fingers.

Even if Buck were pinching his pennies, he was here to teach himself how to make back that less than four dollars in a hurry. Wasn't that the essence of good business? To spend a little to make even more? To risk a dollar over a wrongdoing?

He separated a slice of Swiss from the package. It was smooth and enticing. His mouth watered. His stomach rumbled.

It was cheaper to buy a bag of coffee than it was to visit Park Center Park twice!

Buck shook his head. Then he reached into the pickle jar and selected the ripest one he could find. Even Ronnie Michaels would've spent less than four dollars on a bag of coffee beans if it meant acquiring it legally, and he was a cheapskate.

This practice was an exercise in insanity.

But as he sat at the table and ate his food, he thought less about the Hawaiian coffee and more about winning his bet. Kabuki was a tough trainer with questionable lessons and tactics, but Chet was a horrible bully who no doubt treated his employees like scum. If Buck were to lose the bet, Chet would become the most ruthless employer ever, assuming he'd even pay Buck to work for him. More like a slave driver. But for Buck to win the bet, he'd have to stay in the game, and that meant going along with Kabuki's technique, no matter how morally gray it might get. His conscience would never become as sore under Kabuki as it would under Chet.

There was no easy solution here, but there was the sweeter of two poisons, the softer of two bricks. No matter how much it might sting his conscience, he'd have to lose a little of it to save the rest of it.

Buck finished his sandwich and started on the pickle. He'd stay the course. He'd learn everything Kabuki could teach him.

Maybe he wouldn't like it, but at least he could end his training with his chin up and his pride intact. As long as he won the bet.

Kabuki entered the break room. "How meal?"

Buck looked him in the eye. Didn't flinch. "Excellent. Best sandwich I ever had."

Maybe that was true. Buck saw no reason to challenge it.

"Good. Finish up, then we see Sapphire." Kabuki grabbed the bag of Hawaiian beans off the counter. "We take bag with us."

Sweeter of two poisons, Buck reminded himself.

* * *

DOWNTOWN HYBRID WAS AN interesting plot of town that mixed traditional mom and pop shops with apartment living. The gardens surrounding the buildings were manicured, and the lawns were usually green and mowed. And every shop window had an open sign that was either designed in cursive or fringed with ruffles, or sometimes featured both. Yes, it was the type of cityscape that surrounding towns envied, assuming they ever visited. Even though the streets certainly had their share of litter, especially around the city's public wastebaskets, and no one could travel more than a block without encountering a pay phone or utility pole, the harmony that downtown Hybrid shared with nature was generally even. For every vagrant who lumbered down the street shouting obscenities, there was a mailman ready to tip his hat and say hello. It was a balanced place.

Sapphire's Consignments was the perfect example of this juxtaposition between friendly and abrasive. Sitting across the street from the Shop Down the Street, the store offered much of the same styling—red brick building, conservative sign announcing its name to passersby, trimmed hedges flanking its walls and shrouding the undersides of its shop windows—as well as a feature unique to the businesses on that side of the street, a front lawn. But it also had a popular homeless person camped out by the shop's sidewalk sign. Billy Bob Drake, as the residents knew him, even though he refused to tell anyone his real name, was well-dressed for his situation, clad in a gray felt suit from the fifties or sixties, but it hadn't been washed in a while. His beard, on the other hand, seemed clean today.

As usual, the sight of another human approaching him perked him up. He abandoned his game of jacks to greet Buck and Mr. Kabuki as they moved up the walk.

"Billy-*san*," Kabuki said, as he passed over a small container of food.

"Kabuki-*sensei*," Billy Bob Drake said. "Much thanks, as always."

He opened the container to peruse the contents. A smile crept onto his face.

"Yes, beans! You read my mind."

"What mood today?"

Billy looked up, his smile still vibrant. "Mine or hers?"

Kabuki shrugged.

"Will take both if must."

"Well, I'm in a good mood." He held up the container. "I got beans!"

"And lady?"

Billy tipped his head to the side, and his grin turned impish. "Feisty."

Kabuki grunted. He gave Buck a stern look.

"Careful when Sapphire in feisty mood," he said. "Feisty mean she try cheat boy."

Buck nodded for acknowledgment, though he didn't know what they were doing here. He'd already been cheated on this month. Because he didn't know Sapphire, he figured her cheating wouldn't hurt so much. Probably another lesson that Kabuki had forgotten to name.

"How many people?" Kabuki asked Billy.

"In the store? Good question. Hey, got a fork by any chance?"

"Left at dojo. Round number?"

Billy shrugged. He dug into the beans with his fingers and scooped up a handful. Kabuki had put together a strange mix of baked beans with lima beans and green beans. Billy's ecstatic smile suggested it wasn't too odd of a combination.

"Maybe ten in the last hour." Billy's mouth was full, so his words came out mumbled. Kabuki had to lean in closer to listen carefully. "Definitely busier this afternoon than this morning."

"How they dressed?"

"Some casual like you and me. A couple in suits. Just another Monday."

Kabuki nodded once. Billy's answer must've satisfied him. Buck did not know what to make of any of it. Whenever he went shopping, he just bought whatever he went there for. He'd never bothered asking the locals about the lay of the land of the place.

Suddenly, a dull thumping socked him in the chest from inside. After what he'd witnessed at the Shop Down the Street, Buck worried Kabuki might be casing the joint. He took one step closer to the street. Unfortunately, he didn't know how to talk his *sensei* out of shoplifting another establishment, but he certainly didn't have to play accessory to it. If Kabuki was planning to hit this place, too, Buck would turn toward the street, shove his hands in his pocket, and start whistling as if he knew nothing.

"People in suits leave?" Kabuki asked.

"Yep. One left just ten minutes ago."

"What they carry?"

Billy thought about it. Then he let out a small belch. Took another scoop of beans in his hand.

"Briefcase. Both of them."

"Gut feeling?"

Billy shook his head. "Nah, not these guys. Neither one wore a hat, so, not what you think."

Mr. Kabuki grunted as he stirred Billy's words in his mind.

"Just another Monday?"

Billy grinned. Then he ate the beans. Down the throat they went. Kabuki tapped Buck on the back of his shoulder.

"Come, we go in now." He turned and bowed at Billy. "Billy-*san*."

"Kabuki-*sensei*."

Kabuki headed for the consignment shop. Conversation was over. Billy devoted his full attention to the beans.

"What was all that about?" Buck asked Billy.

"Kabuki likes to figure out how Sapphire makes her money. He thinks men in suits are shady."

Buck wrinkled his cheeks as he processed the information. The answer made no sense. Wasn't this a shop? Didn't that mean she sold inventory to interested customers?

"Does he ever make sense?"

Billy laughed at the question. A bean fell out and caught in his beard. He didn't seem to notice.

"Isn't that how he got the name '*Sensei*'?"

Buck frowned. He was in no mood for a dad joke.

"Why does he even need to know?"

Billy shrugged. "Doesn't ever say. My guess is he's competing for shop worth."

Buck shook his head.

"Okay, why does *that* matter?"

"That's how all the shop owners in Hybrid City act. Don't you know?"

"No."

Billy chuckled to himself.

"Okay, well now you do. Everyone who runs a shop fights to keep it open." He showed Buck his greasy fingers still soaked in barbecue sauce. "That's how I ended up here." He tipped his head toward Sapphire's. "That used to be my shop space. Was a drugstore when I had it. But I was losing the customer popularity contest, and somehow Sapphire got wind of my numbers and bought me out before I could recover. Still don't know how she got them."

Buck didn't know enough about business to offer Billy an idea. But now he was curious himself. He stepped in closer to listen more carefully to the rest of Billy's story.

"Kabuki seemed interested in that detail the moment I told him about it," Billy said. "Probably wants to keep her out of his dojo."

"What would she do with a martial arts studio?"

"Gut it and start a new business. It's a space race around here. The shop owner with the most property wins. The Lease Agent mandates it."

Buck rattled his head.

"Who?"

Billy shook his head and clucked his tongue.

"You apparently have a lot to learn if you're to be Kabuki's understudy." He scooped up another helping of beans. "If you start a business in Hybrid City, you better be ready to play cutthroat rules."

Buck felt that ugly churning in his stomach again. Was *that* why Kabuki five-fingered the Hawaiian coffee? Whatever fire he had in his belly a few minutes ago, Billy figured out how to extinguish it.

Buck wondered if he was filling his fat stack of cash with George Washingtons.

"Donald-*san*! Come!"

Kabuki was standing in the consignment shop's doorway, motioning his head toward its inner guts.

"Thanks, Billy," he said.

Billy nodded. Back to his precious beans.

A faded snapshot of large, cluttered tables filled the interior backdrop of the doorframe's edges as Buck moved up the walk toward the *sensei*. It seemed every knickknack in creation was on sale in there. How Buck had never been curious about it before, he wondered. As he drew closer to the trivial wonderland within, he imagined what he might fill his bedroom with should he find anything impossible to buy in regular retail shops today.

Once inside, the scene played out in full. The reality of what he had assumed was now even clearer. Sapphire's Consignments didn't have just a vast array of forgotten clothing and trinkets of a glorious yesteryear, but it had new stuff, like designer jeans, Atari 7800 cartridges, and even a TRS-80 Color Computer similar to the one his high school's computer department had, or did before it went missing.

When Buck caught up with Kabuki, he found him staring at a table full of VHS tapes and entertainment magazines. The *sensei* was fixated on a copy of *The Karate Boy*, a straight-to-video knockoff of a more popular movie that had been released the summer before.

"Kabuki consulted on movie, but never credited," he said. He picked up the video and flipped it over. "Also never compensated." He shook his head, then returned it to the table. "So, Kabuki never watch it."

"You watch the movie it's based on?"

Kabuki shook his head.

"I hear it's good," Buck said. "Was kinda hoping you'd teach me similar moves."

Kabuki grunted, then continued down the aisle toward the shop counter near the back of the room. Must not have been on the menu anymore, so Buck didn't press any further.

The back of the store was an unusual place for the retailer to position its point of sale, and Buck wondered if it made things easier for the shopkeeper to keep an eye out for shoplifters. But even as he reached the counter, the reality dawned on him. This wasn't even a position for security but the best location for marketing. To get to the counter, the customer had to pass by *every* table, which meant he or she had to view every item along the way. Buck made a note in his head. Tempt shoppers with every item, not just the ones at the front of the store. Might've come in handy whenever he opened his coffee business.

Kabuki pulled the bag of Hawaiian beans from his front pocket and plunked it onto the counter.

"For consignment," he said.

The shopkeeper, a young woman with sharp features and a tinge of blue in her long, dark hair, leaned in for a closer look. She examined the bag's every angle and nodded at every element that passed her mental checklist.

"Unopened," she said finally, as she set the bag on the counter. "How much you pay for it?"

"Shop Down Street sell for three fifty-nine."

The woman brought the bag to her nose and sniffed it.

"Good blend," she said. "You think I should pay you more than market value or less?"

"What Sapphire think fair?"

She read the back label. Smiled at what she saw.

"From the Big Island. That's some rich soil." She eyed Kabuki and looked him over. Then she glanced at Buck. "Who's your cute little friend here?"

"That boy. Too young for Sapphire." Kabuki looked at Buck. "How old boy?"

"Eighteen," Buck said.

Kabuki grunted. "Well, maybe not too young, but still not for sale."

Sapphire folded her arms over her chest and leaned against the counter, now looking Buck over.

"Need a job, kid?"

"I think I already have one," Buck said, thinking about his new employment at the Shop Down the Street.

"You want another?"

Kabuki shook his head. "Boy not ready for Sapphire line of business. Maybe later."

Sapphire shrugged. "Fair enough." She resumed her examination of the coffee.

After the grilling that Kabuki gave Billy over Sapphire's clientele, Buck was surprised at the old man's answer. He figured he'd want an "insider" giving him the latest reports. But he didn't want to bring it up in front of Sapphire. He still didn't understand this arrangement.

"I'll have to consult the chart on market value," Sapphire said. "Off the top of my head, though, I think I can give you base market plus twenty percent. That's probably fair."

Kabuki glanced at the doorway, then back at Sapphire.

"Nice try," he said. "Sapphire make good effort. But Kabuki not stupid. Here counteroffer. Retail value plus ten percent. Sapphire keep for two weeks in back room. Put on table as 'aged to perfection.' Charge retail value plus thirty percent. Everyone go home happy."

Sapphire's left eyebrow raised. She, too, glanced at the front door.

"I assume Billy's been giving you feedback again," she said. "What's his adjective for me this time? Gullible?"

"Feisty," Kabuki said.

Sapphire smirked.

"You're lucky I like you, Kabuki." She glanced at Buck and winked. "And you're lucky I like your little friend here. Fair enough. I'll play your game with modification. Market value plus forty percent and I put the bag on display today."

"Kabuki say he not stupid. Sapphire just level up to retail value. Same price that Store Down the Street charge. Kabuki want retail plus ten percent. Or Kabuki go to Ruby shop."

Sapphire frowned at the mention of "Ruby."

"You wouldn't dare. After all we've been through."

Kabuki reached his fingers toward the coffee bag and pulled it from Sapphire's grip.

"Watch Kabuki," he said.

A smile crept across Sapphire's face.

"Here's my *final* counterproposal. Market value plus thirty percent. I hold for two weeks, sell as 'aged to perfection' for retail plus forty percent. I give you ten percent remainder with your next consignment."

Kabuki thought about the new deal but said nothing. Whatever he was thinking, it must've been overstimulating his brain cells. He turned the bag over in his hands as he contemplated his choice.

Buck, meanwhile, did the math in his own head. Sapphire had essentially produced a more complicated way of reaching the same mathematical conclusion. Regardless of how fancy her wording sounded, she was ultimately giving the same offer as she had from the start. He wasn't sure whether he had the invitation to speak up, but he thought it was the right thing to do. Sapphire was clearly trying to cheat Kabuki.

"The math's the same," he finally said.

Both Kabuki and Sapphire looked down at him. Kabuki had pride in his eyes. Sapphire, on the other hand, expressed a twinge of disappointment. Then she, too, looked upon him with pride.

"Your boy is good," she said.

"Been training just a few hours. Already learning fast."

She nodded. "I definitely like him." Sapphire reached over and pinched Buck's cheeks. "So cute. If I were just two years younger."

Kabuki nodded. "No deal then."

Sapphire reached under the counter and produced a thick binder of spreadsheets. She flipped open to a section with the header "C."

"All right, I'll think of something fair. For now, I'll give you retail value, and once it goes on the table, I'll credit you a percentage that makes sense for both of us."

Kabuki agreed and set the bag of coffee on the counter.

"Deal. Kabuki come back next week for credit."

Sapphire stuffed the bag of coffee under the counter. Then she opened her register and produced three dollars and sixty cents.

"Pleasure doing business with you." She glanced at Buck and rubbed her hands through his hair. "And you feel free to visit any time."

Buck wasn't sure how to feel about her response to him. It was nice to have a young, attractive twenty-something woman paying attention to him after the heartbreak that Jennifer had put him through, and it was definitely nice feeling the electricity from a woman's soft palm radiating all over his scalp, but he didn't like the idea of having someone as cunning as Sapphire showing him that level of interest. If she could talk a customer out of a good deal, what could she talk a vulnerable guy like Buck out of or into?

So, he said nothing and simply followed Kabuki out of the shop.

Once they were outside, Kabuki stopped him and showed Buck the money.

"Lesson ten," Kabuki said. "No such thing as bad deal when base price is zero. Just better deal."

Buck felt his skin crawl at the implication, but he understood the lesson. Sapphire couldn't actually cheat him because he had no previous investment in the product. The challenge here was to get the most return from a free product. Pure profit.

But in a normal world, Buck would have a base price on a product, which meant he'd have to fetch a greater value on sale. Even though Kabuki wasn't offering that lesson as part of the official list, he embedded that idea into his tenth lesson.

So, Buck could modify Kabuki's lesson to: "Any value higher than base price is a good deal." And that would make sense. His high school economics teacher would've passed him on that lesson. Of course, his economics teacher passed him anyway since his only requirement for success was that students show up and prove that they could balance his checkbook for him.

Kabuki, meanwhile, peeled a dollar from the three he'd earned from the sale and passed it to Buck.

"What's this for?" Buck asked, staring at the dollar.

"Commission. Boy earn his first dollar."

"For doing what?"

Kabuki leveled his gaze at Buck.

"Following Kabuki lessons. Now come. Boy have one more lesson today."

Kabuki started down the sidewalk. Buck pocketed the dollar and followed. What more could he do? As they passed Billy, Billy returned the bean container to Kabuki.

"You're going to see him now, aren't you?" Billy asked as they rounded onto the main sidewalk along the street.

"*Hai*," Kabuki said. "Most important part of journey. Boy not succeed without it."

"Good luck, Buck!" Billy said.

Buck thanked him, but he didn't know what Billy was talking about.

"Who are we going to see?" Buck asked once they were out of Billy's earshot.

"Surprise," Kabuki said. "But boy should fix hair before arrive."

Buck ran his fingers through his hair, brushing it back in place after Sapphire had swirled it around. Whoever they were going to see must've been a big deal. For some reason, he wished he'd grabbed that nice tie from Grumpy's parents' closet after all.

* * *

ONE OF THE BETTER things about living in a place like Hybrid City was that most places anyone would've called "essential" were within walking distance of another essential place. Of course, labeling anything as essential was a matter of deciding value according to need, but Hybrid City seemed to have an inherent design perk that one business type was like another. So, it didn't surprise Buck that he and Kabuki didn't have far to walk when they left Sapphire's Consignments for some mysterious place where some "person of great importance" lived.

In fact, the sidewalk wrapped around the building and cut through a small field lined with rows of manicured hedges, and segued into another sidewalk cutting through another field, which wrapped around another building (or maybe the back of the same one), ultimately taking them to another glass door that opened into another business, and it was this business that Kabuki entered and commanded Buck to follow.

So, not far at all.

Inside, Buck found himself in a narrow waiting room with a polished oaken table sitting between three adjacent sofas and healthy floor plants lining along the shop's front windowpane, merging the room's interior aesthetics with the hedges along the window outside. The transition was so seamless that Buck could hardly see the glass. It helped that it was streak-free.

Beside the floor lamp between the sofa along the wall and the one farther from the window was a door. And next to that door was a button. Kabuki instructed Buck to sit. Then he pressed the button. After a few seconds without a response, Kabuki sat on the nearest sofa and picked a real estate magazine off the table. When another minute passed without action, Kabuki opened the magazine and started reading.

"Who are we waiting for?" Buck asked a few minutes later.

"Important man."

That answer didn't satisfy him. He'd already been told that. What he didn't have was concrete details. For example, what man? And how was he important? And why was Buck here to see him?

"Can you elaborate?"

"Kabuki not know what boy mean."

"Who's this important man?"

"Man who let boy have business."

Buck reached for a real estate magazine, identical to the one Kabuki was reading. Perhaps that was the clearest answer he'd have until that door opened.

It took about ten minutes, but the door finally opened. A man in his thirties walked out, crying. As he passed them, he looked at Kabuki, then at Buck. He shook his head, yelled an obscenity at the open door, then continued his way outside.

Kabuki said nothing. He set the magazine down and got off the sofa. He tipped his head toward the door. It was time to go in.

Buck looked out the window. The crying man was shadowboxing at an invisible head.

"Who are you taking me to see?" Buck asked again.

"Lease Agent," Kabuki said as he approached the door. "Man who shape boy's destiny."

The crying man kicked at the hedge. Buck glanced at Kabuki, who was now standing half in the doorway.

Nothing about what Kabuki had said gave Buck any comfort.

Nevertheless, he got off the sofa and followed Kabuki through the door. He crossed his fingers as he stepped over the threshold into his destiny's new great unknown.

Episode 7

The Lease Agent

Aᴆᴛᴇʀ ʜᴇ ᴀɴᴅ Kᴀʙᴜᴋɪ passed through the waiting room door, Buck found himself in a spacious office with marble walls, a mahogany floor, and an arched ceiling rimmed with cantilevered supports.

Buck's breath caught in his throat. On display were objects he'd never expected to find sharing space with each other: a full-sized stuffed bull in the corner with eyes that still looked alive and angry, a bear rug branded with dollar signs that lay centered before the desk, the desk itself being carved from an odd grain of wood, club chairs lined with a dead animal's white fur, and other unbelievable luxuries like a twelve-foot painting encased in an ornate gold frame and ivory lamps in the shape of naked women balancing on either side of the room. The sight of it buzzed in his brain, and he found himself swaying from sudden dizziness.

Behind the desk, an older man in a tailored suit and black cowboy hat was writing something on a ledger. When Buck and Mr. Kabuki approached, he gestured for each to sit in a club chair. There were four to choose from. Buck took the inner one on the right. Kabuki took the outer left, leaving a chair between them. Buck glanced at the empty chair, wondering what was wrong with it.

The cowboy scribbled a final word on his ledger and set the entire writing kit aside. He folded his hands and gave each one a good look. On Kabuki, he lingered for a few seconds and nodded. Kabuki bowed his head. On Buck, the cowboy lingered for longer, sizing him up, raising his eyebrows as he silently inquired about many questions that Buck could not begin to predict.

After nearly a minute of scrutiny, the cowboy finally spoke.

"Your newest trainee?" he asked Kabuki.

"*Hai.*" Kabuki added a nod to his affirmation. Double confirmation.

"What's your name, kid?"

"Buck Star."

"Why are you here?"

Buck almost shrugged, but he remembered he was supposedly in the presence of greatness, so he straightened his back and looked the man in the eyes, this man that Kabuki had called "The Lease Agent." He leveled his gaze as much as the cowboy hat's lowered rim allowed him.

"For you to change my destiny," Buck said.

Buck didn't know the meaning of his own words, but the Lease Agent acknowledged him with a polite nod just the same.

"That's what I'm here for," the Lease Agent said. "How exactly am I doing that for you?"

Buck looked at Kabuki for clarification. Kabuki cleared his throat.

"Boy starting coffee business. Need sell space."

The cowboy glanced at Buck, then pointed at him.

"Him? Running a business?"

"*Hai.*"

"Making coffee?"

"*Hai.*"

"In this summer heat? You crazy?" The Lease Agent scanned Buck up and down. "How old are you?"

Buck didn't understand why everyone cared about his age. But he told him anyway. The cowboy folded his arms over his chest, leaned back, then reached out and slapped his desk. The sound it made was a *thump*, not a *smack*. Must've been really hard wood.

"Hot damn," he said. "Boy after my own heart. Start a business young despite the risks to the throat. That's what I always say. That, and wear a tight collar. You have any experience?"

Buck shook his head. "No, sir."

The Lease Agent folded his arms over his chest again. Now he was looking down at Buck from under the rim of his hat.

"Then what makes you think you'll succeed?"

"I don't know. That's why I'm learning from Mr. Kabuki."

The Lease Agent glanced at Kabuki and nodded.

"Well, if there was ever anyone who could teach a nobody to become somebody, it's this guy." He returned his attention to Buck. "How much business you expecting to pull in?"

"I–I really don't know. This is my first day learning."

Again, the man looked at Kabuki.

"Really? You're bringing him here on his first day of training?" He clucked his tongue. "I always thought you had more sense than that."

"Special circumstance."

Again, his scrutiny was back on Buck.

"What circumstance might be so special that you're here on your first day?"

Buck glanced at Kabuki. The *sensei* nodded.

"Tell Lease Agent what boy tell Kabuki."

Buck swallowed whatever hung in his throat. He looked at the Lease Agent in the eyes.

"I'm trying to impress a girl," Buck said.

The Lease Agent narrowed his eyes at him. His cheeks vibrated as he chewed on Buck's words. Then he gave his desk another fat slap.

"A girl, huh? Well, why didn't you say so?" He leaned forward and widened his left eye. "You know they're trouble, right?"

"I know. That's why I have to win this bet."

"Bet?"

Buck gave the Lease Agent the quick version of his situation, from how Jennifer dumped him for Chet to how he challenged Chet to a "business-off." The Lease Agent seemed to track his every description of the situation, including the term *business-off*. It must've been a thing only rich people understood.

"Yeah, love's a crazy bitch, it is, but it can be worth it. I get you, son. Beat the bully, win back the girl, make a little something on the side. You speak my language. In fact, you kind of remind me a little of myself. You like bourbon?"

"Don't know. Never tried it."

"Want some? Got a bottle under the desk." The Lease Agent reached under his desk and brought up a bottle full of bronze liquid and three whiskey glasses. He set one out for Kabuki, one for Buck, and one for himself. Then he poured a little in each glass. Kabuki bowed in gratitude. Buck just stared at the bourbon, not sure whether to drink it. It had gotten his dad in trouble once upon a time.

The Lease Agent set the bottle down and raised his glass.

"To business." He knocked back his drink. The sound he made afterward convinced Buck he'd burnt his throat.

Kabuki, meanwhile, brought the glass to his nose, sniffed it, then knocked it back. His response was more reserved. The liquid didn't seem to bother him.

Buck picked up his drink and examined it. He didn't know what he was in for. But he was willing to join the club.

As he brought his glass to his lips, however, the Lease Agent reached out and blocked him.

"Wait," he said. "What's the drinking age again?"

He reached for his ledger and thumbed through a few pages. His fingers landed on a story of interest.

"Ah, yeah, never mind. They raised it to twenty-one last year. Thought so." He reached out and took the glass from Buck's hand. "Sorry, kid. Not saying everything we do around here is proper, but we still keep things legal, or legal enough to keep the cops outta here, you know?"

Buck frowned. He was ready to become a man here in this ridiculous office with all this unnecessary furniture.

The Lease Agent drank part of Buck's glass. As he slapped it down, some of the liquid splashed out onto the desk. The cowboy cursed as he reached for a towel.

"I keep telling myself not to drink here." He rubbed at the liquid on the desk's surface. "This desk is expensive." He leveled his gaze at Buck. "Redwood."

And suddenly, Buck understood all he needed to know about this man. At that point, he became aware of the chair he was sitting on. The surface was tough but furry. He dared to ask what it was made of.

"Polar bear," the Lease Agent said. "Finest fur in the world. Hard to get bourbon out. But not impossible."

The Lease Agent put the bottle under the desk, then wiped up whatever bourbon or condensation was left behind.

"Right, well, here's the deal." He lowered the towel out of sight. "Personally, I don't think coffee will ever catch on. But I like your ambition, so I'll strike you a deal. I'll give you a space at the North Park Pavilion at the north end of the lake. You can have it for free while you're setting up, and I'll make sure the park rangers leave you alone about it." He rolled his eyes in thought. "Let's say I give you tomorrow rent-free. Should be plenty of time to get your foundation in place. Then Wednesday, I'll come by first thing to try your coffee. If I'm impressed, I'll work out a leasing contract and you can stay for as long as you need to finish your bet. Sound good?"

Buck nodded. "Sure."

Even as the affirmation left his lips, Buck had no understanding of what he was saying. He couldn't connect to it. Couldn't feel it. It was just a word that existed and was now out in the open. It was a word he also couldn't take back.

"Absolutely," he said as a follow-up. Still no feeling.

Yet, he was starting a business here in this polar bear-fur club chair, at this redwood desk, staring at this drunk cowboy. Three nights ago, he was collecting his high school diploma. Just last Tuesday, Tommy Slick had dunked his head in a toilet (against both of their wills). The whole thing felt unreal.

The Lease Agent extended his hand.

"It's a deal," he said.

Buck didn't know much about business, but he knew handshakes secured actions and commitments, and if he wanted to beat Chet at the end of sixty days, he'd have to shake this cowboy's hand.

So, he did.

And that was that. Business was done. He and Kabuki were back on the sidewalk less than a minute later.

Neither one was crying.

* * *

K ABUKI WALKED BUCK TO the Whipping Shed to review the day's
lessons. Except for Lesson #7 from Shop Down the Street,
Buck wrote everything down on a small notepad that Kabuki had
gifted him for future consultation. (For Lesson #7, he wrote Kabuki's
rule, but with an asterisk and a reminder to come up with a better
lesson later.) Before Buck left, Kabuki showed him how to clean the
coffeepots, told him to set the carafe on the drying rack, and asked
him to clean the empty bean container he'd given Billy.

When all lessons and tasks were completed, Kabuki bowed
before Buck and instructed him to do the same. Buck complied.

"Lesson eleven," Kabuki said. "Always show respect, whether
friend, enemy, or authority."

Buck noted that one, too.

Before he headed home, Buck rode to Ronnie's house to check
whether he could keep the bike longer. Even though he'd technically
paid for four rides, he wasn't clear on whether that equaled four literal
rides or four days of riding. The problem with Ronnie's business
transactions was that they always seemed conditional on the situation,
not on any hard rules. If Ronnie accepted payment for four days but
decided it counted for literal rides only, then Buck was already
pushing his limit. This level of nuance was important to understand
now that every dollar he owned needed accounting and planning.
One of these days, Buck would have to sit down and create a rental
agreement that outlined the exact parameters of the deal. This way,
he could make better plans and allocate his spending better.

After all, that's what a *businessman* would do. Buck smiled at the
thought. Kabuki didn't even have to teach him that one. Just common
sense. And maybe that's all it took to become successful at this crap.

When he knocked on the door, Ronnie's dad answered. He was
wearing pants this time. And a tie. Buck lurched backward at the sight
of him.

"Mr. Michaels," he said, almost choking the words out. "Are you
all heading out to dinner or something?"

"No, you can come in." Mr. Michaels stepped aside to allow Buck passage. "Ronnie's in the bedroom with his new girlfriend."

Buck was halfway through the door when he stopped. What was this now?

"New girlfriend?"

"Yeah, cute girl. Has a name. Can't remember what."

Buck stepped into the dim living room. The television was already on, and the beer bottle was already positioned on the table beside his recliner, so it wasn't as if Mr. Michaels had just come home from the law office where he worked. This girl must've been the reason he was wearing pants.

"Er, should I come back another time?"

Mr. Michaels waved him off as he headed for his recliner.

"Nah, keeps the boy accountable if you stay. Don't know the girl well enough to trust her with Ronnie and a closed door, you know?"

Buck cringed at the thought. Maybe he'd just stay long enough to get the update on his bike rental.

He headed up the narrow hall with the ugly brown carpet, past the guest bathroom, and knocked on Ronnie's door along the opposite wall. The music blaring through was too loud for anyone to hear, so he knocked again, harder.

"What, Dad? We're not doing anything! Go back to your TV!"

"It's me," Buck shouted.

The door opened. Ronnie peeked through. His eyes were rabid, but he looked otherwise normal. Wherever his top hat was, it wasn't on his head.

"Hey, Buckaroo. Kinda entertaining someone right now. What you need? Can it wait?"

"Yeah, yeah. Just needed to find out how much longer I can keep the bike. Gotta start budgeting. To win the bet."

"The bet?"

"Yeah…"

It occurred to Buck that everything was moving so fast that he hadn't yet gotten the chance to tell Ronnie about his bet with Chet.

"I had an interesting day," he added. "A lot going on. Wanted to tell you about it."

Ronnie reached out from the crack in the door and patted his shoulder.

"Sounds great, little camper. Yeah, I've had an interesting turn myself." He checked over his shoulder, nodded at his companion, who was still out of view, then leaned forward and grinned. "I met a girl."

"Yeah, that's what your dad said. How did that happen?"

Ronnie stepped out of the bedroom filled with the loud vocals of Duran Duran and closed the door behind him. Now they could talk normally.

"Remember when Mr. Stamps took you home from Grumpy's?"

Buck nodded. How could he forget? Came home with the worst face-ache.

"While I was waiting for him to get me, the dreamiest lady I'd ever seen came and stood beside me. Naturally, I chatted her up."

Buck smirked. Ronnie didn't know how to talk to girls, and he knew it.

"Wipe that grin off your face," Ronnie continued. "I said hi, and we talked. Then when it became obvious that Mr. Stamps forgot about me, Tiffany took me home."

"Tiffany?"

"Yeah, Tiffany Hadley."

Buck's smirk evaporated.

"Tiffany *Hadley*?"

"Yeah." His face turned serious. "You know her?"

"Dude, that's the girl you were obsessed with in ninth grade."

Ronnie's face was a butter knife, pointed and dull.

"Was I? Hmm." He shook his head. "I guess that's possible."

"You literally went full circle."

Now Ronnie had a bemused look on his face.

"I guess I did. Imagine that." He slapped Buck's shoulder. "I guess dreams do come true. Eventually." He laughed under his breath. "Anyway, keep the bike however long you need. No extra charge. I got a girlfriend now to drive me around, so I won't need it. When Tiffany goes home, I'll call you. Then you can tell me all about whatever this bet is you're talking about."

Buck thanked Ronnie for the free ride. Then he thanked Mr. Michaels for wearing pants, but not loudly enough for him to hear it.

On his way home, he thought about the difference between Ronnie's luck and his own. At the same party where Buck had gotten his butt kicked, Ronnie got his saved. Must've been nice to have everything come together so perfectly.

Of course, that was Buck's dream now. Letting everything come together perfectly. Now that he was about to start his own business by taking the advice of the best trainer in town, his life could come together perfectly, too, even if not entirely in the way he'd hoped.

All he needed now was to win back the girl. Then his life would be as perfect as Ronnie's.

The sun was setting as he rode home. The night was his to enjoy however he wanted. Perfection was already starting.

Once he got to his bedroom desk, he celebrated his newfound aspiration by grabbing a notebook and pencil and writing down his day's earnings and expenses. If he were to run a business, then common sense told him he'd have to account for financial changes on paper, not just in his head. He figured he'd account for all the exchanges made *after* the bet, not before. So, he ruled out every transaction made before the sugar and his commission.

It looked like this:

BUCK'S END OF DAY REPORT:

Earned: $1.00

Spent: $1.49

Net Gain: -$0.49

* * *

AFTER CONVINCING THE GATE attendant that she'd already paid for the day and that it really needed a system for stamping visitors' hands to permit free reentry, Jennifer lumbered into Park Center Park, exhausted but encouraged that her marketing strategy had worked. Even though she wanted to become a therapist when she graduated college, she recognized she could use her powers of psychology now by investigating which marketing techniques produced the best results, and committing to the best outcome by focusing on the most obviously successful tactic.

What she'd determined was that, as a young, beautiful, West Coast blonde, she could get anyone to respond by holding up a sign and sticking out her leg. So, her goal that day was to design and build the best sign possible for gaining leads, using the most inexpensive materials possible. Fortunately, the Office Place was a few blocks from the park, so it didn't take her long to gather her resources. Once she figured out how to navigate the store's gothic aisles, each like the hall of some dank dungeon, getting what she needed was simply a matter of demanding the shopkeeper unchain his slaves long enough to unlock the cells where the poster boards and markers were kept. Fortunately, the shop took regular dollars and cents for payment, so she left with her items easily, but whoever designed the shop sure had leaned into the theme, and when she got in line for checkout, she worried that "buying" the supplies would've required more negotiation and possibly an alternative currency, or worse, a sacrifice. Luckily, capitalism had won over immersion that afternoon.

She just needed one poster board and three markers. With the blue marker, she sketched a drinking glass. With the yellow marker, she scribbled in the representative shading for lemonade. With the black, she wrote out a call-to-action: "Come to Park Center Park to enjoy my lemonade." Once she capped the markers, she brought the sign to the nearest crosswalk and stood there for two hours, flashing the message and absorbing the various honks. She suffered the heat for her art, but when she saw that the Liquid Shack's closing time was drawing near, she rolled up the sign and headed back. Once she regained admittance, she found Chet at the cash box saying "*ka-ching*" repeatedly.

As soon as he looked up, he beckoned her over and squeezed her cheeks between his palms.

"Don't know what you did out there," he said, beaming, "but it was worth every penny."

"Yeah? How did we do?"

He exchanged glances first with Tommy Slick, who was standing against the canopy's metal leg with his arms folded and hat tilted toward his nose, no more excited than when Princess Diana had announced she was having a boy, and then with Pigeon Polluck, whose tongue was hanging out, panting for lemonade, but eyeing the cash box, probably lusting for all the donuts, toys, car parts, or whatever dumb thing he cared about that he could buy with that kind of money.

"We moved over a hundred units tonight," Chet said.

Jennifer felt her chest rising. It sounded as if her marketing efforts had worked.

"How much better was that compared to usual?"

Chet glanced at Tommy. Tommy brushed his fingertips along his temple.

"Off the top of my head," Tommy said, "I'd say five times."

Jennifer's eyes widened. "Seriously?"

Chet kissed her on the forehead.

"Marketing," he said. "Best suggestion ever. After all this time, Dad was actually right! Come, help us pack everything up. We're going out to celebrate our victory."

She broke from his grip.

"Will this celebration cost money?"

Chet shrugged. "Yeah, probably a little. Doesn't matter. We earned it! Well, Pigeon earned most of it."

"Shouldn't we bank the money? To, you know, win the bet?"

"We could, sure. But we're still gonna win the bet because, now that we have a master marketer in our corner, there's no way that twerp has a shot at beating us."

Jennifer considered Chet's statement. She knew Buck better than these goons did—well, better than Chet and Tommy and that one goon—and she believed he was a smart kid who could navigate this field of business if given the will. But she also knew that he was hopeless without support, and she had been his best support until now. Without her in Buck's corner, Chet was probably right to gloat this time. Even so, she wasn't sure, and she thought Chet should play a bit more cautiously.

"Well, let's not spend too much, at least. Deal?"

"Sure thing, babe."

She felt relief swelling through her chest.

"Great, so where are we going?"

Chet winked. "It's a surprise. But let's just say, 'Best Place Ever.' Pigeon's suggestion."

"Best place ever!" Pigeon crooned. "Best place ever!"

Jennifer shrank back. Any place that Pigeon thought was the "best place ever" was probably the worst.

"Do I need to bring my own car?" she asked. "In case I don't want to stay?"

"Only if you don't want to celebrate with us," Chet said. "But today's a great day. You should celebrate."

Jennifer felt that twinge of doubt in her gut, but she'd learned through a popular song that she should always stand by her man, no matter the doubt, and Chet was her man. So, once everything but the canopy was packed and loaded onto Tommy's truck, she got into Chet's car, Pigeon got into Tommy's, and they headed to this "surprise" celebration spot that "Pigeon suggested."

Jennifer frowned the moment she got out of the car and noticed where they were. Of course this was Pigeon's suggestion. Of course! She demanded Chet take her home immediately. Chet told her to lighten up, but she wouldn't have it. Chet said that Pigeon was the top earner, so this was where they would celebrate, and if she didn't like it, she could hitch a ride home with someone else. Tommy, who didn't care either way because he was ultimately responsible for the shop's tables and iceboxes, which were all sitting in his truck's bed ripe for swiping, said he'd take her home, and Chet and Pigeon could celebrate in his place. The suggestion annoyed Chet at first—he wanted both of his employees there with him—but in the end, he relented. As long as *he* got to celebrate his victory, he didn't care if everyone else stayed or left. Besides, he said, Tommy was probably right. They shouldn't leave their entire business exposed in a parking lot if they weren't watching it. Responsibility above team unity.

"So, it's settled then," Jennifer said, as she headed for Tommy's truck. "I guess it's goodnight then."

Chet waved her off and walked toward the building with Pigeon in tow. Tommy, meanwhile, checked that everything in the truck's bed was still secured, then got in and fired up the engine. Jennifer stood by the passenger door, waiting to see if Chet would look back. He didn't. He just walked right in, carrying all the day's earnings in with him.

She huffed, then got into the truck and put on her seatbelt. Tommy backed out before she could hear the *click*.

"Don't let it bother you," he said when they headed out of the parking lot. "Chet will be responsible. Pigeon's the one you gotta worry about."

When Tommy dropped her off at home, she thanked him and asked if he needed water for the road.

"I don't live far from here," he said. "I'll be fine."

She thanked him again, then went inside.

By ten o'clock, she was in her pajamas, ready for bed, but not yet ready to sleep. She'd learned a lot about marketing that day. It took nothing fancy. She didn't need a billboard or a television commercial. She'd quintupled the Liquid Shack's income with one cheap sheet of poster board and three generic fat-tipped markers. And she'd learned that speaking up could do wonders for anyone willing to listen.

But as she sat on her bed, contemplating whether to read the next chapter of her paperback romance or think about more ways to maximize the Liquid Shack's customer base, an empty feeling stirred in her. She had a soul, but she couldn't sense it. She had dreams, but she couldn't grasp them. Something was vacant, and as she worried about making the wrong commitment of time tonight, she couldn't help but know what was bothering her. Watching Chet walking away to celebrate his earnings, with all his earnings, got her asking a new question that none of her female protagonists in those supermarket paperbacks ever had to ask.

Was this new lifestyle really what she wanted?

She decided she wouldn't read anything tonight. Instead, she would write something.

Jennifer got off the bed and opened her desk drawer. There was a notebook inside that she seldom used. She flipped to the next empty page, found a pen wedged in the back of the drawer, and started writing whatever came to mind. It began with two words:

Dear Buck,

* * *

By 2:00 a.m., Chet and Pigeon stumbled out of Piggy's Palace, drunk not on liquid but entertainment. Sure, the saloon-style restaurant had a menu full of meat products, with its specialty of bacon-everything and appetizers full of cheese, but those dancers were something else. Pigeon had made the best choice ever. Best place ever! Between the movie at Hybrid Silver Screen, the free cookies from Pound Cake, making almost fifty dollars at work, and capping the night with the kind of entertainment he could get only when his dad babysat, Chet could hardly believe what kind of day he'd had. And it was only Monday.

As they shuffled toward Chet's car, having little trouble locating it thanks to most of the parking lot being empty, Chet put his hand on Pigeon's shoulder and congratulated him once again for a job well done. Even though Tommy had pulled in a fair number of sales, Pigeon had outsold him by nearly 20 percent, and with his contribution taking in 65 percent of their total income (Chet had raked in 15 percent himself), earned the night's suggested celebration fair and square.

"You've done me proud today, Pigeon," Chet said. "Hope you can duplicate that tomorrow."

Pigeon grinned. "Make me your right-hand man, and you got a deal."

Chet dragged them to a stop. He turned Pigeon to face him.

"You know Tommy's already my right-hand man. He's the one with the truck. Get a truck and I might consider it."

Pigeon's grin flipped.

"You know I don't have that kind of money."

Chet nodded.

"Yes, but keep up this winning streak, and when this bet's over, you'll have plenty of earning potential."

Even as the words came out of his mouth, Chet remembered he wasn't paying Pigeon anything. Part of the collateral for the secret he kept for Pigeon's benefit, and for his own. Judging by the split-second baring of teeth he caught in Pigeon's mouth, it seemed that Pigeon remembered that detail, too.

"Maybe I'll start letting you earn. That would be nice, right?"

Pigeon's face softened. "Yeah. Be real nice."

Chet clapped him on the shoulder and continued toward the car.

"Great. Then we'll talk about that in August. We'll assess your total earnings at the end."

"Fantastic." Pigeon's voice had no enthusiasm, and Chet didn't expect any from him. That secret and the fact that Chet knew it was probably the only things keeping those teeth out of his skin.

They got to the car, and Chet unlocked the door for his subordinate. As Pigeon climbed in, he said something that would undoubtedly cause Chet to lose sleep tonight, and the moment that he heard it, Chet wanted to retract everything he'd just said. But he couldn't unhear it, and it was too late to change the words that Pigeon had heard for himself regarding his future.

Pigeon asked, "You sure it was a good idea letting Tommy, a handsome cowboy like him, take Jennifer home alone when he's had a mad crush on her since tenth grade?"

Chet stared at him. No words. No response. Just a series of silent questions. Was Pigeon saying this to angle for Tommy's spot? Or was it true?

He stared at the steering wheel.

Come to think of it, Tommy *had* always been extra nice to Jennifer whenever she'd been in the room. And he *had* opened the door for her whenever she entered anywhere. Chet always assumed it was just part of being cowboy-adjacent. But what if it wasn't about that at all?

Chet fired up the ignition. The night was now over. Now it was time to account for his day's numbers, including the twenty-five cents he'd spent on ice, that fifteen dollars he'd spent on food, the ten dollars he'd spent tipping the dancers, the two dollars Pigeon had spent on fries, and whatever Pigeon had spent on tips for the dancers. He could worry about Jennifer later.

Chet's End of Day Report:

Earned: $49.34

Spent: $327.23

Net Gain: -$277.89

Episode 8

The Professional Amateur

DAY 2: TUESDAY, JUNE 11, 1985

Buck's Savings Account: $26
Buck's Wallet: $84.51
Buck's Business Funds: unknown
Buck's Expenses: not established
Hours of Operation: not established

BUCK AWOKE THE NEXT morning ready to test his education. Even before he put on a shirt, he reviewed his notes, checked his accounts, and memorized Kabuki's eleven rules. The common thread that bound his information together was "professionalism." If he was to make the most of business and, by proxy, stand the best chance at defeating Chet this summer, then he had to start with mindset. That meant buying the perfect tie. It was a lesson that Kabuki had not yet taught him, but one he'd picked up through observation of every successful man he'd met. Professionals dressed professionally. They looked professional. Acted professional. Portrayed professionalism by being professional. If Buck wanted to win, he'd have to become professional. And that meant wearing a tie.

So, after breakfast and a shower, he hopped on Ronnie's bike and pedaled over to Tailor Made, Hybrid West's premier clothing shop and the place where boys became men. It sat between Pound Cake and that weird office supplies store with the torches on its façade and the strange screams coming from inside, so it was no short ride, and by the time he'd got there, he was sweating. But the shop boasted the highest quality threads within fifty miles, so he didn't disparage the journey. If he could afford it, he would be satisfied.

Fortunately, the shop opened early, so he got in before the rush of wealthy traffic gobbled up his opportunity. And because the floor space was boutique, not department store-sized, it took him no time to find the tie section along the back wall.

He grinned at what he saw. A series of eligible ties lined the shelf marked "50% Off," and any of them could've elevated his game. But the winner, a perfect baby blue silk tie, sat in the middle. A golden clip kept it neat and folded tight. He imagined what it might look like around his neck and smiled. For just thirty-five dollars, it was a no-brainer.

"If you buy a pair of socks with it," Handsome Ted, the shop's owner, said, "you'll be eligible for discounted repairs should your clothing start to show its threading."

So, Buck bought a pair of blue silk socks to go with his blue silk tie. All for just forty-five dollars plus tax.

Excited to join the professional class, Buck went next door to celebrate. He bought one chocolate chip cookie and one peanut butter. While she scooped the cookies out from under the glass counter, Irina Swift asked why he was so happy this morning. Buck showed her the tie.

"Ooh, classy," she said. "What's the occasion?"

"Starting my own business."

Her face lit up as she pushed the cookies into a paper bag.

"That's exciting." Then her face turned serious. "And a bit risky. So, does that mean you've given up on karate?"

Buck told her about his bet with Chet and his new training with Kabuki. She nodded at his every word.

"I see. So, this business adventure is more about revenge?"

Buck wasn't sure he saw it that way, but he couldn't deny his reasons were rooted in vengeance. No matter how he might explain it, Chet's humiliation was the endgame. Earning a stable income was just a side effect, if he were being honest.

"I suppose that's one way to look at it."

"So, your new tie is less about professionalism and more about an accessory to your avenger costume?"

"I—I guess." Buck hadn't really considered the difference until now. He'd figured a tie is a tie, and wearing one made the wearer professional, regardless of his trade. But now he wasn't so sure. "Do you think that's wrong?"

Irina shrugged. "I guess that depends on your conscience. If you just want to humiliate a kid and go back to being a kid yourself once the job is done, then so be it. Hopefully, no one will miss your products when your business no longer serves your purpose. As long as you have someplace to hang your tie at the end of the day, then your money isn't wasted. But if your goal is to become a professional *businessman*, then I'd redirect your thinking to what makes you professional for your business in the long-term, and not a pretender who's only using business to oust a rival." She tapped out the cost of the cookies on her register. "But that's just me. You can do whatever you want, sugar bun. That'll be fifty-three cents."

Buck passed along the change and took the bag from Irina. Even as she passed his purchase over, her smile was warm and friendly. Not an ounce of judgment on her face, even if her words hinted at it.

"Thank you," he said, unsure whether he meant for the cookies or for the advice.

"Of course. And be careful."

Buck didn't understand what she'd meant by that, so he ignored it and left for home to eat his cookies. But as he rode through the streets of Hybrid City, getting sweatier with each passing minute, he thought about Irina's point of view. If he started a business strictly to punish Chet, then he was limited to two outcomes, win or lose, and neither outcome would matter much once the bet was over. The only difference was whether Buck would have to become Chet's whipping boy at the professional level. Obviously, he didn't want that, so he had to win.

But then what? Would he close the business? That was probably the smart move since he had designs on going to college in the fall, and how could he possibly run a business *and* go to college? Had it ever been done? He didn't know.

But what if he were to keep it open? What if he ran the business *instead* of going to college?

Awareness of his surroundings returned, and he narrowly missed a fire hydrant as he swerved to avoid it. Thinking about this right now was dangerous to his health. He'd have to revisit it another time. If it was even worth revisiting. After all, beating Chet was the most important part of this business *right now*. That much he knew. And if he wanted to drag Chet's face through the mud, he'd have to be professional about it.

Maybe he didn't know how to answer Irina's question in a way that would satisfy her judgment, but he knew that he'd made the right choice getting that tie. It made him look so cool and ready to fight, and until the bet was over, he had to fight like a businessman.

* * *

ONCE HE GOT HOME, Buck took another shower, tried on his new socks and tie, and smiled at what he saw. In the mirror was the most professional-looking eighteen-year-old he'd ever seen. Excited to show off his white-collar manliness (even if his shirt was blue), he hopped back on Ronnie's bike and pedaled over to The Whipping Shed, where he found Mr. Kabuki trimming some potted trees in his office.

"Look." Buck self-displayed his new suit. "What do you think?"

Kabuki looked him up and down, making weird guttural noises as he took in the sight. At the end of his scrutiny, he nodded.

"Boy look ready for prom. Good luck."

Buck tugged on his tie, then nudged it forward to offer Kabuki a better view.

"No, it's for business."

Kabuki looked up from his potted tree once again and cocked his head as he reexamined the tie. Again, he nodded.

"Nice tie."

Buck grinned. "You like it?"

"*Hai.* Boy work upscale business?"

"Huh?"

"Where boy get job? TV store?"

Buck wasn't sure if this was part of his training or if Kabuki had already forgotten about yesterday. Even though the dojo master was old, he wasn't quite that old.

"What are you talking about? You're teaching me how to sell coffee. Remember?"

"*Hai*. Not used car?"

"Coffee. We spent all afternoon together." Buck approached Kabuki's desk and leaned closer so the middle-aged man could see him clearly, in case he was going blind or senile. "You showed me how to make coffee. Then you, er, took me shopping. Then we sold what we got. Have you forgotten already?"

Buck must've let his language heat up as he reminded him of their training because Mr. Kabuki stepped away from the tree and raised the palms of his hands.

"Calm down. Kabuki remember. Worry boy take job too serious. Why need tie to sell coffee?"

"Um, because it's professional."

Kabuki nodded while he cleared his throat or said, "Mmm hmm."

"Lesson twelve, dress for success, even when success require no dress."

Buck wrinkled his nose. It sounded like Kabuki was telling him not to wear a dress, which Buck would never do anyway, but given the karate master's cryptic way of delivering lessons, he wondered if it was simpler than that.

"I don't—"

He paused to think. The *sensei* wasn't telling him not to put on a dress. That would've been absurd, and obvious. No, the lesson was something else. This was part of the training. Whatever Kabuki was telling him, Buck would have to remember it.

After a short deciphering session ran through his mind, he dared to ask Kabuki for clarification.

"Do you mean I shouldn't put on a tie for selling coffee?" he asked.

"*Hai*. Fancy tie, to sell fancy coffee, at fancy café, only good for fancy customers. Boy serve coffee at park where dog pee in grass."

Buck grimaced at the thought.

"So, no tie?"

"Unless boy want customers feel small."

"No, I guess I don't."

"Tie better when boy open fancy shop."

Buck considered the master's lesson. Regardless of what he thought—and what he thought was that a suit and tie *always* elevated the conversation—he wasn't the business trainer, and until he had more experience, Buck had to assume the trainer knew more than he did. Even if it made no sense.

In Buck's mind, wearing a suit while delivering coffee meant getting looks of approval from not only customers, but wealthy customers, the kind of people who would not only come back for more, but come back for more *that day*. His dad used to tell him that a suit builds trust, and a tie builds credibility. At the time, Buck didn't get the point because he was still in class and didn't want to get toilet water on his nice shirt come Tuesday. But now he got it. A suit and tie commanded authority, and what better example of authority than proving to his customers that he *deserved* to sell them coffee?

But Kabuki had made a sensible point. He would not offer coffee to rich customers because rich customers would never buy their coffee at a park. To think otherwise was insanity.

And pointing that out was why Kabuki was the master.

"Well, I'm just setting up today," Buck said, "so I can wear something more casual tomorrow."

"If boy like sweating around neck, then boy keep tie on in hot park. Kabuki no judge."

Buck shook his head. He didn't like sweating around anything. He took the tie off and rolled it into his pocket. His neck could breathe easier now. Kabuki gave him a single nod.

"Smart move," he said.

Buck waited for Kabuki to give him more advice, but the older man returned to his potted tree and snipped at a branch with a small pair of scissors. When Buck asked him what he should do next, Kabuki shrugged.

"Go open shop. What else boy supposed to do?"

"Any chance you might guide me?"

Kabuki snipped off a twig and set it in a growing pile beside his elbow.

"Boy know where to set up?"

"I think the Lease Agent said North Park Pavilion. Right?"

"*Hai*. Start there."

Buck thought through his list of questions. He didn't want to mess anything up.

"How many coffee machines do I need?"

"How many boy have?"

"Er, besides the one my mom uses every morning? Um, none."

Kabuki snipped another branch.

"Donald-*san* need at least one. Simple math."

Buck pressed his lips together and let out a raspberry. For all the help that the karate master had given him yesterday, he didn't seem interested in helping him at all today. Perhaps he was on his own now.

"Okay, thanks. I'll leave you to your trees."

"Come back anytime, Donald-*san*."

"Thanks. And it's Buck. Buck Star."

"Not your fault, Donald-*san*."

Buck shuffled out of there, trying to figure out where to go next. The only thought that came to him as he stepped out onto the sun-drenched street was the obvious one. He'd have to buy a coffeemaker.

Even though it was a quick sprint westward, he hopped on his bike and rode over to Shop Down the Street, saving about three minutes of walking time. Once he got off, he opened the door and pushed the bike inside. Usually, the area businesses preferred customers leave their vehicles outside, but Buck always felt more secure bringing it in, and so far, no one had told him not to. The proprietor, Mack Green, nodded at him as he entered. He said nothing about the bike, so Buck assumed it was okay. He parked it by the door. Safer inside, but more convenient out of the way. That was how he liked to operate.

"Ready for business?" Mack asked as Buck headed toward the food aisles.

"Yeah, just gotta get my supplies."

"Yeah? Supplies for what?"

Buck stopped short of the cereal aisle.

"Um, for my business?"

Mack expressed confusion on his face.

"You don't have to buy supplies to work here. Just gotta show up."

Buck squeezed his eyes shut as he recognized Mack's language now. He'd already forgotten he was supposed to work here on Saturday.

"Oh, yeah. I meant my *other* business."

"Other business? Doing what?"

"Er, selling coffee?"

Mack held Buck's gaze for a few seconds as the information reached his brain. Then came the classic flash of realization that Buck must've had himself a moment earlier.

"Right, Kabuki's teaching you how to run a business. I'd nearly forgotten."

Buck smiled. So, he wasn't the only one with a preoccupied brain around here.

"I need coffee products," Buck said.

Mack pointed at the coffee section.

"Let me know if you need assistance."

Buck went to the coffee section to explore the same items he'd looked at yesterday. The moment his eyes locked with the price tag for the cheapest coffeemaker, however, he realized he hadn't planned his expenses well.

The cheapest machine cost fifty dollars. He had barely thirty dollars left after visiting Tailor Made.

"I think I may have bitten off more than I can chew," Buck said when he approached the counter. "Any chance I can purchase a coffee machine on credit?"

"You have a credit card?"

"Er, no."

Mack's face turned grim.

"As much as I'd like to open a store line with you, I don't yet have the proof you'll pay me back."

"Well, I'm coming in Saturday, right? I could work it off."

"Yes, normally I'd agree to that. But you'd have to show up first. If you still need it come Saturday, then we can have this discussion again."

Buck glanced at the coffee section. The offer was tempting, as he would need the coffeemaker if he had any hope of winning this bet and divorcing himself from Chet's wrath forever after. But he couldn't wait until Saturday to buy it. The Lease Agent was coming to evaluate his eligibility tomorrow morning. If he didn't have his workspace set up by then, he'd lose the opportunity. He glanced at Mack and offered him a nervous smile.

"I'll come up with a different plan. Thanks."

"Sorry. I hope you're still coming in Saturday."

Buck nodded. At any rate, he wasn't done shopping, so he returned to the coffee shelf for supplies. Even if he couldn't afford the coffee machine, he could still afford a bag of Store Powder, a box of filters, and a bag of paper cups, so his venture wasn't completely hopeless. Combined, the starter coffee package would cost him just over six dollars.

Once he rang him up, Mack pushed everything into a paper bag and thanked him for shopping.

"See you Saturday," Mack said. "And be careful."

"See you Saturday," Buck said. But he didn't understand the part about being careful, so he just nodded and wished Mack a good rest of the day. Maybe it was the new thing shopkeepers said to their customers before they left. Irina Swift had said it, too.

Buck grabbed his bike, set his shopping bag on the handlebars, and pushed out onto the sidewalk. The sun was bright, but his prospects were dim. The only coffeemaker he had any access to was the one his mom would certainly harangue him over if he took it out of the house for any reason. Now he was out of ideas.

Well, almost out of ideas.

* * *

Buck was examining the coffeepot in The Whipping Shed's break room when Mr. Kabuki came in with his pair of scissors and a plastic bag full of twigs and nettles. The sensei set his items on the counter and reached for a coffee mug.

"Ah, boy just in time to make Kabuki cup of coffee. Want cream, sugar, and dash of cinnamon."

"Yeah, about that. I've run low on money. Would you mind if I borrowed this for the park?"

Kabuki gave him a blank stare, blinking a couple of times. Buck pushed the machine toward the wall.

"Never mind."

"How boy run out of money?"

Buck reminded him about the tie and the socks. Kabuki nodded as he made his guttural agreement sounds.

"Lesson thirteen. Budget."

"I thought looking professional was as important as being professional."

"Where boy learn that?"

"I don't know. TV?"

"Make sense. But bad advice. First, buy items that make money. Then buy items that improve money. Lesson fourteen."

"How do you even keep track of your lesson numbers?"

Kabuki tapped his forehead. Buck nodded as he muttered, "Of course." He wished he could make up rules on the fly and remember their numbering system as if they had always been written in that order. Perhaps with experience he could. It was enough for him to question whether the master had any branded lessons at all.

"So, what should I do? I can't afford to buy a new coffeepot."

Kabuki patted Buck's shoulder.

"May have idea. Be right back."

Kabuki walked out into the hallway and turned left toward the private bathroom. Buck took a seat at the table as he waited. When several minutes passed without the karate master's return, Buck checked the refrigerator for a snack. It was stocked with meat, cheeses, vegetables, and beverages from top to bottom. He wondered how much Kabuki ate because it seemed like it would take two or three men to clean it out in time before anything spoiled. Probably snacks for his other students.

And if the extras were for students, then Buck didn't think swiping a slice of roast beef and cheese would get noticed, nor did he think spreading some mayonnaise across two slices of bread would get noticed.

Buck was just wiping his mouth and throwing away his paper towel when Kabuki returned with a curious object in hand. The *sensei* set the dark, skinny tower on the table.

"This might help," Kabuki said.

Buck looked it over. It had a switch, a basin, and a shallow well with a grill spanning it, but he didn't know what he was looking at.

"What is it?" he asked.

"Coffeemaker."

Buck raised his eyebrows.

"This thing? It's so narrow. Where's the carafe?"

"No carafe. Cup."

"Cup?" It suddenly dawned on him. He nearly pushed it away out of reflex. "You mean it only makes one cup at a time?"

"*Hai.*"

Buck examined it again.

"How long does it take to brew?"

"Same as other coffeemaker."

Buck thought about Kabuki's answer. It sounded suspiciously inconvenient.

"So, I'd have to brew each cup individually?"

"*Hai.*"

Buck wasn't sure what to make of that. He opened the reservoir. Sure enough, there was enough space for water to fill only a single cup.

"What if I get busy?"

"Then people wait awhile."

Buck shook his head.

"I can't brew one cup at a time. If I hate lines, then so will my customers."

Kabuki shrugged. "How many customers boy expect on first day?"

Buck didn't know the answer, but he was hoping for more than one.

"I just need something faster or better. You sure I can't borrow that coffeemaker there?" He pointed at the one on the counter. The one with the carafe.

"Kabuki like that coffeemaker. Make more than one cup."

Buck groaned under his breath.

"What about the one in the dojo?"

"There for training, not for using."

Buck stifled a scream in his throat.

"Please?"

Kabuki patted him on the shoulder.

"If boy don't like one-cup coffeemaker, then Kabuki have another solution."

Buck sighed. "What?"

Kabuki removed a canister from the overhead cabinet. He set it in front of Buck.

"Sanka," he said. "Instant coffee."

In other words, coffee that he stirred into a cup full of hot water.

"Low quality, but faster than one-cup brew," Kabuki said.

Buck was done with this conversation. He decided he'd take his chances with the single-cup coffeemaker.

* * *

RIDING ALL THE WAY up to North Park with a stuffed paper bag on his handlebars was no easy feat, but Buck reached the entrance without crashing or dumping everything. Fortunately, he didn't have to haggle with any gate attendants to get in. Because it was a public park for all to enjoy, he just had to keep to the sidewalks that wound through a series of tiny ponds and keep to the course that brought him to the pavilion. No money exchange necessary.

Finding the pavilion was a different matter entirely, though, and he worried that its obscurity near the back of the park would make discovery problematic. However, when he found it past the park's central lake, atop a shallow hill and nestled in a pocket of dense woods, he sensed his worry slip away. The pavilion was not only discoverable, but a large group of people were already having a party there.

And then the dread set in. It dawned on him that the pavilion wasn't exclusive to him, and to get access as a point of sale would take additional negotiation, if not with the Lease Agent, then with the people who thought they had the right to use it today.

He didn't understand the rules or policies for using a public park's structures for his own reasons, but he thought permission was needed, and now he wasn't sure he had it.

When he rode up to the pavilion and sought the man in charge, he asked, point blank, whether they had permission to use it. The man, a mousy guy with a thin mustache and fancy black tie, simply cackled at the idea.

"Who needs permission to use a public space?" he asked.

Buck raised his hand.

"I kinda thought I did. When I was granted this space by the Lease Agent yesterday." Buck shrugged. "But maybe you know something I don't?"

The man shirked.

"The Lease Agent? You spoke to him? About this here pavilion?"

"Yeah, he said I could have it for my coffee business. I wanted to set up today to prepare for his visit tomorrow."

The man pivoted toward the back of the pavilion, where the storage rooms were located. He gestured to the counter overlooking the covered picnic area. Piles of party gear were stacked on most surfaces. Dozens of adults and children were sitting at the tables. The banner over the serving counter said, *Happy 7th Birthday, Samantha.*

"I mean, if you can find the space, be my guest. But we can't exactly uproot the party, you know?"

Buck nodded. He saw the dilemma clearly. Then he saw an opportunity.

"Would you all like to be my first customers? For free, of course."

The man's mustache twitched as his eyes lit up. Suddenly, his hand wrapped around Buck's shoulders as his other gestured toward a small space near the end of the counter.

"My friend," he said. "I would never turn down a free cup of coffee. Yes, please, let us become your first customers. And welcome to our party."

Buck felt his chest lighten. Perhaps his misfortune was actually fortunate. He could already hear Kabuki muttering the fifteenth lesson in his ear: "When opportunity strike, hit opportunity with sale." Or something like that.

"I'll have it ready for service shortly."

Buck parked his bike beside the serving counter and looked for an outlet near the far end where there was still space. When he couldn't find one, however, he scanned the wall for any available outlets. He found a bank of them near the middle where party supplies and gifts monopolized the counter's surface.

He shoved a few birthday presents aside to make room for the single-cup coffeemaker, catching a toppling box in She-Ra wrapping paper with his foot. His stomach lurched as he realized he'd punctured a small hole in the wrapping, exposing a plastic blinking eye, or an eye he hoped was plastic.

Maybe it came gradually, or maybe it was sudden, but Buck realized in that moment that no one was speaking. All the party chatter he'd heard as he rode up to the pavilion had all but faded. He looked over his shoulder as he put the slightly torn gift on a small pile. Dozens of party attendants were staring at him. No one was speaking.

The mustached man, meanwhile, was ushering him to keep setting up. If there was ever a market for coffee, then this group was the target audience. Several adults licked their lips as they watched him plug in the machine. One woman clapped when the power light came on.

Buck felt his stomach tighten. He'd expected his first test to come with serving the Lease Agent, but he'd serve real people with real return or rejection potential instead. He didn't know which way this would go. Today was all about testing the equipment. He had no plans to serve coffee today.

Nevertheless, duty was calling, and he couldn't blow it now.

Buck nodded as he reached into his pocket. He figured he might as well look professional when he exposed his true level of knowledge. It was time to once again don the tie.

"Get on with it," someone shouted.

Startled, he shoved the tie back in his pocket. Perhaps Kabuki was right. No one cared a lick about how he looked. Maybe he'd dare wear it another day.

Buck opened the top of the basket and inserted a filter. It was designed for a larger pot, so he had to squeeze it in to fit. When he opened the bag of Store Powder, he found no scoop. He frowned at his misfortune. Kabuki's coffee canister had a scoop. Without it, he'd have to pour the powder in directly from the bag, and he didn't know how much was too much or not enough. So, he guessed as he poured. He didn't know the first thing about measuring with his eye, but he thought he'd used a couple of tablespoons' worth of grains. If he were guessing.

Then came his horror. When he reached inside the bag for his next item, he realized he was lacking a critical ingredient: bottled water!

He glanced back at the people with a sheepish grin. They were all so expectant.

"Just one more moment," he said.

He pulled open the plastic bag containing the paper cups and removed one from the stack. Then he headed around the back of the pavilion and entered the men's restroom. Because he couldn't let the people see him using a water fountain, he filled the cup with water from the sink. Fortunately, no one was in there.

When he returned to the coffee machine a moment later, with no suspicion aroused, he poured the water into the reservoir, pretending everything was going as planned. Just enough water to refill the same cup. Maybe it wasn't bottled or filtered, but it was water. Once brewed, no one would detect the difference. He hit the button to start the machine. Then he set the cup under the spout.

Three minutes later, the cup filled with brown liquid. Perfection! Once it finished, Buck had confidence that he could serve his first customer. He gestured at the mustached man.

"Cup's ready," he said.

Buck pulled the cup from the tray and nearly dropped it; it was so hot. He immediately set it on the counter and pointed at it. The man skipped across the concrete floor to claim his prize. Then, just as quickly as he'd snatched the cup from the counter, he tipped it into his mouth. Didn't even wait for it to cool.

And that was all Buck needed to know about his sales potential.

The man's reaction was also all he needed to know about his chance of success.

The man gagged and spat the coffee all over the floor.

"What is this swill?"

As Buck gathered his equipment and returned it to the paper bag, he thought about the ways he might improve his product before the Lease Agent's visit tomorrow. Whatever his decision, one thing was clear. It needed to produce results far better than "this swill."

B Y FIVE O'CLOCK THAT afternoon, Buck had analyzed his business strategy and figured out his mistake at the park. As it turned out, the problem wasn't with the customer, as he'd first assumed, or even with the coffee. His brewing style was neither unusual nor flawed. In fact, everything he'd done at Samantha's 7th birthday party was both appropriate and necessary.

No, the flaw was inherent in the tactics he *hadn't* employed.

As he sat on the beach, listening to the waves crashing ashore and the laughter of bikini-clad college women enjoying summer break as their boyfriends played with their hair, Buck considered why he'd come there to think. Aesthetics.

What was the beach but just a strip of coarse sand alongside the turbulent edge of an angry ocean? *Pacific, my eye!* No one ever came here for the water, despite the advertisements posted in the frosty windows at Surf Legends Boutique. The only sandcastles getting built were the ones Hybrid City Council members commissioned for special events.

No, the beach was a destination for beauty. Not nature's beauty, as the environmentalists often touted downtown every third week in April. But blonde beauty, along with the occasional brunette and redheaded beauty. Sure, the beach in its natural form was fine. Sand here, the occasional bank of rocks there, and the haphazard scattering of palms up in the grassy areas separating the sand from the street. Combined with a daily sunset, the beach was certainly an attractive place without human input. But add in those gorgeous ladies in their tiny bikinis, and the beach became a *destination*, not just a "destination."

Buck failed at Samantha's 7th birthday party because he'd brought only the coffee. If he'd come with cookies, or cream, or cookies *and* cream, he'd have made a much stronger impression. So, if he wanted to impress the Lease Agent tomorrow and get his pavilion space approved, he needed to bring the cookies. And the cream. And, well, the coffee, too. After all, the beach was fine without the women, and the women were sweet without the beach, but bringing both together was a recipe for magic, and Buck needed access to magic tomorrow if he expected to win his freedom from Chet.

* * *

BY JUST AFTER SIX o'clock, Buck knocked on Ronnie's door, and Ronnie's dad answered. When he saw Mr. Michaels wearing pants, Buck assumed the worst.

"That girl here again?" he asked.

Mr. Michaels nodded. But when he stepped aside to allow Buck in anyway, Buck was surprised to find Ronnie in the living room watching television. Alone.

"Hey, Buckaroo!"

Buck headed for the sofa, and Mr. Michaels returned to his recliner. They were watching the news.

"Where's Tiffany?" Buck asked.

"Bedroom," Ronnie said. "Reading a book or something lame. I don't even know."

"How come you're not hanging with her?"

Ronnie scoffed. "I'm not gonna read a book. In the summer? That's crazy."

"I mean, she's your girlfriend, right?"

"Yeah, that's what I'm calling her."

Mr. Michaels shifted in his seat slightly, but he had nothing to add. Just sat there watching the news anchor talk about some festival that was happening further south. Buck's dad had never had any conversations with him about how to keep a woman interested, just how he was better off without them. So, Buck was curious if Mr. Michaels had a different opinion. But given the moment, Ronnie's dad seemed happier staying out of it.

"How's that bet of yours?" Ronnie asked. "You still haven't told me about it."

Buck opened the bag he was carrying and showed him the coffee machine. Mr. Michaels lit up at the sight of it.

"You come to make us coffee, Buck? You want to use the kitchen? Brandy! Can you get Buck some coffee mugs? He's gonna make us all coffee!"

Buck felt his entire butt sink into the couch as he put the machine on the floor. He hadn't even gotten to the Store Powder when the requests started flying at him.

But this wasn't a bad thing. Even as he reached for the filters, he understood that Mr. Michaels was offering Buck the chance to refine his art, to make sure he could practice the lesson he had learned on the beach.

"Do you have cream?" Buck asked. "Because I don't."

Mr. Michaels got out of the chair and gestured Buck toward the kitchen.

"Mrs. Michaels will set you up with anything you need, pal."

"Dad!" Ronnie said. "Don't ask Buck to make you coffee. Come on!"

Buck halted Ronnie with the palms of his hands. "No, it's cool. This is actually perfect. Here, come to the kitchen with me while I make this, and I'll tell you about the weird day I had yesterday."

So, Buck brought everything into the kitchen, and Ronnie followed. Mrs. Michaels, an attractive woman who dressed ten years older than her actual age, helped Buck clear a space for the coffee machine. He put it beside the one they already owned.

While he set up his brew station, he told Ronnie about the bet, beginning with the moment he'd left Pound Cake with the cookies. Ronnie rested his elbow on the counter as he listened, captivated by every word. By the time Buck finished explaining his story, all three members of the Michaels clan had a steaming cup of creamy, sugary coffee in hand, and all three were more interested in his tale than whatever was happening at some festival down south.

"You know what you need?" Mr. Michaels asked as he took his third sip and smiled. "A contract."

"What now?" Buck knew what a contract was, but he didn't understand why Mr. Michaels would bring it up.

"A binding agreement. You conduct a bet with a kid like Chet Armstrong, and you better have the terms in writing. Otherwise, he might—" Mr. Michaels punched his fist forward while making a jerking sound. "You know?"

Buck frowned as he considered what Mr. Michaels was saying. A binding agreement. The kind of thing two parties signed if they wanted to lock into a plan with a consequence attached if one party broke the contract against the other.

"You don't think a handshake is good enough?"

Mr. Michaels shook his head.

"I deal with lowlifes and losers every day, Buck, and most of them are taken to court because they've cheated an even bigger loser. You want to know what happens to my clients when they're taken to court?"

Buck nodded.

"Nothing," Mr. Michaels said. "They go home and don't pay a cent. Why? Because they make deals with wannabe partners on a handshake they have no intention of honoring. Becomes one word against another. Even if my clients are human trash—sorry, I mean, less than upstanding, didn't mean to insult your father like that—they still win these civil cases because the bigger dumbass they made an agreement with didn't sign anything."

Mr. Michaels leaned forward, his coffee cup held suspended over his knees. The steam was billowing up to his jaw.

"Without a written contract, there is no bet."

Buck's frown melted. This sounded like good news.

"You mean I don't have to work for Chet now?"

Mr. Michaels thought about it, then rolled his eyes.

"You *could* look at it that way, yes. But if Chet is physically harassing you, then I don't think reneging on the bet will absolve you from whatever's coming if you don't win, contract or no contract.

No, what I'm saying is that you need a contract to cement the terms of the bet. Meaning, if you're basing your win on *earnings*, not savings, then you just have to outsell Chet to win the bet. Otherwise, pompous rich kid will destroy you on the principle of having a larger bank account by default."

Now Buck understood what Mr. Michaels was saying. According to the present agreement, there was nothing stopping Chet from cheating him. With a contract, Buck could force him to play fair.

"Okay, I get it. So, how do I put this contract together?"

Mr. Michaels circled the living room with his index finger pointed at the floor.

"You bring all of us a second round of coffee, and I'll draw up a contract for you right now."

Buck's cheeks reached for the sky.

"Free of charge?"

Mr. Michaels shrugged.

"Nothing good on TV, anyway. Yeah, let's stick it to that rich kid by keeping him honest. I'll need a few details first. Come to the dining table and we'll talk."

* * *

BY QUARTER AFTER SEVEN, Buck was climbing into the backseat of Mr. Michaels's car. Ronnie got in front. In all that time, Buck still hadn't seen Tiffany emerge from the bedroom.

"You sure she doesn't want to come with us?" Buck asked.

Ronnie shrugged.

"Nah, I doubt it. She's gonna keep reading that book of hers. I guess."

"Okay, just making sure. Jennifer would've been pissed if I hadn't told her I was leaving."

"Well, you don't have to worry about that now, do you?"

Normally, that comment might've stung Buck a little, but if not for Jennifer, then this stupid bet and the contract he was off to sign with Chet wouldn't even be a concern. So, he felt nothing.

"Nope, guess I don't."

Mr. Michaels backed out of the driveway and turned onto the street, still having nothing to add to the conversation.

Mr. Michaels was a safe driver, but not a slow one. Because he knew all the city's traffic rules, and more important, their loopholes, he knew how to get around town in a hurry while staying legal. Ronnie said he'd already taught him those rules, and if he ever got around to getting his license, he'd know how to fast-travel as well. But neither one would ever teach Buck. They called it a "Michaels Trade Secret." But Ronnie had once let it slip that knowing the difference between legal and unofficial stop signs affected how often his dad committed a rolling stop offense. That was one of the secrets. Buck saw it in action when Mr. Michaels cut through a grocery store's parking lot to access an adjacent street without waiting for the traffic light. The elder Michaels ignored the stop sign completely. (But he'd come to a complete stop at the end of a public road beforehand.)

As luck would have it, Mr. Michaels had a lot of friends in this town, and one of his friends was working the gate at Park Center Park that evening. When Mr. Michaels asked him how the family was doing, the attendant told him he couldn't thank him enough for help-ing him beat that extortion charge.

"Want to know how you can thank me again?" Mr. Michaels asked.

The gate attendant pushed a button inside his shack, and the gate rose.

"Already ahead of you," the attendant said.

Not a dime was exchanged between them. Mr. Michaels tipped his head at the attendant and drove through.

Once they got to the end of the parking lot, Buck tucked the contract in his palm and got out of the car. Ronnie and his dad fol-lowed him up the lawn toward the Liquid Shack. As they approached, Tommy and Pigeon looked up from the serving tables with blank faces. They each had a customer. Chet was nowhere to be seen.

"Where's Chet?" Buck asked.

"Wouldn't you like to—" Pigeon was saying until Tommy cut him off with a harsh headshake and a nod toward his customer. "Er, yes. He's in the bathroom."

Buck took a seat on the nearest bench.

"Fine, I'll wait."

Mr. Michaels tapped him on the shoulder.

"We go in. No better time to serve a man a contract than when his pants are down."

Mr. Michaels marched toward the restroom, beckoning Buck to follow. Ronnie, meanwhile, got in line for lemonade. Buck rebuked him from over his shoulder.

"Ronnie, what the hell?"

Ronnie was dumbfounded. "What the hell what?"

"Supporting the enemy?"

A flash of realization passed over Ronnie's face.

"Aw, come on, Buck. They got good lemonade."

Buck wanted to argue Ronnie's rationale, but he didn't know how to dispute good lemonade.

"Just don't let me see you drink it."

Buck was careful not to look back. He was in no mood to watch another betrayal unfold before his eyes.

Mr. Michaels opened the door to the restroom and gestured Buck inside. Nothing about this felt right, but he had little choice. Sometimes the business of being legal required making a deal in unsavory places. His dad had taught him that, and now Mr. Michaels was teaching him that. Mr. Michaels stopped at the sink and shouted into the restroom's darkest corner, where the largest stall occupied space.

"Chet Armstrong," Mr. Michaels said. "You and I have business. Pull up your pants and come on out. Don't make me come in there."

The toilet flushed. Chet came walking out with his hand on his zipper, pulling it upward. His eyes zeroed in on Buck, to whom he flashed an evil grin, then on Mr. Michaels.

"Hey, aren't you my dad's lawyer?"

Mr. Michaels nodded once.

"I am. How's he doing?"

"He's, uh…"

"Taking my advice?"

Chet shrugged. "He doesn't tell me much about his business."

"A shame. Bet he'd have a lot to teach you." Mr. Michaels gestured to Buck for the contract. "You know why we're here?"

"Er, no."

The bathroom door opened. Pigeon walked in. He moved toward the hand dryer and folded his arms over his chest.

"Everything all right in here, boss?" Pigeon's dead eyes had a glaze to them this evening.

Chet nodded. He slipped between Mr. Michaels and Buck at the sink and ran the faucet.

"Everything's fine. I think."

Mr. Michaels smoothed out the contract and set it on the counter beside Chet's sink basin, just outside the splash zone.

"I understand that you and my client made a friendly wager yesterday."

Chet ran his hands under the soap dispenser.

"That's right."

Mr. Michaels pulled a mechanical pen from his shirt pocket. He clicked the top to expose the ink tip and set it on the document. Chet glanced at the paper, but he didn't give it much attention.

"It's my understanding that your agreement is based on a handshake."

"Yes." Chet scrubbed his hands under the faucet stream.

"If you know anything about your own father, then you know that handshakes have gone out with the bathwater."

Chet said nothing.

"So, I'm here to ensure that your little wager has binding circumstances."

Chet looked Mr. Michaels in the eye as he turned off the faucet. Then he glanced at Buck as he shook off the water. He shook so vigorously that the water flew everywhere, including on parts of the contract. Mr. Michaels wasn't fazed by this.

"All you have to do is sign the paper right here on the dotted line, and my client and I can be on our way, and your little wager can continue as planned."

Chet eyeballed the document.

"What's in it?"

Mr. Michaels picked up the pen and pointed it at him, nudging at his hand, signaling him to take it.

"The terms you've already agreed to. Plus, clear language stating that your victory conditions are based on earnings, not bank account. This means you'll need to keep accurate records of your daily sales, as will my client."

Chet moved toward the hand dryer and pushed Pigeon aside.

"I'm not signing that," he said.

Mr. Michaels nodded as he reached through the slit in his dress shirt between two buttons. "I had a feeling you'd say that."

Chet turned and faced him just in time to watch Mr. Michaels slide out another folded document. Buck's eyes bugged. He wasn't expecting a second document!

"I've taken the liberty of drafting an escape clause in the event you or my client does not agree to the written terms. By signing this contract, you absolve the bet, and both you and my client can go on your merry way without further consequence."

Chet was faster in responding this time.

"Not signing that one, either."

He pushed the button on the air dryer, drowning out all sound in the restroom. Mr. Michaels waited for it to shut off.

"Fair enough. You don't want to sign either contract, that's fine. But as my client so astutely pointed out before we came here, by not signing either contract, nothing about your wager can be nor shall be fulfilled. This means that you cannot take his business, and he does not have to work for you, ever. Is that what you want?"

Chet thought about the question for just a moment. Then he marched toward the sink, stole the pen from Mr. Michaels's hand, and signed the first contract. Once he looped the "g" in his name, he tossed the pen at the mirror and turned his back as it tumbled onto the counter.

Mr. Michaels nodded at Buck.

"It's only binding if you sign it, too."

Buck recovered the pen and signed the document under Chet's name. He gave the pen back to Mr. Michaels. Mr. Michaels, in turn, signed a third line across from Chet's, above where it said *Witness*. He wrote the date underneath it.

"And done. On this eleventh day in June, in the year nineteen hundred eighty-five, Chet Armstrong and Buck Star agree to the terms of this contract. As stated, neither of you can claim victory without a proper documented record, with verification from a trusted third-party like myself or my son here…" Mr. Michaels looked around the room but didn't see what he was looking for. "Where the hell is Ronnie?"

"Getting lemonade," Buck said.

Mr. Michaels shook his head. "Traitor. He and I will have to chat about that when we get home." He returned his attention to the contract. "Anyway, the winner of this bet is not officially declared until all figures check out. Finally, this contract asserts that the winner will be judged by the money earned through business actions taken between the dates of June tenth and August eighth. This means pre-existing funds will not count toward the winning value."

Mr. Michaels folded the contract and stuffed it in his shirt.

"Because I hold the contract, know that the terms of this agreement cannot be changed without my knowledge. Therefore, if any part of this contract is violated, then the violator forfeits his right to win, which means the other party will be declared the automatic winner, and all agreements will be fulfilled upon that date."

Mr. Michaels extended his hand to Chet for a handshake. Chet refused to take it.

"Well, that concludes our business," Mr. Michaels said. "Now, if I may add my two cents on the matter, I think neither of you has any idea what you're getting into."

Buck said nothing. He knew exactly what he'd gotten himself into. A path to freedom from his long-term bully, provided he won.

Chet just smirked.

"You sure you want this?" Mr. Michael asked.

"Yeah," Chet said.

Buck shrugged. He wanted freedom.

"Chet, has your dad not warned you of the risks ahead?"

"He supports my juice stand. And the bet. Only winners get to live at my house." He glanced at Buck and, with a wicked smile, drew his thumb across his throat.

Mr. Michaels shook his head. "I shouldn't be surprised." He offered his attention to Buck. "Do you understand the stakes of your decision?"

"I know what I'm doing." Buck would certainly keep learning as he went.

"And you still want this?"

"Why wouldn't I?" He didn't understand what Mr. Michaels was implying. They'd just signed the contracts. What would be the point of second-guessing them now?

"It's not too late to change your mind."

"But it is though," Chet said, putting attention back on himself. "Buck doesn't get a legal pass from my fist if he backs out now."

"Or mine," Pigeon chimed in.

Mr. Michaels shrugged at Buck. His face was sympathetic.

"So be it. Buck, let's be off."

Pigeon whispered something in Chet's ear. Chet smiled and nodded.

"Wait," he said. "Buck, before you go, I have something I wanted to tell you." He glanced at Mr. Michaels. "In private."

Mr. Michaels shook his head. "Whatever you can tell my client in private, you can tell him in front of me."

"This one isn't legal. This one's personal. If you don't mind."

Mr. Michaels glanced at Buck. Buck, meanwhile, felt a tightness in his gut that he didn't like. He wasn't certain how well it showed, but he shook his head at Mr. Michaels not to give in.

"Fair enough," Mr. Michaels said. "I'll be in the car waiting."

Ronnie's dad left Buck alone with Chet and Pigeon. Chet, meanwhile, took a step closer. Pigeon was grinning like a cartoon cat.

"Nice move, twerp," Chet said. "Bringing a lawyer into our bet. I admit I'm impressed. Didn't see that one coming."

"Thanks?"

Chet nodded.

"No, I mean it. I'm impressed. You know what else?"

Buck wasn't sure what else Chet could possibly tell him, unless it had to do with Jennifer, which was probably exactly what he wanted to tell him. But he wasn't expecting a compliment from his chief high school bully, so he didn't know what else to think here. He shook his head for his answer.

"It's Tuesday," Chet said with a smile.

And that's when Buck realized what day it was, where he was standing, and with whom he was standing here. Maybe Tommy wasn't part of the mix this time, but it didn't make the situation any less desirable.

"High school's over, Chet."

"Yeah, but it's still Tuesday."

Chet lurched for Buck's shoulders, but Buck wasn't about to give in this time. As Chet came in for the grab, Buck sidestepped him and kneed him in the groin. Maybe Chet grunted, or maybe it was Pigeon who'd groaned when Buck threw an elbow in his left cheek, but he didn't stick around to find out. He was out the door before he could take another breath.

He caught up to Mr. Michaels outside, just as he was approaching the Liquid Shack, where Ronnie and Tommy were talking about the value of lemonade in a 1980s market.

"Everything good?" Mr. Michaels asked.

Buck nodded. His heart was still racing.

"I'll be fine," he said.

* * *

BEFORE BED, BECAUSE MR. Michaels had spent the drive home lecturing him on financial accountability, and because he'd already figured out the benefit of tracking where his money went, Buck reviewed his expenses and sales for that day. Then he ran through the list of items he needed to pick up at the corner grocery first thing in the morning. If he wanted to honor the terms of the contract and still come out ahead, then he couldn't afford to screw up tomorrow.

He also wrote down his numbers to make sure he complied with the rules of the contract.

BUCK'S END OF DAY REPORT:

Earned: $0.00

Spent: $54.56

Net Gain: -$54.56

* * *

BASED ON WHAT HE'D learned from the father at Samantha's 7th birthday party and from the Michaelses while Ronnie's dad typed up the contracts, Buck was sure his moment of magic required a carton of cream and a box of sugar in his bag of inventory. So, when he awoke the next morning, he turned off his alarm clock, jumped in the shower, and then raced into the world without any breakfast. It was barely 7:00 a.m., the city was just now awaking, and the only store that was ready for business was the corner grocery by Shop Down the Street called, quite unoriginally, Corner Grocery.

When he went inside, the half-bald, portly-but-kind shop owner greeted him from the register. He was still half-groggy.

"Morning, Buck."

"Morning, Sully."

"Here earlier than usual, eh?"

Buck was in a hurry and didn't have time to chat. The Lease Agent was coming to the pavilion at eight o'clock, according to the agreement they'd made on Monday.

"Yeah, where's the cream and sugar?"

John Sully, the store's proprietor, was a businessman first, friend second. He pointed toward the cold-storage items.

"Right next to the milk."

Buck headed in that direction but stopped before taking more than a few steps.

"Any chance milk tastes better in coffee than cream?"

"Hard to say. I take mine black."

Buck frowned. Sully was already busting his theory about yesterday's coffee, and it was only 7:06 a.m.

* * *

BY 7:52, Buck was racing to set up his equipment. Fortunately, the party was long gone, so he didn't have to compete for space. He just had to position everything well. Even though Mr. Kabuki had trained him in the techniques for brewing coffee, Buck assumed that preparation of equipment and placement of inventory were equally important for maintaining top efficiency, especially when the people arrived in droves. Maybe it would become a lesson eventually, but he didn't think it was one he needed to learn. He chalked that one up to common sense.

By 7:56, he'd plugged in the machine, filled the reservoir with water from the fountain, and poured the grains into the filter. Now he was ready for brewing. With his paper cups laid out on the counter and the box of sugar and carton of cream ready for service, all he had left was to wait for the cowboy to come.

And wait, he did.

Five minutes.

Ten minutes.

Twenty minutes.

Buck ran his hand along the side of the creamer carton. It was still cold, but he wasn't sure how long he could keep it unrefrigerated. And he didn't exactly have access to a cooler. Granted, it was still early enough in the morning that it wouldn't go bad right away. But it was summertime. It would go bad eventually.

Thirty minutes.

Forty minutes.

A mom and her three kids wandered by and noticed his setup. She said nothing.

Fifty minutes.

Sixty.

And then a glimmer of hope.

Far down the hill, where the sidewalk wrapped around the lake, a black limousine snaked up the driveway and approached the pavilion. When it stopped at the curb directly across from where Buck was standing, the chauffeur got out, walked around to the back passenger door, and opened it.

A breeze blew in from the west, and a giraffe-skin cowboy boot touched the pavement. A familiar hat emerged from just behind the door.

The Lease Agent had arrived.

He marched up the shallow hill and entered the pavilion. He gave the place the once-over, nodded at no one, and put out his hand.

"All right, kid. Let's see what you got."

Buck, feeling his heart leap while his stomach danced toward his intestines, flicked the "on" switch into brew mode. The hiss of the coffeemaker's boiler against the fountain water churned. Buck glanced back at the Lease Agent and smiled.

And so it begins…

"How's your day so far?" Buck asked, hoping to break some of the tension he was feeling.

The Lease Agent gestured for him to hurry it along.

"Just give me my coffee, kid."

Buck checked the coffee drip. Judging by the machine and its brewing speed, this could take a while.

"Coming right up," he lied.

Episode 10

Into the Deep End

LYING TO HIM WAS probably an irresponsible way for Buck to begin his business relationship with the Lease Agent, but it had to start somewhere. As long as Buck stared at the coffee machine and repositioned the carafe's handle every fifteen seconds, perhaps glancing back and offering a reassuring nod if he sensed him getting anxious—"Yes, everything is perfect"—then he could cast the illusion that the process was faster than what reality was demonstrating. Optics were everything at this stage. But a conversational distraction was also in order if he wanted to keep his customer from walking out empty-handed.

The Lease Agent didn't want to chitchat, however, so Buck said nothing. He just waited for the drip to finish, tapping his foot on the concrete floor, readjusting the handle every fifteen seconds, feeling the lightness in his heart crashing down with his stomach and the rest of his nervous gut, having no clue whether his attempt to shrink time was actually working.

Drip.

Tap.

Drip.

Tap.

Twist.

Drip.

Tap.

"Kid, just gimme what's in the cup. I'm on a tight schedule."

Two minutes into the process. The brew was almost finished, but not quite. Nevertheless, if he waited any longer, Buck would miss his opportunity to impress the most important man in Hybrid City, and with it, his chance to break forever from his high school bully. So, he took an empty cup from the stack and replaced the one being filled on the tray.

While the new cup caught whatever was left of the drip, Buck filled the original with a shot of creamer and roughly two tablespoons' worth of sugar. Before serving, he dumped the contents of the second cup into the first. Compromise through the art of illusion!

It was only then that he realized he had nothing to stir it with, so he improvised. Regardless of the heavy steam billowing from the black liquid warning him not to touch, he dunked his index finger under the surface and swirled. He gritted his teeth to stop himself from screaming at the scalding coffee biting his skin.

Once the coffee was golden, he snatched it from his finger, wiped the runoff on his pants, and handed the cup to the Lease Agent. He waited for a reaction, doing his best not to let the pain register on his face.

The Lease Agent nearly dropped the cup.

"Damn that's hot. Need a glove to hold this thing."

The Lease Agent dipped his own finger into the cup, then pulled it back dripping. He sucked it free of the coffee. Buck held his breath as he watched for a reaction.

At first, there was no reaction. Just a blank expression, as if the Lease Agent wondered whether there was anything good on television tonight. Then he nodded as he stared at his fingertip, then at the cup. He nodded again, then set the coffee on the nearest table.

"Ah, now this stuff ain't very good," he said. "But you're learning, and I'm confident you'll get better in time. I'll start recommending your business. And I'll even give you five bucks to help heat the oil in your new shop engine."

Buck felt his heart leap again.

"But you gotta sign this contract first."

And then he felt slapped across the face. "What?" The memory of signing documents and committing to an unknown outcome was still fresh on his mind.

The Lease Agent reached into his jacket and removed a sheet of paper nearly identical to the one Buck had Chet sign last night.

"If you got a couple of minutes, I'll go over all the essentials. Now, this is important, so pay attention. Without this contract, you have no business."

The Lease Agent slapped the sheet of paper on the table and started telling Buck about all the ways in which he owned him now.

"When we're done, just sign on the dotted line. It'll be fine."

Buck wondered if he should call Mr. Michaels to verify the contract, but then he noticed that some other lawyer had already signed and pre-dated the witness line.

***

Day 3: Wednesday, June 12, 1985

Buck's Savings Account: $26

Buck's Wallet: $30.13

Buck's Business Funds: unknown

Buck's Expenses: not established

Hours of Operation: not established

EARLIER THAT MORNING, BEFORE Buck had visited the Corner Grocery or met with the Lease Agent, he logged his starting funds for the day. This was the amount he already had in his wallet. But he didn't yet know what to do with items like "business funds" or "business expenses." These were just buzzwords that Mr. Michaels had tossed around when he drove Buck and Ronnie home after they had served Chet the contract. How these funds differed from the money in his wallet, he didn't know.

But he figured he could use Mr. Michaels's recommended categories as a starting point for recording his earnings versus his spending. Because the contract specifically outlined the conditions for winning to include business income only, neither his wallet nor his savings would count toward the success or failure of the bet.

What was allowed, however, was using either (or any) source of money to pay for his supplies, which he was doing already. But how that differed from his business expenses, he still didn't know. Perhaps it didn't differ. Or maybe it counted only toward the money he earned from the business. Either way, he'd have to think of something.

Regarding "hours of operation," Buck was also clueless, and he worried he was now standing at the base of a tall mountain without climbing equipment. He knew he needed to establish a schedule of some kind, but he didn't know the best time for opening. And because he wasn't a natural coffee drinker, he didn't understand his clientele or their various consumption needs. On the surface, it seemed Buck was no closer to being ready for business than he was on the night of graduation.

Fortunately, the Lease Agent had a few guidelines about opening hours embedded within the contract, so even if Buck didn't have his financial elements measured out, he could somehow mete out a reasonable opening schedule.

"You can't open if the park is closed," The Lease Agent said. "So, whatever hours you set for yourself, remember that they can't conflict with what's legal. Plan accordingly."

The Lease Agent drew his finger down the left margin and tapped each checkbox he claimed was important. All the points related to Buck's hours of operation clustered near the top of the page.

"Also remember that you're not the only one entitled to the pavilion. My ability to license you the space depends on my ability to respect the park authorities and their rules. Normally, they forbid business exchanges on park grounds, but because I pay for favors, they turn a blind eye to any business conducted in any park I've co-opted. But I can lose that privilege anytime they put the government first. So, you must deny any temptation that might compromise their leniency. That means respecting the clock. I can afford you up to five hours a day. It's up to you to decide when you want those hours. Beyond that, it's a free-for-all. If you stay a sixth hour, it's on you to share with whomever tries to kick you out. In the end, they have the right to claim the space once your time is up. You defy them, and you play with fire. If they complain to the park rangers, I tear up your contract immediately."

"Do I have to decide that now?" Buck asked.

The Lease Agent cast him a sideways glance, but he said nothing more about the topic. If Buck needed clarification, he'd have to make an appointment.

"Down here you'll notice that you are equally responsible for respecting park rules." The Lease Agent was now pointing at a spot halfway down the page. "For example, using the space is not the same as defacing the space. You will set up your equipment before you open, then tear it all down when you leave. Here, this will help you organize."

The Lease Agent pulled a key out of his pants pocket. It was rusty. He passed it to Buck.

"This key belongs to the storage room next to the bathrooms. You can keep your equipment inside. Just don't lose it. I charge for replacements. But be aware that park staff also has access, and you'll be sharing space with their cleaning equipment. I wouldn't advise putting your creams next to their toilet cleaners. Not unless you want a lawsuit in five years."

Buck nodded. He'd figure that out on his own.

"Now, here's the most important part." The Lease Agent was pointing at a body of text near the bottom of the page. "This is your leasing agreement. You are welcome to use this space as long as you want, within the ranges I've outlined, but for a small fee. I expect payment at the start of every month, and I will shut off power to this space during your designated shop times if you do not pay on time. So, put it on your schedule. I also reserve the right to seize your business assets if you continue to operate without paying your monthly fee, power or no power."

Buck felt a twitch in the side of his neck when the Lease Agent mentioned his "fee" and "seizing his assets," but he was relieved to find that the cost was indeed low. Just ten dollars a week, or forty a month. Maybe it had something to do with being a pavilion and not a true indoor shop. He noted the price for his accounts log.

"Because you're starting out, I'm going to waive your initial leasing fee this month. You can pay me your first bill on August first. But listen up, this next part's even more important."

Buck tried to shut out the world around him, but he was now thinking about his free month of occupation. Or was it just deferred? He'd need clarification. Probably by appointment only.

"You need to keep up with my leasing fees, but I'm not the most demanding, or dangerous, man in town."

If Buck was having trouble concentrating, he was listening closely now.

"Let me ask you, have you heard of a being called the Tax Spook?"

Buck shook his head. But the mention of this name caused his skin to clam up.

The Lease Agent studied his face. For the first time this morning, the Lease Agent was slow to respond. His expression was grim. He pulled the brim of his hat down a centimeter.

"He may be the darkest individual in this town, and he comes for everyone, eventually." The cowboy raised his eyebrow. "Everyone. Now, I fear no man, but the Tax Spook makes me drink a fifth of tequila whenever he appears. And if he can do that to me, then he should absolutely terrify the hell out of you. Even if you screw up with me, *never* screw up with the Tax Spook. When he comes knocking, you better deliver what he wants. Period."

Buck's eyebrows rose.

"He'll come knocking?"

"He comes knocking for us all. Eventually. Even me."

"How will I know he's at the door?"

The Lease Agent snickered.

"Aw, don't you worry, kid. You'll know. When that deep chill hits your bones twenty seconds before the knock hits, you'll know. When you scramble for your wallet to find it empty, and that cold voice mocking you, seeping into your eardrums when not a single word has been uttered, you'll know. When the light drains from the fireplace and your steak dinner turns to ice, you'll know."

Buck caught himself rubbing his biceps.

"If you've forgotten everything I've told you, at least remember this. When the Tax Spook comes-a-knockin', it's already too late to run."

Buck nodded, but slowly. He did not want to meet this "Tax Spook," *ever.*

"You've been warned."

The Lease Agent pushed the contract into Buck's hand.

"Now, just sign the dotted line and I'll be on my way."

Buck took the pen from the Lease Agent and wrote his name in cursive at the bottom. The Lease Agent filled in his own name and stamped the date. Then he shook Buck's hand.

"So, I can officially open now?" Buck asked.

The Lease Agent shrugged.

"You can, but you still aren't officially legal. You should make one more stop before you start taking customers."

Buck felt his stomach lurch again. Where else did he have to go to prepare for this new business adventure?

"I may need to draw you a map," the Lease Agent said. "It's not the easiest place to find."

* * *

IF NOT FOR THE Lease Agent's detailed instructions, Buck might not have ever found the Hybrid City Chamber of Commerce, at least not without several hours of exploration and a little trial and error. It was located in a part of town where it probably didn't belong. Even though much of the city's official entities pooled together along the southern edge of downtown proper in the municipal district, the Chamber of Commerce stood alone at the end of a long trail, north of Lake Hybrid, between a scattering of woods and the density of unpaved forest, far out of the way of regular commuter traffic. It was almost as if they didn't want to be found.

But the sign on the door told a different tale. The small rectangular building, made of logs and nails, belonged to the Hybrid City Environmental Council, not the Chamber. The Chamber of Commerce was renting out a room while their own building (in that same municipal pool where Buck had assumed he'd find them) was undergoing a million-dollar renovation. Apparently, they'd been using this space for almost three years. According to the sign, there was no estimate on when the renovations would be complete, but the sign was optimistic. It said, *Will return to normal soon.* Buck couldn't remember seeing any buildings in Hybrid City's municipal district undergoing renovations. He wondered if the Chamber of Commerce had been scammed.

Inside the building, he found a cute but bored receptionist sitting at her desk, messing around with a Rubik's Cube. She was biting her lip as she attempted to solve it. The cube was a kaleidoscope of color and a scramble of patterning, far from being solved. If she were ever to solve it, today was unlikely that day.

When she looked up, she about dropped her toy. Must not have been expecting visitors today.

"Which department are you here to see?" Her face had blanched at the sight of him. It almost matched her blonde ponytail. Buck felt his chest flutter slightly. She reminded him of Jennifer a little. Maybe more than a little.

"Chamber of Commerce," Buck said.

The color returned to her face. She reached for a pen and paper.

"You a contractor, solicitor, marketer, or concerned citizen?"

Buck wasn't sure how to answer that question. Was there a difference?

"Um, I was told I needed a license to run a business."

The receptionist set the cube on the counter and handed Buck the pen and paper.

"Fill out your details here."

"Which details?"

The receptionist didn't answer. Instead, she picked up the phone. A moment later, she nodded at a muffled voice coming through the earphone. Jennifer used to nod that way. Buck felt some electricity running through his system at the sight of her nodding. This girl was cute.

Once the voice stopped speaking, the receptionist hung up. Not once had she uttered a word into the receiver.

"Mr. Perkins will see you now." She withdrew the empty sheet of paper and pen from Buck's grasp.

Buck pointed at the phone. "How did—"

"Just go while you still can. He's got a full plate today."

"But I don't—"

"You want your license or not?"

Buck knew nothing about how the Chamber of Commerce worked, so he fled the desk before the receptionist could rebuke him further. It was only after he passed through the room's lone door and turned the corner that he realized he didn't know where to go. Beyond the door was another small room with no one in it. Except for an adjacent restroom and its open door, there didn't appear to be anywhere else for him to go, or anyone else for him to see.

He ducked into the reception area to clarify her order. The receptionist was once again struggling with her cube.

"I don't know where—"

She glared at him as she turned a portion of the puzzle.

"Have you ever solved one of these stupid things?" She raised the cube up for him to see.

Buck shook his head. "No."

The receptionist twisted another row so hard that Buck was sure she was about to break it.

"Who the hell designed this thing?"

Buck almost said "Rubik," but he held his tongue. He just needed to find this "Mr. Perkins" and didn't want to add to her frustration.

Buck was about to ask his question a second time when the answer came to him. Out of the corner of his left eye, he saw a squirrelly little man peeking through the north window. The man was tall enough to see inside, but everything below his nose was hidden. When he and Buck made eye contact, the man motioned him outside.

Buck thanked the receptionist for her help and walked out the front door and circled the building to the back. He found the man hobbling toward a tent at the edge of the property.

"I saw you go in," the man said, with his back turned. "Assumed you were here for me."

He looked over his shoulder. A smile crossed his white-bearded face when he saw Buck standing there.

"Oh good," he said. "I was afraid I was talking to myself again. Please, follow me."

Buck suddenly wasn't so sure he should follow the man anywhere. Out here in the woods, far from civilization, headed for a tent that hid mysteries beyond his sight. Why wasn't the man in the office where he belonged? Why wasn't the Chamber of Commerce in the municipal corridor where it belonged? And why was this man hobbling?

"Right this way," the man said when he drew the tent flap aside. "Come on, don't be shy."

Buck took a step forward, looked over his shoulder. Took another step, looked over his other shoulder. He was here for a permit. Nothing more. Why did he have to do business in a camping tent?

"Are you the Chamber of Commerce man?" Buck asked as he took yet another step forward.

"Of course. They call me Mr. Perkins. What do they call you?"

Buck wasn't sure he should give the man his name.

"Do you offer business licenses?"

Mr. Perkins smiled. "I do far more than that, my friend. Come inside, and we'll discuss your options. Do you like cookies?"

Buck was ready to turn and run, but as he turned, he saw another man standing at the edge of the building from where he'd come. This man was dressed as a bee.

"You're starting a business?" the bee man asked.

Buck halted mid-step. He couldn't go that way, either.

"When you finish with Mr. Perkins," the bee man said, "I'll need you to come see me. Very important."

The man back-stepped from the corner of the building and ducked out of sight. Not once did the man blink.

Who were these people?

"Ignore him," Mr. Perkins said. "He's just trying to punish you for littering. Come now. I have a busy schedule. Let's see if I can help you."

Buck faced the man at the tent. Now he was holding a cane.

"Please, tell me about your business," he said.

The ground needles crunched under his feet as Buck dared to move closer to the tent. As much as he didn't want to enter, he wanted to re-encounter the bee man even less. He'd take his chances with Mr. Perkins.

Inside the tent, Buck was relieved to find an office-like setting. It was cramped, for sure, with the desk far enough from the canvas wall to allow a spot for Mr. Perkins to crouch on. And the visitor's chair was nothing more than a beanbag. But the tent had a desk, along with a filing cabinet, a pile of papers, and, oddly enough, a phone attached to a line that ran out under a tent fold. The phone was off the hook. Probably a direct line to the receptionist.

Mr. Perkins hobbled to his spot behind the desk and used his cane to lower himself to the floor. Then he reached behind the desk and produced a canister full of candy canes.

"Like one?" he asked.

Buck wasn't ready to accept candy from a stranger.

"I'll pass. Thanks."

Mr. Perkins set the can where he'd kept it.

"So, since you're here for licenses, let's talk licenses. I have a few questions for you. What do you know about business law?"

"Nothing."

Mr. Perkins offered Buck a sympathetic look. Maybe he was supposed to know *something* about business law.

"So, you know nothing about LLCs?"

Buck shrugged.

Mr. Perkins reached behind his desk and produced a tray of assorted cookies.

"Want one?"

They looked plump and sweet, but not as good as Pound Cake's.

"No thanks."

Mr. Perkins put the cookies behind the desk.

"Why do you want a license?" Mr. Perkins asked.

Buck wasn't sure if there was a right answer here. He thought a representative from the Chamber of Commerce asking him why he wanted a license was a bit like Irina Swift asking him why he wanted a cookie.

"Because I'm opening a business."

"What kind of license are you looking for?"

Buck shrugged.

"I know nothing about this, sir. I was told I needed a license and that I could get one here. If there's more than one type, then I don't know what to tell you."

Mr. Perkins nodded as he listened to Buck's words.

"I see," he said. "Interesting. So, I should probably put your mind at ease then. You seem to misunderstand our role here."

Buck sank into his beanbag chair a little further.

"What do you mean?"

"I can't give you licenses here."

Buck said nothing. The Lease Agent had told him to come here. The Lease Agent knew everything about business. He wondered if Mr. Perkins was lying to him.

"What I *can* give you is a business listing and some, er, perks for registering your business with us."

"I don't understand."

Mr. Perkins leaned closer. His elbows were now fully on his desk.

"I can give you business perks. That's sort of our role here."

"But you can't make me legal?"

"I can help you legalize, yes, but I can't make you legal. You'll need an LLC for that. And that's if you want one. If you'd rather operate as a sole proprietorship, then that's up to you."

"Er, what's the difference?"

Mr. Perkins reached behind his desk and produced a carafe of coffee.

"Like a cup?"

Buck felt a jolt in his stomach. He was diving headfirst into a pool he didn't understand when he didn't yet know how to swim. But at least he had an opportunity to find out what good coffee tasted like.

"Yes, please."

Mr. Perkins produced a cup from behind the desk and poured coffee into it. Then he dashed in some cinnamon.

"Hope you like flavored coffee. Something I've been trying."

Buck took the coffee and tasted it. It was…interesting. He noted it in his mind.

"So, what's the difference?"

Mr. Perkins set the carafe behind the desk and folded his hands over a stack of papers.

"Do you have a few minutes?"

"I've got all day."

Mr. Perkins nodded.

"Excellent. Let's start with LLCs. You like the idea of keeping your own money separate from lawyers?"

* * *

After his informative session with Mr. Perkins, Buck was tempted to re-enter the log cabin and flirt with the receptionist—she was so cute—but he didn't want to risk speaking to a man in a bee suit, so he rode straight to The Whipping Shed to plan his next move. But as soon as he walked in, he nearly turned around and walked out. He'd gotten as far as the reception desk when he heard a series of agonizing grunts coming from the dojo room.

Something metallic banged against something hard and wooden, as if a lumberjack had come here to practice his trade. But the scream preceding it was so loud that Buck was almost certain the walls shook. Because he didn't want to know what was going on, he turned for the door.

But he wasn't fast enough. The door finished its closing action as he reached for it, causing the welcoming bell to ring.

"Who's there?"

Buck had his hand on the door.

"Come to dojo!" Kabuki shouted from around the corner.

Buck was tempted to leave anyway, but he didn't want to face embarrassment if Mr. Kabuki came out to find him running away.

At the dojo door, Buck peeked around the corner. Inside, Kabuki was standing at a wooden statue, dressed in a black gi and posing like a fencer ready to parry his opponent. The two katanas that usually adorned the wall were now in his hands.

"You busy?" Buck dared to ask.

Mr. Kabuki rifled off another wall-shaking scream and slashed at the wooden statue. A chunk of wood splintered off as the blade made contact. With a hard jerk, Kabuki dislodged the blade from the wooden body and wiped the fragments off on his vest.

He turned around and bowed to Buck.

"Sculpting," he said. "Boy meet with Lease Agent?"

"This morning, yes."

Kabuki returned the swords to their mount on the wall.

"Go well?"

"He gave me a key to the pavilion. Then he sent me to the Chamber of Commerce for registration. Not sure what to do next."

Kabuki frowned at the mention of the Chamber of Commerce.

"Boy went to Chamber?"

"I did. Was that okay?"

Mr. Kabuki pinched the bridge of his nose and shook his head. Buck felt his skin prickle.

"Boy pay member fee?"

"Didn't leave me with much, but yeah. Was that bad?"

Buck was certain from Kabuki's reaction that he never should've gone, but he didn't really understand why. Mr. Perkins had given him a reasonable pitch. For twenty dollars a month, he could get his business on an official list interested parties could view. According to Mr. Perkins, it could leverage his success if more people knew he existed. Seemed like a good idea.

"Not bad," Kabuki said. "But too early. Better wait when boy know what he doing."

"But it couldn't hurt, right?"

"Depend on whether boy can make more than fee a week."

In other words, Mr. Kabuki clarified, it depended on whether potential customers actually read the list of businesses in the area, and whether they'd respond to seeing his name on the list. Because he didn't even have a name for his business—for the benefit of the list, he'd told Mr. Perkins to list him as "The Coffee Pavilion"—or an official address he knew the number for, he had no guarantee that anyone looking for him would find him. And given how unlikely anyone would even find the Chamber of Commerce to view the list, it seemed probable that he had wasted his money.

"Think it's too late to get my money back?"

"Don't get money back. Benefit in time. Just work hard to make up for it. Listing come in handy eventually. Kabuki on list." Kabuki glanced around the empty room. "Sometime help. Not today, but sometime."

Buck accepted Kabuki's assessment, but now he wondered why the Lease Agent had insisted he get his name on the list. The cowboy had made it sound like he was in violation of the law without it.

"What about an LLC? Should I do that?"

Kabuki thought about it.

"What LLC?"

Buck frowned. Perhaps he was asking questions that went beyond the scope of his training.

"Anyway, I need to know what's next. Do I just open shop now? Should I perfect my coffee first?"

Kabuki gestured for Buck to follow him into the break room.

"Boy train well, but now he must make own decisions. Part of success mean willing to fail. Lesson twelve."

"Aren't we on fifteen?"

"Lesson fifteen. Boy learn from mistake. Boy must be willing to fail."

Buck listened to Kabuki's words while he followed him down the hall. But he wasn't fully on board with this latest rule. He didn't want to fail, nor did he have the time to fail.

"Can't I just skip straight toward success?"

"Impossible. Come, we make plan of action. Look at failure first. Figure out what boy do next."

Kabuki sat him down at the table. A few hours later, they hashed out a plan of action. It was full of if-then statements but no real direction.

"Remember, Donald-*san*, quickest path to success is one that go through failure. Never be afraid to fail. Failure inevitable. If at first succeed, be suspicious. Might be committing crime. Lesson sixteen. Also, stop spending money. Earn first. Then spend."

"Okay, thanks for the advice." He started to stand when something else crossed his mind. "Oh, have you heard of something called the Tax Spook?"

Mr. Kabuki said nothing, but the blood drained from his face.

"Sensitive topic?" Buck asked.

"*Hai!*"

Buck decided not to pursue the question any further.

After he left The Whipping Shed, Buck went straight home. It was the only way he could be sure he wouldn't spend any more money that day. Even when his stomach growled and all he could find in the refrigerator were vegetables, he resisted the urge to run to the store for a frozen pizza. Instead, he reached for a bowl of lettuce and told himself he'd like it. It was the only way he could start making a profit.

Buck's End of Day Report:

Earned: $5.00

Spent: $22.23

Net Gain: -$17.23

DAY 4: THURSDAY, JUNE 13, 1985

Buck's Savings Account: $26

Buck's Wallet: $12.90

Buck's Business Funds: unknown

Buck's Expenses: not established

Hours of Operation: 8 a.m.-1 p.m.

THANKS TO MR. KABUKI'S instructions, Buck had a plan of action today. But it was one he had no intention of keeping. Sure, the master's advice was sensible, and even laudable. But it didn't take the bet's urgency into consideration. And no matter how wise Kabuki's instructions may have been for traditional upstarts like the Coffee Pavilion under normal conditions, it ignored what made its existence relevant in the first place.

Buck may have nodded at Kabuki's words, but they didn't soak into his heart. Even if his goal, according to Kabuki, was not to overcrowd his business with demanding customers, exposing too many cracks and ruining his reputation before it began, but to start slowly, giving him a chance to fix problems before they became a problem, it was still detrimental to the core goal he had set out to achieve.

His goal was to outsell Chet. Period. If he were to run the business as Kabuki had suggested, then he would've wasted half the bet "figuring things out," and that was a guaranteed way to lose. If that meant harming his reputation with certain customers along the way, then he'd have to suck it up and find new customers. The idea was to get those early customers while they could still become customers, and he couldn't let them get away.

For that reason, he decided he would open shop four hours ahead of the agreed-upon schedule. Because it stood to reason that opening a coffee shop in the middle of a hot afternoon was a surefire failure condition, especially when most people preferred coffee the moment they fell out of bed, it made more sense for him to open at eight, not noon.

When he called his mom at work to tell her about the schedule change and why, her reply was telling.

"Well, duh," she'd said.

His mom drank plenty of coffee daily, so she knew the score.

* * *

FORTUNATELY, BUCK HAD A key to the pavilion now, so he didn't have to cart his equipment and supplies in a paper bag across town on a bicycle. He could just unlock the storage room and retrieve the equipment from among the park staff's toilet cleaning supplies.

As soon as he put his workstation together, he stood outside the pavilion to keep watch for customers, determined not to repeat the mistake he'd made at Samantha's 7th birthday party. Thanks to the cream and sugar he had at the ready, he couldn't fail this time.

And thanks to the Lease Agent's involvement, he expected a healthy run of business today. The cowboy had said he'd start recommending him to the public, even if Buck wasn't clear about when or how. Buck assumed the recommendations would've started the moment he got into the limousine and drove off. But he didn't know. The Lease Agent had departed without any instruction beyond his insistence that Buck visit the Chamber of Commerce, which now looked like a waste of time and money, even if it had given him one good idea for coffee and introduced him to a girl that reminded him of Jennifer. But the Lease Agent couldn't have achieved his status by breaking promises, so the customers would come, and soon. That meant Buck would have to prepare for the flood of eager coffee nuts, both physically and mentally.

He started his preparation by chanting over and over that he could "do it." His high school P.E. teacher had once told him that worked. Five minutes later, his mouth got tired, so he practiced his sales pitch instead.

"Welcome to the Coffee Pavilion. What's your poison?"

He liked that one.

Buck waited for twenty minutes at the bottom of the shallow hill, watching for his first customer as he tried out other slogans. The ducks were swimming in the shimmering lake, but no one was jogging up the path. There was a speck of a mother pushing a stroller along the south side of the lake, but she headed in the opposite direction. A few minutes later, an older couple emerged from the path between the pines and started pitching wads of bread at the ducks. But no one was coming to his side.

Five minutes later, he was entranced by the old couple feeding the ducks and wondered if that could've been him and Jennifer sixty years from now, had she not betrayed him.

Five minutes after that, he caught himself thinking about the receptionist from the Chamber of Commerce. By now, he'd given up on trying out new customer introductions.

The resemblance the receptionist shared with Jennifer was ridiculous. She had the same physical form, the same hair, and the same eyes. But unlike Jennifer, she hadn't betrayed him.

Not yet.

Question was, would she?

Buck shook his head at the idea. He was in no mood to run down this road again. Jennifer's wounds against him were still fresh. Even as her face slipped past his mind's eye, he felt that sharp lunge into his chest. Even as he tried to brush her out of his brain, the phantom pain he felt in his back kicked him forward. Now was not the time to think of Jennifer or the receptionist. Now was the time to practice his sales pitch.

"Would you like fries with that?"

Five minutes later, the girl from the Chamber of Commerce reentered his thoughts.

Maybe he could test his equipment, make sure he was genuinely ready for service.

Inside the pavilion, Buck brewed a single cup. After three minutes passed, he poured in the cream and sugar, swirled it around to mix everything together, then waited a few minutes for it to cool. At some point, he dared put the beverage to his lips.

He winced.

Something about it was off, but he couldn't pinpoint the problem. The earthy richness he'd expected twisted into something sharp, like vinegar. Maybe that was normal, but he wasn't sure.

Problem was that he still didn't understand what made coffee "good." Was it all about flavor? Or just the caffeine? Hard to say if this cup would even pass the taste test, but he was confident it wasn't bad. Not really. It could certainly wake a kid.

He put the cup down, giving it time to settle. Chunks of cream floated to the top. Buoyancy was part of the pass-fail test, right? If it floated, then it was smooth. Where had he heard that before? He dabbed at the cream. It bounced.

At some point he'd know the difference between "good" and "not bad," but for now he was satisfied, even if it didn't taste as he'd expected. As long as he got his customers to drink it without spitting it out, he would call it a success. He could modify Lesson #16 without referring to it as a crime. "If at first you sort of succeed, call it good enough."

By nine o'clock, Buck had consumed three cups of his own product, getting more used to the odd taste with each sip, but he had not yet made a sale. He went down to the end of the shallow hill to check whether anyone was in the vicinity, but the park looked quite dead today. If the Lease Agent had recommended him, then it appeared he'd reached out to the wrong people.

By ten o'clock, Buck was sitting on a picnic bench, wondering if Kabuki was right. He didn't know how much sway the Lease Agent had with anyone he wasn't leasing to, but either way, the message was lost. Either way, no one was coming. If Buck wanted to make a sale today, he'd have to return when the park was busier.

But he couldn't abandon shop so early. According to his modified plan, which he'd started with Kabuki and finished in his own mind, he'd work until one o'clock. Originally, he'd agreed to open at twelve and close at five, but as of this morning he thought that was ludicrous. Now the idea of twelve-to-five sounded reasonable. But he wasn't about to sit under this hot pavilion for nine hours straight. Tomorrow, he'd do it Kabuki's way.

By eleven o'clock, Buck was sweating through his shirt, but he was still zero for zero. Staying another couple of hours seemed pointless. The heat was giving him a headache. Who would even come? Five minutes later, ten minutes later, still no customers. Kabuki had mentioned a period called "dead hour," a time when no one would show, and it seemed his entire day had fit into that window pretty comfortably.

It was unlikely to change now.

That was it then. If business were adaptable, then he would adapt his schedule to what worked, not what *could* work. Eight-to-eleven. Not eight-to-one or twelve-to-five. Not great, but good enough.

He unplugged the coffee machine and wrapped up the cord. Then he twist-tied the bag of cups. Thankfully, he hadn't lost the twist-tie. Those things were so easy to misplace.

Meanwhile, the girl from the Chamber of Commerce reentered his mind. As he gathered the cream and sugar together, he visualized her lovely face. He wondered what her smile might've looked like.

As he sealed up the canister of Store Powder, a soft voice spoke to him from over his shoulder.

"Oh, are you not giving away any more coffee today?"

Buck turned around to find a disheveled man in ratty clothes staring back. He looked as if he hadn't bathed in years. Not in any place that didn't have ducks swimming on it, at any rate.

"You're here for coffee?" Buck asked, suddenly realizing the man and the coffee smelled exactly the same.

He smiled, showing off whatever teeth he still had.

"A man in a limousine told me I could come here."

So, the Lease Agent *had* sent out the call to check out his business. Fair enough.

"How do you take it?"

Buck plugged in the machine and fished out a cup from the bag.

"Cream and sugar," the customer said.

Buck put two scoops of Store Powder into the filter and poured a cup of fountain water into the reservoir. He pressed the button and listened to the churning begin.

"You from around here?" the customer asked.

"Yeah, I live near the edge of town. What about you?"

The man pointed at the ground.

"Live right here." A look of confusion crossed his face. He pointed out across the lake. "Actually, my camp is that way. But I live on the grounds."

"Year round?"

The man shrugged.

"Depends."

Buck considered the implications of what he was saying.

"Er, do you have any money?"

The customer shook his head.

"Nah, haven't had my own money since the seventies."

Buck watched the coffee drip into the cup. The man must've thought the coffee here was free. And Buck didn't have the heart to tell him it wasn't.

Of course, as he watched the coffee fill almost to the top, he realized he had no idea what to even charge for it. For all the planning he and Kabuki had spent mapping out his business, how to price the coffee wasn't on the list. They'd spent most of it talking about marketing, outreach, and record-keeping—all the stuff he'd do later.

The brew finished. Buck removed the cup from the machine and filled it with cream and sugar. Once he swirled it around for an even mixture, he passed it to the homeless man.

"What do I owe you?" the man asked.

This caught Buck by surprise.

"I thought you said you don't have money?"

He shook his head.

"Nope. But I have favors. Need me to run an errand for you?"

Buck thought about it. He would've liked someone marketing for him. But he wasn't sure a smelly guy in ratty clothes would've made the best partner for that kind of work.

"Nah, this one's on the house. Enjoy."

The man sipped his coffee, then spat it out.

"Ick. I think your cream is spoiled."

Buck sniffed the carton. Smelled just like vinegar.

"Damn."

"Do you not have a fridge to store it in?"

Buck closed the carton and tossed it in the trash.

"I guess I need to get something to keep it cold."

He didn't know how much a bag of ice cost, but he was certain he'd need to buy one next time he bought cream. He'd probably need a cooler, too.

"Thanks for spotting that," Buck said.

The homeless man smiled.

"Glad I could help."

The homeless man walked off with coffee in hand, perhaps disgusted by the taste but grateful for the opportunity to have coffee today. And he'd paid for it with a favor. Buck no doubt would have unknowingly served a paying customer that same spoiled cream, and that would've ruined his reputation quickly, especially if that customer told all of his friends about it.

Buck smirked. So, that was why Kabuki had wanted him to take it slowly today.

* * *

THE HOMELESS MAN'S ARRIVAL had encouraged Buck to stay open for the rest of his shift. After all, if he showed up, then others might, too. As long as he didn't serve anyone cream, he'd have a shot at turning a nickel today.

But at one o'clock, the park was still dead, so he packed up his equipment and supplies and locked everything in the storage room. Today could've been an off day, and he didn't want to jump to any conclusions about the location or opening schedule just yet. At the same time, he wondered if his results would've improved closer to evening. Perhaps the problem was with Thursday, and that tomorrow would present better results.

For now, though, he had other things on his mind, namely a cute receptionist who manned the front desk at the creepiest place in Hybrid City. He wanted a chance to talk to her again, to see if she was in a better mood. Jennifer may have been out of bounds now, but the cute receptionist was still a possibility, hopefully.

As he rode his bike toward the remote log cabin northeast of the pavilion, he wondered how this might go. Because Jennifer was his first girlfriend, he knew nothing about rebounding or how it worked. He just knew that loneliness sucked and that talking to the receptionist might fix it.

The path to the log cabin connected to the street network of the Lake Hybrid area, which connected to North Park, so it took Buck hardly any time to reach the El Camino in the shallow parking area beside the building, which gave him little time to practice what he might say once he saw her. Even as he dropped his kickstand behind the car, he was still thinking through the possibilities, none of them sounding as impressive as he'd like.

As his hand touched the wooden door, however, he froze. The handle might've been solid, but his fingertips melted into its surface. Beyond was a girl he didn't know and couldn't predict and, therefore, didn't know how to approach. His pulse raced as his elbows refused to bend. This might've been a mistake.

What was he supposed to say to her? *Hi, I was in the neighborhood and thought…* Why would anyone be in *this* neighborhood? Whatever reason he'd offer her for daring to interrupt whatever she was doing at her desk, she'd see right through it. If he wanted to talk to her without being obvious, he'd need a different approach.

Buck backed away from the door and returned to his bicycle. He'd have to think this through. Girls could smell fear, if they were anything like their high school counterparts. The receptionist would be no different. The only reason Jennifer ever bothered to talk to him was that he had something to offer her (free homework solutions). What could he offer the receptionist? To this day, he had never solved the Rubik's Cube.

Then, an idea came to him. If this didn't work, nothing would.

* * *

"As a woman," Irina Swift said, passing the cinnamon roll and Buck's change over the counter, "I'd happily accept a gift this sweet. But as the girl who works the desk at the Environmental Council, that's probably all I'd do."

Buck pocketed the change. He'd check his account balance later.

"But it would give me a reason to talk to her, right?"

Irina rested her elbows on the counter and used her knuckles to prop her chin.

"I suppose. You sure you want to talk to *that* one?"

Buck thought about the question. It seemed kind of a stupid one to ask.

"Yeah. She reminds me of Jennifer."

Irina's eyes rolled a little. She tried to mask the movement by shaking her head slightly, but it was too late. Buck caught the gesture. He didn't understand why she'd done that.

"Is that a bad thing?" he asked.

Irina took a breath before speaking. "Doesn't have to be. But it could be, depending on the girl. Knowing Lila as well as I do, which I admit may not be well enough, I'm not confident."

"But if she gets me to stop thinking about Jennifer…"

Irina nodded.

"I hear you. She broke your heart. Never a fun thing, regardless of how old you are."

"Yeah. You had your heart broken?"

"Oh, sure, several times. And it probably wouldn't surprise you that I've done the heartbreaking plenty more. It's something we all deal with and do. In different ways, of course. In my case, a cinnamon roll is part of that healing. Not really the source of attraction."

Buck thought about that. It was too late to give back the cinnamon roll, and he didn't know it *wouldn't* work on Lila, if that was really the receptionist's name. Now that he'd bought it, he'd still need to use it. Or eat it himself, which was also a possibility.

"What do you usually want?" Buck asked.

"A puppy. Can't go wrong with a puppy."

Buck wrinkled his lips. There was no way he could afford a puppy.

"What are the odds Lila hates puppies?"

"Knowing Lila, probably high. I see her more as a lizard girl."

"Just any kind of lizard, or do I gotta go to a pet store?"

Irina stared at him. Her cheeks wrinkled a little.

"Do you really think Lila will patch that wound for you?"

He wasn't sure. The wound was still fresh. But Jennifer was compromised. Even if she wanted him back, the stain of Chet was on her now. Buck had to move on. He just wasn't sure how big of a leap in the other direction he was willing to take. Lila was close enough to the original that she could satisfy some of the ache inside. He was pretty sure of that. But if she was into lizards…

"Probably," he said, doubting his words, but still willing to test them.

* * *

BUCK RETURNED TO THE log cabin with the packaged cinnamon roll in hand. He still didn't know what to say, but saying anything was better than saying nothing. With his hand once again on the handle, he took a deep breath, then pulled the door open.

Inside the murky cabin, the man in the bee suit was hovering over the reception desk, barking orders at Lila. As the space between the door and the frame widened, both she and the bee man glanced at the entrance where Buck was standing.

Before Buck could blink, the bee man swiveled fully in his direction and marched toward him. Even though his words related to the existing conversation, other words crept into his sentences, sounding as if they were transforming into a new topic. These new words were directed at him.

Rhyme and reason fled with Buck as he released the door handle and stepped backward. His heart pounded when he hopped on his bike. Behind him, all he heard were words. Buzzwords. Meaningless words. Something about litter.

He pedaled away as fast as he could. Within minutes, he was at the entrance to Lake Hybrid, suffering for breath. Hopefully, the pursuit stopped the moment he rode out of sight—that bee suit couldn't have been comfortable in this summer heat. But Buck couldn't take the chance that the bee man was hovering at the front door, waiting for him to return. At the same time, he couldn't let the cinnamon roll go to waste. He'd paid over half a dollar for it.

So, after a deep breath, Buck crept into the woods and followed the path back to the cabin, just out of view of the road.

He'd gotten halfway when he spotted the bee man still walking south toward Lake Hybrid. Buck tipped the bike and dropped to his stomach, crawling as fast as he could toward a patch of tall grass.

The bee man, still on the road, passed by without noticing him. Buck felt his breath return to his lungs the moment the man turned the next corner out of sight. He got to his knees, ready to sprint the rest of the way until something else turned him into a statue.

"You here to see me?" a voice said from behind.

Buck's heart thumped so hard that the propulsion caused him to leap right out of the grass patch. Then it decelerated the moment he turned to face his surprise guest.

"No, I…"

"Okay, no hard feelings," Mr. Perkins said. "So, I'm getting your first business perk together. Isn't that exciting?"

Buck nodded slowly. What was he doing here?

"I expect to have it ready for you by next week." Mr. Perkins's eyes drifted down toward the bag in Buck's hand. "That for me?"

"No, the receptionist."

Mr. Perkins smiled.

"Ah, you have the eyes for her?"

"I, um…"

The kindly, bearded man put his hand on Buck's shoulder.

"I'm sure she'll love it. But I wouldn't expect much in return. She's, well, she's Lila." He tipped his head toward the log cabin, which was still hundreds of feet up the path. "Better hurry, though. She goes home soon."

Buck grabbed his bike and scrambled out of the woods before any other weird things happened around here.

* * *

ONCE AGAIN, BUCK TOOK a breath as he palmed the door handle. His heart was still racing from anticipation, and he

155

didn't think it would slow until he got this over with. But thanks to all Irina and Mr. Perkins had said, he was no longer sure this was a good idea.

The door swung right at him, nearly bending his wrist. The receptionist bumped his shoulder so hard that he nearly dropped the cinnamon roll. Her backpack smacked him in the chest as she marched past.

"Oh, hi," he said, trying to play it cool while he rubbed out the shock of pain in his shoulder from the impact.

Lila stopped and turned to face him. She wore an impatient expression.

"Everyone's gone," she said. "We reopen tomorrow."

Buck smiled.

"You solve your Rubik's Cube yet?"

She slid her backpack toward her front and unzipped the top. Inside, she pulled out the jumbled color cube and tossed it to him.

"Be my guest," she said, and turned toward the parking lot.

"My name's Buck. What's yours?"

She stopped again. Turned to face him.

"Look, dude, I don't mean to be rude, but I'm trying to get out of here before that weirdo returns. Is there something you need, or can it wait 'til tomorrow?"

Buck stepped forward, holding up the cinnamon roll.

"I brought you a sweet," he said.

Lila groaned.

"I just got through losing ten pounds. I don't really want to gain it back."

Buck frowned. He opened the bag to peek inside. The roll was still fresh.

"It's a cinnamon roll," he said.

Lila's expression changed. She was no longer impatient. In fact, it looked as if a smile might've crept onto her face, if she were to allow it. She moved toward him and snatched the bag out of his hand.

"Can't resist that," she said. "Okay, you win. I'll take it. Buck."

"Do you need a ride home?" he asked as he pointed at his bike. "I'm pretty good at doubles."

Lila cocked her head toward the El Camino.

"I have a car. But thanks for the offer."

Buck was running out of things to say. He'd understood her reason for wanting to run, and he wasn't sure he wanted to risk those weirdos coming back, either.

But he had to keep her attention.

"Think you could drive me home?" he asked without thinking through the question.

Even stranger than the men who worked at this log cabin was Lila's answer to his question.

"You can toss the bike in the back," she said. "Just don't crush the plastic doll in the bag."

Buck was careful not to damage anything as he loaded his bike.

"Where do you live?" Lila asked.

Buck told her.

"Okay, that's not too far from where I'm going. Get in."

Buck opened the passenger door and peeked inside. A large pink bra stuck out from the joint where the seat and the backrest met. He stared at it, not sure what to do.

Lila noticed what he was looking at and snatched it out of the crevice. She tossed it into the footwell.

"Don't mind that," she said. "It's not even mine."

Buck looked at her. She noticed.

"My boyfriend takes the car out at night when I'm asleep. That one belongs to one of his friends." She stared at him. "He assures me it's not what I think."

She peeked into the cinnamon roll bag as she turned on the engine.

"Anyway, this looks really good. Thanks for thinking of me."

"No problem," Buck said.

"You getting in or what?"

Buck nodded as he climbed in, almost certain he'd never talk to this girl again.

"Thanks for the ride."

"Yeah." She backed out of the parking spot without checking behind her. "Say, aren't you the kid that was dating Jennifer Mills?"

Buck said nothing. How would this girl even know that?

"What happened with that? I keep seeing her with that douchebag. What's his name? Fart?"

Buck looked at the side of her face and smiled. Maybe she was cooler than everyone had given her credit for.

"Yeah, that's his name."

Lila reached into the bag and broke off a piece of cinnamon roll. She popped it in her mouth and nearly melted from the taste.

"This is awesome. Man, you get me."

Buck nodded. Maybe. Hopefully.

Episode 12

Priming the Rebound

"YOU KNOW WHO'D BE perfect for you?" Lila asked as she swerved around the bee man, who was still patrolling the road toward Lake Hybrid. "My friend Nina. She's nothing like Jennifer."

Buck was clutching the armrest as the shallow hill toward the lake got shallower by the second. He whipped his head around as the bee man slipped in and out of sight, soon to disappear inside the cloud of dust the El Camino kicked up in its wake.

"She's actually nice, you know." Lila dipped in for another piece of cinnamon roll. She offered it to Buck. "You want a piece?"

Buck was afraid to reach out and take it. The trees were flying by so fast he could hardly see them.

"Here, open your mouth. I'll shove it in there."

Buck opened his mouth, but not for the cinnamon roll fragment. Lila stuffed it in before he could scream.

"Oh, or I know who you'd like. You like girls who don't speak much English? There's this French girl who waits tables at my favorite tea place. You'd *love* her. French people never cheat."

Buck leaned against Lila's shoulders. She'd just turned a corner and was now headed for North Park.

"Yeah, I'm gonna introduce you to her." Lila checked her watch as she pushed Buck off her. "Not sure when she starts work, though. Tell you what, meet me there tonight, about eight o'clock. I'll warm her up for you if she's there tonight. What's your name again?"

Buck was now pressed up against the passenger door. Lila had turned another corner, this time left into the park's back entrance. She was taking the shortcut home.

"I'll bet she'll like you, too. You seem like a decent guy."

The homeless man, to whom Buck had served coffee earlier, was picking up a glass bottle off the side of the road. Buck blinked. Now he was distant in the side mirror.

Lila glanced at him. "Why are you so stiff? Relax. We're friends now." She reached over and pinched him on the biceps. "I'm gonna help you get over that chick if you'll let me."

But clearly not in the way he'd imagined.

* * *

A FTER LILA DROPPED HIM off at home, Buck thanked her for the ride, then caught his breath, then checked his wallet for the latest damage. He had barely eight dollars left. Plenty to buy more cream and a bag of ice, but it was questionable whether he had enough to buy adequate cold storage. Last time he'd checked the price of a cooler was about never ago. He'd probably have to go to the bank, assuming it was still open at this hour. But he didn't have much left in there, either. Less than thirty dollars.

Either way, he was doomed to serve crappy coffee if he didn't take care of his creamer problem, so he hopped on his bike and rode off to Happy Homewares, the local home goods store that shared plaza space with Pound Cake and Tailor Made, to see how much the price might set him back.

He found a plastic cooler in the camping aisle. It cost $39.99 plus tax. Even if he'd gone to the bank, he still wouldn't have enough to cover the cost. He'd need some way to fill the price gap.

Outside the shop, on the sidewalk where pedestrians could ignore him, he conducted a mental checklist of every lesson Mr. Kabuki had taught him in case any of them could help solve this latest problem.

Lesson #1: "Never give in to the enemy." In this case, the enemy was poverty.

Lessons #2 and 3 didn't apply to his current situation, but Lesson #4 was essential: "Quality matters. Better quality means better money." Made sense.

The problem, however, was with Lesson #5: "When supplies run out, buy more." This brought him back to the core issue. Money required quality, and money was something he didn't have yet.

But then he had an ace up his sleeve, the lesson that made the rest of them possible. Even though it was halfway down the list, it was still the most important lesson for the current situation.

Lesson #7: "When in need of supplies, money is just a hurdle, not a wall."

Buck recalled the incident where he'd learned this lesson. Mr. Kabuki had taken the Hawaiian beans without exchanging a dime for them. But instead of keeping the bag, he'd brought it to Sapphire for consignment.

"When in need of supplies…"

Buck glanced at the entrance to Happy Homewares. The proprietor, Marvin Brewer, was kind of a dope. But he was also good at observation. Kind of a hit-or-miss proposition.

Buck shook his head at the idea. What was he thinking? Kabuki's solution was not the point of the lesson. It couldn't have been. The message was in the wording itself. "When in need of supplies, money is just a hurdle, not a wall." Buck considered that statement more. What if the *method* of earning money was also a hurdle, not a wall?

That was the lesson that had introduced him to Sapphire. It was also, perhaps, the only part that had made it valuable to him now.

* * *

Buck sniffed the carton of cream to see if anything had changed. It was worse than he'd remembered, and he'd yanked it from his nose. It had been in the trash since eleven o'clock this morning, but thankfully the park custodians hadn't yet emptied it. He could still use it.

He unlocked the supply closet where he'd kept his coffee equipment and found a box of trash bags on a shelf beside it. He pulled a bag loose and stuffed the carton of spoiled cream in it. Then he checked the closet for other supplies that might've helped him get closer to the goal. He snatched the bottle of toilet cleaner that he was certain was changing the taste of his Store Powder. Hopefully, the park's custodial staff wouldn't miss it.

A short time later, he rode past Billy Bob Drake and parked his bike at the door to Sapphire's Consignments. Hopefully, she was interested in what he offered today.

* * *

"NOT SURE I CAN resell this one," Sapphire said as she closed the creamer and set it on the counter.

Buck stared at her for a second longer than usual. Either he was still surprised by her sudden change in hair color from dark brunette with a blue streak to a more normalized but still unconventional redheaded state, or he was stunned by her lack of confidence in the product.

"I thought you could sell anything," Buck said.

"I can sell fresh things and unopened things, but what you've brought me is harder to move. If you'd brought this to me just before Halloween, I could probably get you good money for it. But in mid-June? Can't think of anyone who'd want it."

Buck frowned. He'd dug in that trash can for nothing.

"What about the toilet cleaner?"

She cocked her eyebrow at that one.

"Industrial strength. Not bad." She picked it up and shook it. "Feels almost empty though. Doubt it's worth more than fifty cents."

Sapphire unscrewed the top and peeked inside. The intense fumes forced her to push it away.

"Yikes. Where'd you get this stuff?"

"I'd rather not say."

"Well, it's definitely near empty. But I can give you twenty-five cents for the jug and fifteen cents for what's left of the chemicals."

"You just said you could give me fifty cents."

"Prices are fluid. Markets shift."

"Over ten seconds?"

Sapphire shrugged. "Thirty-eight cents now."

"Fine, I'll take it. Sheesh!"

Sapphire winked at him.

"I like you. So gullible. Here, I'll give you sixty for being a good sport. No, a dollar. Good faith. Hope you come back with something else for me soon."

Buck rolled his eyes.

"What else could I possibly bring you? I just gave you the only thing I can afford to part with."

Sapphire shook the jug of toilet cleaner.

"You could bring me more empty jugs. Or glass bottles. The recycling center comes to me for supplies, and I always compensate anyone who helps me."

"How much?"

Sapphire leaned across the counter and pinched Buck's cheek.

"Ten cents for glass bottles, like soda bottles and wine bottles. Twenty-five cents for jugs like this one. Except milk jugs. Only give five cents for those."

"But you'll pay me to bring you junk?"

"Specific types of junk, yes." She raised her eyebrows. "Recyclables."

Buck thanked her for the information and the dollar and headed out to retrieve his bike. How had no one ever told him about recycling before? As he gazed across the lawn and watched Billy Bob Drake pick at something on his shirt, he wondered if anyone had bothered to tell him about it, either. Seemed like he could use the extra money.

"Hey, Billy," Buck said. "Want to help me with a job?"

* * *

Buck and Billy checked for glass bottles along the shore at Hybrid Beach, first skimming the sand for glittering objects, then pacing the nearby park. Collectively they found a couple of dozen beer bottles, but most of them were broken, and Buck wasn't sure what Sapphire's standards were for bottle integrity. Either way, he bagged up what he could find and pooled it with whatever Billy had found.

They moved toward the shops and checked the alleys. Buck recovered a plastic paint spray bottle. Billy brought him a milk jug.

"You can keep that one for yourself," Buck said.

Billy thanked him for the charity.

They headed north to Wild Trends, where the proprietor, Rory Stickmeyer, was out dumping his own collection of empty bottles. His business was in alcohol sales, and his product was worth about five bucks on Sapphire's economic scale.

"Be my guest, little man," Rory said, when Buck asked if he could take the bottles off his hands. "Not sure when the city last collected the trash. If you want, you could search the dumpster for more. I'm sure you'll find some."

Buck asked Billy if he'd like to do the honors. Billy wasn't keen on the idea, but because he was sharing in the profits, he was willing to take the plunge.

"Try not to cut yourself, bro," Rory said to Billy as Billy climbed in. "Gotta be some broken glass in there, too."

While Billy hunted around the dumpster, Buck told him he'd be right back. Because Tealeaf Central was so close to Wild Trends, he figured he'd hop over to see what all the hype was about this French girl that Kabuki, Mack Green, and now Lila kept talking about.

He hitched his bag over his shoulder, got on his bike, and rode toward the tea café, checking down alleys for other items of interest in case Wild Trends wasn't the only hotspot for profitable trash around here. As he got closer to Tealeaf Central, however, he noticed something odd poking out of a metal trash can next to an apartment building. It was rectangular and brown, but alluring. Buck steered closer for a better view of the mysterious object.

Wads of packing paper covered parts of it, so he had to dig a little to uncover what hid beneath. But it wasn't until he saw the first button that he gasped in delight. The sight of it sent adrenaline through his system. He dug faster, revealing more of the item, exposing a cord, then a plug, until there was nothing mysterious left about it.

His heart started pounding.

He'd found a VCR!

An actual VCR!

With all its buttons intact! In fact, the only noticeable thing missing was the face shield protecting the loading deck.

Buck didn't want to damage the buttons or the casing, so he emptied the trash of anything that might scratch it, then pulled the video recording device out of its chariot to the landfill.

He couldn't wait to show Sapphire his new discovery.

* * *

BUCK WAS CAREFUL TO set the plastic bag on the counter when he'd told Sapphire that he'd come bearing treasures. The bottles inside clinked as the bag settled into place. He opened the top and pulled each bottle out one-by-one. A beer bottle here. Another beer bottle there. Oh, here was a nice, skinny soda bottle. Oops, another beer bottle.

This went on for several minutes until it was time to retrieve the grand prize. Then he set his hand on the plastic casing that kept the machine from spilling out all its circuits. He locked his eyes with Sapphire as he studied her imminent reaction. With his fingers gripped tightly around the nearest corner, he slid the VCR out of the bag.

A shallow smile crept onto Sapphire's face when she cast her gaze on the machine.

"Interesting," she said, as her own fingers moved toward the object. "Interesting indeed. Where did you find this?"

"Apartment building."

Her fingers moved immediately toward the exposed loading tray. She felt around inside.

"You sure this thing still works?" she asked.

Buck held her gaze.

"Only one way to find out."

Sapphire nodded, then brought the unit up to a television that she kept behind the counter. She also stole an adapter from a box of gadgets that she'd kept around for convenience.

After hooking the machine up to the television, she told Buck to grab a tape off the table. He found a beat-up copy of *The Beastmaster*.

"All right, let's see what it does," she said.

She plugged in the machine and then inserted the tape. Or tried.

Not only did nothing happen, but the machine refused to accept the cassette. Sapphire pushed on it harder, but the gears inside were not grinding.

"Looks like it's broken," she said.

Buck nodded.

"But it's still worth something, right?"

Sapphire offered him a wry smile.

"Not here, it isn't."

Buck's gaze fell. Now he was looking at his shoes.

"Sorry, Buck. I sell only things people want. But don't give up yet. You might want to take it over to Disinterested Pawn. It's on the next street. Benny might offer you something for it. He's less picky."

Buck nodded, feeling all his enthusiasm racing out of his chest. He was so sure this VCR was worth the price of an icebox.

"Do I still get something for the bottles?" he asked.

"Sure. Sure. Just give me a few minutes to do the calculations. But hey, Benny's not far from here if you want to try him while I count. I should have something for you once you get back."

Buck agreed, so Sapphire helped him load the VCR back in the bag.

Fortunately, the Disinterested Pawn was a short ride away, on the street behind Shop Down the Street and The Whipping Shed. It was also the only shop on the street that had bars on the front door and windows. Buck didn't understand why. It wasn't that dangerous of an area.

Inside the pawnshop, Buck could smell the musk of old socks and tobacco, and a parrot was squawking from somewhere in back. And a haze of smoke permeated the air. It made him dizzy.

The walls were a deep green, like money, and old posters saying *Mondale 4 Prez* cluttered them from end to end. Each table was as junk-filled as the ones in Sapphire's consignments but kept an inventory focused primarily on electronics and weapons. The floor was stained with rusted water spots. And a chain-link fence straddled the counter that separated the clerk from the customer. It was the kind of place that didn't bother laying down a welcome mat.

An older gentleman with no hair and in military fatigues sat on a stool behind the counter, chomping on a cigar. He was watching a game show on a thirteen-inch black-and-white television.

He tilted forward on his stool slightly when Buck approached the fence.

"Are you Benny?" Buck asked.

"Sumthin' like that, kid. Whatcha got for me?"

Buck showed him the VCR.

"Ah, that's a beauty. Does it work?"

Buck shook his head.

Benny nudged his head sideways toward an empty table beside the counter.

"Set it over there," he said.

Buck did as he was told.

Benny went through a door behind the counter, then came out another door right to the table. He took the VCR in his hands, then headed for the door again.

"Back in a sec," he said.

A few minutes later, he returned to the counter with a fistful of cash in hand.

"Here's ten bucks. Cost you twelve to take it back. You got thirty days to come get it before I put it on the tables."

Buck raised his eyebrows.

"You gonna fix it?"

Benny smirked at him.

"Sheesh, kid. What do I look like? A repairman? Here, take your money and get outta here. I'm missing my show."

Buck asked no more questions. He stuffed the money in his wallet, then went back to Sapphire's Consignments to collect whatever she owed him.

In total, he'd made seventeen dollars and twenty-eight cents for his scavenger hunt. Combining that with the rest of his savings, he had just enough to buy a cooler, some ice, and a new carton of cream for tomorrow.

Of course, now that the banks were closed, he'd have to make that run first thing in the morning. Too late now.

* * *

ON HIS WAY HOME, Buck stopped by The Whipping Shed to give Mr. Kabuki his first day's report. Kabuki offered his usual confirmation grunt as Buck recounted the events. When he'd told him about the spoiled cream, the old man merely laughed.

"What Kabuki say about failure?"

"Has to happen before I can succeed."

"*Hai*. Boy learn valuable lesson today. Worth celebrating."

Buck noticed the clock on the wall. It was already after seven o'clock. He was supposed to meet Lila at Tealeaf Central soon. Hardly any time for him to shower or change his clothes.

"Can we celebrate tomorrow? I have a date in a little while."

Kabuki's eyebrows and mouth turned upward simultaneously.

"Boy have date? Shopkeeper's daughter?"

"No, the girl from the Chamber of Commerce. Lila."

Kabuki frowned.

"Ah, Lila trouble. Shopkeeper daughter better."

"Yeah, she's the French girl, right?"

"*Hai.*"

"Yeah, Lila's trying to set me up with her, too. Everyone's insistent on this."

Kabuki nodded. "Then Lila smarter than Kabuki think. Good. Kabuki put on tie, and we go meet Lila and French girl."

Buck shook his head.

"What? No, *Sensei*, let me do this one myself, okay?"

Kabuki put his hand on Buck's shoulder.

"Have boy ever been married?"

"No." What a dumb question. He was eighteen.

"Kabuki have. Boy might want advice."

"I mean, Lila's supposed to help me with this."

"Have Lila ever been married?"

Buck shrugged. How was he supposed to know?

"Maybe. I think she's my age, though. I know she has a boyfriend who's cheating on her, even though he says he isn't, even though he clearly is."

"*Hai*, but Lila boyfriend musician, so…"

Buck wrinkled his brow.

"How does everyone around here know each other so well, but I don't know any of you?"

This time, Kabuki shrugged.

"Business network. Become businessman, meet everyone. Donald-*san* get his day."

"Whatever. Look, Mr. Kabuki, I need to go home and get ready. Just do me a favor. If you come, can you sit at a different table? I don't want Lila or the French girl spooked by you watching us."

Kabuki bowed.

"*Hai.* Will take notes from behind plant and give report after."

Buck bowed in return. That seemed fair.

* * *

BY EIGHT O'CLOCK, BUCK was racing across town to meet Lila at Tealeaf Central. Despite his shower and nice tie, he was sweating out of his armpits from pedaling so hard. Once this bet was over, he'd have to start saving for a car.

He got as far as Wild Trends when he spotted Billy Bob Drake coming out of the alley with the bag of bottles he'd scavenged from the dumpster. Billy, in turn, spotted him and flagged him down. Buck didn't want to be a jerk, so he rode up to where Billy was standing. Billy was covered in sludge and had a banana peel hanging from his head. But he also had a smile on his face.

"I found more than a dozen in there," he said. "What do you think that's worth down the middle?"

Buck shrugged. He knew the answer was the bottle count times ten, divided in half, but he didn't have the time to analyze the exact numbers, especially now that he had what he needed for tomorrow, so he didn't care about the bottles anymore.

"Twenty cents maybe? Thirty? I'll talk to you about it later."

"Aw man, imagine what I could get for thirty cents. Hey, you ready to head back to Sapphire's?"

Buck was rocking his bike forward, trying to get to Tealeaf Central. It was so close.

"Billy, I appreciate the help, really. I have to—"

Before he could finish his response, though, Buck considered what he was walking into. Tealeaf Central wasn't expensive, but it also wasn't free. Whatever he ordered tonight, he'd have to pay for. And if Lila expected him to pay for her, too, then he needed all the money he could get.

His eyes fell on the plastic bag in Billy's hand. He examined the decrepit soul standing before him with the expectant smile and the banana peel on his head.

"Get on the handlebars," Buck said.

* * *

LILA WAS NOWHERE TO be found when Buck finally walked into Tealeaf Central almost forty minutes and two dollars later. But Kabuki was sitting at a table behind a plant, just as he'd said he would.

Buck glanced at him and raised his eyebrows as he passed. Kabuki shook his head. Lila hadn't been there. Buck wondered if she'd forgotten about him already.

He sat at an empty table and waited for the waitress to greet him. A smarmy twenty-something dude with big teeth came to his table instead.

"I'm Stevie, and I'll be your waiter tonight." He pulled out his notepad. "Can I start you off with an egg roll?"

Buck craned his neck toward the plant. Kabuki was leaning sideways, studying Buck's actions. This was nothing at all according to plan.

"Um, give me a few minutes to decide."

The smarmy kid winked and gave him the finger gun, then headed back into the kitchen where Buck hoped he'd stay.

Buck, meanwhile, hurried over to Kabuki's table.

"Have you seen the French girl?" Buck asked.

Kabuki shook his head. "Just boy with teeth."

Buck studied the room. The dining area was filled to half capacity. The clientele covered all ages.

"Should we get out of here?" Buck asked.

Kabuki shook his head. "Kabuki like this place. Gonna stay and have sandwich and oolong."

Buck was so exhausted from failure that he decided to stay, too. Only, instead of getting his own table, he figured he'd hang out with Kabuki. Fortunately, Kabuki understood Buck's exhaustion and offered to pay for his meal.

"Know what boy's problem is," Kabuki said, when the smarmy kid brought them each a ceramic mug of oolong tea. "Need advertising."

"You mean like commercials?"

Kabuki nodded. "*Hai*. Word-of-mouth good for business, but bad for ignorance. Boy need paid advertising before he get word-of-mouth advertising."

Buck made a mental note.

"Is that one of your rules?"

"*Hai*. Don't remember number."

"We're on seventeen now."

"Rule seventeen. Buy word-of-mouth."

"How do I do that?"

"You hear of place called Ad Hut?"

Buck nodded. It was next door to the Lease Agent's place.

"That where boy should go for help. See Ad Guy in morning. He get customers for business."

"How much does advertising cost?"

Kabuki shrugged.

"Never use it myself. Word-of-mouth already strong."

Buck raised an eyebrow at Kabuki. Not once had Buck seen another student at The Whipping Shed since he'd started.

Kabuki shied away from Buck's gaze, as if he knew what he was thinking.

"Maybe Kabuki could invest in flyer or two."

A slender hand with pink nail polish slipped in between them, dropping a plate full of crackers. Buck lurched backward at the surprise intrusion.

"Sandwiches come soon," the owner of the hand said. Her voice was thick and accented. "Need anything while wait?"

Buck noticed Kabuki nodding and smiling at him, nudging his left hand toward this mysterious server. Buck felt the pit of his stomach drop. He knew what was coming, but he dared to look up, anyway.

The pundits were right. The French girl was magnificent.

"I, uh, um…"

Kabuki kicked him from under the table.

"I'm Buck," he said.

"*Oui*, I'm French Girl. Need more tea?"

Buck glanced at his cup, not because he wanted more tea, but because it was safer that way.

"I'm good. You say your name is French Girl?"

"*Oui*. Yes."

"Do you have a real name?"

"Yes, but Americans have trouble with it. So, they call me French Girl. Need cream or honey?"

Buck dared to cast her another glance. Her face was angular, but soft. And her hair was dark and curly, though it was pinned back in a ponytail, probably to keep it out of people's crackers. Her eyes were also dark, but no less intoxicating for it. Maybe they were bronze. Or hazel. Whatever they were, they were lovely. And her lips, boy, weren't those the most luscious things he'd ever seen?

"Yes, please," Buck said, forgetting the question.

He watched her walk toward the kitchen. There was nothing intentionally sexy about it. She didn't exactly shake her hips or anything. But her curves were so perfect that she didn't have to walk sexy to be sexy.

And everyone thought she was perfect for him? Were they crazy? Perfect, yeah. But what business did he have attracting anyone perfect, especially that perfect?

"Mr. Kabuki…"

"*Hai*. Boy like?"

"*Hai. Oui*. Like indeed."

Buck's palms began to sweat as he reached for a cracker. He shoved it in his mouth and chomped so hard that he'd nearly bitten his tongue. He reached for another, this time coming close to wearing a hole in the inside of his cheek.

"What do I do, *Sensei*? I've forgotten everything about girls."

Kabuki gestured for him to calm down.

"Start with heart," he said, as he pointed at his own chest. "Not with crotch."

Buck noticed the kitchen door swinging open and French Girl strolling out with a tray and two cups sitting on her fingertips.

"She's coming back. Help me."

Kabuki leveled his gaze at him.

"Lesson eighteen," he said, "don't panic."

When French Girl approached and set the cups on the table, Kabuki bowed his head and thanked her. Then he kicked Buck and nodded at him. He'd wanted him to do the same.

"Thank you," Buck said.

"Yes," French Girl said. She nodded once and smiled. "Anything else?"

"Uh, boy have something to say," Kabuki said. He tipped his head in Buck's direction.

Buck was taken aback by this. "I do?"

"*Hai*, boy pay girl compliment."

Buck glanced up at French Girl, who was now looking down at him. She wasn't exactly tall, but she was tall enough to feel like she was several feet away. Something about her was intimidating. And yet, she cast a smile, or something like a smile.

"Compliment?" she said. "That's good thing, right?"

Buck nodded.

"Still learning English," she said. "Want to make sure."

"Yeah, er…" he glanced at Kabuki for advice, but all the old man did was tap at his chest. "Yeah, so I wanted to compliment you…"

French Girl was still watching him, her face expectant but unsure. This probably wasn't the first time someone had tried to compliment her and failed.

"I just wanted to say…" and then, just like that, the words came to him. "I just wanted to say that Hybrid City is better for having you, and I hope you'll be here a while."

His eyes fell toward the table as he delivered his words, but then he dared to look up at her when he finished.

She was smiling. And her hand was over her heart. Buck didn't know a thing about her, other than that she was French and lived with the shopkeeper at Shop Down the Street, but in that moment, he knew that he'd said the right thing, especially once he spotted that tear rolling out of her left eye.

"Thank you," she managed to say, failing to look away. "That make me feel better. Was starting to hate this place."

Buck smiled. The connection was now made.

"Need anything else?" she asked.

Her hand was still on her chest, and that was when Buck noticed the name on her nametag.

"No, Maggie," he said, his eyebrows raised to signal that he'd learned her name.

Her face narrowed for a moment, but then she laughed when she noticed him looking at her nametag.

"That not my name. This Maggie's nametag. I borrow when she not here."

Buck frowned. "Don't you have one of your own?"

"Never got one, no. But boy sweet for noticing."

She winked at him. Buck's chest fluttered again. Why was he so resistant to meeting this French girl before?

Buck's End of Day Report:

Earned: $20.28

Spent: $0.64

Net Gain: $19.64 + French Girl's interest

* * *

EARLY THE NEXT MORNING, as Buck prepared to head to the bank and withdraw money from his savings account so he could purchase the icebox, he checked his mailbox for the latest coupons and special offers for anything else he might need today. But what he'd found instead was a letter addressed to him.

"The hell?"

He flipped it over in his hand to make sure he wasn't imagining things. But no, it was real. It was a letter from Jennifer. And there was a smudge of lipstick on it.

Episode 13

Clean Water, Polluted Memory

IT WAS TOO EARLY in the morning to suffer a crisis of the heart. But if he didn't read Jennifer's letter now, he'd spend the remainder of the day thinking about it, wondering how she'd intended to torture him. So, he opened it. To get it over with. But also to stoke his curiosity. This was, after all, the girl he'd wanted to graduate and celebrate his eighteenth birthday with. He also wanted to make sure she was the one who'd written it. It would've been worse if Chet had forged her name on something he'd written to torment him.

Fortunately, her handwriting was unmistakable. No jock could ever mimic it. The "J" in her name had that swoop that rounded in on itself and dashed under the other seven letters. The foot of her "f" stretched lower than her J-dash, dipping into the next empty line. The "r" was shaped almost like a heart, as it often was, though resembling less of one now than it had in signatures past. The passion she'd had in her pen was almost as evident as ever before, and if Buck hadn't known better, he'd have thought she was trying to lure him back in. And that worried him now that he was trying to move on. But at least she'd written it. Not Chet.

He took a deep breath as he started reading.

Dear Buck,

I don't know where to begin, but I feel like I should write you something. I hope this comes across well. But I'm not sure. So, I'll just say what's on my mind. Things between us went in a direction neither one of us expected. I'd say that's normal, but I don't know. Being with you was nice, and I liked nice. But the idea of being with Chet was a once-in-a-lifetime opportunity that I couldn't pass up. I hope you understand. It's like if Molly Ringwald came to you and asked you out. Would you really turn her down? I know you wouldn't. That's what happened to me. Chet may not be Jake Ryan, but he's pretty close. That's a Sixteen Candles reference if you forgot. Such a good movie.

I just wanted to let you know that I don't hate you. You probably think I do, but I don't. I just like Chet more. He's successful, you know? Or at least that's the way it looked when this started. But who knows? Some of his choices seem irresponsible. Makes me wonder if he really knows what he's doing. I can only guess.

I don't know why I'm even writing this. I guess I just need to vent. He says he loves me, but then he abandons me to hang out at a strip club. Is that what guys do? I don't remember you ever doing that to me.

Thank you for never doing that to me.

Anyway, I shouldn't be writing you. It's not fair to Chet. But what I did to you isn't fair either, especially since

The next part was smudged beyond recognition, as if she had tried to erase it, but Buck could still make out the remains of the words *night*, *trick*, and *birthday* under the phrase that replaced them.

you did nothing to deserve it. I should've told you I liked him.
I guess that's still true. Even if he is looking at naked strangers as I write this.
Okay, I'm going to stop writing now before I start crying.

Your friend,

Jennifer

Buck sat at his desk for several minutes as he stared at and through the letter. Maybe he was so tired from staying up most of the night, dreaming about French Girl, that nothing before his eyes made any sense. But reading Jennifer's words felt like studying a brick for the grand meaning of life. If he'd thought hard enough about it, he could have seen the value. But he wasn't energized enough to commit to that level of analysis. The problem was he was putting his toes into a new sea of fish, and if he looked back at his memories of her, it would pollute his dreams.

After all, betrayal was betrayal, regardless of how bad she may or may not have felt about it.

Maybe if last night had never happened, he'd care more about what she had to say. Or maybe if he'd never met Lila, Jennifer would still keep the real estate in his mind. Three days ago, that would've been the case. But a lot happens in three days. Three days ago, Buck didn't have a coffee business. Three days ago, he didn't have a contract defining the terms of his bet with Chet. Three days ago, he wondered if Chet might've even been right about him—that he was a loser.

But a lot changes in three days.

He shook his head. Maybe her effort to reconcile was laudable. But she'd written this too late.

His trash can was down by his feet, maw opened, ready to be fed. He glanced at the letter again and that swirly, swishy signature.

But no. As much as he wanted the betrayal she represented out of his life and mind, he was willing to give her credit for acknowledging the horribleness of her choice. So, he refrained from crushing the lined paper with jagged spiral edges between his fingers and slam dunking it in the wastebasket. Instead, he refolded it into its envelope and tucked it in the back of his school supplies drawer where he kept his notebooks and his new business tracking ledger. Maybe someday he'd use it to warn his kids about whomever they'd give their hearts to. He was confident those kids would never call Jennifer "Mom."

While he was digging around in his drawer, trying to find the best place to keep the letter without having to ever look at it again, he removed his business ledger and set it on the counter. In contrast with what he wanted to ignore, his business ledger was the exact opposite of that.

Day 5: Friday, June 14, 1985

Buck's Savings Account: $26
Buck's Wallet: $32.55
Buck's Business Funds: unknown
Buck's Expenses: $2 a day*
Hours of Operation: 12 p.m.-5 p.m.

As Buck looked over his accounts, he realized he hadn't yet figured out how his monthly fees would factor into his expenses, so he did a quick bit of high school math and decided the forty dollars the Lease Agent wanted each month broke down to $1.33 a day. Likewise, his twenty-dollars-a-month Chamber of Commerce fee boiled down to $0.66 a day. So, he'd have to set aside two dollars each day to remain active as a business owner.

Of course, the Lease Agent had said he'd defer the first month's rent payment, so maybe he didn't owe that first forty dollars? Buck wasn't certain how to handle that—forty dollars could still make the difference between winning and losing the bet! So, he put an asterisk beside it to remind himself to ask. Hopefully, he wouldn't forget.

He also thought today was a good day to test the afternoon crowd at the park. Yesterday proved the morning crowd wasn't nearly as addicted to coffee as he'd thought or hoped, assuming they even knew he was there, so today he'd have to switch it up and cross his fingers that the lunch folks were rabid coffee drinkers.

With his day now planned, Buck headed off to the bank to withdraw the money he needed for the icebox and replacement of fresh cream. Then he was off to buy his needed supplies at Happy Homewares as soon as it opened at ten o'clock. Between the bank and the home goods store, however, Buck paid Irina Swift a visit and tried an egg and bacon croissant that she was testing. Irina was nice enough to let him eat it for free. While there, he told her about French Girl.

"She sounds exquisite," Irina said. "Did she show the same interest in you?"

"I think so." Buck wasn't actually sure. More like he'd hoped so. "She came to my table, like, three times."

"Why didn't you ask for her number?"

Buck had wanted to. When French Girl asked him if he "needed anything else" as she handed them the bill, he almost said, "Your phone number," but his tongue got stuck to the roof of his mouth. Even Mr. Kabuki tried spurring him on when he kicked him under the table. It just wasn't enough to get his mind and mouth to reach an acceptable agreement. His mind wanted one thing, his mouth another, and Kabuki's foot couldn't help them mediate.

"She's too perfect," he said.

Irina smirked at him.

"No, she's not. She's flesh and blood. Like you." Irina handed him a bottled water to help him wash down his breakfast sandwich. "You don't have to fear her."

Buck washed down the bacon. Then he glanced at the water bottle. Something about it was…cleaner than he was used to.

"Hey, this is good." He was now staring at the generic water drop image on its label. "Where'd you get it?"

"Water Monkey," she said. "Ping's got a sale going on this week. Couldn't resist. He sells the best water."

Buck took another swig. He couldn't detect a single trace of rust or lime. Just pure water.

It gave him another great idea.

* * *

BUCK HAD LITTLE LEFT to his name after buying the cooler from Happy Homewares and the bag of ice he needed to keep it cool. Replenishing his supply of cream also set him back another half a dollar. But he wanted to check out Water Monkey's sale in case it could help him make better coffee.

The shop was boutique in size, but it had a dedicated product focus. Wall-to-wall empty water bottles for athletes, prepackaged bottles of water with the generic water drop labels, and watercoolers for offices. It also sold jugs for refilling the watercoolers. In the back of the store, next to the bathrooms, was a public watercooler stocked with paper cups and a sign on its body that said, *Floor Model, Not for Sale.* Buck poured himself a cup and smacked his lips with delight.

Just as clean as the bottled water Irina had given him. This place was the best.

"See what you're looking for?"

Buck looked over his shoulder to discover a small Asian man staring at him from beside a display of carbonation pumps. The stitched nametag on his lapel said his name was Ping Sierra. This must've been the store's owner.

"Irina Swift said you had a sale this week."

Ping nodded. "Yessir. Fifty percent off everything in the store, except watercooler. Can't give those away too cheap, you know?"

Buck shrugged. What did he know?

"What you here for?"

Buck pointed at a case of bottled water. "How much for those?"

"Fifty percent off regular price."

"Which is?"

"Cheaper than regular price."

After a quick clarification, Buck concluded he couldn't afford a case right now, which was a shame, considering the discount. But Ping agreed to sell him a dozen bottled waters individually, at ten cents each.

"You like, you come back."

Buck bowed in gratitude. Ping offered him a confused look.

"What you bowing for? We shake hands here."

Buck shook his hand. Then he took his bottled waters to the pavilion where he finished setting up shop for the day. Now that he had a cooler, he could keep not only his creams chilled but also his water. His clean, not-rusty water.

* * *

No one had stopped by in the time he'd spent setting up, so Buck waited until noon to open officially. This decision caused him some trouble a couple of hours later when a family drove up to the pavilion in a van stuffed with party supplies. After a short back-and-forth about "fairness" and "rental agreements," the family's patriarch relented and gave Buck the middle finger. Then, as his wife shuffled the children back to the van, the dad bought a cup of coffee for the road. He offered Buck two dollars and a hearty insult. Buck thanked him for the two dollars.

By three o'clock, more recreationists were jogging or bicycling around the lake, and Buck straightened his back in preparation to serve them. Nothing invigorated a man or woman drenched in sweat more than a steaming cup of caffeine, and he was ready to hand it off as they ran by. In fact, to ensure he didn't miss anyone, he went down to the trail where everyone was running, holding out a cup for anyone willing to take it.

In the course of an hour, four people stopped to talk, but none was interested in hot coffee while on a jogging spree. Two, however, said they'd come back once they finished. Buck made another four dollars on their return. They each ordered coffee with cream and sugar. Both were impressed by its quality and told him they'd consider coming back for more.

"The secret is fresh cream and *bottled* water," he told them.

It wasn't until he packed up for the day that he realized he shouldn't have been sharing trade secrets with anyone who didn't work for him. But at least he'd made six bucks.

* * *

ON HIS WAY HOME, Buck did some math and determined he was bleeding cash faster than his old locker roommate, Garrett Nedmeyer, bled nostrils after slamming his face against the locker door too many times. "Just try the latch," Buck would always shout at him. Even though he was brand new to practical economics, he didn't have to stretch his imagination to realize he was spending almost eight times what he was earning. And now that his bank balance was down to a dollar, he didn't have any fallbacks.

As he rode through Hybrid West, watching all the colorful shopfronts race by, he considered stopping at each one to check whether the shopkeepers needed any errands run, for a fee, of course. With every store that slipped by, however, he talked himself out of it—what did they need him for? But by the time he'd gotten to Novelties Plus, a shop dedicated to trinkets and tchotchkes, he'd given in to his temptation. How would he know if he didn't ask anyone? So, he asked the shopkeeper, Danny Goodboy, if he needed anything.

"I wouldn't mind a cup of coffee, actually," Danny said. "Been on my feet all day, moving products around to freshen the place up, all for nothing since nobody shops here much, but I could really stand to wake up. Gonna be a danger on the road if I don't, you know?"

Buck was about to tell him he knew just the coffee from just the place, when Danny provided a place for him. "Here's a dollar. Melty's Ice Cream makes a great cup."

Buck pocketed the dollar, then left without a word. His gut had fully sunk by the time he reached the sidewalk. He knew Melty's Coffee and Ice Cream Bar well. He wasn't a fan.

It was nothing against Melty's as an ice cream shop or even as a coffee dealer. Both were fine products, as far as he knew. Buck's problem was that Jennifer worked there, and unless she was helping Chet today, she would probably be the one to serve him. He didn't even need a scoop of vanilla in his bloodstream to give him those chills, especially if she wanted to talk about the letter. There was no way he was ready to have that discussion.

As he got on his bike, he weighed his options.

On the one hand, he could just leave. Danny had given him a dollar. One measly dollar. Would he really miss it? Most people wouldn't.

On the other, Buck wasn't like his father. If someone gave him a dollar for a job, then he'd have to complete it. Danny wanted coffee from Melty's. It mattered nothing to him that Jennifer Mills might be working there today. That meant Buck would have to confront her. After that weird letter she'd sent him, he really didn't want that. And now that French Girl was on his mind, he didn't even see much point in talking to her, period. It was a bad hand.

That left him with the third hand. Coffee from the pavilion. It was certainly the easiest and safest option, as well as an opportunity to show off his product, and thus the most obvious for the situation. But Danny had given him a dollar. After his sale to the disgruntled father, Buck had figured out his pricing point. He was charging a minimum of two dollars for a cup of coffee with cream and sugar.

Now that he was hemorrhaging cash, he couldn't afford to take from his own supply if all he'd get for it was a dollar. Plus, the pavilion was much farther away. By the time he'd return to Novelties Plus, the coffee would be cold.

So, there was no good choice. He should've just kept riding.

Buck closed his eyes and pedaled onward. Sometimes the best decision was the random one. And the random one brought him to Melty's, anyway.

As he opened the door, he peeked across the dining room, past the serving counter, into the depths of the kitchen. Jennifer was nowhere in sight. Perhaps he was in the clear. Or maybe she was just in another room. Either way, he had to be quick. His hands moistened as he marched across the dining room floor.

The girl standing at the counter frowned as she recognized him. Buck always had trouble remembering her name. Fortunately, she was wearing her name tag this time, so he didn't have to guess.

"Hey, Emmy."

"Marcy," she said, shaking her head as he reached the counter. "Emmy's not here."

Buck pointed at her name tag. "Then why—"

"You're in trouble, pal. Jennifer told us not to serve you if you ever came in here."

So, the name tag conversation was already over. Fair enough. Buck reached in his pocket and slapped Danny's dollar onto the counter.

"I'm running an errand for someone," he said. "So, I'm not the customer here."

"You sure look like one."

"Small coffee, black."

"You've got some nerve ordering me around after what you did to my best friend."

Buck raised his eyebrows. Best friend? Jennifer had a best friend?

"What are you talking about?"

"Do I have to spell it out for you?"

Buck needed to hurry this along. Even if Jennifer wasn't here, he couldn't risk her showing up and asking if he'd gotten the letter or why he'd come to Melty's. How would he respond? She wouldn't believe the truth. Too simple. Too obvious. They had too much history.

"She cheated on me. Not the other way around."

Marcy took the dollar and shrugged. "Not the way I heard it."

She stormed into the back without another word. Then she returned with a small paper cup. It was steaming. She passed it over.

"I spit in this, just so you know."

Buck shrugged.

"Told you, it's not for me. Spit in it again if you want. I don't care."

Marcy took the cup back and poured it down the sink.

"You're a jerk. Hold on."

As Buck returned to Novelties Plus with the new cup of coffee in hand, he couldn't help but wonder what else Jennifer had said about him, and what else she had kept from him. Not once had she ever talked about a best friend or that her name was Marcy or Emmy or whatever. Made him wonder if he ever really knew her, or if he'd just thought he did.

Kinda made him wish she was at Melty's today. Then she could've answered those questions for him. If he'd even known to ask about them. If she would've bothered to answer.

He gripped his forehead and winced. He was getting an ice-cream headache just thinking about how complex his life had gotten since graduation night.

Episode 14

The Ad Guy

AFTER HE DELIVERED THE hot coffee from Melty's, Buck told Danny Goodboy about the new business he'd started and asked him to consider stopping by sometime. Danny, sipping his current beverage, didn't seem so interested now that his needs were satisfied. But as he shifted his focus from his cup to Buck, back to the cup, then back to Buck, his hedging of thoughts suggested he was too nice to put it totally out of mind.

"If it's better than Melty's," Danny said.

Buck fought to hide his disappointment. He was almost certain his coffee wouldn't compare. Melty's had been around longer and understood its clientele better. Buck learned the value of using fresh cream over spoiled just this week.

"Of course it's better," Buck said, turning away to avoid making eye contact.

Danny smacked his lips after taking a long swig and closed his eyes to savor the taste. The luxurious peace that passed over his face said it all. Buck had a long way to go if he wanted to poach Melty's customer base.

"I'm open Monday through Friday," he said anyway. "North Park Pavilion. About noonish."

Danny peered at him from over his cup.

"Who drinks park coffee at noon?"

Buck was tempted to say "no one," but he said nothing.

In truth, there was nothing he could say that would raise his confidence. Everything about this business was ill-conceived. Kabuki's training was good enough to teach him how to make coffee but not how to sell it. Until he got his target customer base to believe in his product, there wasn't much he could do to make them his customer base, Danny Goodboy included.

The only thought he had left was to make a special delivery.

"Would you like me to bring you a cup of my own blend?" Buck asked. "So, you can try it for yourself?"

Danny brought his Melty's cup to his lips. As soon as the hot liquid entered his mouth, that look of pleasure returned. Buck sensed the disinterest returning. His perfect customer's heart was already spoken for.

"Well, thanks for the dollar at least."

Danny offered him a thumbs-up. Buck walked out of Novelties Plus wondering if there was such a thing as the perfect customer. If so, he had yet to find it. Certainly not here.

He stood on the sidewalk outside, unclear about what to do next.

Evening was setting now. Traffic along the street was thinning now that the workweek was over. Drivers passed him, giving him no attention, neither knowing nor caring about what he offered. To them, he was some random kid with nowhere to go.

Then came the harsh reality he'd tried ignoring all week.

Money had been escaping his wallet too quickly and finding its way back in too slowly. His financial security was a lake ebbing itself away into dryness. If Buck continued to work for what amounted to lost parking lot change, then he'd have to close his coffee business before it ever got a chance to grow.

He hopped on his bike and started for home, asking himself the critical questions for survival.

How could he change the tide? What did he need to improve his situation? Could he improve his situation? Fortunately, Mr. Kabuki had sucker-punched him into starting a job at Shop Down the Street tomorrow. But how would that lead to an uptick in coffee sales? At best, it would give him more cash leverage to keep up with supplies, but according to the contract he'd signed with Chet, he couldn't use an outside source to pad his bet earnings.

Granted, he'd have to review the contract to be sure. He remembered that any savings prior to the bet were out of bounds, but it was unclear if earnings he'd made from any source during the bet were eligible. Could he add his employee earnings to his ledger? On that same note, was it possible Chet might do the same?

As he rode through downtown, considering his options for improving his chances, a possible answer to his questions reached the corner of his eye: a poster in the shop window for Outdoor Chores & Crap, "The Place for All Your Yard Needs." The glossy sign invited him to check out the shop's latest discount on ladders: "Now 50% Off the Retail Price."

Even though he never understood why the shop owner had named the store as he had, Buck knew the business was popular among yard enthusiasts. Dads of all ages could be seen entering and exiting the shop on a minute-to-minute basis. Ronnie's dad had even raved about its selection and prices. If Buck had kids of his own, he'd probably patronize the shop regularly, too.

Buck had no need for a new ladder right now, but knowledge of the shop's success led him through a spiderweb of interwoven thoughts, and at the center of his construction was a piece of Kabuki's advice that he wished he'd remembered sooner. If that poster could lure in the town's majority of middle-aged men, then it stood to reason that Buck could use something similar for his own business.

Fortunately, he knew where to find it.

A few minutes later, Buck found himself back at the Lease Agent's place, but not really. He'd gone next door to a tiny advertising agency called The Ad Hut, where a wave of green architecture hit him in the eyes on entry. The color drowned out the obvious intended focus on red, white, and blue, and the six-foot dollar bill awkwardly hanging from the American flag behind the sales counter reemphasized the clash of ideas here. This place was all about money and freedom, but which was more important? That question had no answer according to the shared dominance of symbols. It drowned in both.

Buck hardly had time to take in the rest of the shop when a scrawny guy with a bushy beard and luscious smile approached the sales counter from the back room. His eyes were bright at the sight of Buck, and his hands rose for an embrace or a showcase.

"Comrade!" the man said with a thick Russian accent. "Who's Ad Guy, you ask? Why I'm Ad Guy. Never see you here before."

Buck shrugged.

"Never been interested in your store until now," Buck said.

"Understand. You must fear democracy, for my shop all about democracy."

Buck noticed a banner along the right wall. In big red letters, superimposed on an American flag background, it said, *Sell Your Propaganda Cheap*. The Rs were all backwards.

"I can see that."

"America greatest nation," the Ad Guy said. "Burn commies."

"Right, so I assume you sell ads here?"

"That what sign says." The Ad Guy squinted at the sign on the wall. "Good English."

"Right. So, I'm looking to improve my business. Got anything that can help me generate interest? I'm technically a beginner."

The Ad Guy winked and gave him the finger gun.

"Lucky you ask. I have stuff to hand red-blooded American types. Stuff to hand red-blooded American trees and buildings. And stuff for make you popular. Like Reagan and not Comrade Gorbachev."

The Ad Guy retrieved a small flyer from behind the counter and showed it to Buck. On it was a list of advertising options, including flyers like this one, oddly enough.

"Flyers small and end up in trash. But they get message across quickly." The Ad Guy pointed at the next item on the list. "Handouts better for spreading message as they do better to catch eye. Get people to remember message longer than flyers. Some people hang them on bedroom wall, or should."

Buck shot the Ad Guy a quizzical look. "How would you know that?"

The Ad Guy shrugged. "KGB secret. Now posters best investment. Hang them on trees and park benches to attract attention. Last as long as it take for authorities to tear them down." He flashed his gaze at Buck. "Watch out for bee man. Bee man and Ad Guy mortal enemies."

Buck shivered at the memory of "the bee man." As far as he knew, he was still out looking for him.

"Any tips on where best to hang them so they'll last?"

The Ad Guy thought about the question.

"In store?"

"What if my business is in the park, out in the open?"

"Maybe handouts better."

Buck glanced at his list of options.

"How much for those?"

"Print two dozen for three dollars."

Buck's chest tightened. That was more than he'd earned per glass bottle at Sapphire's.

"Any chance I can get a fifty percent discount on that, like ladders at Outdoor Chores and Crap?"

The Ad Guy thought about it.

"With coupon, yes."

Buck tapped the counter.

"Can I get a coupon?"

"Can get lots of coupons. Whole book even." The Ad Guy pointed at the next item on the list. "Six dollars."

Buck weighed the pros and cons of purchasing advertising options with the Ad Guy and decided that even a handout worth twelve and a half cents was worth it if it meant finding a repeat customer. So, he ordered a pack.

The Ad Guy told him it would be ready Monday evening.

"You can't give them to me now?" Buck wanted to generate interest as quickly as possible before he bled any further.

"All ads custom-made," the Ad Guy said. "Take time to print."

Buck frowned at this slap in the face by reality once again, but he understood the need for a time delay to get a higher quality product. If his potential customers got their hands on glossy paper with shiny, typed words, then they were more likely to become his customers. If the tables were turned, Buck would want his solicitor to care enough to hand him a professional piece of advertising than an amateur job on cheap paper and handwritten words. Easy psychology. So, he thanked the Ad Guy for his help.

The Ad Guy saluted him.

"Thank you, Comrade, for choosing most patriotic store in city for shopping. Now I sing 'Patriotic Song' in your honor…"

"Yeah, you don't have to do that. I'm fine. Thanks."

* * *

As Buck formed a plan for distributing the handouts once he picked them up next week, something honked and crashed behind him. The racket was so sudden that he swerved within inches of the nearest building, then fell as he corrected himself. His bike clattered behind him as he skidded off the sidewalk and into the grassy swale.

A car door opened and shut behind him.

"Hey, you still want to get tea?" a woman's voice called out.

His knees were bruised, but fortunately his pants saved him from getting scraped. The pain was minimal. Even so, he was stomach-down in the grass.

"I'll buy," the woman continued.

Buck got to his knees and spun around to face his assailant. Lila was marching toward him, silhouetted in the headlights shining from her El Camino behind her. Buck barely made out the bright smile on her face, but he could tell she was wearing a tight dress and party beads around her neck. The beads glowed in the ambient light around them.

She reached out for his hand as she got within range and helped him to his feet when she took it.

"Sorry to stand you up last night," she said. "My boyfriend and I had a big fight, and I didn't feel like going anywhere afterward."

Buck said nothing. Just brushed the grass off his knees.

"But we're cool now. So, you wanna get tea or what?"

Lila didn't wait for Buck to answer. Instead, she pivoted on the balls of her feet and reached down to pick up his bike. Before Buck could tell her he'd get it himself, she had it upright on both wheels and started walking it toward the car, which was halfway on the sidewalk.

"Here, you can tell me on the way there," she said. "How's your day today?"

Buck scratched his head to check for blood. There was none.

"My day was good," Lila said. "I scored negative on a pregnancy test. So, I'm in a happy mood."

Buck stared at her as she lifted his bike into the back of her car. What the hell had just happened here?

"Come on, get in the car. I wanna tell you all about it."

His feet started moving toward the headlights, even though his brain told him to run the other way. She had his bike, though. Where was he supposed to go?

So, he got in the car. Then she told him all about the pregnancy test she'd passed, as if she'd just earned an A plus.

***

TEALEAF CENTRAL ON A Friday night was busier than on Thursday. Buck and Lila sat outside waiting for a seat for almost twenty minutes. When they were finally allowed in, the host sat them in the middle of the room where everyone could see them.

Within seconds, Buck sensed eyes on his back, even if there was no one giving him attention. This was the first time he'd been out with a girl since Jennifer had cheated on him, and he didn't know how he was supposed to feel about it. Even if she and Lila resembled each other physically, there were still clear enough differences between them that Buck's body imploded a little at the awkwardness of sharing this public space with a girl he barely knew.

Where Jennifer was soft-spoken, Lila was loud. Where Jennifer insisted on focusing on herself, Lila roped Buck into the discussion. Where Jennifer was happy to remain unseen, Lila was animated. Where their physical attributes drew parallels, their character attributes diverged. Buck struggled to match a familiar face to a strange personality. And he couldn't understand why Lila was suddenly so friendly. All eyes were watching him now.

He must've been lost in his thoughts because he failed to notice her holding his hand until she slapped the table beside it.

"So, what do you think?" she asked.

"It looks good," he said.

Lila kept his hand, but she retreated a little.

"Huh?"

Buck shook his head. Noticed the feeling of her palm in his. How had it gotten there? Why was it there? Why was there no special sensation between his legs in connection with this moment?

"Can you repeat the question?" he asked.

"I was asking if you think I should marry him?"

Again, Buck glanced down at his hand in her hand. Ever since he'd gotten into the El Camino, he'd become lost in a storm of thoughts. Could he ever get customers to take him seriously? Would his wallet bleed out before he could apply the tourniquet? Would his coffee ever measure up to Melty's quality? And now he wondered how he'd gone from pining for Lila to feeling ambivalent towards her. What was he even doing at this table?

High school had never prepared him for questions like these. As much as he hated spending the better part of his teenage years wedged behind a metal locker door, at least it shielded him from having to answer such tough questions like the ones he was asking now.

Likewise, his sheltered life among schoolbooks and a grouchy Garrett Nedmeyer never presented him with such serious questions as the one Lila was asking now. What was the right answer here? And what would happen if he'd given her the wrong one? Would she still like him? Would he still care?

Before the words to an empty response could leave his mouth, another woman's voice whispered in his ear, or at least it sounded like a whisper in his ear, even though it was probably spoken at a natural volume from a couple of feet away.

"What would you like this evening?" the woman asked in her sexy accent.

Buck's carotid pulse thumped in his neck. It somehow modeled his heart, which also accelerated. The skin of his palm was moistening, and he sensed Lila pulling away finally. He glanced up to face his interrogator: his lovely, brunette interrogator.

"Hi," Buck said. It was all he could manage.

French Girl nodded and smiled at him. "We have special on herbal tea. Would you like?"

Buck said yes. It was all he could say.

French Girl scanned him from his eyes to his hand, the one in Lila's palm, then up to Lila's eyes. Lila was beaming.

"Herbal tea is awesome," she said. She darted her spare finger between her and Buck. "I'm buying both."

French Girl twitched a smile, then wrote something on her notepad.

Even though he had been caught in a spell since falling off his bike, Buck was now aware of his position, whom he was sharing it with, and the optics he was displaying to not only everyone around him but also to the lovely French waitress beside his right shoulder. He pulled his hand out of Lila's and withdrew it into his own lap before she could grab it again.

"As friends," Buck said.

French Girl glanced down at him. Her expression was confused. "Sorry?"

Buck nudged his forehead in Lila's direction.

"We're friends."

French Girl twitched a smile.

"Okay. Like food with tea tonight?"

Buck glanced at Lila. Lila was smirking at him. She must've sensed his discomfort.

"I need to think about it," Buck said.

French Girl asked Lila the same question. Lila gave her the same answer.

When French Girl retreated to the service station, Lila kicked Buck in the shin. The look on her face couldn't have been more amused.

"I called it, didn't I?" she asked.

"Called what?" Buck knew exactly what she was referring to, but he wasn't sure he should give her the ammunition.

"It's written all over your face. You Casanova."

Buck was about to respond, but the words caught in his throat. Lila leaned forward and reached out for his biceps.

"Come on, level with me. You were here last night, right?"

Buck averted her gaze.

"That's a yes," she said. "You talk to her?"

Buck kept his attention on the service station door. French Girl hadn't emerged yet. He felt the strain in his chest rising and the skin of his neck tightening.

"You're not going to embarrass me, are you?" he asked.

"Now, why would I do such a thing?"

"Not an accusation. Just a question."

Lila's hand crept up to his shoulder and then to his cheek. She forced him to face her.

"I would never do such a thing," she said. "I'm a fan of love, both as receiver and as instigator."

"Instigator?"

"I'm a girl, so I know girls. I know how we think. Act. Love." She tipped her head toward the service station. "You want her, I can help you get her."

Buck's heart accelerated another few beats per second. The sensation between his legs returned. Anything that got him French Girl's notice was worth the extra help.

"How?"

Lila winked at him. "You just got to make her think you're worth it."

Buck shrugged.

"Okay, how?"

Lila glanced at the service station.

"Like this."

Buck followed her gaze. French Girl was coming back to the table with two saucers and cups in her hand. She was staring at Buck as she advanced, her hands delicately balancing the cups on the saucers. Her hips swayed with every motion of her feet. Her elbows remained locked, protecting the containment of the tea she carried. Her hair bobbed on her shoulders, teasing him with an invitation to dance. It was all he could do to——

Lila's fingernails dug into his cheek as his face jerked to his left. Next thing he knew, her face was just inches from his. And then it was pressed against his, her nose fencing with his. Something peppermint-flavored hit the back of his throat. His eyes must've popped open, even though he saw nothing but a pair of closed eyes filling his view.

Even with all the comparisons he'd made between Jennifer and Lila, there was no comparing this. Jennifer had always reserved her affections, even when she called herself "girlfriend." This was incomparable. It was brand new.

And he knew French Girl was witnessing every second of it.

Episode 15

Shop Down the Street

EVEN AFTER LILA PULLED her lips away, the ghost of her kiss lingered on Buck's mouth. Peppermint and lipstick, the latter of which he knew neither the brand nor the flavor. There might've been the taste of bubblegum left behind. Definitely a splash of fluid that didn't belong to him. And the essence of a smile burned in his retinas.

So that's what it was like to be kissed. He wondered where the fireworks were.

Something hit the table. Just as Lila returned to her side of it, two cups of tea touched down on the surface. Anchored to their handles were two sets of fingers belonging to a lovely European woman who hadn't yet kissed him. Would her flavors be similar? Or would she leave behind the taste of red wine? Maybe some French dressing?

He dared to raise his eyes to meet French Girl's. She was staring at Lila. Nodding at her. Then she turned her attention to Buck. Nodded at him.

"Enjoy your tea," she said.

And that was it. She turned on her tiptoes and headed back to the kitchen. Never looked back.

"She's so jealous," Lila said.

"What?" Buck said.

"You have to call her. Tonight. While she hates me."

Buck faced Lila. She was tipping her head toward the kitchen. Not even a trace of romance in her eyes. Just matter of fact. The kiss was strictly for show.

Buck said nothing.

* * *

WHEN BUCK GOT HOME, he fetched the family phone book from under the breakfast counter and searched for Mack Green's number. He wasn't sure what to say once French Girl answered, but he rehearsed some possibilities. The top idea was "we're just friends," referring to Lila, but French girls came from the land of romance, and "just friends" probably had a different connotation than whatever he thought. After all, French people kissed with their tongues. That's what his math teacher used to say whenever the topic of algebra got too boring. Surely, "just friends" translated into French meant "sleeping together." If French Girl was jealous, as Lila believed, that would just throw salt in the wound.

So, he'd need a backup.

Other possible topics included the weather, old girlfriends, and his favorite color, but when each starting phrase ended with him giving up, he decided it was better, perhaps, to say nothing and let French Girl do all the talking. It had worked with Jennifer, and Lila seemed to enjoy controlling the conversation, as well. If he held silent for a few seconds, chances were French Girl would also take command. Besides, it would give her plenty of practice speaking English. Buck already knew English, so he didn't need the practice.

Satisfied with his decision, he continued searching for Mack's number. He'd been so consumed with how to say hello that he'd somehow ended up in the H section of the phonebook, so he backtracked to where he belonged.

Mack's name was listed among a hundred other Greens, including two other Macks, but most belonged to neighboring towns. Buck called the only one listed with a Hybrid City address. Mack answered.

Buck hung up. It was Mack's phone. Why did he expect French Girl to answer? Maybe he assumed that as a teenage girl she'd snag the handset off the cradle the way a dog snatches a biscuit out of the air. Wasn't that what girls did in the movies and on TV? Obviously, they did it in real life, too. Right?

Must've been a fluke in timing. Buck called again. Mack answered.

"Yello."

Buck hung up. He looked at the clock. It was almost nine. Maybe she was still at the tea shop. He hadn't seen her since she'd dropped off his tea, so he thought she'd left. But maybe she was just avoiding Lila. Because of jealousy. That had to be it. Buck decided he'd try again at ten.

"Yello."

At eleven.

"Yello."

Buck didn't want to torture himself anymore, so he spoke.

"Is French Girl there?"

"Yep, who's this?"

"Um…"

"Ouch."

"Huh?"

"Sorry, sat down too hard. Gotta get a cushion for this chair. Let me tell you, kid, you better take care of yourself as you get older. When I was your age, I was cruisin' for chicks at the beach. Now I'm contemplating whether to buy hemorrhoid cream. Not to say I have hemorrhoids, but I don't know that I don't, you know?"

"Um…"

"Been calling around for expert advice. Pharmacy. Dime store. Doctor's office. They all support different brands, which tells me they're all taking kickbacks. You know what a kickback is, kid?"

Buck said nothing. Mack didn't give him a chance. He spent the next twenty minutes going down a rabbit hole of medical information before circling back to the original question.

"So, what're you calling for again?"

"I wanted to talk to French Girl," Buck said.

"Oh, yeah, no, I don't let her use the phone."

"Sorry?"

"Teenage girl. Probably talks too much, you know? I don't want her tying up my phone. In case someone needs to call me. I don't have call waiting."

"Um…"

"Who shall I say is calling?"

"Buck."

A few seconds passed.

"Wait a minute, I know that voice. You're Kabuki's student, right?"

"Um…"

"Yeah, that is you." A brief pause. "It's late, kid. Shouldn't you be in bed by now? You're starting work tomorrow, remember?"

"Um…"

"Go to sleep. I'll tell French Girl you called. See you in the morning. Don't be late."

"Okay."

Mack Green hung up, leaving Buck alone with the dial tone.

He stared at the handset. Then he put it in the cradle. He didn't know what to expect from the phone call, but at least it didn't go as badly as he'd thought it would. Not that it was particularly great, either.

BUCK'S END OF DAY REPORT:

Earned: $7.00

Spent: $46.78 ($25 from savings; $21.78 from wallet)

Net Gain: -$39.78

* * *

BUCK CONTEMPLATED LEAVING THE pavilion closed today since he was scheduled to work at Shop Down the Street until early evening. But he had two concerns. First, nothing he earned from Mack Green could count toward his bet, which translated into a wasted day. But second, and worse, leaving the pavilion vacant meant someone else could take it, and if they took it today, then there was no reason they wouldn't take it tomorrow. If that trend were to continue, then he'd have to fight for the space on Monday, and that would've wasted more of his moneymaking time for the rest of the week, especially if he'd lost the battle.

He couldn't afford either scenario, but he couldn't break his trust with Mack Green, or Mr. Kabuki by proxy, either. He'd have to show up to work today, at Shop Down the Street. But he'd also have to fulfill his shift duties at the Coffee Pavilion. And he couldn't split his body in two.

As he set his milk-layered cereal bowl in his kitchen sink and rinsed it out, he figured out the solution. He'd ask for help. It was the only way. And as far as he knew, the rules didn't forbid it. So, he fetched the phone from the wall and dialed the number he knew best.

"Hey, Ronnie," he said when his best friend picked up. "Want a job today?"

"Hey, little camper." The frog in Ronnie's voice signaled that he was still half-asleep. "I don't work Saturdays. Or any day."

"But you could!" Buck didn't mean to shout, but he had limited time to haggle. He was due to arrive at Mack's shop by nine o'clock. "What I mean is, I need your help."

"Doing what?"

Buck explained his situation as quickly and accurately as possible, covering every operational task and contingency he could think of. Ronnie, meanwhile, didn't offer Buck much confidence in his understanding of the job's complexity since he zoned out and snored a couple of times during the sales pitch. But when Buck finished his spiel and asked Ronnie if he could count on him, Ronnie offered him a simple reply.

"I'll ask Tiffany if she wants to help. It's her call."

At that point, Buck was willing to risk her answer.

"I'll leave the key to the equipment closet under my front doormat," he said. "I'll stop by after my shift to check in."

"Tiffany will want payment if she helps."

Buck felt something drop in his chest. Might've been a lung. But it was probably the cost of business stinging him in the heart.

Of course, she'd want to get paid. Nobody in 1980s America ever worked for free. What choice did he have but to agree?

"How much?"

Ronnie laughed. That question seemed to wake him up.

"That'll depend on how popular she is. Obviously."

Buck hung up. Why did everything sound like extortion? The cereal in his stomach turned. Tiffany was an attractive young woman. Of course, she'd be popular. He sighed. There was no getting around the inevitable. Today was about keeping the business open, not about earning his own keep. But if he could scrape anything out of this deal, he'd have to try.

He called Ronnie back and apologized for the abrupt disconnect.

"Can you talk her down to the lowest possible amount at least?"

Ronnie laughed again. Buck hung up. He had no time left to negotiate. Either they'd help him for a fair price, or they wouldn't. Either way, he had to brush his teeth and get to the shop. It was already 8:30.

Day 6: Saturday, June 15, 1985

Buck's Savings Account: $1.00

Buck's Wallet: $17.77

Buck's Business Funds: unknown

Buck's Expenses: $2 a day*

Hours of Operation: ???

* * *

BUCK RODE HIS BIKE into Shop Down the Street at 8:57 and parked it beside a cardboard cutout advertising West Coast Cola, a regional soft drink that tossed a few competitive blows at the global giants during their war for dominance. According to the sign, all bottles were marked ten percent off. Buck made a note in his head in case anyone asked about it later. So far, the store had no customers.

Mack was standing on a ladder behind the sales counter, stringing up a banner between two support posts that also advertised West Coast Cola. The caption below asked consumers why they should pay more for the national brands when they could enjoy "almost as good" local brands for ten percent less. Buck didn't need to address the question, as he already knew the answer. The national brands tasted at least twenty percent better, which, thanks to Coca-Cola's new formula, made both Coke and Pepsi almost equally sweet. But as long as no one asked him his opinion, he wouldn't have to lie to make a sale. Plus, what was he supposed to say? He rarely drank West Coast Cola himself, as he suspected one ingredient was fertilizer. That's what his math teacher had once said about it at any rate.

Buck approached the counter. "I'm here."

Mack, who had his back turned and hadn't noticed him walking in, glanced over at the clock on the wall.

"Ring you up in a sec. Where is that kid?"

"No, it's me. Buck."

Mack reached for the pole to stabilize himself for balance and glanced over his shoulder to confirm Buck's presence. His eyes lit up at the sight of him, then flashed toward the cardboard cutout.

"Ah, good. Why don't you park that bike of yours in the back room, then come up here and help me?"

Buck walked his bike around the soft drink display and down the nearest aisle toward the entrance to the back room. As he opened the door, he cast a glance at the coffee aisle. A trickle of sweat popped out of his neck. There were fewer bags of Hawaiian coffee than of other brands. He passed through the door before he could give it another thought.

The back room, or stockroom, as Buck discovered it to be, was roughly the same size as the sales floor, but full of pallets and crates, not displays. Most were marked. A cubic outcrop with an open door and a single square window stood in the corner at half the height of the rest of the room, beside the door to the checkout zone. A desk was visible through the window inside. Mack's office. Between the two doors, a high-powered motorized floor fan oscillated from side to side, blowing warm air into the storage area. The air-conditioning ducts running across the ceiling were quiet.

Buck parked his bike outside Mack's office and headed through the main door into the checkout zone. He found Mack with one foot on the second-to-highest ladder step and the other dangling over space. Mack was leaning against the support pole as he tried tying a banner string around it. The ladder was tipping a few inches away from him.

"What should I do?" Buck asked.

"Just need you to hold the ladder so I don't break my neck," Mack said.

Buck stood on the side of the ladder opposite the pole and pushed it so all four feet touched the floor.

"Much better. Thanks."

"This the big promotion?"

"You catch on quick. Yeah, we sell a hundred bottles, and West Coast will double our next supply for the same cost."

"Anyone buy any yet?"

"A few. But Coke and Pepsi are still dominating, as expected. Gotta hand it to West Coast for trying, though. Hard to compete with those two. Especially when everyone knows you spike your drink with fertilizer."

Buck said nothing. He was already thinking the same thing.

"So, what do you need me to do today?"

Mack knotted the string and tugged on it. The banner shifted a little to the left.

"Well, gotta get you to clock in, fill in some paperwork, and do the legal stuff. Then I'll have you put out some stock."

"More West Coast Cola?"

"Eh, we'll see how it goes. Not the hottest seller, to no one's surprise, so I'm hoping the advertisements will tip it in our favor. But it's Saturday, and people love soda on Saturdays. Might get lucky. No, I need you to stock some of our dry goods first. Twenty-pound bags of dog food. Boxes of cereal. Things like that. You strong?"

Buck shrugged.

"Strong enough to lift twenty pounds of dog food? Sure."

"Can you move a crate's worth of dog food? Got a few dozen bags for you. This job will require a strong back."

Mack had brought his dangling foot back onto the step, and now he was angling toward the other pole to his right. Buck had to move to avoid getting kicked.

"I suppose."

"Well, make sure. Can't give you work insurance if anything goes awry."

Buck remembered Ronnie's agreement to help him with the Coffee Pavilion today. Mention of "work insurance" caused him to shake the ladder slightly.

"Is that a thing businesses have?"

"Hold the ladder tighter, please. Yeah, some do. Incentivizes workers who can't pay for it themselves. But it's more for older workers. Thirty-somethings. People old enough to break and smart enough to sue when they slip on a puddle. Nothing I need to worry about with you, hopefully."

And nothing Buck needed to worry about with Ronnie, hopefully.

"Hopefully."

Mack wrapped the banner string around the right-hand post. He struggled with tying it.

"Almost done," he said. "We'll get you nice and legal in just a moment."

"Okay."

"Then you can get started on the dog food."

"Sounds good."

"Then I'll have you stock the coffee area when you're done with that."

Buck felt a lump in his throat.

"Coffee area?"

"Yeah. Needs a refill." Mack hovered between the ladder and the pole as he meditated on his thoughts. "It's weird. I keep running low on Hawaiian coffee, but I don't seem to sell much of it. According to the books, I should have more."

The ladder shook. Mack pitched sideways and caught the post with both elbows. His right foot kicked at it. The right side of the sales banner touched down on the top of his head. Buck corrected himself immediately and fixed the ladder's stability.

"Hold the ladder tighter," Mack said. "If you don't mind."

"Sorry." Buck's words caught in his throat. He wasn't sure if he'd apologized out loud or in his mind.

Mack, meanwhile, reached his foot to the ladder step and eased his way into his previous position, just before he'd slipped. He resumed tying the banner as if nothing unusual had just happened.

"Need to double-check the accounting," Mack said. "But yeah, I'll need you to stock the Hawaiian coffee. Popular item. Either that or I'm losing my mind."

Buck, meanwhile, felt his heart speeding up. He still didn't know how to tell Mack about Kabuki's Hawaiian coffee habit without admitting himself as an accomplice.

"Okay" was all he could muster in response.

* * *

THE FIRST FEW BAGS of dog food were easy to transport. They couldn't have been over fifteen pounds, even though they claimed twenty, and the distance between the supply crate and the shelf was half the length of the store. Thirty steps on average. Buck lifted with his legs and carried the bags close to his chest. Comfortable work.

But it got tougher as the shelf quantity grew and the supply crate diminished. After ten bags, Buck felt a strain on his knees and lower back. After fourteen bags, he felt it in his elbows. The wind was still in his lungs, but the early stages of burning in his side were beginning. By the twenty-second bag, his shoulders stooped, and his pace slowed. Sweat soaked the back of his shirt. But he was walking, and carrying, and panting. Easy-ish.

"How you doing there?" Mack asked as he looked on from the security of his checkout zone.

"Fine," Buck said.

"You sure? Your face is turning red."

"Doing great."

The supply crate contained over fifty bags, but Mack had assured Buck he wouldn't have to unload everything. Just enough to satisfy customer demand. The problem was that Mack hadn't defined what customer demand looked like.

"How many is that?"

"Thirty, I think," Buck said, overselling the mark in case thirty was enough. He'd counted twenty-two.

"Get it up to forty, and I think we'll be okay for the weekend."

Buck plopped the latest bag onto the rising pile, then trudged back to the stockroom, grateful that his own business wasn't this demanding on supplies.

But that was a problem, too, wasn't it? Even though hardly anyone had come into the store since Buck's shift started, the Shop Down the Street still had a clientele, peak hours, and a net worth in its favor based on Buck's previous experience as a customer. It had the components needed to stay in business. Did the Coffee Pavilion have that? And would it have that before his bet with Chet expired? As Buck reached for dog food bag number twenty-three, he wondered how Ronnie and Tiffany were doing.

Unfortunately, he couldn't check on them. Not until his shift ended at six o'clock. He could only assume they'd gotten there on time, if at all. Ronnie hadn't exactly confirmed he would show up or do the job. He'd left it up to Tiffany to decide.

As Buck carried another bag to the pile, he had another disturbing thought. Ronnie had never claimed to know how to make coffee, either. Even if he had gone to the pavilion to do Buck's job, there was no guarantee he'd know what to do once he opened it. Would he remember to add a filter before putting in the coffee grounds? Would he ensure the cream was fresh if anyone asked for it? Would he remember to put the pot back on the warming tray after pouring a cup?

Buck's stomach knotted as he dropped bag number twenty-three onto the pile. What if he had made a terrible miscalculation in asking for Ronnie's help? Businesses lived or died by their customers' responses. If Buck's customers were pissed at Ronnie's service, then Buck would no longer have a business by the time he clocked out for the day. Six days to fail. Had to be a new world record.

Buck wiped his forehead. Stared at the dog food pile. Wondered if he'd still be allowed at North Park by Monday morning.

"How many is that?" Mack asked.

"Thirty-four," Buck said.

* * *

Mack spent the lunch hour instructing Buck on how to fill out his employment forms. To work legally for Shop Down the Street, Buck had to provide his full name, address, citizenship, tax code, whatever that meant, and his hours of availability. He also had to sign a waiver assuring the company of his ability to lift at least forty pounds and that he wouldn't sue if he injured himself on anything less than that. Then, he had to put his signature on all documents and write today's date. When Buck handed the paperwork back to him, Mack looked everything over and nodded.

"Good, you won't sue me. Maybe I can get my wife an anniversary gift this year."

"You're married?" Buck asked.

Mack glanced up at him from the desk and smirked.

"Course I'm married. Why wouldn't I be?"

Buck shrugged.

"Dunno. Just surprised by it. Didn't think wives let their husbands take in hot foreign exchange students for the summer."

Mack held Buck's gaze for a moment. His smirk turned into a full-on smile.

"Hot, huh? You got a thing for French Girl?"

Buck shrugged.

"Dunno."

Mack squinted at him, then nodded.

"Yeah, all right." He grouped the papers together and set them aside. "Tell you what I'll do. Because I can't pay you for two extra weeks, I'm gonna do you a favor. Provided you—"

"Wait, what did you say?"

Mack caught his words and did a double-take.

"Sorry?"

"What's this about not paying me for two weeks?"

Mack's face relaxed.

"Oh, yeah, legal requirement. Everything takes time to process. You'll get a check for your work, but not at the usual time. Another two weeks. Maybe three, depending on how quick everything moves." Mack lowered his gaze. "That's not a problem, is it?"

Buck suppressed his rising stress. He needed money now. This weekend. Not in two weeks! He had supplies to buy, bets to win,

French girls to take to dinner, maybe, hopefully. Of course, this was a problem. It was a huge problem.

He shook his head. "Nope, it's fine."

But who was he to rock the boat? Getting paid eventually was still better than getting paid never.

"So, what's this favor?"

Mack nodded. "French Girl. I'll let you talk to her on the phone next time you call. Least I could do to keep your morale up."

"Morale?"

"Yeah. If the roles were reversed, I'd be pissed to have to wait for a paycheck for an entire month."

"A month? You said two weeks."

Mack tipped his head sideways. He was studying Buck now.

"Yeah. When I say two weeks, I'm talking about the two weeks on top of the usual two weeks you get paid normally. So, four weeks from now. Maybe five, depending on how quickly things move."

Buck's stomach knotted. Four to five weeks for his first paycheck seemed like a death sentence for him. Then again, it also sounded like a large starting paycheck with a French Girl bonus.

"Okay," Buck said. No reason to throw away his bonus by complaining. He'd just have to work harder at the Coffee Pavilion, if that were even possible.

"Great. Just make sure you don't screw anything up today, and French Girl can talk to you this evening."

Buck's elbows trembled. What did it take to screw something up? Another undefined condition, courtesy of Mack Green.

"How are we doing on the Hawaiian coffee?" Mack asked. "You started on that yet?"

* * *

BUCK WAS HALFWAY THROUGH the Hawaiian coffee resupply effort when the front door chimed. Mack greeted the incoming customer almost immediately.

"Ah, my favorite *sensei*. Welcome. How's life at your end of the street?"

"Usual," Kabuki said.

Buck's stomach twisted as he knelt to better position the bags. *Not now. Not now.* If Kabuki were to sneak over here to support his habit while Buck worked the area…

"Got more employees for me to consider? Your latest suggestion's working out pretty well, I must say."

"Good. You talk about…"

Kabuki's voice lowered out of Buck's hearing range. Sounded like he was asking a question. Mack responded with an equally low volume.

Buck wanted to get closer to hear what they were muttering about, but he also didn't want to get caught eavesdropping, nor did he want to act as the accomplice to another theft if Kabuki came over, especially now that it would upgrade him from accomplice to insider, so he returned to the stockroom where he couldn't hear the conversation. He stayed back there for several minutes, digging through the coffee supplies, giving himself ideas for his own business.

When it seemed like enough time had passed, Buck finally grabbed another handful of Hawaiian coffee bags and headed onto the main floor. He found both Mack and Mr. Kabuki standing beside the coffee shelf with stern looks on their faces. They were staring right at him.

Buck stopped at the end of the shelf and stared right back.

"Anything you'd like to tell me?" Mack asked, tapping his fingers against a loose bag of Hawaiian coffee.

Buck's heart pounded as his eyes flicked over to Kabuki, who was also staring at him.

"What do you mean?" Buck asked.

Mack nodded at the bags in Buck's hands.

"I think you know," Mack said.

Buck felt a queasiness in his stomach. Mack and Kabuki were standing side-by-side, scrutinizing him, likely quizzing him about the missing bags of coffee, together. But it made no sense. Kabuki was the one who'd stolen them. Why was he staring at Buck like that?

Unless…

"Are you trying to frame me?" he asked Kabuki.

No one responded to the question. Just stares.

A cold wind could've blown through at that moment and no one would have blinked.

Then Mack glanced at Kabuki and nodded.

"I guess that's the best we're gonna get out of him," Mack said.

Kabuki nodded once.

"*Hai*. Good enough."

Kabuki approached Buck and put his hand on his shoulder.

"Pass test, sort of," he said. "Ready for next lesson."

Buck shook his head. What was going on?

"Sorry?"

"Lesson ten. Always protect reputation, even if expose other guilt."

Buck frowned. How was this a lesson? What exactly was the lesson? And why did Kabuki have such terrible counting skills? This would've made for lesson nineteen if there was an actual lesson here!

Kabuki glanced at Mack and nodded.

"He understand," Kabuki said.

"Glad I can help."

Then it all made sense to him.

"Wait, this *whole thing* was a lesson?" Buck asked.

"*Hai*. Always pay for what boy need, even if thief-ing only option. Never be thief, and never associate with thief. Always other option."

Buck glanced at Mack.

"Am I to assume then that you know what Kabuki did?"

Mack nodded.

"He didn't do what you think he did. He prepaid for that bag, but he wanted you to think he was stealing it. Your job was to tell me he took it. Prove your integrity. Kabuki says you wrestled with it, as expected, but you should've been faster at ratting him out."

Buck turned his attention back to Kabuki.

"You *wanted* me to rat you out? Seriously?"

"*Hai*. Boy not in gang. Boy businessman with reputation. Loyalty to Kabuki not worth ruining reputation. Bad reputation lead to other legal problem. Lead to more stealing. Nobody win."

Buck frowned. He couldn't believe he was getting played this whole time by both men.

"So, does that mean I don't actually work here?"

Mack chuckled at that one.

"What? Of course, you work here. You filled out the paperwork."

Buck nodded. He agreed the ruse would've gone overboard if it had included him filling out legal paperwork. So, he still had a weekend job away from the Coffee Pavilion to earn extra spending money, which meant he still had to show Mack some respect if he wanted to keep his job and his reputation fully intact.

"Okay. Do I still get to talk to French Girl tonight?"

Mack exchanged glances with Kabuki, then shrugged.

"I'll think about it," he said. "You sure took your sweet old time telling me about that Hawaiian coffee, and, well, you didn't *actually* tell me in concrete terms, did you?"

"Kabuki stole Hawaiian coffee from you and apparently tried to frame me, or something, I don't know."

Mack shrugged.

"Okay, you still took your sweet time telling me, so I'll have to think about it."

Buck dropped the bags of Hawaiian coffee on the floor where he stood and headed back for the stockroom. He was about due for a break anyway, even if Mack hadn't yet approved it.

A few weeks into adulthood, and it was already confusing the hell out of him.

Episode 16

The Security Question

ONCE BUCK FINISHED HIS shift at Shop Down the Street, he rode his bike to the Coffee Pavilion to check on Ronnie and Tiffany. As he pedaled down the network of sidewalks, however, questions about their success hit him at the speed of asphalt moving under a tire.

The questions were simple at first. How many cups had they sold? Would anyone become a repeat customer after their service? Who was friendlier to the customers, Ronnie or Tiffany?

But as he got closer to the park, his questions darkened. Had Ronnie accidentally injured anyone? Had he injured himself? Had he forgotten to charge for each cup?

Before Buck knew it, he was imagining every worst-case scenario possible:

1. They opened shop but couldn't attract any customers. Even with Ronnie using his belly-pat-head-rub combo to gain attention, no one wanted coffee, least of all from him. But he'd still want to get paid for his time.

2. Because Ronnie knew nothing about making coffee, he'd toss grounds in the well without using a filter first, clogging the machine and breaking it.

3. Neither Ronnie nor Tiffany would show up, leaving the Coffee Pavilion vulnerable to customer frustration, especially if any repeat customers were to arrive.

4. Ronnie would accidentally burn the pavilion down. Why he'd play with matches near a wooden surface, Buck didn't know, but it *was* a worst-case scenario.

5. Ronnie and Tiffany would make out in front of the customers, making them so sick that they wouldn't want to come back.

With every corner Buck shot and every intersection he dashed through, his stomach lurched from the inevitable horror he'd face when he arrived to find that one of his fears had come true.

But when he reached North Park, his stomach calmed. The park was crowded, even at ten past six.

That was the beauty of summer. Because the sun fell later in the evening, families and fitness junkies could stay longer, getting their fill of nature and recreational joy long past dinnertime. It also, hopefully, made them thirstier for adrenaline, and what better source of adrenaline than caffeine? And because Saturday was the busiest day of the week for parks and picnic grounds, even the often-isolated north end had the potential to load up with customers.

Under these conditions, it was possible that Ronnie and Tiffany had actually turned in a decent performance today. As Buck rounded the sidewalk onto the southern shore of the big lake, he crossed his fingers. Across the water was the hill on which the pavilion sat, and though it was too far from the southern shore to see clearly, it was nevertheless visible. And unless those were dogs scavenging the trash stations, it appeared that people were using the space.

Of course, his worries returned as he rounded the lake and witnessed the size of the crowd fading fast. By the time he reached the northwest bend, the number of potential customers scaled down to just those countable by hand. And by the time he reached the hill, they'd reduced to three.

But all three had paper cups in their hands. And whatever they had in those cups, they were drinking it.

Buck stopped riding and caught the sidewalk with his left foot. He released his tension with a single exhalation. Even though Ronnie was sitting at a table counting a small stack of cash, Tiffany was marching around the back counter, removing parts from the coffeemaker and cleaning them with a damp rag. At least one of his fears could be checked off as illegitimate. Ronnie and Tiffany had definitely shown up. Actually, two. Ronnie hadn't burned the place down.

Buck parked his bike behind a tree and did his best to stay hidden. One customer trekked down to the trash station and tossed his cup. Then he turned and offered Ronnie a thumbs up. Ronnie waved him down as if it were no big deal. Another customer who was watching the exchange clapped. Again, Ronnie turned his attention to the clapper and delivered his sheepish "what more can I do?" shrug.

Tiffany, meanwhile, reassembled the coffee machine and set it to the side. Now she was packing the cream and sugar into a box. It was hard to tell from this distance, but it looked like there were more cream and sugar supplies than when he'd last opened shop.

Unable to restrain his curiosity any further, he rolled the bike out from behind the tree and marched it up the hill into the pavilion. Ronnie glanced up from the wad of cash in his hand and grinned.

"Welcome back, little camper. Boy, what a day we had!"

The stress in Buck's stomach melted. None of his worst-case scenarios played out. Now he could find out the truth.

"Sit down," Ronnie said. "Let me tell you about it."

Buck parked the bike and took the bench across the table from him. The cash bag sat unzipped by Ronnie's pinkie.

"It all started after you hung up on me. Tiffany was like, 'What do you want to do today, babe?' and I was like, 'You in the mood to sell coffee today, babe?' and she was like, 'What-evs, babe,' and, let me tell you, Buck, we had a hell of a 'what-evs' today. Look at this!" Ronnie fanned out the wad of cash so Buck could see it better. Buck tried to count it, but Ronnie, glancing around as if suspicious of onlookers, tucked it away before it drew unwanted attention. "Have you ever seen so much cash in your life?"

"How much is it?" Buck asked.

Ronnie passed the wad across the table.

"See for yourself."

Buck took the wad from Ronnie. He also pulled the cash bag closer. As he counted each bill, he stuffed it in the bag. But even as he tucked them away for safekeeping, he couldn't help but grin at each bill he counted. Maybe they were just ones and fives. But there were plenty of them. And the cash bag was heavy with coins.

One-one-one-five-one-one-five-one-one-one-and on it went until there was nothing left to count. Then Buck dumped the bag's coins onto the table. Multiples of every denomination fell out, adding up to more than ten dollars in change.

In all, Ronnie had collected $131.30 from customers.

"Twenty of that is petty cash," Ronnie said. "Tiffany thought it would be smart if we offered people change."

Buck nodded. It would've been smart, and he was surprised he hadn't thought of it himself. Then again, he hadn't had enough customers before today to consider it, so it was an easy oversight to make.

Ronnie had collected $111.30, though Buck wasn't clear where the thirty cents had come from. He usually asked for rounded dollars, thus eliminating the need for coins. When Buck asked about it, Ronnie said, "Taxes."

"If you don't collect it from your customers, then it comes out of your own pocket when the IRS and the bad man comes-a-knocking. That's what my dad always says."

Again, Buck nodded. He'd forgotten about sales tax. Of course, someone was going to pay for it. If not the customers, then Buck. And Buck didn't want to owe more taxes, especially not to the "bad man," whatever that meant.

"So, what do I owe you for helping me out?" Buck asked.

Ronnie gestured to Buck to pass the bag back.

"Depends on Tiffany. She did most of the work. I basically just collected the money."

As it turned out, Tiffany was the reason they'd had any business today. Ronnie explained she had not only made the coffee—because she was good at it, not because Ronnie was lazy or incompetent—but she also drew in the customers. Ronnie certainly did his part to find any interested parties, but Tiffany was the one who sealed the deal. Ronnie attributed her short shorts and cut-off blouse to their success.

"I mean, would you buy coffee from *me*?" Ronnie asked. "Or *her*?"

As Ronnie pointed at her, Tiffany was marching a cardboard box toward the storage room. Maybe the box stunted the way she walked, but her feminine curves were not exactly shaking with seduction. She looked more like a professional mover whose uniform showed more skin than the competition's. Certainly more attractive than Eddie Furrow's Uncle Fred, but not quite showing her full potential as a hot young blue-eyed brunette woman who could sell a sports car with a smile. Buck took Ronnie's word for it.

"Hey, babe," Ronnie said when Tiffany came out of the storage room empty-handed. "Tell Buck your secret."

Tiffany approached the counter and picked up a cooler. She shook it. It still had ice in it, though judging by the sloshing around inside, it was melting.

"You're selling the wrong kind of coffee," she said.

Buck stared at her dumbfounded. What other kind was there?

"It's summer. No one wants hot coffee in the summer." Again, Buck stared at her. She nodded at the two customers still hovering around the pavilion area. "Ask them what kind of coffee they got?"

Buck shrugged. He didn't understand the game she was playing, but he was willing to play it. He climbed off the bench and approached the nearer of the two customers milling about. It was the same middle-aged man who'd clapped for Ronnie.

"Excuse me," Buck said. "Is that coffee you're drinking?"

The customer stared at him from over the rim of his cup. His throat wasn't moving, so he wasn't drinking anything. He just had the cup to his lips. Judging by the hands on his waist, it seemed he was securing the cup with a bite.

"What kind is it?"

"What other kind is there?" The customer spoke through his teeth.

"I don't know. I was told to ask what you got."

"Black coffee," he said. "Iced."

Buck's head trembled. It was as if the ghost of reality had just slapped him upside the head with a fish.

"Iced?"

The customer nodded once. The cup bounced slightly.

"You can put ice in coffee?"

The customer pointed at his cup. "This one's got it."

Buck bit his lip as he contemplated the description.

"Is it any good?"

The customer shrugged.

"It's cold, and that's what matters."

"Thanks."

Buck shuffled up the hill toward the pavilion. Ice in coffee. What a novel idea! He had to think this one through. If customers liked ice in their coffees, then what else did they like? Soft drinks? Brown sugar? Pepperoni? The field of possibilities had just grown exponentially.

"Think you can come back tomorrow?" Buck asked Ronnie as he entered the pavilion, even though he was really asking Tiffany by proxy.

"Sure, we had fun today," Ronnie said. "Though the price is the same."

Buck's train of thought stalled on the tracks.

"Did we ever decide what that is?"

Ronnie thought about it.

"Let's see. Five hours. Forty-two cups. Sacrificed dignity. I'd say between us, a hundred dollars would be fairest."

In other words, Buck thought, *I get to keep twelve dollars for myself.*

"Doesn't that come out to ten dollars an hour?" Buck asked.

"Gross, yes. Net, more like five."

"Net?"

"We had to replenish our supplies early on. You didn't leave us with much to work with. We had to shut down for an hour just to buy new supplies. So, it's more like five hours plus an hour. And then there's lunch. We had to eat, so that's another—"

"Fine, I get it. Take a hundred. I'll keep the rest. Can you still come back tomorrow? I have to do another shift at Shop Down the Street."

"Course I can," Ronnie said. "Not sure if Tiffany can, but I can make it. No problem. Just gotta learn how to use the coffeemaker first."

Buck forced a smile.

"Yeah, see if you can have her teach you how to actually do the work, if you don't mind."

Ronnie winked and pointed. "Will do, little camper." Then he lowered his gaze and glanced to his left and right and left again. "Though, I do have one concern after having spent the day doing this."

"Yeah?"

"When Tiffany and I went to the store, no one was here to watch the equipment."

Buck felt his stomach doing that worst-case scenario freefall again.

"You mean you left it on the counter?"

"We were coming right back. But nevertheless, the situation got me thinking. You should invest in security. Even that storage room is susceptible to vandals, you know?"

"You left the equipment unattended on the counter?"

Ronnie leaned forward and put his hand on Buck's shoulder.

"It's fine. No one was around. And we were coming right back. But still. You should consider hiring a security guard. People around here are crazy." Ronnie leaned forward. "They actually put ice in their coffee. Can you believe it? Who puts ice in their coffee?"

Buck understood Ronnie's point, but he still hated the way he'd reached the conclusion.

"Do me a favor," Buck said. "Maybe don't leave my equipment unattended if you help out again tomorrow?"

Ronnie tapped Buck's shoulder, then gave him the thumbs up.

"Will do, little camper."

There wasn't much else to discuss, so Buck helped Tiffany clean up the rest of the station, then thanked them for their time and told them they could leave. Meanwhile, he considered Ronnie's advice. Even as the sunlight dimmed to dusk, Buck considered the people who'd come to the park at night. Drunks. Homeless. Vandals. Even though he had little to lose right now, the potential damage grew the more his assets increased. At some point, he'd have to take security into consideration.

But where would he go? And how much would it cost?

And then he remembered that he already had the answer. Mr. Stamps, the bouncer at Grumpy Balser's graduation party. Buck could call him.

But that was an expense he couldn't afford right now. Besides, he had a key to the storage room, which meant he could keep it locked. In reality, he was fine. Nothing to worry about. Nothing at all. Why else would he even need a key?

* * *

His day at Shop Down the Street had left him with little confidence, but his indirect success at the pavilion had given some back, so that night after dinner, Buck took another shot at calling French Girl. This time, true to his word, Mack let her talk.

"Who this?" French Girl asked when she picked up the phone.

Buck swallowed the excess saliva building in his throat. The time had finally come. He had her attention now.

"French Girl?" he said.

"No, I'm French Girl. Who this?"

"Buck. Buck Star."

French Girl said nothing.

"We met at the tea shop earlier."

"Maybe."

"No, we did. I was with a blonde girl. She kissed me in front of you." Buck squeezed his eyes shut as the words left his mouth. He wasn't supposed to say that part.

"Oh, *oui*. Yes. I remember."

"It wasn't what it looked like," Buck said. "We're just friends."

"Okay."

Both were silent a moment.

"That all you wanted?" French Girl asked.

"No." Buck wanted this conversation, but he didn't know what to talk about. He knew nothing about French people or their culture. Was it polite to say so? If only he could see her face right now.

"You like America?" he finally asked.

"It fine. You?"

"Do I like America?"

"Yes."

Buck liked his home, if that was what she was asking. He'd never been elsewhere to compare experiences.

"I live here, so…"

"Okay."

Another moment of silence.

"Have you made any friends since you got here?" Buck asked.

"Girl at work nice. Boy who bring me flowers every day also nice."

What boy?

"What boy?"

"Ken? Kahn? Kone? Forget."

"You like him?"

"I like flowers. Boy nice."

Buck said nothing.

"You have friends?" French Girl asked.

"No one who brings me flowers, but I got a few, yeah."

"You like flowers?"

Buck hadn't given it much thought.

"I guess so. I don't hate them or anything."

"Okay." A brief pause. Then French Girl put a chime in her voice. "You like me bring you flowers?"

"Yes. Yes, I'd like that very much."

"Then I also be your friend?"

"Yes. Yes, I'd like that very much."

More silence. A fan was buzzing on the other end. French Girl must've liked it cold. Or windy.

"So, need anything else?" French Girl asked.

Buck had no plan. Everything he'd considered about this phone call was for exploration and hope. His only agenda was to get her interested in him somehow. But he couldn't say that, not directly. He had to improvise.

"I was hoping you could tell me about France," he said.

"Okay. What you want to know?"

"Ever been to the Eiffel Tower?"

* * *

MEANWHILE, IN ANOTHER, FANCIER part of town, Pigeon Polluck was so excited about his unexpected plunder that he skipped along the walkway up to Chet's front door. Because Chet's parents were out of town, he also had no fear about knocking so late at night. Everything was coming together perfectly.

He knocked. Checked the bag of coffee under his arm. It was still there. He knocked again. This couldn't wait. The bottle of cream was getting lukewarm from the summer night's heat. He knocked a third time. The two rows of fifty cups each teetered under his other arm, both inches from falling.

The door opened.

Someone other than Chet was standing on the other side.

"May I help you?" the young brunette asked, a glazed look in her eye.

Pigeon's tongue got stuck between his teeth. The cups hit the ground. The woman was dressed only in a business shirt, and she wasn't even wearing a tie. Last time he'd seen her, she was dancing on a table at the club where they had celebrated their successful sales day. Her hair was a mess.

He tried to say something, anything, but the words weren't coming out.

Didn't matter. Chet pushed the woman aside.

"What?"

Pigeon's eyes followed the woman as she tilted out of view. Then he remembered where he was standing. He displayed the loot under his arms.

Chet didn't seem impressed.

"Too late for coffee. Go home, Pigeon. I'm busy."

"Not here to make coffee. Here to share booty."

Chet glanced off to where the woman had drifted. He shook his head.

"Nope, I'm keeping this one to myself."

Pigeon forced the bag of coffee and the bottle of cream into Chet's stomach.

"No, I'm saying this is…"—he raised his eyebrows for emphasis—"stolen."

Chet examined the bag. Rolled it around in his hands.

"You know we sell juice, right? What am I supposed to do with this?"

"No, no. You miss the point. This was *Buck's* bag of coffee. It came from his shop." He scrambled for the two rows of cups rolling at his feet.

Chet seemed more interested now, but he still didn't invite Pigeon inside. At least he was listening.

"How'd you get it? You were at the Liquid Shack all day."

"Sent my little brother in to spy. He noticed that Buck's friend, that weird kid with the big hat, left the place unattended, so he took what he could carry."

"You ask him to do that?"

"Not specifically. Told him to improvise." He tried passing off the cups.

"So, he took supplies." Chet shook his head and closed the door behind him.

Pigeon didn't understand Chet's reaction. He'd thought Chet would be grateful. He knocked on the door again.

"He can't make coffee if he don't have it," Pigeon said when the door reopened.

"So, you turned your little brother into a thief? What the hell's wrong with you? What is he, ten?"

"Almost."

Chet tossed the bag of coffee to the side. It landed on a nearby table, judging by the soft thud and the clattering candles.

"Look, I appreciate the effort, but we're not turning a kid into a thief just to win this bet. Don't do it again."

Pigeon edged closer to the door. He wanted to get another glimpse of the woman before Chet slammed it in his face again.

"You want me to take the coffee back then?" he asked.

"Well, no. What's done is done. I mean, one bag of coffee—what is that? Fifty dollars in sales? Plus cream? Another ten easily. And cups? No, we'll take the advantage. Plus, we could use the cups. But from this point forward, you don't involve your brother in our business."

Pigeon was just about within range of seeing the woman's toes when Chet slammed the door again. This time, Chet was within inches of smashing in his nose.

So, the message was clear. Pigeon couldn't involve his little brother. But Chet said nothing about involving bigger, less related people in this lucrative business of sabotage.

Pigeon headed back for the street, ideas once again streaming through his happy-to-please mind.

BUCK'S END OF DAY REPORT:

Earned: $131.30

Spent: $129.14 ($120 absorbed; $7.14 resupply costs; $2.00 for daily fees)

Net Gain: $2.16

Paycheck Accrued: $19.93 (7*$3.35)-15%

Paycheck Total Due: $19.93 in 27 days?

DAY 7: SUNDAY, JUNE 16, 1985

Buck's Savings Account: $1.00

Buck's Wallet: $19.93

Buck's Business Funds: unknown

Buck's Expenses: $2 a day*

Hours of Operation: 12 p.m.-5 p.m.

Money on Hold: $19.93 (26 days)

ON SUNDAY MORNING, BUCK kicked his sheets to the side and leapt out of bed. Although he didn't want to appear cheesy to the invisible eyes peeking at him through his windows or walls or other surfaces he couldn't understand but science fiction movies had convinced him were watching, he couldn't help himself. He spun around with his arms outstretched and sang the popular line from *The Sound of Music*.

French Girl liked him. It was unmistakable. They'd spent past midnight talking, and not once did she hurry him off the phone (except for when she had to go to bed). Of all the things she'd said last night, the most lyrical words of all were also the loveliest.

"I don't have boyfriend," she'd told him. She'd also said something about avoiding attachment since she was an exchange student and would eventually return to France. But Buck couldn't remember the details. The important thing was that she was single. Incidentally, so was he.

When Buck went to Shop Down the Street for his shift, he smiled at Mack Green and offered him a thumbs up.

"So, all's forgiven about the Hawaiian coffee?" Mack asked.

Buck had already forgotten about that. Of course, now that Mack had mentioned it, he still wasn't happy to play the pawn in some test of loyalty. But because he'd allowed him to speak to French Girl all night, Buck had no reason to hate him.

"Resentment is for cats," Buck said. "The birds are out singing today."

"I guess that's a yes?"

Buck was certain to show off his teeth when he smiled. Mack nodded.

"Good, we're even then."

"I'm going to call her again tonight. So much more to say."

Mack shook his head. "Better if you just see her at the shop. Couldn't sleep with all her gabbing on the phone all night, and I don't want to go through that again."

Buck frowned. "You could hear our conversation?"

"Nah. The idea that no one can get through in an emergency makes me worry I'm missing an emergency."

He understood. If the phone was busy all night, then who could tell Mack the shop had burned down? Buck would just have to see French Girl in person. Nothing wrong with that at all.

Buck worked his seven-hour shift without a shred of anger. Just thoughts of French Girl. By the time he left at four o'clock, he headed over to Tealeaf Central to check in with her.

"Work 'til nine," she said. "Call after."

Buck felt a knot in his stomach. Thanks to Mack's rules, he wouldn't get to talk to her after work. It had to be now. Or never.

"Yeah, I can't. Mack won't be happy if we're on the phone all night again. How's your day?"

"Can't talk now. Got tables." Her gaze was already drifting toward one of them.

"Want to meet somewhere after?"

"Like where?"

Buck thought about the question. He couldn't think of any place that stayed open past nine on a Sunday night.

"Not sure. Everything's closed by then."

"Then maybe I come over when done, if okay."

Buck's words caught in his throat. *Come over? To his house?*

French Girl waited a few seconds for his response, but she was then pulled away by a customer who wanted a refill. Buck stood there with an empty head. Calling her was one thing. Spending time together in person was another. And in his house, no less. Because his mother worked until past midnight, he'd be alone with French Girl for hours. In his house. Alone. With French Girl.

A few minutes later, she returned, this time holding a sheet ripped from a notepad.

"Write address."

She handed Buck the note and a pen but could not wait for him to fill it out. Another customer wanted a bagel.

After five minutes of people demanding her services, Buck felt awkward standing around in the middle of the dining room without a place to sit, so he left the slip of paper on a vacant table beside a cash tip. Given that French Girl was the only one serving tonight, it seemed safe to leave it there for her.

* * *

RATHER THAN RETURN TO the pavilion and interfere with Ronnie and Tiffany's job performance, Buck headed to the beach to think about his good fortune. Less than a week ago, he was challenging Chet over his girlfriend-snatching. Now he was on the verge of getting a new girlfriend. If not for the terms of the bet, Buck would have no need to continue down this silly road. Jennifer's betrayal meant nothing now. French Girl would bring him restoration.

Of course, the terms of the bet meant he couldn't just quit. Giving up his coffee business and Jennifer's respect to spend time with a new girl would inevitably lead to him working for Chet, which was unacceptable. But maybe French Girl could repurpose his pursuit. Maybe she'd even quit Tealeaf Central and work with him at the pavilion!

Once the sun touched the edge of the ocean, Buck retrieved his bike and headed home. On the way, he stopped at Ronnie's to collect his coffee earnings. Ronnie and Tiffany had sold forty-seven cups that afternoon. Today's profit was double-digits higher than yesterday's.

"We're busy tomorrow," Ronnie said. "But today was fun. Three dads got in a fistfight over a barbecue pit."

"Cool. My day's still better, though," Buck said.

* * *

By 9:30, Buck was sweating. He sat by the front door, waiting for the soft knock of a gentle European girl's fingernails—no, European *woman's* fingernails—and checked his breath every minute she'd failed to show. He'd prepared his house for her arrival forty minutes ago by pulling the wrinkles out of his doormat and setting a bowl of peppermints on the welcoming table. He'd also taken a quick scan of the house for embarrassing left-behinds, like wadded tissues on the floor where he'd missed the trash, or his underwear sticking partway out of the laundry basket. But he couldn't think of every contingency she might find awkward or insulting, so he crossed his fingers and called it okay.

More time passed. The repetitious *tick-tock* of his mom's grandfather clock drove Buck to nod along with it. It was the only sound in the room. The ticking rattled his brain between his ears. If it didn't stop, it would give him a headache.

By 9:45, he was hooking his fingers around the phone's handset, preparing either for her to call, or for him to call her despite Mack's wishes. Although he was certain he'd placed his address on one of her tables at Tealeaf Central, it was also possible that she'd missed it. Or worse: that the table actually had belonged to another server, and she never got it.

Tick. Tock.

The living room was getting stuffier. The birds outside had gone to bed a long time ago, leaving behind a sound vacuum as quiet as space. Other than a group of kids talking too loudly as they walked down the sidewalk, or the obnoxious engine sputter of some driver's old clunker coasting up the street and cutting off as it parked at a neighbor's house or died, the neighborhood outside had also gone to sleep. All that was left to listen to came from inside the house. His shoulders heated.

He turned on a fan to generate cooler air and white noise. It was the only way to distract himself from the unhampered cacophony of his worried thoughts.

The grandfather clock was still *ticking* and *tocking*. Buck's head was still rocking. The fan offered him minimal relief. French Girl's shift had ended almost an hour ago.

Tick.

Tock.

At 9:55, he walked outside to get some air. His house was air-conditioned, but it was still stuffy. A summer breeze passed over him. The scent of petunias rode with it. No more *ticking*. No more *tocking*.

An old Volkswagen he didn't recognize sat in his driveway. It was gray or powder blue, but under the amber lights it was the color of jewelry. A soft gold or bronze. Like an Olympic medal. Or an engagement ring.

From behind the windshield, a woman with long hair and a slender face sat in the driver's seat with her fingers on the steering wheel and her bottom lip under her teeth. She was staring back at him, unmoving. Buck didn't move, either.

They held each other's gaze for seconds, if not minutes. Even with the gentle breeze coming through, Buck's neck continued to sweat. Would she get out? Would she drive off?

She did nothing. Just sat still. Looked at him. Maybe weighing her options.

Buck dared to step forward. Her right hand moved off the steering wheel, toward the gearshift. He took another step. She turned on the headlights. Another step. The car's engine fired up. Buck ran before she could back out.

"Wait!" he said.

But it was irrelevant. The car didn't move. The engine was running, but the Volkswagen stayed parked where it was.

Buck approached the driver-side door and waited for French Girl's move. The window was up, so he couldn't speak to her. He could only wait. She held his gaze for much too long without a word or an action.

And then the window rolled down.

"Don't know why I'm here," she said.

Buck wasn't sure how to respond to a statement he wasn't ready to hear. For the time he'd spent eliminating awkwardness from his home, he hadn't considered the awkwardness that might come from conversation. So, he went with the obvious.

"I invited you out after work," Buck responded.

French Girl nodded. "*Oui*. Yes."

Buck said nothing. It seemed that neither of them had anything to add.

"Want to come in?"

French Girl said nothing.

She was here, but Buck sensed she was about to leave. Whether he'd ever get to talk to her after that, he didn't know.

"We had a nice talk last night," Buck said. "I was hoping we could do that again."

French Girl nodded. "It was nice."

"Yeah, so I wanted to talk again. Or maybe watch a movie together. You like movies?"

"It's late."

In other words, she couldn't stay long. So, no time for a movie.

"Well, either way, Mack won't let me call you, so…"

"So, we talk here?"

"Yeah."

French Girl turned off the engine and got out of the car. The breeze on Buck's neck returned.

"I don't know you well."

"Right."

"So, we sit at dining table. Opposite sides."

Buck understood the line she was drawing. Whatever hopes he had for a romantic evening were dissolving by the second.

"Okay," Buck said.

"Okay," French Girl responded.

By 11:05, Buck and French Girl were sharing a laugh at the dinner table over an incident that had happened to him at school involving Garret Nedmeyer's locker and a firecracker that Garret had used as a security measure for keeping others out of it.

"The fire department showed up and everything," Buck said. "I had to check my fingers to make sure I still had them. Last time I try borrowing a book from Garret."

French Girl laughed so hard that she knocked her water glass over and didn't even notice.

* * *

BUCK HADN'T EXPERIENCED MUCH of a life outside of high school in his last eighteen years, so his conversation with French Girl that evening focused mainly on school stories. Coming from France, she had little experience with the American school system. Perhaps the education in both countries was similar, but something about an American high school was more glamorous. Each time he finished one story, she asked him to tell another. And when his imagination and memory of his personal experiences gave up talking to each other, he brought out all four of his yearbooks to remind him of more.

His freshman yearbook reminded him he wasn't popular, as the only picture he found was the one he took for the portraits page. Having a dozen signatures out of a class of hundreds, including eight from teachers, further cemented his obscurity. His sophomore yearbook was almost as bad, except he showed up in the background of one photo where the Chess Club had taken out an ad. He hadn't been part of the Chess Club, but given his motion blur, it was likely he'd routed through their remote corner of the school during a chase sequence between him and a bully, when he was the hunted. When he got to that page, he glossed over it. As far as French Girl needed to know, that blurry figure wasn't him.

His junior yearbook was more interesting than the previous two, but not for Buck. As he flipped through the pages, trying to recall the classes and events that French Girl would find fascinating, he landed on and almost blew through a memorial.

"Who's that?" French Girl asked as Buck was halfway through the turn for the next page. She pointed to the portrait at the top.

Buck reset the page and followed her finger. In the black-and-white photo was a portly blond kid named Lester Biggins. He was a sophomore. And deceased. He was also smiling in the photo. It was unclear how much time had passed between getting his picture taken and needing it for the memorial. Two months, maybe three?

"Poor sap," Buck said.

"Says he died?"

Buck nodded. "Yeah, that was last year. His name was Lester. Lester Biggins. Not at all popular. Died anyway."

French Girl pulled the yearbook from Buck's hands and studied the page for herself. Under the portrait was a lifespan indicator: 1968-1983.

"Doesn't say how. Was he sick?"

Buck remembered the story well. It was one of those incidents that had the potential for urban myth, but because a cafeteria worker had found him at the bottom of the gulch, there was no myth. Lester had begun the morning physically healthy but died a broken body.

School authorities hadn't spoken much of it that day. They'd announced it that morning as "a tragedy" and that "Lester Biggins was no longer with us." Because he was a nerd, everyone had thought he'd committed suicide after failing shop class or something. But Buck had never believed that. As far as he knew, Lester was just minding his own business, maybe getting a little intense with his calculator, and got too close to the railing. When the cafeteria worker had found him, Lester was still holding his calculator close to his chest.

"Investigators spent weeks interviewing us," Buck said, after giving French Girl the short version. "Months even. As far as I know, they'd never ruled on a cause. Like me, they didn't buy the suicide angle. But they didn't rule it out, either. It was still possible. Too many unknowns surrounded the case."

"You say he really liked his calculator?"

"Huge math geek. Obsessed with it. Studied algebra like a mad scientist. Didn't spend as much time with trigonometry."

"So awful. How his family take it?"

Buck didn't know Lester personally, so he didn't know how to answer the question.

"Badly, I assume."

"He have friends?"

Buck took the yearbook back from her.

"Could we talk about Lester another time? It's kinda depressing, you know?"

French Girl nodded. "*Oui.* Yes."

Buck stared at Lester's photo one last time, then closed the book.

"So, let's check out my senior yearbook."

French Girl thanked him for a nice evening and headed home just five minutes later. He didn't ask her to stay. Just thanked her for stopping by and for getting out of the car when she could've just left. It was all he could do to put the focus back on them. But it wasn't made to last. The night was over. Lester Biggins had clearly robbed the evening's magic from both of them.

BUCK'S END OF DAY REPORT:

Earned: $144.55

Spent: $122.00 ($120 absorbed; $2.00 for daily fees)

Net Gain: $22.55

Paycheck Accrued: $19.93 (7*$3.35)-15%

Paycheck Total Due: $39.86 in 26 days?

DAY 8: MONDAY, JUNE 17, 1985

Buck's Savings Account: $1.00
Buck's Wallet: $42.48
Buck's Business Funds: unknown
Buck's Expenses: $2 a day*
Hours of Operation: 12 p.m.–5 p.m.
Money on Hold: $39.86 (25 days)

MAYBE IT WAS OUT of high school habit, or maybe last night had ended on too dour of a note, but Buck was less eager to fly out of bed on Monday morning than on Sunday. The birds were out chirping, probably, but he couldn't hear them. Or, if he could, they sounded like street traffic or distant alarm clocks.

As much as he'd loved hanging out with French Girl at the dinner table, he couldn't help but wonder if he'd handled the Lester Biggins tragedy with enough grace. It wasn't as if he'd wanted to gloss over the story. At the time it had happened, it was a big deal. Students who never knew him cried their eyes out. Those who did walked around like zombies. Even the school bullies were sad. The mood in those days was worse than on a typical Monday morning. Last thing Buck wanted was to relive them.

"It's not your fault, little camper," Ronnie said, when Buck called him and told him about his date with French Girl. "Lester Biggins will bring down the mood in any room. You're kinda bringing me back down, if I'm being honest."

"Sorry, I just don't know if I handled it right. How do French girls handle tragedy? Are they more sensitive to it than us? The same?"

"Well, she wasn't there, and she didn't know him. I'm sure it was worse for us."

"I mean, does she think I'm insensitive for sweeping it under the rug? You don't have to be there to have an opinion about it."

"Maybe. I don't know. Then again, who wants to talk about a dead kid on a first date? That's a little weird if you ask me. I would've avoided the conversation altogether."

"Problem is, we talked about him, and then she left. We were having a good time until we weren't."

"Well, Lester Biggins had that reputation. Even in death."

Buck considered Ronnie's words. Maybe it wasn't his fault. Either way, he'd have to stop by Tealeaf Central later and salvage the mood.

"They still haven't ruled his death out as a suicide, you know," Ronnie added. "Not sure if you knew that."

"No, I haven't been keeping up with the story."

"My dad knows some stuff about it. Can't divulge the details, even with me, but he doesn't think Lester was being a klutz, either."

"Are you saying…?"

"Maybe. Nothing has been ruled out."

As Buck sat by the phone, anchored to it by its cord, he wished he could get up and retrieve his yearbook for a second look. But he didn't want to be rude. Not again. One of these days, he'd have to ask his mom to buy one of those new cordless phones, or maybe get one himself, so he could roam the house more freely while talking.

"That's really interesting."

"Lester might've been a mood-killer, but he wasn't the only killer in the room. Allegedly."

"I should tell French Girl," Buck said. "She might also find that interesting."

"Great way to get back on her good side."

"Yeah. I feel better now."

"Awesome. All right, little camper. I've got things to do. Don't forget, Tiffany and I can't help at the pavilion today, so you're on your own."

"I know. Thanks. I won't be out there until later, anyway."

"I keep thinking there's something I have to tell you. But I can't recall what. Tiffany mentioned something important, so she says, but I was trying to bite a splinter out of my thumb, so I wasn't listening too closely."

"Let me know if you remember."

They hung up. Buck hoped this "something important" wasn't an emergency. Ronnie would've remembered the details if that were the case. Hopefully.

* * *

BUCK GRABBED SOME BREAKFAST. Normally, he'd head out for the pavilion to prep his workstation the moment he put on his shoes, but thoughts of French Girl, Lester Biggins, and the possibility that Lester's death wasn't an accident grounded him to his thoughts, and eating gave him time to meditate.

At the time, no one had suggested Lester's death was anything more than a distracted teen walking too close to the edge of a cliff, but Buck couldn't remember anyone marrying themselves to the idea that it was strictly bad judgment, either. Lester was a klutz, but he was also a target for bad behavior. While it was always a silent question whether he'd purposely thrown himself over the railing to avoid ridicule or harassment—such an extreme reaction to either—not many people believed it enough to establish it as the official rumor. His lack of attention to his general surroundings whenever he'd have his devices in hand was always the accepted cause of death. Not much different than walking into traffic before checking either direction for oncoming vehicles.

But now that he thought about it, he couldn't remember Lester ever being down on himself for the way the other kids treated him. He was never mopey nor overly stressed about his situation. Like Garret Nedmeyer, and even Buck himself, Lester just took his role like a champ. He understood he was awkward, took the occasional mental abuse, and then went back to his calculator once the dust settled. The more Buck thought about it, the more he believed the idea that Lester would intentionally throw himself over the railing was absurd.

That left him with a bigger question. *What if…?*

Buck's phone rang. The thought vanished.

"Hello?"

"Yes, looking for American patriot, Buckster, er, Star."

"This is Buckster, er, Buck. Who's this?"

"This Ad Guy at Ad Hut. Order ready. Five boxes of handouts for red-blooded American boy. All hail capitalism."

"Five boxes? I thought I'd ordered one."

"*Nyet.* One box not good enough. Five boxes put bread on table. Boy thank me for ordering more."

"So, you're saying I did order just one box?"

"Ad Guy want boy successful. One box like tickle bear when five box kill and stuff it."

Buck winced at the thought of tangling with a bear. They weren't common in this part of town, but they weren't zero, either. Either way, he got the point.

"Do I have to pay for all five?"

"*Da.* Not expensive, though. Boy make back money when customers see advertisement. No time at all. All hail capitalism."

"Okay, I was expecting the order tonight. Guess I'll be there shortly."

Half an hour later, Buck had five boxes containing two dozen handouts each lashed together on his handlebars, doing his best not to tip them all over the street as he rode.

* * *

THE HANDOUTS WERE SIMPLE but to the point. They showed the name of the business, the location and hours of operation, and a simple graphic of a blue coffee cup and saucer tilted just enough for the liquid inside to reach the rim. The headline above it said: GREAT COFFEE TO PERK YOU UP.

To make his life easier, Buck kept one box with him and stored the rest at home. Then he rode around various sections of town, passing out the information to anyone who would take it, or posting anywhere he thought pedestrians would look—streetlights, park benches, trees, wherever. Once he emptied one box, he rode home for the next. By the time he finished sharing every handout—120 sheets in all—he was drenched in sweat, parched in the throat, and heaving for breath. But he'd finished before noon.

His strategy had been simple. As a benevolent marketer willing to talk about his business to anyone interested without being pushy about it, he gave the handout to the passersby who'd made eye contact, and he answered inquiries when asked. When they questioned what a kid like him was doing selling coffee, he answered with the same response:

"Living the American Dream." Then, in a silent tribute to the Ad Guy, who had nudged him in the right business direction, he finished with, "All hail capitalism."

His soon-to-be customers said nothing. They just took the handout and moved on.

Happy that more people now knew about his business, Buck stopped by Pound Cake for a soda. While there, he told Irina Swift about his dining room date with French Girl. She told him not to worry about the yearbook incident.

"If anything, it shows that you're not full of yourself. The important thing is that French Girl sees the real you, not the pretend you."

"What's the pretend me?"

"The person you become to gain customers for your business."

Buck waited for clarification, but Irina offered him none. She just shrugged and returned to counting her cupcake stock. Buck decided he would figure out what she meant once he found himself faced with it.

Satisfied with his refreshments, Buck stepped outside and felt a chill wind coming through. A handout promoting the Coffee Pavilion rode in with it and slapped him in the shins.

* * *

DESPITE THE WORRY THAT crept into his chest after three more handouts promoting the Coffee Pavilion floated past his bike tires on his way to the park, he discovered on arrival that his worries were unjustified. A half-dozen customers were already waiting for him, hanging out at the picnic tables under the roof, casually checking their watches.

"Place isn't open yet," a middle-aged man said, when Buck marched past him toward the serving counter.

"What time is it?" Buck asked. He'd looked at the clock at Pound Cake before leaving at 11:40, but he wasn't sure how long it had taken to ride here.

"Three minutes after twelve," the man said as he stared at his watch. "Not sure where that kid with the top hat or his cute girlfriend are. Thought this place opened at noon."

"It does. I'm actually the owner. The other guy was helping me out."

The middle-aged man perked up, as did the other people within earshot.

"So, you can make me a small iced cup with cream and sugar?"

Buck walked his bike to the nearest post and parked it. "Just give me a few minutes to set up, and I'll get you anything you want."

The man checked his watch again, as did the others who were waiting.

"I'm in a hurry. On my lunch break. Thought you'd be open by now."

"Yeah, just give me a few minutes. Still gotta set up the equipment."

"Most coffee businesses open first thing in the morning, you know. On time and ready to serve."

"It's my first week doing this. Still learning."

The man shared an unhidden eye roll with another man standing near him. The sigh in his voice was also conspicuous.

Buck said nothing. It was obvious he'd misjudged his sudden popularity.

When he'd gotten up this morning, he didn't expect anyone to show up by noon, given that he'd spent most of last week ushering one dead hour after another. So, he didn't bother racing over when the clock at Pound Cake edged closer to twelve. But now that his assumptions were clearly wrong, his feet moved faster, almost at a run, and his hands trembled at the storage room lock as he fit the key to it. These people were losing patience, and he still hadn't set up his station.

As he dragged the cooler to the counter, he noticed two people had left, including the man he had been talking to. If he still wanted that small iced coffee with cream and sugar, he wasn't getting it here. But four remained. And three more were coming up the hill. And some kid was playing in the bushes off to the side, probably not a customer. Either Ronnie and Tiffany had built an exceptional reputation over the weekend, or Buck's handouts were working faster than he'd intended.

"You open?" a customer asked when Buck plugged in the coffeemaker.

"Almost," Buck headed for the storage room to get the bag of store powder.

"Thought you opened at noon."

This time, it was Buck who rolled his eyes. He would not be this late tomorrow.

For the next three minutes, he set his filter, filled his coffee powder, and poured the water bottles into the reservoir, preparing for the brew. He noted that among his change in inventory, which he still hadn't counted completely, his bottled waters were as he'd left them. Apparently, Ronnie and Tiffany weren't using them, which left him wondering what they'd used instead. Water from the fountain? It had a bitter taste. Water from the lake? It had algae in it.

It worried him they'd likely compromised his coffee's water quality over the weekend, but his thoughts on the topic derailed the moment he counted the rest of his supplies. While they had left him with enough coffee to serve a few dozen customers today and almost enough cream, they hadn't left him with many cups.

In fact, they'd left him with just three.

That couldn't have been right.

"How much longer?" a customer asked from behind.

"Almost ready." Buck checked over his shoulder. Another middle-aged man in a suit was coming up the hill. Must've been one of Ronnie's weekend guests. Not anyone who had taken his advertisement earlier. Why weren't these people getting their coffee at Melty's? He was sure Melty's had a limitless supply of cups on hand.

"Black with sugar," another young urban professional said from over his other shoulder. "Got any donuts?"

"No, I just sell coffee."

Buck located the source of the demand. On the picnic table to his left was a guy in his mid-twenties who kept an oversized briefcase by his side.

"You should sell donuts," the man said. "Coffee and donuts, you know?"

The coffeemaker was percolating louder as it slowed its brew. Almost done.

Meanwhile, off to the side, Buck couldn't get the image of the cup trio out of his peripheral. Even when he turned his head, he remembered the sight of them.

Down near the lake, two joggers veered around a family of ducks. As they rerouted their paths, their faces turned toward the pavilion where the swell of customers hung out in plain view. The sign promoting cheap coffee, which Ronnie must've mounted on a support beam over the weekend, was facing back at them. It was enough to draw them in because, a few seconds later, they committed to the new direction and started up the hill.

Buck dashed inside the storage room for a second look. Maybe he'd overlooked a stack of cups and was about to shoot himself in the foot for nothing. Maybe he had fifty-three ready to serve, not three.

But his fears were confirmed. Every cup he had available was already on the counter, and for the first time since he'd opened this business, the supply was far lower than the demand.

He stared out the door as he contemplated his situation. The kid who was playing in the bushes down the shallow slope and off to the side had no idea how much easier his life was with the bugs.

Buck had visited enough shops in his life to know that businesses ran out of things before closing all the time. It was rarely a big deal.

"Just come back tomorrow," the proprietor would say. If he'd gone to an ice cream shop two hours before closing and the shop owner had just run out of Neapolitan ice cream, he could just order a scoop of vanilla and a scoop of chocolate and call it a day. As long as the shop owner still had a cone or a bowl to serve it in, all was fine.

The bowl, after all, was the business. Not a specific flavor.

Buck's problem now had nothing to do with lacking a flavor. Running out of the delivery mechanism at the *start* of the workday was not just a rookie mistake; it was a straight-up idiot move.

"That kid coming back?" A customer said through the wall. "Coffee's done."

"Maybe it's self-serve?" Another one replied.

"Is the coffee free?"

Buck had to put a stop to this. He returned to the serving counter, reminded everyone that the coffee had indeed cost money, and that he would serve them in a timely manner if they'd just be patient.

"We all have jobs to get back to," the young urban professional said. He was reading over a sheet of paper as he held his briefcase lid aloft. "No time for patience."

Buck slid the first cup out of the plastic bag and filled it with fresh coffee.

"Who wanted black with sugar?"

The same guy raised his hand and the paper he was reading along with it.

"Two bucks," Buck said. He reached for the sugar container.

"I want cream in mine," said the man to his right, one of the originals who had been waiting for him when he arrived.

"Also two bucks."

Buck had all three cups standing straight on the counter within seconds and three-quarters full within seconds more. Sugar, cream, cream and sugar, ice. Three orders, with three individual needs. Six dollars, no tax.

But there were still seven customers remaining. By now, the joggers had taken seats under the pavilion.

"Iced coffee and cream," one of the two joggers called out to him.

"There is a line here," Buck said. "I realize it may be invisible."

The remaining customers exchanged glances. There was no pickup station at which to gather, nor was there a register marking the official ordering spot. Without a system of queues and customer numbers, getting coffee at the Coffee Pavilion was a free-for-all. Buck pointed at a spot that he thought could symbolize the start of the line.

"If you want coffee, stand here."

Of course, even as they gathered in a tidy row, Buck had no way of serving the remainder. He'd just sent out all his cups. To get more, he'd have to shut the place down, and none of these people would've been happy about that. Bad word-of-mouth would spread within minutes. He'd be run out of town by nightfall. This was no way to win a bet.

"Iced coffee and cream," the jogger repeated himself.

Buck nodded and smiled. "Coming right up."

He didn't know how to make this true. What was he supposed to do? Bring the carafe to the customer and order him to tilt his head back and say "ah"? Maybe dunk a couple of ice cubes in first to minimize the scalding bean water flowing onto the man's tongue? Swirl in the cream afterward? The whole thing was absurd.

"We're in a hurry," the jogger said, pointing at his lady partner.

"Just a minute."

Buck returned to the storage room. Sometimes, the thing he needed most had a habit of appearing at the time he needed it most. Perhaps this would be one of those situations.

But it wasn't. There were no fresh cups. Just the used cups still in yesterday's trash behind the building. All the fresh cups were still at the shops downtown.

"You coming back?" Yet another customer was getting impatient at the picnic area.

Buck jabbed both of his index fingers into the sides of his forehead and rubbed out the pain that was growing from inside. Whether his next move was madness or relief, he didn't know, but he'd become weary of the harassment. If these people wanted their coffee, then they were going to get their coffee, no matter what, or how.

A few minutes later, Buck cleared out the pavilion, satisfying every waiting customer and earning twenty-two dollars to boot. Fortunately, none of them had noticed him digging used cups out of the trash prior to his bringing them to the counter and filling them with fresh coffee. Only one had noticed an odd flavor they didn't expect.

Crisis averted.

Now that he could take a second to breathe, he packed up his supplies, stowed them in the storage room, and made a ride into town to buy more fresh cups. As it turned out, he was also short of cream.

* * *

MEANWHILE, NORTHWEST OF THE pavilion, under a low-hanging shrub, a nine-year-old boy chased an ant with his fingers. The ant was fast, but the boy was faster. Every time he smashed his fingertips into the dirt just inches ahead of the ant's path, he laughed at the small creature's confusion. A simple obstacle and the ant's entire plan for the day was ruined. The ant would have to veer around his fingers in the hope of rediscovering the path it was on, only to once again get derailed by another unfortunate smashing of fingers into its trajectory.

If the boy hadn't been having so much fun torturing the bug, he'd have brought his fist down right on it, kind of like what his older brother would do to that older kid at the pavilion once he handed his disposable camera over to him.

The boy wasn't sure why his brother Pigeon wanted these pictures, but knowing him, his reasons were probably demented. Either way, turning them over meant not having to endure a massive titty-twister when he got home, and that was perfectly fine by him.

* * *

WHEN HIS SHIFT ENDED that evening, Buck was exhausted. His detour to Corner Grocery for another package of paper cups and a bottle of cream had eaten up almost 45 minutes of business hours, and by the time he'd returned to the pavilion and reset his station, another dozen customers were standing around getting mad at him for wasting their time, as if he'd made them come in the first place. It was enough to get his neck vein throbbing. But he got through it. Although he hadn't pulled in the numbers that Ronnie and Tiffany had gotten that weekend, he'd still improved over his previous week's performance, and that was all that mattered. It was a victory.

He stopped by the Whipping Shed to report his progress, but Mr. Kabuki was too busy tending to something in the back room to listen, so Buck quietly swallowed his pride and continued home. Once there, he logged his progress for the day. He'd gotten half of his statistics written when a knock at the front door interrupted him.

When Buck answered, the man from the Chamber of Commerce who dressed in a bee uniform was standing on the other side. He was still wearing that bee uniform. The breeze caused his wings to shake.

"Mr. Star? Remember me?"

Buck checked over his shoulder to make sure his mom wasn't spying on this potentially weird conversation.

"Er, yes."

"You were supposed to come see me after your meeting with Mr. Perkins. What happened?"

"Um…"

"No matter." The man reached behind his back and produced a flyer. It was the same flyer Buck had posted earlier that morning. "Recognize this?"

Buck's eyes lit up. "Yes, of course. I'm promoting my new coffee business. Did you want to stop by and try a cup?"

The man crushed the flyer between his cartoonish "bee hands" and tossed the paper ball over Buck's shoulder. It landed somewhere inside his living room.

"If you wish to litter, start with your own place," the man said.

Buck frowned. He didn't know what that was about. He looked behind him to find the paper ball on the floor, swimming in the dog's water bowl.

"How can I help you?" Buck asked.

"You can help me by not littering."

Buck said nothing.

The man produced another form from behind his back. This one was unfamiliar.

"According to the Hybrid City Environmental Council, you are allowed to post flyers in shop windows, but you may not use them to desecrate our trees or sidewalks."

Buck tried to read the paper held before him, but the man waved his hands while he spoke too much for the letters to resonate with him.

"I didn't post any flyers on the sidewalk," Buck said. "You're making things up."

"Did you hand any out to people today?"

"Well, yeah. How else am I supposed to advertise?"

The man produced another flyer from behind his back.

"I found this in the gutter, on its way to the park. Surely one of your 'customers' tossed this the moment you passed it out."

Buck failed to see how that was his problem.

"Then shouldn't you yell at the person who dropped it?"

The man shoved the flyer into Buck's chest.

"You don't cure the disease by healing its symptoms. Now, what I have here is an advertisement allotment plan." He thrust his personal information sheet in Buck's face. "It tells you how many flyers you're allowed to post and where without accumulating a fine. Follow this plan, and you and I won't have any problems. But you go past the quota, and you can be sure you'll hear from me again. And I'll come with a lawyer. Understand?"

Buck shook his head.

"Who are you?"

The man locked eyes with Buck. His face was deadpan as he took a backward step toward the road.

"Ernest Bee, Hybrid City Environmental Council, champion for our trees." He tossed the sheet of paper at Buck's feet. "Read it carefully. The Environmental Council demands your obedience."

Buck picked the paper off the ground and skimmed its contents. According to the information, he was allowed no more than a dozen handouts in the streets before the litter police came after him.

"This seems kind of unfair," he said.

But when he looked up for a response, Ernest Bee was already halfway down the street, flapping his arms as if he were flying.

Buck crumpled the paper and tossed it into the bush. If he needed it later, he knew where to find it. But if it blew down the street and into the woods, that was fine, too.

Buck's End of Day Report:

Earned: $50.00

Spent: $21.64 ($15.90 for promotions; $1.05 personal; $2.69 supplies; $2.00 for daily fees)

Net Gain: $28.36

Paycheck Accrued: $0

Paycheck Total Due: $39.86 in 25 days?

DAY 9: TUESDAY, JUNE 18, 1985

Buck's Savings Account: $1.00
Buck's Wallet: $70.84
Buck's Business Funds: unknown
Buck's Expenses: $2 a day*
Hours of Operation: 12 p.m.–5 p.m.
Money on Hold: $39.86 (24 days)

THE NEXT MORNING, BUCK had a headache. As much as he'd wanted a good night's sleep, he couldn't shake the image of a grown man in a bee suit haranguing him over his advertising methods. How else was he supposed to promote his business? Were there other promotional methods that the Environmental Council would overlook that he could've employed? And how had Ernest Bee even figured out where he lived? Buck shivered at the question.

Regardless of the answers, his headache wasn't going away, so he searched for a bottle of aspirin. But he'd barely got through the bathroom door when his kitchen phone rang.

"Dude, did you read the papers this morning?"

Buck rubbed his eyes as he tried keeping the handset to his ear. Ronnie's voice sounded like a normal, albeit enthusiastic teenager most hours of the day, but first thing in the morning it sounded like a foghorn.

"Why are you shouting?"

"Did you read the paper this morning?"

"When do I ever?"

"Dude, my dad showed me page three of the local section. It ain't good, man."

Buck rubbed his other eye. It was too early in the morning for him to get yelled at.

"Fine, hold on."

He found the morning newspaper still in its plastic wrap halfway up his empty driveway. His mom must've already been at work, as usual.

Once he returned to the phone, he removed the paper and leafed through to the local section. He spread page three open across the kitchen table.

If he were eating cereal right now, he'd spit it out.

"Dude!" Buck said. "What the hell am I looking at?"

"I know, right? What were you thinking?"

Buck was thinking he was desperate.

At the top of the page, in glorious, faded color newsprint, four images painted an ugly story about Buck's coffee business. In the first panel, Buck's feet were planted firmly on the ground, but his body was tilted out of sight, into the depths of a big, barreled trash receptacle. In the second panel, he stood beside the receptacle with a cluster of disposable cups cradled in his arms. In the third, he was inside the pavilion pouring coffee into a cup while a customer stood in line waiting for it. And in the last panel, Buck was counting the customer's money as the customer brought the cup to his lips.

The headline and article beneath the photos were no less friendly. According to the article, Buck Star, owner and proprietor of Hybrid City's newest coffee shop, willingly served his customers trash coffee while trying to keep it a secret from them. It claimed that he took their money, then spat in their faces as a thank you for nothing. Due to the investigation of an anonymous source, *The Hybrid City Post* could break the story before this "insult to the coffee industry" could strike again. The article ended with a promise to update the public on future developments as they unfolded.

"Dude, seriously," Ronnie said. "What were you thinking?"

Buck's headache was getting worse. It was moving behind his eyes. The whole world at that moment was a vacuum of recognition, where space was meaningless and objects had no texture or existence. His thoughts couldn't find an anchor.

And just as quickly, they did.

"I was out of cups." Realization dawned on him. "You'd left me with three and didn't tell me."

A moment passed in silence. Then Ronnie spoke up.

"Oh yeah, that's what I'd forgot to tell you Sunday night."

"Dude, this is your fault."

"Aw, come on, little camper, don't blame me for this. You open late enough in the day to check your supplies first. Don't you?"

"I had to pass out my handouts to get customers. Marketing. Took all morning. But I would've waited if I'd known I *needed more cups.*"

"Couldn't you have just bought more when you saw you were almost out?"

"Customers were already in line. I had to do something. Couldn't just walk away. How would that look?"

"Better than what I'm looking at now, if I'm being honest."

Buck shook his head. How was he supposed to recover from bad PR like this? He hadn't been open long enough to counter any claims against his quality. On the same day he was hyping his business, some "anonymous source" was actively destroying it.

"What am I supposed to do now?" Buck said. "First, that guy in the bee suit and his threats. Now this?"

"Guy in the bee suit?"

"Long story. Dude, why couldn't you just tell me about the cups?"

"Look, Buck, my dad's a lawyer. He can give you good advice. Want to talk to him? He hasn't left yet."

"How much will it cost me?"

"Ha ha. No, really. Here, hold on."

"No, Ronnie, don't—"

But his refusal didn't matter. Mr. Michaels was on the phone before he could finish the thought.

"Hey, Buck," Mr. Michaels said. "So yeah, this is a pickle, but not a turd. You can recover. Stay out of the news and the public will forget. Rebuild your reputation one customer at a time. Or invite the Coffee Critic to write you a review. That helped Melty's come back from the dead a few years ago."

"The Coffee Critic?"

"Yeah, nice guy. A little hard to please, but pleasing him will remove all stains from your reputation. Even give you a gold star medal for doing an impressive job. If you want, I can give him a call once I get to the office. Will even do it for free."

"You will?"

"Yeah, if it means cutting Ronnie a break, sure."

In other words, Buck thought, the lawyer was bribing him to ignore his son's oversight. Then again, if this worked, then the bribe was worth it.

"Okay."

"Great. I'll let you know when to expect him. Or I'll try. His arrival can be unpredictable, which is sort of the point, I guess. In the meantime, can you recall who took those pictures of you?"

Buck hadn't seen anyone with a camera. He was too busy trying not to touch dirty baby diapers while he was fishing those cups out of the trash.

"Wasn't paying attention."

"Think back to that moment, Buck. It's important."

"Why? The pictures are out. What difference does it make?"

"Whoever submitted those photos didn't get them by chance. They were waiting for you to fail."

"Huh?"

"Classic dirt dig. This wasn't an amateur bird photographer horrified by an accidental angle while waiting for a condor to land on the pavilion roof. Someone was staking you out, watching your every move, and capturing it once you made the wrong one."

Buck's heart skipped.

"You mean—"

"Your anonymous source is an enemy, intentionally waiting for you to fail, and seizing it the moment he spotted it. Most likely, given my experience with bad people."

Buck thought back to that moment. The only person interested in his failing at his coffee business was Chet, and he was nowhere on the scene, nor were his cohorts.

So, if not Chet, then who?

"How cutthroat is the coffee industry?" Buck asked.

"Don't know. But it seems to be rising, doesn't it? When you go to work today, keep an eye on your surroundings. Yesterday won't be an isolated event."

* * *

WITH HIS REPUTATION IN the toilet, Buck didn't visit Shop Down the Street or Corner Grocery just to restock his coffee and an extra bag of cups. He also searched the shelves for ideas for improvement. He still had plenty of cream and sugar to get through the day—probably enough sugar to even get through the summer—but that was all. At some point, his customers would begin judging the quality of his coffee against his competitors', especially Melty's. With Buck charging two dollars a cup and Melty's charging one, it wouldn't be long before his surge in customer base would die for reasons beyond bad press.

"As a business owner," Buck asked Mack, "what would you do to bring the customers back?"

Mack was still reading page three of the local news section and hadn't yet made eye contact.

"Not what you did. That's for sure."

"Okay, I get that. But assuming I can't turn back time, what would get you more interested in my coffee than in Melty's?"

"You mean, how would you make your coffee more attractive?"

"Yeah."

Mack lowered the page enough for Buck to see his eyes.

"Add some spice. Don't limit yourself to just cream and sugar."

"Spice?"

"Yeah, like cinnamon powder. Or nutmeg. Just something in addition to sugar. The whole reason Melty's keeps its coffee so cheap is because it doesn't do anything special to it. You do something special, and you'll win the coffee war." He pointed to the top of the page. "Assuming people forget about this."

* * *

BUCK TOOK MACK'S ADVICE and bought a bottle of cinnamon powder. Just one. Because his reputation was stained, he didn't want to risk tarnishing it further with a bad idea, and using cinnamon in coffee was an untested gimmick. So, one was enough. And it was a small bottle.

Of course, it was also a fringe idea, so he wasn't yet sure how he'd use it. Would he sprinkle the powder into the cup, then pour in the liquid? Or would he stir it in like sugar? Or would he take a third approach and mix the powder in with the coffee grounds? And would his customers even notice the difference?

To enhance his offering, Buck also bought a can of whipped cream. He figured if his customers liked cream inside their coffee, then they'd also like it on top. After all, if it worked for pie, then it would work for black wakeup water.

Then came the hard part: convincing people to give him another shot. Given how clear the photos were, he knew most people would be disgusted at the very thought of giving him their money or drinking his coffee. So, his hope for turning things around was to find the people who didn't read the newspaper.

He'd start by seeking kids his own age.

He also didn't bother seeking people out in the park as he normally would but went right for the downtown districts. Even though he had no more handouts to offer people on the street, he could still talk to them, see what kind of beverage mood they were in, and steer the conversation according to their responses.

"Hey, nice day we're having, right?" he'd ask. "Great day for a coffee break, am I right? Have you seen the newspaper today? No? Well, let me tell you, it's a slow news day. Not even worth a look. Say, you know what would make this day even better? Coffee at the park.

You should swing by the North Pavilion just after noon and grab a cup. It's better than Melty's."

Alternatively, if they said "yes" to his newspaper question: "Well, that stuff will rot your brain, and you shouldn't believe a word of it, not even if it comes with pictures. I hear they manipulate images to tell the story they want, not the one that's true. How can you even trust them? I tell you, I don't trust them to even spell my name right, much less tell me the truth. I'm Buck Star, by the way. I sell coffee at the park if you're interested. I totally sell fresh cups, and only fresh cups, never used. Don't trust the papers."

This new strategy earned him a dozen visitors that day, but no more. Most of the people he'd talked to had seen the photos and didn't believe his rebuttal about the newspaper's reporting ethics. In fact, several people spat in his face or on his shoe. They'd told him they'd never visit his coffee stand, and they'd tell all their friends and family not to visit, either. And the conviction on their faces had convinced him they were serious. They would never be his customers, and if they were to follow through on their threats, then their networks would also never be his customers.

So, he made the most of the dozen who hadn't seen the news story. He wowed them by telling a story about the coffee he was making for them.

"The secret to coffee this superior," he said, as he nestled the cup against the carafe, "is to cultivate the beans myself. You'd think I'd buy it from a shop or a supplier. And I can assure you that would be much easier. But as a customer, you shouldn't have to put up with something so simple. For two dollars a cup, you deserve something more special than that. You deserve fresh beans from the richest soil on Earth. And lucky for you, I'm fresh off my trip to Hawaii, where I spent days marching up and down the fields, picking these beans special for you. And when you've got big game hunters hunting humans for sport at the other end of the field, you've got to work fast, let me tell you."

And once he handed them the cup, he'd top it with whipped cream and top that with cinnamon powder.

"The only thing better than coffee picked by a man running for his life is coffee served like a dessert. Tell me what you think."

To Buck's relief, all twelve customers said they'd come back for more. A couple of them even gave him a tip for making such excellent coffee. Not bad, considering the first seven cups were reheated from the previous day's leftovers.

But it was still just $24 in revenue, plus the tips. And with nine days out of sixty already in the can, as well as most of the city repulsed by yesterday's desperate decision, he wasn't sure how to turn his earnings into a win in time. Chet must've been pulling in at least double that amount every day, and his reputation hadn't yet been ruined.

As Buck headed to the Whipping Shed to seek further advice on how to salvage his chance for success, all he thought about was the word *yet*.

Maybe there was still a way to turn the tables on him, if only he could figure out what that might be.

Of course, as Ronnie's dad had said, Chet might not have been the only entrepreneur out to get him. If so, then he'd have to watch both his back and his front. And maybe even his side while he was at it.

Episode 20

The Boon Suggestion

THE NEON SIGN OVER the Whipping Shed's door was flashing, beckoning new visitors to enter. It must've worked because several complete strangers were hanging out in the lobby, waiting for an audience. As Buck put his hand on the door handle, he wondered whether he'd move to the front of the line or be forced to wait with them. Mr. Kabuki had never made his policies clear about who received priority audience.

However, Buck had gotten as far as cracking the door open when he let it fall back into place. What more could he learn from Mr. Kabuki that he couldn't from doing the work? The Master had already gotten him this far on nineteen on-the-spot lessons. What good were those lessons if Buck didn't put them into practice?

And what of Lesson #15, "Part of success means a willingness to fail"? Maybe he'd fail, and he certainly had approached that line with his trash cup stunt. But what did that actually mean? Buck wondered if the answer lay in the follow-up Lesson #16, "If at first you succeed, be suspicious, for you might be committing a crime."

The lesson, Buck realized, was that success came from experimentation, not luck. Digging in the trash was not the ideal solution for resupplying his cups—he'd learned that the hard way. Instead of earning a hundred dollars today, he'd earned less than thirty. If that metric continued, Chet would beat him. So, he had to change his strategy. He didn't need Kabuki to remind him of that.

Buck headed down the sidewalk. He didn't know what his next move was, but he'd learned that adding whipped cream and cinnamon powder to the top of the coffee was a step in the right direction. Over time, he could probably rebuild his reputation, especially if he stayed out of the trash.

Of course, he'd gotten as far as the alley when he realized he didn't have time to wait for his reputation to improve. Even if he could retain the dozen customers he'd kept with his bright idea for tomorrow's income, they alone wouldn't save him. If each shared positive word-of-mouth with one of their friends, essentially doubling his income, he was still scraping half of Ronnie's sales. And that assumed they all returned, which they never did. There was no way he was breaking fifty dollars tomorrow.

Buck leaned against the wall and stared across the street at Sapphire's Consignments. Cars glided past him as he watched the glitter of traffic in the shop's windows. Kabuki's Lesson #10 entered his mind: "No such thing as a bad deal when the base price is zero."

He also remembered the terms of his contract with Chet. Neither could involve his personal bank account as a condition for victory. All values determining the "win condition" were based on sales. But the contract had never stated explicitly that sales had to come from his coffee business.

Thank lawyers for loopholes.

Buck closed his eyes. Thought of his room. What did he have that he no longer needed? What about his mom's things? She was never home anymore. What would she miss?

The images of his house emptying to win a bet were giving him a headache.

No, there had to be a better way.

But what?

As his ideas for growth escaped him, he surrendered to the reality that he had nothing to offer Sapphire. All his possessions were necessary. If he were to claim a victory in fifty-one days, he'd have to do so on the strength of his impeccable sales skills. He leaned sideways against the wall and drifted around the corner into the alley.

A dumpster stood along the opposite wall, one lid open, the stench not yet unbearable. Buck's eyes locked on it.

Images of the *Hybrid City Post* flashed in his mind. But so did images of the Disinterested Pawn and the ten dollars Benny had given him for the broken VCR.

Buck rolled his body back toward the sidewalk. Sapphire's Consignments was just across the street. But his hands were empty. He rolled into the alley. The dumpster was right there, ready for exploration.

He closed his eyes. High school had never prepared him for this kind of life.

But he knew what he had to do. A sale was a sale, no matter the cost.

"I'll give you five bucks for this," Benny said, when Buck handed over the blender he'd found in the dumpster. "Might want to see if Sapphire will give you something extra for that bit of apple still inside."

Outside the Disinterested Pawn, Buck once again leaned against the wall. Now smelling like rotten fruit, he wondered if there was still a better way to earn a dollar in Hybrid City.

The sky was dimming. The neighborhood shops would close soon. The workday was just about over.

Then, just like that, an idea came to him.

Who better to ask for advice than the richest man in town?

* * *

"You know," the Lease Agent said, as he threw the local news section across the desk and into Buck's lap, page three flapping open and forcing the images of his trashcapade to reenter his sights, "I have a mind to burn your contract right now over what you did. I trust you to represent my space, and you pull this garbage? You know how that looks on me?"

"Sorry, I just—"

"I didn't give you permission to speak."

The Lease Agent yanked the cigar out of his mouth and dropped it on the ashtray. As the charred end sizzled and a waft of smoke rose past his nose, he pressed both palms on his desk and stood from his chair. Despite being clad in a dress shirt, bolo tie, and tweed jacket, the Lease Agent had on just his boxers underneath his waist. Buck wasn't sure whether to shirk in fear or cringe in laughter.

"When you rent a space from me, I expect you to perform at your best. When my name is on a structure, you honor that. And when the rent comes due, you pay it. Got me?"

Buck nodded.

"So, for whatever reason you're here, you can save your breath. I'm not interested. Fix this nightmare, and then I might listen to you."

"I'm trying," Buck said. "But that's the point. Mr. Kabuki can teach me how to make coffee, but he hasn't really taught me how to sell it."

The Lease Agent lowered himself into his leather chair and reached for his cigar.

"If he *had* taught you, I could guarantee he would've left out the part about you digging in the damn trash for your damn inventory."

"I know. I can't succeed until I fail first, but—"

"You fail and learn by making sensible mistakes. Not intellectually baffling ones."

"I was desperate. I ran out of cups, so—"

The Lease Agent's face changed. Now his eyes were much wider.

"Oh! Well, then why didn't you say so? *That* changes everything."

Buck straightened his back. "Does it?"

"No!" His face returned to that awful glowering state.

Buck curled up in his chair again. Why had he come here?

"Look, I don't know what you think you're doing. But whatever it is, you need to exercise intelligence." The Lease Agent pointed at the newspaper still in Buck's lap. "That there was just plain stupid. I don't want to work with or support stupid people."

"I know. I'm sorry. I just—"

"Get out now. I'm tearing up our lease agreement. Clean out the storage room and bring back the key tomorrow evening."

Buck's stomach imploded, or at least it felt like it had. If he had no shop, then he had no way to recover his sanity.

He was now staring at the floor. The rug at his feet was fancier than anything he'd ever stepped on. The Lease Agent must've spent the price of a house to acquire it.

Stupid Ronnie and his stupid paper cups. What was he supposed to do now?

"I'd figured out the perfect coffee today," he said, lamenting the futility of his small victory. But even as he dwelled on his wasted discovery, he recognized the salvageable statement embedded within. He straightened his back, giving himself a few extra seconds to think through his comeback. "I can sell a lot of it, too. I just need a chance to get the people back. Mr. Michaels even agreed to get the Coffee Critic to my shop. Just need time to—"

The Lease Agent chomped on the back of his cigar.

"What's the perfect coffee?"

Buck dared to make eye contact.

"What?"

"I said, what's the perfect coffee?"

"Oh. Well, cream, sugar mixed in, topped with whipped cream and cinnamon powder. Customers loved it. Just got to—"

The Lease Agent held up his palm in a halting position.

"That does sound good." The Lease Agent lowered his hand slightly as he paused in thought. His fingers curled into a fist. He brought it to his chin. Looked off to the opposite wall. His eyes swiveled back down onto Buck. Then he pounded the desk. "Dammit, you can keep your shop if you keep selling coffee that good." He pointed at Buck. "But don't you dare get caught serving customers cups from the trash again. You hear me?"

"Yes, sir."

"All right. What's your question then?"

"Huh?"

"You came here to ask me something. What is it?"

Once again, Buck sat straight and smoothed out his shirt. He knocked the newspaper out of his lap to avoid the reminder of his worst moment since the bet began.

"It's going to take me a while to rebuild my reputation. I know that. I can do it one cup at a time. But it won't be fast enough. Remember that bet I told you about?"

"No. Remind me."

Buck recounted his terms with Chet, including the part where he'd have to become his employee and subject to his abuse if he'd lost.

"So, you don't think you'll outsell Mr. Armstrong?" The Lease Agent asked.

"I don't know. I just know I won't get enough sales momentum to pass him in time, not without a miracle."

The Lease Agent leaned forward with a smirk on his face.

"So, you're here for a miracle?"

Buck nodded. "If you got one, yeah."

The Lease Agent winked.

"Yeah, I got one. How much time do you have?"

"How much time do I need?"

"It amazes me how complete idiots can still ask the perfect question."

Buck said nothing.

"I got some donuts in the next room. Why don't you grab one? This won't be a quick lesson."

"Okay."

"Anyone might miss you if you don't come home tonight?"

"No, Mom works late. Usually goes right to bed, I think. Maybe my dog. But he disappeared with my dad, so I don't expect to see him tonight."

"I should feel sorry for you. But I don't. No time for that."

"Thanks."

"All right. What do you know about investments and hostile takeovers?"

* * *

WHEN BUCK HAD ARRIVED at the Lease Agent's office that evening, he wasn't sure what type of advice the drunk cowboy would offer. But he certainly hadn't expected a lecture. Advice, sure. But not a seminar's worth of information. Nevertheless, a complete education in the stock market and how it worked had followed his simple question, "How do I earn more money faster?" And now Buck was getting tired.

"Can you just give me the introduction?" Buck asked. "Teach me the ins and outs as they become necessary?"

"Do you want to succeed in life or not, kid?"

"I just want to wrap my brain around all of this."

The Lease Agent glared at him.

"How old are you?"

"Eighteen."

"I was running three businesses out of my daddy's garage when I was eighteen. Your generation has no capacity for enterprise."

"I'm just tired. What time is it?"

"Clock's over there. Do you not see it?"

Buck turned his head. Found the grandfather clock rocking its pendulum in the corner. It was after eight o'clock. He'd been here for not even two hours. He rolled his eyes. If he had to endure another two hours of this…

"So, if I understand you correctly," Buck said, sinking deeper into his chair as he rubbed his eyes, "I have to check the price of a business's stock each day…"

The Lease Agent had the newspaper's business section open to today's stock trading information. The page had several names circled in ink with lines connected to prices enclosed in other ink circles.

"First, you have to find one that's cheap but profitable. Never choose a stock from one report. You have to follow the trends."

"Okay, but why? What's the point of all this?"

The Lease Agent leaned back in his chair and folded his hands over his belly. His eyes were serious.

"Have you ever taken an economics class?"

"Yeah…"

"You ever learn the stock market?"

"We got tested on it, but I don't remember much about it."

"You remember the part about *investing* in the stock market?"

"Vaguely."

"What about selling?"

"Not really."

The Lease Agent leaned forward.

"You collect baseball cards?"

"Long time ago."

"You have any you wanted to keep?"

"Sure. At the time."

"What would it have cost your friend to buy your prized card from you?"

"Never thought about it. Wasn't up for discussion."

"Think about it now. If you still had your collection, and if you still cared about that one special card, how much would it cost me to buy it from you?"

"Based on the time, I wouldn't have wanted to sell it. It was my favorite card."

The Lease Agent took his cigar in his hand and pointed it at Buck.

"So, how much would I have to spend to get it into *my* collection?"

Buck nodded. He thought he understood the Lease Agent's point.

"More than I would've charged you for the others," he said. "A lot more."

"That means your card had value. Companies have the same metrics. To buy into a company, you have to match their value. That's why you always start with one that has low value. It could become more valuable over time. Once it gets valuable, you sell it. Pure profit. You get me?"

Buck nodded.

The Lease Agent got up from his chair and approached the wall with all the animal heads. Between the two deer was a framed painting of a forest scene. The Lease Agent pulled the painting off the wall to reveal a safe.

"I wanna show you something in case you don't actually get me."

Because the Lease Agent wasn't clear about whether he wanted to meet at the safe or at the desk, Buck got up from his chair for a better look. Unaware of being observed, the Lease Agent entered his combination—Left 2, Right 10, Left 8—and opened the safe. From it, he removed a document. There was a spiral notebook with gold wire sitting at the bottom.

"You ever hear of the Gravestucker Winery?" The Lease Agent was studying the sheet of paper.

Buck shook his head. "No."

"It's a small chateau in the middle of Napa Valley. Five years ago, no one had heard of it. In fact, I'd discovered it by luck. I was out for a joyride one Saturday afternoon and wound up in a ditch."

Buck sat down. It didn't appear the Lease Agent was interested in showing him anything.

"After stumbling across one vineyard after another, I found myself nose-to-wood with the chateau's front door. The proprietor invited me in, offered me some wine, and showed me around the place.

"It was a dump. But the wine was excellent, so I offered him a trade. On the condition that I get a three-year-old bottle or older sent to my mansion every weekend, I'd invest in his business and bring it out of obscurity. With the money he and I would both earn on the deal, he could fix up his building and start inviting visitors to sample the wine for themselves. He agreed. And for the privilege of spending a night with his best-looking daughter, I told him I'd help him go public immediately."

The Lease Agent paused in thought.

"Unfortunately, he wasn't quite as happy about the follow-up condition as he was the initial, and our deal went sour."

He ambled back to his chair and plopped down behind the desk. As he plunged into the seat, he smacked his desk with the document in hand. It was a chart full of monetary figures.

"This sheet is based on the stock prices of his direct competitor, Tart Bottler Farms. After the proprietor refused me his daughter's audience, I went to Tart Bottler instead. With five daughters to choose from, Tart's proprietor had no problem giving one up for the cause. Sure, none of them were as attractive as the one at Gravestucker Winery, but no one ever said business is perfect. Sometimes you just take what you can get if it means the difference between deal or no deal. You hear me, kid?"

Buck said nothing.

The Lease Agent slid a second sheet out from under the first. The template was the same, but the figures were different.

"This here is the balance sheet for Gravestucker Winery. Never mind how I got the info. What you'll notice by comparison is that Tart Bottler's revenue increased like a pregnant cow's belly, whereas

Gravestucker Winery remained flat. Sure, they managed to squeak by, and even now you could visit their farms and sample their wines. But their building is still uninviting, and their women are still chaste. No way to grow a business. Tart Bottler's, on the other hand…" The Lease Agent inflated his cheeks as he raised his arms from his sides as if expanding. "All from joining the stock market and gaining investors."

He pointed to the column on the right.

"You notice this side here? That's my monthly earnings. Notice how it keeps climbing? Gravestucker on the other hand…" He flipped his thumb upside down. "If they'd kept the terms of the investment, they'd be putting Tart Bottler out of business, and I'd be getting a new bottle of wine each weekend."

"Is there a point to all this?" Buck asked.

The Lease Agent slapped the Tart Bottler Farms report.

"Money, kid. I'm rich because I invest in other people's businesses. And you can, too. Give me three hundred dollars, and I'll get you over the finish line with your bet with Mr. Armstrong. How old's your mom?"

"Not for sale."

The Lease Agent squinted at him.

"Okay, then, five hundred dollars will get you over the finish line."

Buck said nothing. He was nowhere near earning five hundred dollars. He would need a miracle just to afford the Lease Agent's miracle.

Buck's End of Day Report:

Earned: $31.00

Spent: $13.67 ($11.67 for stock; $2.00 for daily fees)

Net Gain: $17.33

Paycheck Accrued: $0

Paycheck Total Due: $39.86 in 24 days?

* * *

Just before nine o'clock at Tealeaf Central, Jennifer Mills stirred her water with her fingernail as Chet once again berated her over that incident from a week ago. Tommy Slick had driven her home without incident, but because they had been alone in his truck together, Chet couldn't let it go.

"You don't know his reputation," Chet said. "You should understand why I'm so upset."

Jennifer sucked the water off her nail, then dipped it in the glass for another round.

"He's got that cowboy hat, and you know how much girls like that," Chet complained.

Jennifer made eye contact with him but said nothing.

"If you'd just come to the club with us and let me take you home—"

"You wouldn't have met your new girlfriend?"

Chet's voice caught in his throat.

"I don't know what you're talking about."

Jennifer sucked her fingernail.

"Don't let Tommy lie to you about that." Chet's feet were tapping like a drummer's against her toes. "What else did he say? What else did he *do*?"

"You're paranoid," she said. "I keep telling you that, but you refuse to listen. Tommy and I are friends. Period. Let it go."

"According to Pigeon—"

Jennifer slapped the table with her hand. The people sitting next to them looked over in response.

"I told you not to speak his name in front of me. I hate that kid. There's something really wrong with him."

Chet nodded. "More than you know. But still, he makes a good point."

"No, he really doesn't. You need to stop listening to him. There's nothing between me and—"

The door to the tea shop opened. Chet had his back to the door, so he couldn't see who was coming and going, but Jennifer had the perfect view.

"Buck."

Chet shook his head. "I'm not accusing you of being with that—"

Jennifer grabbed Chet by both cheeks and kissed him full on the mouth. Keeping her attention past his forehead, she watched Buck slip off to the side behind the plants and disappear into another part of the dining room. He hadn't seen her. The kiss was a waste, so she released Chet and resumed her position.

Chet, meanwhile, said nothing. He just stared back at her. They hadn't kissed since the incident with Tommy.

Jennifer looked off to the side. She didn't want to explain herself, so she thought it better not to address it. But the silence was awkward, so she excused herself.

"I'm going to wash my hands," she said.

Without waiting for a response, she slipped out of her chair and headed for the plants. Once around the corner, she spotted Buck again. He was sitting at a table with that French waitress. What was her name? French Chick? French Girl? Francesca?

Jennifer stood there watching. Buck said something to the waitress, but he was too far away for Jennifer to hear. The waitress smiled at him. And laughed. And she stroked her hair! Her sexy curly hair!

Something fiery hit Jennifer in the pit of her stomach, and it wasn't the tea. She took several steps forward. She felt like a charging bull inside.

But then she stopped, grabbing the nearest chair to squelch her rising momentum.

What did she care who laughed at Buck's stupid jokes? She was no longer dating him. Even if he looked happy right now to be in the French girl's company...

Jennifer didn't want to watch anymore. He looked too happy next to her, like he had the first time he and Jennifer were alone together doing her homework. She also had no interest in walking past him or into the restroom to fake-powder her nose or whatever. She had no more interest in washing her hands. In fact, she had no more interest in drinking tea, or eating croissants, or—

She put her hand over her mouth to stifle the scream that wanted out. Before it could leak through the gaps in her fingers, she turned from her table and hurried out the front door. As far as she knew,

Chet would think she was still in the restroom fixing herself and would amuse himself by checking out the other girls in the room while he waited.

Little did he know, he would be waiting a long, long time.

Episode 21

Desperation

DAY 10: WEDNESDAY, JUNE 19, 1985

Buck's Savings Account: $1.00
Buck's Wallet: $88.16
Buck's Business Funds: unknown
Buck's Expenses: $2 a day*
Hours of Operation: 12 p.m.-5 p.m.
Money on Hold: $39.86 (23 days)

WHEN BUCK CHECKED HIS mailbox the next morning, he found yet another weird letter from Jennifer. There was no stamp on the envelope, so she must've hand-delivered it. But why she'd choose to come here instead of mailing it, he didn't understand.

More baffling, however, was the letter itself:

Dear Buck,

I'm glad you're getting back on your feet. Maybe once you can afford it, we could have a milkshake for old times' sake.

Your friend,
Jennifer

It had been a week and a half since the bet began, and he was much too far from winning or losing to garner her attention or sympathy now. For whatever reason she was sending him this letter, it made no sense.

When had they ever shared a milkshake together?

But it didn't matter. He stared at the letter for several minutes or more, hoping to crack the code, checking it front and back for any secret messages or warnings she might've sent. Surely, Jennifer wasn't writing him because she wanted to go out for a milkshake "for old times' sake." She preferred lemonade.

It must've been a trap.

But who was setting it?

Buck's fingers squeezed the edges of the letter, but he relaxed them before crushing it into a ball. He decided he would store the letter in his desk instead. He needed a record of her insanity in case she was planning something awful for him.

Or, in an unlikelier case, if she were trying to save him from someone else's awfulness.

* * *

WEDNESDAY CAME AND WENT like Tuesday, with fewer than a dozen people visiting the shop all day but more praising his cinnamon whipped cream coffee and leaving him tips. Then Thursday saw a small increase in customers but with fewer tips now that some were repeat visitors and no longer wowed. Friday saw a drop in both, returning to a dozen customers with no tips.

Because his low volumes with his income-to-supply cost ratio was keeping him from earning that second hundred dollars quickly enough, Buck spent Friday night scouring the beach for more plastic bottles he could recycle at Sapphire's. He stayed out past midnight, inviting French Girl to help him for double the quantities. Fortunately, she was happy just to stay out on a Friday night and didn't ask for payment.

Saturday and Sunday, Buck was back at Shop Down the Street pulling his weekend shift, and Ronnie and Tiffany agreed to cover his spot at the Coffee Pavilion. He'd instructed them to recommend the cinnamon and whipped cream topper to all customers, and the results did not disappoint. As an experiment, they added a third topping, peppermint candy. The customers raved about the new addition. By Sunday night, the Coffee Pavilion had once again pulled in a hundred-dollar day. Minus Ronnie and Tiffany's cut, Buck still did better than he had all week.

But it was nevertheless too slow. The Lease Agent had promised a miracle at five hundred dollars. Buck was still under three hundred. Even if it were possible to reach the five-hundred-dollar mark before the last day, the Lease Agent had made it clear that the miracle could happen only if Buck had time to sell stock at a profit. If he continued at this rate, the odds of him making that deadline were low.

Monday and the days to follow saw better sales than the previous week had seen, but it was obvious now that business was best over the weekend. Whether the strength of the weekend was in the timing or in the staff, Buck didn't know, but according to the graph paper he'd bought at the Office Place, that strange dungeon of a shop near Pound Cake and Tailor Made, his financial trajectory was not sloping high enough or fast enough to make a difference. No matter what he did, he was still below the growth arc he needed, which meant he was losing.

On Friday, June 28, which was now Day 19 and just shy of the bet's one-third mark, the dread of his future failure must've shown on his face because Sapphire finally called him out when he'd brought in his fifth bag of plastic bottles for the week.

"For all the advice you got these last few weeks," she said, "you're still doing it wrong."

Buck dropped the bag of empty bottles on the counter. He was exhausted, but he looked her in the eyes without blinking.

"Please don't tell me yet another lesson. Everyone just gives me lessons. No one wants to walk me by the hand. I just want my miracle."

"Miracles don't come easy," she said. "Or cheap. You need to bring me bigger items."

"I don't have access to bigger items. I've had my eye on a coffee bean grinder since last weekend, but I can't afford to spend thirty dollars on it right now. I need to save five hundred dollars for my miracle."

Sapphire folded her arms over her chest.

"Five hundred dollars? Is that what you think will win your bet?"

"I don't know. That's the price the Lease Agent fed me."

Sapphire leaned on her back foot. Now she was studying him.

"The Lease Agent? What's he demanding five hundred dollars for?"

"Says that's the price of investment. He wants me to get into the stock trade. Says that's a quicker way to increase my income."

Sapphire said nothing.

"You don't think it'll work, do you?" Buck asked. "You think I'm wasting my money?"

Sapphire looked at her blue fingernails.

"Not at all. But I think you're naïve."

"Why?"

"Oh, I don't know. Maybe I'm naïve myself."

Buck looked around the room. Just about every knickknack imaginable had representation in her consignment shop. She was no idiot to business actions.

"Go on. I know you want to give me advice. What is it?"

Sapphire lowered her hand and smiled at him.

"The Lease Agent knows his way around the stock market. And whatever his advice about investments is probably a good one."

Buck leaned against the counter as he waited for her to finish.

"But he's got a secret that even I haven't cracked," she said. "The true spice to his wealth lies in a secret he refuses to share. But we all know it has nothing to do with the stock market."

"What is it then?"

Sapphire shrugged.

"No one knows. That's the problem. I've asked Billy out there to spy on him every night until he figures it out. So far, he hasn't caught him in any unusual acts. He goes out to the saloon every Friday and Saturday night"—she glanced up at the clock—"which should be soon, but he just goes out for a drink, then comes back home. Billy hasn't learned a thing, and frankly, neither have I."

"So, how do you know he's even keeping a secret?"

"Because no one can find his name tied to any business, yet he gets substantially richer by the day. How does he do it?"

Buck thought about it.

"You think he's involved in the Mafia?" Buck had seen *The Godfather* a few months ago, and it was still on his mind.

"To a degree," Sapphire said. "Though, it may be even worse. I have my suspicions, don't ask me why, but I can't find out without seeing his records, and he won't let anyone inside his building without an invitation or a chaperon."

"I've been inside. I've seen his office. It's weird, but…"

Sapphire shook her head.

"I've been in his office, too. We all have. You can't own a shop here without first signing the documents that he makes us sign at the office. But what I haven't seen is the inside of his desk. That's where I'm trying to get Billy to look."

"What would he have in his desk?"

"The answer."

Buck stared at Sapphire, but he wasn't sure what more to say. It was then that he remembered the painting on the wall.

"He kept some papers in a safe on his wall," Buck said. "I saw him open it when he told me about the stock market. Showed me his investments in two wine places."

Sapphire's eyes lit up.

"Did he now?"

"Yeah, he was trying to make a point about the stock market, I think. I was kinda lost if I'm honest."

"What did they look like?"

"Just charts full of figures. His point was that he invested in one and it made them both lots of money, while he snubbed the other and it barely survives."

"I see. Well, that would make sense to me if he'd invested venture capital. Did he specifically say he invested in their stock?"

Buck shrugged.

"I don't understand any of this."

Sapphire put her hand on his shoulder and nodded.

"It's okay. You said he'd opened the safe. Did you see anything else? Like gold or stacks of cash?"

"No. Just a small pile of papers. And a notebook, I think. Nothing else."

Sapphire's face hardened.

"Notebook?"

Buck nodded. "Near the back."

"What color was it?"

Buck hadn't paid that close attention to it.

"I don't know. Black, I think. Maybe dark gray."

"With a gold spiral?"

Sounded familiar.

"Pretty sure, yeah…"

Sapphire slapped the counter. She whispered something under her breath.

"What?" Buck asked.

"I said, 'So that's where it went.'"

"Huh…"

Sapphire turned her back and headed for the room behind the counter.

"Uh, are we done here then?" Buck shouted into the void.

She peeked her head around the door.

"You want to earn an extra twenty bucks?" she asked.

"Yeah, sure."

"Go to the Meerkat Saloon by the hospital. See if you can get a seat next to the Lease Agent and keep him busy. Take Billy with you for backup."

"What? Why?"

Sapphire ducked out of sight again. She emerged a moment later with a crowbar in hand.

"I need to get into his office. Where's the safe?"

Buck told her.

"You wouldn't by any chance know the combination, would you?"

Buck had seen the Lease Agent enter it, but he couldn't recall the numbers exactly.

"I remember a left-right-left combination. None of them were past ten. Wait, no, one of them was ten. I don't remember the other two."

"Which one was ten?"

"Right, I think."

"You don't remember the others?"

Buck shook his head.

"Okay, that's fine. I can figure it out. But I need you and Billy to keep the Lease Agent occupied for as long as possible."

"Why? What's in the notebook?"

Sapphire held his gaze.

"Your five-hundred-dollar miracle. It's the secret to how I got my wealth, at least until I'd lost it. Now I know how he got his, that thief."

Buck wasn't sure how to respond to that.

"I was wrong, by the way," Sapphire said.

Buck said nothing.

"This *is* about stocks. It's about the high-performing stocks I've been playing. He must be piggybacking off my research."

Buck understood now. Sort of.

"I've been struggling for months to piece together the information I'd lost. It's been tough. No one wants to give up their information easily, and it's been a pain trying to rebuild my list of tradable companies." She sank against the wall and let out a deep sigh. "I really want my book back. He can do his own research if he wants to get rich."

A moment passed between them. Sapphire looked Buck in the eyes.

"Twenty dollars if you help me get it back. Plus information toward your miracle."

Sounded reasonable.

"Can I bring French Girl instead of Billy? He smells."

Sapphire thought about it.

"Yeah, I suppose Billy would be better with the crowbar, anyway. You can bring French Girl."

"She's not off 'til nine."

"Just make sure the Lease Agent doesn't come back to the office while we're there, and I won't care what time she gets off."

Buck agreed. Looked like he had a side mission now.

And twenty more dollars, assuming this went well.

Episode 22

The Meerkat Saloon

FRENCH GIRL AGREED TO meet him at the saloon once her shift at Tealeaf Central ended. After the busy day she had serving tea, she couldn't wait to visit the bar. Buck hadn't told her why they were going, just that it would be something different from the usual, even though their relationship was too new to even have a "usual." French Girl was happy to try something different.

She reminded him, however, that just because she stopped taking tables at nine didn't mean she would be ready to leave by then. She told him not to expect her before ten, in case she had a lot to clean up at closing time.

Buck couldn't go to the Meerkat Saloon alone, but he also worried ten o'clock would be too late to finish the plan, so he called Lila Deerborn for backup. Fortunately, Lila was home to take the call and all too eager to get out of the house. Getting her to agree to the plan was easy. Her only condition was that he bought her a drink first.

At 8:30, Buck returned to Sapphire's Consignments to confirm everyone's part. Sapphire and Billy Bob Drake would take a crowbar to the office door at sundown, and Buck and Lila would infiltrate the Meerkat Saloon and watch the Lease Agent's movements. To ensure all parties had time to fulfill their roles, Buck agreed to distract the Lease Agent if he tried to leave before ten. Sapphire didn't think they'd need longer than that.

As the sun raced for the horizon, however, Buck had second thoughts about inviting French Girl to the saloon. Although Sapphire was simply reclaiming what was hers, her method was still illegal, and Buck was helping her get away with it. Nothing about the plan would link him to the upcoming break-in, but he still didn't want to risk tying French Girl to the plan should something go wrong and fingers pointed back at him. Not to mention, he didn't want French Girl and Lila interacting. He wouldn't know how to explain that. So, he returned to Tealeaf Central to change her involvement.

"I have a headache," Buck said, hoping she'd take the bait. "Going to turn in early. Let's take a rain check on the saloon. Maybe next week instead."

French Girl looked confused.

"Rain check?"

"It means we'll meet there another night. Just can't do it tonight. Thought I could."

French Girl frowned. "Oh, but it sounded like so much fun."

He put his hand on her shoulder and stroked it. Her shoulders were so slender and smooth, even under a long-sleeved dress shirt.

"Maybe we can go tomorrow night," Buck said.

French Girl shrugged.

"I guess so. Feel better then."

Buck kissed her on the cheek. She didn't shy away, which was great. Everything between them was getting better by the day.

* * *

LILA WAS STANDING BY the door chatting up some dude in a biker uniform when Buck rode up to the Meerkat Saloon just before nine o'clock. He attempted to wave at her to get her attention, but she didn't notice, so he rode on for the parking lot, passing a parked limousine with black windows inside the entrance. A row of motorcycles stood along the side of the building. Buck parked his bicycle in a free spot between two Harleys.

Unlike in the movies, where a popular center of nightlife had lines of waiting patrons a block out the door, Meerkat had a small bump of stragglers standing outside. Most were engaged in conversations, taking the occasional puff of a cigarette, and it wasn't clear if they were waiting to get in or just getting fresh air while they smoked. Lila was among them, and she shared a cigarette with the biker dude.

"Oh, my friend's here," she said when she spotted Buck coming up the walk. "Wanna meet him?"

Buck, aware that she was referring to him, stopped and waved at the biker.

"No," the biker said.

Lila handed the cigarette back to the biker and reached out to embrace Buck. She kissed him full on the mouth. Buck had never sucked on a tailpipe, but he imagined it would've tasted a lot like Lila's mouth had that moment.

After Buck coughed, he patted Lila on the back and thanked her for coming. He also reminded her she didn't have to kiss him anymore. He and French Girl were officially together, most likely. Kissing him was unnecessary now, maybe even detrimental.

"Did she say it's official?" Lila asked.

"Not yet, but I know she will."

Lila stroked his cheek.

"Sweet boy. So dumb. It's never official until she says it is. So, until it's official—" Lila kissed him again. Buck coughed.

"I thought we were just friends."

"We are. Friends kiss."

"No, they don't."

"Well, I kiss my friends. Get over it. Sweet boy." She kissed him again. Buck coughed.

Buck shrugged. Smoke inhalation or not, Lila was still attractive, so a kiss from her from time to time was probably okay. She kissed him a fourth time, making her point.

"Have you seen the Lease Agent arrive yet?" he asked, struggling to clear his throat of smoke burn.

Lila peeked around the front door and scanned the room inside.

"He's at the bar. Got a pitcher of beer beside him."

"Is he alone?"

"Of course he is."

Buck watched the traffic drift by. Now that he was here, he needed an action plan.

"We can't let him leave before ten," Buck said. "I've never been to a bar before. Not sure how this works."

Lila backhanded him on the clavicle.

"That's why you invited me. I'll take care of it. Follow my lead."

Lila showed the bouncer her ID and walked right in. Buck reached for his wallet and flashed the bulky door guard his life stats and was ceremoniously denied.

"To enter, you either need to be twenty-one or hot," the bouncer said. "You're neither."

Buck watched Lila march deeper into the crowd. "I thought the age limit was eighteen."

"It was last year. Change in law, change in policy."

Some dude grabbed Lila by the arm as she passed him, twirled her around, and drew her close. She smiled at the guy. Her hips shook in sync with his rhythm.

"But I have to get in there. I have a meeting."

"Yeah right. Come back in three years," the bouncer said.

The big guy pointed at the sidewalk. His message was clear. Buck belonged outside with the smokers and rejects, not inside with the drunks and the hot girls.

"It's an emergency."

The bouncer shook his head. "No, it's not." The big guy reached in his pocket and produced a business card. He passed it over to Buck. The card said *Twelve Steps for Alcoholics*. "We meet every Monday at the hospital."

"I'm not—"

Buck could still see inside the saloon. At the bar, the Lease Agent was pouring himself another glass from the pitcher, leaving himself with over half of it full. On the dance floor, Lila was grinding her hips with the dude who had pulled her in from her advance.

"Never mind."

Buck returned to his bike. There was still time to fix this, but not by conventional means. He'd have to improvise now.

* * *

MEANWHILE, DOWN AT THE Lease Agent's office, Billy Bob Drake was having trouble with the crowbar. Although the sun was basically down for the night, a tinge of baby blue still lingered low in the skyline to the east, making the remaining light a bit too bright for the occasion. It also didn't help that the moon was almost full. Even if it were a couple of days from complete fullness, it was full enough to keep the night sky shiny. And with the amber streetlights standing among the shrubs every fifty feet along the sidewalk, casting their radial glow onto every crack, there was no way they could do this job in complete darkness. Their only hope of getting in undetected was to work on the lock while no one was around.

For this reason, Sapphire stayed hidden behind the hedges, but she watched both sides of the sidewalk for unexpected travelers. Fortunately, this side of the building did not sit along any public street, just a concourse and sidewalk between two buildings. She didn't have to worry about passing vehicles betraying them tonight. Her only real concern was with the businesses across the field. Their entrances faced the Lease Agent's office, and three of them still had lights on.

"How's that lock coming?" Sapphire asked.

Billy, crouched low enough to gaze directly at the lock, had his elbows up at an awkward angle, sliding the crowbar blade up and down between the door and the frame.

"Can't seem to catch it," he said.

"Come on, Billy. There's a hamburger and fries waiting for you if you get this done."

"I'm working on it. Just keep an eye on the sidewalk, please."

Sapphire hadn't taken her eyes off of it. She was just good at using her peripheral vision to detect motion. The sidewalk, so far, was clear. Unfortunately, it was also as bright as a Las Vegas park at midnight.

* * *

BUCK HAD RIDDEN HIS bike through the streets of Hybrid City's beach sector as fast as he could and dumped it at the front door of Wild Trends. Fortunately, the shop was still open.

Rory Stickmeyer was restocking a shelf full of flavored syrups when Buck finally found him.

"My dude," Rory said when Buck shouted at him for attention. "How's the coffee business going?"

"Never mind that. I need to know how—" Buck's eyes fell on the syrups. "Hey, is that caramel?"

Rory picked a bottle of caramel off the shelf and twisted it so Buck could see the label. "Sure is. And over here I got peppermint. And here's some hazelnut."

Buck entered a trance as he scanned the shelf's bottles. Each flavor would've gone perfectly with some cream and sugar.

"Customers are baking pastries with it," Rory said, "but I bet you could do something even more clever with it."

"Yeah…"

Then Buck snapped out of it, remembering why he'd come here.

"I'll come back for some of this stuff another time. Right now, I need a fake ID."

Rory shrugged.

"Aw, dude, you can't tell me that. I sell alcohol here. Now I know you're not twenty-one."

"It isn't for you. It's for the Meerkat Saloon. I need to get in. Like now. Where can I get one in a hurry?"

Rory thought about it.

"There's a guy who calls himself Shady Derek over near Pound Cake. Runs a place called The Un-Shop, if you've seen it. It's basically a black-market dive. Keeps his business in the dark. But he seems to be the source of all the fake IDs I encounter around here. Given that the sun is down, he's probably open now."

"Where is it?"

"Not sure exactly. Never had reason to visit it myself. I just know it's near Pound Cake. Irina might know."

Buck agreed. Irina Swift knew a lot of things.

"I'll be back for the syrups tomorrow," Buck said. "Save your favorites for me."

"Will do, buddy."

* * *

"WOULD YOU PLEASE SPEED it up?" Sapphire demanded her assistant. Her heart was pounding, and the night's heat was drawing sweat from her neck. Billy Bob Drake was still fiddling with the lock and making no noticeable progress on it. And the stench coming from his shirt reminded her of eggs. It drove her mad.

"Just shove it in and pop the lock," she said.

"It's not that simple," Billy said. "To leave the least amount of damage, first you have to—"

"Fall back!"

Sapphire had noticed movement coming from inside one of the businesses across the street. Billy fell backward and rolled behind the hedge just as a young woman exited the candle shop across the sidewalk and to the left one unit.

The woman was smiling at her bag as she reached the sidewalk but stopped for a moment to look toward the Lease Agent's office. Her face went blank as she stared. Maybe she'd noticed something odd about it. She made no motion indicating otherwise.

But then she continued, returning her fixed gaze to whatever she'd bought at the candle shop.

Sapphire was now breathing on the back of Billy's neck, and his neck was casting the scented remains of an old breakfast at her nose. Once the coast was clear, she shoved him out onto the office doorstep, ridding herself of his foul stench immediately. Time to get back to work.

* * *

MEANWHILE, AT THE MEERKAT Saloon, the Lease Agent poured himself another glass. The pitcher was below the halfway point now.

Lila, who had intended to join the Lease Agent at the bar and distract him with idle conversation, had instead gotten pulled into the corner, where she was now square dancing with a group of bikers and cowboys. Every time she tried edging closer to the bar, someone else had reeled her farther away.

She still didn't understand why Buck hadn't followed her in. This was his plan, after all.

* * *

Irina Swift was arranging what remained of the day's pastries under the glass counter when Buck hurried in. She waved at him as he approached.

"Have you heard of the Un-Shop?" he asked her.

Irina rose above the glass and stared at him from across the counter.

"Yes, what do you want with that place?"

"Rory at Wild Trends says the kids get their fake IDs there. I need one."

Irina shook her head.

"You're better than that, Buck."

"Normally, yes. But tonight is different. It's an emergency."

Irina reached into her pouch and produced a small business card. It was another one promoting Twelve Steps for Alcoholics.

"It's never an emergency," she said.

"What is it with—never mind! I don't need a drink. I need to get into the Meerkat Saloon so I can distract the Lease Agent from going back to his office before ten."

Irina gave him a look she'd never given him before. This one was mixed with confusion and accusations.

"Why?" She was clearly suspicious of his behavior now.

"It's personal," he said.

"So personal you need to visit the Un-Shop? Do you even know what the Un-Shop is?"

"Yeah, fake ID place. Look, I didn't come here for judgment. I just need to—"

"Aren't you also trying to win a bet?"

"Yeah, I—"

"You know how much a fake ID costs?"

Buck was about to respond, but he stopped himself. He admittedly didn't know, nor had he given it much thought until now.

"A hundred dollars at least," Irina said. "You have a hundred dollars in your pocket?"

Buck shook his head.

"Can you afford to spend a hundred dollars if you did?"

Buck shook his head. He needed every penny toward buying his miracle and winning the bet.

"Would you ever see a return on investment of that hundred dollars if you were to buy that fake ID?" she asked.

"I don't know."

Buck needed it to stall the Lease Agent from heading back to the office before ten. With all the running around he'd been doing, however, he'd lost track of the time. According to the clock on the wall, it was already 9:30, and by the time he'd recover a hundred dollars from his cash bag from under his bed and get to the Un-Shop and make the request for the ID and wait for the printing, it would probably be after midnight, and that was definitely too late to justify spending that kind of money.

In short, he would've been wasting it, something he should've realized before even leaving the saloon.

"Let me give you another piece of advice," Irina said, her tone now harsh. "The Un-Shop is no place for good kids like you. Shady Derek is a lunatic, and his shop is nothing more than a gateway to a life of crime. He sells more than fake IDs. A lot more. And none of it's good. Don't go."

Now that Buck had done the math, he couldn't see the point in going anymore.

"Okay." Of course, he still had no better plan for getting into the Meerkat Saloon. He just understood that his current plan wouldn't have gotten him inside, either. "Any advice on how I can stall the Lease Agent without it?"

Irina's face softened. A smile crossed her face.

"You don't. The Lease Agent will do what the Lease Agent wants to do. If he wants to stay, he'll stay. And if he wants to leave, he'll leave. Your job is to stand by and watch."

She reached under the glass counter and handed him a macadamia nut cookie.

"On the house," she said.

* * *

French Girl finally finished her shift. Now that she was off the clock, she could go home and rest her feet.

But she really didn't want to listen to her exchange dad talk about his day. And she really didn't want to spend another Friday night watching the last ten minutes of TGIF on TV. She really wanted to do what teenagers did on a Friday night.

She wanted to go to a movie.

Or go to a party.

Or go to…

Buck had gotten her interested in the idea of visiting that saloon. She nodded to herself. Just because he was at home sick with a headache didn't mean she had to go home, too.

There was no reason she couldn't go to the saloon herself.

* * *

Down the sidewalk from the Lease Agent's office, another flash of movement entered Sapphire's peripheral vision. She reached out, grabbed Billy by the belt buckle, and pulled him behind the hedge. Then she put her hand over his mouth as they waited for the traveler to pass by. Billy slobbered all over her palm.

Now she was ready to kill the Lease Agent for taking her notebook.

"Don't say anything," she whispered, trying not to gag.

Sapphire pulled her hand away and wiped it on her shirt. Then she dared to peek over the hedge as the person drew closer.

She ducked and held her breath.

It was a Hybrid City police officer on patrol.

He was ambling along the sidewalk, shining his flashlight at every front door of every business along the way. His movement was crisp and determined. This was his turf now.

"And don't move," Sapphire whispered in Billy's ear. She felt for the crowbar and pried it out of Billy's hand. She lowered it to the dirt between her and the wall.

The cop shuffled toward the candle shop; shined his light at the door. Seemed satisfied, so he pivoted toward the north side of the concourse and aimed his light at the Lease Agent's door.

The cop paused.

His face stiffened.

There was something about the door he didn't like.

* * *

Buck finished the cookie and thanked Irina for the reality check. Then he raced back to the Meerkat Saloon. It was almost ten o'clock.

Traffic thickened the closer he got to the entertainment district, but it didn't slow him down. Because he was on a bicycle, he just had to veer around pedestrians, not cars. Didn't take him long to scoot across town.

He'd returned to the saloon within fifteen minutes, but something was different from before. Whatever it was, he couldn't place it.

Giving the anomaly no more thought, however, he dropped his bike in the same open parking spot as before and dashed for the front door. The bouncer still wouldn't let him in.

"What time is it?" Buck asked.

The bouncer checked his watch.

"Nine fifty."

Not yet ten o'clock. He still had time to catch the Lease Agent on his way out. The crowd of smokers had gotten thicker since he'd left before. So had their smoke.

But something didn't feel right about this, any of it.

Buck peeked inside the door to check on the situation. Lila was dancing with a group of guys near the restrooms. And the bar was now full of cowboys and bikers. So far, so normal.

But the Lease Agent was not among them.

So far, less normal.

He scanned the crowd for evidence that the Lease Agent was dancing. But there were too many others choking the dance floor. If he was in there, he was consumed by them.

Suddenly, he realized what was different about the parking lot. The limousine was gone.

He closed his eyes and cursed.

"I thought you were sick," a young woman with a French accent said in his ear from behind him.

LIKE THE PROVERBIAL WOODLAND creature that shared his namesake, Buck was caught in the headlights. Nowhere to run. Too late to hide. French Girl stood before him, still in her work uniform and with her hair pinned back, here, free from serving and ready to be served, but not all smiles, and not much grace. She was rigid, her left hand on hip, right hand under her jaw. Lovely eyes searching him, but not at all soft.

She was expecting him to respond. That was obvious.

According to her, Buck had said he was sick. But what had he told her? Was it a stomachache? Sounded about right. He had invited her to a saloon, after all, a place where they served greasy fries or onion rings or possibly other items tough on the stomach lining. He had no idea what they actually served because he'd never eaten here, but this place seemed like it would have grease on the menu. Regardless, he was sure it would've aggravated his stomach in healthy times, so he must've told her he'd had a stomachache and couldn't tolerate the food here.

"I started feeling better on my way home," he said. "Must've been something I ate."

French Girl's thoughts were racing. She muttered something under her breath in French.

"What?" Buck asked.

"So, you came without me?"

"I figured you'd meet me here." He gestured to her. "And I was right."

French Girl spoke something else under her breath.

"I don't know what you're saying," Buck said.

"I thought you had a headache."

Buck winced. He *had* said it was a headache.

"Ice cream headache. I keep forgetting they're not real headaches. Better now."

French Girl's face softened.

She erupted with laughter.

"What?" Buck asked. She'd gone crazy.

"You American boys are so funny and stupid at the same time." She reached out and pinched his cheeks. "No wonder so many movies made about you."

She released him and patted him on the shoulder.

"So, we go in?"

Buck eyed the bouncer. The guy was sitting on a stool, one foot on the rest, the other on the sidewalk. His arms were folded across his stomach. No one was going in, so he had nothing better to do than watch the crowd.

French Girl grabbed Buck by the arm and pulled him toward the door.

"Two please," she said when she reached the bouncer's post.

The bouncer scanned her up and down. Nodded. Then he held out his hand for Buck.

"ID, please."

Before Buck could hear his formal rejection for the second time tonight, French Girl had gone in without him. By the time she was halfway toward the bar, her hips were shaking to the music of Duran Duran's latest hit, "A View to a Kill."

There wasn't much reason to chase her down. He couldn't get in. Odds were better that Lila would dance with French Girl before he'd ever get the chance.

The thought of it made him sick to his stomach.

* * *

SAPPHIRE'S CONSIGNMENTS HAD ALREADY closed for the night, but Buck knocked on the front door, anyway. They'd agreed to meet here after ten o'clock to review the notebook and plan the next step. But judging by the state of the darkness and silence inside, Buck wasn't sure the plan was still in motion. The lights were off, and Buck was already twenty minutes past due. And he couldn't detect any movement inside. Nevertheless, he waited.

He knocked again.

A fissure of light split the darkness deep inside the shop. After a second's pause, something bulbous broke the seam further, at about the height of an adult human head. Then nothing.

Buck knocked a third time and waved.

The crack widened, now revealing a female silhouette in the doorway. The back office was illuminated behind her. Then it wasn't.

Buck checked over his shoulder. What was going on here? When nothing else happened, he knocked a fourth time.

She appeared right in the doorway, an apparition with dirty, matted hair and wrinkled clothing. Buck leapt backward.

The door unlocked. Before Buck could react, Sapphire lunged forth, grabbed him by the forearm, and snatched him inside. She locked the door behind her.

"To the office," she whispered. "Did anyone see you?"

"Why are you acting like this?"

"*Whisper!*"

"Why are you acting like this?" he whispered.

"Watch out for the table. We'll talk in the office."

Sapphire led him through the mini-maze of display tables before circling the counter and entering a dark room behind it. The office. She must've turned off the light before crossing the room.

Once the office door was closed behind them, Sapphire flicked on the switch. The room was once again visible. Billy Bob Drake was sitting in a chair across from her desk. Both were caked in dirt and leaves.

"Did, er, everything go well?" Buck asked.

Sapphire took the seat behind the desk, folded her hands over some invoices, and looked him in the eyes.

"No," she said.

Buck sank into the only vacant chair left in the room, an orphaned member of a dinette set.

"But you got the notebook, right?"

Sapphire's silence said it all.

Buck pressed his forehead to his palm and sat hunched in the chair until his stomach tightened. He'd kissed Lila and lied to French Girl for this book, and none of them had access to it yet. This was *not* part of the plan.

"Do I still get my twenty bucks?" he dared to ask.

Sapphire said nothing.

"Okay. What happened?"

Sapphire told him everything up to the moment the cop appeared on the scene.

"So, the cop, in a rare act of detective work," she said, "investigated the scratches near the lock. Twice in his random swings of the flashlight, he nearly exposed us in that shrub. I swear he must've been avoiding going home to his wife because he just parked it by that door, scratching his head, running his fingernail over the lock, and spending an absurd amount of time analyzing what could've just been someone hitting it with the side of a couch on moving day.

"*Then* he rang the doorbell. When nobody answered, he knocked. When that didn't get an answer, he finally stepped away. But did he continue on his merry way? *Of course not.* He got as far as the main walk before stopping again and consulting his notepad. Must've wanted the lamplight, because now he was writing something on it. Really thought through his words, maybe even his ten-dollar vocabulary, because he took a long-ass time figuring out what he wanted to note. Barely got his pen scratching when you-know-who came staggering up the lot."

"Who's you-know-who?" Buck asked, knowing the answer but wanting the confirmation, especially now that the night was over, and he was tired, and he couldn't believe he'd wasted his evening on this stupid plan, not to mention kissed a girl with chimney breath who wasn't French.

Sapphire confirmed it for him, without scoff or irony. Perhaps she was tired, too.

"So, we give up then?" Buck asked.

Sapphire was now clutching her own forehead, shaking it softly.

"We'd almost committed a felony," she said. "And we came within inches of getting caught. I still want my book, but to tempt fate again…"

To Buck's surprise, the next words he heard were not from Sapphire, but from Billy Bob Drake, who had been listening to the conversation with no sense of reaction. Now he was alive, and his hands were searching for something to grab.

"We never give up," he said. "If there's anything I learned after losing my business, it's that we never let anyone steal our stuff, especially when it's all we got."

He pointed at Buck. "You don't let anyone steal your girlfriend."

He pointed at Sapphire. "You don't let anyone steal your book."

Then he pointed at himself. "And you don't let anyone steal your adventure."

Billy Bob Drake rose from his chair and beat his fist against his chest.

"We don't let anyone steal our victory. Ever. We go back. Tonight." He picked up the crowbar he'd been sitting on. "Now."

Sapphire shook her head.

"Sit down, General Patton. We think of a new plan."

Billy brandished the steel rod.

"But the lock! It must be picked!"

"Prison will steal a lot more from you than your adventure. Now, sit down and think. Three current and former shop owners here. Surely one of us can think of something that'll not only work but keep us out of the law's scrutiny."

Minutes passed without a response. Even as Buck and Billy were each about to say something, they swallowed their words. Sapphire, meanwhile, said nothing at all. Just sat there, staring at her desk.

No one was ready to admit that the Lease Agent had defeated them without even trying. Any plan they could think of would have to outsmart the most formidable business mind in all of Hybrid City. The fact was, the notebook was in the safe, and the safe was protected behind a combination lock, and a landscape painting, and a drunk man with a cowboy hat who probably also carried a gun if his persona and wall trophies were of any indication.

And then, just like that, the solution presented itself.

"The cop rang the doorbell?" Buck asked.

Sapphire pointed her index finger at Buck and made a buzzing sound with her mouth.

"Think you could do the same?" he asked.

Sapphire said nothing.

"If you can," Buck continued, "then I have a plan that might actually work."

Sapphire sat up in her chair. Her pointed finger twisted upside down, and her palm opened to him.

"Go on," she said.

Buck told them what he was thinking. When he finished, Sapphire nodded.

"That's painfully simple. But it might work." She slapped the table. "Fine, we'll try it. Better plan for Monday, though. Won't be as believable if we try over the weekend."

"Would Tuesday be better? More time to plan our steps?"

Sapphire shook her head. "No, just come see me Monday morning, and we'll work out the details. The less complicated we make it, the better the chance we have."

"Will I still get my twenty dollars?"

Sapphire smiled at him. "Let's see how it goes first. On that note, I need to shower. Both of you, get out. I'm going home."

* * *

SATURDAY AND SUNDAY CAME and went as they had the previous two weekends, with Mack Green teaching Buck how to run a shop properly, and Ronnie and Tiffany ensuring the Coffee Pavilion didn't implode or scare off what few customers Buck had kept in the wake of his publicized Dumpster dive. He remained calm for the most part, but the anxiety of bringing his plan against the Lease Agent on Monday caused his neck to tingle and his gut to gurgle.

Mack had to snap his fingers before Buck's eyes on a few occasions, but he'd recovered his senses when it mattered.

"Right," Buck said. He'd caught himself in a daze for the fifth time. "Health inspectors are the worst."

Mack handed him a mop.

"That's why I need you to pay attention when you clean the floors. Come on, Buck. This is insider stuff. Gold material. I don't see Kabuki teaching you this crap. Leave no mess behind."

"I'm trying not to."

Monday's plan had to work. It was too simple to fail. As long as everyone did his or her part exactly…

"Be extra careful with that spilled milk," Mack said. "Don't want some kid coming in here and licking it off the floor."

"They do that?"

"The ones who think they're cats do."

Buck tried to put Monday out of mind as he neared the end of his Sunday shift, but it wasn't easy. Something about his idea that it was "so simple" bothered the heck out of him. What was ever truly simple?

And that's when his stomach cramped. It was a message.

Nothing about tomorrow's plan was simple, and that was the problem. Even if Buck and Sapphire did their parts, they still relied on the Lease Agent doing his. And he was the only one unaware of the game they were playing. He could've broken character and wrecked the whole thing at any time.

The problem with rich eccentrics was that they broke character all the time. That's what made them eccentric.

"Better do a thorough job with that egg yolk, too," Mack said. "Health inspectors don't generally like to see animal products smeared across interactive surfaces when they come to visit."

After his shift, Buck checked in on Ronnie and Tiffany, collected his cut of the earnings, then went off to see French Girl at Tealeaf Central. She told him she was busy. When he asked if they could meet after her shift, she gave him the same answer.

"Having a girls' night out," she said. "That what it's called?"

"Again?"

"*Oui*. Yes."

French Girl had a girls' night out last night, too, leaving Buck at home with a frozen dinner and episodes of *Gimme a Break!*, *Mama's Family*, and *Hunter* to enjoy alone.

"I can't believe you and Lila are friends now."

"Yes, Lila fun. You know she at saloon other night?"

"Yes, you told me."

"Hit on lots of boys."

"Yes, she does that."

"Her boyfriend seem okay with it."

"Probably doesn't even know."

"That why he okay with it."

Buck glanced at French Girl. She winked back at him. His stomach grew even tighter than before.

* * *

On Monday, July 1, or Day 22 of the bet, Buck finalized the plan for the day. Because everything relied on the Lease Agent's schedule, Buck finally bought that card stock open sign from the Office Place he'd had his eye on for a couple of weeks and rode off to the pavilion to use it. He drove a nail into the pavilion leg where customers were most likely to see it and hung the sign over it. He flipped it to "Closed." No one would get any coffee until Sapphire got her notebook.

Once he confirmed that everything at the pavilion was locked down, he returned to Sapphire's to check in.

"We're still on for later?" he asked.

She was handing a bearded guy a wad of change after he had given her a small hula girl lamp.

"Just give me a time," she said.

Buck nodded. "It has to be you, just to remind you."

"I know."

"Don't send Billy in your place."

"I won't."

"It won't work if he's the one ringing the bell."

Sapphire thanked her customer. The bearded guy gave Buck a funny look. Buck nodded at him.

"Enjoy your money," he said to the man. "And stop by the Coffee Pavilion tomorrow for your coffee pleasure. Second of July special. All cups just two dollars plus tax."

Ronnie had reminded him to collect tax with each cup last weekend. He'd finally started doing it that Wednesday.

"Isn't that what you normally charge?" Sapphire asked when the customer had moved out of earshot.

Buck shrugged. "Marketing. Both Kabuki and Mack said I needed to master it."

Sapphire smiled at him.

"It's scary how quickly you're learning the tricks of the trade. Anyway, yes, tell me when you need me. I'll do my part."

Buck's stomach was now at the tensest it's been all weekend. Now was the time to set the last piece in place.

"I'll be right back," he said.

* * *

THE LEASE AGENT WAS still in his morning bathrobe when he opened the office door, but his cigar was already halfway down to a stub.

"What you need, kid?"

The Lease Agent took the cigar in hand and waved it around in tiny circles as he awaited an answer. A nearby fly buzzed off.

Buck swatted smoke out of his face.

"I was wondering if I could make an appointment to meet later this morning or afternoon."

"What for?"

"Need more investment advice. There's still something I don't understand. Just wanted time to clarify before I start making big decisions, you know?"

The Lease Agent studied him.

"What's your question?"

Buck shuffled where he stood. He hadn't really considered what to ask yet. He was just trying to get the appointment. Whatever his question would be, he'd present it at the meeting.

"It's a bit complicated. I know you're busy, so I can come back anytime today. Just need to plan a time and—"

The Lease Agent stepped inside the hall and gestured for Buck to enter.

"You seem free now," he said. "I'm preparing breakfast. Come to the kitchen. I can give you twenty minutes."

"I—"

Buck looked off to either side of the office building.

A beagle was chasing a squirrel down near the cross street at the end of the field.

Some birds were flying from tree to tree, hunting for bugs or seeds.

A tall policeman was patrolling the main walkway between buildings, swinging his nightstick, whistling some tune only he could hear. Buck wondered if it was the same cop who had spent the evening investigating the scratched lock.

He looked at the latch. Just as Sapphire had described it, the frame had a few notches where the door would've caught. His attention floated upward.

The Lease Agent was watching him.

"You coming or not?" he asked. "Got bacon on the fryer. Don't wanna burn it."

"Could I meet with you later this morning, in the office?"

"Kid, my slate is full today. You want my attention, now's the time. You're down to nineteen minutes."

Buck considered whether he had to do this today. Maybe tomorrow would be better.

"What's your schedule this week?"

"Tomorrow, busy. Next day, busy. Day after that, busy. Every day, busy. You're here now. You got a question for me or not?"

Buck wondered how far down the road he could kick this can to make sure he got it right.

But no. Time was running out. Today was already twenty-two days into the bet. The halfway mark would be upon him before he knew it. A moment would come when it would be too late to invest if he still wanted the upper hand. In fact, it might've already been too late. He didn't know how fast this stuff worked.

It had to be today.

"Just give me a moment," he said. "I'll be right back."

He stepped away from the door, but the Lease Agent beckoned him forward.

"Kid, once this door closes, I'm going back to my breakfast, and this opportunity will be gone. Whatever your complicated question, now's the time. Come in or forget about it."

Buck squeezed his eyes shut and nodded.

The Lease Agent was definitely *not* fulfilling his part of the plan.

* * *

"I'VE ONLY MADE ENOUGH for myself," the Lease Agent said as he rotated the sausage link he was frying over the stove. "So, I won't be sharing."

Buck took the seat closest to the door. He'd have to make a run for it should the time present itself.

"Might have an old box of cereal lying around if you're hungry, though." The Lease Agent shifted from side to side as he reached for a salt shaker, then a spatula to flip an egg, then a tub of butter for the toast. His bathrobe swayed along with him and kept going even as he changed direction. "You like Corn Flakes?"

"I'm not hungry," Buck said.

Compared to the main office and its museum to woodland creature massacres, the office kitchen was plain. Not much different from Kabuki's kitchen. In fact, except for the oven and stove set, plus the six-seater oak dining room table across from the serving counter, there was no difference at all. They sat in opposite positions in relation to the main hall connecting all rooms—the Lease Agent's kitchen was up front and to the right of the main hall, in about the same position as Kabuki's training room—but that was it.

It took some of the magic and mystery out of his lair.

"What about coffee?"

Buck said nothing.

The Lease Agent glanced over his shoulder and noticed his face.

"Oh, right," he said. "Dealers never partake of their own product. Milk?"

Buck wasn't sure if the Lease Agent was playing the gentleman to his guest or playing a head game to a possible enemy. But it sure felt like stalling. Did he suspect why Buck was here?

"Sure," Buck said.

The Lease Agent pulled an empty glass out of the cupboard and set it on the counter.

"It's in the fridge," he said. "Got three kinds to choose from."

So much for the gentleman's game.

Buck checked the refrigerator as the Lease Agent continued serving himself his breakfast. Sure enough, there were three jugs. Two were marked with colorful store logos. The third just had black marker scrawled across it.

"You have unpasteurized milk in here?" Buck asked.

"Yep, got connections. Don't tell anyone, or I'll have to shoot you."

Buck made a mental note of it. The FDA had deemed unpasteurized milk illegal. Possessing it was almost as bad as having drugs. No one had explained why, as far as Buck knew, but they'd all agreed it was forbidden.

"Is it safe to drink?"

"Of course it's safe. Wouldn't have it otherwise."

"Won't give me cancer or anything, will it?"

"Only one way to find out, kid."

In other words, Buck thought, drinking unpasteurized milk wasn't guaranteed safe. Just maybe safe. He popped the lid and sniffed it for freshness.

"How's your pavilion business since our last chat?" the Lease Agent asked.

Buck set the unpasteurized milk aside and tested the other jugs. One was store-bought whole milk. The other was two percent. Both smelled fine.

"Making a killing," he said. "Really turning things around."

Over the last couple of weeks, Buck had been working on fixing his reputation, but he had hardly been killing it. More like flicking it in the ear.

"That's good to hear. I've had my doubts."

The topic of investments still hadn't surfaced, which Buck was grateful for given how little he had prepared his question. But it wouldn't be long. The spatula was already scraping along the surface of the pan to scoop up those scrambled eggs. Once the plate was full, the real conversation would likely begin. Buck reached for the unpasteurized milk. It made him curious.

"You ever get sick off this milk?" Buck asked.

The Lease Agent pivoted from the stove. His cigar hung from his frown.

"If you want the two percent, just grab that. You're one of the most overly cautious kids I ever met. You want to succeed in business, just go for it."

He returned to the sizzling meat sitting on his burner. The kitchen had gone from smelling like sausage to smelling like burnt sausage.

Buck poured the unpasteurized milk into the glass. He'd have all his questions answered as soon as he drank it.

"All right, kid, I'm about done here. If you're gonna ask your question, ask it now."

Buck put the glass to his lips. Tilted it back enough to taste the first drops of milk on his tongue.

It was sweet.

But he still didn't know what to ask. So, he improvised whatever he hoped would get a long, drawn-out answer. He started by chaining as many buzzwords together as he could from what he remembered watching rich Texas nighttime soap opera stars talk about on TV.

"What's the average failure rate of a stock bought with minimal research?" he asked. "And how will it affect my bottom line during a price drop?"

"Unknown and badly," the Lease Agent said. "Is that all?"

Buck set the glass down.

He had nothing else to add. His mind was blank. Even in his greatest moment of subversion, the Lease Agent had popped his balloon. Now what?

"No, um, there's more."

But there was no opportunity for him to ask his next fake question. The sound he'd been waiting for had finally come.

The office doorbell rang.

Sapphire must've figured out the situation when he didn't come back right away.

The Lease Agent grumbled as he turned off the stove.

"Hold that thought, kid. Wait here."

The Lease Agent stomped out of the kitchen and headed for the front door.

Buck wasted no time. He dashed out behind him and raced for the office, hoping the Lease Agent was too distracted by the front door to notice.

Episode 24

Field Games

BUCK RAN ON TIPTOES across the shallow carpet. He made no sound, but his footsteps were still too loud. At any moment, the Lease Agent would sense him a few body lengths behind, either through sonic vibrations or through plain inconvenient intuition.

But he did no such thing. As Buck turned the knob of the office door, the Lease Agent turned the knob of the front door. Maybe he was more in sync with the plan than Buck had earlier assumed. Maybe Buck was just lucky.

"To what do I owe the pleasure?" the Lease Agent asked.

"You and I need to talk," Sapphire said.

Buck closed the office door behind him and braced himself against it. His chest was pounding, and his breathing shortened, and the unpasteurized milk hit his stomach hard. But he was in the Lease Agent's inner sanctum now, free to search it.

The mounted deer heads on the wall were staring at him.

He had no time to second-guess his next move. Sapphire would tell the Lease Agent an incredible fake story, but it wouldn't be a long one.

"You won't remember it," Sapphire said, "because you were really drunk. *Really* drunk."

Buck lifted the landscape painting off the hooks and lowered it to the floor. It was heavier than it looked. The right corner touched down before the left, and it was not a soft landing. And it clapped against the wall as it fell to rest.

He checked over his shoulder. Watched the door for a few seconds. Listened to what was happening outside.

"I was drunk, too," Sapphire said.

The conversation was still active. He was in the clear for now.

The safe was basic. Nothing particularly complex about it. Just a classic wall safe with a combination lock and a latch. If the Lease Agent had any serious valuables like gold bars or savings bonds, he'd probably stash them elsewhere, perhaps at home in a bigger safe with more challenging locks.

"You got a little flirty with me," Sapphire said. "I might've flirted a little back."

Buck put his hand on the combination lock and turned it once to the left, then ten to the right. He remembered the Lease Agent spinning ten to the right.

"You flirted some more."

Buck turned one to the left and tried the latch. Locked. He turned one left, ten right, and two left. Locked.

"I flirted back some more."

One left, ten right, three left. Locked. One left, ten right, four left. Locked.

"We started to dance to some jazz."

"The kid ain't mine," the Lease Agent said. "My meat's gettin' cold."

Buck's hand slipped off the dial.

The front door slammed shut. Buck's heart about leapt out of his chest. It might've been his imagination, but he was certain the walls shook from the impact.

He reached for the painting and lifted it by its left corner, struggling to hold its frame, trying to get it up to the hook, careful not to let it slam against anything, not that it mattered if the Lease Agent returned to the kitchen and didn't find him there.

He'd raised it halfway up when the doorbell rang again.

"I said the kid ain't mine!"

"That's not what I'm trying to tell you!" Sapphire's shout was even louder.

The front door reopened. Buck froze, uncertain whether to hang the painting or to resume seeking the right combination.

"Get to the point, then. I've got a busy day."

Buck chose the combination lock. No time to waste. One left, ten right, six left. Locked.

"Where did I leave off?"

"We were both drunk."

"Oh, right, really drunk. Really, *really* drunk. Deadly drunk."

Each rotation had room for up to thirty clicks, and Buck raced through as many as he could as quickly as his fingers allowed. By the time he'd gotten to his twelfth attempt, his fingers slipped, and he had to reset the combination. He couldn't remember if the combination zeroed out on the first miss, or after he turned past zero. He assumed the latter.

"I feel like you're trying to tell me about a pregnancy," the Lease Agent said.

"Why would you think that?"

"This entire conversation is heading in that direction."

"You assume, then, that I'd actually sleep with you?"

"I mean, why even bring up how drunk we were if that's not the payoff?"

"I'm actually insulted right now."

"I could always go back to my breakfast. Don't really have time for whatever this is, anyway."

"Fine, would it make you happy if that was the payoff?"

"I'd be happier if I could actually remember that."

Buck's hands slipped off the dial again. He was up to twenty-seven clicks, just four away from starting a new chain.

"Do you think I'd want to remember that?"

"You talk to me as if I'm some kind of repulsive creature. You'd be so lucky to remember!"

"I didn't come here to share in your revelry of some sexual conquest. I came to tell you a story."

Two left, ten right, one left. Locked. Two left, ten right, two left. Locked.

"But one that depends on our state of lucidity. Just give it to me straight, Sapphire. Did we or did we not break a few springs—what night are we even talking about?"

"If I said yes, is that what would make this conversation interesting to you?" Two left, ten right, seven left. Locked. "Only if I told you that you've sampled my best goods?"

Two left, ten right, eight left.

"Yes."

The safe opened.

Buck wasted no thought on what he was looking at. He snatched the notebook, tucked it under his shirt, and closed the seal and spun the lock.

"You want to know the truth?" Sapphire asked.

The Lease Agent said nothing.

Buck, meanwhile, set the painting on the hooks so quickly that he'd hardly been quiet about it. Once again, the frame clapped against the wall. His heart raced faster as he listened for a reaction.

"Where are you going?" Sapphire asked.

"You're wasting my time," the Lease Agent said.

"Don't close the door on me. You want to know the answer or not?"

"Just tell me, woman. Did we do the mattress shuffle or not?"

Buck dared to peek out the office door. The Lease Agent was standing at the door, his back facing Buck, and his bathrobe flapping in the gentle breeze. Just beyond his shoulder, Sapphire was leaning against the door frame, her eyes flickering between the Lease Agent, the waiting room inside, and somewhere off to the side.

When her eyes flashed past Buck, he nodded at her.

Sapphire switched her attention back to the Lease Agent's face.

"No," she finally said. "We never slept together."

Buck tiptoe-dashed across the floor and reentered the kitchen. He took his seat and leaned on his fist as if bored. His neck was sweating, and his heart was still pounding.

"Sorry I wasted your time," she said.

Buck reached for a paper towel and wiped down his neck. He couldn't leave any evidence behind. He put the towel under his milk glass.

A moment later, the Lease Agent stormed back into the kitchen and knocked his cabinet door open. He yanked a plate out of the stack and nearly smashed it on the counter. He dumped his eggs out onto the plate, then the sausage. The toast sat in the toaster, forgotten.

The Lease Agent marched to the table and dropped the plate onto a placemat. He sat down, reached for the eggs, then cursed as he looked at his fingers.

"Need a damn fork," he said.

"Should I go?" Buck asked. "You seem upset."

The Lease Agent nodded and waved him off.

"Yeah, kid. I don't have time for this anymore. You can ask me your questions another time."

Buck got up from the table.

"Okay."

The Lease Agent reached inside his silverware drawer and removed a fork.

"By the way, you can leave that here," he said.

Buck's neck throbbed.

"Leave what here?"

The Lease Agent nodded at his hand, which was just over his belt. "You know."

Buck felt his stomach drop. Even despite all his planning and secrecy, the Lease Agent still knew. But how could he? Buck had been extra stealthy.

Then again, he was dealing with the Lease Agent. Could anyone pull anything past him?

As he reached for the lower part of his shirt to lift it up, he noticed he was still holding the milk glass.

On a whim, Buck set it on the table.

"Thanks," the Lease Agent said. "Had that glass since I lived on the ranch. Makes me nervous to let visitors drink out of it. But I gotta show my trust and hospitality somehow, you know? Prove I'm not the cold bastard everyone thinks I am. Not first thing in the morning, anyway."

"I see." Buck's stomach dropped again, for a different reason.

"You like the milk?" he asked.

"Yeah, it was sweet."

The Lease Agent nodded. He returned to his breakfast, a little calmer now. When he set his fork down, he did so like a normal human being.

"Can't tell you my supplier," he said, "but if you ever need an item of special quality, let me know, and I'll see if I can arrange a meeting for you. By proxy, of course."

Buck shrugged. He had no idea what any of this meant. He just wanted out now.

"Sounds good. I should go now."

The Lease Agent swatted the air as if a mosquito had come for his eggs.

"Yes, yes, you should."

BUCK PLAYED IT COOL when he stepped foot outside of the Lease Agent's office but turned on the gas once he rounded the corner and knew he was out of sight. Halfway down the intersecting walkway between the courtyard and the main road, he fell against the nearest wall to catch his breath.

He'd gotten away with it.

Just to be sure, he checked over his shoulder for pursuers.

Sure enough, he was alone.

No spies.

No cops.

And most importantly, no drunk cowboys.

His heart slowed over the course of the next couple of minutes. Even though the air was hot, the sweat on his neck evaporated. His skin was still sticky, but the signs of guilt for breaking into the most powerful man in Hybrid City's safe were melting away.

Everything was going to be all right.

Nevertheless, he wanted to know what he'd risked his future on.

Checking over his shoulder once more, he ducked low behind a hedge and freed the notebook from under his shirt. It was smaller around the edges than the notebooks he'd used in school, but twice as thick.

He opened the front cover. On the first page, Sapphire's name was crossed out in red marker. Just above it was a name he didn't recognize. Probably the Lease Agent's real name.

On the next page was a series of bank account numbers. Beside those numbers were the names of shops he recognized.

Page 3: Melty's Coffee and Ice Cream Bar.

Page 8: Pound Cake

Page 14: The Whipping Shed

Buck wasn't familiar enough with financing to understand what he was looking at, but it seemed that Mr. Kabuki was bleeding money. A lot. According to the line chart at the bottom of the page, he had a red year at the start of 1984, but it spiked into green late that summer. An asterisk over July noted that the sudden rise coincided with the theatrical release of *The Karate Kid*.

The movie had made martial arts popular, at least until the start of this year, when the line fell again.

Karate out, coffee in, he remembered Kabuki saying. Perhaps he was being more than metaphorical with that statement.

Buck continued scanning the accounts represented in each book. How the Lease Agent knew all this information, he didn't know, but it worried him. Whatever the cowboy's methods, they exposed him as something of a spy. The notebook noted all of a business's vitals: name of owner and operator, rent price, address, phone number, monthly income, and bills owed. According to page 32, Shop Down the Street was also bleeding money. Mack was three months behind in paying his rent.

By page 40, Buck closed the book. His stomach was queasy again. Having so much personal information at his fingertips didn't seem right. Looking any deeper had to have violated a sense of confidentiality somehow. He wasn't sure about the legality of possessing such information, either, but it sure didn't seem ethical. The sooner he got rid of it, the better.

As he moved toward the road, and by proxy, Sapphire's Consignments, he had another realization enter his mind.

The Lease Agent had put his name on the book, but it wasn't his to begin with. These records went back three years. How long ago had he stolen it from Sapphire?

Sapphire hadn't implied losing the book over three years ago.

She'd said that this book was the secret to her riches. But it was also the secret to the Lease Agent's riches.

It still wasn't clear to Buck how either got rich off the information.

By the time he reached the front door, he had second thoughts about handing it over to her. Sure, it was her notebook. But what would he unleash by giving the power back to her? And what power would he give? She was no more trustworthy than the Lease Agent with cutthroat business practices. Billy Bob Drake was a testament to that.

Buck changed direction and headed for the Whipping Shed. Before he made any decision, he wanted to seek advice.

* * *

Fortunately, there were no classes scheduled for this time, so the dojo was empty when Buck entered. Mr. Kabuki was spending the free moment crouching at the end of the hallway, painting the bottom of the door to the back room. His wrist moved up and down in fluid motions as he spread the white-tipped fibers of his paintbrush over its surface.

Buck moved halfway up the hallway but stopped at the kitchen. Student or not, he still had to respect the boundaries of the training hall.

"Do you have a minute, *Sensei?*"

Mr. Kabuki nodded. "*Hai.* Just fixing door."

"Time to spruce the place up?"

"*Hai.* Kabuki miscalculate situation. But everything fine now. Just repairing damage. Kabuki not underestimate situation next time."

Buck didn't understand the context of what the Master was saying and saw no need to pursue it. If Kabuki wanted to clarify, he could, but Buck had a more important concern in the meantime.

"Have you seen anything like this before?"

He held up the notebook for Kabuki to see. Kabuki narrowed his eyes as he studied it from ten feet away, then nodded once.

"Notebook," he said. "Office Place have many like it."

"No, I mean, have you seen anything like what's inside?"

Kabuki held out his hand. "Come, show Kabuki."

Buck knew not to go to the end of the hall without an invitation. Now that Kabuki had extended one, he quickly scooted up close enough for him to share his findings. Kabuki took the notebook from him.

"Yes, interesting," he said as he flipped through the pages. "Irina Swift do well."

He got to page 14 and stopped.

"Hmm. This accurate."

"You recognize those numbers?"

Kabuki nodded once. "*Hai.* Bad year for Whipping Shed until last summer. Went from cruel summer to cool summer. Book accurate."

He handed it back to Buck.

"Is it bad that I have this?"

"Do book belong to boy?"

"It belongs to Sapphire. But I took it from the Lease Agent."

Kabuki resumed painting.

"Then boy should give book back to Sapphire. But not before studying rival business."

Buck looked at the front cover.

"Study how?"

"Lesson eighteen. Rival research."

"We're on twenty now."

"Lesson twenty. If want to be top in industry, spy on rivals for information and use found knowledge to beat them. Melty's, page three."

Buck stroked the front of the page. He'd already seen the stats for Melty's. The ice cream and coffee shop was on a constant rise. It had made several thousand dollars last month. He did not know how to use that information to his advantage.

"How does this work?"

"See sales. Outsell. But that not beauty of book. Look at last figure."

Buck flipped open to page three. The last figure was the three-year graph showing sales records versus bills and the resultant profit.

Melty's on an average day earned as much as twenty times what Buck had earned on his best day. There was no way he could outsell Melty's on those metrics.

"Yes, the lines are well-drawn. Not sure how it helps me, though."

"Not graph. Look above. Last figure."

Buck looked above the graph. Suddenly, he understood what Kabuki was referring to. His eyes had passed through the numbers so fast that he hadn't registered their meaning until now.

"Share price," he said. "It's a stock value. Right?"

Kabuki winked at him.

"*Hai*. Local stock market, but still powerful. Use found knowledge to beat rival."

"You're saying they can be bought out?"

Kabuki winked at him again. "Stock exchange hold key."

Buck read the stock price again. Almost ten dollars for a single share, with thousands of shares available. Local or not, it was still way out of Buck's price range.

"How many shares does it take to buy a company?"

"Depend how many shares for sale. Fifty-one percent required to own."

Above the stock share price was share availability. Melty's had over three thousand shares, with most of them belonging to the company.

Based on the math, Buck would need at least fifteen thousand dollars to buy it from the current owner.

"Yeah, I'll never afford this," he said. "But it's interesting."

"*Hai*."

Buck thanked Kabuki for his advice, but he didn't see how it could help him. In the end, it was better left in Sapphire's hands. It was hers to begin with, anyway.

It wasn't until he'd gotten within ten feet of Sapphire's Consignments that he thought of searching the notebook for information about the Liquid Shack.

* * *

BUCK SEARCHED THROUGH EVERY page of the notebook for signs of Chet and his lemonade stand. He scanned every business's name and owner's information, but it wasn't until he flipped to the last ten percent of records that he found Chet's name.

Maybe it was buried under most of Hybrid City's businesses, but it was there.

The grass under his butt was prickly, and he wanted to find a park bench to ease his discomfort. But he couldn't turn away. Nor could he afford to have Sapphire march out and snatch the book from him after looking out the front door and seeing him alongside the road. He had to keep reading, right here, right now. At least where he sat, the bushes along the shop wall provided him with shade.

He couldn't believe what he was looking at. Yeah, Chet was making a profit, and he was raking in more than Buck had each night. But not much more. The difference could be counted in the tens. With a robust marketing campaign, Buck could possibly edge ahead. Over the course of thirty days, he might even get within striking distance.

The problem, Buck realized, was that Chet could also invest in marketing and ensure his place in the lead.

The solution to victory had to come with investments—if possible, by investing in that 51% of shares.

But Chet's share value was a dollar each, and Buck would have to buy over five hundred of them to win the majority stake.

No matter what, Buck needed that $500 as soon as possible if he expected to win.

Buck held the page between his fingers as he considered the situation. The goal was attainable. But he had to kill it in sales. And fast. The way the Lease Agent had described it, he needed at least fourteen days to collect on an investment. That left him with just under three weeks to earn the acquisition fee.

Fortunately, he'd collect his Shop Down the Street paycheck by then. That would reduce his coffee sales requirement by a significant chunk.

Relieved that this quest was no longer impossible, Buck got to his feet and brushed off his jeans. But he didn't move yet.

Something in his gut continued to stir.

He flipped closer to the back of the book.
Closer.
And then he saw it.

Name: Buck Star

Business: Coffee Pavilion

Address: North Park

Monthly Income: Pending

The page was largely incomplete compared to the other businesses logged in the notebook. But there it was in pure black ink.

The Coffee Pavilion was listed in the Lease Agent's stock tracker even though Buck had never put it up for trading.

He realized there under the dying shade that he knew nothing about the stock market, perhaps to his detriment.

* * *

A FEW MINUTES LATER, Sapphire brought Buck into the back office and told him to sit down. She gave him a cup of water.

"You're a bit late getting back," she said. "Everything all right?"

Buck hadn't even considered the time that had passed since the heist.

"Had to make sure he wasn't following me."

Half true.

Sapphire nodded and extended her hand across the desk.

"May I have it?"

Buck wasn't sure what else he could get from the book, so he passed it over. She thanked him.

"Did you have a look inside?" she asked.

Buck said nothing.

"It's okay if you did. You might've learned something."

Buck nodded.

"I may have peeked at it."

Sapphire winked at him. Then she opened the book and frowned at the title page.

"That bastard."

She continued thumbing through the pages. At first, her face softened. But as she skimmed past page twelve, her expression changed.

"The Whipping Shed is in here," she said.

"I noticed."

"That's not one of my investments." She continued on, and on. "None of these are. This guy has really raped the city here."

"What do you mean?"

She flipped the book around so Buck could see, even though he'd already seen it.

"My investments are for incorporated businesses, like Melty's and Hybrid Wholesale." She pointed at the entry for Tailor Made. "This isn't a corporation. Handsome Ted is the sole proprietor."

"Okay."

She turned the book back to herself.

"You don't get it, do you?"

Buck shook his head.

"He shouldn't be listed here."

The pit of Buck's stomach jerked. If Tailor Made wasn't supposed to be on the list, then what did that mean for Buck and the Coffee Pavilion, or even Chet and the Liquid Shack?

"Why?"

Sapphire said nothing. She just read the page. Buck waited for a response.

She flipped to the next one.

"William Hollander and the Office Place. Sid Sachs and Over There Pizza. Did these guys go corporate?"

"I don't know."

Sapphire closed the book. Gave him a weak smile.

"Thank you for bringing this back to me. But now I have to figure out what's going on. You should go now."

"I don't understand."

Sapphire paused. "Something about this is really, really wrong."

Buck said nothing. He'd either slept through much of his economics class or spent a good chunk of it stuck in his locker. He remembered little about playing the stock market game.

"Should I be worried?"

"Maybe. But realistically, I think we all should be."

Buck nodded. He trusted Sapphire's perspective, but he understood none of this.

"Do I still get my twenty dollars?" he asked.

* * *

ON THE OTHER SIDE of town, Lighterhead's Fireworks Superstore was having its annual 4th of July Blowout Sale, and Chet and the gang were marching up and down the aisles planning for the festivities. Jennifer was hardly interested in rockets or firecrackers, and she would've much rather spent the morning at the beach, but she was getting dragged along from explosive to explosive, anyway. Chet had spent the last few nights begging her to forgive him for whatever he'd done wrong, and he thought spending more quality time together would fix it. Because it would've shut him up, she finally agreed.

She just didn't understand why Pigeon Polluck and Pigeon's new girlfriend, some brunette he'd met at the strip club the night they'd all celebrated their day of hot sales, had to come along with them. Likewise, she couldn't figure out why Pigeon tagged along but Tommy Slick wasn't invited. In fact, she'd wondered why Tommy wasn't invited to any of the before- or after-work activities anymore. She thought she'd made it clear to Chet that she and Tommy were just friends.

Chet didn't seem to get that, though.

"I'm not paying for all of that," Chet said, when Pigeon ran his hand across the backs of several boxes of M80s and dumped them into the shopping cart. "We're here for sparklers and bottle rockets."

"Aw, come on, Boss," Pigeon said. "Ain't nothing like a good boom-boom, you know what I'm saying?" He winked at his girlfriend, but the woman just rolled her eyes and emitted a sound of disgust.

Weird reaction coming from his girlfriend, Jennifer thought. She must not have been a fan of explosions, either.

"Yeah," Chet said. "But I'm not paying for it. You can."

Jennifer kept her thoughts to herself. As long as *she* wasn't the one paying for it, she saw no reason to add her input.

"You'll thank me for it," Pigeon said.

Jennifer's stomach lurched. Pigeon Polluck was drooling over the boxes he'd scooped up as he knocked more into the cart after them. For some reason, he was really excited about those M80s.

She also didn't like the fact that Pigeon's girlfriend kept shifting her attention to Chet.

Episode 26

Fourth of July

DAY 25: THURSDAY, JULY 4, 1985

Buck's Savings Account: $1.00

Buck's Wallet: $328.85

Buck's Business Funds: unknown

Buck's Expenses: $2 a day*

Hours of Operation: 12 p.m.-5 p.m.

Money on Hold: $119.58 (8 days)

SAPPHIRE'S WORDS HUNG LOOSELY in Buck's mind for the next three days. He continued business as usual, crafting fresh coffee and pouring it into fresh cups for anyone visiting the Coffee Pavilion during operation hours, as well as barking his product to anyone running alongside the lake whenever business was dead. And each new day had gained him either a few customers or leads, making him a little more stable as a coffee merchant and less damaged from the fallout from his *Hybrid City Post* story. But there was still something about her words that scratched at the back of his mind.

Something about this is really, really wrong.

She'd never clarified her thoughts on the matter. Just warned him that he should've been worried about it. It was vague. Borderline forgettable. But it had planted a seed.

321

With each hour that passed, Buck kept his eyes on the sidewalks that crossed the bottom of the hill on which the pavilion stood. He'd half-expected the Lease Agent to send a liaison to check on his progress. But he wasn't sure how to identify a lackey from a park regular.

He wished he were old enough to drink. Might've eased his stomach a bit.

So far, the Lease Agent had kept his hooks out of Buck's ledger, but somehow, he knew roughly where Buck sat on the profitability bench. Or rather, Buck's entry in the Lease Agent's notebook suggested he would have that information soon.

Monthly Income: Pending

What method did the Lease Agent use to turn that "pending" into a number? And how accurate a figure would it be?

When Buck wasn't watching the sidewalk, he monitored the access road that ran up to the side of the pavilion. Odds were better the Lease Agent or his goons would approach in a limousine, not on a bike or on foot. Nevertheless, Buck wouldn't rule out any possibility.

Some guy's voice broke him out of his spell.

"What?" He turned from the counter to face the customer.

"I said I want a large iced coffee with cream and cinnamon." The skinny middle-aged man in the tracksuit must've been standing there for a while, but Buck was just now aware of his presence. He had sweat puddles running down from his neck. Taking a break from a run, most likely.

"We just have one size," Buck said. He showed the man a paper cup that represented the size all his coffee was served in.

The man nodded. "Fine, I'll take that. But you should get bigger cups. That's large enough to get me home, but not enough to get me through the day. I don't really want to come back here for a second cup."

Buck filled the man's order.

"How much more would you be willing to pay for a larger size?"

The man offered his feedback. Buck took a mental note. Next time he ran to the store, he'd have to buy a bag of larger cups.

"I'd like a donut, too," the man said. "You should sell donuts with your coffee."

Buck noted that, also.

After Buck thanked the man and handed him his coffee, his thoughts trailed back to the Lease Agent and his notebook. He still couldn't figure out why his name and business were even in there.

* * *

ON HER WAY TO Melty's Coffee and Ice Cream Bar to begin her shift, Jennifer spotted Chet waltzing out of a gardening shop with a bag of fertilizer over his shoulder. His back was straight, and his gait was confident, but his car was not parked along the curb. She expected to watch him stride into the neighboring parking lot, but he went to a pile of fertilizer bags by the loading dock.

It was when he tossed the bag onto the pile that she realized he was wearing khakis and a burnt orange polo shirt—the shop's uniform.

He went back inside. She ran up to the door and waited beside it. He came back out with another bag.

"Hey!" she barked.

Chet fumbled it when he saw her standing there, but he caught it before it landed on his foot.

"What are you doing here?" He was looking this way and that.

"Gonna ask you the same question. Who's running the Liquid Shack?"

"Tommy, Pigeon, and Pigeon's, er, girlfriend. Shouldn't you be at Melty's?"

"On my way."

They locked eyes, but Chet said nothing. He just stood there with the bag of fertilizer cradled in his arms.

"You gonna tell me why you're working here?" Jennifer asked.

"Extra money," he said. "It's a free country."

She folded her arms across her chest.

"Is it for you, or for the bet?"

Chet gave her the stink-eye.

"For me. What do you care how I win?"

"So, for the bet then." She smiled. "Okay. Have a nice day."

Jennifer turned her back and continued down the sidewalk.

"It's for me!" Chet cried.

Jennifer said nothing.

"It's a free country!" Chet said again.

Jennifer said nothing. Just kept walking.

* * *

As was the tradition of every American boy and girl on the Fourth of July, Buck Star packed up his supplies, closed his shop, and ran over to Tealeaf Central to pick up his French companion for a little celebration at the beach with fireworks and fun. Because French Girl was still new to the country, she hadn't yet experienced an American Independence Day, and Buck wanted to make sure she got her chance tonight. Fortunately, she was all in.

"Beach at night sound fun," she said.

"There will be fireworks, too," Buck told her as he helped her round up the dirty dishes on her tables so she could get out of the café faster.

"Okay."

French Girl was perhaps too busy to let the moment sink in. Buck wasn't sure whether France had access to fireworks or if French Girl had ever seen them. But in case she hadn't, he couldn't wait to see her eyes glitter in wonder.

"Fireworks are awesome," Buck said. He took a towel from a nearby table and wiped down another for her.

"Uh-huh." She dumped the contents of three teacups into a pitcher and set them all in a plastic bin.

Total wonder, just a while longer.

However, once they got to the beach, French Girl's wonder turned to horror.

"So many people," she said. "Where we sit?"

Buck understood the question. She wasn't asking where they *should* sit. She was asking where they *could* sit. The shore was packed from the ocean to the parking lot with the town's residents awaiting the big show. Most years, Buck had gotten to the beach early enough to pick a comfortable spot by the central palm tree, not far from the stairs. But because it had taken them so long to close the café, they didn't arrive until just before the fireworks show was scheduled to begin.

"We can hang back here." He pointed at a park bench that was still empty despite the fringes of beach visitors meandering in front of it. "The show's good no matter where we sit. It's just better on the beach."

French Girl frowned.

"We try to go down there? Maybe by water?"

The sea of spectators was thicker than the sea of saltwater alongside it. There was no getting down to the beach now unless they wanted to crowd surf. All three stairway access points were clogged. Those on the beach were locked in, and those on the boardwalk were locked out.

"Park bench is more comfortable," he said. "You'll like it up here."

They sat beside each other on the park bench. Buck dared to put his arm around her shoulders. She pouted.

"They look like they having good time down there."

So many faceless people in the crowd. Buck couldn't see what she saw.

The first flare shot up over the ocean and exploded into a dandelion of red light. Buck "oohed" and "ahhed" for French Girl's benefit. She just sat there with her arms folded over her chest, looking down at the crowd.

Another one shot to the sky and exploded. She glanced at it but said nothing. Didn't make any kind of reaction.

Buck shrugged. Maybe she wouldn't be dazzled by this after all. But at least she let him keep his arm around her.

"Hey, Little Camper!"

Buck and French Girl glanced to their left. Ronnie and Tiffany were coming through the wispy crowd on the edge between the boardwalk and the street.

"Got room for two more?"

Buck and French Girl squeezed close together and pulled right to make room for them. Ronnie and Tiffany squeezed in beside them so that Tiffany and French Girl were in the middle and Buck and Ronnie were on the edges.

"Guess you guys were late getting here, too," Ronnie said.

"What?" French Girl and Tiffany both asked. A sonic boom had cut off Ronnie's voice, though Buck had watched his mouth move.

"I said, guess you guys—" Another boom. "Here, too!"

"Yes, we here," French Girl said.

"Pretty obvious," Tiffany said.

Ronnie tried to repeat himself a third time but gave up when two more fireworks pounded the cloudless twilight sky above.

Typical Fourth of July. Everyone comes to party, but no one gets to talk.

French Girl was now watching the sky as trails of smoke drifted south. Her face was still without a reaction. But, just as Buck had expected, her eyes glittered with each new blast of color.

Tiffany, meanwhile, was fidgeting where she sat. She slid forward an inch after every explosion. When Ronnie tried to put his arm around her, she shook him off.

"No room for that," she said between sonic booms.

"Aw, come on, Babe. Romance is what makes this fun."

"We're both sweaty." She squirmed again. "And this bench is too small."

French Girl agreed. "Yes, too small. Beach better."

Tiffany nodded to her.

"Yeah, that's what I've been trying to tell him. He spends so long trying to pick out the right pair of pants for the sand that we get here too late to sit on it."

"Aw, come on, Babe, no one wants to wear the wrong pants on the beach. You ever get sand in your ass?"

"No, but I'm getting a pain in it right now."

Ronnie smirked at her.

"Wanna sit on my lap to comfort it?"

Tiffany rolled her eyes and stared off at the sky. Ronnie glanced at Buck and shrugged.

Neither of them had had girlfriends this time last year. It was obvious to Buck that neither one knew what to do with having girl-friends this year.

The girls watched the fireworks. Buck decided it was better to watch it with them. Even French Girl's shoulders were getting tense under his forearm. A moment later, she also squirmed away.

"Your arm hot," she said.

Buck understood. He set both hands in his lap.

Now all four of them were sitting stiffly on that bench. The continuing fireworks did nothing more for the mood. But at least they were all together.

Buck smiled. It was an improvement over last year, when it was just Buck and Ronnie standing pressed against fat strangers under that palm tree by the stairs. Being pressed against French Girl would always be better than that old alternative.

* * *

DAY 26: FRIDAY, JULY 5, 1985

Buck's Savings Account: $1.00

Buck's Wallet: $381.73

Buck's Business Funds: unknown

Buck's Expenses: $2 a day*

Hours of Operation: 12 p.m.–5 p.m.

Money on Hold: $119.58 (7 days)

THE NEXT MORNING, AFTER having his best Thursday yet thanks to the holiday, Buck did his resupply shopping at Sassy Supermarket out in the western part of town. As much as he liked Shop Down the Street, and its position on the way to the park, his options there were limited, and he realized he needed to expand. By visiting Sassy Supermarket, the largest locally owned grocery store in Hybrid City, he could buy not only a hundred-count bag of large paper cups but also a bag of polystyrene cups, which he'd intended to get since the first time a customer had burned his hands holding a scalding hot paper cup. While he was there, he also bought plastic stirrers, so he wouldn't have to stir customers' coffees with his finger anymore, and a box of store brand donuts. It came with a dozen glazed.

After paying almost seven dollars for his latest stock, he hopped on his bike and headed for the park.

And once he arrived at the edge of the hill below the pavilion, he lost control of his wheels, spilling everything on the grass, including the bike and himself.

Buck picked himself up, but he couldn't believe what he was looking at. It must've been a dream, but it wasn't. Unless his eyes had deceived him, he was witnessing his earliest business nightmare come to life, and it was much too late to wake from it now.

Episode 27

Firework Fallout

Rom the bottom of the hill, it was hardly noticeable to the untrained eye. But Buck spotted the pavilion's state of change immediately. The storage room door was wide open. Unless the park rangers had commissioned a routine maintenance or safety check and never bothered to tell him, it should've been closed. And given that there were no service vehicles in the area, Buck did not assume this was a safety check. But he also didn't know how they operated. Maybe it was fine.

Leaving the bike where he'd dropped it, Buck lumbered up the hill, keeping careful attention on the open door. He wasn't sure what to expect here, but he readied himself for some dude in an official park uniform to stumble out and check a clipboard. *All clear. See you next month.*

But his relative unease hit the gas, turning into full-blown dread when he crested the hill and saw the door's true state. It was damaged. There was also a bloom of black soot plastered all over it. When he'd left for Tealeaf Central yesterday, the door was closed and locked. Whatever he was looking at now, it was not the result of his oversight. And given the state of damage, he didn't think it had much to do with a park-commissioned safety check, either.

He took a deep breath. Clearly, he'd have to investigate this.

Nervous about what he'd find, he marched up to the counter to deposit his new supplies, then steadied himself. His ability to operate today depended on what he was about to discover. He chanted under his breath that it would be all right, as if everything that had gone wrong last night would fix itself in the next two seconds. It was a calming technique he knew wouldn't work, but he tried it anyway.

Down the east side of the hill, a couple of joggers ran past his bike. They were probably the twentieth set of people to come through here already today. Any of them could've investigated the open storage room and helped themselves to the equipment inside. But they kept running. Maybe the nineteen before them had, too.

He couldn't delay the inevitable any longer. The pavilion would be open for business in twenty minutes. If he still owned a coffeemaker, he had to move it to the counter and plug it in. If he still had water, he needed to fill the basin and heat it up.

Just like the first time he dared to say hello to Jennifer, or more recently to Lila or French Girl, Buck struggled to take that last step toward the storage room door. From where he stood, he could already tell the door had been forced open. Splinters were crumbling off the tongue and the catch, as if some giant had kicked it open from the inside. And the splattering of soot indicated an explosion where the giant's foot would've landed.

Of course, there was no giant trying to escape from such a tiny prison. And Buck hadn't stored any explosives with his coffee equipment when he'd last closed for the evening. But even if these things *had* happened, they wouldn't have altered the end result. Reality wasn't the product of what could've been, but the result of what was.

He dared to look inside.

Flecks of red paper littered the storage room, swimming in a puddle where the black soot mark trailed off the door and continued along the floor under the burnt southern shelf, right under where he'd kept his cooler—his cooler that now had a wet, inch-thick crack racing up its side to the lid.

He knelt and picked up one of the soggy scraps floating in the ice-melt puddle.

"Em-eighty," a voice said from behind.

Buck clutched the side of the rickety shelf as he recovered from his fright. A man in a white suit and hat was standing just outside the doorway.

"Looks like a whole bunch of them." The man examined the doorjamb. "This here was a crowbar. Whoever blew this place to hell wrenched it open first. The explosions came after."

Buck was still trying to slow his heart. "Who are you?"

The man extended his hand.

"Rhett Rowe, Downtown Insurance. I represent the Lease Agent's investments."

Buck stared at the man's piano-white loafers. They were next-level class, far beyond the sophistication of the tie he'd bought at Tailor Made last month.

"Why are you here?" he asked.

"I check on all his properties once a week before lunch to make sure everything's on the up and up. But in today's case, the park ranger called me over to investigate. Looks like this one ran into some trouble this week. You party too hard last night?"

"I have a key. Clearly this wasn't my doing." Buck popped the lid off his cooler. The plastic bag holding the ice was now crumpled and drenched in water. The cream inside had spoiled. He ran his finger along the crack from its interior. "I paid forty dollars for this."

Rhett Rowe leaned forward and put something on the shelf beside Buck. It was a small card.

"My number. Make an appointment with me this weekend to discuss your losses. In the meantime, I have to close this place down for a few days while my team and I figure out the damage." He pointed at the blackened walls.

Beside the cooler, Buck's open sign sat along the shelf's edge. The spot above the "O" was singed.

"Can you do it after five o'clock?" Buck asked.

The man shook his head. "Afraid not. Need to check for other damage. No telling how structurally sound this place is after"—he motioned with his hand—"all of this." He shook the shelf. A piece of the wood came off in his hand. "Or before all of this, for that matter."

In other words, Buck wouldn't be able to open the shop today.

Not that he could anyway, given that half of his supplies had been blown up overnight.

* * *

By one o'clock, Buck was sitting in Ronnie's living room with a box of his surviving equipment and supplies on the couch beside him. The insurance adjuster had tried convincing him to leave everything in the storage room to tell the most accurate story for the investigators once they came in to do their part, but Buck insisted on taking it all with him. Maybe he couldn't operate his business for the next few days, but he certainly wasn't about to risk shutting it down for the rest of the summer.

Ronnie sat across the box, examining the coffeemaker. He flipped the lid open and peered inside the basin.

"Doesn't look broken." He sniffed it. "But the flash powder residue might change the flavor a bit. Much earthier now."

"That sounds like a positive."

"Could be. Have you tried plugging it in yet?"

Buck shook his head. "Mr. Rowe ran me off before I could test anything. Told me it would look bad if I stuck around."

"That makes no sense. Here, we'll try my kitchen."

Buck set up the coffeemaker on Ronnie's kitchen counter and ran through the brewing process. The coffeemaker made a strange squealing noise that Buck had never heard before, but the dark liquid dripping into the carafe eased his concern. Once it finished, Buck checked the glass container for leaks. There was a hairline crack near the top, but as long as he didn't pour ice water into it, the carafe would hold. Judging by its position, he would also have to tip it sideways to prevent premature leaking when transferring liquid to a cup, but it wasn't career-ending. The carafe would last the season. Hopefully.

"Seems fine," Buck said.

"You have an extension cord at home?" Ronnie asked.

Buck didn't know what he had. He rarely went into his garage.

"Maybe."

"Then who needs the pavilion? I'll bet you could sell coffee from your driveway. As long as you have somewhere to plug in the coffeemaker."

Buck straightened his back. That didn't sound entirely hopeless. Stupid, sure. But hopeless? Maybe not.

"You think people would visit?"

Ronnie lifted the lid of the water reservoir and looked inside.

"No leakage here." He closed the lid. "Yeah, why not? Eight-year-olds do it all the time."

Buck shrugged.

"I think they sell lemonade, not coffee. And they're eight, not eighteen. Most of them are cuter."

"Yeah, and they're eating into Chet's business, too. Who's your competition?"

"Melty's Ice Cream."

"Besides Melty's?"

Buck thought about it. He had no answer.

Ronnie picked up one of the surviving water bottles and examined it. "So, set up a table in your driveway. See how it goes. You might be surprised. Worse thing, you learn no one wants to come to your house. Say, I've been meaning to ask. Are these for me and Tiffany to drink? That water fountain at the park tastes bitter, and every time I look at one of these things, I want to suck it down."

Buck stared at the side of his face but said nothing.

Ronnie put his fingers around the cap and twisted it, breaking the seal, but Buck stopped him from removing it.

"Please don't drink that," he said. "I still need it."

* * *

IT WAS TOO LATE to justify setting up a home station for today, but Buck wanted to test its viability as a business solution, so he rummaged through his garage for supplies that might help him make it work.

As Ronnie had suggested, Buck not only had an extension cord coiled in a box by the washing machine but also two card tables folded up and stashed along the back wall. He even had a metal folding chair, likely left over from the last time his mom had hosted a yard sale.

When he set the larger table up at the end of the driveway, he was pleased to find that the extension cord could reach.

Another happy discovery was the realization that he could reuse his water bottles by filling them at his own kitchen sink. Fortunately, his mom had invested in a filtration system, so the water came out clean. By running his business out of his driveway, he wouldn't have to stop at the Water Monkey anymore. That alone would save him several dollars a week.

He also had the brilliant idea of saving money on cups by letting customers use his mom's mugs, but he shot it down when he realized they'd probably leave with them. For now, he'd keep using paper and polystyrene cups. Thankfully, the paper cups had been sitting on the opposite shelf and survived the explosion.

Regarding creamer, he'd just keep it refrigerated until he needed it. Or he could find an empty flowerpot, fill it with ice from his freezer, and leave the creamer chilling inside for the duration of the workday. If he wanted a second flowerpot, then he could also experiment with using real milk as a garnish. But he wouldn't do that unless the customers asked for it. He still used milk for his cereal, and he wanted to ensure he had enough for tomorrow's breakfast.

Buck was convinced. This could work. He could drive a nail into his mailbox post and hang the open sign on it. Even though it was damaged, it was still functional, unlike his poor cooler. The blast had eaten the sign's top edge above the "O," but not the corners where the string was attached. He could still use it.

Buck felt better now. Not relieved, because he was still losing money today, and Ronnie and Tiffany wouldn't be able to enter the house while he was at Shop Down the Street, so he wouldn't have the weekend sales he'd normally have. But he would have Monday. Rhett Rowe, the insurance adjuster, had suggested that the pavilion wouldn't reopen to the public until Wednesday at the earliest, depending on what the inspectors concluded, so he probably had Tuesday, as well.

Buck unplugged the coffeemaker from the extension cord. As he did so, an older man rode past his mailbox, stopped, and backed up to greet him.

"Whatcha doin' here?" the old man asked.

Buck told him about his coffee business and why he was setting up a table here. The old man's knees were wobbly, and Buck worried he would fall over trying to hear the whole story. But he'd kept his stance, and his patience. The old man didn't seem like he was in a hurry to go anywhere.

Once Buck had finished his story, the old man nodded.

"Yeah, that's a good decision here, running a business outta yer own home. I did that once. Retired at forty-five as a result. Granted, my industry was a bit hush-hush, if ya know what I mean, but it paid the bills and then some. Not sure coffee will get you on a Caribbean island anytime soon, but you got great ambition. Just make sure that ol' Lease Agent don't try to buy your house as a result of yer success, you know? That man will try to own anything."

Buck understood. He hadn't forgotten about Sapphire's notebook, and he still didn't know how he himself had ended up on its latest page.

Buck told the old man about that, too.

"Yep, probably getting his intel from the Chamber of Commerce," the old man said. "Once you get on their books, you get on his. Seems to be the way it works, from what I hear."

Buck's stomach dropped. On the day he'd met Lila, he'd given the Chamber of Commerce twenty dollars to register his business.

If the old man's story was true, then Buck had gone onto the notebook page the same day he became a member of commerce. He'd have to talk to Sapphire about this as soon as possible, see what she knew about it.

"Gotta do it like my son Derek does it, just like I myself used to do it. Run yer business in the dark."

Buck didn't think that was plausible, given that his was an early morning to midday business, but he thanked the old man for his advice.

"Want a coffee for the road?" Buck asked him.

"Nah, pretty sure that stuff's bad fer ya, if it's anything like what I use ta sell. Gotta keep up mah health, you know?"

Buck asked no more questions and let the old man ride off. The last thing he wanted was to find himself witness to a cold case if the old man's words had more bite to them than just bark.

Episode 28

The Legend of Jasper Sage

BUCK PACKED UP HIS driveway test shop and stored the pieces in sections of the garage where he could access them quickly. With the extra time he had that afternoon, he returned to the shops around town to restock his lost supplies—creamer, whipped cream, a bag of ice, paper cups—along with his nearly depleted supplies—coffee store powder and peppermint candy. He also kept a lookout for new items that might go well in or with coffee. Although he already had a box of donuts, he thought it was a good idea to have a box of cookies on hand, too.

By Friday evening, Buck paid Sapphire a visit and asked her about the Chamber of Commerce. He described his encounter with the old man on the bike and what he'd said about the Chamber's connection to the Lease Agent. Sapphire, however, didn't seem convinced.

"Sounds like your contact might be a bit shady." She was wiping down the sales counter while preparing to close, but she was still listening. "I wouldn't trust him."

Buck said nothing.

"Tell me again what he said about the Chamber."

Buck told her. Sapphire nodded and hummed, but she still wasn't convinced.

"This man look a bit crooked?"

Buck shrugged. "He was old. So, yeah."

"Dark beard? Matted hair? Grizzled but with an unusually high voice?"

"He was graying and a bit thin up top. But yeah, he looked like he'd been through a few rounds with Rocky Balboa. Didn't really notice his voice. It was cracked, I think."

She ran her cloth over the register and jammed her index finger between the buttons.

"Well, either way, I think you ran into Old Man Jasper Sage," she said. "Devious little man, cunning as hell. Slips through the cracks just when you think he's cornered. We all thought he was dead. But maybe his death is just legend."

Buck said nothing.

"He's been out of the picture since the seventies. Likely in hiding. Police have looked all over town for him, but no one's caught him at his last known address since his home business went under." She said *home business* with air quotes. "No one knows exactly where he lives these days. You say he was on his bike?"

"Yep, rode right up to my driveway."

"Might be one of your neighbors now. Or he's squatting nearby. You get cops down your street?"

"Rarely."

Sapphire nodded.

"That explains it." She thought about what she'd say next. "I don't know. Maybe he's right. I suppose a criminal mind *would* know a criminal mind. But he's really good at manipulating people, so I hear. I'd be careful if he ever comes back around. And I'd definitely be careful about what he says."

"How do you even know it's him and not just some old man on an evening bike ride?"

Sapphire considered her thoughts.

"Back in the seventies, Jasper Sage didn't have a driver's license. Rumor had it that he'd lost his right to get one. If that's true, then he wouldn't want to risk exposure by getting into a wreck."

"So, you think because this old man rode a bike to my house, and not a car, it automatically makes him this old fugitive?"

Sapphire shrugged. "It's a theory." She popped open the register and cleaned the tray inside.

"Okay, so if this *is* Jasper Sage, then what if his words are true? It adds up, doesn't it?"

"There are holes. For example, Mr. Perkins of the Chamber of Commerce was the one who'd caught on to what Jasper Sage was doing out of his garage. He's also the one who tried shutting him down. After Sage threatened to burn the entire forest where the Chamber stands, Perkins agreed to pull back the reins, but not before telling the police where Sage was operating.

"Jasper Sage proved cleverer in the end, though. When the police raided his home, they found no evidence of his business. And they couldn't find him anywhere to talk. Every time they came to question him, he was missing. They eventually declared him dead and turned his property over to the state.

"That was the last anyone had heard from him." She stopped scrubbing and looked Buck in the eyes. "A few years later, that old shack in the grass lot behind the Office Place went up. That's where Shady Derek runs his operation now. Rumor has it he's Old Man Jasper Sage's son, continuing the work his father started."

Buck said nothing. Sapphire began scrubbing the counter.

"Funny thing, of course," she said, "is that the Chamber hasn't done a thing to shut the Un-Shop down, and the cops haven't bothered to raid it, even though everyone knows it's the spawn of Jasper Sage's old garage business. Makes you wonder why, doesn't it?"

"Yeah."

"Sage has a vendetta against the Chamber of Commerce and will do anything to discredit it. So, I don't believe what he told you is true. The more young business owners who doubt the Chamber, the fewer members they'll have in the future."

Buck considered what she'd said. Now it was he who wasn't convinced.

"But it adds up. I go into the notebook right after the Chamber signs me up. Is that just a coincidence?"

"Maybe. But when you signed up with the Chamber, hadn't you also just signed up for the leasing agreement?"

The two events did happen in the same week.

"Yes."

Sapphire tossed her cloth into a nearby bucket. She folded her hands on the counter and leveled her gaze at Buck.

"Mr. Perkins is a good man. Highly reputable. He'd never sell us out to the Lease Agent. I agree that he's up to no good. But Mr. Perkins isn't the one helping him. I don't think we're going to find what we're looking for at the Chamber of Commerce. If we're to solve this mystery, we have to look elsewhere."

"Where?"

"That's what I'm trying to find out. I'm thinking of asking a few of the neighborhood shop owners to help me. You're working for Mack Green, aren't you?"

Buck nodded.

"I think we should start with him."

Buck would see Mack in the morning. Maybe he could put a bug in his ear. But Mack wasn't the only one on his mind.

"What about Mr. Kabuki? He's part of the neighborhood. And he's wise."

Sapphire shook her head.

"I like Mr. Kabuki, but I wouldn't trust him with this one."

Buck deflated.

"Why?"

"He's got secrets of his own. Some really dark ones if the whispers are true."

Buck said nothing.

"But they're just whispers," Sapphire said. "Whispers and lies often go together."

Buck was seeing some truth in her words now.

* * *

After he left Sapphire's Consignments, Buck went to Tealeaf Central to see if French Girl wanted to come by after work, but she said she had other plans, so Buck went to Ronnie's house and told him about Sapphire's story. Ronnie's dad, who was in the living room listening to the whole thing, sighed in wonder when Buck came to the end.

"So, that's where old Jasper's hiding. I didn't think he was dead."

"Should I be worried if he comes back?" Buck asked.

Mr. Michaels thought about it.

"Yeah, probably."

Buck felt no reassurance from his answer.

"So, what do I do about it?"

"Eh, maybe don't run your business out of your garage longer than you have to, since he clearly hates anyone who succeeds at it. For obvious reasons."

Buck noted the advice.

"Think I'm good 'til Tuesday?"

Mr. Michaels shrugged.

"Do what you gotta do, Buck. But if you still have Mr. Stamps's card, you might want to consider calling him, especially after what happened at the pavilion last night."

Buck noted that advice, too. Security was probably a good idea, but he wasn't sure he could afford it.

Mr. Michaels shrugged at his own reasoning. "It's all speculative, of course. An urban legend. No one has actually caught Jasper Sage in the act of selling illegal wares. His business presence just happened to coincide with some really sketchy things about a decade ago. The main concern has always been less about him and more about his associates, if you want to know the real truth."

"His associates?"

Mr. Michaels scratched his chin.

"He'd get his wares from someone, somewhere. Whoever supplied him was of even shadier substance. Of course, the same could be said of his son Derek nowadays."

Buck's spine shivered. The old man knew where he lived. Maybe he'd come back. Was he too quick to assume that running a business out of his driveway was a good idea?

"Would he send his associates after me?"

Mr. Michaels sighed. "I don't know, Buck. As I said, it's all speculative. His past could very well be behind him now. Or a product of hearsay. Sometimes, a man stays in hiding to prevent the past from returning. Sometimes he's not even in hiding, just forgotten. For all we know, he could be supportive of homegrown businesses today.

Assuming, of course, that it was in fact Jasper Sage you met and not, as you suspect, just some old man on a bike."

Buck stared at the ceiling. "I'm so confused."

"It's good to keep you on your toes, though. That's the real lesson here. Don't give up in the face of vandalism. You had a good thing going at that pavilion."

Buck agreed.

"Let me tell you," Mr. Michaels continued, "there's no sense in derailing your entire business by moving it to a location that no one but old men on bikes will visit. We gotta get you back in action, back to the real market where you have a shot at defeating Chet Armstrong."

Mr. Michaels had an expression of inspiration on his face. His fists were clenched and slowly rising. If Buck didn't get back to work at the pavilion, he believed Mr. Michaels would likely take his place.

"Okay," Buck said. He didn't want to disappoint the fired-up lawyer.

"Now, enough of that," Mr. Michaels said. "Let's get back to Sapphire's notebook. Tell me more about that."

Buck asked him what he wanted to know.

* * *

THE NEXT MORNING, BUCK went to Shop Down the Street to start his shift. As soon as he clocked in, he helped a few customers locate the items they were looking for while Mack looked over the week's accounts. Once business slowed for them, Buck told Mack everything Sapphire had said the night before. Mack listened without judgment. Once Buck finished his story, Mack poured himself a cup of coffee and started his response.

"I disagree with Sapphire if you want my opinion. She's right that Mr. Perkins is respectable. But she's wrong to paint him as some perfect saint. He's not. Kindly? Sure. Incorruptible? Not a chance."

"So, you think he's feeding the Lease Agent information about our businesses?"

"Someone is. The Lease Agent may require that we pay him rent, but not one of us is required to share our books. If our information's in his book, then someone told him about it. Mr. Perkins is the best candidate for that."

"You think so?"

Mack sipped his coffee.

"Yep. Unless…"

"Unless what?"

"Nah, it couldn't be him."

Buck leaned in for a better listen.

"Who?"

Mack looked around the shop for eavesdroppers, though it was kind of pointless. The store was empty of customers, hence their free conversation time.

"It could be Ernest Bee."

Buck gasped. He remembered the scary bee man from a couple of weeks ago, the man who tried to fine him for other people's litter.

"Isn't he part of the Environmental Council?"

"He *is* the Environmental Council. But he works out of that office. It's possible he'd have access to the Chamber's member information."

Buck considered the possibility. Mack was on to something.

"Would he have a vendetta against the city's businesses?" Buck asked.

"Hard to say. He hates anything and anyone who pollutes his sacred town. Miss a trash can? It's your ass. Your car spits one too many dark clouds from its tailpipe? It's your ass. Fart in the wrong direction?" He pointed at Buck to finish the answer.

"It's your ass," Buck said.

"With Ernest Bee, it's always your ass."

"Sounds like he *is* the ass."

Mack pondered the idea further.

"Of course, he's not really into the success or failure of businesses. As far as I know, he has no incentive to keep financial tabs on us, not unless he wants to know how much he can fine us for. But in his line of work, income has no bearing on the size of a fine. Big or small, he just wants our ass."

"So, are you saying it's not him?"

"It's someone. Just not sure who. Maybe it's him. Maybe it's Mr. Perkins. Maybe it's someone we haven't considered. Until a few minutes ago, I'd assumed Jasper Sage was dead. Now you tell me he's alive and lurking. Anyone could be responsible here."

"Maybe. And he *might* be lurking. No confirmation."

"With Shady Derek gaining some traction in the darkest corners of town, I wouldn't be surprised if old Jasper Sage is alive and back to work."

"If you say so."

Buck was ready to cast the blame on the bee man. Anyone who dressed like a bee for fun was clearly up to no good.

But then again, examining the relationship between Ernest Bee and Mr. Perkins wouldn't be complete without considering all proxy relationships. After all, they weren't just two figures in the woods who remained isolated from everyone. Anyone who owned a business would've gone through those doors at some point, and maybe even made friends with them. Then again, those same people were the victims here, not the culprits. They had other cohorts.

Thinking about their associates pricked at Buck's mind, as a formless face lingered in the shadows of his thoughts, though he didn't want to acknowledge whom it belonged to. He tried thinking of every negative name that had ever crossed his memory bank, but none he wanted to condemn had any known ties with the Chamber of Commerce. Nevertheless, the image sat there in the forefront of his thoughts, and as it sat there moving toward the light, the darkness peeled off its face.

Clarity was already there, but he didn't want to acknowledge it. But he'd have to. If a mosquito landed in a bowl of peanut soup, and the person eating the soup reacted to a peanut allergy, then he or she couldn't blame the reaction on the mosquito. Truth was, if Mr. Perkins had access to the city's business owner information, and if Ernest Bee had access by right of being in the same building, then it stood to reason that…

Buck felt his stomach growl. Even though it was lunchtime, it wasn't hunger that upset him.

He pinched the bridge of his nose. He was embarrassed even to consider asking his next question.

"Have you met French Girl's new friend yet?" Buck asked, only sort of changing the subject.

Mack shook his head.

"She's not my real daughter. I try not to get to know her friends."

"Okay, because she may be hanging out with the enemy, and you and me both may need to keep an eye on her if anything you or the old man posing as Jasper Sage say is true."

Mack stared at Buck from over the rim of his coffee cup. He seemed intrigued.

* * *

Just after three o'clock, the Shop Down the Street's front door opened. While this was not an unusual occurrence for a Saturday mid-afternoon, especially considering this was a neighborhood mini-mart that specialized in kitchen items, and dinnertime was a couple of hours away for many, it did catch Buck by surprise when he realized who had entered.

Tommy Slick's cowboy hat rode low over his brow as he stared at the milk display inside the entrance. The special discount was still active as part of a post-Fourth of July special. But he made no move toward the cold storage section. Instead, he made a beeline for the paper cups.

"Hey, Buck," he said, when he passed by.

Buck, who was mopping the next aisle but could see into any aisle thanks to the shelves standing at shoulder height, nodded back at him.

"Howdy."

Tommy picked up a couple of bags of cups and headed for the counter. Buck watched him but said nothing. He just held the mop motionless, dripping dirty water onto the floor.

When Tommy noticed Buck staring, he tipped his hat to him.

"Bet going well?"

"Not really. No."

Tommy's eyes refocused on the mop handle, which was higher than Buck's head given how he was holding it.

"Earning extra money here to make up for it?"

Buck lowered the mop until it was below the top shelf. He wasn't ready to answer that question.

"How's Chet? Any idea where he stands?"

Tommy shrugged.

"Not sure if I should give up that information. Business secret."

"But do you know it?"

Tommy tilted his head sideways. He considered what to say.

"Yeah, more or less. I run the register."

"More than five hundred?"

"Yeah."

"More than a thousand?"

Tommy tapped the side of his nose. Buck wasn't certain if that was confirmation or negation.

"Fifteen hundred?"

Tommy raised his thumb and tilted it downward. So, it was less than fifteen hundred, but maybe more than a thousand.

Buck liked Tommy enough to keep him out of trouble with Chet, so he didn't press the issue any further. Whatever the answer, he had to clear fifteen hundred dollars by August 8th if he expected to win. And that assumed Chet wouldn't cross that threshold first.

"Any word on how Jennifer is doing these days?" Buck asked.

Tommy lowered his hat to the bridge of his nose.

"We're just friends."

Buck didn't understand the context.

"Okay."

"Sorry, force of habit. Chet's been paranoid about us lately. She's fine, but she's unhappy."

Buck perked up. Even though he had moved on to French Girl and wasn't really looking to win Jennifer back, he was glad she was unhappy with Chet.

"That's great," he said.

Tommy smirked at that one. Buck suspected he agreed. An unhappy Jennifer was a ready-to-move-on Jennifer. Buck had learned that the hard way. Perhaps Chet was about to learn that, too.

"Anyone running this register?" Tommy asked.

"Oh, right. Mack's in the office." Buck dropped the mop against the shelf and ran to the front counter to help Tommy with his cups.

Before Tommy left, he nodded at Buck.

"You say the bet's not going well. This place not paying you?"

"It does, but just forty a week. Almost broke three hundred at the coffee pavilion, but someone tossed some em-eighties into my storage room and destroyed half of my supplies. Can't go back until insurance tells me I can. So…"

Tommy's gaze drifted to the side.

"Interesting," he said. "You know how many?"

"How many em-eighties? No. Enough to kill my cooler and half my water bottles. At least they missed the coffeemaker. Mostly. But they singed the floor and destroyed the door, so I can't keep anything there. Not until insurance clears me."

"Yeah…"

Buck studied his face.

"Unfortunate, right?" he asked.

"Sure is," Tommy agreed.

Tommy was staring at the floor, thinking about something. Buck's stomach tightened.

"You have any thoughts about that?"

Tommy shrugged.

"When did it happen?"

"Fourth of July. Sometime after I closed."

"That's too bad."

Buck pressed the issue. "Any thoughts?"

Tommy nodded.

"Yeah, I have an opinion about that." He pointed his cups at Buck. "You might want to talk to Chet about that one. Not saying he's responsible. But I have a feeling he'll know who is." He nudged the door open with his shoulder. "Seeya around, Buck."

"Yeah, seeya around, Tommy."

And with that, Tommy left as he had entered, head low, hands in pockets, except for the two fingers he needed to hold his cups, and into the sunlight where his body would become a silhouette.

Episode 29

Girls' Night Out

AFTER WORK, BUCK CALLED Rhett Rowe to discuss his property losses. But the insurance adjuster wasn't in his office. His secretary told him he was out on assignment and that he should call back on Monday. Buck thanked her for her time, but he didn't mean it. The insurance adjuster had told him to call this weekend. Not Monday.

Next, he called Mr. Stamps for a consultation, but he was careful about the hidden fee attached that wasn't so hidden. With his money depleting faster than he could earn it back, he refused to exchange any bank or credit card information with Stamps's secretary until he agreed to sign Stamps on for protection duty. That meant knowing the service fee upfront. The secretary sighed, but she gave up the information. It would cost Buck over a hundred dollars a night to hire him. Buck hung up without a goodbye. He had to end the call before she could find some other way to squeeze cash from him.

With his options evaporating like a Popsicle melting off its stick, Buck sat in his kitchen with no idea what to do next. His pavilion situation was put on hold. On Mr. Michaels's advice, Buck also decided not to open his driveway coffee shop for the evening joggers in case Jasper Sage rode by. And he'd already stocked up for his next business day, which was Monday.

With nothing else delaying the inevitable, Buck sighed and picked up his phone. Calling Lila was the last check on his list of matters to address for the day.

But when she answered, he realized he had no plan for confronting her. What was he supposed to say? Both of his thoughts about her proximity to the Chamber's list of business information were accusatory in tone, and he didn't want to put her immediately on the defensive. She was already wound up by default.

So, he started with the softest version of the more innocuous question he could think of.

"What you up to tonight?" he asked.

"Girls' night out," she said. "Wanna come?"

Buck shook his head. "No."

Lila took a breath. "You're no fun."

"Not a girl."

"What are *you* up to tonight?" she asked.

"Not much. Just trying to solve a mystery. Stuff like that. Calling to see if you and French Girl wanted to help."

"Yeah? What's the mystery?"

Lila apparently didn't catch the hint that she was stealing his new favorite girl away and that he wanted her back.

"How I ended up in the Lease Agent's notebook."

"Oh, fun. But how's that a mystery?"

This was an unexpected response. He leaned onto his kitchen table to brace himself for whatever came next.

"Are you saying you know the answer?"

"Well, sure. Who doesn't?"

Buck sat up straight. His fingers hooked around the phone cord. Was she actually about to give herself up?

"Okay."

"I mean, it's pretty obvious, isn't it?"

"Is it?"

"Well, sure. It's a notebook. If he's got a pen…"

Buck rubbed his temples. This whole thing was giving him a headache.

"I'm trying to find out how he knows everyone in town's business information," he said. "He's got all our financial records in there and uses it for stocks or something. It's how he gets rich. I want to know how the hell he got all of that, and how it's making him such a money monster."

Lila whistled as she listened. Once Buck finished his diatribe, she let out another heavy breath.

"That is quite the mystery. I'll see if French Girl wants to explore that instead."

"Okay, but—"

Lila hung up. Buck stared at his handset, then set it on the hook. A few minutes later, the phone rang.

"French Girl is out," Lila said. "So, I guess I am, too. Hope you solve the mystery though. Big stuff."

Buck felt a dull stabbing pain in his chest.

"Why doesn't she want to hang out with me anymore?"

"Hang on."

"Wait, no—"

Dial tone.

Ring.

"So, she wants a date, not an adventure. You never bring her roses. Just tasks to accomplish."

"When do I ever—"

"That's what she says. I don't know what any of that means. I just know that girl loves to dance. Maybe you should learn how to dance if you can't afford roses."

"Then what? I never see her anymore. She's always out with you."

"That's why you should come out with us. She'll be there, too."

Buck grumbled under his breath.

"Fine."

Looked like he was going on a girls' night out tonight.

"Where are we going?" he asked.

"Oh, the perfect place."

As soon as the call ended, he squeezed his eyes shut and growled. He had a date with two girls, but still no straight answer about how he ended up in Sapphire's notebook. Looked like he would have to think of some other way to get the answer, assuming there was an answer other than "not guilty."

* * *

Buck retrieved his tie for his night out even though there was nothing professional about the event. Going out with not one, but two hot girls at once qualified as a special occasion worthy of dressing up, and he wasn't about to waste it on jeans and a T-shirt. Well, he'd still wear his jeans; he never went anywhere without them. But the shirt would have long sleeves and buttons. And he'd have his trusty blue tie from Tailor Made around his neck.

He'd told Lila he'd meet them at Lucky's Roller Bowl-A-Rama at eight o'clock, but Lila offered him a ride instead.

"Every time you take that bike anywhere," she'd said, "you arrive sweaty. Why don't you just enjoy the drive for a change?"

Buck remembered the terror of riding with her in the El Camino last time, but he relented when he sensed her flashing him her toothy smile. Through the phone, she could've just as easily been glowering at something on television. But he gave her the benefit of the doubt since her inflection was cheerful.

"I guess…"

"It'll be fine," she said. "I'll make sure you don't wind up face down in a ditch."

A short time later, the horn blasted through his entire house when he stood at his bedroom mirror, trying to set the tie at the right length. Even though he was still getting to know Lila, she didn't strike him as the type who would wait long for him to finish getting ready. The engine was running, and he'd have just seconds to catch that ride.

He ran out the bedroom door with his lights still on. Once he patted his pockets to verify his keys were with him, he locked the front door and raced for the driveway. His shoelaces flopped around as he jogged for the car, his left shoe still hanging halfway off his foot. If given a couple more minutes, he would've tied them, too.

Twilight was setting in, but there was still enough light to see inside the cabin to the passenger seat. French Girl had already taken that spot, and she finger-waved at Buck when she looked up and saw him. Then, on Lila's suggestion, she rolled down the window. Lila leaned over her.

"You're in back," she said to Buck, pointing her thumb at the bed of the car.

He checked behind the window for a better view. Buck would share bed space with a lawn mower and gas can.

"My boyfriend asked me to get it fixed," Lila said when Buck pointed at it. "Just picked it up an hour ago and didn't have time to drop it off at home. It'll be fine. Just don't accidentally start it up."

Buck frowned. He didn't want to spend the first part of his evening dodging a lawn mower or gas can in the back of an El Camino, especially when French Girl would be just on the other side of the rear window, separating him from the quality time he'd hope to share with her in the back of a car like this.

But at least he wouldn't arrive at Lucky's Roller Bowl-A-Rama sweaty.

Hopefully.

* * *

THE DRIVE WAS MOSTLY peaceful. Lila kept her word for much of the drive, staying fixed to a single lane of traffic, maintaining the speed limit, and stopping at every red light. There was one instance, of course, when a driver cut in front of her, then decreased his speed down to a crawl, which prompted her to speed up to his bumper, veer around him until she was level with him, give him the finger, then cut in front of him and slow to a stop, forcing him to slam on his brakes and make eye contact with Buck through his windshield, which then led to him giving Buck the finger and a possible death threat, if the angry expression and finger across his throat had any indication. But Lila floored it as the man stepped out of his car holding a bat, so it had ultimately turned out well.

When they got to Lucky's Roller Bowl-A-Rama, the city's roller rink and bowling alley hybrid, Buck kicked the lawn mower away, vaulted over the bed wall, and scrambled to open the door for French Girl before she could open it herself.

"*Merci*," she said. "Thank you."

French Girl smiled at him as she stepped out of the car. For all the evenings since the Meerkat Saloon lockout, this was the first time she'd shown him genuine warmth. He smiled back.

"*De nada.* You're welcome."

Judging by the number of cars in the parking lot, Lucky's was crowded tonight, probably twice the volume of the Meerkat Saloon, but easier for teenagers to access. It had an admissions girl sitting in a glass booth, selling and ripping tickets for anyone who wanted in. The only requirement for entry was money. No ID needed. At just a dollar for a ticket, entrance was guaranteed.

"Three dollars," the ticket girl said.

Buck glanced back at both Lila and French Girl. Lila shrugged while French Girl studied her nails.

"You're buying," Lila said. "If you're a gentleman, that is."

Buck grumbled under his breath. Paying French Girl's way? Sure. Paying for Lila? He wondered what else he'd be on the hook for tonight.

He checked his wallet. He could spare three dollars.

Once the ticket girl pressed a button under her desk, the entrance swung open, and the three of them were given passage into the greatest teen hotspot in all of Hybrid City.

Lucky's Roller Bowl-A-Rama understood the deepest desires of western youth—they wanted access to skates, and they wanted access to bowling balls. As long as no one bowled down the middle of the rink while skaters went round and round, no one would see this combination as a mistake. To Buck's knowledge, this separation of activities has remained respected since its inception.

Lila led them to the skating half of the complex, where the disco ball was already spinning stars on the dark oval floor. Because Lucky's had such a low-cost admission, it assumed that visitors would choose their activity and pay for it once inside. The skate rental window had a short queue of customers wrapping around its carpeted half wall. They lined up at the end.

"You have roller rinks in France?" Buck asked French Girl.

"*Oui.* France first-world country."

"You ever been to one?"

"Of course. Skating fun."

Buck nodded. The more he spoke to her, the more he realized he didn't know what to talk about.

"What's your favorite part?"

"Couples' skate," she said, smiling.

Buck's heart sped up a fraction. It appeared to him that she might've been flirting.

"You?"

"Couples' skate," he said, even though he'd never actually skated with anyone as a couple, Jennifer included. He normally preferred the racing portion of the night, even if he usually lost.

They smiled at each other. Then, out of the corner of his eye, he sensed an intrusive presence hovering close. He dared to look. Lila was leaning on the half wall next to them, chin resting on her hands, hips swaying side-to-side, eyes staring wide at the romantic comedy that unfolded before her. Her mouth spread cheek-to-cheek in thick-lipped bliss when she noticed him glaring at her.

"Don't mind me," she said. "I'm not even here."

The skate rentals cost Buck nine dollars, three per person, but the night was still young. Soon, there would be pizza and soda. And maybe a few arcade games if either Lila or French Girl had any interest in them. And if Buck was really unlucky at Lucky's, then there might've been some bowling to round out the evening, which would've been another dollar per person per game, plus three dollars per person for shoe rentals. If Buck wasn't careful, this girls' night out, or as he liked to think of it, this date with two hot girls, would've eaten more than a tenth of his savings. Now that he was locked out of doing business at the park until the insurance adjuster allowed him back in, spending that kind of money would've been reckless.

But he was willing to risk it to improve his relationship with French Girl. After a cold Fourth of July, he needed to inject some fire back into her heart. If she liked bowling, he would pay for bowling. But for now, he was just paying for skating.

The three of them headed onto the rink the moment they laced their skates, and they kept within a few body lengths of each other. Buck checked over his shoulder whenever he got too far ahead of French Girl, making sure she hadn't fallen or dipped so far back that they'd end up with different people. Lila was also there, never far away, and Buck worried that if French Girl had fallen, Lila would be the first to her rescue.

But that never happened. French Girl was an excellent skater. Every time she rounded the corner, her legs crossed in and out effortlessly. Whenever a peppy song hit the loudspeakers, she would dance and bob along with the beat. Not even Lila could mimic her moves. Of course, Lila didn't have much grace to begin with. She was a good skater, but inasmuch as she didn't fall. Her skills were wooden at best.

After several songs came and went, they rolled off to the barrier wall and walked themselves up to the main floor where they'd find a table to crash for a short time. Lila would threaten to dance whenever a new song came onto the sound system, but she never followed through. Too much trouble taking off the skates. Fortunately, French Girl had enough skill that she didn't have to remove her skates to dance. Even if Lila stayed in her seat, French Girl would hop up and do a jig beside the table, impressively staying upright, not once losing her balance.

"Where did you learn to move like that?" Lila asked.

"Ballet," French Girl said. "Back home."

Buck wondered what other moves she could do with such balance and grace.

After a few minutes of catching their breath, they were back out on the rink, keeping up with the music, and dodging the bad skaters who had the misfortune of proving their lack of skill to the public. It was continuous fun until the moment Buck collided with a blonde girl who demonstrated the skating prowess of a crippled duck when she went from skating with traffic as a newborn walks, to falling, to tripping Buck, to causing him to tangle with her on his way to the floor.

He fell hard on his knees and collapsed against her stomach as they both skidded a foot across the polished plywood floor. A soft puff of breath went out of her. But she hadn't lost it completely.

"Buck?" the girl said when he rolled off her lap and sat upright, trying to remember how to balance himself.

He looked toward his saboteur and found her struggling to roll onto her knees as her feet kicked in and out, unwilling to grip the floor beneath her.

It was Jennifer. Of course it was her. Of course! Who else in all of Hybrid City could have possibly been there at that exact moment in that exact place to trip him up? Of course, that also meant Chet wasn't far away. The back of his neck tingled at the thought of something sharp striking it from behind, but he didn't dare look. He didn't want to know the truth yet.

"What are you doing here?" he asked. Other skaters were zipping past his head.

"I came here with Chet and the boys. And Pigeon's girlfriend. What are you doing here?"

"Same, but with French Girl and the girls, or girl. Lila."

Jennifer glanced past Buck's shoulder. He sensed Lila and French Girl hovering nearby, watching them. Maybe Chet, too. And Pigeon. And Pigeon's girlfriend? That part made no sense. Jennifer waved at whoever was behind him as she continued to struggle with her feet. He didn't dare look behind.

"You all right?" Lila asked when she skated up to them.

"Pretty typical of me," Jennifer said. "I'll be fine."

Lila leaned down and helped her up. Buck helped himself up. Seconds later, French Girl came up beside them and put her hand on Buck's shoulder.

"You good?" she asked.

Buck nodded. Across from him, Jennifer was studying her. Buck wondered if he'd told French Girl the truth. He had to change the subject, fast.

"You said Chet's here?"

Jennifer pointed her thumb at the bowling alley part of the building.

"He doesn't skate. Not competitive enough."

Buck narrowed his eyes as he tried to scope out the other end. In contrast with the roller rink, the bowling alley was lit brightly. But he couldn't spot his nemesis anywhere among the lanes.

"You sure?"

Jennifer carefully spun herself to look.

"I thought he was there. I mean, he's somewhere."

Buck noticed Tommy's hat near the last lane and Tommy standing underneath it. Though he was blurry this far away, Pigeon was also distinguishable as he dry-humped a bowling ball on his chair. A familiar-looking kid of about nine or ten was also sitting next to him, laughing. But Chet was not among them. And neither was Pigeon's girlfriend—if such a woman existed.

"I see Tommy's here," Buck said. "They on speaking terms?"

"Sure, why wouldn't they be?"

Buck shrugged.

"Don't know. Saw Tommy earlier. Sounded like he was in the doghouse. Over you, apparently."

Jennifer struggled to turn herself around. Lila's hands were inches away, ready to catch her if she fell. She was blushing.

"There's nothing going on between me and Tommy. Promise."

Buck raised his hands.

"Hey, no judgment. You and I are the past. If you and Tommy want to become a thing, be my guest. I've got French Girl now."

Jennifer eyed her again. French Girl's light touch got even lighter when her hand lifted from his shoulder.

"How you have me?" French Girl whispered in his ear.

Buck felt a chill on his skin. He wasn't sure of the question. After weeks of talking to each other, he figured they were official. Certainly seemed that way given how often he'd visited her at Tealeaf Central and how often their talks lasted beyond midnight. Had he miscalled their relationship?

He dared to look into her eyes.

"Aren't we together now?"

"*Oui*. You, Lila, and me are here together. But how you have me? What you mean?"

"Phone calls. Dates? You know, together?"

"Dates?"

Buck searched Lila's face for help, but she was playing the voiceless observer. Her mouth was agape, but not in any way that suggested advice. More like a need for popcorn.

"I thought you and me are a couple now. Right?"

A bemused expression crossed her face. "Are we?"

She wasn't angry. He relaxed. "Aren't we?"

French Girl glanced at Lila. Then at Jennifer. She kissed Buck on the cheek and smiled.

"*Oui.*"

Buck's heart returned to his chest. All was right with the world. Except, now he felt the chill of rejection coming from his other side.

"Congratulations," Jennifer said.

Buck put his arm around French Girl as he turned to face Jennifer. Her face was neither amused nor angry. Just plain.

"I owe it all to you," Buck said.

She smiled, thin-lipped. "Maybe Tommy and I should become a thing after all, if everyone seems to think that's inevitable."

"You could certainly do better than Chet." He stared across the room toward the bowling alley. Pigeon was dry-humping a different bowling ball. Tommy was now sitting across three chairs, hat over his brow, as if about to fall asleep. The kid was struggling to carry a heavy ball up to the lane. No one else on that team was present. "So, where's Pigeon's girlfriend? I don't see her."

Jennifer shrugged.

"Is it really that big of a mystery?"

"I don't know what—"

Lila smacked him on the biceps and gave him a look. *Get a clue*, her face was saying.

Buck connected the dots in his mind. He nodded. Of course.

He offered Jennifer a weak smile. Maybe she deserved it. Maybe not. But there was no point in their torturing each other anymore. The past was the past. It was time to forgive and move on. The resignation on her face was too heartbreaking to look at if he'd given any time toward feeling an ounce of sympathy for her.

"You should give Tommy a chance," Buck said. "You deserve much better than that bastard you're with now."

"That Pigeon's girlfriend is with now, you mean." She raised her finger in air quotes when she said *girlfriend*. Her cheeks quivered, and her face shaded toward red.

"Yeah," Buck said.

Before that first teardrop could find its way out of Jennifer's eye, Lila had her arms around her. She patted her on the shoulders.

Jennifer, no longer trying to stand on her own, hugged her back. And then came the free-flowing of tears. It was worse than when Buck had brought her a single rose for Valentine's Day.

"You can skate with us if you want," Lila said, soothing her with a gentle stroke through her hair. "Forget that douche."

Remarkably, none of the other skaters stopped to see what was going on. Maybe Van Halen's "Jump" was just too peppy for them to bother with the situation.

"That okay with everyone?" Lila asked.

Buck shrugged. He was too inexperienced in juggling three ladies to question whether this was a good idea. Then he jumped.

French Girl had just pinched him on the butt.

"This boy mine," she said. "Remember that, and we fine."

Judging by the expression on Lila's face, she was torn between laughter and sympathy. Jennifer, meanwhile, nodded. Hers was the pink face of sadness and ongoing resignation.

"Great," Lila said. "Buck, would you mind getting us some food and drinks? I think she deserves some comfort."

Episode 30

Confrontation at the Roller Bowl-A-Rama

J ENNIFER'S PRESENCE PRICKED BUCK'S skin for the next twenty minutes. It was bad enough that she couldn't skate without taking out the random passerby and forcing him and his two female companions to help her and her unfortunate victim off the floor. But the dueling of glares she shared with French Girl whenever she'd straighten her blouse and regain her composure somehow created a force beam that redirected at him and left him feeling exposed.

His dad had failed to prepare him for many events in life, one of which was what to do when an ex-girlfriend tagged along with him and his new girlfriend. Was she a third wheel or a broken one?

Fortunately, Lila was there to balance the growing tension, and whenever the primping of invisible feathers became noticeable, she would step in and crack a joke or point at some guy that Jennifer could date if she wanted to, which Buck should've been fine with given their new situation.

But the stigma of exposure refused to leave, so after Jennifer's fifth fall and French Girl's subsequent reluctance to help her stand as Jennifer glanced in Buck's direction for assistance, Buck told the three of them he needed to use the bathroom and would be right back. At least there, he could be alone for a minute and not feel like he was seconds away from getting clawed.

Except, he wasn't alone. Once he rolled into the restroom, he found three other guys taking up space at the urinals, each one staring at the wall but none wearing roller skates. They each wore bowling shoes.

The problem with Lucky's was that the restrooms and locker area were centralized, so every visitor gathered at the same places regardless of entertainment focus. That meant if three guys from the roller rink and three guys from the bowling alley needed to pee, then three guys would have to wait their turn or use a vacant stall, if there were any, because Lucky's had only three urinals to cater to its entire clientele.

Unfortunately for Buck, not only were the three urinals in use, but so were the stalls, so he had to float awkwardly by the sinks as he awaited his turn, trying not to stare at anyone peeing, but at the same time having nothing else to look at but the floor or the ceiling, since the men's restroom was not designed for hanging out but for taking care of business.

Fortunately, he had to wait only a few seconds before a stall door opened, removing awkwardness from the equation.

He inched forward as he waited for the occupant to leave. Then he about fell to the floor when the first sign of motion reached his sight.

A sexy brunette in a small blue dress and non-matching bowling shoes stepped out, pulling the hem of her skirt down as far as it would go, which was barely halfway down her thighs. Buck grabbed the side of the neighboring stall to regain his balance. But then he about lost it again.

Chet followed her out of the stall, fastening his pants. He stopped short when he saw Buck standing there.

He and Buck made eye contact, but neither said a word for several seconds. The only sound in the room at that moment was of water running, or of water hitting the back of a urinal. Amid the confusion, Buck wasn't sure what he was listening to. If they were out in the desert, it would've been the howling of wind. And that roll of toilet paper on the floor would've been a tumbleweed. But they were in a men's room. Not a desert.

Chet was the first to break the silence between them.

"You saw nothing, twerp."

Buck watched the woman sashay out of the men's room. He couldn't help but stare at her hips until she rounded the corner and disappeared into the main room.

"Was that Pigeon's girlfriend?" he asked.

"She's not—" Chet caught himself. "Yes."

Buck dared to look Chet in the eyes.

"Jennifer already knows about her, I think."

Chet ambled toward the sink and looked at himself in the mirror. He ran his hands under the faucet and used the water to straighten his messy hair. Then he checked his zipper.

"She doesn't, and I'll kill you if you say anything."

Buck shrugged. "Honestly, I don't care anymore. You can make out with whomever you want in whatever gross place you decide. It's none of my business."

Chet studied him through his reflection in the mirror. Buck raised his hand.

"I just came here to pee and get away from my two dates for a bit."

Chet turned around and nearly laughed at him.

"Two dates? You?"

Buck shrugged again.

"Maybe I'm not the loser you think I am."

Chet checked his watch. Then he moved to let one of the previous urinal occupants use the sink. Buck edged toward the new vacancy.

"Guess we'll find out in a month, won't we?"

Right. The bet.

Buck had come to Lucky's to enjoy his night with French Girl, not to discuss the bet or anything else that had threatened to give him heartburn. But Chet's presence reminded him of what Tommy had told him regarding the M-80 attack on his storage room.

You might want to talk to Chet about that one. Not saying he's responsible. But I have a feeling he'll know who is.

"What do you know about an attack on my business the night of the Fourth?"

Chet's face blanked. "Not sure what you're talking about."

Buck paused his advance on the urinal. A guy who had walked in behind him took that opportunity to take his spot.

"Someone broke into my storage room. Tossed in some em-eighties. Destroyed my equipment."

Chet's mouth tightened. He was suppressing a smile.

"What's that got to do with me?" His belly was trembling, and his cheeks were going pink. At any moment, the laughter would find its way out. Buck wouldn't give him a chance.

"Tommy fingered you."

The belly jiggle stopped. The undulating motion of his throat ceased. His body tamped down on whatever remained of the laughing fit that was trying to find its way out.

"What are you talking about?"

"He didn't say you were responsible. But he said you would know who was."

"I know nothing about that." He tilted toward Buck. "When did Tommy talk to you?"

"Earlier today. At the Shop Down the Street."

Chet pinched the bridge of his nose. He shook his head.

"He and I need to have a serious discussion, it seems." From behind his fingers, Chet was once again glaring at Buck. "Let me get something straight with you. Just so we're clear. The bet is still on. And I still plan to kick your ass and own it." He pointed at Buck. "But I am no cheater. Whatever happened to your storage room, I'm sorry. That's not cool. But it has nothing to do with me. And I know nothing about it. Well, except now."

Buck waited for the suppressed laughter to return, but no such thing happened.

"You promise?"

Chet raised his hand.

"I have more honor than that. The bet is to out-earn you, not to destroy your equipment and then out-earn you. That's like tying your shoes before the footrace. Why bother? Not even a challenge."

"You used to tell Tommy to dunk my head in a toilet." It wasn't until the words had left his mouth that Buck remembered where he was standing. Fortunately, Chet made no moves to expose the irony or take advantage of it.

"I take competition seriously, as well as business. If I have to cheat to win, then I don't deserve to win."

Buck expected a follow-up or a clarification, but there was none. Meanwhile, another urinal was getting abandoned. If he didn't take his spot soon, French Girl and the others would wonder what had happened to him.

"Fair enough," he said. He drifted toward the new vacancy. "If that's true, then you'll let me add a few days to the bet."

"What are you talking about?"

"I can't serve coffee from the pavilion until the insurance inspectors let me back. That could be days. Maybe more."

Chet thought about the situation. He shook his head.

"Nope. A deadline's a deadline. If you can't serve at the pavilion, then you'll have to find somewhere else to serve. Bet's still sixty days. Not sixty plus a few days."

Buck took his spot at the urinal. Unzipped his pants.

Of course, Chet wouldn't want to extend the bet. His idea of honor wasn't the same as Buck's, apparently.

"Fair enough," he said, and then he started to pee.

Chet washed his hands and headed for the exit. But Buck called out to him before he rounded the corner into the main room.

"If you're looking for Jennifer," he said, "she's hanging out with me, having a great old time. So, I'm actually out with three girls tonight. Just thought you'd like to know."

Chet grimaced, then bolted out the door.

Who needed honor, anyway?

* * *

BUCK RETURNED TO THE roller rink with an empty bladder and full confidence, but the moment he noticed the mass exodus from the skate floor, he nearly pulled a one-eighty. The time for general skating was ending. Lucky's DJ was prepping all skaters for a change in programming. And given the lowering of the lights, he wasn't about to launch a racing series.

Ladies and gentlemen, and especially ladies, it's the moment you've been waiting for. Buck's stomach lurched. Amid the throng, French Girl,

Jennifer, and Lila between them were hovering by the barrier wall, with all three looking in his direction.

It is time for couples' skate. Gentlemen, please grab your partner, and head to the floor. Prepare for your night to remember.

All three women were watching him, though only one could be chosen. It wasn't quadruples' skate.

The love theme from *The Breakfast Club* was playing over the loudspeakers, getting the crowd energized for the roller romance ahead. Buck had never skated as half of a couple before. In groups of two or more, sure. But couples' skate was different. During couples' skate, everyone watching knew that this was your girlfriend. The two of you were together. That was the point of couples' skate. It had nothing to do with skating with your partner. It had everything to do with telling the world who your partner was.

And Buck had three ladies staring back at him. Each was vying for his hand, it seemed. But only one could be chosen. Those were the rules upheld by Lucky's, society, and women in general.

Even though the choice should've been obvious by now, the looks on their faces suggested differently. To pick one meant rejecting two others. Pairing him off with one woman meant forcing the others into isolation. Other girls who didn't know them would stare at them, judging them, mocking them for being alone. Like old maids. Society's outcasts. That's what their faces were saying to him right now.

Obvious choice, but not one so easy to make.

Then, like the parting of rain clouds on a summer evening at the beach, Lila nodded and skated for a nearby table. She knew she wasn't in the running. A few weeks ago, she was the only one in the running. But time and reality changed the score for her, and for Buck. By grace, she was willing to acknowledge her inferior position, judgment by other girls be damned.

That left just Jennifer, the ex, and French Girl, the brand new but current, still available to become his chosen one.

Both were watching him. Both anticipated his choice. Jennifer's relationship with Chet was on the decline, if not already dead. And Tommy had made no moves toward her, according to her, and according to Tommy. And she and Buck had been a thing until just over a month ago. A month was hardly enough time to get over anything, much less a change in thinking.

French Girl, meanwhile, had just reciprocated his feelings with a public kiss on the cheek and her native word for agreement, *Oui*, when he asked her if they were together. According to the rules of love and war, French Girl was the new flame, even if they hadn't made out yet. So, even if his thoughts about Jennifer were raw, his feelings for French Girl were fresh.

All right, lovebirds. Last call.

French Girl nudged forward, as if to make a run for him and take his decision into her own hands. Jennifer noticed and followed suit. French Girl noticed Jennifer matching pace, so she pushed with her other foot. Jennifer mimicked her action, but did so clinging to the barrier wall to ensure she didn't fall.

The rink was filling up. The disco ball was spinning stars onto the purpling wooden floor below. The music was changing. The opening chords of "Heaven" by Bryan Adams filled the air.

The girls were now skating at him, French Girl effortlessly, Jennifer as a woman fleeing a zombie attack. Clearly, they both wanted to be chosen. But Buck didn't understand why he had to choose. French Girl was here with him. Jennifer was here with Chet.

But that probably explained everything. Even if Jennifer were here with Chet, Chet was here with Pigeon's girlfriend, or "girlfriend" if the truth had any say. In effect, Jennifer was here alone, and she hated being lonely.

Buck would have to choose. Maybe break Jennifer's heart.

Just like she'd broken his on the night of his birthday.

He remembered how painful that had been. Never again would he go through that if he could help it.

It would've been cruel for him to do the same to her.

He nodded. The choice was obvious now. No more fear. Besides, the song had already started.

Buck placed his hand on his stomach, winced as if suffering from a cramp, and raced back to the bathroom where he'd hide until couples' skate was over.

It wasn't until after his retreat that he realized the consequences of his choice. He'd condemned not two but all three women to the judgment of other girls who didn't know them. Unless he knew nothing about women, there was no greater public rejection he could've given them.

* * *

To the relief of Buck's wallet, the girls weren't interested in bowling, so once they returned their skates after spending twenty minutes making sure Buck wasn't sick, they headed for the car. Jennifer followed them as far as the exit, then turned back for the roller rink as they passed through the door. French Girl seemed relieved to be rid of her. But Lila paused on the sidewalk as she held the door open.

"You seriously going to ride back with them?" she asked.

Jennifer glanced over her shoulder. The look on her face was as resigned now as it had been all night.

"I appreciate the commiseration, but it would be weird if I didn't."

"It would be weird if you did. You made such progress tonight. Don't blow it."

Buck looked at Lila with horror. What was she thinking? Pitting Jennifer against French Girl was fine for the roller rink. But for the ride home, too? She couldn't do that!

Jennifer changed direction and headed for the exit. Once again, dread entered Buck's stomach. If he wasn't sick before, he was sick now.

"Honestly, it doesn't matter," Jennifer said. "I never wanted to come here. But Chet insisted. Then he abandoned me to Tommy, Pigeon, and Pigeon's little brother the moment we took a lane because Pigeon's fake girlfriend fake lost her fake earring near the lockers. I went skating afterward just to get away. He can sweat it out wondering where I went, if he even notices I'm gone."

So, that was it then. Jennifer would ride back with Lila. And French Girl. And Buck. All of Buck's ladies in one confined space, each once owning a portion of his heart, each now declaring a spot within his personal space. Now they were merged, like Voltron, but a super hot girl-bot designed to complicate his ride home, combined to rip even greater chunks of his heart from his chest if he gave any of them the strength.

"I have an El Camino," Lila said to Jennifer. "So, unless French Girl wants to ride in the back with Buck, would you mind?"

"Or they could both ride in the back and I could ride up front," Buck jumped in and offered.

Lila glared at him.

"Ladies up front. You're in back." She exchanged glances between Jennifer and French Girl, both of whom refused to stand within six feet of each other or even look at one another. "So, who's willing to ride in the back?"

French Girl, her eyes fixed on Buck, stepped forward. But when her eyes moved to the El Camino's bed, she stepped back. "Don't want to ride with mower."

Jennifer stroked her hair as she took a step forward. "Guess it's me then."

On the ride home, Jennifer gazed out at the passing streetlights. Through the back window, French Girl kept turning her head to look at them. Buck, meanwhile, pinned his back against the window as he held the lawn mower at bay with his foot.

Jennifer said something, but the wind had a dampening effect on her voice.

"What?" Buck said.

"I said French Girl seems nice." She shouted this time.

"Oh, yeah. She can be!"

Jennifer leaned toward Buck and put her hand on his knee. He flinched. Then he checked over his shoulder to see if French Girl was watching. Fortunately, she was facing forward.

"I'm happy for you," she said.

"Are you?"

She shrugged. "I think so."

Buck said nothing. He just willed her to move her hand before French Girl looked back.

"I've spent the last month wondering if I'd made a mistake," Jennifer said. "I sent you a couple of letters. Not sure if you got them—"

"I got them." Buck remembered finding them odd, and maybe even suspicious.

"Yeah, I just…"

Buck pulled his knee out of her reach. Her hand flopped onto the bed, but she didn't seem to notice. She was off in another world.

"Nice night, right?" she said.

"We don't have to talk about this," Buck said, trying to steer the conversation back to silence. The less he talked to Jennifer, the better his relationship with French Girl.

Jennifer glanced at him and offered him a weak smile. She seemed to understand.

"I blew it," she said. "I never should've gone with Chet."

"But you did, and now I'm with French Girl, so…"

"I'm happy for you." She'd said this almost automatically. Buck didn't buy it.

"Are you, though?"

She held his gaze. A moment passed in silence. Then she nodded.

"Of course."

"Then I don't understand your regret."

A thought came to her. Jennifer chuckled to herself.

"Oh, sorry. I think I'm giving you the wrong impression. I'm not suggesting you and I should still be together. I'm just saying I never should've gone with Chet."

Buck frowned. She was making no sense. Unless…

His focus trailed to the lawn mower, which his foot was still anchoring to the gate. The gas can, which sat light on his shin, was trying to roll off.

He'd listened to what she said. But now he was beginning to hear her, too.

She never should've gone with Chet. But that didn't mean they should've still been together now.

He looked at her. She was looking back. But there was no desire on her face. Nor anger. Just a girl looking at a boy that she was no longer dating.

"You never loved me, did you?" Buck asked.

Jennifer returned her attention to the passing streetlights. If there were an answer to that question, tonight wasn't the night she'd offer it.

Buck pulled his knees into the fetal position as he wedged himself between the window and the bed wall. As his left cheek pressed into the glass, he noticed French Girl looking back at him. Her expression was neither happy nor sad. Just questioning.

It seemed no one had answers for anyone tonight. And maybe that was okay for now.

The lawn mower, meanwhile, crept toward him and once again found security against his feet.

Buck's End of Day Report:

Earned: $0.00

Spent: $43.64 ($41.64 for entertainment; $2.00 for daily fees)

Net Gain: $-43.64

Paycheck Accrued: $19.93

Paycheck Total Due: $139.51 in 7 days?

Episode 31

The Unexpected Visit

Once Lila dropped Jennifer off at her house, Buck stretched his legs across the bed of the El Camino and cracked the tension out of his knees. Riding in the back of a car like this wasn't quite the same as riding in a truck. The space was smaller, or at least it felt that way. And because that lawn mower had taken up so much room, he'd been cramped most of the ride. Now that Jennifer was home and standing in her driveway, he could relax again.

Jennifer tapped the side of the bed panel and offered Buck a smile. There was nothing seductive about it. Just gracious.

"This was fun," she said. Clearly, she'd forgotten the part where she cried in Lila's arms, or where she'd spent half the ride home not answering his most pressing question. "We'll have to do it again sometime."

He smiled back. Nothing about tonight was fun.

Meanwhile, Lila slipped out of the car and gave Jennifer a hug. French Girl stayed in the passenger seat, looking in the opposite direction.

"You need anything, you call," Lila said. "I have no problem kicking a cheating ex-high school jock's ass."

Jennifer flashed her eyes at Buck, then back at Lila.

"I'll be fine," she said.

And with that, Jennifer thanked Lila for the ride and headed for her front door. Once she was inside, Lila turned to Buck and offered him one of her dreamy smiles.

"I love a happy ending," she said.

"Any chance the lawn mower can ride up front with you?"

Lila said nothing. Just drifted around the back of the car and headed for her side.

He'd hoped French Girl would take Jennifer's spot, but he had no such luck. For the next few minutes, he rode in the back of that El Camino alone, wishing for the company of his new French girlfriend, but having a window dividing the space between them. He could already see the night's ending: he'd get home, they'd say goodnight, and he'd once again be alone for the rest of the night.

It seemed unfair to have his date so unceremoniously intruded upon, even if technically he was the one who'd crashed the party. Tonight, after all, was supposed to be a girls' night out. But he was invited, and after several nights of missing each other, he wanted to spend time with her. He just wanted to spend it with her alone.

Buck leaned his elbow against the bed panel and propped his cheek in his palm. Maybe this was what becoming an adult was like. Maybe modern dating wasn't like it was in the movies, where a boy and a girl went to a soda shop and sipped a milkshake out of the same glass. Maybe modern dating included ex-girlfriends crashing the party, and obnoxious sidekicks interrupting potentially romantic moments with awkward stares and misplaced lawn mowers.

Maybe modern dating was supposed to suck.

Fortunately, Buck didn't have long to suffer through the questions. He and Jennifer lived a few minutes apart. By the time his dismay considered flirting with anger, Lila pulled into his driveway. He hopped out before she'd even brought the car to a stop.

"You want to come in?" he offered them when he leaned toward the passenger window. He still had an important question for Lila, and he didn't want to lose sleep waiting for an answer. "I got milk if you're thirsty."

Lila smiled at him, but French Girl said nothing.

"That your idea of a nightcap?" Lila asked.

"A what?"

"Drink before bed? Usually hot? And boozy?"

"Hot boozy milk? You serious?"

Lila winked.

"You'll learn. But no. I gotta get home to my boyfriend. Otherwise, he'll think some other dude is getting me pregnant. Plus, I gotta get French Girl home."

Buck glanced at French Girl. She twitched a smile at him. The problem with getting around by bicycle was that he couldn't take her home himself, not easily.

"I guess Mack's got a strict curfew."

"He not my dad," she said.

"So, I guess that's it then?" Buck said. "Night's over?"

"Afraid so, champ," Lila said. "But we had a lot of fun."

Buck waited for French Girl to offer her two cents, but she said nothing.

"All right," Buck said. "I guess I'll see you later."

"How long you two date?" French Girl finally said. Now she was staring at him.

"Me and Jennifer?"

"*Oui*. Yes. How long?"

Buck did the math in his head. They'd started dating around Thanksgiving, if he recalled.

"A few weeks maybe," he said. "Not long."

"Six months," Lila unsolicited her help. "That's what she told me."

French Girl nodded, then stared out the front window toward Buck's garage.

"Plenty of time," she said.

"Plenty of time for what?" Buck couldn't read French Girl's mind, but he was desperate to know what she was thinking.

"Anything." She looked at him. "Like couples' skate?"

Buck wasn't sure whether to feel angst or relief here. Was that *really* what was on her mind?

"Jennifer's a terrible skater. I'd never go out on the rink with her voluntarily."

"Promise?"

"I…yeah, I guess." Buck glanced at Lila for unsolicited help, but she was too busy checking her watch. "I wanted to choose you, if that's what you're wondering."

French Girl nodded.

"You just feel sorry for her, that all?"

Buck wasn't sure of the right answer, so he said yes.

"She dumped me for Chet, so I didn't want to give her the satisfaction. But I also didn't want to hurt her the way she hurt me. Is that okay?"

French Girl considered his question, but she offered no answer. Maybe she didn't have one.

Lila, meanwhile, looked up from her watch and flashed Buck apologetic eyes.

"Dude, I have to go. If I don't leave now, my boyfriend will get another girl pregnant. I'll have French Girl home in a few minutes if you want to call her. Sorry."

Buck backed away from the car and offered them a wave. He would never understand Lila's situation, but he understood her urgency to leave.

As the car backed out, Buck headed for the front door. But he'd barely got his hand on the doorknob when he heard a familiar voice calling out to him.

He turned toward the street. French Girl was running up the sidewalk toward his driveway.

The breath ran out of his lungs, and for a moment he gasped for air. She was coming for him.

"What are you—" he stammered out when she got to the driveway.

"No curfew," she said. "So, you take me home tonight. After we drink milk."

Buck smiled. It was a dream come true.

"Just milk?"

"See how night goes."

Buck was so elated by her gleaming face, a real expression of interest, or happiness, or something he couldn't properly describe, that he barely registered turning the doorknob or opening the door. In fact, he was so thrilled to have her enter his home on a Saturday night with no parents around that he didn't realize until after they'd reached the couch that he'd got in without his keys.

But the moment French Girl got her arms around his neck and closed her eyes, as if in preparation to kiss him (maybe the way the French do it?), Buck recognized the improper entry.

"Wait," he whispered. "Something's wrong."

She opened her eyes, just inches from pressing her lips to his. So close! But this was serious.

"I'm sure I locked the door when I left."

"Good."

She closed her eyes again and started opening her mouth, but Buck, with the torturous fire of regret searing through every cell of his gut, put his hand up to her face to stop her from moving any closer.

"No, not good. The door's unlocked, but my mom's at work. I'm sure I locked it before I left."

French Girl opened her eyes and closed her mouth. She retreated slightly, then looked around the room.

"Anything missing?"

Buck pulled away from her, again hating every moment of it, and tiptoed around the back of the couch. The lights had been on when he'd left, but only the kitchen light was on now. The rest of the house was dark. He moved toward the lamp but drew short of flicking the switch. Shadows crisscrossed the living room, masking vaguely the objects that still populated the floor. A part of him was afraid to investigate any further.

The problem was that everything else looked as he'd left it, in its proper place. But given that he rarely took inventory on his way out the door…

"I can't tell," he said. "Wait here."

He took a couple of steps and accidentally kicked the dog bowl, causing it to skid across the floor.

He cursed under his breath. The clatter probably echoed through several rooms. But his sharp concern turned to curiosity. His mom had always kept the bowl full for sentimental value. But when Buck kicked it, there was hardly any water left to drench the floor. Buck wasn't sure whether to consider this strange or a normal thing he rarely paid attention to anymore. Perhaps she'd tired of filling it and he'd just failed to notice.

After looking around for other inconsistencies, he moved toward the kitchen but thought better of it. Instead, he reached for the table lamp, unplugged it, and handed it to French Girl.

"Just in case we're not alone."

French Girl nodded. She pressed it to her chest as if carrying a dagger.

Buck kissed her on the cheek. Maybe not the romantic gesture he was about to experience a few seconds ago, but it was good enough for the moment. She smiled at him.

"Come back to me," she said.

Buck planned to do just that. But first he had to see why the kitchen light was still on when the others were off.

Whenever someone entered Buck's house, they'd first step foot into the living room where they could end the journey and take a seat in front of the television and enjoy a night of laughter or suspense. But if they chose to continue, then they had three new choices: move right into the hallway where the guest bedrooms and bathroom were, or move forward and left through the dining room and into the kitchen where they could access the back door or the garage, or climb the stairs to the second floor where the master bedroom took up most of the space.

The dining room had split shading from the living room's darkness and the kitchen's brightness. The closer he moved to the arch separating the kitchen from the dining room, the more he became exposed to whatever or whomever was watching him. To be safe, he grabbed a chair from the table and used it as a shield.

At the edge of the archway, Buck took a deep breath. Then he swung himself around into the kitchen.

No one was in there. He exhaled, and his neck pulse suddenly raced. His adrenaline was still spiking, but now it was facing a crash.

He set the chair down and leaned against it. He needed to calm himself.

And then he noticed the kitchen's main oddity.

Someone had turned on the coffeemaker.

He abandoned the chair and went for the machine, opening the filter and smelling the grains. Had someone made coffee from his personal inventory? Or was this from his mom's stash? After all he'd been through, if this was part of his stock…

Something nudged his right ankle from behind. It was cold and wet. On split-second reflex, he pulled his ankle away—

French Girl screamed.

Buck hardly had time to glimpse what had touched his ankle—

"Whoa! Who are you?" a man shouted. A man with a familiar voice.

"Who are you?" French Girl shrieked.

Buck dashed into the dining room and barely stopped himself from hitting a table corner as he pivoted to the side and stumbled toward the bookcase. A shadowy figure, dull and dark, stood near the couch. Dark, yes, but not too dark to identify.

"Dad?"

The man he'd lived with throughout childhood but had since grown up seeing only twice a year, usually around the holidays, was standing in the semi-darkness by the light switch, frantically flipping it up and down without result, likely because the source of that light was held aloft and unplugged over French Girl's head in preparation to strike.

"What the hell!" Buck shouted.

"What the hell right back at you," his dad said. "Tell this girl to stand down."

Buck gestured with his palms at French Girl to lower the lamp, but she ignored it. She kept bobbing the lamp over her head, ready to swing it.

"It's okay," he said to her. "This is my dad. He's home for some reason. You can set the lamp down."

She eyed him, clearly unsure whether to comply. Buck tried gesturing to her with his palms again.

"It's my dad," he said again. "Not a killer."

French Girl straightened her legs and locked her knees in place. She brought the lamp close, but she stopped threatening to swing it.

"Could you please plug that back in?" his dad said, pointing at the lamp. "That cost me a hundred dollars once upon a time."

French Girl stared at the lamp, then at him. She dared to set it back on the table where it belonged. Buck swooped in and plugged the lamp in for her. Relieved that the danger had passed, Buck's dad flipped the switch again, this time casting the living room in light.

"Okay, everyone calm?" His dad's hands lowered.

"Yeah," Buck said. "What are you doing here?"

"I live here." His dad glanced at French Girl. "Who's this?"

"My girlfriend."

His dad's face registered something between pride and regret.

"She have a name?"

"French Girl," Buck said.

"French Girl?" His dad stared at her. "That your name?"

"*Oui.*"

"Your real name?"

"No," she said.

"You have a real name?"

"*Oui.*"

Buck's dad waited for a follow-up, but French Girl offered none.

"Care to share?"

French Girl glanced at Buck and shook her head. "Secret."

"Secret?" His dad leaned forward and jabbed Buck in the shoulder. "Your girl a spy or something?"

"She's a tea waitress."

His dad frowned. Not the exotic life he'd hoped his son would date into, apparently.

"No one know my name," French Girl said. "Just way it is."

"Why?"

She shrugged.

"No one know how to pronounce it. So, I don't tell them."

"Yeah? Is it one of those complicated French names with X's and U's?"

"Not complicated to me," she said.

"Just to everyone else?"

She shrugged again. "I not want to make life harder on everyone. I okay with 'French Girl.'"

His dad extended his hand to her. "Jim."

She hesitated. When he didn't back down, she shook it. Everyone's shoulders dropped after that.

And then the cold, wet thing nudged Buck's ankle again.

"Pudding?"

Buck's half-poodle, half-cocker spaniel was sniffing his feet. He hadn't seen the dog for months. Buck dared to reach down and pet his head, but the dog growled. Pudding trusted some people, but not everyone, and not all the time. Sometimes Buck could pet him without incident. Sometimes the dog would growl if he got too close. Perhaps being away for so long increased his distrust. Buck withdrew his hand before the dog could snap at it.

"I made coffee if anyone wants some," Buck's dad said.

"Not from my stock, I hope."

"Your stock?"

Buck dared move his hand toward the dog again, hoping to touch his curly fur for old times' sake, but Pudding didn't seem ready for a reunion, so after another tense growl from his dog, Buck withdrew his hand again. "I run a coffee business now. I had to bring my supplies home after some vandal blew up my storage room a couple of nights ago."

His dad stroked his chin as he considered Buck's news.

"A coffee business? Really? How old are you now?"

"Eighteen."

Buck's dad mouthed some calculations as he stared at the ceiling and nodded along with his numbers.

"Yeah, okay. Adds up. All right. Happy belated birthday then. Should I assume you graduated, too?"

"Last month."

"Guess I got a lot to catch up on. Here, take a seat. Let me get my coffee. Are the grains in that blue jar your stock?"

"No, those are Mom's."

His dad glanced at his watch. "What time does she get off work?"

"Two."

"All right, so I've got just over two hours to get out of here." He pointed at the front door. "By the way, you need to do a better job locking that there. I still got my key, but I didn't have to use it."

Buck was certain he'd locked it on his way out. Then again, he had been in such a hurry to leave that it was possible he'd misjudged his locking job.

Buck took a seat on the couch beside French Girl while he waited for his dad to get his coffee. He wanted to put his arm around her, but he didn't know what the protocol was for interacting with girlfriends in front of parents. When his dad had been home for Christmas, Jennifer was at home with her own parents, so they had never met, so he couldn't find out then.

Either way, it didn't matter. Pudding decided for him when he jumped onto French Girl's lap and licked her cheek.

"Nice doggie," she said, scratching his ears. Pudding had no problem with her petting his head.

Buck dared to pet his head, too, but the dog growled. "Aw, come on."

His dad came out of the kitchen a moment later with three coffee mugs and placed one before each of them.

"Make sure you wash these before your mom gets home. I don't think she'd be happy with either me or French Girl here this close to midnight, and I wouldn't want her asking questions."

"I guess not." Buck was too busy staring at his dad to worry about the coffee mug. "Why are you here? It's not Christmas."

His dad sipped his coffee, then set it on the table.

"Nope, you first. You graduated and got yourself a girlfriend and a coffee business, and it's barely July. What's the story here?"

"I think you already told it."

His dad gestured to him to elaborate.

"Fine. It started with a bet."

So, Buck spent the next twenty minutes or so telling his dad about the bet, the business, and everything but the part about Jennifer cheating on him. His dad, however, noticed the hole in his story.

"Why would this rich kid want to out-business you?"

"It's complicated."

His dad glanced at French Girl. "Is it a pissing match over her?"

Buck shook his head. "Chet hardly knows French Girl."

"You sure?"

"He sure," French Girl said. "Blond boy douche."

Buck nearly spat out his coffee. For a girl who was still learning English, she sure understood how to prioritize certain words for certain occasions.

"Some other girl then?"

Buck said nothing.

"*Oui*," French Girl said. "Blonde girl crybaby."

Buck squeezed his eyes shut. He couldn't get anything by these people.

"Jennifer Mills," he said.

"Oh, that girl you were dating last time I was here? Was that her name?"

Buck explained to French Girl that his dad and Jennifer had never met. She told him she'd put the pieces together and assumed as much.

"Well, this one seems much better," his dad said. "What's your name again, sweetheart?"

French Girl shrugged. "Better I don't say. Embarrassing how many say it wrong."

"Is it Marguerite?"

She shook her head. "No."

"Margeaux?"

"No."

"Etienne?"

"No."

"Dad, she's not going to say. And you're running out of time."

He checked his watch again. "I see that."

"Your turn. Why are you here?"

Once again, his dad took a sip from his cup. By now, Pudding had hopped off French Girl's lap and gone to sleep by Buck's dad's feet.

"It's possible I may already know a little something about that bet of yours."

Buck was holding his own cup, but on hearing that, he set it down for fear of dropping it and spilling coffee all over the couch.

"What do you mean?"

"It's complicated. But I have my ear to the ground. I wouldn't call it a perk to my business. More like a curse."

Buck said nothing.

His dad sighed. "I came here by cab, if you're wondering why my car's not out there."

"Get to the point, Dad."

"No one knows I'm here, and it needs to stay that way."

"I wasn't planning on telling Mom. I think you already made that clear."

"Good. But you need to tell no one, including Mack, or Kabuki, or even Irina Swift."

Buck felt his stomach drop. How could his dad possibly know about any of these associations? He was living on a farm outside of town. His life was sowing seeds or milking cows for some ranch owner. He didn't own a phone, much less a phone book. Buck hadn't wondered where his car was because he'd come to Christmas on a bicycle.

"How do you—"

Buck's dad held up his hand to silence him. He looked at French Girl and nodded.

"Can you keep a secret, too?" he asked her.

"No one know my name."

He nodded. "Good." He took a breath. "Buck, buddy, I suppose you're old enough for me to tell you the truth."

"Yes, please do, because you're talking like a lunatic."

His dad picked up the coffee cup, but Buck stopped him from drinking it.

"Mom's still coming home soon, no matter how many times you put that thing to your lips."

"Right." He set it back on the coffee table. "She and I are not on bad terms, by the way. We agreed I needed to stay away. To keep you and her safe."

"From what?" Buck didn't ask this with surprise or wonder. More like frustration.

"I work for some…difficult people."

"Yeah, I hear farms can be rough. But what's that got to do with—"

"I don't work on a farm. Never have."

"But Mom says—"

"Your mom is protecting you from the truth."

Buck said nothing.

"We decided that it's better that I never come home. That way they can't hurt you when they come for me. Why come if they know I'm not here?"

Buck was trying to process his dad's words as he spoke them, but time was limited, so he had to keep the conversation going whether he understood any of it or not.

"Who? What are you talking about?"

"We thought holidays were safe because they'd be too busy celebrating their own to worry about where I'd be spending mine."

"What. Are. You. Talking about?"

"You ever hear of an organization called Rising Sunshine?"

"No."

Of course he hadn't. If it wasn't on TV or a shop sign, why would he hear anything about such a thing?

Buck's dad glanced at French Girl. She shook her head.

"Why would she know?" Buck asked.

"I figured Mack might've mentioned it in passing."

"Why would *he* know? What is it?"

Buck's dad eyed the front door. "You ever lock that thing?"

Buck got off the couch and checked the doorknob. He locked it just to get the story going. It was almost one o'clock.

"There." He dove onto the couch. "Go."

"Right. So, Rising Sunshine operates out of Chicago in an old neighborhood that used to be a centerpiece during the bootlegging era. You ever learn about that in school?"

"Maybe. I don't care. Get to the point. Please."

His dad raised his hand to the back of the couch, flicked it forward as if to gesture his train of thought, then held it there frozen.

"No, I can't tell you that," he finally said. "Not even your mom knows all of it."

Buck was ready to scream. His dad lowered his hand.

"Here are the two things I came here to tell you. Then I have to go. You have to trust me that what I tell you is enough for now. Understood?"

Buck's guts wanted to burst through his belly. His knees were jittering up and down. His hands and knuckles shook in his lap. What the hell was his dad keeping from him? Why was he here five months before Christmas?

"I heard Jasper Sage stopped by yesterday."

Buck's body froze. How could his dad know *that*?

Then again, after all the name-dropping he'd done with all of his business owner friends, how would he *not* know that?

"That's the rumor."

Buck's dad leaned forward and put his hand on his shoulder.

"I'm going to ask you to pack up your business."

"Someone blew up my storage room. I can't get back to the pavilion until the insurance inspector lets me reopen. I have to run it here in the meantime, even if Jasper Sage is jealous of it. Or I lose the bet."

His dad shook his head.

"Jasper Sage isn't jealous of anything. And I'm not asking you to pack up your business here."

"Okay…"

"I'm asking you to pack up your business, period. Don't reopen."

Buck's stomach dropped.

"I have to reopen. What—why are you saying this?"

Buck's dad leveled his gaze at him.

"Because I don't want Rising Sunshine to know about you."

"Okay, but—"

"You don't get it," his dad said.

"Of course I don't get it! You won't tell me anything."

"The less you know about them, the better."

"Why?"

"Because the less they know about you, the better."

Buck stood up. He couldn't take this madness any longer.

"Dad, spit it out! Why are you telling me this?"

His dad glanced at his feet. At his knees. At French Girl. Then back at Buck.

"You went on Rising Sunshine's radar a few weeks ago, and I don't want them to investigate you further."

Buck said nothing. His chest was burning now.

"Your run-in with Jasper Sage yesterday moved you a notch higher on their list. If you don't quit now, they're going to start researching you. And that'll bring their attention back to me." He leaned in close. "And none of us want that, I promise."

Buck said nothing.

"You understand me?"

Buck understood none of this. He just tried processing the squirrel-diet story his dad had fed him, however much that was possible.

But it wasn't exactly possible.

He still had a bet to win. And a cryptic story about some mysterious group in Chicago wasn't reason enough for him to give up now.

"Buck? You understand?"

"Yes." He didn't.

"These people are bad news. Stay off their radar. And keep them off of mine."

Buck caught himself staring at his lap. He was supposed to trust his dad. That was the unwritten contract signed between fathers and sons for generations and millennia. Dads were always supposed to know best.

But Buck's dad hadn't been around much the last few years. All this time, Buck thought his dad was a farmer's assistant and his dog had been turned into a goat herder or something. But now…

"Fine, I'll pack it up," Buck said.

Except, even as the words left his mouth, he knew he would do no such thing.

Episode 32

A New Ultimatum

N O FATE WAS WORSE than becoming Chet Armstrong's slave, no fate under *any* rising sun. As Buck uttered, "Fine, I'll pack it up," he leveled his gaze at his dad. Whether or not his words had landed, he'd finalized his decision. After years of living a lie away from home, his dad's words meant little to him now.

"Thank you," Buck's dad said.

There wasn't much else to discuss after Buck's dad had said his piece. As far as his dad knew, Buck would dismantle the coffee business, and his dad would move back to whatever secret life he was having without much worry for his son's wellbeing.

"I'm sorry if this messes you up," he continued, "but the alternative would be much worse."

"I understand," Buck said.

Of course, despite his assurances, Buck would make no such change to his plans. Whatever this man's warning, it sounded like smoke, not fire. If there was some group—probably a cult judging by its name—that wanted to cause him trouble for merely daring to sell coffee to townsfolk, then he'd fight back as needed. Let them come! But Buck wasn't about to throw away his livelihood on the musings of a man who'd basically abandoned his family. No, Buck would surrender to his request in word only, just to get him out of the house. By Wednesday, he would return to business as usual, assuming the insurance inspectors cleared him. His dad would be far away by then and wouldn't know any better.

Unless, of course, his ear remained pressed to the ground, as it seemed so already.

"If you signed a leasing agreement with the Lease Agent," his dad said, "I can help you cancel it."

"I can do it myself. Thanks."

"I'm sure I can make him understand."

"I'll handle it."

His dad fumbled once again for the coffee cup. Now that he'd said everything he'd planned to say, Buck let him drink without protest.

"All right, well, I know you still need to earn a living. If Mack's not paying you enough, I could talk to some of the other owners out there. Since you like coffee so much, I could probably get you a job at Melty's."

Buck shook his head.

"You've helped enough already. Thanks."

He still didn't understand how his dad knew about his employment at Shop Down the Street, or even about Mack adopting French Girl during her exchange season, but seeing as how both details pointed simultaneously at Mack, the answer didn't seem so mysterious.

His dad set the coffee cup down.

"Okay, so I guess I'll let you get back to your life. Congrats on graduating and turning eighteen. See you at Thanksgiving?"

"I guess."

His dad patted him on the shoulder.

"Remember, remove any trace that I was here tonight. And don't tell your mom." He checked his watch. "I'm counting on you."

"I'll forget you were here the moment you leave."

His dad gave him a disappointed look.

"Buddy, don't say it that way. I know I haven't given you much reason to respect me over the years. But that's by choice, not irresponsibility. Understood?"

Buck shrugged. He didn't understand any of this.

"We'll catch up again Thanksgiving." He glanced at French Girl. "Any chance you'll tell me your real name before I leave?"

"I hate when people mispronounce it."

"I won't mispronounce it."

French Girl stared at Buck. She bit her lip.

"What if Buck hear and mispronounce it? Devastating."

Buck said nothing. He didn't want to give her ammunition to hate him.

"Whisper it in my ear then," his dad said. "I won't say a word."

French Girl thought about it, then shrugged. She leaned across Buck's lap and whispered into his dad's ear. When she resumed her position, she had a mixed look of fear and relief on her face.

"Really?" his dad said. "That's your name?"

"*Oui.*"

His dad shook his head. "People mispronounce *that?*"

Again, she shrugged. "Americans not French."

His dad stood up from the couch and straightened his shirt. He checked his watch.

"How unfortunate." He looked her in the eye. "Well, if I see you again, I promise not to mispronounce your name. Not even sure how that's possible, but, well, I'm not stupid. For some, maybe it's possible."

He turned his attention to Buck. "Your mom will be here in less than an hour. I'd suggest you take this nice young lady home before she gets here."

"We have a date," Buck said.

"Yeah, well, I don't think she's ready to find you home alone with a girl after midnight, so you should make sure that doesn't happen. Next time, date earlier."

Buck sighed. "Fine."

This time, he'd do exactly as his dad suggested. Buck may have known nothing about Rising Sunshine or his dad's secret life, but he knew everything about his mom, and his dad was absolutely correct about what he'd said. As much as he wanted French Girl to stay the night, he couldn't let that happen. He had to walk her home.

So, once his dad and Pudding left and headed one way, Buck took French Girl by the hand and walked her the other way.

It wasn't until he got to her doorstep that he finally leaned in for that kiss.

The porch light went on before he could finish the job.

"Mack…" he muttered.

French Girl touched him on the cheek.

"That okay," she said. "Anticipation make heart grow fonder. That the saying?"

French Girl opened the front door and slipped inside before Buck could respond. He didn't know what the saying was. All he knew was that he really wanted to kiss her, and now she was out of reach.

* * *

DAY 28: SUNDAY, JULY 7, 1985

Buck's Savings Account: $1.00
Buck's Wallet: $311.57
Buck's Business Funds: unknown
Buck's Expenses: $2 a day*
Hours of Operation: Closed until further notice.
Money on Hold: $139.51 (6 days)

BUCK HAD SPENT SEVERAL hours during his shift at Shop Down the Street trying to figure out how to broach the topic to Mack about his dad's visit, but he wasn't sure what to say. Somehow, his dad had known what was going on, and given the intimacy of certain details, like French Girl's temporary stay at Mack's house, for example, it seemed like Mack was the one informing him.

But there could've been other connection points involved, like third parties or none-of-their-business partners informing on Mack to his dad. If Buck brought up the visit, then he'd also have to mention the discussions they had about these shady entities who seemed to have their claws in every business in the greater Hybrid City area. Maybe Mack had already known the details about Rising Sunshine, Jasper Sage, and even Buck's dad himself, but what if he didn't? If not, then Buck would unwittingly bring up a topic that should've remained unbroached, and he would have no way of taking it back.

As Buck carried the latest stock of milk from the back to the refrigeration station, he rehearsed a mock conversation in his head. He needed to consider the best approach if he were to take any approach. The problem here, however, was that Buck needed trustworthy guidance, and his dad was not the one to offer it. Mack was a pillar in the neighborhood and an upstanding member of the small business community. If anyone had sound advice for Buck, it was Mack. Or Mr. Kabuki. Or Irina Swift. Pretty much all the people his dad had warned him not to talk to about this.

He reached for a jug of milk and slid it into the refrigerator.

-So, what do you think about me running my coffee business out of my driveway?

--Why run it at all when you could work here seven days a week like I do?

The milk fit perfectly. He reached for another.

-Would it be wiser if I continued operating my coffee business out of my driveway, or should I wait for the pavilion to reopen, or should I just pack it up completely?

--Depends on whether you're okay with Jasper Sage and Rising Sunshine showing up at your house while your mom's at work and your dad's away and killing you dead right there on the street in front of your house where all of your customers can see it happen and then steal your coffee because who are they supposed to pay now?

Buck shook his head. The conversation definitely wouldn't play out that way. He reached for a third jug of milk. The milk crate was almost empty, and he'd have to return to the back room for the next one.

-Have you ever met my dad?

--Of course I have. He and I play poker every weekend.

Buck placed the last jug of milk in the refrigerator. The cool air hitting him in the face whenever he opened that door was not doing much to stimulate his pretend conversation. He had no great ideas here.

The crate was empty, so he brought it back to the storage room and retrieved the next one. While he was counting what remained of the milk stock, the shop's front door dinged. Someone entered.

Because Mack was in the office doing paperwork, Buck had to man the register. So, he went through the sales door to reach the counter. The new arrival, some blond dude, was half-stooped at a pyramid of soup cans with his back to Buck. Buck leaned his elbows on the counter and called out to him.

"You need help with anything?" he asked.

The blond guy stood up and folded his arms across his chest. After a moment's breath, he turned around, slowly as if on a lazy Susan. Chet Armstrong's face materialized from under that head of hair, and he was now looking Buck in the eyes.

"So, the rumors are true," he said.

Buck lurched backward, as if he'd been punched in the gut. He caught the counter's edge before he could commit to losing his balance.

"What are you doing here?"

Chet held up a can of bean soup.

"Shopping," he said. "What are *you* doing here?"

Buck's mouth opened, but he had no words.

Chet approached the counter and slapped the can of soup on the counter.

"When you told me you ran into Tommy here, you didn't mention that you *worked* here."

Buck said nothing.

Chet spun the can around to point the label at Buck. He tapped the lid.

"You earn decent pay to run that register?"

"Are you buying that can or not?" Buck asked.

"As a customer, I do believe I have the right to control the conversation. So, I'll ask again, do you earn decent pay to run that register?"

"Pretty sure that's my business."

Chet nodded. "Yes, that's why I'm asking. Because, you know, you and I have a *financial* bet in progress, and every penny we earn contributes to the result." He leaned on his own elbow. "The understanding, of course, is that every penny we earn is tied to our business. Our *own* business."

"Shall I ring up your soup, or are you just here to harass me?"

Chet picked up the soup and hurled it across the sales pen, nearly dinging Buck in the shoulder. It crashed into a rack of newspapers and magazines, bounced up against the wall, then fell and rolled onto the floor. Buck stopped it with his foot.

"You're going to pay for that," Buck said. He picked up the can and scanned it into the register. "A dollar, to start."

"I'm not here to buy anything, twerp! I'm here to give you a message. According to the rules—"

"Chet Armstrong!" Buck swirled around to find Mack standing in the doorway to the stockroom. "That you making all that racket?"

"I was just here to buy some soup," Chet said.

"Yeah? You normally yell at my employees and throw things at them when you buy soup?"

"I just—I'm just here to—"

"How's your dad these days? Still corrupt?"

Buck dared to look in Chet's direction. The look on his face was hostile but submissive.

"My dad's not corrupt."

"Oh, but of course he is. Everyone knows it. Don't you?"

"He does what he has to, to survive."

"Yeah, is that what he tells you?"

Chet said nothing. Mack swiped a magazine from the rack and pointed it at him.

"Is that what *you* do, too?"

Chet glared at Buck, even though Mack was the one spitting out all the venom. He pointed his index finger at him.

"A bet's a bet," he said. "Honor the rules, or forfeit the win. Keep this up,"—Chet waved his hand over his head—"and you dishonor the rules."

Chet turned from the counter and huffed as he hurried for the exit. As the glass door closed behind him, he remained standing in the frame, looking this way and that, as if unsure where to go next. Before finally ducking off to the left, however, he turned toward the door and looked inside. He pointed at Buck, then jammed his finger downward and brushed his hand side-to-side, the signal to quit whatever it was he was doing, so it seemed.

Once he was gone, Mack patted Buck on the shoulder.

"Trouble in coffee town?" Mack asked.

"In more ways than one," Buck said.

"Does the other way have anything to do with your dad's visit last night?"

Buck turned to face him but said nothing.

Mack closed his eyes and smiled.

"French Girl told me everything," he said. "Was trying to figure out how to talk to you about it. I guess you were hit with some whoppers last night, huh?"

"You could say that."

"If it's any consolation," he said, "I don't think Rising Sunshine will interfere with your business before your silly bet with Chet ends. They're a pain in the ass for sure, but they move slowly. When does your bet end?"

"August eighth."

Mack offered him a warm smile.

"I think you have time to finish before they start hitting you with needles. You could always decide what to do with your business afterward."

"You think Chet is on their radar, too?"

"We all are," Mack said. "We just don't all know it. If Chet knew, then I don't think he'd be challenging you to anything like this. He'd be too scared to risk his business that way."

"Why? Who or what is Rising Sunshine?"

Mack rolled his eyes as he considered how to answer the question.

"You remember Prohibition?"

"No. Wasn't that in the thirties?"

"Twenties and thirties, yeah. It made alcohol production and sales illegal. But like all things made illegal, certain groups found ways around the laws and produced and sold alcohol, anyway."

Buck said nothing. He wasn't sure why this history lesson mattered.

"Rising Sunshine is the surviving splinter group of a splinter group of a splinter group that thrived during the era of Prohibition. It follows the same general action guide as those who operated back then. Get support to fulfill its needs in whatever way possible, even if that way is aggressive."

"You're saying Rising Sunshine is a mob group?"

"Something like that."

Buck leaned against the counter to steady himself.

"Wait, are you saying the mob has its eye on my coffee business?"

Mack glanced at the ceiling and shrugged.

"Not necessarily."

"Not necessarily?"

Mack looked him in the eye.

"Keep it open long enough, and they will. But they don't necessarily know you exist at the moment."

"But they will? In time?"

"If you're wondering why I pay you so little, well, now you have some idea. They demand a hefty service fee. So, now you know where half my money goes."

Buck felt his breath leaving his body. This was news he wasn't ready for.

"You think Rising Sunshine was the one who destroyed my supply room at the pavilion?"

Mack shook his head. "No, I think that was just a prank. Probably some kids who were bored and needed someplace to blow off their fireworks."

Buck clutched the side of the counter and leaned forward as if to wretch all over the floor.

"This is too much," he said. "This is all too crazy."

"Yeah, but you get used to it after a few years."

Buck shook his head.

"I have to quit," he said.

"Sure. That may be wise. But that's also part of business in Hybrid City. You don't have to close the Coffee Pavilion. You just need to keep as far below the radar as possible."

"Not talking about the Coffee Pavilion." Buck gestured at the front door where Chet had left.

Mack's eyes followed his hand. Now it was his turn to say nothing. Buck noticed the silence and looked his employer in the eyes.

"Not because of Rising Sunshine," Buck assured him. "Because of Chet. He's giving me an ultimatum. If I don't quit this place, I lose the bet."

"Is that what he said to you?"

"According to the rules, I can count only what I earn from coffee, not what I earn from here."

"Were you planning on using what you earned here toward your bet?"

"I don't know. I mean, I'm technically selling you my time, right?"

"Absolutely."

"And I thought the bet included all income. But I was also hoping to use what I earned here to pay for my coffee supplies."

"For higher profit margins."

"Yeah. I think so."

"But Chet thinks you should devote all of your resources to the bet for it to count."

"Yeah."

Mack looked at the clock on the wall.

"You sure he's not just pulling a fast one on you to gain the edge?"

Buck shrugged. "I don't know. But even so, my business does best on weekends, when I'm not actually there to drive it. I have to pay my friend Ronnie and his girlfriend to operate in my place, so everything they earn ends up going into their pockets, not mine."

"So, by being here, you're actually losing money."

"I think so."

Mack nodded.

"Makes sense. Okay, then how about this? You finish your shift today, and we'll put your employment on pause until August eighth. Then, once your bet ends, you come back to work, and I'll give you two additional shifts during the week. How's Wednesdays and Thursdays sound?"

"I'll have to think about it. You're only giving me twenty dollars a day."

"I'm also giving you refuge from Rising Sunshine. They don't harass employees like they harass owners."

Buck looked off toward the refrigeration station where he still had milk to stock.

"I guess we could put that on ice for now."

Day 29: Monday, July 8, 1985

Buck's Savings Account: $1.00
Buck's Wallet: $309.57
Buck's Business Funds: unknown
Buck's Expenses: $2 a day*
Hours of Operation: 9 a.m.-3 p.m. (at home?)
Money on Hold: $159.44 (5 days)

DESPITE RECEIVING OPERATIONAL WARNINGS from multiple sources, Buck decided not only to open the coffee shop in his driveway Monday morning but also to get an earlier start and stay open longer. He had to make up for lost time. But more importantly, he had to retest his market.

The fact was noon was too late to open a coffee shop, regardless of its location. Melty's opened its doors at six in the morning, and it was the star coffee shop in town.

While there was no way Buck would get out of bed before six, he certainly had no excuse for staying in bed until noon, especially if some people refused to drink any caffeine past breakfast. But he had been up at seven most mornings this summer. The only reason he had for opening late was to ensure he could get his daily supplies in time, as well as respect the pavilion schedule he had to share with the rest of Hybrid City, given that it was still a public structure.

That was a logistics detail, though. He could always reschedule his priorities. Prepare coffee in the morning and shop for supplies in the evening. Doing it any differently was probably nonsensical the more he'd thought about it.

Before Buck opened the garage door and dragged out the card table, he wanted to check the neighborhood transportation routes for traffic. Selling coffee was the priority after having been out of action all weekend, but getting the customers was also important. He checked the street and sidewalk for the likelihood that he'd get any customers today.

The situation looked grim.

Buck lived on a quiet road near the eastern edge of town. His house was not part of a development, nor was it near a commercial area. While he had neighbors and a neighborhood, neither saw much activity between eight in the morning and six at night. In fact, the only people driving through were those who either lived east of him, as few as there were, or wanted out of town. Most residents of Hybrid City, unfortunately, weren't interested in leaving town after nine o'clock on a Monday morning.

He returned to his living room and plopped onto the couch. If he hauled out that table and set up that coffeemaker, not only would he risk sitting in his driveway for hours without making a sale, but he'd do so under a July sun without the luxury of a canvas top to give him shade. He'd end the day with a headache and most of the same stock he'd started with.

Even without the multiple warnings about opening shop in his own driveway, this sounded like a bad idea.

But he didn't have much time to dwell on the negative. Just as he closed his eyes and contemplated saying "screw it" and sleeping until noon, his living room phone rang.

"Hello?"

"May I speak to Buck Star?"

"This is him."

"Hi, this is Rhett Rowe from Downtown Insurance. Remember, we spoke at the park last Friday?"

Buck sat up straight.

"Yes."

"So, I apologize for not taking your call this weekend. Something came up, and I had to take care of it."

"Did you win?"

"No, I scored just over—that's confidential. But I just wanted to let you know that I'm meeting with the insurance inspector this morning. Afterward, I'll be speaking with the Lease Agent since it's his property that was affected. Once I've had my meetings, I'll have a better idea of what to tell you about reopening. Sound good?"

"So, you don't have an answer for me yet?"

"Working on it. These things take time."

Buck dug his feet into the floor as he tried smoothing the tension out of his thighs. He'd spent all weekend waiting for this call. So far, it had been a letdown.

"Okay. Are you calling me, or should I call you?"

"I'll call you. You'll be home, right?"

"I guess I'll have to be."

"Good. No idea when that'll be, though. These things are unpredictable. I'd clear your calendar in case it takes a while. That okay?"

Buck no longer understood the purpose of this call. Was the point simply to piss him off? Was that why his mom would always complain about insurance agents and other bureaucratic entities after meeting with them? Did that explain why she had so many headaches?

"I guess it'll have to be."

Adulthood was really starting to suck, way more than high school ever had.

"Great. I'll call as soon as possible."

So, it looked like Rhett Rowe would make the final decision for him. Buck would stay inside until the insurance adjuster called him back. That way he wouldn't miss the phone call.

He turned on the television and watched a morning talk show. By nine o'clock, that talk show became a game show. Then that game show became another. And another. Then news. Then a soap opera. Between every commercial break, he looked at that phone. But it didn't ring. Wouldn't ring.

And then it rang.

"Mr. Rowe?"

"Who?"

"Hello?"

"Hi, are you behind on your mortgage payments?"

"What?"

"This is Dirk from Awesome Mortgages, and today I have the offer of a lifetime. For just fifteen minutes of your time—"

Click. Buck went back to watching his soap opera.

It was almost two o'clock when Rhett Rowe finally called him back.

"So, you want the good news or the bad news?"

"The good," Buck said. He'd been watching some other Dirk (not the mortgage guy) seducing Francesca away from her husband, and it was causing him tremors of the heart. The lack of regard people had for other people's feelings—

"As I suspected, you'll be able to return to the pavilion on Wednesday, possibly."

"Possibly?"

"With certain conditions, yes. Most likely."

Buck wasn't in the mood to push the issue further. The deeper he dug with this guy, the uglier the dirt.

"Okay, and the bad?"

"You'll be responsible for part of the damage."

Buck nearly dropped his phone.

"Pardon?"

"It's complicated. Some bureaucratic mumbo jumbo in the insurance contract language—let's just say it's not all paid for. We'll have to wait for the official report before I can cut a claim together, but it won't be too bad. Just a small fee."

Buck's rising blood pressure found its level.

"How small?"

"Eh, we'll make sure it's manageable. Don't worry about it. You'll be fine. I just wanted to make sure you're aware that it won't be zero."

"Will it be one?"

The insurance adjuster laughed.

"No, it'll be higher than one. But like I said, don't worry about it. I should have the final amount for you tomorrow morning. Be sure to pick up your phone."

"What if I can't afford it?"

The insurance adjuster laughed again.

"It's really not a big deal. Super affordable. Sorry to have worried you about it."

"Except now I'm worried."

"There's honestly nothing to fear. Promise. It's just my job to inform you that you'll have to pay something. Really, it'll be affordable."

"But you can't tell me how affordable?"

"Super affordable. I'll have the amount tomorrow. Just, have a good day, Buck. By Wednesday, you'll be laughing at how ridiculous all of your worrying is. I just wanted to get back to you before the day got away. And, you know, it's part of my job to keep you in the loop."

Buck wasn't relaxed, though. The moment he hung up, he went to his garage and dragged the card table onto the driveway. Whatever this "small fee," he wanted to make sure he could cover it. Come hell or high water, he'd sell out of his entire coffee stock this afternoon if he had to.

* * *

BUCK DIDN'T SELL OUT of his entire coffee stock that afternoon. In fact, he sold nothing. Not a single customer stopped by to check out his coffee. A few people walked by the table, but not one was interested in what he was selling. They were all in a hurry to get to wherever they were going. No time to support a neighborhood business. No time even to say hello.

He was tempted to keep the shop open past five to get the slower evening crowd's business, but Jasper Sage entered his thoughts, so he packed up and shoved everything into the garage. He didn't want to face him again.

And he packed up not a moment too soon. Just as he pressed the button to close the garage door, the old man rode by. Buck made eye contact with him as the door began grinding downward, but he pretended not to notice. As the old man started raising his hand to wave, the garage door cut off the visual. Buck headed into the kitchen before any further action disrupted his plan to avoid him.

Just after six o'clock, Buck reviewed his sales ledger. Now that he was a day shy of the halfway mark, he wanted to chart his progress and project his likelihood of winning the bet.

The results were bad. No question about it. According to Tommy, Chet had earned over a thousand dollars. But according to his ledger, Buck had earned over three hundred. Sure, he'd gotten off to a slow start as he learned how to make coffee and run a business where he'd sell coffee. And he was still trying to build a clientele despite Melty's cornering the market in Hybrid City and gaining the loyalty of nearly everyone in town. But he was progressing. His sales were trending upward. As long as he started tripling or quadrupling his sales over the next thirty days, he stood a chance at winning. But just a chance. A small chance.

However, it was Ronnie and Tiffany who had gotten him most of his sales. And he was about to lose that small chance thanks to a "small fee" that Rhett Rowe had promised "won't be a big deal."

Buck closed his ledger. Maybe he hadn't been at this game for very long. But he'd been at it long enough to know that nothing in business or bureaucracy was a small deal. After all, two nights ago, he'd thought his coffee shop was his business only. Now he had to consider Rising Sunshine. And then there was Sapphire's notebook and all it had revealed.

No, the world of business in Hybrid City was far too complicated for anything to be of "no big deal."

The truth was, Buck had lost the bet long before he'd ever made it. And now it was too late to stop the incoming train wreck. All he could do now was brace for it.

* * *

DAY 30: TUESDAY, JULY 9, 1985

Buck's Savings Account: $1.00
Buck's Wallet: $307.57
Buck's Business Funds: unknown
Buck's Expenses: $2 a day*
Hours of Operation: pending
Money on Hold: $159.44 (4 days)

"MR. STAR?"

Buck had waited until one in the afternoon for that blasted phone call. What was it with these "professionals" who made him wait for hours past the promised appointment time to get back to him?

"Speaking."

He held onto his phone cord as he waited for Rhett Rowe to get past the formalities and get to the point. The man wasted an entire commercial break and at least three minutes of soap opera drama asking him how his day was going and telling him about his.

"So, the Lease Agent and the insurance inspector and I all reached a conclusion. You'll have to visit the Lease Agent's office to work out your payment. But as I promised you, you won't have to pay much. Very affordable."

"Okay. Will it be two dollars?"

The insurance adjuster laughed. Why he kept finding this funny, Buck didn't understand.

"Higher."

"Three dollars?"

"So, insurance will cover most of the damage. Between the Lease Agent and the Hybrid City Parks and Recreation Department, the insurance is powerful and can pay for basically everything, including the damage to the walls."

"Okay."

"However, remember that little bureaucratic entanglement I told you about yesterday?"

"Yes."

"The fine print says that insurance will cover all unpreventable damages, including those caused by acts of nature, like lightning or bear scratches."

"Bear scratches?"

"Just a formality. Insurance assumes that the mere act of existing poses certain risks for damage, so it covers all costs in the event of nature rebelling and destroying property. It's no one's fault but nature itself, and insurance hasn't figured out how to make nature pay. So, it pays for nature."

"Hooray for bears."

"Right. So, that covers unpreventable damages. For preventable damages, insurance will cover costs beyond the deductible."

"Deductible? What's that?"

"Ah, I guess your mom, dad, or school never taught you how insurance works. Essentially, the deductible is what the insurance company will not pay, so the policy owner pays. Most plans come with low deductibles as a form of trust. Trust in the company to pay the difference, but also trust in the policyholder not to do anything reckless. The best way to avoid paying anything is to prevent anything from happening."

"Okay."

"So, because the Lease Agent is owner and the Parks and Recreation Department is host, they are absolved of any payment beyond the standard deductible, but one of them is on the hook for the deductible. Typically, the one paying the bill is the one most responsible for it. But again, that's where the fine print comes with fangs."

"Let me guess…"

"Right, so the byline in the insurance agreement is that the Lease Agent is on the hook for any structure that the Parks and Recreation Department claims belongs to him. This applies to your pavilion. That means the Parks and Recreation Department is completely off the hook from paying even a dime."

"But because the Lease Agent is no idiot…"

"Yes, I'm pleased to hear how quickly you catch on. The Lease Agent didn't get rich by being stupid. He got rich by understanding language. The fine print goes on to define preventable damage as anything that could've been prevented. This includes nature if a tree falls on the structure because no one had to plant the tree next to a pavilion or build the pavilion next to a tree. But it also includes acts of men who can be reasoned with.

"In your case, somebody vandalized the property. According to the fine print, that could've been avoided had you employed competent security. Key word here is 'competent.' Obviously, if you hire cheap security, you're likely to get cheap results. The fine print discourages underpaying for security."

"Because expensive security prevents vandalism."

"Exactly."

"Except for when it doesn't."

"There's always better security. So, because the pavilion did not have adequate security in place on the night of July fourth, the fine print says that damage caused to the storage room was preventable, and therefore worthy of the deductible."

Buck took a deep breath as he waited for the final punch to the stomach. He knew what was coming. He just needed to hear it so he could hang up and start planning for his comeback.

"Go on," he said. "Hit me."

"Sounds like you already know the ending. Yes, the Lease Agent has rewritten and notarized the fine print to take responsibility off the owner if the damage is caused under the care of a renter. In this case, the renter becomes sole owner of the deductible."

"And I'm the renter."

"Yes, you are the renter."

Buck waited to hear whether there was additional fine print that might defer the hook to another party, perhaps back to the Parks and Recreation Department who had the gall to offer public park property to a private owner, but there was no such follow-up. So, he sighed as he listened to the insurance adjuster flipping the page on whatever script he was reading.

"So, what do I owe for this?"

"Not much. Just…let me find the price here…"

Buck gripped his handset so tightly now that he worried he might crack the plastic.

"Okay, found it. It's only two hundred and fifty dollars."

In other words, Buck realized, most of his earnings since the bet began.

"Only?"

"Like I said," Rhett Rowe said, "super affordable. Barely two days' pay. Nothing at all to worry about. Just take a check to the Lease Agent this afternoon, and you'll be cleared to return to the pavilion, hopefully by Friday morning."

"Friday?"

"Yes, it'll take a few extra days for the Parks and Recreation Department to repair the damage. Permits and red tape and things like that. Friday at the earliest. If not by then, then certainly before the month ends. Just check in periodically to see if it's ready."

"Not Wednesday?"

"No, whatever gave you the idea that—"

"Thanks for the info."

"Sure thi—"

Buck slammed the phone on the cradle so hard that he was sure he'd cracked some buttons.

* * *

Because Buck paid for everything in cash, he'd almost forgotten that he owned a checkbook. But there it was at the bottom of his desk drawer, hidden away in a manila folder that his mom had given him a year ago when she'd helped him open his own account. Until now, he had had no income worthy of a weekly bank visit, nor bills that required a monthly withdrawal, so he'd had no need for checks. So, it seemed almost unfair that his first check in almost a year would be written for such a stupid payment.

But he had to write that first check, eventually. Perhaps the reason for that check was always destined for something ridiculous.

He removed the checkbook from the folder and discovered a small booklet with tiny boxes inside. His mom had called this book "the register." Despite it having just a few lines filled in from earlier bank visits, he knew both its purpose and its usage instructions. He kept a similar document for his coffee sales reports. Essentially, he had to write his deposits and withdrawals inside the tiny boxes and practice his second-grade math skills to determine how much money he still had in the bank by the close of the business day.

Since the bet began, Buck had made a transfer from his savings account to his checking account, but he hadn't logged it in the register. Reconciling that difference now gave him the practice he needed to ready himself for the big play—the bill to kill all savings.

Once he found his coffee sales sheet and his daily ledger documenting his spending, he recorded the relevant numbers into his bank register. Then he counted his cash to make sure everything balanced with his ongoing records.

Everything matched. So now it was time to face the gut-wrenching decision to throw it all away on a bureaucratic rule he couldn't fight. But first he'd have to make a bank deposit. His check was useless if there was no money in his account.

The Bank of Hybrid City had its air-conditioning cranked up to just above freezing. On a scorching July afternoon, nothing beat standing in an icebox. Even though he dreaded the idea of losing most of his summer earnings from a single pointless transaction, he felt like a member of high society standing there in that queue with three other businesspeople—a plumber, a maid, and a car salesman judging by their uniforms—and for a moment, he felt proud standing there. He was an adult now, making money and spending money like everyone else, free to earn and spend without limit, no longer subject to the barriers surrounding a fixed weekly allowance. Once he dumped his bag of cash onto that bank counter, the bank teller would offer him a wink and a smile and say to him as he'd say to any bank customer who deposited his stacks of cash:

"Enjoy it while it lasts."

And then Buck fell back to earth. Just like his mom would always complain, he wouldn't actually get to keep the money or use it on anything he wanted. It was just there long enough to keep the mortgage companies from tossing him on the street or the tax authorities from throwing him in jail. Or in his immediate case, to keep the Lease Agent from suing him for the damage done to the pavilion by some careless third party.

* * *

The Lease Agent had a smile on his face when he opened the door and gestured Buck into his office. Once he sat Buck down, he reached for two glasses and filled them both from a pitcher of water.

"You understand now the risks of owning a business, right?" the Lease Agent said.

"Everything costs more than I have," Buck said.

The Lease Agent tapped his glass against Buck's. The resulting chime filled the space with a dull echo.

"It'll get better if you keep at it. The trouble with starting a business is that it requires momentum to get out of the red. You have expenses that outweigh your income. Without investors' contribution or help from your parents, you'll be out of business before you know it. Unless, of course, you can generate a miracle."

The Lease Agent took a sip of his water and sighed as it went down his throat.

"But given why you're here, I don't suppose miracles are in your favor."

"I've never written a check this big before," Buck said. "How do I do this?"

The Lease Agent handed Buck a pen and pointed at the small box to the right of the blank check.

"Just write the value there. I believe you're giving me two fifty, plus a convenience fee of twenty-five dollars."

Buck glared at the old cowboy. Surely the man hadn't just tacked on yet another fee.

"Repeat that?"

"Two fifty, plus the twenty-five-dollar convenience fee."

Buck nodded, then sent the pen back across the desk.

"No," he said.

"No?" The Lease Agent leaned against the back of his chair and folded his arms across his chest.

"No. I was told two fifty. That's what I came here to pay. And that's all I'm paying. Period."

The Lease Agent pushed the pen back to Buck. Buck refused to take it.

"You do business with me, boy, you play by my rules. Two fifty plus a convenience fee."

"Two fifty plus nothing."

The Lease Agent pawed at the blank check. "Perhaps I'll just fill this out for you."

Buck snatched the check out of reach. He got up from his chair.

"Maybe I'll just leave and give you nothing."

The Lease Agent had looked amused until this point, but he was amused no longer. He stabbed his finger downward.

"Sit back down. We're not done here."

"It's two fifty, or we're done."

"Boy, I can kick you out of the pavilion and make it so you earn nothing the rest of the summer."

"You're already taking everything I've earned. What difference would it make?"

"The price of business is to manage all incomes and outcomes. You sell a cup of coffee, you pay for damage to a storage room. It all counts."

"You already own the town, according to Sapphire's notebook, so why do you need to bleed me dry with your stupid convenience fee?"

The Lease Agent locked eyes with Buck.

"What did you say?"

"I said—" Buck suddenly realized the information he was giving up. The Lease Agent had probably realized the notebook was gone by now—it had been over a week since Buck had taken it—but he wouldn't have known why it was gone. As far as Buck *should've* been concerned, the Lease Agent got drunk one night, took the notebook out of the safe, and accidentally flushed it down the toilet. But more accurately, Buck shouldn't have been concerned at all because he shouldn't have known it existed.

"I said…"

He wasn't sure how to follow up his mistake. Whatever momentum his anger at the situation was building, his faux pas knocked it off track.

The Lease Agent was now looking at the painting on the wall that hid his safe.

"You saw Sapphire's notebook?" he asked.

"Sapphire's what?" He had to get out of this somehow.

"Boy, what game are you playing right now?"

"What are you talking about? I'm not trying to play a game. I just want to be done with this insurance nightmare."

The Lease Agent turned his attention to Buck.

"Then pay the convenience fee and get the hell out of here. You're already eating into my money time."

Buck's stomach was on fire. He had to get the Lease Agent's attention away from the wall safe long enough to get out of there. And there was only one way to do that.

He took the pen. Filled in the check. Signed it.

Then he handed the pen back to the Lease Agent. He slipped the check across the desk after it.

"What the hell is this?" the Lease Agent said when he picked up the check and looked at it.

"Two fifty, just as I'd agreed to. Nothing more. You want extra, take it up with my lawyer."

The Lease Agent's look of amusement returned to his face.

"Your lawyer? You have a lawyer?"

"I call him Mr. Michaels. But you can call him the Grim Reaper if you come after me with your convenience fee."

The Lease Agent slapped the check onto the desk and offered Buck a huge grin.

"Well played, my boy. Well played." He pointed the pen at him. "But we're not done here. Far from it. Now get out. Every minute I talk to you, I lose a dollar."

Buck got up from his chair, happy to oblige.

On his way out of the office, he heard the Lease Agent getting out of his chair. Just before he slipped out of the main entrance, he heard something heavy hitting against the office wall. It sounded like it had come in from the direction of the painting covering the safe.

Episode 34

Hustle and Crash

BUCK COULD HARDLY CONTAIN his tears of anger when he came barging into the Whipping Shed during one of Mr. Kabuki's training sessions. If this ground were a place for managing emotions, he was about to fail. But he wasn't taking a test. This was the real world.

Nevertheless, he was stampeding onto respectable territory, so he suppressed his rage long enough to wrench his shoes off his feet before approaching the mat, as was required according to the signs on the wall. Once on, however, he stomped toward the middle and forced a bow before the master and his dozen or so students who, for some reason, were learning karate. As he folded at the waist, the weight of his despair raced into his sinuses.

Mr. Kabuki held up a fist to the class and jerked it sideways.

"Practice stretching," he said. He turned to Buck. "What boy upset about out?"

Buck wiped his nose. He wasn't crying, but only through sheer will. The backlog of waterworks needed at least one outlet, however, and it chose his nostrils for escape.

"I lost my money to the Lease Agent," he said. "Everything I worked hard for all summer…it's all gone."

Mr. Kabuki put his hand on his shoulder and leveled his gaze at him.

"*All* gone?"

"Most of it. What do I do? I can't beat Chet under these conditions."

"Always more favorable conditions on horizon if boy look for them. Lesson twenty-one."

"I don't know. Everything I do just invites the leeches to steal my money."

"*Hai.* That why boy kill leeches."

Buck wiped his nose.

"That's metaphorical, right?"

Mr. Kabuki said nothing.

Buck shook his head. "I just want this bet to end. I don't know what I got myself into."

Mr. Kabuki nodded.

"Wait in break room. Class end in hour. Then Kabuki talk strategy."

Buck obliged. He grabbed his shoes and went into the break room, where he sat at the table with nothing more than his thoughts and his broken heart to torment him.

All he could think about was a giant hand that had popped out of a whirlpool in the Pacific Ocean, scooped up all his cash, and pulled it back under. Like a disappearing act that wasn't magic. He grabbed his hair and pulled it. This weak act of self-mutilation would do nothing to bring back what he'd lost, of course, but it hurt enough to match the misery he felt in his soul.

Lesson #1: Never give in to enemy.

And as he sat there, dreaming of ways to shove the Lease Agent in front of a passing truck without consequence to himself, his thoughts segued to a cascade of business lessons Kabuki had taught him throughout the last month, as if having the audacity to solicit their fake help:

Lesson #2: Always have a guard dog.

Lesson #4: Quality matters. Better quality, better money.

Lesson #7: When in need of supplies, money is just a hurdle, not a wall.

Lesson #10: No such thing as a bad deal when the base price is zero.

Lesson #13: Budget.

Lesson #15: Part of success means a willingness to fail.

Lesson #18: Don't panic.

Lesson #21: There are always more favorable conditions on the horizon if you look for them.

There were other lessons instilled in him, of course, but these had come at him like a pack of cards exploding in his face.

And they seemed to follow a theme.

Do what must be done to succeed.

Buck checked the time. Kabuki's class would last another fifty minutes. Buck's knees fidgeted under the table. He would never last that long without bursting into a fit of madness. Something had to be done to turn his bad luck around. He needed out of this nightmare.

His gaze fell on Kabuki's spare coffeemaker. It was sitting on the counter beside a station containing coffee cups, sugar, and stirrers for the creamer. It looked like it hadn't been used for a few hours.

Lesson #5: When supplies run out, buy more.

Lesson #6: Always show leadership, even when subordinate.

Lesson #7: When in need of supplies, money is just a hurdle, not a wall.

Lesson #8: Always know the product being sold.

Lesson #10: No such thing as a bad deal when the base price is zero.

Lesson #16: If at first you succeed, be suspicious, for you might be committing a crime.

Lesson #18: Don't panic.

Lesson #21: There are always more favorable conditions on the horizon if you look for them.

His knee hit the underside of the table and caused a salt shaker to tip over. Another bit of normalcy destroyed. What was next, the pepper?

He pushed his chair away. Got to his feet. His shoulders heaved from his heavy breathing. His gaze remained fixed on the coffeemaker.

That damn coffeemaker.

He wanted to throw the salt shaker at it. And the pepper. He wanted to run at the counter and sweep the whole ugly contraption right onto the floor, crushing the carafe as a bonus. He wanted to swipe that sugar away and make it snow all over the floor. Then do it again with the salt. And the pepper.

He was in this mess because of a coffeemaker. *That* coffeemaker. Or one just like it.

Lesson #11: Always show respect, whether friend, enemy, or authority figure.

Lesson #19: Always protect reputation, even if it means exposing others' guilt.

Buck pounded his fist against the table.

"No! Screw that!"

Nobody deserved his respect. And what reputation did he even have to protect? He was just a loser, doomed to fail if he didn't turn his fate around, right here, right now.

Lesson #9: Burnt mouth is bad mouth.

Buck no longer wanted a burnt mouth. It was time to turn this whole thing around.

Lesson #21: There are always more favorable conditions on the horizon if you look for them.

* * *

BUCK KNEED THE DOOR open and stormed into Sapphire's Consignments with a salt shaker, a container of sugar, and Kabuki's spare coffeemaker under his arm. But when he set all the items on the counter, he absorbed the sensations of a fitful conversation coming from the back room.

After taking a deep, calming breath, he tiptoed around the counter and peered into the office. Inside, Sapphire was yelling at someone from across her desk, but Buck couldn't see whom. So, he cracked the door open wider.

And that's when his feet reacted with a backward step. That force of anger that had encased his body for the last few minutes bounced back at him. His breath squeezed as high as his throat and stopped.

The Lease Agent was sitting in the guest chair. And he turned his gaze right at Buck.

Buck lurched backward, then ran for the counter. He'd kept enough control of his momentum not to crash into it, but barely.

He wasn't about to wait for a reaction. He gathered his emergency loot and ran right out of the store.

* * *

AT TEN MINUTES TO three o'clock, Buck was sitting on a bench in a small grass lot behind the Whipping Shed, his stolen supplies taking the space beside him. And he was crying. Now that no one was watching, he had to get the stress out of his system.

Fortunately, it didn't take long. Once the tears stopped flowing, he wiped his eyes with his shirtsleeve and followed it with one gnarly sniffle-snort, or a snortle. As his nose cleared, he felt calm enough to rethink his situation.

The grassy lot overlooked the road leading off to Pine Alley Drive, a vast residential neighborhood where many of Hybrid City's housebound residents lived. It was a place where many young high school graduates got a taste for entrepreneurship whenever the residents needed someone to mow their lawns.

That same road also moved westward into a small shopping area where a young entrepreneur could buy wholesale items, provided he had membership, which Buck didn't, pawn useless crap he no longer needed or wanted, or fulfill other meaningless transactions that would leave him both empty and broke after the exchange of money was made.

At one end of the street, a boy could become a success.

At the other, a failure.

And Buck was sitting here on a park bench at the point where the road required a choice.

Beside him, Kabuki's spare coffeemaker sat unplugged and removed from its ideal environment. Where it had sat before Buck swiped it, it had function and purpose. But here on this park bench, it was just dead weight and a cheap dollar on consignment.

Buck looked at his watch. Five minutes to three.

It was never in his best interest to betray his master this way, anyway.

* * *

"OKAY, TELL KABUKI WHAT happen," Mr. Kabuki said, as he brushed aside the door and entered the break room.

Buck watched Mr. Kabuki approach the counter. The master opened the basin to his coffeemaker and placed a filter inside. As far as Kabuki knew, it had never left the building.

"The pavilion was vandalized on the Fourth of July," Buck said. "I just paid the Lease Agent for the damages. And now I've got barely fifty dollars to my name. I don't know what to do."

Mr. Kabuki nodded. "*Hai. Hai.* Kabuki had similar problem when buying Whipping Shed. Lease Agent wanted additional five hundred dollar for security deposit on top of regular security deposit."

"For no reason?"

Mr. Kabuki thought about it.

"Good reason. Lease Agent think Kabuki injure customers with weapons. Didn't want liability."

"Well, he tried charging me a convenience fee. Twenty-five dollars!"

"Did boy pay it?"

"No, I threatened a lawyer on him if he tried."

Mr. Kabuki pressed the button on the coffeemaker.

"Maybe not smartest reaction. But Kabuki understand. Would've done same if also inexperienced. Boy have some time to prepare for fallout."

"Fallout?"

"*Hai.* If Lease Agent demand convenience fee, then boy better pay. More trouble later if refuse."

"Yeah, I got that feeling."

Buck reached for the salt shaker and spun it around between his fingers.

"Does business ever get easier?" he asked.

Mr. Kabuki nodded. "*Hai.* That why Kabuki keep katana in dojo. Sword reason Lease Agent leave Kabuki alone."

Buck frowned. He didn't have a sword.

"Am I screwed?"

"Depend. How hard boy willing to work to turn ship around?"

"However hard it takes. I can't become Chet's slave."

"Then do. Advertise. Make great coffee. Get friends' help. Do whatever takes to win. Become best coffee boy in town. Make customers know it. Feel it. Sell enough coffee, Lease Agent convenience fee become nothing more than mosquito seeking a bite if boy work hard enough."

"And what about security? I have to hire Mr. Stamps if I'm to avoid having my storage room damaged again. I've already lost almost a week's worth of work because of it."

"If boy sell enough coffee, then security affordable."

The coffeemaker finished. Mr. Kabuki prepared Buck a cup and brought it to him.

Buck was taken aback by its taste. It had a richness greater than anything he was selling.

"What kind of coffee is this?" he asked.

"Hawaiian bean," Mr. Kabuki said. "Best coffee in town."

Buck made a mental note to pick up some Hawaiian bean coffee as soon as possible.

* * *

As it turned out, as soon as possible was the moment Buck had left the Whipping Shed and headed for Shop Down the Street. Fortunately, Mack had several bags of Hawaiian coffee in stock, so Buck bought all three. But before Buck turned for the door, Mack asked him an important question.

"Do you have a coffee bean grinder to chop those beans up?"

Buck stared at the advertising decals on the front of each bag. Each one displayed a scoopful of roasted beans as the sales image, not a pile of dark powder. It suddenly became clear to him that he'd bought three bags of coffee he couldn't use in a coffeemaker.

"No."

He imagined his kitchen as he thought through his answer. His mom didn't own a bean grinder, either, if his memory was accurate.

"I can give you an employee discount on the one at the end of the aisle if you want."

For as long as Buck worked at Shop Down the Street, he noticed that cylindrical device bookending the coffee section but never considered whether he needed it. He'd been building his coffee empire on store brand powder since the start and thought he could run out the summer on that alone.

Having three bags of coffee beans with nothing to transform them into powder seemed foolish.

"How much?"

"Discount's usually ten percent off for devices. Comes out to about twenty-seven dollars plus tax."

Buck considered what remained in his wallet after the huge insurance payment and the three bags of Hawaiian coffee beans.

"I honestly don't think I can afford it."

Mack closed his eyes and nodded.

"I thought so. In that case, I've got an alternative for you. Come in back for a second."

Mack led him into the office where he had his own coffee bean grinder on display next to a coffeemaker. There was also a stack of paper cups on the table leaning against the wall and a container drizzled with coffee grounds beside it.

"You can use mine for now. I also got a Tupperware container in the storage room you can use until you replant your feet."

Buck felt a sense of relief washing over him. Thank God for Mack Green and his generosity.

So, Buck took Mack up on his offer and spent the next two hours grinding his bags of Hawaiian bean coffee into powder and dumping it into the plastic container to keep it fresh. Of course, that meant letting another sales day get away from him. But now he was ready to make a major comeback once he regained access to the Coffee Pavilion this month…if not sooner…and at some alternative but equally lucrative location in the meantime.

* * *

Day 31: Wednesday, July 10, 1985

Buck's Savings Account: $1.00
Buck's Wallet: $45.10
Buck's Business Funds: unknown
Buck's Expenses: $2 a day*
Hours of Operation: pending
Money on Hold: $159.44 (3 days)

"Hybrid City Chamber of Commerce, Lila Speaking."

"Hey, it's Buck. Do you want to leave work early and help me kick Chet Armstrong in the balls?"

"Sounds fun, but Mr. Perkins is out today, so I have to take down all his messages."

"Anyone ever call him?"

"Sometimes."

"Any chance you could get away with leaving the phone off the hook until tomorrow?"

"I could. But Ernest Bee is always listening. He probably hears me talking now. He would detect the busy signal all the way from his office."

"I thought of a way to get my business back in serious action, but I need the El Camino. You sure you can't call out sick or anything?"

A few seconds of silence.

"Both of these guys hate it when I bring up menstrual cramps. I'll see if I can leverage it this time."

Buck hung up. Thirty minutes later, someone knocked on his front door.

"Okay, what are we doing today?" Lila asked when Buck opened the door.

Episode 35

Temptation Coffee

BUCK AND LILA LOADED the card table in the back of the El Camino and wedged the coffeemaker and supplies on the bench in the space between them. Then they were off. Buck spent the next few minutes staring at his inventory, a bit worried he was robbing himself of great potential now that he was down a cold storage container, but his attention soon waned when he realized they were headed up the wooded path to the Chamber of Commerce.

"What are we going here for?" Buck asked.

"Your plan gave me an idea," Lila said. "I think I know how to maximize sales and undo your little insurance problem."

Buck said nothing. Just nodded. The thought of returning to the Chamber of Commerce with Ernest Bee flitting about, as well as the still-unsolved mystery of how Sapphire's notebook acquired secret information related to businesses that had dealings with the Chamber, left him with a stone in his stomach. Plus, he still hadn't figured out how to broach the notebook topic with Lila without making things awkward, if not dangerous between them, and part of him wondered if he even should, given how well they were getting along. And with the stigma of Rising Sunshine now hanging over his head, he wondered if Sapphire's notebook was even of concern anymore.

When Lila parked the car, she asked Buck to wait in the passenger seat. A moment later, she came running out of the building with a roll of raffle tickets spilling out of her hand. She tossed it onto the inventory stack as she hopped into the driver's seat.

"Got money for markers and a sheet of poster board?" she asked.

"No, and I really don't want to step foot inside the Office Place if I can help it. That place gives me the creeps, especially those fiery-eyed, skull-shaped endcaps."

Lila tapped him on the shoulder and offered him a look of agreement.

"Thought so. Be right back."

And into the Chamber of Commerce she went. A moment later, she raced out of the building with a poster board and markers.

"If Ernest Bee asks, this is for an environmental awareness seminar." She wedged the poster board under the card table. "Okay, let's make a killing."

Buck assumed she'd meant for them to sell lots of coffee now.

* * *

Their destination stood on the make-or-break model of success. If they couldn't turn Buck's economic fate around with the clientele they had the potential of reaching here, then he was finished and the bet was Chet's to win, period. So, Buck understandably swallowed his breath when Lila turned the corner onto the target street and saw hardly anyone walking on the sidewalk.

Not all was lost, however. No one ever spent their day at the beach hanging out on the sidewalk. Buck and Lila could still turn a decent profit if they marched down to the sand and lured sunbathers to their table, provided they found a power outlet.

"How long is that extension cord of yours?" Lila asked.

Buck shrugged. He'd never measured it.

"Because I don't think we're going to find an outlet anywhere outside of ten feet of the bathrooms."

"Then we set up by the bathrooms."

"It'll smell like urine. Do we want to associate that with coffee?"

Buck thought about it. Lila had a point. But the bathrooms had a power outlet.

"Coffee leads to urine. Dehydration leads to thirst. Cycle of life. Don't overthink it."

Lila shrugged.

It was settled then. They set up on the patio where people could sit on benches while their friends or partners relieved themselves. Just like at a real outdoor cafe. The day was looking up.

*　*　*

ONCE EVERYTHING WAS SET, Buck and Lila worked on getting customers' attention. Because most beachgoers were more interested in bottled water, soft drinks, and beer than hot drinks, Buck's pitch for coffee was difficult, just as it had been all summer. But Lila had a plan to get the people drinking, anyway.

"It's simple," she said. "Buy a coffee, win a prize. Marketing 101."

She ripped a raffle ticket from the roll and handed one to Buck. She dropped the other into a paper cup.

"The pageantry is important. Make sure they see you drop it in. Then, once the day is over, we draw the winner from the cup." She dumped the cup ticket in her hand and flipped it over for Buck to see. "Hopefully, he wrote his phone number."

"So, is there one prize, or do they all win prizes?"

"One prize," Lila said. "That's why it's a raffle."

"Okay, I don't know how these things work. I never win anything."

"It's common sense."

"Sure. Maybe we change the wording then? 'Buy a coffee, *maybe* win a prize'?"

"We'll adjust as needed. Right now, the important thing is to make sure we give them a prize they want."

"Free cup of coffee?"

Lila leaned against the table and tapped her fingers against her hips.

"No, that's lame. We need something that'll move tickets. I mean, like rocket fire. How many days are left in the bet?"

"Less than thirty."

"And how far behind are you?"

"Over a thousand, I think."

"So, mathematically speaking…you need…"

Lila snapped her fingers and grabbed the marker from the table. She got to work on the poster board. Buck couldn't see what she was writing or drawing. She angled herself to keep it a secret.

"Do I have to buy something expensive?" he asked.

"It should be expensive, but no."

"Do I have to give away something I already own?"

"Nothing *you* own, no."

Buck tried to peek over her shoulder, but she noticed and nudged him away with her hip.

"Don't distract me," she said. "This requires perfect penmanship and a few swirls."

Buck backed off. Gave his attention to the people strolling along the sidewalk. Most ignored him. Those who made eye contact nodded, but they made no offer to check out his coffee. An attractive woman in a bikini walked by and smiled while tussling her hair, but she kept moving along, failing to stop for a flirt or even a chat. The half-naked muscle man walking beside her noticed her smile and grunted. Didn't look like either would stop for coffee today.

"And just about…" Lila gave her poster message a swoop of the marker. "Done!"

Lila bounced where she stood as she slid the poster board off the table. She aimed it in Buck's direction.

"What do you think?" she asked.

Buck stared at the poster board, studying each meticulous letter, saying each one in his head. As he converted the scrambled alphabet into word comprehension, he lost control of his jaw—he couldn't keep it locked to his upper lip—but he also couldn't make a sound. He was just mute at that moment.

Apparently, he was promising his customers one hell of a prize, despite having no stake in it.

"I–er…"

"Pretty great prize, right?"

Lila had a huge smile on her face. Buck wasn't sure how to take that.

"You sure that's legal?" he asked.

Lila shrugged. "Guess we'll find out."

Buck studied the poster board's message. It didn't seem like anything they should've put on display, certainly not where the public could see it.

"I feel like this could get us in trouble," he said.

"Not if we do this quickly."

"What if the cops stop and ask questions?"

"Simple." Lila turned the poster board facedown. "We're just here to sell coffee."

Buck stroked his chin. Maybe it could work.

"Won't your boyfriend get mad?"

"Only if I fulfill the prize."

Buck glanced at her.

"Are you fulfilling the prize?"

Lila scoffed at the question.

"Hell no. You see the dudes walking this place? And what if a woman buys a coffee but wins the raffle? This is just the lure. There is no prize. Not anymore."

"So, we're lying to them?"

Lila shrugged. "We're selling them coffee. That's all they really want, right?"

Buck stared at the roll of raffle tickets. His customers would buy coffee *and* raffle tickets. "The coffee seems lame by comparison."

"Thank you." Lila's smile rivaled sunshine, the weirdo.

"What if they ask who won?"

"We say it wasn't them."

Buck felt a headache coming on. It could've been the heat from the sun causing him discomfort. But it was likelier that it was something else.

"I guess it's like you said." He stroked his forehead. "At least it's like rocket fuel, even if the rocket never gets off the launch pad."

"When we're done here, Chet won't know what hit him."

"I think he will, actually. Ouch."

* * *

THEY SOLD THEIR FIRST cup within minutes. Then their second. And their third, fourth, fifth…it just kept going. Buck checked the extension cord every other sale to make sure no one had kicked it loose from the public restroom block. If they were to keep coming, then he was to keep brewing. Some customers returned for a second cup. Did they love the Hawaiian coffee? Or did they just want the "prize" that badly? Whatever the reason, Buck found it difficult to keep up with the demand.

Regular coffee. Iced coffee. Large iced coffee. He was selling it all. And running his inventory into the ground. At one point he had to take Lila's car to Sassy Supermarket for a refill of cream. While he was out, he picked up a dozen packs of bottled water.

Without missing a beat, the customers demanded portions of his new inventory. One, two, three, four…

And then the record screeched to a halt.

Down the sidewalk, Buck discovered the papercut to his tapping finger, the ketchup to his ice cream. A uniformed police officer was moving up toward the restroom block and mini-courtyard, almost dead center to his serving table. He was still half a football field away, but given how fast he was walking, he'd be on them within the minute. Lila, who was bent over the table as she poured a fat guy a fresh cup of coffee, hadn't noticed.

"Speed it up," Buck whispered to her. "We might be seconds away from trouble."

Lila straightened her back and pinched tight the V in her open neckline. Her face wrinkled at the sight of the approaching officer.

"I can take him," she said.

"I don't want you to take him. We need to—" Another half-naked customer with a doll's figure and a magazine cover model's attire swooped in from the side and ordered an iced Hawaiian coffee with peppermint candy. Buck had lost his train of thought once he started nodding at the customer's request.

Fortunately, Lila caught the hint that Buck had failed to deliver eloquently. As soon as she wished the fat guy luck and shooed him away, she hid the sign under the table and stashed the raffle tickets under the upside-down storage box. By the time the cop approached the table—about twenty seconds later—he was unaware of any prize. But he nevertheless came bearing bad news.

"Hey guys, this isn't really a place for hawkers." He pointed towards the nearby businesses. "They don't like independent competition so much."

Lila leaned forward, allowing her neckline to sag once again. "Aw, but it's delicious coffee."

"Even so…"

"Wanna try some? It's on the house." She smiled with a wink.

The police officer was about to say more, but his eyes fell on the Hawaiian coffee-filled carafe. Like a bird responding to a blanket drawn over its birdcage, he suddenly went quiet.

"Tempted?" Lila chirped.

"What flavor is it?"

"Hawaiian. The best in town." She touched the back of his hand.

The cop shrugged. "I guess you aren't technically selling it to me, so I guess it isn't against any ordinances if I just take a few small sips."

"We won't count the sips if it turns into a few more." Lila winked at him. "Promise."

So, after getting his free cup of coffee, the cop turned his back and pretended they weren't there. Lila had the poster board back on display within seconds.

They operated for another couple of hours before another unexpected visitor dropped in on them, seemingly from out of a palm tree, but more likely from Sweet and Golden, the honey shop across the street.

"Lila Deerborn, prodigal receptionist," Ernest Bee said as he stepped in closer. He was still wearing that ridiculous bee uniform. Must not have owned a pair of jeans. "You seemed to disappear from work this morning." The bee leaned forward and squinted at her. "We needed you. Thought you got lost on your way to the bathroom. Yet, here you are." He offered her an open-armed gesture. His bee mittens were absurdly palms-up. "How odd."

Lila pointed at the restroom block behind her. "Yep, found it. Would you like a cup of coffee?"

"Miss Deerborn, I'm afraid—"

"Buy a cup, maybe win a prize?"

Before Ernest Bee could get in another word, Lila showed him the sign.

At first, he merely glanced at it. But as he was about to speak again, he gave the sign another look. This time, he read it, then studied it, a bee caught in a jar of honey, unable, or perhaps unwilling to escape. He stroked his chin as he muttered his thoughts out loud.

"Very entrepreneurial," he said. "The type of spirit the Chamber of Commerce is proud to have representing it." He glanced at the roll of raffle tickets. "Those, of course, could lead to litter." His eyes once again focused on the poster board. "But who's going to litter with such a prize on the line?"

Lila put her hand on her hip and shook it as she raised her other hand and shrugged. Her voice went silky as she batted her eyelids. "I have *no* idea."

No elaboration followed. Just another nod at the sign.

"Fools," he finally said.

So, Ernest Bee bought a cup of coffee.

As he took the foam cup between his oversized palms and tried not to crush it, he brought it not to his lips, as Buck might've assumed, but to his nose and breathed in the aroma. His eyes squeezed shut in a moment of ecstasy.

"Smells delicious," he said. As if by automation, his hands floated away in a hovering circle, giving the coffee an artful swirl. "The taste must be exquisite."

"You should try it," Buck said, wishing this guy would just leave. His bee suit was killing the buzz that the prize had generated.

He glanced at Buck and the stack of polystyrene cups lying sideways on the table. "I can see why you'd want to advertise this place." He sipped the coffee. His face melted with delight. "Fantastic."

Buck felt a rise in his chest. Did Ernest Bee just see the light?

As his eyes reopened from the euphoric reaction, Ernest Bee stared at the poster board advertising the raffle prize. Between the coffee and the promotion, he was mesmerized. Another minute would pass before he spoke again.

"Yes," he finally said, "this is coffee worth bragging about. Delicious."

Buck straightened his back as he gave this unlikely helper his attention. The weird bee man was about to give him the green light to advertise as he saw fit; he could sense it in his gut. It was the breakthrough Buck needed not only to survive, but to keep his head high above water. Suddenly, his initial visit to the Chamber of Commerce was reaping an investment.

"But I'm afraid rules are rules," Ernest Bee finally said.

And once again Buck deflated. "What do you mean?"

Ernest Bee took another sip. "This is excellent. Other worldly." He swallowed and savored the moment. Buck, meanwhile, was holding his stomach to nurse the volcano that was getting ready to erupt from inside. *What do you mean???* Buck dug his fingernails into the table as he awaited Ernest Bee's response.

"I just mean you still can't throw your handouts all over the sidewalk," the bee man finally said. "I can see why you'd want to advertise. Getting the word out about this excellent coffee…it would be a service, not just an act of commerce. But, well, you still can't. Not in a littering way, at least." He smacked his lips. "You could always buy a commercial, of course."

Buck was certain a commercial would've cost him hundreds, if not thousands of dollars. And for what? A cup of coffee cost a couple of dollars. He'd never make that back in time.

Ernest Bee sipped his coffee and licked his lips. "I guess that's it. This has been a fantastic visit." He glanced at Lila and winked. "'Stepping out for a moment.' Ha! Good one. Maybe we won't tell Mr. Perkins about this side business, huh?"

Lila gave him the finger guns. "You know it."

"Would you like another for the road?" Buck asked, lost in a trance of his own.

Ernest Bee took another sip.

"Oh my, I—"

"It's worth another ticket," Lila said with a smile.

Ernest Bee bought a second cup before he'd even finished his first.

The instant purchase broke Buck out of his spell and gave him an idea.

"I'll give you an extra coffee plus a ticket on the house if you promise to let me advertise my flyers without interference," Buck said, as he handed back Ernest Bee's change. "Hell, I'll give you five free tickets for extending me that courtesy. Ten tickets!"

Ernest Bee thought about it. "Twenty tickets and you have a deal."

And so, Ernest Bee had three cups of coffee and twenty-three raffle tickets to juggle as he prepared to leave. Judging by the smile on his face, he couldn't have been happier with the condition.

"Carry on, Miss Deerborn. See you at work Monday."

"If not sooner!"

Ernest Bee's cheeks turned red as he buzzed off.

"Well, that was awkward and gross," she said when Ernest Bee zipped through a crowd and fell out of earshot. Her shiver that followed was blatant.

"This whole thing is awkward and gross."

"Yeah, well. At least you're killing it. Where do you stand so far?"

Buck counted the money. He found it difficult to put all the numbers together. It seemed unnatural.

"This can't be right," he said.

But it was right. Thanks to Lila's prize idea, Buck had already sold over a hundred cups of coffee that day, and they weren't yet finished.

At least not until another cop came marching in from the street and scolded them for violating a local ordinance. This one, unlike the first one, seemed to prefer tea to coffee, so Buck and Lila had to shut it down. Buck also had to pay a small fine for breaking the ordinance.

But, after the sales he'd raked in that day, as well as the reputation he'd built in his new, hopefully-to-return customers' minds, this latest fine wasn't about to crush his soul, especially since he'd basically erased his insurance fee and added back a dollar to boot.

It may have been a tiny increase to his bottom line, but it was still an increase. Once he'd checked his ledger for the night, he'd get to mark his graph green again. It was a victory. He was finally back on the upswing.

This would require a celebration of some sort.

This would require, he guessed, some kind of house party.

Buck's End of Day Report:

Earned: $320.23

Spent: $68.52 ($50.00 in city fines; $16.52 in inventory; $2.00 for daily fees)

Net Gain: $251.71

Paycheck Accrued: $0

Paycheck Total Due: $159.44 in 3 days?

BUCK WAS PROBABLY DELUSIONAL, riding off the natural high of his stellar sales day—the best he'd ever had, in fact—but the thought of celebrating his over two hundred dollars in sales at Tealeaf Central, or some other quiet corner of the city, bored him. Sure, they were intimate places, designed for any group that could fit at the same table and smell each other's breath as they listened to jazz and consumed tea and cookies. But they were too small. For the amount he'd pulled in today, he wanted to go big or go home.

Or maybe go big *at* home.

Yes…the answer was obvious…

"I have an idea how to celebrate our victory," he said.

Lila stared at him as she waited for him to answer. Fortunately, the road was empty of other drivers, but that wouldn't last long, so he had to tell her the plan quickly.

Kids at school had called them house parties, but they'd never invited him to the ones they threw. Other than when he'd crashed Grumpy Balser's on graduation night, where he'd spent most of the night trying on ties and not mingling with guests, he'd never attended a house party, so he didn't exactly know how to throw one.

But based on the stories he'd heard from friends who'd heard from other friends who'd eavesdropped on conversations between the cool students, the house party was a major life event, if not a rite of passage, where anyone who was anyone—or popular—would come together independently of classrooms and locker rooms and enjoy an evening of music, potato chips, and high school drama with one another. It was a place where boys could make girlfriends and girls could fight over boyfriends, and everyone could have a good time in the safety of the host's home, usually whenever the parents were away on vacation, and no one nearby had the phone number for the police.

The house party was an event that Buck had often wanted to attend himself, as it meant someone in power was paying attention to his value and considered him worthy of the invite. But no one had ever mailed him that card, so tonight he would change the tenor of that dream. Now he'd become the one sending out the invites.

And the obvious first invite would go to Lila, since she was the reason he'd sold so many cups of coffee today. She was also the one sitting immediately beside him when he'd thought of the idea.

"Depends on my boyfriend," she said when he told her the idea. "He doesn't like going anywhere."

"So, leave him at home. You don't need a date, do you?"

"Nah, not usually. But we've been apart a lot lately. Plus, you know, Gina Groach has been sniffing around the premises lately, and I don't trust her. She's been looking for someone to put a fourth kid in her I'm pretty sure."

"You have weird domestic issues."

Lila shrugged.

"Even so, I have to protect my home and hearth, as they say. Damon's not going to keep his pants zipped up forever, especially if Gina Groach comes a-knockin'."

Buck pinched the bridge of his nose. He had so much to say to Lila right now, but he reminded himself that she'd chosen this life of her own free will.

"I'd still like you to be there. You're the reason I'm not redlining my financial chart right now."

She reached over and rubbed his biceps. Buck had preferred she'd kept both hands on the wheel given how fast she was driving, but he appreciated the affection.

"No promises, but I'll see what I can do." She hit the intersection at full speed and nearly spun the car out as she rounded the corner.

The sedan she'd nearly sideswiped wailed its horn at her. "Have you ever thrown a house party?"

Buck admitted to being a virgin in party hosting.

"Make sure you have plenty of paper towels available," Lila said.

"Lots of spills?"

"Lots of vomit."

Buck leaned his head against the passenger window. Maybe this wasn't the best plan after all.

* * *

IT TOOK HIM UNTIL almost six o'clock to get in touch with everyone he knew, but the mission was a success. He'd throw the party tonight while the euphoria was still head-high. Perhaps it wouldn't last until the wee hours of the morning as a weekend party might do, but it would do the job he wanted. His friends would gather at a central location where no one had to spend money or risk getting kicked out because someone wanted to close shop. The only time limit was their ability to drive home safely. Or two o'clock, when his mom was due home—whichever came first.

With the plan settled, Buck went to work setting up his living room for his guests. He brought every chair he could find to the coffee table and arranged them in a circle. Maybe they'd sit in them, maybe not, but the option was there if they wanted it.

Then he checked the kitchen for snacks. He didn't have much to choose from, but he did have a popcorn maker. So, he popped enough corn to fill a mixing bowl. He also melted butter over it and poured on the salt. But it didn't look like enough. He needed some food padding.

Fortunately, he had a half bag of cheese curls wedged in the back of his dry food cabinet. They'd gotten stale, but he wasn't about to waste them. He poured the remaining contents in with the popcorn. Now he'd had a snack bowl.

And that was the extent of his party-planning efforts. Given that he was never popular in high school, he hadn't had much experience in throwing the types of parties people would want to stay late for, unless those people were the sort he'd call friends. Fortunately, those were the people he'd invited tonight. But he had no illusions regarding the level of wildness tonight's party would reach. He was not a high school celebrity, so he had a small mountain to climb.

Nevertheless, a piece of his stomach ached when he gave his living room a once-over and realized he was so green as a party planner that he hadn't even prepped his stereo with good music. Even as it sat in the corner by the television, ready to serve its listeners to the best of its ability, it had one working speaker and a broken tape deck. If he wanted music, he'd have to play one of his mom's records or listen to commercial radio. And it would play his choice in monaural sound. Definitely not the soundtrack of an excellent house party, and probably not even a fun one.

Buck collapsed on his sofa as he skimmed the rest of his sad effort to entertain his guests. The more he thought about it, the more he figured this was a bad idea.

* * *

WHEN BUCK OPENED THE door for the fourth time tonight, the skinny kid on the other side stood there wearing a blank expression on his pimple-lined face. His shoulders were hunched and his glasses glazed, but he was dressed to party, with a suit, tie, and everything.

"I don't know what I'm doing here," Garrett Nedmeyer said, with his finger still poised over the doorbell.

Buck stepped aside and gestured for him to enter.

"Welcome to my home," Buck said.

Garrett leaned forward enough to peek inside, as if to look for where the traps were hiding.

"What's going on here?"

"I told you on the phone."

He took one step in and halted. He tested the carpet with the tips of his dress shoes. When it didn't suck him into a black hole, he looked over Buck's shoulder and froze.

"Why are there other people here? And girls?"

"Because it's a party. That's how parties work."

Garrett didn't seem to register his situation. The toe he'd brought forward didn't move any closer inside. Buck turned his attention to his other guests to see if they could offer some help. Ronnie Michaels simply shrugged and shook his head. Tiffany was looking at her nails.

"We have popcorn," Buck said. "You like popcorn?"

"With movies. You have movies?"

"Well, no. This isn't that kind of party. But we also have cheese curls."

"No, you don't," Ronnie said. He was chewing something.

Garrett peeked around the door in the other direction, toward the dining room and kitchen. Buck once again gestured for him to step inside.

"No one's going to shove you into a locker, if that's what you're worried about. We're just hanging out. I had a big victory today, and I just wanted to share it with friends. And then I thought I should also invite you, you know, because we all deserve to go to a house party every once in a while."

Garrett smiled. "You see me as a friend?"

Buck once again felt his stomach eating itself. Former locker roommates didn't make them friends. But now he'd opened the door and couldn't close it without making a fuss.

"Sure."

Garrett's face turned suspicious.

"And you're not just saying that to tee me up for a wedgie?"

"No, Garrett. No one's going to give you a wedgie tonight. You're a guest here."

"Because my mom just washed this suit, and she'll be really mad if anything happens to it."

"Will you just come in so I can close the door and stop letting the air-conditioning out?"

So, Garrett Nedmeyer joined the party. He took a seat on one of the dining chairs, about as far from Ronnie and Tiffany, who were on the sofa, as possible. He was also apprehensive about getting anywhere near French Girl, likely because she was hot. The pizza that Buck had ordered and Ronnie had paid for was the only thing he seemed to feel any comfort with. His eyes focused on the pizza box the moment he found his balance and adjusted his pants. But he was still too nervous to make a move.

Meanwhile, Ronnie stared at him, mouth agape. Tiffany flicked her attention at him in the second between staring at her index fingertip and her middle one, but she wasn't bothered by him one way or the other. And French Girl had yet to even notice him. If she had an opinion about him, she hadn't expressed it yet.

And that was the extent of Garrett Nedmeyer's effect on tonight's party: present but nonintrusive; timid but existing. Buck had gambled on his popularity by inviting him, and now he could see that he'd broken even.

With that, Buck stood by his front door and took an inventory of the scene before him. Minus Lila, everyone he'd wanted in attendance was now here. As far as Buck was concerned, this was about as good as the party needed to get. Of course, he had some board games lying around upstairs if he needed to spice things up a little. Nothing energized a group of friends like a heated game of Monopoly. But he'd break that out only if he needed it.

* * *

THE NIGHT STARTED OFF slowly enough, with Ronnie and Tiffany thumb wrestling between conversations about fake vacations they'd take together, French Girl wandering around the living room, looking at any object she could comfortably put in her hands, and Garrett staring at his lap, doing all he could to avoid looking at French Girl, probably because she was hot. But that slowness lasted only until someone knocked on Buck's front door for the fifth time that night.

At first, Buck didn't give it much thought. The lights flashing through his living room window had gotten his attention, but not enough to break him from his laughter at Ronnie and Tiffany's exploits. But as he got closer to the door, he wondered why anyone was even knocking. Unless Lila had changed her mind about attending, which was possible but unlikely given her home situation, whoever was knocking on the door wasn't invited.

He opened the door. And he about had a heart attack when he saw who awaited him.

"Grumpy Balser?"

The chunky rich kid from a few blocks away, high school-famous for hosting every party that mattered senior year, was standing on the other side, dressed in a slick white disco suit, and was accompanied by dozens of teenagers that Buck had never spoken to throughout all his student career.

"Someone tipped me off that there was a party here tonight. So, I'm here to populate it for you." He turned to the crowd and pointed them at the door. "Here you go."

Before Buck could step aside or protest, the crowd that was gathered on his lawn marched forward and pushed him out of the way. Next thing he knew, Ronnie and Tiffany were being edged off the sofa, and Garrett Nedmeyer was getting pushed into the kitchen. Meanwhile, every slice of pizza still in the box was now in a stranger's hand, while every loose object within view was getting examined or handled. Some girl had even taken it upon herself to turn on Buck's one-working-speaker stereo and dial in to some station that was playing Michael Jackson's "Thriller."

"I don't—" Buck was having trouble hanging on to the nearest surface as party crasher after party crasher swept past him.

"Don't mention it," Grumpy Balser said. "If you need anything else, I'll be home."

And with that, Grumpy returned to his car and left.

* * *

THE FLOW OF TRAFFIC into his two-story home was endless, or so it seemed, with two guests arriving for every one that left. If Buck had hired a ticket collector to man his front door, he'd surely have counted enough people to fill an entire high school by the time eleven o'clock rolled around. This was definitely not the party he'd envisioned earlier that day.

"You have so many friends," French Girl said as she fought against the tide of teenage bodies to reach Buck. Buck, in turn, was struggling to step more than five feet into his own living room. "Thought you had just one."

Buck wasn't sure how to respond to her comment. Technically, she was right.

"These aren't his friends," Ronnie said as he also struggled to meet Buck by the sofa lamp. "Buck, I don't know what to say. This feels like a disaster."

"Does anyone know how to get this crowd under control?" Buck asked. "Grumpy Balser just abandoned ship."

"Feed them barbiturates," Tiffany said. She crept up from behind the sofa and fell in step beside Ronnie. "Fall asleep in minutes."

"That doesn't get rid of them, babe," Ronnie said. "That just gives Buck a human carpet. Not what he needs right now."

"Chase them out with broom?" French Girl asked.

"Or you could lure them outside with a keg," Lila said.

Buck spun around and did a double-take.

"Lila? When did you get here?"

She was standing on the other side of a kid that Buck had vaguely remembered from geometry class.

"Few minutes ago. Had to park at the end of the street. Didn't think you were so popular."

"Me, either."

An older, taller guy, roughly in his mid-twenties with shaggy hair and a scruffy beard, was standing past her shoulder, casting his eyes on every attractive woman in the room at chest level, including French Girl.

"This is Damon," Lila said. She slapped him on the cheek. "Hey, you're here with me. Eyes off the competition."

The scruffy guy refocused his attention on Lila. Then he smirked and rolled his eyes at her. "Guy can dream. What's the harm?"

"You'll go broke with all those paternity suits if you dream too hard."

"You know I got eyes only for you," Damon said, as he once again studied the bosom of the nearest attractive woman who wasn't Lila, Tiffany, or French Girl.

"I was hoping we could just hang out tonight," Buck said. "I wasn't expecting this insanity."

"How much is it costing you?" Lila asked.

"Well, so far, nothing. Ronnie bought the pizza. But I'm afraid to check the fridge. My mom's gonna be pissed if she comes home to find it empty."

"I still say you use the 'growing boy' defense," Ronnie said. "I'm telling you, it'll work."

Buck said nothing.

"So, you didn't blow all your earnings today on this monstrosity?"

"No."

Lila nodded. Then she cast her gaze off toward the kitchen, where several dozen people were blocking the path.

"So, I didn't waste my day?"

"No."

She reached past the kid from geometry class and patted Buck on the arm.

"Fun party then," she said.

"Yeah, but I still don't know what I'm supposed to—what the?"

Ronnie, Tiffany, Lila, French Girl, and the kid from geometry all followed Buck's gaze. A few feet to their south, Jennifer Mills was passing through the front door, which had been wide open since before ten. She didn't seem to know what to look at to find her footing, so she was looking at everything.

Jennifer was careful not to touch anyone as she edged her way into the house, but it was a losing proposition. Even as she held up her hands and maneuvered her shoulders around the human obstacles before her, they bounced into her like bumpers in a pinball machine. She got knocked this way and that for several feet before she lifted her eyes and saw Buck a couple of arm-lengths away. The anxiety on her face switched to relief when she saw him.

Buck's heart raced in that moment. Jennifer's hair was tied back, but her face was painted to accent her cheekbones. Normally, she worked at Melty's Wednesday nights, but she'd since changed out of her uniform and donned a pink dress that matched her lipstick. The sight of her reminded Buck of why he had been so infatuated with her during high school.

The sight of her also generated an unexpected heat radiating against the back of his right shoulder, from exactly where French Girl was standing.

"How dare you!" somebody screamed to his left.

Buck flinched. It wasn't the sexy voice of a hot European girl violating his ear, as he might've expected at that moment, but the nasally voice of a nerdy kid still trying to find its bravado. Garrett Nedmeyer lurched into Buck's view and barked at him. "You promised me!"

Buck didn't know how to respond.

"What's the matter?" Ronnie asked him.

"You promised me no one would give me a wedgie. You *promised!* My mom's gonna kill me!"

Garrett forced his way past the kid from geometry class, then Lila, Jennifer, and Damon, who was staring at Jennifer's chest. Lila watched Garret wiggle his bony ass free of his wedgie as he struggled past her, then noticed Damon's new line-of-sight and once again slapped him across the face.

"Dude!" she yelled.

"Let's play a game," Damon said. "Truth or Dare."

"Dude!" Lila slapped him again.

Jennifer, meanwhile, slipped past Lila and the kid from geometry class and found her spot between Buck and French Girl.

"Hi," she said, reaching out to rub his biceps. "How are you?" She nodded at French Girl, then set her sights back on Buck. "This seems fun. I didn't know you had so many friends. Thought you had just one."

Buck said nothing. He was too busy watching French Girl turning her back on him to have even a thought about how to respond to his beautiful ex-girlfriend's comment.

"Where's she going?" Jennifer asked.

The way tonight was going, Buck would've been lucky to have even one friend remaining by sunrise.

"Maybe she'll come back later." Jennifer smiled at him. "So, how are you? Anything new? You look great tonight."

All Buck could do was stare at her. Unfortunately, she looked great tonight, too. And that had the potential to become a big problem.

Buck was now convinced, officially, that tonight's house party was a bad idea.

Episode 37

Broken Things

Each room in the house was packed with party guests, but Buck felt distant from everyone. Even as he stood crushed among his small parcel of friends within the mass of surrounding strangers, having Jennifer once again standing so close after so many weeks of separation made him feel like an alien inside his own home, and he didn't know what to do with that feeling.

"Why are you here?" he finally asked, after struggling to find the words to say.

"Grumpy Balser invited me," she said. Her smile was nervous but hopeful.

Buck tried looking over her shoulder and ultimately at the front door.

"Probably should've expected that. Anyone come with you?"

"No, just me. Really, you look great tonight."

Buck wasn't ready to believe her, not about being alone. Even though things between her and Chet were tense, Buck remembered how quickly she'd switched allegiances to his nemesis that first time. Chet might not have come here with her hand-in-hand, but that didn't mean he hadn't followed her in shadow. If they were fixing things, then it was possible he would exploit that trust to gain a foothold into Buck's private world and destroy him if he'd known Jennifer was coming.

"You sure?"

"Yeah, I love that tie on you."

"I mean, about coming alone."

Jennifer reached for his chin and turned it toward her.

"I'm alone," she said, as half a dozen people flowed in around her. "Promise."

"You say Grumpy invited you?"

She nodded.

"Did you know it was going to be at my house?"

She nodded.

"And you came anyway?"

She stroked his shoulder.

"I'm your friend now. This doesn't have to be weird."

"You're wearing that dress that I…well, you know how much I like it when you wear it."

"You like it now?"

Buck said nothing. He searched the crowd for French Girl, who had since retreated into the human depths of party darkness, drifting further into the black edges of the living room, where she'd soon get sucked into the turbulent wilds of the dining room, never to be seen nor heard from again, at least not tonight.

"Dare!"

Damon's voice broke Buck out of his desperate situation.

"No," Lila said. "We're not playing. Too many people around."

Damon's sudden intrusion also stole Jennifer's attention. "Ooh, Truth or Dare." She elbowed Buck in the ribs. "Fun game, right? So many possibilities."

Lila, meanwhile, pleaded with Damon to let the suggestion die.

"Come on," Damon said. "I dare you to get some Action Jackson with me on the couch in front of all these people." He gyrated his hips at her to emphasize his request. "Imagine the stories to follow. We'd be legends."

"I said no."

"Think about it! What a memory that would give us, am I right? Call the newspaper. We're gonna set a new town record. Don't say no. Say, hell yeah."

Lila slapped him across the face. "Draw a line, jerk. We're not having playtime in *this* sandbox."

"Didn't stop you at my boss's party last week."

Lila growled at him.

"What we did at your boss's house didn't involve a spectacle."

"You sure about that?"

"It was in the garage, on the hood of his Mercedes, and it was really, really fast. It wasn't in a living room, on a couch, in front of the *other guests*. What you're suggesting now is inappropriate. The answer is no."

"My boss loves that car. How is this worse?"

"Okay, then, let's be decent guests *this time*. Unlike your boss, I actually like Buck and his friends."

Damon growled back at her. But his growl fizzled out. Lila was standing firm in her decision. She had the hands on her hips to prove it. Damon had to back down—it was clear in his eyes—but he still backhanded a ghost out of frustration.

"Well, if you won't do it, then I'll find someone who will. I didn't come here just to sit around and talk to people."

Lila threw her hands up. "Shall I get a camera then?"

Damon said nothing. His eyes had already gone back to search and destroy mode.

Buck stood frozen as he processed the scene he had witnessed, but then he realized what was about to happen. He snapped out of his trance and took Jennifer by the hand. He pulled her toward the stairs.

"Let's get out of here, quick," he said.

* * *

A FEW MINUTES LATER, Buck was sitting on a sheet-covered recliner in the attic, with Jennifer sitting across from him, and Ronnie and Tiffany, who had also sensed danger from Damon's new mission and had to get the hell out of there, fast, sharing an adjacent polyester sofa between them. They each exchanged glances, but none of them said a word.

Meanwhile, at the edge of the nook where they'd found the furniture, a clock was ticking, reminding them that the night was getting later, even though the party was nowhere near dying, as was evidenced by the thrum of chatter and stereo music on the floors below. Buck's grandfather's old clock (just a wall clock with mechanical arms and a cracked frame, not an actual grandfather clock) was sitting on a rickety wooden table, still counting the minutes to midnight, as it had done nonstop since the late 1970s.

Buck got up and checked the time. His mom would be home in a little over two hours.

He sat back down without a word.

A few minutes after they'd escaped to the attic, Buck had heard footsteps beating on the stairs beneath the entrance. His spine went rigid as he worried that another hundred people would suddenly burst into the space and shove them all into a corner where the roof dipped toward the boarded floor. But the footfalls reversed course, leaving them once again to claim the space as theirs alone. That was the only reminder they had of what was going on beneath them since taking refuge in the attic. From that point on, it was uncomfortably quiet, save for the constant mud of party noise setting the ambiance from below.

After another round of awkward silence, Ronnie was the first to make a noise. He cleared his throat.

"Are we having fun yet?" he asked.

Everyone glared at him. Buck's face was wet with sweat. Jennifer's dress was darkening around her neckline. Tiffany was fanning herself with a magazine she'd picked up from a pile of literature beside the attic's entrance hatch. Ronnie himself was soaked through his armpits.

"Who even tipped Grumpy off?" Buck decided now was the time to ask.

Ronnie's hand twitched, but he made no commitment to raise it.

"Wasn't me," he said.

Buck examined his friends' follow-up expressions, looking for a tapping foot or an eye pointed in the wrong direction. Everyone who knew about the party either was sitting in the attic or wandering around aimlessly in the wasteland of compressed teens below. None of the party crashers themselves could have tipped him off. Buck wasn't ready to believe him.

"You sure?"

Ronnie sank deeper into the couch and pinched the bridge of his nose. He looked like he might've been getting a headache.

"Grumpy and I don't talk." He glanced at Tiffany. "Babe?"

"I don't even know the guy."

Buck felt a tightness in his gut. The stress of the situation was building inside now.

"Someone tipped him off," he said. "This is crazy."

"Was it Garrett?" Ronnie asked, loosening his shirt from his skin.

Buck stared at him. "Really?"

"I mean, besides me and Tiffany, who else knew?"

Only two other people, Buck realized. One of them was a foreigner who didn't know anyone from Hybrid High, except for Buck and his circle of friends. The other invitee knew more people locally, but she was also a few years older and less likely to have associations with students from the high school as they did.

If Lila was the leak, then she likely leaked by association.

Either way…

"I have to get these people out of here," he said after another moment of silence.

"How do you expect to do that?" Tiffany asked. "If you can't get them to drink your coffee, what makes you think they'll listen when you ask them to leave?"

"They drink my coffee."

"After *we* sell it. You think Ronnie and I can convince these people to leave when they're having so much fun?"

Buck was too tired to argue with her. Whether she had a point, he didn't care. He just wanted everyone to go home. Throwing a house party of any size was a bad idea.

"I dare you to try," Buck said.

Ronnie, whose back was gradually slouching into the couch cushion, perked up.

"You dare us?" he said. "You *dare* us?"

Buck knew Ronnie too well to ignore what he was doing here.

"Yes," Buck said. "I dare you. *Dare* you."

Ronnie got to his feet and tugged at his shirt collar. The front of his shirt unstuck from his chest.

"Challenge accepted. Babe, we have a mission to accomplish."

Tiffany rolled her eyes at him, but Ronnie didn't take the slight. He took her hands and pulled her off the couch. "Come on. Let's tell 'em we saw a skunk run in."

Tiffany's feet skidded along the floor as Ronnie dragged her toward the attic's entrance. Each footfall creaked under their weight, stabbing at the dull stillness punctuated by the distant commotion beneath them.

Once the door hatch closed behind them, Buck was once again alone with Jennifer.

Jennifer was rubbing her hands together between her knees. Buck, meanwhile, couldn't help but notice that her legs were close together, but not crossed. He fought the temptation to look toward her upper thighs.

"So, anything new since the last time we spoke?" Jennifer asked.

Buck forced himself to look in her eye where his gaze was safer.

"Had a pretty good sales day today."

She lifted her hands to make room for crossing her knees.

"I'm glad," she said.

Something was ticking in his ear. He thought it was his grandfather's clock. But it could've been his heart. Or maybe a time bomb.

"How are things between you and French Girl?"

Buck said nothing. He was too busy trying to figure out whether he'd heard something explode. According to the placid expression on Jennifer's face, he was probably just imagining it.

* * *

WHEN BUCK WAS IN high school, he'd shown competence in math and the sciences. He rarely missed a class or a homework assignment, and when he showed up, he sometimes raised his hand and answered a question correctly. If the teacher called on him, he still answered the question, sometimes correctly, even if he was nodding off.

But he was never a straight-A student. Sure, he'd acquired his fair share of A's, especially in the classes he'd grasped rather quickly, like math and science, but he didn't stick the landing in every instance. For example, during his first semester of chemistry, Buck had written on his test that the oxidation state for iron with three ions was *ironic*, not *ferric*, which was the correct answer. He realized his mistake after he'd turned in the exam, but by then it was too late.

That was often the way he'd fallen short of perfection in high school: he generally knew the answers (like that a chemical losing three electrons gives it an *–ic* ending), but he'd sometimes get his wires crossed. In the case of his chemistry test, he was thinking about the English literature test he had to take later that afternoon. An easy mistake, but a mistake nonetheless.

English was, of course, another course he understood well enough to pass, but never really excelled at. With English, he had to think through arguments and synthesize reading materials. Not his strength by any measure, but not outside his range of competency, either. Any time he had to express his thoughts on paper, he'd get a B or a C. Passing, sure, but not stellar. As a student at Hybrid High, passing was good enough.

So, Buck was a decent student in high school. But like all students, he had his trouble spots, and his primary source of pain came from the social sciences. In particular, Buck struggled with psychology. Even though he understood how the human body worked, hence his B in biology, the mind was a different beast, one he'd found himself tangled with whenever he thought too much about it.

Taming the human mind required understanding it, and Buck had a difficult time keeping up. He often earned a C for the homework he'd completed, but his test scores kept him on the lower threshold for most of the semester. He'd avoided a D because he earned extra credit by attending a few therapy sessions and writing a report about his experiences. But that C wasn't because he'd demonstrated an aptitude for psychology. The human brain just wasn't his thing.

As he sat in that attic across from Jennifer, trying to think of the answer to her tough question while he avoided looking at her thighs in relation to the length of her dress, all he could think about was the fact that he knew nothing about a woman's brain.

"Things are fine," he finally said.

Jennifer said nothing. On hearing his words, she glanced back down at her knees and nodded.

Almost a minute passed before she continued the conversation.

"Have you kissed her yet?"

Buck squirmed in his chair. She was getting too personal now. Why did she care?

And what if he hadn't? Or had? What business was that of hers?

The attic really was getting hotter by the minute. He tugged at his collar to separate it from his soaking neck.

"I came by Melty's a few weeks ago," he said, as he let his collar fall back in place. "Your coworker spat in my coffee."

Jennifer stared at him for a moment before bursting into a chuckle fit.

"Did you drink it?"

"It was actually Danny Goodboy's coffee. You know, that guy who works at Novelties Plus? She just thought it was mine, even when I told her it wasn't."

"But did you drink it?"

"Wasn't my coffee."

Jennifer gave him a look he knew all too well—that "are you sure" look.

"Wasn't my coffee," Buck reiterated.

She reset her knees as she readjusted her position in her seat. Now she was sitting sideways and stretching her legs over her chair's armrest. She used to do this whenever she wanted to get comfortable, especially when confronting entertainment. Most likely, she did it tonight for the same reason. She propped her elbows on the chair's backrest and angled herself to see Buck better.

"Why were you there then?"

"I told you, to get Danny his coffee."

"You sure you weren't there to check up on me?"

"We'd broken up by then."

"Obviously. Yet, you still dropped by knowing I could've been working."

"Danny paid me a dollar to go. I was doing a job."

"A dollar? You came by my work for a dollar?"

"I was desperate."

Jennifer studied him.

"You sure you weren't there to check up on me?"

"You kidding? I didn't really want to go. I was afraid you'd be there."

She recoiled at that comment. Her rising amusement suddenly fell away. Perhaps that was the wrong thing to say.

"Because I didn't think you'd want to see me," Buck clarified, taking a stab at damage control.

Jennifer nodded. His amendment seemed to appease her.

"That's fair," she said. "And maybe true at the time."

She slid her hip backward so that she could sit fully on her side. "But it's not true now. If I'm being honest, I've missed you. As a friend, of course. I know you're with French Girl now. But I still missed you." Even as she confessed her feelings, her face soured at the sound of French Girl's nickname escaping her mouth. "So, I'm not trying to move in on you or anything."

"Then why bring it up?"

She shrugged.

"I don't know. French Girl doesn't seem to like me. I shouldn't blame her, though, given my history with you. But you know. You might still like to know. Maybe."

Buck wasn't sure what the safe answer was, given his situation, so he went with the one that best represented the truth.

"Maybe," he said.

Jennifer smiled. But her smile was short-lived. Not even three seconds later, Buck's attic door burst open. Ronnie came stampeding in.

"Buck, you gotta get downstairs," he said. "Like, now."

"Why? What's going on?"

Ronnie was out of breath, but he tried to calm down by lowering his hands and centering himself.

"Well, a good thing and a bad thing has happened."

Buck waited for him to clarify.

"The good thing is that people are leaving, in a hurry."

"Great. That's what we wanted. You told them it was a skunk?"

Ronnie rolled his hand at Buck, indicating that there was more to the story.

"No. That brings us to the bad thing. Come on, you gotta get down there."

"What's the bad thing, Ronnie?"

Ronnie jabbed his thumbs into his eyes.

"That Damon guy."

"Oh no, what?"

"Just…"

"Dude, get a broom, fast!" Tiffany screamed as she came bursting through the attic door. "He's almost got her pants off!"

Buck leapt from his chair. He didn't like the sound of that.

"Lila? What's he doing to her?"

Ronnie waved his hands at him.

"Not Lila. Samantha. From chemistry class."

"Samantha?" This was a new one. Buck couldn't recall…

"That really pretty dark-haired girl who always bragged about the guys she'd slept with? Samantha."

And that was all Ronnie needed to say. Now he remembered Samantha.

"Where are they?"

"On the couch. Where else? Buck, I don't know, man. We might already be too late."

Buck found an old lamp sitting on a dusty table by the attic door.

"I'll get them out. You guys finish kicking out the spectators."

He descended the stairs, muttering to himself just how bad an idea it was to throw this house party tonight. And to think it was only Wednesday.

* * *

B_Y JUST AFTER ONE in the morning, Buck had cleared out everyone who was left standing in plain view, but he didn't have time to check the hidden places in his house, like behind his mom's clothing racks or inside the kitchen pantry. His mom was due home a little after two, so he had to clean up as much of the house as he could to cover his tracks. That meant putting the nook and cranny search on pause.

Before sending Ronnie, Tiffany, and Jennifer home along with the stragglers, he asked them to help straighten the place.

In reality, however, it was a fool's task. The house was a mess from top to bottom. Even if his mom came home at two in the afternoon, he still wouldn't have had enough time to clean up. With tables overturned, sofa cushions in the plants, and a small flood coming out of the upstairs bathroom and down the stairs, Buck was in for a rough night. She was going to find out.

And then there was the living room sofa itself. Buck still shuddered at the memory of what he'd seen. Not a second passed that he didn't want to apologize to Ronnie and Tiffany for having to witness the travesty of what had transpired on that couch alongside him. But he decided that the less they spoke of it, the better. They could each process the nightmare in their own way.

"You want me to hang this picture of your dad back on the wall?" Ronnie asked. He was standing on the stairs' lowest step.

"Sure."

Ronnie struggled to find his footing as he reached up to the nail where the photo used to hang. His hand trembled as he tried setting it in place. Then he dropped the picture frame onto the step below.

"Sorry," he said, as he bent down to pick it up.

"Sure."

Tiffany, meanwhile, sat in the corner of the room, staring into space. Her knees were pressed against her chest, and her arms were wrapped around them. She was also shaking. Jennifer knelt beside her, trying to rub some comfort into her shoulders. Unlike the others, Jennifer had stayed behind in the attic during the…incident, so she'd missed all the horror.

Buck plugged the living room lamp back in. It was chipped but not broken. He could still turn it on, though he didn't want to for fear of seeing the sofa more clearly. He turned his attention to the dining room in case he needed to fix anything in there.

"You want me to hang this picture of your dad back on the wall?" Ronnie asked.

"Sure," Buck said.

Truthfully, he didn't care where Ronnie hung his dad's picture right now because Ronnie was just going to drop it again.

* * *

Buck sleepwalked through the house, looking for furniture to set right, but he was still aware of the time. By 1:45, he had to send his remaining guests home. The house was still a wreck, but he could blame it on himself if his mom got mad. She often complained that he was becoming a careless teenager, so he figured he could bank on that assumption this time. But it would work only if his friends were gone. So, he escorted them out to their cars.

And that's when he saw the El Camino parked along the road a few houses down.

The four of them shambled down the street to investigate. When they got to the car, they found Lila resting her head against the wheel.

Buck knocked on the window. She lurched backward in surprise, then relaxed when she saw him looking in. She rolled down the window. Her eyes were blotchy from sleeplessness. Or something else.

"Hey," she said.

"Hey, are you all right?"

Lila rubbed her eyes and smiled.

"Of course I'm all right. Never better. Just got really sleepy all of a sudden. Thought I'd crash here until I recovered. Why do you ask?"

"It's just—"

"Your boyfriend's a bit of a…" Ronnie added but couldn't finish the thought. He looked at Tiffany for help, but she offered none, as she was still in a daze. "He's a bit of a…"

"Chet," Jennifer said.

And with that, Lila nodded and burst into tears.

SEVERAL MINUTES PASSED BEFORE Lila calmed down enough to reenter a reasonable state of communication, but even then she was snorting and sniffling too much to complete her sentences. Through the tangled mess of her choked-up words, Buck could extrapolate from her an apology and regret for bringing Damon to the party, but something else hid behind her words, and she wasn't making much effort to conceal it.

"I need to (sniff) just be alone (snort) for a little while. If you don't mind."

Jennifer and Tiffany each took turns patting her shoulders, telling her it would be all right, that she was beautiful, and that she'd get through this, whatever this was. Buck and Ronnie, on the other hand, took progressive steps backward until they could no longer see Lila through the gap between Jennifer and Tiffany's arms.

"What do we do now, little camper?" Ronnie whispered.

Buck's head was full of uncertainties and scenes of abstract confusion. Between having his house crashed by almost an entire high school's worth of teenagers, spending time in an attic alone with Jennifer a month after their breakup, and witnessing…whatever the hell happened on his sofa, Buck had no sensible words to contribute to the situation.

He simply felt dead inside.

"Seek therapy, I think," he said.

Ronnie stared off into the night shadows outlining the neighborhood's trees, cradling his top hat to his chest. He rocked it like a baby.

Buck patted Ronnie's shoulder. They'd all get through this. But regardless of the mess made of his mind, Buck remembered his mom was due home any moment now. They had to wrap this party up once and for all.

"Can you get home all right?"

Ronnie shrugged. "I'll manage."

Buck nodded. Then, a moment later: "Hell of a night, right?"

"Hell of a night, little camper."

And with that, they said nothing more.

Buck turned toward the El Camino one last time to make sure everyone was calming down and able to leave safely, but something distant under an amber streetlight stole his attention away.

A young brunette in a flowery dress was sitting alone on the sidewalk just shy of the stop sign. Like Ronnie, she was staring off into the sky, seemingly unaware of her own existence.

Buck patted Ronnie's shoulder again, then headed off toward the brunette. Once he got within speaking distance of her, he called out her nickname.

French Girl offered him a quick glance but then turned her back on him.

"I thought you'd left," he said, as he sat beside her.

"I did."

"Then why are you sitting here?"

She shrugged.

"Afraid to walk home alone."

"City's not that dangerous at night, at least not around here."

She turned her head enough to offer him a sidelong glance.

"Not what scares me."

Buck looked at the tiny El Camino, which was now a block away, and wondered if he understood French Girl's private fear better than she'd thought.

"How long have you been sitting here?"

"Don't know. Hour, maybe?"

"Did you see anything strange at the party before you left?"

This question prompted French Girl to turn and look at him directly. Even under the amber light, her face was ashen and hollow.

So, she'd seen what Buck had seen.

He dared to put his hand on her shoulders to comfort her. But she squirmed out of his reach. Message received. He put his hands back in his lap.

"Want me to walk you home now?"

"*Oui.*"

So, Buck took French Girl home, but they spoke very little along the way. Either she was exhausted or pissed at him, and Buck had no desire to ask which was truer. But when they finally got to her front door, she thanked him for keeping her safe.

"So, are we okay then?"

She shrugged.

"Need time to think. Tonight bad. Don't like your friends."

"Those people weren't my friends. My friends were the ones there before the chaos."

"Also don't like blonde girl."

"Jennifer?"

"*Oui.*"

"I don't know what to say. I didn't invite her. She just showed up."

"But you spend night in attic with her?"

Buck froze where he stood. How did French Girl even know about that? Unless Ronnie or Tiffany had found her and told her…

"We just talked while riding out the storm. Nothing else."

French Girl put her fingertips against Buck's cheek and smiled.

"Still not happy."

"You could've joined us, you know. If you knew I was up there…I don't know why you didn't just come up and join me."

"Don't want to be around blonde girl."

Buck said nothing. He was too tired to press this issue any other. French Girl removed her hand from his cheek and reached for the front doorknob.

"Well, I home," she said. "*Au revoir.*"

"Can I call you tomorrow?"

She unlocked the door and slipped inside. Before she closed it, she held his gaze.

Buck waited for her to answer. But she said nothing. Just closed the door behind her and locked it.

So that was it, then. That was her answer.

Buck made it three steps down the front walk before he collapsed sideways into the grass and let the tears pour out. But he'd hardly gotten a drinking glass's worth of water out of his eyes when something clicked behind him. The front door creaked open in the night stillness.

Buck wiped his eyes as he spun around, but he felt his spirits drain away again when he discovered it wasn't French Girl who came out to meet him. Mack lumbered down the walk and knelt in the grass beside him.

"Rough night?" he asked.

"You have no idea."

"French Girl raced into her bedroom and slammed the door shut, so I figured something had happened between you. What's wrong?"

Buck told Mack briefly about his day at the beach and the party to follow, then went into vivid detail about the incident that had killed the night for everyone. Mack nodded along at every turn, as if everything Buck had said was house party clockwork. When Buck finally got to the part about Lila crying in her car, Mack held up his hand and told him that was enough.

"It could've been worse," he said.

Buck shot him a look. "How?"

"Your mom could've come home early."

Buck was too horrified by his memories to imagine how it might've been made worse. But he knew, intellectually, that Mack was right.

"Will we ever get past this?" he asked after a short pause.

Mack gave him that "yeah, sure" look that signified everything would be okay.

"Not likely you'll forget. I still remember when it happened to me. But once you flip those cushions over, you'll return to normal in no time."

"It happened to you?"

"Of course. My wife and I laugh about it to this day."

Buck frowned. Now he wasn't sure which side of the couch Mack was speaking from, and he didn't want to find out. At any rate, he was done talking about it.

"Will Lila be okay?"

Mack thought about the question.

"Not for a while," he said. "She'll need her friends."

"Because her lifestyle—"

"She'll need her friends. She's not well. Hasn't been for a while."

Buck rubbed the last tear out of his eye.

"Okay. Thanks for the talk."

Mack squeezed the back of his neck and rocked him forward and back as a dad might've rocked his teenage son after hitting a home run or, perhaps, someone else's car, depending on the situation.

"Sure thing. By the way, you still not coming in this weekend?"

"Yeah, like I said. I have to win this bet with Chet. Can't jeopardize it. My freedom's on the line."

Mack nodded.

"I understand. All right then. Position's still open when this bet expires." He got to his feet. "By the way, tomorrow's Thursday, right?"

"Yeah."

"Need any folding chairs or anything for your business?"

"Um…maybe? I don't know."

"Fair enough." Mack tapped him with his toe. "Do yourself a favor. No matter your plans, go to Happy Homewares tomorrow. Maybe they'll have a sale on lawn chairs. Maybe not. Either way, go there tomorrow, just in case. Make sure you go to the lawn department, and make sure you're there about three o'clock."

"Is it time-sensitive?"

"Sure is."

"Any chair in particular?"

"You'll know it when you see it." Mack helped Buck to his feet. "Good luck."

Buck thanked him for the tip, though he didn't know why Mack thought he needed lawn chairs. Or good luck. Regardless, it wasn't a bad idea. Maybe he could fit a couple into his budget. After all, people who drank coffee also liked sitting in lawn chairs.

He headed home after that, but he was in no hurry to get there. His mom was surely through the front door by now, and the last thing he wanted was to endure her exhausted rage after she'd seen the state he'd left their house in. If he walked slowly enough, he could probably get in after she'd gone to bed. But there was no guarantee she wouldn't develop a cleaning obsession on her way to her bedroom. If she had, then he'd have to face her no matter how late he got home.

It took him almost an hour and a half to get back, so he was surprised to see the El Camino still camped where Lila had parked it. When he approached the driver's side door, however, he found the car empty and her things gone.

He glanced up and down the road to see if she was sitting on the sidewalk as French Girl had a couple of hours earlier, but she was nowhere to be found.

"Lila?" he said into the darkness, in case it spoke back to him.

He got no answer.

Maybe she'd decided she was unfit to drive and walked home instead. Or maybe someone had picked her up. Either way, she wasn't here, so Buck had no more excuses standing between him and his front door.

He had to go inside now.

* * *

THE NEXT MORNING, BUCK awoke later than usual, but he still hadn't gotten much sleep. After his mom had spent almost an hour screaming at him for wrecking the house, he climbed into bed at five o'clock and passed out from exhaustion. Not even the fear of what may have transpired in his bed during the party crippled his willingness to conk out in it, and sleep stole him from the world of the conscious within seconds. But when he awoke after ten o'clock, the fear invaded his stirring mind, and he leapt out of his bed like a frog abandons a lily pad.

He brushed off his entire backside, just in case. Then he ripped the sheets off the bed and marched them into the garage, where the laundry machines were waiting. He shoved them into the washer and doused them with soap. Buck didn't do his own laundry often, but today would be the exception.

Once he got the washing machine started, he returned to his bedroom to pick out his clothes for the day. He preferred having them ready to wear when he got out of the shower.

But when he opened his closet, the wall of jeans split open, and three people from the party spilled onto the floor at his feet, forcing him to jump out of their way. They were so smashed from the night before that they'd hardly registered their impact with the ground. Their grunts were the only clue they gave to indicate they were even still alive.

Buck recalled his mom's reaction to the mess he couldn't clean in time, as well as the various events that had ruined his house party fantasy and degraded his soul. The shadows of his recollection suddenly angered him to the point that he hated these people, whoever they were, and he would make them pay for his lingering misery.

Either that or just ask them to leave.

"Go home!" he shouted, kicking them until they awoke.

The people, two guys and a girl, were clad in their underwear and were in no hurry to pick themselves off the floor, and they were in even less of a hurry to shuffle off into the hallway where they'd be excised into the living room and ultimately out the front door where the sun burned the eyes of the groggy.

"You see our pants anywhere?" one of the guys mumbled.

"I don't care," Buck said. "Get out."

The guy reached for one of Buck's jeans, but Buck swatted at his hand.

"Don't take mine. If you can't find yours, then keep them on next time."

The girl, meanwhile, found her skirt and pulled it on. She didn't know where her blouse was. The other guy grabbed a white tank top off Buck's dresser. Buck didn't recognize it, so he let him have it.

"Ten more seconds and I get the broom," Buck said.

The girl found her blouse under the bed, and the second guy found his shorts beside it. The girl headed for the door as she pulled her blouse down over her head and toward her waist. The second guy hopped after her as he put on his shorts. The first guy, meanwhile, was still looking for his clothes. They weren't under the bed.

"I can't find them, man."

"Five seconds."

"Dude, I can't find my clothes."

"Then stay home next time."

And so, by 10:15 on a Thursday morning, Buck had ejected a guy, a girl, and a dude who was still in his underwear onto his front lawn and locked the door behind them. By 10:18, he had found a mysterious set of clothing that was too big for his body inside a pillowcase when he'd stripped his pillows for the laundry room.

He threw the clothes out onto the street. Then he went back in to take his shower.

***

Day 32: Thursday, July 11, 1985

Buck's Savings Account: $1.00

Buck's Wallet: $296.81

Buck's Business Funds: unknown

Buck's Expenses: $2 a day*

Hours of Operation: pending

Money on Hold: $159.44 (2 days)

WHEN BUCK STEPPED OUTSIDE a little after eleven o'clock, he looked down the street to see if Lila had come back for the El Camino. But it was still there. He checked the driver's side in case she'd returned and fallen asleep, but it was still empty. He went back inside and called the Chamber of Commerce's office phone. Ernest Bee answered, so he hung up.

When he called Lila's home phone and some dude answered, probably Damon, Buck pulled the plug out of the phone dock, then hung up.

If Lila was out of commission for the day, then Buck would have to sell coffee on his own skill. But because she was the one with the keys, he couldn't exactly load up the car as he had yesterday. So, once again he'd have to figure out how to get sales out of his driveway.

Or go somewhere that he could set up without needing a car to get there.

* * *

THE ALLEY OF PINES was the strip of road that ran north and south between Buck's neighborhood and the east side of downtown and stretched as far north as the Pine Alley Drive settlement. It was a commercial gray zone where people could hawk their wares if they really wanted to, but they had no guarantee of success thanks to how few people were interested in any business east of downtown.

It was close enough to Buck's house that he could drag a card table and a box of coffee equipment to the nearest corner without too much strain on his body, but not so close that people would think he was running a neighborhood coffee stand. Depending on traffic through the area, it had about as much sales potential as the Coffee Pavilion had at the park.

Buck found a shaded spot comfortable enough to justify his setting up his table a few blocks north of his street and on the corner opposite the old newsstand that resident old-timer, Noah Nash, was still running. When Buck pulled the table legs into place, old Noah called out to him.

"Hey, Buck! Haven't seen your dad in a while. He stop reading the news or something?"

"Or something." Buck set the table upright, then reached down for the coffeemaker. But he didn't know where to plug it in. "Hey, you have an electrical outlet over there?"

"Sure do. Whatcha selling?"

"Coffee. Want a cup?"

Noah Nash waved Buck over. "Sure do. Why don't you come set that table over here? Coffee and a newspaper. What a novel idea!"

And so, Buck crossed the street and set his table up next to Old Man Noah Nash. By two o'clock, he'd learned that pairing coffee with a newspaper was worth twenty-six sales and over fifty dollars.

* * *

After packing his shop and thanking Mr. Nash for sharing a power outlet for his coffeemaker, Buck returned home to get his bike. While there, he called Lila to check that she was all right, but he still couldn't reach her.

Meanwhile, the clock was nearing 2:30, and Mack had suggested Buck visit Happy Homewares at around three, so with nothing else on the agenda for the day, he hopped on his bike and headed off to see what was so special about these lawn chairs.

Once Buck arrived and headed for the lawn and garden department, he went straight for the outdoor furniture aisle. According to the tags, most of them sold for between forty and two hundred dollars, but none were on sale that he could see.

When he asked the department's cashier for more information, she told him she hadn't heard of any sales, but it didn't mean there weren't any coming soon.

She used the intercom to call the floor assistant over. A moment later, the assistant slipped into the aisle behind Buck and asked the cashier what she needed. She told him "the gentleman," meaning Buck, wanted information on upcoming sales. The assistant told her, sure, let him just consult his sales book.

Buck closed his eyes and shook his head. He'd "know it when he saw it," Mack had said. When Buck finally turned to face the assistant, he confirmed with his eyes what he'd already recognized with his ears. Chet in the store's uniform leaned over a glossy advertisement full of yard items that one might buy at Happy Homewares.

CHET WAS FOCUSED ON the advertisement, so he didn't notice Buck watching him at first. But the moment he set the literature down to address his customer, his skin flushed almost to the color of his hair.

Buck tapped his fingers against the counter as if to tell him he was waiting for an answer. Chet said nothing. His countenance steadily moved from surprise to defensive. Within seconds, he was edging on his heels, either in preparation to dodge a punch, or to run.

The cashier, meanwhile, gestured to Chet to answer. He made no such response.

"Would you like me to consult your advertisement for you?" the cashier asked him.

Chet said nothing. He just kept his eyes focused on Buck as he threw the advertisement at the cashier's chest. The glossy pages flapped open and split off into loose layers as it smacked her.

"That was rude."

"This twerp's no customer." Chet, now rocking forward on the balls of his feet, stepped closer to Buck. "He's a trespasser."

"Actually, I came here for information about lawn chairs," Buck said.

"Wrestlers use them in battle," Chet said. "Shall I demonstrate?"

Buck had seen too much horror in the last twenty-four hours to fear this guy anymore. He stepped closer, almost enough to see the pores on his pasty face.

"Yes, please do, you conniving liar."

"What's going on here?" the cashier asked, no longer interested in the advertisement.

Chet pushed Buck against the chest, sending him backward so hard that he had to spin and catch himself on the counter to stop himself from falling.

"Guy talk," Chet said. "Doesn't concern you."

"Sir?"

Buck corrected himself and gestured to the cashier that he was fine.

"Guy talk," he echoed. "This is how we chat."

Before the cashier could react, Buck lunged forward and ran his shoulders into Chet's stomach. Chet let out an audible gasp, but he caught Buck's momentum and threw him back into the counter. Thanks to all the bully outsourcing Chet had done senior year, Buck had forgotten how strong he was.

"Wow, Tommy must've been going easy on me," Buck said, catching himself and correcting his stance. "He never threw me against a wall like that."

"I've been working out."

Chet lunged forward to attack, but Buck hopped over the queue railing to avoid him. Chet overstepped his intended resistance point and had to catch himself on the counter to prevent falling.

The cashier, meanwhile, apparently no longer interested in "guy talk," directed her attention back to the advertisement.

"You shouldn't have come here, twerp," Chet said, as he came stomping around the metal queue. "I've got allies."

"You shouldn't have come to the Shop Down the Street. I've also got allies."

Chet was now on him. Buck had to step backward to avoid a leg sweep.

Guy talk just got serious.

Chet was several inches larger and almost twenty pounds heavier. Buck shouldn't have come here. But now that he was here, he realized it was time to run.

Without another thought, Buck sprang away as Chet righted his stance and lunged forward with a fist to the cheek. He missed him by a few inches, but it was enough to put Buck into flight. Rows of garden plants raced by as he sought shelter in the tools aisle ahead.

A potted orchid hit him in the back, launching him forward and sending him to his knees. He rolled across the floor on impact.

His body ached now, but he didn't stay grounded. Adrenaline now spiking, he jumped to his feet and scrambled forward as another potted orchid came crashing down to his right, splattering soil all over his jeans.

"Why are you running?" Chet asked. "What are you afraid of?" He sounded out of breath.

Another pot launched over Buck's head and came down six feet ahead. He leapt over the explosion of dirt to follow.

"I hear you're trying to win Jennifer back. Why would she ever go back to a twerp like you?"

Buck wasn't sure where this information had come from, but the idea was scandalous enough that he almost stopped to deny it. But in his state of adrenaline, his body wouldn't allow for such a momentum shift. His feet, responsibly, overruled his pride.

When Buck crossed the boundary into the yard tools aisle, he dared to look over his shoulder. Chet was so close that flecks of his spit were landing on his neck.

Buck reached to his left and grabbed for the nearest item with a stick. He snatched a rake off the shelf.

When he turned and held the tool in a defensive stance, he discovered, to his regret, that Chet was pulling a machete down from the higher shelf, which Buck couldn't reach without a stepladder.

Chet brandished the machete over his head as if he'd already won the battle.

Buck took a step back. He had a much longer reach with the rake, but the ends were made of flexible metal and would hardly scratch Chet, much less cause him injury. The machete, on the other hand…

"Yield," Chet said, as he pointed the saber at Buck.

Buck pointed the rake at Chet.

"Never!"

Chet lowered his machete and roared with fake laughter. Then he grabbed the rake by the handle and yanked it from Buck's grip and flung it aside.

He pointed the machete at him again.

"I said, yield."

Buck balled his hands into fists.

"Then what?"

Chet said nothing.

"Then what?" Buck asked again.

Chet stared at him for several seconds. He had nothing to say.

"Then what?" Buck asked a third time, now frustrated.

Chet closed his eyes and shook his head. He tossed the machete to the side.

"Man, I don't know. That's just what you're supposed to say when you draw a blade on someone's throat."

Buck unclenched his fists. His eyes focused on the machete on the floor. Then on the rake. Then back onto Chet. Chet's shoulders were heaving as he tried to catch his breath, but the fire in his eyes was dimming.

"Does that mean we're done now?"

Chet ran his fingers through his eyes and stretched his back.

"Yeah, I guess so." He stared at Buck for a moment. "Were you seriously going to hit me with a yard tool?"

"You've spent most of high school torturing me. I'm done with that crap."

Chet nodded.

"Fair enough."

Buck relaxed a little now, but he wasn't yet ready to drop his guard.

"Were you seriously going to cut me with that machete?"

"Dude, get real. I'm at work." Chet's eyes turned fiery again. "But don't think this is over. I won't be at work forever."

Buck moved closer now, but he sidestepped Chet as he got within striking distance. He was ready to leave Happy Homewares.

"So, now that I know about this, are you going to keep working here?"

"Of course. I take my job seriously."

"Then we agree that if you stay here, then I get to work at Shop Down the Street a couple days a week?"

Chet said nothing. Buck was now past him and moving closer to the garden plant display.

"Do we have an agreement?" Buck said.

Chet bent down and picked up the machete. The rake was out of Buck's reach.

"Chet? Do we have an agreement?"

Chet stared at the machete and flipped it around in his hand. He tossed it into a spin and caught it by the handle. As it landed in his palm, he glanced at Buck, then cocked his arm back as if to throw.

Buck flinched as Chet flung his arm forward.

But Chet never released the machete. He just turned on the balls of his feet and put the weapon back on the shelf as a stock boy would, laughing his ass off.

Buck returned to the counter without an answer. On his way past the queue, the cashier told him that the lawn chairs wouldn't be on sale until Labor Day.

"Have a great day," she said, as Buck headed for the exit. "Thank you for, er, shopping at Happy, er—"

* * *

BEFORE HEADING HOME, BUCK swung by Park Center Park to spy on the Liquid Shack, and as he suspected, Tommy and Pigeon were running the place in Chet's absence. Tommy spotted him from across the parking lot and waved him over. But Buck pretended not to see him. At least not at first. Just as he was about to ride out of the park, however, he felt a nagging at the back of his mind that he shouldn't be rude to Tommy, especially considering Tommy was usually nice to him when not taking orders from Chet. So, he made a U-turn and crossed the parking lot to greet his sometimes friend.

Once he parked his bike, he asked him if Chet was there, knowing full-well that he wasn't.

"Yeah, Chet hasn't been around much lately," Tommy said. "His dad is sick or something."

"That's too bad," Buck said, knowing full-well that it wasn't.

Buck noticed out of the corner of his eye Pigeon leaning forward at the serving table and staring at Buck with an intense expression on his face, as if he were about to kill him. It was uncomfortable enough that he didn't want to look.

"Says he'll be here this weekend." Tommy poured Buck a cup of lemonade. "Want one on the house?"

Buck drank it. It had a grapefruit-raspberry taste.

"It's our latest, hottest seller."

Pigeon grabbed a raw lemon from a cooler by his feet and threw it at Tommy's head, knocking his hat loose.

"Don't give away our secrets," he said.

Tommy caught his hat before it flew off his head. Once it was fixed in place, he glared at Pigeon.

"You do that again, and I'll give away all of *your* secrets, including that ugly one."

Pigeon grew stiff. Without another word, he shuffled off to the restroom block.

"What secret is that?" Buck asked, when Pigeon was out of earshot.

Tommy shook his head. "Sorry, can't give that chip away for free. That one's my emergency card."

Buck almost asked him how much he wanted for it, but he stopped himself when he remembered every dollar counted, and he'd already spent two of them getting into the park.

"Fine, I'll drop it."

Just as he was about to turn and walk away, Buck had an epiphany. Since Chet and Pigeon weren't around, he figured he was safe to ask Tommy his thoughts.

"Any chance you'd want to work at the Coffee Pavilion for me when I'm allowed back in?"

This caught Tommy off guard. He nearly spilled the cup he was holding.

"Serious?"

"Just a thought. I could use more help. I'd be willing to pay you a little better than these guys."

Tommy glanced over his shoulder toward the bathrooms. Then he looked at the cup in his hand.

"I'll have to think about it. It's tempting, but maybe not so wise."

"How much would you want per hour?"

Tommy lowered his hat over his brow.

"It's not the money that keeps me here," he said.

"Then what is it?"

Tommy looked him in the eye.

"It's better for my health if I stay here." He handed Buck another cup of lemonade. "Yours, too, especially if you stop making those kinds of offers or inquiring about certain kinds of secrets."

* * *

BUCK RETURNED HOME THAT night after six o'clock. Once again, he checked the El Camino on his way by, and once again he found it empty. He tried calling Lila at the same places and got the same answers. Wherever she was, she'd disappeared off the map.

Now worried about her, he called Ronnie to check whether she'd gone to his or Tiffany's house, and when Ronnie said no, he called Mack to check whether she'd stayed the night with French Girl. Mack reminded him he was the one who had walked her home last night, not Lila. So, that left Buck with just one other person.

He dared to call Jennifer.

"Haven't seen her since last night," Jennifer said. "She asked us to leave her alone, so we did."

"Okay, thanks."

"How are you today?"

Buck hung up. He wasn't in the mood for small talk.

* * *

BY NINE O'CLOCK, BUCK had finished cleaning the house. In all, he'd counted fifteen broken items, which was far fewer than he'd expected or feared. Other than the sofa cushions, which he'd flipped on Mack's advice, though he really wanted to burn them, the house furniture survived the ordeal. He found a few scratches on the walls, and three of the picture frames were cracked. But most of them could be polished or replaced.

The worst damage appeared to be Buck's psyche, but he also found a broken pot in a corner of the family room past the dining room when he'd gone in there to clean. The plant that had called it home was leaning over the ping-pong table when he found it, and Buck didn't have an alternative container for it, so he left it there to deal with later.

Now that the house was mostly back to normal, Buck kicked off his shoes and turned on the television. He needed a good Thursday-night laugh. Fortunately, all the week's best sitcoms were on, so he was set for a good time.

And that good time lasted for about twenty minutes until someone knocked on his door.

When Buck opened it, he found Lila standing on the other side. She was wearing the same clothes from the night before, and she was carrying a duffel bag.

"Mind if I crash here tonight?" She entered the house without waiting for an invitation. "My car's hard on my back after a while."

She swept over to the sofa and was about to sit on it when she changed her mind and took the chair that Buck had been sitting in. "Yeah, this'll do."

Buck stood in the doorway, gobsmacked.

"Where have you been?" he asked. "I was starting to think you were kidnapped."

Lila's face softened as she glanced at him. She moved her hand to her chest.

"That's sweet, I think."

"Are you all right?"

She waved him off.

"Of course, I am. I just need a change of scenery for a minute, you know?"

Lila bounced in the chair a few times to test its durability.

"Think your mom would be okay with me sleeping in this chair tonight?"

Buck reacted to her question on instinct.

"No. I mean, I don't know. I'd have to explain to her who you are and all of that. She's already mad at me for last night's aftermath."

"You get grounded?"

"No, I'm eighteen. She's not going to ground me. But she might start charging me rent."

Lila nodded. "Yeah, I can see that."

"How long do you need to stay?"

"Just tonight, hopefully."

Buck considered the situation. He was glad she was safe. But he wished she were safe elsewhere.

"Would you mind sleeping in the attic? There's furniture up there, and my mom never goes up there. It would be more peaceful for you, and less combative for me."

Lila thought about the offer.

"If that's what it takes not to spend the night in my car, I'll take it."

"Okay then."

"Okay then." Lila smiled. "Thank you."

"Sure." Buck already hated the idea. His mom never went into the attic, but there was always the potential for a first time. "Enjoy your stay."

And so, Lila Deerborn would sleep at Buck's house tonight, in his hot attic where the dust gathered and the mice also slept.

"Great," she said. "So, where's your shower?"

* * *

A LITTLE AFTER TEN o'clock, Buck turned off the television and headed for his bedroom. But before he locked himself in, he climbed upstairs and listened to the ceiling. Lila had made a bit of a racket getting into the attic some time ago, but she seemed to have found her spot, so all was quiet now. He didn't want to go to bed until he knew she would be silent enough to avoid attracting his mom's attention.

When he was certain she had fallen asleep, he returned downstairs to his bedroom and retired for the night. After changing into his shorts and updating his ledger for the day's earnings and losses, he climbed into bed and turned off the nightstand lamp.

The digital clock under his lamp was now flashing the time in bold red letters through the dark. The window on the opposite side of the room had the shades drawn, but the neighborhood's ambient light seeped in through the edges. All was dark, save for the usual slivers of glowing things. Everything was as expected.

It was almost 10:30. Buck drifted off to sleep.

But his slumber didn't last. Something had woken him from a forgotten dream at 11:10.

Buck lay in bed listening to the stillness. The silence lingered for a moment, and he wondered if something in his dream had startled him.

But it happened again. A knock on his bedroom door.

He climbed out of bed. Shuffled across the floor. Unlocked the door and opened it.

Lila was standing on the other side. She was wearing just a gray T-shirt that extended halfway down to her knees. There was a picture of a kitten on it.

"It's too hot up there. Can't sleep a wink." She pushed past him and headed for his bed. "Hope you don't mind being short a pillow tonight because I'm taking one or two."

Instead of stealing a pillow, however, she hopped into the bed and shoved her legs under the sheets. Buck stood by his door, incredulous.

She noticed him staring at her, so she patted the space beside her.

"I'm not kicking you out of your own bed. Just need to share it for the night. More comfortable here."

Buck said nothing.

"Dude, it's fine. I'm just taking up a spot. No need to look at me like I'm a leper."

She patted the space on the bed again.

"We're friends."

Buck hesitated, but he decided she was right. No need to freak out right now. Nothing was going to happen. Besides, it would've been worse if he'd slept in the living room recliner. His mom would've found him there and asked why he wasn't sleeping in his own bed.

"Okay."

He locked the door and returned to his bed. As he pulled the sheets down to make room for himself, he noticed her shirt riding a little higher, but not so high that it betrayed anything. He hesitated moving any closer but then reminded himself that he also needed a pillow and a comfortable place to sleep. Regardless of who was lying there beside him, he needed his space so he could get his rest.

He climbed onto the bed and slipped his legs under the sheets, ignoring the thumping of his heart. Then he pressed his back against the mattress and held still.

Lila's breath reached the side of his neck, but just barely. She was keeping a respectable distance. Maybe this would be okay.

He turned his head slightly to glance at her in the neighborhood's ambient light. She was angled toward him, but her eyes were closed. She was already drifting off to sleep.

Buck relaxed a little. This was fine.

Lila opened her eyes and smiled. Then she lunged at him and pretended to bite him. He recoiled so hard that he almost knocked his lamp off the nightstand.

"Just kidding," she said, laughing. "Sheesh, you're wound up. Go to sleep."

Buck lay there for the next hour doing no such thing, not until he knew she was far off in dreamland. And then he parked his pillow on the floor because he still didn't want to take the chance that she'd wake up in the middle of the night and torment him.

But now he couldn't sleep, so an hour after that, he returned to bed, this time placing his pillow between them. He fell asleep the moment he turned his body away from her.

Then at 3:22, he awoke again. This time, he made no mistake about what had roused him from his newest dream. Lila was weeping just over his shoulder, and judging by the sound of it, she was doing so into her pillow.

Episode 40

The Park Bouncer

THE KNOCK ON THE door in combination with the continuous pressing of his doorbell late Thursday night was so loud and persistent that Chet was tempted to fling the door open at the intruder just to shut him up. But the door opened inward, not outward, so he was forced to suppress his fantasy and greet the obnoxious visitor the normal way.

Pigeon forced his way into Chet's living room the moment he turned the door handle.

"Some manners, Pigeon," Chet shouted.

But Pigeon ignored him. Just sat on the living room couch and parked his ass on the crocheted throw pillow Chet's mom had bought years earlier. He glanced around the room.

"Where's that hot chick you're dating?"

"At work. Don't worry about her. You and I need to chat."

"Got any beer?"

"Focus, Pigeon. We have a problem."

"What's that, boss?"

Pigeon bounced on the pillow, his hands between his knees. He was like a Doberman Pinscher tied to a fence just three feet shy of a steak.

"Buck came to Happy Homewares today."

"Yeah? So?"

Chet told Pigeon about how Buck had attacked him with a machete while he was trying to be a good employee to a dissatisfied customer.

"What a monster," Pigeon said. "Bastard!"

He elbow-jabbed the back of the couch and countered with a fist to a throw pillow.

"I need you to talk to our monster tomorrow," Chet said. "About whatever you think is important. But you *cannot* tell me how the conversation goes."

Pigeon saluted Chet and bounced right off the couch.

"Our conversation will be my secret alone," Pigeon said, getting to his feet.

"Good. Hopefully, you'll start making a habit out of keeping your secrets to yourself."

"So, how about that beer?"

"How about you go home now before you get me in trouble?"

Pigeon saluted Chet again. Without another word, he was out the door.

Chet spent the next five minutes pacing in his living room.

* * *

ON FRIDAY MORNING, BUCK awoke to two problems. The first was that a blonde woman lay beside him in bed, digging her face in the pillow, rubbing her left knee and most of her thigh along the mattress sheet less than a foot from his own thigh. Given that he was supposedly dating a brunette, this bore an aesthetic problem should French Girl come marching through his bedroom door. "It's not what it looks like," he'd say. But she'd never believe him. The rope they'd been walking since Jennifer had made a return in his life had tightened. Getting caught in bed with yet another blonde girl would bode unwell for him, even if his girlfriend was European and allegedly kissed with her tongue.

The second problem was that he didn't know how to get rid of the blonde girl.

Lila's face was half buried behind a baby blue pillowcase, but the visible part was experiencing an uneasy peace. Her eyes were closed, and her lips were flat, but the bags under her eyes were still puffy. She'd spent several minutes crying herself to sleep hours earlier, and Buck was in no hurry to invite those tears back into action. But he couldn't let her stay. At some point, he'd have to risk sending her into another emotional fit.

Buck went out to the kitchen to make himself some breakfast. He figured he'd deal with this conflict of interest later.

He'd gotten halfway through his bowl of cereal when his living room phone rang.

"Hello?"

"Buck Star? It's Rhett Rowe. You got a minute?"

Buck took another spoonful of frosted cornflakes. Started chewing. This guy had already cost him two hundred fifty dollars he couldn't afford to lose. He didn't care if he had to hear him chew his food.

"Shore." *Sure.*

Rhett Rowe spent the next five minutes telling Buck the situation with the Coffee Pavilion and its state of repairs. Apparently, things had moved along faster than expected.

"There's still a bit of red tape," the insurance adjuster said. "But unless something ridiculous happens, you should be able to set up shop again Monday."

Buck set his bowl on the coffee table. He'd been doing so well at the beach and the newspaper stand that he wasn't certain he wanted to return to North Park's most isolated pavilion on a hill.

"Will the Lease Agent refund me for the days I was out of operation?"

Buck had to hold the handset away from his ear when Rhett Rowe laughed so hard that he had a spasm.

"Okay," Buck said, once Rhett calmed down. "I'll plan to return then."

"Just be aware the storage room still has damage. You can store your stuff in it—as long as you don't put anything on the burnt parts of the shelf, nothing should hit the floor. But the lock is flimsy."

That nervous pang Buck sometimes got in his gut zapped him.

"I thought the pavilion was closed all week specifically to fix the damage."

Rhett Rowe laughed again, but with less heartiness. "No, this week was about assessing the damage and deciding when to reopen. The park, the bureaucrats, and the Lease Agent all agreed that it could return to operation Monday. As far as fixing it goes, they figure that'll take longer. Maybe a few months."

"To fix a few shelves and a door lock?"

"Welcome to adulthood, kid."

The conversation ended soon after that. Buck was left holding onto his phone and with no sense of peace. He would return to the pavilion on Monday, but he wasn't confident his inventory would remain safe overnight.

The best he could hope for was that Fourth of July was a special occasion, and no one would bother messing with it again for the rest of the summer.

He turned on the television to distract himself from everything he was thinking about. Hopefully, by the time the game shows ended, everything would've solved itself.

* * *

By just after ten o'clock, nothing had solved itself. Worse, Buck now had a third problem to deal with. Someone was knocking on his front door.

His heart raced. It could've been a door-to-door salesman making his daily rounds. His dad had once warned about them and the money they were likely to snatch if Buck was off his guard. *Just tell them you already own a vacuum*, he'd say. But now that Buck had learned something about the art of sales, he was confident he could send the guy off without a penny.

As he set his feet to the floor, however, he knew there was no salesman on the other side. Just a French girl looking to catch him in some dirty act that he wasn't committing, but one he had no way of proving otherwise.

He contemplated changing direction and heading for the kitchen—avoid conflict entirely—but French Girl kept knocking, and he didn't want her waking Lila. He'd have to answer the door and somehow convince her to leave. It would've been worse if she'd kept knocking, woken Lila, and Lila answered the door while still dressed in nothing but a long T-shirt. Because someone had to.

So, he would answer it first. Beat her to the punch.

Buck balled up his fists, took a deep breath, and opened the door, ready to face the accusatory stare of a European brunette who got jealous easily.

A strange but meaty fist arced at him and smashed him in the solar plexus. Buck gasped as the wind rushed out of him. Another fist followed, narrowly missing his cheek as he bowled over.

As his knees hit the floor, he looked up to find an enraged Pigeon Pollock standing outside his doorway, eyes wild and nostrils flaring, and his hands preparing for another strike.

Buck leaned sideways to grab the door with both hands. He was struggling for air, but his mind was now clear.

Pigeon took a step closer as Buck flung the door in his face. But Pigeon caught it and sent it back.

Buck rolled onto his back and kicked both feet into Pigeon's ribcage. This time, Pigeon fell backward and took a tumble into the grass. Buck slammed the door again, this time sealing it. He reached up and locked it before Pigeon could get up off his ass and retaliate.

The wind was finding its way back in as he grabbed for the umbrella stand to steady himself. Something pounded against the door. Buck crab-walked to his living room window to assess the situation.

Through the curtains, he watched Pigeon running halfway into the yard and running back with his shoulder angled in a battering position.

Thump!

Buck fell onto his recliner and sank into the cushions. The bullies had never come to his house before. They'd always kept it at school or somewhere public. He didn't know what to do now.

Whomp!

"You shouldn't have come to Happy Homewares!" Pigeon shouted at the door. "You should've stayed off our turf!"

Buck wondered if Pigeon understood the irony of what he was saying, if he understood irony at all.

"You crossed the line!"

A moment of silence. Then, *thump!*

"I'll make you pay!"

Thump!

Whomp!

Thump!

"What the hell is going on out here?" Lila rubbed her hair as she came into the living room on her tiptoes. Her shirt was about to betray her privacy.

Thump!

She glanced at the door. "You gonna answer that?"

Buck shook his head. "Go back to sleep. He'll get bored and wander off. Hopefully."

Whomp!

"Who?"

"Pigeon Pollock."

Lila was now alert. "The psychopath?"

Buck gestured at the door.

"He's mad about something that happened between me and Chet yesterday, or so it seems. I have no idea what he's on about."

Thump!

"He sounds like he wants to kill you."

"What else is new?"

Lila marched across the living room and peeked through the curtain.

"Something is glinting in his hand," she said. She glanced at Buck, worry now on her face. "A knife."

Whomp!

"Seriously?"

She bit her lower lip. Her eyes were fearful. No longer puffy. Just frightened.

"If he gets in…"

Buck slipped out of the chair and checked the window for himself. Lila wasn't lying. Pigeon was now racing at the front door with a knife in hand, angled at the door like an overhead dagger.

Thump! Skttch!

Buck went to the phone.

"Who are you calling?" Lila demanded.

"Police," Buck said. "Or he's going to hack up my door."

Whomp! Skttch!

Lila bounded onto him and forced the handset back into its cradle.

"No. If the police come, there will be witnesses."

Buck studied her face. She was scared. But also pissed. Her sad eyes were now mad eyes.

"What do you mean?"

She nodded at him. "You have a back door?"

Thump! Skttch!

"One out the family room, the other out the garage to the side, if you can get past the junk."

She kissed him on the cheek. "I'll go out the family room. If I don't make it back, thank you for everything."

"What do you mean if you don't make it back?"

Lila smiled at him, patting him on the cheek. Her eyes were softening, but they weren't anything close to peaceful.

Whomp! Skttch!

"I hope we can laugh about this someday."

"Laugh about what?"

She didn't answer. Just raced off to his bedroom, then the family room, as wild and pantsless as ever.

Thump! Skttch, skttch, skttch.

Buck looked through the curtain, clutching it in his palm. Pigeon was now carving at his front door.

Lila didn't want him calling the police for some reason, but that didn't mean he couldn't prepare himself for the worst. He searched his bedroom for a weapon. When he couldn't find one, however, he searched the garage. His choices were a golf club or a baseball bat.

He took both.

Back in the living room, he perched behind the window with both weapons in hand. Pigeon was once again in the yard, one shoulder in the battering position, the other supporting a raised dagger. Once again, he came charging at the door. Once again, the door banged against the doorjamb. How much longer it could endure his assault, he didn't know. At some point, it would splinter and break.

Whomp! Skttch!

Just past Pigeon to his left, presumably out of his line of sight, Lila was creeping across the front yard, low alongside the border hedge. Pigeon was too focused on the door to notice her. Once she made it to the sidewalk, she got on her bare feet and started running. She was out of sight within moments.

Thump! Skttch!

"I'm coming to get you!" Pigeon crooned. "Come out, come out, wherever you are!"

Buck watched the door. Daylight was showing in its upper right corner.

The phone was a few feet away. All he had to do was pick it up and call the police. The station wasn't that far away.

But Lila didn't want him to.

Except, now she'd left. Whatever she was thinking…

Whomp! Skttch!

"I'm almost through, you bastard! Hope you said your prayers!"

Skttch! Skttch! Thump!

Pigeon was right. The doorframe was splintering.

Even if he called the police, they'd never get here in time. Buck's stomach was clenched. The whole time he'd been Mr. Kabuki's student, he could've been learning karate. What was he supposed to do now? Throw hot coffee in Pigeon's face?

Actually…

Buck was just about to race for the kitchen when something obnoxiously loud stole his attention: an engine roaring, tires squealing.

He peeked through the curtain. His eyes went wide.

The El Camino bounced over his driveway, nearly wiping out his mailbox, and carved two deep tire tracks into his front lawn as it raced for Pigeon's position.

Thump!

Pigeon somersaulted backward onto the hood, over the roof, and into the bed in back as the car came to a stop less than two feet from Buck's window. Buck lurched backward out of reflex.

Lila sprang out of the driver's side and hopped over the bed wall.

Buck ran outside with the bat and golf club in either hand. Lila was in the back, shoving her heel repeatedly into Pigeon's gut. She was screaming something at him, but it was unintelligible. If they were curse words, they were new.

Buck held the bat up, ready to swing, but he didn't need to. Pigeon was trying to hold off Lila's kicks, but his defense was weak. He'd already submitted in defeat. His face was no longer angry. In fact, he had a weird smile on his face.

He was looking up her shirt.

* * *

AFTER LILA PUT ON some pants and she and Buck dumped Pigeon unconscious in some random shopping center parking lot twenty miles out of town, she took Buck home, thanked him again for being kind to her during her time of stress, and told him she'd spend the day looking for apartments. If she needed him, she'd call, but she expected to have a new place to stay by nightfall. Buck spent the rest of the morning cleaning up the mess Lila and Pigeon had made on his front lawn.

The front door would require a bit more effort, though. He called Ronnie over for help.

"I don't know, little camper. This is bad."

Ronnie had spent the better part of five minutes studying the damage done to Buck's door.

"I mean, it can be fixed, sure. But it'll take effort. Maybe more wood. Or wood glue. You have any wood glue?"

"I'm no carpenter."

"Yeah, me either. I could call my dad."

Buck shook his head.

"I don't want to involve your dad in this."

"Yeah, all right. He's at work, anyway. Apparently, there's another claim in the Lester Biggins situation. Someone else saying it's murder."

"I thought your dad handled fraud or theft cases."

"He does. But he's really interested in murder. Likes to know what's going on in those cases."

"Well, if it is murder, I hope it gets solved. But I still think it's just Lester getting too close to the edge when he should've been watching where he was going."

"Yeah, he was a klutz, wasn't he?"

Buck stared at his front door. Pigeon had gashed it good. But he was never getting all the way through with his knife. It was the shoulder-bashing that had caused the greatest trouble.

"Can't believe Pigeon came to my house," Buck said. "When does this end?"

"When he gets arrested for assault and battery."

Buck frowned.

"In other words, not until he gets caught in the act."

Ronnie put his hand on his shoulder.

"Aw, buck up, little camper. He lost this round. He'll be too humiliated to come back here." Ronnie was consumed with thought for a moment. "Although…"

"Although you know that statement is ridiculous?"

"No, although he'll want to change the battleground when he reengages."

"Awesome."

Ronnie nodded, confident in whatever he'd say next. "You'll need backup."

"Lila won't be there all the time."

Ronnie chuckled. "Not talking about Lila."

"You can't fight."

"Not talking about me, either."

Buck glanced at him. "Then who are you—"

But Buck didn't need to finish the question. Given all that had happened in the last couple of weeks, he already knew what Ronnie was driving at. It was the very thing Ronnie had been suggesting since the graduation party and the very thing Buck had been putting off since the bet began, the thing that could have or would have kept him out of trouble if he'd listened to Ronnie in the first place, the thing that he couldn't ignore or delay any longer, the thing that would've cost him significant money but would likely keep him out of insurance hell or the hospital if he'd just take the chance.

Buck closed his eyes and nodded.

"Mr. Stamps," he said, the name rolling off his tongue. "You want me to consult with Mr. Stamps."

"You need a security guard," Ronnie said. "Maybe even a bodyguard."

Buck ran his fingers through the gashes in his door. They were deep cuts. Buck realized these could've been in his chest or gut if he hadn't locked Pigeon out of the house in time.

"How much do you think that'll cost?" he asked.

"Less than life support at the hospital," Ronnie said.

Buck agreed.

So, he called Mr. Stamps for help.

The fee wouldn't be cheap, he soon discovered.

* * *

IT WOULD COST HIM twenty dollars an hour for security or fifty for personal protection, neither of which he could afford at his business level.

"Just name the time and the place, and I'll be there," Mr. Stamps said over the phone.

Buck decided fifty bucks an hour was too much for his income—not that twenty wasn't also, but fifty was unsustainable—so he agreed to door security.

"Someone vandalized my storage room on the Fourth of July. I want to make sure that doesn't happen again."

"How'd they get in?"

"Firecrackers, I think. Maybe a crowbar. Don't know. They just did a number on my shelves."

"How'd they get into the building?"

"What building?"

"Your business. How did they get in?"

"Just walked up to it. There's no 'in.' It's a park pavilion."

"A park pavilion?"

"With a storage room, yes."

Brief silence on the other end.

"So, I'm guarding a storage room?" Mr. Stamps finally asked.

"The last time they blew it up, I had to serve coffee out of my driveway. No one came. I need security."

A sigh.

"All right. Then I guess that'll make me your park bouncer. Fee's the same though, whether fancy nightclub or park pavilion. I'll need a special permit if you expect me to remain on the grounds at night."

"Why?"

"Parks close at dusk. I'm not special to the parks department. They'll want to know why I'm there, then charge me for permission to stay."

Buck rolled his eyes. Everything was a racket.

"I suppose I'll be paying for that, too?"

"Given that you're eighteen and probably a virgin, I'll absorb the permission fee. But if this somehow turns dangerous for me, I'll be tacking the cost back on. Got it?"

"I—I don't know what being a virgin has got to do with anything, but fine."

"Then we have a deal. When would you like me to start?"

"I'm going back Monday."

"Then I'll see you Monday."

"Given what you're charging, I'd rather not. Can you just guard the door during peak vandalism hours?"

Silence.

"Mr. Stamps?"

"Okay, you're clearly in over your head here, so I'll help you out. I'll send a few guys out to observe your business and monitor its activities over a twenty-four-hour period. We'll do it every day for a week, see if there's a pattern or risk beyond a holiday freak event. It'll cost you an extra hundred dollars, but it'll be a onetime fee, which you can pay after your bet ends. If there's a threat, we'll let you know. Then we can pick the best time. But based on experience, I'd say you'll want me between ten and three overnight."

"Sounds like we have a deal."

Buck was too tired to overthink the offer. If Mr. Stamps was deferring the reconnaissance fee until after the bet, then he had no reason to challenge it.

"I'll get the paperwork to you on Monday."

So, it was official. Buck now had himself a park bouncer.

Vandals beware!

But he didn't yet have a bodyguard. After what Pigeon did to his front door, he wished he could afford one now.

DAY 33: FRIDAY, JULY 12, 1985

Buck's Savings Account: $1.00
Buck's Wallet: $358.42
Buck's Business Funds: unknown
Buck's Expenses: $2 a day*
Hours of Operation: pending
Money on Hold: $159.44 (today)

AFTER HIS PREOCCUPATION WITH Lila, Pigeon, and Mr. Stamps—three people who took him from calm to anxious in the space of minutes—Buck had gone the morning forgetting about his accounting ledger, and more important, the significance that today held on his personal journey to financial victory.

He'd forgotten that today was payday. Not from his own coffee shop, which had a payday every day as long as customers showed up. But from his moonlighting as a shop clerk at his neighborhood convenience store, Shop Down the Street.

But now that he had a moment to himself, the reminder returned. The long-awaited paycheck Mack had been promising since his hiring date was now ready for collection, provided Mack's estimation on delivery was correct.

This was perfect timing, of course, considering he was about to blow the whole thing on one night's worth of security.

But when he'd got to Shop Down the Street to collect his earnings, Mack seemed unprepared for it.

"I mean, I had a feeling you'd come for it eventually," Mack said, as he gestured Buck toward the supply room. "It's just after four weeks of conversations about everything else, I'm a bit surprised you're asking about it now."

"But you do have it, right? You told me that in four weeks, everything should be good to go."

"Sure, sure." Mack disappeared through the door behind the sales counter. Buck caught up with him after going through the supply room. "I just have to make sure everything's square."

Buck took the sole plastic chair across from Mack's desk while Mack rummaged through an accordion folder full of documents.

"How's everything going with the other business?" he asked.

Buck didn't want to think about the other business. He rocked in his chair with his hands between his knees as he considered just the snapshots: the threats, the warnings, the occasional sales.

"Pavilion's reopening Monday," he said.

"That's great. Any word on who broke into your storage room?"

Buck shook his head. The investigation hadn't gotten to that point. Maybe it never would.

"Ah, here we are." Mack plucked a rectangular card with perforated tear tabs on each end and handed it over. Another company's name and address appeared on the return label. Buck's eyes bugged at the sight of it.

Rising Sunshine.

Buck pointed the name out to Mack. Mack rolled his eyes.

"Yeah, that's a can of worms," he said. "You'll find that they 'own' many of the companies under the Lease Agent's purview. I doubt it's a coincidence. But like I told you before, you don't have to worry about them as an employee. It only starts getting hairy when you're an owner."

"Like of a coffee pavilion, for example?"

Mack shrugged.

"At least you don't make much. They're less interested in owners with temporary locations and small revenues than in those like me."

Buck tore off the tabs from his paycheck. "Speaking of…"

He unfolded the pay stub and scanned the check. He was silent for a few seconds after reading the amount in the payment box.

"Is this right?" He turned the check upside-down to see if the office's lighting affected the printed value.

"Should be. What were you expecting?"

Buck had memorized the value he thought he was owed, down to the cent.

"A hundred fifty-nine, and change," he said.

$159.44, to be exact.

Even as he said the number out loud, he saw it printed on the pay stub. Just not on the check itself. The check itself had a lower value, much lower. Forty dollars lower.

He pointed at the expected value on the stub and showed it to Mack.

"See?" Then he shuffled through the other numbers that removed money from his expected income, all leading to his actual paid income of $119.58. "What's all of this?"

Mack leaned in for a closer look. His expression changed to an all-knowing smirk.

"Ah, yes. Taxes."

Buck closed his eyes as the realization slapped him across the cheek. Of course. Taxes, the thing both his parents had complained about every few weeks, seemingly randomly, especially in the spring. The thing his economics teacher had allegedly warned his students about every class period, even if Buck wasn't paying much attention to why it mattered so much. The thing he never really understood but always seemed to show up on his sales receipts after buying anything.

Every time anyone complained about taxes, Buck figured they were talking about the twenty cents added to his hamburger combo meal, which always bothered the hell out of him, too.

Why was it also showing up on his pay stub?

"The thing I have to pay extra for when I buy stuff at the store?"

"One and the same."

"I have to pay it here, too?"

"Yes. Well, a different tax here."

"A different tax?"

"But a tax nonetheless."

Buck folded the stub over the check and tucked it under his shirt.

"How many taxes are there?"

Mack whistled.

"How many indeed."

"What the hell, Mack?"

"Yep."

Buck did the math in his head. "Twenty-five percent?"

Mack took a seat at his desk and folded his hands over his belly.

"A bit much, right?"

"That's a quarter of my work. Gone! Where?"

"Not just yours, Buck. Not just yours."

Buck dared to look at the value printed on his check again.

"How many hours did I basically work for free?"

Mack rested his elbow on his desk. His demeanor was calm and understanding, like that of a father who'd just found out his son accidentally crashed a car into a mall trying to impress a hot girl with his driving skills.

"You didn't work for free. You just didn't make minimum wage, as advertised. More like seventy-five percent of minimum wage."

"Nice way to spin it." Buck opened his check again. Couldn't believe what he was looking at. "Twenty-five percent. Why so much?"

Mack's face grew serious. "Keeps the Tax Spook happy."

Buck closed the check again. He was tired of the stomachache the lie had given him.

"The Tax Spook? Where have I heard that name before?"

"It gets around, to everyone's dismay."

He paused for thought. Kabuki may have mentioned him once. Or maybe Mack had himself. Either way, he didn't like the guy.

The whole discussion was rotting his insides.

He pounded his fist against the desk, then leapt out of his chair. "Doesn't matter. I work for a living. You can be sure I earn *every* dollar at the Coffee Pavilion, unlike here. No one gets a single cent but me and maybe my friends. I wish you had the same attitude."

"That would make the Tax Spook very unhappy," he said, still serious. "You *have* been setting aside twenty-five percent of your shop earnings, *haven't you?*"

"Of course not. I'm trying to earn a living. I'm trying to survive. I'm trying"—Buck was ready to choke on his saliva from feeling such frustration over the idea of losing a dime to some mysterious force he couldn't control or reason with—"I'm trying to win a bet!"

Mack's face went grave. Buck's internal temperature lowered. He was used to seeing Mack acting casual, not like this. He sat back down.

"Is that bad?"

Mack blew words through his mouth as if someone had untied the balloon containing his thoughts.

"Hoo-boy-is-it." Mack could no longer make eye contact with Buck.

"Okay. What happens if I don't give the Tax Spook twenty-five percent of my earnings?"

"You know that thing that happened on your couch a couple of nights ago?"

"Please don't remind me." Flashes of the most horrifying images Buck had ever witnessed, anywhere, dotted his mind, and he forced them out even faster through a split-second silent exorcism, though it was too late for his stomach, which churned the moment his brain fed it the memory.

Then, terror gripped him: "You're not suggesting…"

"Yeah, well, between the couch and the Tax Spook's penalty, if given the choice, you'll beg to experience the couch incident again, might even learn to appreciate it."

Buck shuddered where he sat. Nothing in this world, or the next, would make what had happened on his couch preferable to *anything*. If Mack could identify the one thing that was less preferable, then maybe he would have to take it seriously.

"Is there a chance the Tax Spook doesn't know I exist?"

Mack pointed at the check in Buck's hand.

"Maybe before. Unlikely. But definitely not now."

Buck cursed under his breath.

"So, I'm in it now. That's what you're saying? No going back."

"There are two certainties in life. Death and taxes. The Tax Spook guarantees both will come for us one day." Even as the words left his lips, he looked nervously at the ceiling, as if the conversation was being overheard by someone.

Buck said nothing. He just wondered how he'd missed all this valuable information in high school. Must've been discussed on those days he'd spent stuck in his locker thanks to Chet Armstrong's antics.

"And then there's the IRS," Mack said, now sounding exhausted. He just shook his head at that one.

Perhaps it was time to change the subject, Buck thought. Give his stomach a chance to recover.

"How's French Girl?" he asked.

Mack snapped back to attention. "Still bothered by the other night. Won't look me or my wife in the eye."

"Sorry."

"Maybe you could check in on her yourself. Maybe she'll at least look *you* in the eye."

"It happened at my house, on a couch we both shared once. So, unlikely."

Mack shrugged. "Even still…you might have better luck than we did."

Buck agreed it was worth a try. So, after he went to the bank and deposited his much-smaller-than-expected paycheck into his savings account, which he would access only in an emergency, or when cream aged out faster than his customers could pour it into their coffees, he stopped over at Tealeaf Central to check on French Girl.

Only when he got there, he couldn't find her. After asking around, her manager, an attractive redhead in a pink dress named Bridget Sachs who rarely conversed with the customers unless she was looking for solid word-of-mouth—something of which Buck had to deal with a few times as a customer himself—confessed French Girl was on break.

"There's a small gazebo a couple of blocks down that she likes to visit. You could check to see if she's there," Bridget said.

"Thanks."

"Who are you again?"

When Buck asked why that mattered, Bridget said it was "for safety."

"If she doesn't come back in one piece, I need to know whom to report to the authorities. You a brother, a friend, or a stalker?"

Buck shook his head. "Boyfriend. Sheesh."

Bridget took a step back. She suddenly looked surprised.

"Boyfriend? You sure?"

"Of course I'm—" Buck self-evaluated his body for a moment. Surely, he was good enough for French Girl. Right? "Why? Is that hard to believe?"

Bridget shrugged and walked away. Maybe she had other work to do. Or maybe she just didn't like telling the truth.

Either way, Buck started feeling self-conscious but took Bridget's advice anyway and went down the street a couple of blocks to search for the gazebo. When he didn't find it, he went another way, and then another, checking himself out in the reflection of every window he passed. As far as he could tell, he looked fine and datable. What was Bridget Sachs even talking about?

After another few minutes of wandering around the area, Buck found what he was looking for: a tent-sized overhang between clustered pine trees in a shaded neighborhood park north of the tea shop.

Just as Bridget had suggested, he found French Girl sitting on a bench at the far side of the gazebo. His heart sank at the sight of her. She was dressed in her Tealeaf Central uniform, skirt hemmed above the knee, sitting with a paper bag lunch in one hand, and a rugged guy's cheek in the other.

And she seemed happy.

FRENCH GIRL WAS AS lovely as ever, the way she crossed her knees and angled them ever so slightly away from public view. Keeping herself conservative while being forced to wear a short skirt for work was just her style. But now she was angling them at another man. Perhaps her knees, as crossed as they may be, were a bit loose.

And her hair, though normally wavy and bouncing on her shoulders, tousled often by the gentle breeze passing off the ocean each evening, seemed straight and untouched now, thanks in part to the stillness of the surrounding pine trees but more likely a trick of the eyes caused by the shadow from the gazebo top. Even if the shade worked separately from the wind, it nevertheless absorbed her hair's sexiness.

And those lips, as luscious as they were, were a work of art drawn now as a smile, not at Buck, but at another man.

And just who the hell was this other man?

As Buck stood there in plain daylight, barely outside the rim of the gazebo's shadow, the one thing that really irked him, perhaps more than anything else, was that French Girl, who could clearly see him out of the corner of her eye, ignored him, as if they had no history together.

And look how she gripped the guy's cheek, as if it were something worth gripping! It was like a stone carving, not at all soft, or plush, or resembling a teddy bear. The dude's face wasn't even bearded! Just some plucky paperback romance cover model, of the kind one might find at a grocery store between the magazines and the bags of charcoal! What was coming next? A kiss?

Buck and French Girl had gone through so much together. Roller rinks! House parties! Other stuff! What did this guy have that Buck didn't?

Someone touched the back of his shoulder. He nearly leapt out of his jeans.

"What you doing here?"

Buck turned to face his assailant. French Girl was looking at him now, somehow, in the light. But she was also still under the gazebo, under with…

Though, now that he looked more carefully at her, or what he could tell from the adjustments his eyes made transitioning from light to shade, the version of her in the gazebo wasn't actually wearing a Tealeaf Central uniform but a Grab Those Cakes uniform from a rival bakery and beverage shop that sported similar brand colors. And her hair, while definitely not wavy or bouncy, was as such because it was straight and clearly ironed. And her breasts…well…even on this impostor, they were lovely, but they didn't belong to French Girl!

Buck squeezed his eyes shut as he slapped both of his cheeks.

"I was told you'd be here," he said.

"*Oui.* Bridget said you came asking about me. Told me you be here." She paused. "Why you watching Trisha and her boyfriend?"

"Trisha?"

Buck opened his eyes and followed French Girl's finger. Trisha, who had been inches from kissing the guy, as Buck predicted was coming, stopped mid-move and glanced in his direction.

"Hey, French Girl," the attractive straight-haired brunette said. "Back so soon?"

"French Girl." The chiseled guy with the half-open shirt and the rocky pectoral muscles peeking out of the collar nodded at her. Then at Buck. "Dude."

"Sorry," French Girl said. "My boyfriend not as cool as yours."

She elbowed Buck in the ribs.

"No judgments," Trisha said. "People watch us all the time. Gives them hope for a better life, even when they know they'll never have it, or us."

French Girl leaned sideways and whispered in Buck's ear. "They have syphilis. But they nice."

Buck smiled at the two figures under the shaded canopy. He suddenly felt ridiculous for having thought Trisha was French Girl. Now that he was staring at her, he decided Trisha looked nothing like her.

"But they have someone," French Girl said loud enough for Trisha to hear.

"And that's what's important," Trisha said. "Everyone should be happy. Your boyfriend have a name?"

"Buck," Buck said.

"Nice to meet you, Buck." She stopped in thought. "I actually know nothing about you."

"Well, I'm eighteen, from the Pine Alley section of town, live with…"

Buck glanced at French Girl. It suddenly occurred to him why Trisha knew nothing about him.

"How often do you two talk to each other?" he asked French Girl.

But it was Trisha who answered: "We eat a late lunch together most days, since our shifts are similar. Donovan joins us from time to time, but only when he's lonely. Right, baby?"

"Happens often," the chiseled guy said.

"What do you talk about?" Buck asked.

"Anything, sweetie," Trisha said. "Life, bunnies, tea, whatever."

"But not boyfriends?"

"Oh, Donovan pops into conversation *all* the time. We also talk about a guy named Johnny, but I thought…"

Trisha put her hand over her lips. Instead of finishing her sentence, she reached into her paper bag and took a bite out of a sandwich. Donovan turned away so he wouldn't have to watch her eat.

"Johnny who?"

When no one answered, he turned to French Girl. "Johnny who?"

She shrugged.

"Nobody. Just a boy at work. Dumb kid."

"But handsome," Trisha said, her mouth half-full. When everyone looked in her direction (except for Donovan), she once again covered her mouth with her hand, as if she'd said the wrong thing. "Not that I'd noticed."

"Should I be worried?"

"No," French Girl said.

"Hell yeah," Trisha said. "I mean, no. Sorry."

French Girl nodded and smiled at Trisha. Then she turned back to the sidewalk. Buck chased after her.

"Should I be worried?" Buck insisted. When she didn't answer, he asked again, this time reaching for her arm.

"No!" she said, stopping where she was and facing him. Her face was fierce, but then it softened and somehow morphed into embarrassment. "Maybe."

"Maybe?"

She shrugged.

"Johnny nice boy. Handsome, but stupid. Not what I want. But he pay attention to me."

"I pay attention to you. You know how hard I had to work to get your attention?"

"You kiss Lila night we meet."

Thunder struck Buck right in his chest. If the trees had been still before, they were horizontal from the blast now.

"You remember that?"

She shrugged and nodded, as if it were old news. Then she laughed.

"Just friends, you say. Didn't matter at time. Me, you not together then, so why I care who you kiss?"

"We *are* just friends, for the record. The kiss was supposed to get your attention in some twisted Lila kind of way. I guess it worked."

French Girl shrugged. "Maybe. But soon as I become your girlfriend, you don't kiss me, not like Lila."

"Lila kissed you? What the hell?"

French Girl's expression blanked. "No, I mean like you kiss Lila."

Buck suddenly couldn't shake the image of Lila and French Girl kissing, even if it never happened. He smacked his head to get it out of his head before it went "somewhere French."

"I tried, several times," he said, now that he had regained control of his thoughts. "We were always interrupted."

French Girl nodded. "*Oui.* And that point. Something always in way. Lila. Blonde girl. Coffee. Tea. Exchange dad's rules. Then there couch…not sure how describe it."

"Please don't try. I can't bear to hear the words it would take coming out of your precious mouth."

French Girl offered him a weak smile.

"Johnny listen to me. Make time for me."

"This the dumb handsome kid you work with?"

"Yes."

"Does he listen to you *because* he works with you?"

"He still there when I need boy talk to. You there sometimes. Johnny there most times."

Buck felt that pang in his stomach again, and it had nothing to do with hunger.

"So, if I blow off work, hang out at Tealeaf Central all day, and pretend I don't have a life or other friends, then you and I will be good again, and I won't have to worry about this interloper Johnny kid?"

French Girl held his gaze. Her lips twitched, as if she had something to say in response, but nothing was coming out.

Buck helped her: "You can say yes, if it's the truth."

"No," she said. "Problem not that you have a life outside of me. Problem is your life is almost entirely outside. How many times you see Lila this week? And for how long?"

Buck didn't want to admit the answer, especially since she woke up in his bed this morning—a detail French Girl did not need in her head, even if the reason behind the reality was innocent.

When Buck didn't answer, French Girl continued. "What about blonde girl?"

"Her name is Jennifer."

French Girl grimaced. She really didn't like hearing her name, apparently.

"Not often," Buck continued, this time having no need for remorse.

"Your ugly friend with the uglier hat?"

"Ronnie? He's not ugly, is he?"

French Girl shrugged.

"Okay, well, I see your point. You and I don't spend enough time together. We can fix that. Maybe you can serve coffee with me instead of tea for Bridget Sachs. We could go into business together. We could be partners. We could be…"

Her eyes were glazing over. None of these seemed appealing to her.

What the hell did she even want?

"Help me figure out what you want?"

French Girl rubbed his shoulder. Her eyes were searching and beautiful, but they were also dull, like going from the noon sky to a pair of jeans in the hamper at midnight. Or maybe fresh wet grass to a piece of wilting lettuce. Or a new penny to a tarnished one. Whatever she wanted to say, she wasn't saying it. She just held him there with a smile and sad but beautiful eyes. Or were they beautiful but sad?

He wondered if they always looked different in daylight…

Then she did something he wasn't ready for. She leaned in and kissed him right on the lips. Her mouth was sweet, like a bag of fruit candies, but there was no passion in it, no tongue. Just a mere pressing of the lips and a slight grinding of the teeth, and nothing more. It was there, then gone in under three seconds.

A bit like kissing a friend if that friend were exceptionally close.

It was a lot like kissing Lila.

"I want to figure out what I want," French Girl said finally.

"Which is?"

Again, she shrugged.

"I don't know. That the point. But until then…" She tapped him on the cheek and ran her fingers through his hair. "You really try, don't you?"

"Try what?"

"Handsome but dumb."

"I don't…"

She lowered her hand to his elbow and stroked it. Her smile was strong, but it weakened over the course of a few seconds. Buck suddenly became aware of the traffic cruising by just a few feet to his left.

This whole time they'd had an audience of a hundred strangers on the way home, or to the bar, or to the beach, or to wherever.

"You nice boy. A friend."

And there was that thunderous blow to the chest again, this time hitting him hard enough to knock him back a step.

"Friend?"

Something in French Girl's face changed in that moment, as if she'd figured out the mystery to her own question about what she wanted. She'd gone from uncertain to certain, confused to clear.

"Yes, friend. Good friend."

"But not…" He couldn't bring himself to finish the thought.

She wrapped her arms around his shoulders and held him close.

"Now you can kiss Lila or blonde girl all you want." She released him from her embrace and winked at him as if this was the very thing he'd been pining for since the day they'd met.

"Her name's still Jennifer," he said after recovering his step.

French Girl nodded. "*Oui*. Jennifer. You free to kiss Jennifer as much as you want."

Buck listened for the pain in her voice as she spoke "the blonde girl's" name, but he couldn't detect it. No sadness, no joy. No emotion at all. Just contentment.

Her decision, then, was final.

Episode 43

Training Ends

BUCK WANDERED AROUND THE streets aimlessly for the next couple of hours, kicking pebbles, taking one foot into the crosswalk before checking for traffic, and searching trash cans for discarded items he could sell at Sapphire's Consignments or the Disinterested Pawn—whatever kept his mind off his breakup with French Girl.

On the one hand, he should've been relieved. For the entire time they were "together," Buck never got the feeling they were truly together. Sure, French Girl demonstrated the jealousy he'd expect from a woman who called herself his girlfriend, but they rarely went out, and they hardly kissed, and, well, as of today, the relationship was too short for it to really count. Her jealousy may have been real, but it had the hallmarks of something forced given how little they connected with each other.

On the other hand, he should've been pissed. Or felt betrayed. Or something leading to a deeper anger or resentment at her for putting him through this. But what was she putting him through? Again, as much as he wanted "them" to work, nothing about them was working. The odds had piled on them by the gallon, not the fluid ounce. He'd gone after her because Jennifer had left him for Chet, and Lila was already in a dysfunctional relationship. Now, it seemed, Jennifer and Lila were coming out of their chains, and French Girl was looking for a new one to tie herself with.

Buck sat on a nearby bench and watched traffic coast by. Two hours after a breakup with a hot European girl and he felt like someone's grandpa.

Nothing made sense anymore. For all its problems as an institution for young minds, at least high school had exhibited some level of structure and sanity, with a social infrastructure that most teenagers could handle, regardless of their positions in the hierarchy. Post-high school, everything had devolved into the plot for a daytime soap opera or Saturday morning cartoon.

And that senselessness continued the moment he got home and checked his mailbox.

For much of the last month, Buck had gotten the usual bills addressed to his mother and advertisements addressed to his house. But other than the occasional solicitation from a branch of the military asking him to enlist, the mail hadn't come for him.

Today was different, though. Today, he'd gotten another letter from Jennifer.

The knot in his stomach returned. Her timing couldn't have been worse. Now that he was back on the singles block, he couldn't think of a palatable reason to keep avoiding her. If he opened the letter, read it, or even acted on it, whatever that might require, French Girl would no longer get upset over it. No one would. Except perhaps for Jennifer, and only if he didn't open, read, or respond to the letter.

Problem was, he couldn't deal with the constant cycle of betrayal. Quite frankly, he didn't have time for it. If she wanted to get back together with him—a possibility, considering she was still sending him letters—then he'd have to make time for her again, and set himself up for heartbreak again, and pour himself into the coffee business to get his mind off of her again. Never mind that she was the reason he'd even entered the coffee business; it actually seemed unfair how she continued looking for ways to pick her way back into his life.

But still, she'd already apologized for hooking up with Chet. It probably wouldn't hurt to open the letter to see what she had to say. Maybe he'd find he'd gotten her all wrong. Maybe she was offering him a business proposal. It wasn't her style, but it also wasn't out of her reach.

As he pulled the letter from the pile, deciding whether to read it here or inside, a piece of card stock fell out from under it and landed on the grass by his feet. On its front was solid black coloring. No words or images. Just an empty rectangle, like a magazine insert keeping the issue crisp. But there were no magazines or glossy advertisements waiting for him today. The card was random.

Except, it wasn't. Once he flipped it over to check whether it was the same on both sides, he discovered words in white lettering printed on its face. His stomach lurched at what he read. As if by some ominous force of magic, the words echoed precisely the terrible message Mack Green had warned him about just hours earlier, as if the warning itself was the beacon this postcard needed to find him. The sight of it sent an actual chill down his spine.

See you soon.
—The Tax Spook

* * *

FOR SOME REASON, THE Whipping Shed was locked, and the lights were off, but Buck pounded on the door, anyway. The day might have been getting late, but it was not yet over. Kabuki should've been there, either teaching a class or preparing for one. Having the shop closed so early was unusual.

Buck flipped the black card over in his palm. The ominous white letters on the dark canvas beckoned him to look, even as he tried to avoid it. *Look at me!* it shouted at his brain. *Look at me and weep!*

He kicked at the door, slapped at the glass, screamed into the void. Then, as if by call or by miracle, a light down at the end of the hall appeared. Then another closer light, making the dull hallway brighter. Soon, the reception area lit up.

Kabuki emerged, his face stern as he approached the front entrance. His face had a sheen of sweat.

"Why boy in panic?"

Buck scrambled inside the moment he could fit through the door, then checked over his shoulder to make sure he hadn't been followed.

"Someone chasing you?"

Buck shook his head. Couldn't speak. Just showed Kabuki the black card.

Kabuki took the card, letting his sight fall upon the white words. He dropped it as if it were freezing to the touch. His focus went immediately to the ceiling.

"What do I do?" Buck demanded. "Who is this guy?"

Kabuki held up a palm but said nothing.

"Mr. Kabuki?"

Kabuki shook his head, then lowered his hand to silence him.

Without a word, Kabuki turned and headed for the hallway. When Buck tried to follow him, the old man, without glancing back, held up his fist in the halting position. *Stay here* was his silent message to him.

A moment later, Mr. Kabuki returned with a broom in hand. Before Buck could blink, Kabuki swept the card out onto the sidewalk where the wind might take it away.

"Lesson twenty-two," he whispered as the door fell closed. "Some forces inevitable. And unstoppable. Tax Spook come for all men. Eventually. Nothing boy can do about it."

Kabuki held his gaze but said nothing more. The temperature in Buck's chest fell. Even his stomach was now too cold to ache. The reception room doubled in size. Tripled. Something at the end of the hall groaned.

It all came back to him now. It wasn't Mack Green who had warned him about the Tax Spook. The Lease Agent had done it at the signing of the lease. Even the man who owned the town feared the Tax Spook. And if that were the case, then what courage could Kabuki offer him in the face of his mysterious upcoming arrival?

Buck collapsed onto the nearest chair. None of his mentors could advise him on how to handle this sudden invasion into his financial life. It seemed they had all fought against the Spook and lost themselves. Perhaps that was what had kept them humble.

"So, what now?" he finally asked.

"Would offer boy sake, but not old enough for drink yet."

"I won't tell anyone."

Kabuki put his hand on Buck's shoulder.

"Kabuki have nothing left to teach boy. Time to become man. Boy must face Tax Spook on his own."

The room shrank again. Buck glanced up at his mentor. Kabuki nodded back. The look on his face was clear.

Buck had finally graduated from his business training.

* * *

THE TAX SPOOK'S CARD of warning had vanished by the time Buck returned to the sidewalk, and he had no interest in looking for it. With luck, the Tax Spook would get delayed suffering the ire of Ernest Bee, who might berate him for littering, assuming Ernest Bee had the guts to cross his path. But now Buck had nowhere to be, so he went to Ronnie's to decompress.

But before Buck could say hello, Ronnie reached out through the door and pulled him into the living room. Ronnie's dad was parked on his recliner in the corner, but he seemed just as eager to see him.

"Dude, I've been calling you for the last two hours," Ronnie said.

"Sorry, I haven't been home. The day I had—"

"Yeah, ignore it. None of it matters."

"Huh?"

Ronnie's dad gestured at the couch across the room. "Sit down, son."

Buck wasn't sure what was happening, but he complied. As the adult in the same house he owned, Ronnie's dad had complete authority here.

"How's business going?" Mr. Michaels asked.

"Not well. I've had a couple of good runs, but they've been ruined by bad days."

Ronnie's dad leaned forward.

"Well, all of that is about to change. Real soon."

Buck glanced over at Ronnie, whose face was now beaming. He was hopping up and down where he sat.

"Are you well stocked with your supplies?" Mr. Michaels asked.

"Trying to be. The pavilion's reopening Monday, and I just called security."

"Mr. Stamps," Ronnie clarified. "The best in the business."

"He's expensive?" Mr. Michaels asked.

"More than I can afford."

"Not anymore."

Buck said nothing. Mr. Michaels had already got Buck's attention, but now he was also getting his curiosity.

"I made some calls on your behalf. Made one important connection." Mr. Michaels pressed his palms together. "Have you heard of the Coffee Critic?"

The name was familiar, but Buck didn't know much about him.

"He writes for *Coast Life Weekly* magazine. A lot of people in Hybrid City read it."

Buck said nothing. If that were true, he wasn't one of them.

"He's always on the search for the region's best coffee."

The weight in Buck's chest lightened. He understood where Mr. Michaels was going with this. Ronnie had already mentioned once that his dad would make some calls.

"I don't know when he's coming," Mr. Michaels said, "but your coffee shop is now on his radar, and sometime in the next thirty days, he will stop by. So, get ready. Make sure you start each day prepared. Then give him the best you got. If he likes what you're selling, I can guarantee his article will give you the clientele needed to put you well over the winning line."

If Buck had failed to breathe for the last twenty seconds, it was all rushing in now. Even as Mr. Michaels grew silent, Buck found himself on the verge of hyperventilating. After all the horrible turns of events lately, this was very good news.

"Oh, thank God," Buck said. "Because I'd just gotten a note from the Tax Spook and—"

"Tax Spook?" Ronnie's dad was now out of his chair. "He found you?"

Buck's breath once again stilled.

"Yeah…"

Mr. Michaels wiped his forehead with the back of his hand.

"Okay, no problem. This can still work. It's just…"

Buck exchanged glances with Ronnie, who seemed just as in the dark about what Mr. Michaels was saying as he was.

"You're going to have to be *really* impressive now. You need to make the Coffee Critic sing your praises if you want to earn enough from his readers to survive the Tax Spook's visit." Mr. Michaels clapped his hands together. "I'd suggest you get a team together. Yesterday, if possible."

* * *

BUCK WAS EXHAUSTED BY the time he'd got home, but he considered Mr. Michaels's advice. Starting tomorrow, he'd have to scout for additional help. He'd been getting helpers to assist him all month, but now that he was entering a Saturday where he could actually focus on his business and not on Shop Down the Street, he could work on assembling his perfect staff, consider their strengths and weakness, and figure out how to pay them fairly without bankrupting himself or ruining his chances at winning the bet.

As he lay in bed, something in his gut convinced him to open Jennifer's letter. He'd been ignoring it since its arrival for fear of what it might say. But as he opened it and skimmed its contents, he was glad he had taken the chance. Her words this time were simple. But they were meaningful. Among the various apologies and delicate dances around what had happened at the house party a couple of nights earlier, Jennifer had ended her letter with a very important question, one that Buck would kiss her for if she were here in his room with him right now.

How can I help you win?

Love,

Jennifer.

Episode 44

Jennifer's Confession

DAY 34: SATURDAY, JULY 13, 1985

Buck's Savings Account: $120.58

Buck's Wallet: $356.42

Buck's Business Funds: $119.58 (from SDTS Earnings)

Buck's Expenses: $2 a day*

Hours of Operation: pending

Money on Hold: none

BUCK STOOD AT THE entrance of Melty's Coffee and Ice Cream Bar, unsure whether he wanted to step inside. Across the tiny dining room, Jennifer rang up an ice cream sale for a young mother and her four-year-old daughter. She was smiling at the woman but stealing glances at Buck. So far, neither Buck nor Jennifer had said a word to the other. But any hostility between them had evaporated. Their glances were amiable. Soon, they would talk. But for now, he waited for her to clock out.

Of course, he hoped he wasn't making a mistake by coming here. Sharing peaceable glances was a step in the right direction, but it wasn't the same as having nice things to say to each other. Jennifer's letter, while sounding hopeful, still had the potential of baiting him into something cruel. If she wanted, she could take this opportunity to kick him even harder in the nuts, metaphorically or physically. He tapped his fingers against his upper thighs as he debated whether to stick around or run.

But he was too curious about her motives. She'd written that she wanted to help him win the bet. And, assuming she was telling the truth, he was interested in knowing how she'd planned to help. If he left now, he'd be stuck in perpetual suspense.

That was not an option he was willing to take.

Once the young mother and her daughter left, Buck, deciding it would be awkward to keep standing in the doorway, took a seat inside. He chose the one closest to the door. Jennifer, meanwhile, went into the back room, either to prep for the next order or to chat with her coworkers. But Buck remained alone in the dining room, inches from the exit, unsure of the wisdom of sitting not only a short distance from his ex-girlfriend, with whom his relations were currently questionable, but also in the seat of one of his better funded rivals.

Melty's Coffee and Ice Cream Bar was not just an ice cream bar; it was also a coffee shop, hence the name. And it was the most popular coffee shop in town. With its one-dollar coffees, its prices could not be beat, not for a profit at any rate, certainly not one that would win Buck a bet. But it also served good coffee. And that was the real challenge. How did he beat Melty's at both price *and* taste for a single cup?

The caramel syrup and peppermint candies he'd started putting in his premium three-dollar coffees had certainly helped him gain a foothold in the market. But now that he had the Coffee Critic in his sights, and vice versa, he had to figure out how to make that combination more appealing than what Melty's offered.

While he waited for Jennifer to clock out, he watched Melty's as an operation. He'd certainly visited the place many times in the past, but only ever as a customer. Now that he was a competitor, he wanted to see how it handled products, transactions, and service. Covert intelligence, but not in a sexy way. He just wanted to watch what they did and see if he could do better.

"Five more minutes," Jennifer said when she returned to the counter. Buck was the only person in the shop, so she was talking to him.

He nodded but said nothing. He still didn't know exactly why he was here. And given that he was the shop's sole patron but not a customer, he wasn't sure exactly what else he might learn by sitting here.

When Jennifer finished her shift, she thanked him for stopping by but told him she didn't want to have the conversation here. Buck insisted they stay longer—his verbal excuse was that he'd just gotten there and didn't want to move again, but his silent excuse was to gain competitor insights—but she didn't think it was appropriate, something to do with fraternizing with the customers. He explained that he wasn't a customer. She said the boss didn't know that, or care.

Buck understood. She was right. Even though it would've been helpful to see how the enemy worked, it would've been more helpful to convert a new enemy back into a friend. If securing the latter meant ignoring the former, then he'd agree to the terms.

So, Buck and Jennifer left the frosty dining room of Melty's Coffee and Ice Cream Bar and went to the blazing beach where their onetime love affair had first come to an end.

* * *

"I HAVEN'T BEEN HONEST with you," Jennifer said, as she leaned back on her elbows and gave Buck a quick glance, as if her message had been as normal as admitting to buying him the wrong-sized socks for Christmas. Buck stared back in silence, uncertain how to interpret her statement.

"I didn't start dating Chet because I was interested in him," she added.

Jennifer had been watching the ocean waves for the last five minutes without a word, either lost in thought or lost in the beauty of the Pacific at sunset. But now she had nothing but shockers to utter. Buck continued studying her, aware that she was telling him something important, but not sure how just yet. So far, it sounded absurd. What was she even saying?

She lowered her elbows further until her back touched the beach towel underneath them. Her hands went up over her forehead and through her golden hair. The hem of her shirt rose to her belly button. Buck tried not to look, but he couldn't help it. So much mystery on either side of the fabric.

"Just thought you should know," she said.

"Know what?" Buck still didn't understand her message. What did it matter why she'd dated Chet? Didn't change the fact that she had dumped Buck to do so.

"I started dating him to help you."

Buck's eyes diverted back to Jennifer's face. As interesting as her exposed belly may have been, the ideas hidden in her brain now caught his attention.

"You're gonna have to explain that one," he said.

"That's why I brought you here. I figure I still owe you a proper birthday party. Without lessons to teach."

"Lessons? What? The Hell?"

She reached over and rubbed his biceps.

"I know you're with French Girl now, so I have to be careful about what I say, but—"

"She broke up with me."

Jennifer sat up, letting her shirt fall back into place.

"What now?"

Buck gestured for her to continue. "Not important information. Yours is more important. Say it."

Except now Jennifer seemed to catch her words in her throat.

"I mean, that's horrible, or wonderful, or…"

"You stopped at dating Chet, not because you were interested in him, but because you wanted to help me. Nothing about that statement makes any sense. So, please explain what you mean, as if I'm an idiot. Please."

Jennifer slowly nodded, either to process what she was about to tell him or to figure out how to lie to him again.

"You were bullied. A lot," she said. "And it's not like you're a natural target."

"You mean like Garrett Nedmeyer."

"Exactly."

"Or Lester Biggins."

Jennifer glanced at him, her expression dark.

"That's super sad, Buck."

"But that's what you're saying."

She glanced off at the ocean. "You didn't have to be bullied. You chose it."

Buck smirked.

"That's ridiculous."

"Why you chose it is something for a psychologist to figure out. But you didn't have to, and I wanted you to stop. You know how embarrassing it is to date a guy who spends half the day in a locker because someone else put him there?"

"Who cares? You chose it."

Jennifer paused for a moment, apparently lost in the orange ocean beyond her feet.

When she spoke again, her throat sounded dry. "I went after Chet partly to stop him torturing you. But when I realized he wouldn't stop, I tried provoking you to fight for yourself. So, I planned your birthday around that goal, to make you so mad at him that you'd bare your fists and throw a punch, make him see he can't push you around." She chuckled under her breath. "But you didn't do that, did you?"

"No." Buck considered what she was telling him. "Are you saying you were with him even before my birthday?"

Jennifer said nothing.

"Jenn?"

She closed her eyes and covered them with her palms.

"How long before?" Buck asked.

"Since Christmas."

Buck didn't wait for an explanation. He picked himself off the towel and headed for the parking lot, grateful he'd ridden his bike here.

* * *

THE BIKE DIDN'T MATTER, though. Jennifer followed him the entire way home. Even when he took side streets to avoid her, he couldn't shake her. The problem with bicycles, he realized, was that they could never outrun a car. And the problem with him as a bicyclist was that he still couldn't ride up and down stairs. There was simply no escaping her. By the time he'd gotten home, she was already pulling into his driveway.

"I'm sorry for lying to you." She caught her skirt in the car door as she closed it but stopped dead in her tracks when she noticed. She freed herself before it caused her more embarrassment. Buck raced for the front door when she started moving again. "I thought I was doing the right thing."

"By betraying me?"

"I didn't see it as a betrayal."

After some fumbling with his keys, Buck got the front door open.

"What you see isn't always what you get."

He leapt inside, but he couldn't close the door fast enough. Jennifer slipped in through the crack before it got too thin. She backed away before he could grab her and throw her out.

"No one has to bully you," she said, now moving toward the couch. *Please don't sit on it*, Buck thought. "If I have to pull the right lever for you to get that, I will."

"And so you did."

She was inches away from the couch and was about to sit on it. But she stopped herself. Having been at the party, she must've remembered what she and everyone else saw happen on it. She corrected her position and moved to the dining room table instead.

"You and I don't have to be enemies," she said, as she chose her preferred chair. "We can put our mistakes behind us."

"*Our* mistakes?"

"You didn't fight back. You made a bet you couldn't win. We both were stupid."

"I made that bet because of you."

"Right motive. Wrong action. Just throw a punch, Buck. Tell the bully to move on. Haven't you been seeing that karate guy? What did he tell you?"

"To go into business for myself."

Jennifer said nothing. She put her elbow on the table and sighed.

"Can you go home now?" Buck asked.

"No. I want things right between us."

Buck wasn't ready to believe her. But he was willing to get himself closer to belief, especially now that it was evident she had no plans to leave his house. He just had to ask the right question. But what was the right question?

He shook his head. There could be only one.

"How do you feel about Chet?"

She flicked her bangs.

"For a while, I may have forgotten my mission a bit. Jerk or not, he's still handsome. And demanding."

"I don't want details."

She leveled her gaze at him.

"I don't love him. Never did. He's still a jerk. And now he's cheating on me with some dancer."

"He can't cheat unless you're still with him."

She nodded thoughtfully.

"You're right. So, I guess he's not cheating then."

Buck was still standing by the front door, but now his feet edged him closer to the dining room table. His stomach was growling. Jennifer was staring at him from the darkened half of the room. The light from the kitchen illuminated her from behind, giving her contrast amid the deep shadows etching along the opposite side of her face. If she had had any blemishes, they had since vanished.

"Are you hungry?" he asked.

"A little."

"I've got a couple of frozen dinners in the freezer if you want me to make you one. I assume you'll be staying a while."

She smiled slightly.

"I'd like that."

"Okay. In the meantime, tell me more about how you're going to help me win this impossible bet."

Her smile brightened.

"Thought you'd never ask," she said.

Episode 45

The Grand Reopening

Buck and Jennifer sat at the dining room table for over an hour, eating frozen dinners and conspiring over methods for bringing Chet and his Liquid Shack down to their knees. Jennifer had come to Buck's house with a central plan, but Buck, getting caught up in the moment, expanded that plan well into the absurd. At one point, he'd discussed the possibility of heading out to sea, catching an octopus, and hauling it back to Park Central Park where he'd dump the poor aquatic creature right on Chet's serving table.

But when the ideas ran out, and the laughter died to an awkward silence, Buck conceded to Jennifer's original plan. It was the best they had, not because it was unique, but because it was effective.

"Just don't break his heart in the process," Buck said.

Jennifer touched her fingers to her neck. "Who? Me?"

With nothing more to discuss, Buck asked if she wanted to watch TV: a simple invitation that didn't come so easily. Trepidation over Jennifer's original betrayal had cast a shadow over his momentary joy, and he feared regret over his decision to ask her to stay. But before he could fight his tongue and beat it into submission, the words came out, and he was left with a question in need of an answer.

Rather than give him an answer, however, Jennifer dragged her dining room chair into the living room—between the couch and the coffee table—and turned on the television for him. Buck pulled his dining room chair beside her. A charity concert was already playing on the screen.

"Want to watch this?" she asked.

"Who's playing?"

Jennifer studied the screen.

"Looks like everyone."

According to the clock on the wall, it was almost seven. He didn't know how long she'd stay.

The open-ended evening stirred his anxiety, but it failed to send him into a panic. Maybe he'd survive the night with her beside him. Maybe he'd even feel numb to her past behavior.

That would've been all right with him.

"*Airwolf* starts at eight," Buck said. "We could watch this until then."

Buck's vote didn't matter, though. The concert had the makings of something historical. The room seemed to disappear around them. They watched it well past eight o'clock. And nine. And ten.

By eleven o'clock, the televised concert had raised millions for feeding African nations. Buck had seen nothing like it before. The event had to have broken a record or two. Maybe a few.

As the concert came to an end, Buck tried to think of anyone he knew who might've belonged to a band. They wouldn't be able to help him feed a series of distant nations, of course, but they could help him sell some coffee during his grand reopening.

Seemed like a good enough cause to him.

* * *

Day 35: Sunday, July 14, 1985

Buck's Savings Account: $120.58

Buck's Wallet: $354.42

Buck's Business Funds: $119.58 (from SDTS Earnings)

Buck's Expenses: $2 a day*

Hours of Operation: pending

Money on Hold: none

THE NEXT MORNING, WITH just one day left before the Coffee Pavilion's grand reopening at North Park, Buck picked up the phone. He needed to reach anyone he knew who might've known something about music. He started with Ronnie.

But as soon as Ronnie admitted he knew nothing of the sort and ended the call, Buck hit a dead end. It occurred to him he hadn't gotten any of his former classmates' phone numbers. Even as he scoured old yearbooks for KITs (keep-in-touches), he found none except for one from the P.E. teacher, and he didn't expect Mr. Grablet to know any musicians.

He called Ronnie back.

"Do you know *anyone* in a band?" Buck asked.

"Let me check," Ronnie said.

A few minutes later, Ronnie returned the call.

"So, it looks like I've got a friend of a friend who has a cousin who plays the saxophone."

Buck's anxiety lifted. He felt a smile creeping onto his face.

"Can you get him to come to the Coffee Pavilion tomorrow around noon?"

"I'll see what I can do."

Buck bit his fingernails as he waited for Ronnie's next follow-up call. As much as he knew asking for a musician to play at the grand reopening was the right move, as no passerby could resist the smooth sounds of a saxophonist's bluesy melody, he was still nervous about the cost. With Ronnie, Tiffany, and Jennifer helping him during the day, and Mr. Stamps starting his security shift at night, Buck was already on the hook for a large outgoing payment. Adding a musician to the roster would've taken that payment even higher, perhaps much higher. It was inevitable. The best Buck could hope for was the musician not asking for much.

"Johnny Bones will be there at twelve sharp," Ronnie said when he called back with news about the saxophonist. "He wants cash up front."

"Of course he does."

Buck would have to tap into his savings again. Looked like he needed to return to the bank in the morning and withdraw all that money he'd deposited on Friday.

* * *

Later on Sunday evening, Buck reviewed his current stock and double-checked that his equipment was still working. Because he didn't want to get caught off-guard during the height of business, he also topped off any item he might deplete before closing time. Then he stopped by North Park to check on the pavilion to ensure everything was indeed ready for business.

The damage was still visible near the storage room's door frame, especially close to the lock. Even though the wall had been touched up with paint, it had received just one coat of a slightly off-shade color. The burn marks were still visible through the paint, just not as pronounced.

He tugged at the door to ensure it wouldn't splinter the frame. Nothing broke, but it jiggled a little.

Two hundred fifty dollars for a half-assed repair job. Matched perfectly with what his dad used to rail on about insurance companies. But at least it secured the room again.

He unlocked the door and checked inside. To his satisfaction, he found the shelves had been replaced, this time with metal racks. If anyone were to toss in another firecracker in the middle of the night, they'd have a harder time sending the whole thing to the floor.

Buck locked the door and returned to his bike. Looked like he was ready for tomorrow's grand reopening. Hopefully, it would be a success.

* * *

DAY 36: MONDAY, JULY 15, 1985

Buck's Savings Account: $120.58

Buck's Wallet: $339.77

Buck's Business Funds: $119.58 (from SDTS Earnings)

Funds-to-Wallet Refund Due: $14.65 (spent on supplies)

Buck's Expenses: $2 a day*

Hours of Operation: pending

Money on Hold: none

ON MONDAY MORNING, BUCK called Ronnie to meet him at the pavilion by nine o'clock. Because Ronnie had no job or other important place to be, he had no issues getting there on time. To Buck's delight, Ronnie also brought along Tiffany, who had brought with her a box of party supplies.

"You can't have a grand reopening without festive banners," she said.

Without waiting for thanks or a rejection, Tiffany got to work decorating the pavilion with her papier mâché designs, many of which contained the colors of the American flag. She began by smoothing out a vertical "grand reopening" pennant down the front pillar where Buck usually hung the open sign. If Buck didn't know any better, he'd think she was promoting him for public office.

"We figured I'd post some flyers at the park's front entrance," Ronnie said. "Hope you don't mind them written in marker. Business could be much better if people actually knew you were back here."

"Makes sense," Buck said. "But we also need a sales strategy. I was thinking—"

But Ronnie was already halfway to his car before Buck could finish his thought.

Looked like they already had a plan for the day. That left Buck to set up his station and stock the storage room.

"What do you think?" Tiffany asked when Buck turned toward the pavilion. She was displaying her handiwork with the vertical grand reopening pennant.

At two feet long and bright with primary colors, the sign could attract attention from as far away as the lake at the bottom of the hill.

531

Anyone who passed by would have to take notice. Considering they had a musician coming to add to the attraction, Buck had no reason to criticize their chance of success today. The pennant was perfect.

"I approve."

Tiffany gave him the "A-okay" sign, then moved to the next pillar to post a twin pennant. No one was going to ignore them today.

Whether Buck won or lost the bet, he was definitely about to give Chet a run for his money.

Then Tiffany said something in passing that nearly gave Buck a heart attack, in a good way.

"By the way," she said as she looked at him from over her shoulder, "Ronnie's dad suggested we work as volunteers this week. Something to do with keeping ahead of the Tax Spook. Ronnie's not for it, but I'm sure I can talk him into it if it'll help you get ahead."

Buck couldn't believe his ears. Was Tiffany suggesting that she and Ronnie work *for free* this week?

"Um…yeah."

"Great. I can't promise you forever, but I can probably sway him to agree to volunteer work until Friday. That should put you ahead by at least five hundred dollars."

Buck was speechless. Even in his thoughts, he didn't know how to respond.

"If worse comes to worst," she said, "I may get him to agree only to a payment delay until after the bet."

Buck's head came back down to earth. This sounded much more like a Ronnie kind of deal.

"If you guys help me win," Buck said, "I might pay you back with interest."

Tiffany breathed a sigh of relief. "That sounds like an easier argument to win. Consider it a sure thing then."

* * *

BEFORE SHE LEFT BUCK'S house Saturday night, Jennifer had promised that she'd help with the Coffee Pavilion's grand reopening. By 10:30, she made good on her promise.

She also brought with her a box of pastries.

"In case you need breakfast," she said.

Ronnie and Tiffany each grabbed a donut from the box, but Buck was hesitant.

"Think we could flip them to our customers?" he asked. "How much you pay? I bet we could charge our customers double."

Jennifer gave him a dirty look.

"These are *our* donuts. This is *our* breakfast."

Buck scanned the box. She had brought them a dozen assorted flavors.

"I'm not going to eat three donuts. Ronnie?"

"I might," Ronnie said, his mouth half-full.

"Tiffany?"

Tiffany licked her fingers clean of the sugar that came off her first donut. "One for me."

"Unless you're going to eat half the box, some of these are going to waste." Buck waited for Jennifer's reaction, but she offered him none. "So, can I sell a couple of them? Every dollar counts."

Jennifer folded her arms across her chest. "Don't you have a musician coming today?"

"I doubt he wants to get donut powder on his instrument."

"You don't know that."

"Jenn, come on. Help me out."

She grabbed the box from the table and pulled it close to her chest.

"I am helping you out. It's gonna be a long day. I'm bringing you breakfast." She started down the hill. "But if you don't want to eat it…"

"Bring them back. Maybe I'll want one for lunch."

She came back up the hill with a smile on her face.

"That's all I ask."

The next twenty minutes were back to business, filled with equipment testing, quality checking, and other pre-opening logistics. As the clock drew closer to eleven and eventually noon, Buck sweated more and his stomach grew tighter. It had been a while since his last sale at the park, and he had no clue if any of his efforts would pay off.

Some hope arrived in pockets, however, as a few park visitors stopped by to find out what "these kids" were doing. But Buck had nothing to offer when they asked for a sample. Normally, he'd give in to the marketing practice of letting customers try before they bought. But he needed every cup to count today, and he wasn't about to give any away for free.

At least, that was the case until a mother and her young son veered off the sidewalk and came up the hill. She was mousy in appearance and conservative in dress. But her eyes focused on them with intent. She walked right up to Ronnie.

"You're Jack Michaels's son," she said as a statement, not a question. "The lawyer."

Ronnie straightened his back and adjusted his hat for a perfect fit.

"I am. Do I know you?"

"I saw you posting flyers at the front of the park and recognized you from Hybrid High."

"Oh, were you…er, I don't recognize you. Were you a teacher I had? I don't—"

"You went to school with my son. My older son." She nodded at Buck and the others. "I suppose you all did."

Buck couldn't help but sneak a few sidelong glances at the woman as she made small talk with Ronnie. It sounded as if she were angling for free coffee. The little boy with her was dancing at the end of her hand, trying desperately to break free. He had his eye on a squirrel hanging out at the base of a nearby oak tree. She probably needed more energy to keep up with him. Buck readied his denial of free samples speech.

"It's possible," Ronnie said. "I still don't know—"

She reached her free hand out to Ronnie. Ronnie stared at it, not sure what she wanted.

"Your dad is a saint for all he's doing," she said.

Ronnie, with a look of mixed confusion and gratitude on his face, shook her hand, as if that was the intention she had for sticking hers out.

"Okay. What is he doing?"

"He's looking into my son's case after the school's lawyers refused to touch it."

"Oh. What case?"

The woman hesitated to answer. Her skin lost a bit of color. But her gaze was nevertheless intense.

"My son died at school," she said. "I'm sure you've heard about it."

Buck, Ronnie, Jennifer, and Tiffany simultaneously gasped at her words. Ronnie added to his surprise with a finger-point at her.

"You're—you're Lester Biggins's mom?"

She nodded.

"My son did not commit suicide, despite what the school alleged. I'm sure of that. And your dad agrees with me. I know he's not that kind of lawyer, but his involvement in finding me the right team has been a godsend to our case, and we think we're going to hit a breakthrough soon. So, I don't know what kind of relationship you have with your parents. Lester was always open with us about his problems and concerns, and nothing in his words or attitudes ever suggested he wanted to throw himself off a cliff. So, I don't believe he threw himself off. But I wanted you to be proud of your dad, just in case. He's a good man. And I also wanted to clear my son's name, just in case you've heard and believed a lie."

Ronnie took off his hat and held it to his chest. He was speechless.

Buck, meanwhile, had started brewing the woman a cup of coffee, free of charge.

"Before I go," Lester's mom said, "I also have one request. From all of you. If you hear of *anything* that might give my lawyers ammunition against the school or whoever's responsible for his *murder*, please contact me. We've been at this for so long, the resistance has gotten exhausting. But we believe someone is hanging onto the truth."

Ronnie and Tiffany nodded. Buck was so busy dashing his attention back and forth between her and the coffee pouring into the polystyrene cup that he didn't react. But he understood. Jennifer, meanwhile, was quiet after hearing the woman's words. She just stared at the ground, chewing on something that wasn't physically in her mouth.

Lester's mom released her younger son's hand to reach into her purse. While he ran off after the squirrel, she pulled out a small card and handed it to Ronnie.

"Your dad already has my information. But you should have it, too, just in case."

She retrieved three more cards, one for each of them.

When Buck took his card from her, he passed her the cup of coffee.

"On the house," he said. "If you want it."

She accepted. He also offered her and her young son a donut.

* * *

THE FIRST PAYING CUSTOMERS of the day trickled in a few minutes before noon. Buck's mind had buzzed so much over Lester's mom's request that he'd almost forgotten why he was there. That people showed up also caught him off guard since Ronnie and Tiffany were still hanging out under the pavilion and not yet patrolling the park for potential recruits. As a result, he wasn't yet ready to serve.

He was tempted to tell the early arrivals that the shop wasn't open yet. But he thought better of it. They were here, and they were ready to spend money. Money on coffee that he would make them. What moron would turn them away?

"Just one moment," he said to the first customer, a jogger who had already sweated a gallon through his T-shirt.

And just like that, Buck Star was back in business.

Taking their cues, Ronnie and Tiffany each patted him on the arm and ran off to start their marketing gigs. Jennifer, meanwhile, stayed behind to take each customer's order on a notepad. As a coffee server at Melty's, she had experience with coffee and customer service.

Once they'd served and seated the starting line, five customers in total, Buck whispered his thanks to Jennifer. She winked in response.

The initial rush, however, was just that: initial. Once the first five customers drank their coffees and tossed their cups in the trash, the pavilion was quiet again.

Too quiet.

Buck checked the time. It was a quarter past twelve.

"Where's the saxophonist?" he asked.

Jennifer glanced down the hill, but she had nothing to offer but a shrug.

Five minutes later, a black car cruised up the access road and parked by the storage room. A slick man with the hair to match stepped out in a dark suit and dark sunglasses and marched up to the pavilion with sax and amplifier in hand.

"You pay before I play," he said without a hello.

"Pardon?"

"You the owner of this joint?" The saxophonist lowered his sunglasses just enough to reveal the upper slivers of his dark eyes. This must've been Johnny Bones.

"I run the business, yeah. But—"

"One-twenty, in cash. Then I start the jam."

Buck scanned the pavilion. For now, it was just him and Jennifer present. No one else was coming up the hill.

"How experienced are you?"

"Good enough to do what I came here for."

Buck winced at his answer. More like a non-answer. But he went with it. Time was wasting.

"You need to set anything up first? There's a plug by the coffee equipment."

"I've already done you one favor. Now it's time to pony up. Make sure you're good for it. With businesses like these…" Johnny Bones lowered his sunglasses to the tip of his nose. He studied the pavilion and the surrounding situation. "No telling how much you'll have left at the end of the day."

Buck understood his point. He'd had plenty of days like that already, and he'd been at this for just over a month.

"What favor? I'm hiring you."

"I got out of my car. Normally, you come to me. But you're new to this jam, and frankly, your operation here seems, how shall I say, pathetic."

"Thanks."

Buck was ready to send the guy home, but Jennifer swooped in beside him and offered the saxophonist a toothy smile, one of her best.

"One-twenty is fine," she said. "Could you start setting up? We're expecting more customers to arrive any moment."

She elbowed Buck in the biceps. Buck snapped out of his flash of resentment and went to the money pouch to retrieve six twenty-dollar bills.

"The agreement was for five hours," Buck said, as he handed over the money, bidding it a silent farewell as it got sucked out of his hand and instantaneously slurped into Johnny Bones's pocket. "Or twenty-four dollars an hour."

"I'm aware," the saxophonist said in an insulted tone.

"Just saying, you're twenty minutes late, and we close at five."

Johnny Bones tapped his sunglasses back in place. "Then stay open 'til five-twenty. You'll get your money's worth. Chill, dude. I got this riot."

Buck's jaw tensed. He glanced at Jennifer for wisdom, relief, or validation—he wasn't sure what he needed that moment. Her expression was calm as she nodded at him.

"Thank you," she said to Johnny Bones. "We'll be happy with whatever you play. Please start playing."

Ten minutes later, the saxophonist completed his equipment installation and warm-up set, just in time for the next wave of customers to arrive with Ronnie and Tiffany leading them up the hill.

Finally, Buck could relax. Every necessary component of this grand reopening was now in play. By closing time, he would be well on his way to becoming a solid competitor against Chet and this ridiculous bet once again.

"Any requests?" the saxophonist asked the people standing in line.

One person requested "Baker Street."

"Coming right up."

And with one smooth transition from standing upright to leaning against the side of a picnic table, left knee up, chin tilted down, Johnny Bones slid the instrument's mouthpiece into his mouth and belted out the worst version of "Baker Street" Buck had ever heard.

Where the original version's sax solo sounded like velvet sadness treading water in a rainfall, Johnny Bones's version sounded like the ducks from the nearby lake having an orgy.

"What the hell…" Buck couldn't think of any words to follow his shock.

Johnny Bones stopped the song midway and apologized to the crowd.

"Just warming up, folks. Not the easiest song to play without the lyrics or the supporting band. Just gotta find my rhythm."

He started again. This time, the geese joined the fowl fornication fest.

"Anyone want to request an easier song?"

No one had any suggestions.

"Here, I'll play you 'Careless Whisper.' You'll love it."

Buck gritted his teeth. "Careless Whisper" by Wham! wasn't exactly his favorite song, but it was high on the list. If Johnny Bones's cover was anything like the one he'd just played…

Buck braced himself. But not well enough. Out of the saxophone's horn came the entangled cries of ducks and geese creating a mutant nest of quacklings. Violently.

Buck stuck his fingers in his ears. But it was no use. The sound bled through.

"There's something wrong with my instrument," Johnny Bones said. "Let me run home and get my backup. Don't go anywhere. I'll be right back."

He ran to his car and drove off.

He never returned.

"Yeah, that was Billy Durk's friend," Ronnie said, when an hour passed and Johnny Bones hadn't come back. "Billy Durk's an idiot."

Buck considered the $120 he'd given the guy for nothing.

"Billy Durk isn't the only one," he said.

Jennifer, who was patrolling the picnic tables to check on each customer's needs, must've overheard their discussion because she came over with a knowing look on her face and an idea in her head.

"I think I know how to fix this," she said.

Like Johnny Bones, she raced off without another word. But unlike Johnny Bones, she returned half an hour later with a boombox and a stack of mixtapes in hand.

The rest was like magic.

She plugged the music player into the outlet. Found a tape that triggered her delight. Popped it into the tape deck. Hit PLAY.

And then came a moment Buck hadn't prepared for: absolute beauty pouring out of Jennifer's mouth as she lent her surprisingly angelic voice to the music.

Everyone under the pavilion stared. Buck's heart melted. If Ronnie and Tiffany were also entranced, Buck didn't know.

There were no ducks or geese having angry sex anymore. This time, it was a songbird.

For the next hour, everyone who walked by stopped to listen to her sing.

Most of them bought a cup of coffee while they listened.

But Buck forgot to count how many there were.

Jennifer kept singing.

Episode 46

Crack Security

DOWNHILL FROM THE PAVILION, crouching behind a prickly shrub, Dodo Pollock found himself torn between maintaining lookout duty and making a run for it. His job, as he understood it, was not supposed to be complicated, even for him. He just had to listen to any comments spoken among visitors, regardless of whether they bought coffee or served it. If they discussed "business strategies" or "secret ingredients" or "something useful," whatever that all meant, he had to write it on his arm. Or if they talked about pricing or coffee quality, Dodo had to jot that down, too. Then he had to take his list to Pigeon and Pigeon's scary blond jock friend for further discussion.

As long as he didn't miss a word, he'd earn his ten minutes at the arcade this weekend. Nothing in the assignment suggested he should make a run for it.

But all that singing made him cringe. That blonde girl was hot, no question about that. Even at ten years old, Dodo knew the difference between a girl who was gross and a girl who wasn't, and the girl singing by the pavilion was most definitely not gross. But she had nothing on Madonna. Her voice was like a bicycle bell, ringing, and ringing, and ringing. No rhythm or pop. Just high-pitched squealing.

Strangely, the people around the pavilion seemed in awe of her singing, but Dodo was not so easily charmed. Maybe he didn't understand the appeal—everyone often said he was too young to understand this or that, and this could've been one of those cases. But it was equally possible that she had put some magical chemical in the coffee she was serving to keep them listening. Dodo noted "chemicals in coffee" on his arm. She had to be poisoning them to keep them interested in her song.

After several minutes of fidgeting behind the bush, Dodo made his decision. He'd stick his fingers in his ears until she finished. No one was saying anything that Pigeon would care about, anyway. If he knew his older brother well, Pigeon would rather someone repeat what Dodo had done on the Fourth of July. What difference did knowing the enemy's strategy even make when you could cripple them with yet another explosive to the equipment supply?

Of course, Pigeon had forbidden Dodo to go anywhere near his explosives after he'd failed to destroy the storage room completely. "Stop wasting my stash on a half-assed job," he said. That was the main reason Dodo was on listening duty now. But Pigeon would've been grateful if Dodo had brought the whole pavilion down.

So, if Dodo dared to try again, he'd have to be more thorough in the destruction. And he'd have to keep quiet about it until he knew Pigeon would approve of the result.

It was the best way to ensure he'd never get suckered into listening duty again.

* * *

Dodo must've fallen asleep behind that shrub because the world around him was suddenly quiet. No screeching masquerading as singing at the pavilion. No poisoned customers pretending to like what they'd heard. Now that the sun was low on the horizon, the only jogger left in sight was rounding the lake and heading south.

Beyond that, no one was around. Just Dodo and the bugs crawling at his feet. The pavilion was his now.

He crawled out from behind the bush and crept to the nearest picnic bench. Even though the place looked abandoned, he wasn't ready to believe it. That singing girl and her friends could just as easily be hiding on the opposite side, right behind the wall by the bathrooms. He had to make sure.

Nope, they'd all left. He was alone now.

Dodo sneaked around to the storage room and tested the door handle. It was locked. Just as before.

He checked his surroundings. The jogger was gone. None of the park rangers were on patrol in this area.

They had made his job really easy.

He checked his pocket to confirm what he'd already known. Just the pen he'd been using to mark up his arm. No explosives this time.

But he could get more if he found his brother's stash. And if he did a thorough job destroying all the equipment this time, Pigeon might even promise him twenty minutes at the arcade. That is, if he dared to even tell him what he'd done.

In the distance, a coyote howled. Dodo dashed for the sidewalk leading out of the park. It was time to meet up with his brother and his brother's scary jock friend to report what he'd found.

* * *

"WHAT DO YOU MEAN she poisoned them?"

Pigeon's scary blond friend edged closer to Dodo, forcing him to shrink back. His eyes displayed more disbelief than anger, probably in line with the tone of his question. But Dodo didn't know him personally, so he didn't trust him. Pigeon's friends often had that reputation. Normally, Dodo would just run away, relieving himself of the personal torture that comes with big kids threatening him with their harsh questions. But now that he was on the scary friend's turf, he had nowhere to retreat. He had to ride this one out, tell the big jock what he wanted to hear.

"She sang to them, and they didn't hate it," he said.

Pigeon's scary friend tossed his hands up and spun away. "Why are you even giving him a job?" he asked Pigeon, who was standing a few feet away.

"Because he's my brother, and I have to give him things to do to keep him out of trouble."

Pigeon did his best to keep a straight face, but he wasn't good at it. Even if he was serious and meant every word, those same words wouldn't come without a strain of laughter laced beneath them. The first time Dodo noticed this quirk about his brother happened the first time Pigeon killed one of Dodo's goldfish, on accident, of course, as Pigeon asserted again and again. As the years went on, Pigeon proved he was accident-prone.

"Jennifer's not a bad singer," the scary friend said. "And she didn't poison anyone. This is a waste of my time."

"Well, he can't go home. No one's there."

Pigeon and the scary friend exchanged glances. The scary friend looked unhappy.

"How much trouble can he really get into being away from you?"

"He'll find a way."

The scary friend waved Pigeon off. "Somehow I doubt you're blameless in that." Now he was looking at Dodo. "Go home, kid. You're useless to me."

Finally, a concept Dodo was familiar with. The sooner he got away from the scary friend, the better.

Without a word, Dodo raced out the front door, hardly interested in all the cool statues on the scary jock's front lawn. Well, except for that pink flamingo by the driveway. He had to kick that one before hopping on his bike and riding into the night.

* * *

WHEN DODO GOT HOME, he ditched his bike in the backyard and knocked on the door for someone to let him in. When no one answered either the front or back doors, he found his dad's trusty crowbar at the bottom of the tool pile and used it to latch open his bedroom window. Once inside, he swatted away the flies buzzing over his bed, turned on a few lights to keep from tripping over Pigeon's pile of metal in the dark, and searched the room for Pigeon's secret stash, which seemed to change locations every night.

Dodo had to look inside every box and run his hand through every mound of unwashed linens before he found the prize he was searching for. Underneath Pigeon's stack of unread textbooks was an envelope stuffed with M-80s. Dodo grabbed a couple and stuffed them in his pocket. He found a lighter in the kitchen.

***

Shortly after midnight, Dodo returned to North Park and hopped over the gate to the parking lot. Just as it was the night of the Fourth of July, the park was nothing more than shifting shapes and shadows, with a few amber lights glowing over sections of the expansive sidewalk winding its way into the depths. Somewhere out there, the park rangers were on patrol, but they were also in cars. Dodo would have to ride fast and stick close to the shadows if he wanted to get to the pavilion without being noticed.

His first close call happened almost immediately at the entrance. As he dashed across the illuminated parking lot, he spotted movement out of the corner of his eye. A pair of headlights was rounding a corner from behind a low hill and coming into the lot. He pedaled hard and fast, streaking onto the sidewalk and into the safety of darkness before the headlights moved level with the start of the trail and the vehicle's driver stepped out to investigate. Dodo checked over his shoulder to see if he had attracted attention.

The patrol car had stopped at the sidewalk entrance, but no one got out. It was possible the driver was watching his shadow, but because no one was taking action, it was equally possible the driver had simply reached his next station and would spend the next five minutes eating a sandwich.

Because the driver hadn't made any new moves, Dodo cast the vehicle out of mind. He had a mission to fulfill, and he'd rather do it with the ranger camping at the front of the park, not the back where Dodo was headed.

His second close call happened three minutes later when a stray dog dashed out of a bush and started chasing him down the sidewalk.

The dog, likely a Doberman or Rottweiler, was fast. Really fast. No matter how hard Dodo pushed on his pedals, the animal's snarls were inches behind his heels, and a couple of times Dodo could've sworn he'd felt a nip and a subsequent sheen of hot liquid dripping onto his skin.

But onward he rode.

The dog did not tire, however, and Dodo yelled at the animal to leave him alone as his own exhaustion set in. Whether the dog heard him, though, was uncertain. It barked so loudly that Dodo could barely hear his own voice.

Yet onward he rode.

Dodo's calves burned, and his lungs were nearing a similar discomfort. Fortunately, the snarls grew quieter every few seconds. Maybe the dog was slowing down. If only Dodo could afford to slow down himself.

But he couldn't.

He wouldn't.

So, onward he rode.

The sidewalk was coming up on a crossing where the park's main road cut through two hills. A pair of amber streetlights kept the intersection safe for anyone who hadn't yet gotten to their cars by the park's closing at nightfall. Dodo was about to race between the hills, through the sidewalk intersection, when another pair of headlights increased the road's brightness ahead.

With the angry dog drifting farther but still close behind in pursuit, Dodo had to make a decision: keep going and risk exposing himself to the owner of those headlights or ride up the hill to stay out of sight but risk drawing the dog within biting range.

He glanced over his shoulder. The dog was too scary. Dodo chose the headlights.

His stomach was on fire, but he pushed on his pedals as hard as he could as he lined up his handlebars with the gap between the two posts separating the trail from the road. The headlights were brightening, and he was certain he was about to play a game of chicken with the driver. But he raced on. And he punched through the gap.

The ranger's car was just to his right. There was no way Dodo had blasted past his nose without being seen.

The car tires screeched to a stop behind him, and the flashes of red and blue lit up the grass around him. But it was the bloodcurdling squeal of the dog in pain that almost knocked Dodo off his bike.

Now that he was tens of feet past the road, he dared to look over his shoulder again.

The car had come to a stop. And its lights were on, as Dodo had assumed. And the driver, a bona fide park ranger, was getting out of his car.

But the ranger was not giving his attention to Dodo or the sidewalk. He was attending to the dog he'd just hit.

Something in Dodo's gut stung him that moment. But he tried to suppress it. The dog had threatened to bite him. Dodo did nothing to deserve its agitation. And the ranger wasn't going that fast. The car might've been going fast enough to hurt it, but not to kill it. The dog would survive. It just had to shake off the car's sudden bite and forget it ever happened. The dog would turn out fine. He was certain of that. He had to be. At worst, it would need to see a vet. At worst.

Dodo rode on before the park ranger turned his attention to the dark where he was lurking. He was already close to his destination. He hoped the dog would be okay.

There were no other close calls after that. Dodo reached the lake where no road was visible. From there, he had to ride along its shoreline until he found the hill where the pavilion stood. He could ride at a leisurely pace. He could even catch his breath.

Ten minutes later, Dodo dropped his bike near the shore and marched up the hill to the spot where that girl had sung earlier that day. And just like before, the place was empty. He had the pavilion all to himself.

After checking the bathroom door to find it locked, he marched around to the other side of the building where he could pee on the side of the trash can. Once he finished, he reached into his pocket for the first M-80. Fortunately, it was still dry, despite how badly he was sweating after his hard ride.

The M-80 was an awesome little piece of explosive joy. Smaller than a stick of dynamite, but more powerful than a firecracker, it did serious damage at an affordable price. Once the wick was lit, the mystery of its upcoming destruction would soon reveal its secret. Dodo giggled in anticipation every time he lit one.

With no dogs or park rangers getting in his way, Dodo set the explosive on the door handle and readied the wick. Then he reached for his lighter and flicked it.

Then came the explosion of sound. But not from him or his firecracker. And not from a barking dog.

"Get away from the door, kid!"

Dodo lost control of the lighter, letting it fall to his feet. His spine tensed. But he saw no one.

"I said, back away, or the next bullet goes in your ass!"

Next bullet? Was there a first?

Dodo reached for the lighter, but another explosion ripped the silence. He fell backward as he failed to take it.

"Last warning, kid! Time to go!"

It was at that moment that he noticed what he hadn't seen before. Just on the edge of the light surrounding the pavilion, a dark car was parked at the edge of the access road, and a hulking figure was stepping away from it, into the light.

The figure had a handgun pointed right at him.

Dodo didn't know what to do. His feet failed to move. And his body had no more feeling he recognized. It was possible that his butt was sliding along the concrete away from the storage room door. But he could've just as easily felt the current of blood in his body pushing him as if he were a boat. He was getting seasick sitting there.

The hulking figure in black leather and vicious smiles stamped his way across the road as he approached the trashcans and storage room. His weapon remained fixed on Dodo's head.

"I'm going to count to three," the man said.

Dodo noticed his clothing lacked the usual park ranger patches he'd expect to find on a park authority figure this time of night.

"There will not be a four."

This man was scruffy. Angry. Not the man he'd seen attending to the dog.

"One…"

Nor was the car on the edge of the access road a ranger's vehicle. This car was black with a sheen on its paint, as if it were owned by a rich man, or a gangster.

"Who are you?" the man demanded.

Dodo's tongue froze. He didn't know what to say.

"I said, who are you?"

Silence.

"You start talking or you'll never speak again. Who are you?"

His tongue dislodged from the roof of his mouth. "Dodo."

"What did you call me?"

Dodo stammered. "That's my name."

The man cocked his head to the side.

"You making fun of me?"

"No–no…"

"What's your *real* name?" The man's eyes were turning red, as were his cheeks.

"That is my real name."

The man considered his answer.

"Dodo what?"

"Pol–Polluck."

"Your parents must hate you. Get up." The man gestured at him with the gun, but Dodo was stuck to the pavement.

"I said, get up. Two…"

"I can't move." Dodo noticed his zipper was wet. He must not have finished peeing earlier.

The man pointed the gun at Dodo's feet and fired a round. Chunks of concrete leapt up and fell against his shoes.

Dodo found his motion. Less than a minute later, he was on his bike and speeding for the park exit.

As far as he knew, the lighter was still by the trashcans and the M-80 was still on the storage room door handle. At this point, they could stay there forever for all he cared. He just wanted to go home and crawl into bed and cry.

Pigeon owed him a whole day at the arcade for this one.

* * *

DODO NEARLY PISSED HIS pajamas again when his bedroom window slid open. Fortunately, it was his brother sneaking in at what must've been three in the morning. When Pigeon saw him staring back, he growled at him.

"What are you still doing awake? Turn off the light."

"I can't sleep." Dodo was still shivering under his sheet, which was wrapped tightly around his body.

Pigeon winced as he stepped over his pile of metal to reach the lamp. Apparently, he was still in pain from all the bruises he'd suffered earlier falling down a flight of stairs. "Well, you aren't gonna keep me awake."

Pigeon turned off the lamp. The only light casting shadows around the room anymore came from the street outside.

"Chet didn't scare you, did he?" Pigeon asked.

"No." Pigeon's friend did scare him, but Dodo would never admit that.

"Then, I don't know why you can't sleep."

Dodo knew why, but he couldn't tell Pigeon. His brother had forbidden him to take his stuff after the Fourth of July incident, especially his M-80s. If he told him what had happened tonight and admitted to failure, his brother would definitely get mad. And when Pigeon was mad, he was accident-prone. Several goldfish and a few cats and dogs had already learned that the hard way. There was no reason little brothers couldn't learn the hard way, too.

"Me either," Dodo said.

* * *

DAY 37: TUESDAY, JULY 16, 1985

Buck's Savings Account: $120.58

Buck's Wallet: $427.16

Buck's Business Funds: $119.58 (from SDTS Earnings)

Funds-to-Wallet Refund Due: $14.65 + $7.59 (spent on supplies)

Buck's Expenses: $2 a day*

Hours of Operation: pending

Money on Hold: none

THE NEXT MORNING, AFTER what might've been his most successful sales day yet, Buck was getting ready to head out the door when the phone rang. He considered ignoring it, but curiosity got the better of him.

"Would you like to accept a collect call from…?"

Buck was about to hang up when a semi-recognizable voice came through.

"Mr. Stamps," the voice said.

Now Buck was even more curious.

"Okay."

"Buck Star," the man said, once the operator got out of the way. It sure sounded like Mr. Stamps. "Had a really successful night last night. Stopped a vandal and everything."

Now he had to sit down. "Really?"

"Yeah, little brat with an M-80. Scared him off before he could blow the lock."

Now he shifted in his seat. He wanted to get comfortable for this. "When was this?"

"Just after midnight. Let me tell you, buddy boy, you sure paid for your security fee last night. That kid was about to wreck your world."

Buck screwed his face in thought. He wondered if this was the same vandal that had destroyed his storage room the first time.

"Can you describe him?"

"Yeah, just a punk kid. About nine or ten. Pocket full of explosives. Came to do serious damage. Made him piss his pants. Don't think he'll bother you again."

"That's good. Did you turn him in to the police?"

"Nah, kid made a run for it. But I got a name if you want to track him down."

Buck didn't love the idea of chasing after a nine- or ten-year-old kid with the law. But he also didn't want the kid attacking him a third time if he was the same person who'd attacked on the Fourth of July.

"Probably not a bad idea." He reached for the notepad. And the pen.

"Dumb name," Mr. Stamps said. "Calls himself Dodo."

Buck dropped the pen. His throat was suddenly dry.

"Dodo Polluck?"

"Yeah, how did—"

"Thanks for the info."

"Yeah sure. Say, I need another small payment from you, if you don't mind."

Buck cast his eyes toward the front door. He had to get his workday started.

"Didn't we already agree you'd cover tonight, too?"

"Yeah, about that. So, I'm in jail at the moment. But not to worry—"

Buck pitched forward, nearly knocking his knees into the coffee table.

"Jail? Why? What happened?"

"Yeah, so, that kid was up to no good. Needed a proper fear of God in him, you know?"

"No, I don't. What did you do?"

"So, nothing injurious or anything. Just a warning shot at his feet. Not a big—"

"Warning shot?" Buck reached for the first thought in his head. "You mean like from a gun?"

"Yeah, you know. Farmers use it to scare the birds. I scared my own bird. But let me tell you, those park rangers…"

Buck had heard enough. He wasn't about to put a reckless bouncer's bail on his growing tab of insane expenses. So, he hung up.

After the handset hit the cradle, Buck buried his head in his hands and shook it. Things were definitely out of control now. Pigeon's brother was part of the sabotage game. The boy was a miscreant like his brother, but he was still young and had a chance for a better path. This was not it. Everything was a mess.

And that's when an even more horrible realization finally hit him. He'd spent the last few minutes sitting on the couch, in full contact with the cushion, and didn't even notice.

* * *

A FTER HIS SECOND MORNING shower, Buck got dressed and headed for his garage. He decided that before he opened the Coffee Pavilion this morning, he would stop by the Liquid Shack for a quick word with the owner. And he'd bring a golf club with him just to make sure his message was clear.

T HE ALARM CLOCK SCREAMED at him for the sixth time that morning. Fed up, Pigeon reached under his pillow and hurled a knife at it. The hilt knocked it right in the face, forcing it off the TV tray. But it kept whining.

Agitated by the noise, Pigeon pressed the pillow against his ears.

"Dodo, shut that damn thing off!"

His little brother must've been in the room because the alarm eventually stopped, and something shuffled along the floor back to Dodo's bed.

"What time is it, anyway?"

"Dunno," Dodo mumbled. "Didn't look."

Pigeon, knowing he'd regret his next move, peeked out from under the pillow. Although it was lying on the floor on its back, he could see the clock's face as plain as his usual bread sandwich lunch.

Nine o'clock. Time for work.

He contemplated sleeping in for another few hours since his body was more important to him than his job, especially since Chet and he went way back, and Chet would understand. But Chet's been extra aggressive with the sales lately, probably because of that twerp Buck Star gaining some ground on their stupid bet, so he could've just as easily earned his ire for being late.

Pigeon cursed at his bed sheet. He'd have to get up and go to work now.

"All right, I'm out," he said to Dodo, who was probably already fast asleep. "Don't burn the house down while I'm gone. Mom and Dad will kill me when they get back from Tahiti or wherever the hell they went if you do. And you know what that means."

Dodo didn't answer. But he knew.

Pigeon rolled onto his back and took a breath. The deeper he inhaled, the worse his lungs ached. He'd take it like a man.

He was still in pain from the beating he'd gotten from that blonde girl when he'd gone to Buck's house last Friday, and even more so from the beating he'd taken late Friday night from the trucker who'd found him in a ditch on the side of the highway a hundred miles north of town and brought him home for a fee he couldn't pay. So, he had extra reason to stay in bed this morning. But the pain wouldn't hinder his moving like a cat today. Only the weak slept off a series of bruises instead of walking it off, and Pigeon was no weakling.

So, he slipped out of bed and searched his pile of metal for a companion tool of the day as if there was no such thing as pain. A crowbar was too large to hide in his waistband, and his swords were meant mainly for intruders and the tree out back. That left him with just one of his knives or his half-dozen shurikens, also called throwing stars, to take with him to work today.

Today was Tuesday. Torture Tuesday. Good day for the knife if Chet were to bring him lemons to cut and slice and skin alive. Not so much for the ninja stars, which were better on days he used the lemons for target practice, days like Wipeout Wednesday or Throwing Thursday, but perfect for a knife.

Of his knives, most were great at cutting, but the gold butterfly knife best matched his belt. He flicked his wrist to spread open its handles and reveal its blade. Smooth.

Then, ignoring the sharp throbs drilling into his body from his numerous bruises, he threw it at the side of Dodo's mattress, startling the boy awake. The blade had wedged into the bottom sheet, just inches from Dodo's hand that was draped over the side. Even if it wasn't Throwing Thursday or Slasher Saturday, the knife was still a fine companion for the day.

Dodo, realizing what had happened, flung his pillow at his older brother.

"What'd you do that for?"

"Wakey, wakey. I'm leaving. Don't burn the house down, or you know what will happen."

Pigeon plucked the knife out of the mattress and headed out through the bedroom window before Dodo could retrieve his pillow and throw it again. Last thing he wanted was to encourage that kid's violent streak.

* * *

He'd broken a few speed limits and run most stop signs and red lights to get there, but Pigeon made it to the Liquid Shack on time, or his version of on time, which was 9:23 on the dot. He knew that because Chet showed him his watch when he came hiking across the grass to meet him.

"Do you need an alarm clock?" Chet asked.

"No, I've got plenty already. Thanks."

Chet shook his head and returned his attention to the cash box. He was in the middle of his ritual morning funds review when Pigeon arrived.

"Get to work," Chet muttered.

Pigeon swung the flat edge of his hand to his forehead in salute, then winced from the pain of his sudden motion. Not only had he inflamed his bruises in that move, but he'd accidentally smacked himself. Chet didn't seem to notice.

Pigeon's main job at the Liquid Shack was to assemble the canvas tent and set up the tables with supplies. Whenever he arrived, he'd assess the current wind direction and velocity and set the first tent spike in whichever spot around the tables was most against the wind. Today, that position was next to Tommy.

Tommy, who was squatting over a plastic juice dispenser with the hose from a beer keg in one hand and a canister of lemonade powder in the other, was busy prepping the juice bar and offered Pigeon neither acknowledgment nor notice when he approached. He just kept his attention on the concoction he was making. With every pump from the keg, water squirted from the hose, and Tommy would sprinkle some powder into the stream. He often called it "the perfect mix." Pigeon never understood why he couldn't just pour the powder in, then tip the keg upside down into the container. It would speed up the mixing process. But Pigeon wasn't the mixmaster of the group. He was the tentmaker.

After giving him an unrequited hello, Pigeon drove the first tent spike into the earth just inches from Tommy's right foot with a lunge from chest height. Although the move hurt like hell, it got Tommy's attention.

"If that had hit my foot…"

"So, what's the poison today?" Pigeon wrapped a thin rope attached to the canvas's closest corner through the metal loop on the spike's head in preparation to stand the tent's first leg.

"Same as every day. Why are you still asking?"

Pigeon leaned closer and barked in Tommy's ear. Tommy glared at him. Pigeon chuckled.

"Just erect the tent," Tommy said, as he returned his attention to the juice-making.

"How was breakfast?" Pigeon asked with a toothy grin. He loved asking this question. Tommy always hated it. As Tommy rolled his eyes, Pigeon knew he'd got him yet again.

"For the last time, I don't eat roadkill. Just set up the tent and leave me alone."

Pigeon reached into his belt and brandished the butterfly knife.

"Don't tell me what to do." He pushed one foot back to make sure he got the ninja action star pose right.

Tommy stepped away from him, his eyes falling on the knife handle. Pigeon hadn't yet flicked it open, but he was certain Tommy knew he could.

Tommy's hand remained firm around the hose as he slowly aimed it in Pigeon's direction. Pigeon laughed and shoved the knife back in his belt.

"The look on your face…" Pigeon said.

"You're asking to get shot, you know," Tommy said, no humor in his voice.

"I'm sure I could take a squirt of water to the chest. I'm so scared."

Pigeon turned his attention to the tent leg he had to stand. He was already growing bored with Tommy's seriousness. The guy rarely cracked a smile, and today was no different.

Maybe he should've flicked the knife open. That would've sparked Tommy's fire better, making the morning worth waking up for.

Or it would've at least done a better job distracting him for when Pigeon performed his daily ritual with the ice scoop. The ritual was always harder when Tommy was focused or in a good mood.

* * *

BY TEN O'CLOCK, PIGEON had driven the last tent stake into the ground, Tommy had prepped the third and final juice container with ice and their latest flavor, purple lemonade, or maybe it was grape, and Chet had finished accounting for the day's supplies. So, they were ready to serve. And it was a good thing because three people in business suits were already hovering near the tables, and, as Chet would often say, people in suits didn't like to be kept waiting.

But these same three businesspeople didn't see the bigger picture. They just saw lemonade. Or grape juice. They completely missed the hard work that went into serving them their juices. Not one of them glanced up at the tent or bothered to admire how well each of its legs stood against the wind. They looked only at the juice. Deep down, Pigeon found their oversight infuriating. And inconvenient.

The Liquid Shack was a shop made for utility, not aesthetics. Under the plain white canvas tent were three plastic tables arranged together like a horseshoe. The head table displayed the three juice containers with their spigots turned away from customers to prevent self-service, as well as several rows of paper cups ready for filling and the cash box with its contents turned away to prevent self-service. For an advanced market lemonade stand, it was all straightforward.

Under the table, several iceboxes awaited orders, along with a metal scoop for large hauls and an ice pick in case a customer wanted to negotiate the price, or as Chet suggested, to break off stubborn chunks for easier loading.

Again, all very practical and utilitarian. But also unassuming and convenient.

In the early days of the business, Chet insisted they use one of the paper cups to scoop ice into each juice cup. He said it would save them money. But as they gained business and paper cups became more precious, Chet had changed his mind and upgraded to the metal scoop. The side effect was they shoveled more ice into a cup and supplemented it with less juice. That meant more sales.

As a result, Chet proved himself wise as a shop owner. But he was also a brilliant marketer. He had figured out that printing and displaying his sales figures for each month where businessmen might see them showed the Liquid Shack's popularity, leading to more word-of-mouth, and more customers trying it out. That meant more numbers on the graph the following month. This rise in popularity meant that Chet could raise the prices of a cup by a nickel after every new graph was printed.

When they'd opened the business at the beginning of their senior year, in part to convince the community that they were decent people just trying to make it in this crazy world, but also to make some extra money for booze and strip clubs for once they became old enough to partake in them, they were charging a dollar per cup. Now they were over a dollar fifty. Or maybe two. Pigeon paid little attention to the current price. But for however much they were charging, they were using less lemonade than they had at the start. That was the beauty of the ice scoop.

But the ice scoop had other uses, too.

Neither Chet nor Tommy knew about the stash of cash Pigeon had hidden behind the bathrooms under the power line marker, which he'd buried with the ice scoop. Chet often complained that the cash box was short twenty bucks by Saturday each week, but he never figured out why. He usually blamed it on bad calculations and had even brought a calculator to keep track of incoming and outgoing funds. Because Tommy was in charge of sales, he was blamed for the bad math, and Chet demanded that he start using the calculator.

Tommy always insisted that his math was fine. Chet would then suggest he stop letting twenty bucks go missing if that were true.

Pigeon loved the conflict between them. But he also loved that neither one had figured out he was the one skimming the top, especially since he turned out his pockets before leaving each night but after burying his bonus.

The problem with skimming, though, was that he needed the perfect moment to sneak away and dig up the hole. That meant having at least one part of the day where he moved unnoticed. Some days, the arc and flow of business gave Pigeon the perfect cover to sneak away. But on other days, he had to stimulate conflict to distract them.

As long as he kept Tommy on edge, he could generate that opportunity. Tommy was often so concerned with quality and honor that he gave little attention to anyone other than himself. That made his buttons easy to push.

In times he couldn't get away, however, he'd put the money in a temporary location. This was generally riskier, as his temporary locations were easier to spot not only by Chet, but by any random park visitor who was looking in the right direction. Examples included behind the toilet or under the playground slide next to the bathrooms. In the year since he started working at the Liquid Shack, he'd lost only fifty bucks to bad positioning, and only ever to children. Fortunately, Chet hadn't caught on yet. But Pigeon and his knife were ready for the day he did.

"You gonna serve them or not?" Tommy barked, snapping Pigeon out of his reverie.

All three businessmen were lined up at the serving table, each one demanding a drink. Pigeon offered his best grin, the one he gave people he hated right before adding a drop of stomach-convulsing poison to their beverages of choice—in his fantasies, at least, not in reality, as he had not yet access to such poisons, nor had he the skill to squeeze in a drop without them noticing. After flashing a fake smile, he dug the metal scoop into the ice and shoveled so much into each cup that half of it spilled back into the cooler. Then he dug even deeper to grab some melted ice off the bottom to fill the cup's lowest centimeter with water. This allowed the cup to fill with lemonade much faster.

"Two bucks, please," Pigeon said through his teeth, as he passed the cup along to the first businessman.

The businessman stared at the cup and grimaced. He must've noticed how clear the lemonade looked in contrast to what was in the juice container.

"This just looks like flavored water," he said.

"Good, then you understand what you're buying. Two bucks, please."

The businessman slammed two one-dollar bills onto the table and stormed off. The other two businessmen watched with concerned looks on their faces. They were next in line.

Tommy, who was manning the cash box, took the money and filed each bill in the appropriate slot. Once he deposited the money, he gave Pigeon the evil eye.

Pigeon smirked. Everyone was starting the day in a bad mood, and he couldn't have been more pleased. He'd earn his extra five bucks for the treasure trove in no time.

By eleven o'clock, Pigeon had served a dozen cups of lemonade, mostly to businessmen or children, and skimmed his first dollar. He kept the dollar in his pocket for safekeeping. It was still too busy for him to sneak away to the burial spot unnoticed, or even to grab the ice scoop when there were no cups in need of filling, so it would stay in his pocket for the time being.

Ten minutes later, as the twelfth customer marched off cursing something under his breath, a new visitor arrived on the scene. But this one was already in a bad mood. This customer, a dork he often helped torture in high school, who never appreciated the life lessons Pigeon and friends were teaching him, was approaching the table with a scowl on his face and a golf club in hand.

* * *

CHET KICKED HIS CHAIR back as he rose from the table, nearly knocking aside all his precious sales charts. His eyes locked with Buck Star's, who was marching toward them and shaking his golf club at his side. A skirmish was coming, and Pigeon would watch it in 3D. Just the moment he was hoping for. He trembled with delight as he once again set his palm to his butterfly knife, ready to brandish the blade and rip some gashes into the skin of an angry dork in case Chet needed backup. And, boy, did he want to assist in this fight!

But Buck did not charge Chet nor the table he was hovering over. Rather, he came angling for Pigeon. What a pleasant surprise!

Pigeon flicked his butterfly knife's handle open, exposing the cold, metal blade. *Dork Dejour, coming up.*

The angry dork didn't keep on his trajectory, however. As soon as he made his way to Pigeon, he set his path for the drink table. His attention darted from one focal point to another. The only constant was that golf club bouncing by his side as he advanced.

"What are you doing here?" Chet asked, his voice strained but cautious. Buck was almost within spitting distance.

"I've had enough of your sabotage," Buck growled. "You mess with me, I mess with you."

"What are you talking about?" Chet's focus moved to the golf club.

Pigeon, meanwhile, tilted his hand back, preparing to throw his weapon. As long as he said nothing, the dork wouldn't suspect the attack.

"You tried to blow up my storage room. Again!" Buck smacked the side of the table with the club. "I've had enough!"

Chet stepped forward, his eyes still on the golf club. Buck was now within striking distance.

"I didn't—what are you even talking about?"

Pigeon was about to throw the knife when Buck spun around and pointed the golf club right at him.

"You sent your little brother to do your dirty work, you frickin' ass-nugget."

Pigeon relaxed his hand. What was he saying?

Buck, meanwhile, swung his club in Chet's direction.

"On your orders," he continued.

"Not my orders." Chet struggled to remain calm. "You're dreaming. And you're trespassing."

"It's public property, and I paid my entrance fee. You. Are. Lying."

Chet held up his palms in protest. "I think you and I need to discuss something here. I did not—"

"Pigeon's little brother snuck into the park last night with the same heavy-duty firecrackers that were used to blow up my storage room on the Fourth of July, intending to repeat the vandalism. Fact! Tell me you didn't send him. Tell me, you filthy *liar*!"

Chet was once again eyeing the head of the golf club, which was now inches from his throat. He could've reached out and snatched it from Buck's hand. Why he didn't, Pigeon didn't understand.

He also didn't understand Buck's accusation about Dodo. Pigeon's little brother would *never* smuggle his M-80s out of the bedroom, because he *knew* not to touch his stuff after what had happened on the Fourth of July. The story didn't add up.

It had better not add up.

"Pigeon," Chet said, his eyes still fixed on the weapon pointed at him. "Did Dodo try to blow up Buck's storage room last night?"

"Of course not." *He'd better not have.*

"My security officer says otherwise," Buck said.

"Your security officer?"

Buck's attention moved to the cups of ice on the table. His golf club hovered over them.

"The guy I hired to ensure you and your goons—not you, Tommy—stay the hell out of my business."

"Something you should be doing now with mine?"

Buck lowered the golf club head onto the table, right in the middle between the cups. Pigeon tightened his wrist again in case Chet asked him to lunge the blade into Buck's rib.

"Give me one reason I shouldn't wreck your operation right now," Buck said.

Chet glanced at Tommy, then fixed his attention on Pigeon. Pigeon felt his throat tighten.

"I'll ask again," Chet said. "Did Dodo try to blow up Buck's storage room last night?"

"I said no." Pigeon didn't like these kinds of accusations. These were the kinds of accusations dorks got stabbed over.

"Are you sure?" Chet asked.

"You're gonna believe this dork over me, your best friend?"

Chet shook his head. "You're not my best friend. And it depends. If Dodo didn't try to blow up Buck's storage room, then what was he up to last night after he left my house?"

"I don't know. Watching TV, probably."

"Can you find out before we have an incident here?"

"There's no need for—"

"Go ask your brother if he tried to blow up the damn storage room, Pigeon! Now!"

Pigeon took a step backward. This wasn't the first time Chet had snapped at him, but it was the first time he'd believed that dork over him.

He didn't know what to think about that, or what to feel.

Over his shoulder, Pigeon sensed Tommy watching the whole thing, calm yet judgmental. Pigeon spun around and pointed his knife at him.

"What are you scoffing at?"

Tommy stared at the knife's point.

"Get that out of my face if you care about your life."

Pigeon closed the knife and shoved it back under his belt. He stormed off towards the park's exit to get to the bottom of this mess.

* * *

ONCE HE GOT HOME, Pigeon found Dodo still in bed, wrapped in his top bed sheet, shaking and mumbling "stop" at something in his dream. Whatever he was dreaming about, it would stop. Right now. Pigeon grabbed him by the neck and forced him into a sitting position. Dodo's eyes shot open as his back slammed against the wall.

"Did you steal my M-80s last night?" Pigeon demanded.

Dodo's eyes bulged, then looked toward Pigeon's stash.

"No…"

"Then why was that dork claiming that you tried blowing up his storage room last night?"

"I don't—"

"He said there was a security guard and everything. What were you doing last night?"

Pigeon pushed his little brother harder against the wall. He wasn't ready to strangle him, so he released his neck and grabbed him by the shoulders instead.

"Answer my question!"

"I–I–"

Pigeon pulled him from the wall, then shoved him into it even harder.

"Answer the question!"

Dodo started to cry. Pigeon released his shoulder and slapped him across the face.

"Stop crying. Boys don't cry. What happened last night? Did you steal my M-80s?"

Through his choked sobs, Dodo got a few words out. Perhaps not enough to tell the whole story. But enough to paint a clear picture.

"I just–just wanted to help. That cop…"

"What cop?"

"The–the security (sob), the security guard…(sob), he pulled a gun on me and (sob)…he—"

Pigeon released his brother's shoulders. With his hands free, he wrapped his fingers around his butterfly knife and squeezed the hilt until his knuckles strained. "What did he do with the gun?"

"He–he pulled the trigger and—"

Pigeon pounded the mattress next to Dodo's knee with his other fist.

"The cop did what? He shot you?"

"He shot the ground (sob) by my feet, but—"

"At the park pavilion?"

"Y–yeah, when he caught me by—"

"That bastard!"

Pigeon wouldn't stand around waiting to hear the rest of the story. He'd leave his brother there to cry alone. Maybe he didn't know which cop he had to kill for shooting a gun at his little brother, but he did know which dork had hired that cop to do it. So, he knew who'd have to pay for this.

"Here, quit your crying." Pigeon reached into his pocket and tossed the dollar he'd skimmed from the Liquid Shack onto the bed. "Go to the arcade. Make a day of it."

Dodo took the dollar, but he didn't stop crying.

Despite his continuous physical pain, Pigeon climbed out the window and returned to his car. There was no follow-up plan in his mind, and there was no guarantee one would surface. He just knew what the outcome would be.

There would be blood.

* * *

AFTER SEVERAL HOURS OF stalking North Park for his prey, Pigeon found the dork leaving on his bicycle. Buck kept to the sidewalk as he rode out of the park entrance and rounded the park's outskirts and headed north, unaware of the eagle that was hovering at close range behind him ready to swoop down and strike. Pigeon had no idea where Buck was going, but wherever it was, he'd make his move once no one could see him.

Buck was in a hurry. He rode at a fast pace, his golf club sitting precariously across the handlebars. But then he slowed, as if time no longer mattered, as if he had reason to rest. It looked as if he was getting tired.

Pigeon held a modest distance back from Buck as they reached the edge of known civilization. Because he was in his car, he could keep up with the dork with no trouble, but because Buck was on a bike, Pigeon had to drive a bit too slowly for comfort. He convinced himself that all predators moved at less than twenty miles an hour before they made the kill, so the reduced speed was tolerable. But it wasn't comfortable. Driving that slowly could attract attention.

He decided to compromise his position a little to throw suspicious onlookers off the scent. Pigeon turned down a side street at his first opportunity and sped up to almost double the speed. Then he took the next street north and looped back around to the main road, just in time to watch Buck ride on by, oblivious to his presence.

This would be easy, Pigeon realized. Buck didn't know what was coming to him. So, he just kept on riding, as if he had no care in the world, as if he wasn't about to have his worst day ever.

* * *

Pigeon had never seen this road before. Wherever it led, it would offer no witnesses. It was like a mouse scurrying right into the jaws of the cat.

Buck continued riding up the winding road, never checking over his shoulder. This was good for Pigeon. He could drift up behind him unnoticed.

But a remote place like this came with certain risks. Because it was isolated, save for a small forest on either side of the narrow road, it wouldn't be difficult for Buck to hear Pigeon's engine sneaking up. That would give his position away immediately.

So, he couldn't tease his prey any further. It was now or never.

Pigeon floored it. His old beat-up Datsun raced up the road, closing the gap between him and Buck within seconds. The dork glanced over his shoulder inches before Pigeon's front bumper struck the back of Buck's wheel. Not enough time to figure out which bird had just eaten him.

Pigeon felt the force of the impact through the whole car, but he kept driving. The important thing was that the bike spun off the road, and Buck and his stupid golf club flew off into the trees with it, down into the ditch below the road's shoulder. Whether the dork stayed lifeless in the ditch, Pigeon wouldn't worry about it. His job now was to get the hell out of there before anyone connected him to a hit and run.

He kept driving down the road, hoping it had an outlet. But he discovered too quickly that there was neither an outlet nor much distance between the end of the road and the impact location. There was just a small rustic building with a sign by the door. The Hybrid City Chamber of Commerce. There was an even smaller parking lot in front of it. It was the only place Pigeon could turn his vehicle around.

Pigeon pulled into a space beside an ugly blue El Camino and threw the gear into reverse. As he backed out onto the road to face the opposite direction, however, he couldn't help but think the car was familiar. Really familiar.

He put his foot on the gas. He couldn't stick around to find out why.

But he couldn't stop dwelling on it, either. The El Camino tantalized him through his rearview mirror as its reflection shrank from view. He was pretty certain he knew that car, like a dream made real, or a peripheral predator coming into full view. If not for Buck lying in a ditch a few hundred feet ahead, he would have stopped to investigate further.

If not for Buck…

Pigeon tapped the steering wheel as he watched the El Camino drift out of sight. It was too familiar.

He felt a smile creeping across his lips. Maybe he could come back a little later once the heat faded to figure out why.

Buck's mood was still hot after Pigeon raced off in his ugly old beige Datsun, and his fury burned the back of his shoulders. But now that Pigeon was beyond the reach of his golf club, he had nothing left to damage. Even if he wanted to destroy every cup and every juice dispenser in retaliation for the near catastrophe against his storage room, he couldn't rightly punish Chet or the Liquid Shack for the crime. The blame fell squarely on Pigeon and his little brother.

With no other reason to stick around, Buck shook his head at Tommy, grunted at Chet, then marched off to his downed bicycle in the grass. As he stood the bike upright, Chet shouted at him.

"I swear I had nothing to do with it!"

Buck didn't look back. He just rode on for the park's exit. His fight would always be with Chet. But today, it was Pigeon who'd scheduled the meeting with his fist.

For the next hour, Buck rode around North Park, calming himself down, but also getting a sense for the day's clientele at the Coffee Pavilion. So far, the park had little activity, barely enough to get excited about, but that didn't surprise him. Given it was just Tuesday, he didn't expect yesterday's business. But he did anticipate its continuing upward trend towards a daily net profit. Even with the park looking bare across all fields and trails, he was confident traffic would pick up by afternoon.

He just wasn't confident about his sustained attendance today.

Pigeon had crossed the line letting his little brother attempt a second round of vandalism against the Coffee Pavilion, and Buck couldn't get the outrage out of his mind. Now that Mr. Stamps was in jail for threatening a minor with a firearm—what was he thinking?—Buck didn't have the overnight protection to prevent Pigeon or Dodo from striking a third time. To leave his business exposed to damage was unthinkable, yet he was out of ideas for protecting it. The last thing he wanted was to hire another lunatic to keep watch, especially if he could be held responsible for the outcome.

Buck shuddered at the hell that would've rained upon him if Mr. Stamps had actually struck Dodo with a bullet. The kid might've had absentee parents, but they'd step up in a heartbeat if it meant suing somebody out of house and home.

Either way, he needed a solution to his new problem.

By noon, Buck ended his nervous ride at the Coffee Pavilion and got the machines ready. Fortunately, Ronnie and Tiffany were already preparing the advertisements, so his tasks for the day were minimal. He could brood over his encounter with Pigeon in peace.

By three o'clock, however, Buck's concentration had finally given way to his frustrated daydream, so he asked Ronnie and Tiffany to finish out the day for him. He needed help in dealing with his vandal problem, and he needed peace of mind knowing that his solution wouldn't send another ally to jail.

As he left North Park on his bike, Buck thought through his list of contacts for someone who might connect him with a reliable security force. After running through his mental shortlist, he decided he would visit Mr. Perkins at the Hybrid City Chamber of Commerce. If anyone in town had the connections to help him without pillaging his bank account first, it was Mr. Perkins.

With lead in his feet, Buck pumped his bike pedals harder than ever, taking to the northern streets of Hybrid City as fast as he could. In part, he wanted to push the anger out of his system. But he also wanted to ensure he got to the Chamber of Commerce before Mr. Perkins left for the day. He didn't know the man's schedule.

But his fast ride didn't last long. After just a few minutes of heavy pumping, his calves burned, his feet ached with the thousand stabs of needles where his blood wanted to escape through his shoes, and his lungs heaved. He had to slow down to regain his breath and feel his feet again.

As he decelerated, however, a strange presence nipped at his back. He attributed the sensation to regulating blood flowing through his body, but the feeling wasn't comfortable. At one point, he checked over his shoulder to see if he was being followed, but there was nothing there. Just the street he was on, and the side street that bisected it. The back bumper of a beige vehicle was disappearing down the side road, but whomever it belonged to, they were likely headed home. Buck rode on.

Hybrid City was a relatively easy town to navigate if the bicyclist stuck to its central and southern regions. But once he got north of the parks, he'd have to deal with a network of residential roads at the base of a gradually steepening hill, and these roads demanded what little energy he had left. By the time he'd gotten out of the neighborhood and up to the bottom of the final stretch taking him to the Chamber of Commerce, Buck was out of breath.

But he rode on, pushing against one pedal and the other, as a Viking raider might push against the oar of a longship, or an Olympian might train into the dead of night. Left, right, left, right, *huff, huff, huff.* Up the hill he rode.

Up the hill, and through the woods, to the Chamber of Commerce he went.

It was a ride he'd taken several times before, but he'd always done it slower and steadier than he did now. This one was siphoning his energy. With little power left in the rest of his body, he couldn't maximize his sense of sight or sound, and now his sense of touch was failing. Only his sense of smell remained in a heightened state, and the scent of bad gas and burnt rubber grew stronger the higher up the hill he rode. It overpowered the natural pine scent coming from the surrounding woods, and it certainly didn't fit the environment.

He also felt his sixth sense creeping onto his back again. That feeling he'd gotten down in the neighborhood minutes earlier returned, this time with a stronger discomfort. He thought he could also hear an engine approaching.

Buck was about to turn his head and check whether he should ride along the shoulder, but a great force bumped him from behind, making that decision for him.

Next thing he knew, his world turned blurry and topsy-turvy.

He might've blinked. But that was it. As he looked down, the road was no longer beneath him, nor was his bike. He was, for a moment, just like Superman, flying without wings, but also like Humpty Dumpty, fragile on landing.

Buck's golf club hit the ground first. He came down into a patch of high grass right past it, smashing his shoulder into the earth, followed by his hip, and rolled hard down the shallow hill until he nearly cracked his ribs at the base of a tree.

Between the impact with the ground and the exhaustion he felt from riding hard all day, Buck's lights blew out.

But then they came back on. And he found his side throbbing with pain.

He tried to get to his feet, but he collapsed after rising to his knees. He tried again, this time lifting himself on his right elbow. Even though his left side was screaming at him, the pain in his right side was duller, so he could keep himself propped.

Up the hill, his bike had gotten caught on a tree. From the looks of it, it hadn't taken much damage. Just a slightly bent back wheel. But the frame was still good. He also found his golf club lying in a patch of grass much further from where he'd thought it had landed. Fortunately, it had also taken little damage, if any.

So, it seemed he was the only one who really suffered on impact. Good thing he could self-heal. He breathed a painful sigh of relief as he realized this setback wouldn't cost him much. He could probably hammer the bike wheel back into its proper shape once the pain in his side eased away.

If only he understood why he'd crashed. He hadn't felt a bump under his wheel. Just behind it. But he saw nothing. Only smelled it. Maybe heard it.

If there were a car, he'd missed identifying it.

Nothing he could do about that now.

The road was about thirty feet from where he'd stopped rolling. Because it was also about six feet up the hill, he'd have to punish his body further to get to the shoulder. But he couldn't risk lying immobilized in the woods for the rest of the night, so he had to push himself into motion.

He dug his elbow into the earth and pulled himself forward as he kicked out with his right leg, inching little by little toward the golf club as a fallen infantryman might crawl for the safety of a bunker after getting shot. The grass and the dirt took turns eating into his flesh as he scraped along, but up and along he went, wincing at every bite.

Soon, inches turned into feet, and seconds turned into minutes. After about five minutes of snaking up the hill, he wrapped his fingers around his golf club and stood it upright.

Now he had a cane.

Using the golf club to help him redistribute his weight, Buck got on his right knee and then onto his right foot. His knee wobbled slightly, but he held firm. With the club's help, he could stand and stay standing.

Next, he hobbled toward his bike, clenching his teeth in pain with every step.

It took Buck another ten minutes to reach the road with his bicycle wobbling beside him. Now that he could lean fully onto the bike, he used it to steady himself. It would be his crutch as he walked the remaining journey to the Chamber of Commerce.

Fortunately, the El Camino was still parked in the dirt lot once he got there, and the building's main entrance was still unlocked when he tried to open it. He stumbled inside.

"What the hell happened to you?" Lila raced over from her desk to help him. "Someone run you off the road?"

"I think so," Buck said. "Didn't catch the plate. Or the car."

Lila glanced at the front door as she took him by the wrong arm. "Ow."

"Sorry." She reached for the other side and tested his pain threshold. He nodded that it was safe. She walked him to the counter.

"I briefly glimpsed someone using the parking lot to turn around about thirty minutes ago. Figured it was just someone who had made a wrong turn. Didn't give them much attention. Maybe I should have."

Buck grabbed hold of the counter and propped himself up. As long as he didn't put any weight on his left side, he was fine.

"Too late now. Think you could drive me home after work? There's no way I'm getting anywhere by bike tonight."

"Yeah, five o'clock okay?"

"I have no choice. How are you doing, by the way?"

Lila returned to her chair.

"Don't change the subject. You need any aspirin? Ice pack?"

"I'll survive. I've been worried about you. Seriously, how are you?"

"I'll also survive."

"Lila, help me out. Give me some peace of mind in case I die."

She considered the question. Then nodded.

"I've been better. But the worst is behind me, I think." She picked up a pen and wrote something down in her notebook. "I decided I can't crawl in a hole and disappear from the world. Whatever that means, I just have to keep moving forward, you know?"

Buck nodded. The head motion gave him a slight headache.

"So, I figured I'd start by coming back to work. At least that's one normal thing in my life, if my life can have any sense of normalcy."

"It's good to see you," Buck said. He realized his jaw also hurt. He winced from the pain.

"You look miserable. You sure you're okay? You look like you fought a tree and lost."

"Had a rough morning. And afternoon, it seems. I actually came to see Mr. Perkins. Didn't think you'd be here."

"Yeah? Want me to get him?"

"If you don't mind. It hurts to walk."

Lila nodded at the sofa along the eastern wall.

"Why don't you have a seat over there? The cushions are soft. Here, I'll help you."

Lila was right. The sofa was better than standing. While she was off looking for Mr. Perkins, Buck tilted to his right side and lay down.

Ernest Bee came out of his office just as Buck got comfortable.

"Take off your shoes first if you're gonna do that," he said. "Nobody wants to sit on your muddy footprints."

"Can you just…I'm in pain here. Badger me another time. Please?"

Ernest Bee eyed him suspiciously.

"We don't house vagrants here. What are you playing at?"

Buck rolled his eyes. The headache grew a little more intense. He winced.

"I'm not a vagrant. You know that. You've been to my house."

Ernest Bee stroked his chin as he considered Buck's story.

"Aye, yes. I have been there." He marched over and swatted Buck's feet off the sofa. Buck cried out in pain, but Ernest didn't seem to notice. "Doesn't change the fact that you need to keep your damn feet off the couch."

"Hey," Lila shouted as she reentered the room from the back door. "Leave him alone. He was just hit by a car."

This seemed to get Ernest Bee's interest.

"You trade insurance?"

"Car didn't stop."

"Ah, a hit and run, was it?"

"Yeah," Lila said. "Some beige car, if it was the same one that U-turned in the parking lot half an hour ago."

"You get the license plate?"

"No, I was at my desk."

"Did you get the plate?" Ernest was now asking Buck.

"No, I was too busy hitting a tree."

"Unfortunate. Bet we could sue the bastard. Committing a crime on city property. Ooh, the legal playground we'd enter."

Buck tried to sit himself up. If he couldn't put his feet on the sofa, then there was no reason to lie on it.

"Your eagerness to weaponize your position gives me the creeps," Buck said. "But in this case, I think I agree with you."

Ernest Bee pointed his puffy gloved index finger at him. "That bastard tries to hit you again, you come find me, got it? We'll fry his ass together."

Buck did something in that moment that he'd never thought he'd do. He smiled at Ernest Bee.

"Thanks for not making this my fault."

"Ah, there's my visitor now." Everyone glanced toward the back to find the jolly old Mr. Perkins pulling himself through the door with his red and white striped cane. "To what do I owe the pleasure?"

Buck told Mr. Perkins the story involving the Coffee Pavilion and Mr. Stamps and mentioned the danger his business was in by not having adequate security. Mr. Perkins nodded at the story thoughtfully.

"Yes, yes, I can see how that's a conundrum. Anyone have any thoughts?"

Ernest Bee, who was still hanging around, tapped his forehead with his glove.

"Sounds like Mr. Stamps had the right idea."

Buck frowned at him. He'd almost won Buck's trust. But at least now the world had returned to equilibrium with that comment.

"I've had my own defensive problems lately," Lila said. "Not sure I'm the best person to ask."

"Yes, yes, we still need to discuss that if you're willing. But it's your business, not ours." Mr. Perkins leaned heavily on his cane as he hummed under his breath. "As for Buck Star's problem, the solution may also not be so simple. Buck, let me ask, why have you come to us with this problem?"

"I figured you'd know of all the legit businesses around here who might help. Maybe you know of a reputable security firm. Maybe you've worked with businesses that could make a recommendation. Hybrid City isn't exactly squeaky clean of all crime."

"No, no, it's not. But your business is in the park, yes?"

"North Park, yes."

"It still surprises me that the park rangers permit that. It used to be illegal to conduct business in our public parks."

"It still is," Ernest Bee chimed in. "But the Lease Agent has pockets deep enough to fill with park rangers. From my under-standing."

"Yes, yes, well either way, I'd think the park rangers would be all the security you'd need."

"They aren't, though," Buck said. "Someone, likely the same kid, blew up my storage room on the Fourth of July. I got stuck with the insurance bill. I need better security."

Mr. Perkins stroked his chin. "Yes, yes, I see why you may think that." A moment passed in silence. Something was entertaining Mr. Perkins's mind. He kept humming in a pitch that grew increasingly optimistic in tone until finally, "But maybe the better solution is to make so much money that no amount of vandalism can stop your success."

Everyone in the room gave him his or her undivided attention. Mr. Perkins was lost in thought until he noticed everyone staring at him.

"Buck, have you ever visited my specialty shop, Perks Outlet?"

Buck tried to shake his head, but then just said no. He didn't know Mr. Perkins had a store. Or if he did, he'd forgotten.

"Come with me. I'll show you something that can turn the tide of your fun little bet. Do you believe in magic?"

Buck almost laughed. "No."

"Neither do I, but what I have at my store is almost as good as magic." He nodded at Lila and Ernest Bee. "Will you two help Buck to my truck?"

They walked Buck to the parking lot outside while Mr. Perkins headed out the back door. Two minutes later, an engine with the voice of a monster roared to life behind the Chamber of Commerce building. A truck painted fire-engine red with six-foot wheels came rolling out from the access road on the side and bounced as it stopped.

"Hop in, my boy. We're off to embark on an odyssey." From the driver's side window, Mr. Perkins looked down at the others. "Anyone else want to come?"

Ernest Bee shook his head. "We still have work to do. And so do you."

"I shall return in a jiffy. Now, help the boy up. That first step is a beast."

* * *

Mr. Perkins parallel parked the truck alongside a hot pink building that had thick bars on its windows and an even thicker chain blocking its boarded-up entrance. Above the door was a broken sign that said PRKS OUTLE, with the E and the T clearly the main victims of the vandalism. Buck asked about it.

"Yep, not the nicest neighborhood in Hybrid City," Mr. Perkins said. He set the emergency brake and cut the engine. It made a sound resembling a monster's last snore before entering deep sleep. "Keeps the looky-loos out."

"Looky-loos?" Buck scanned the immediate area to find that none of the other stores were any better off.

"Don't want the wrong people knowing about the secrets of Perks Outlet. Only those who earn the right."

"Earn the right? The right for what?"

Mr. Perkins winked at Buck.

"A good businessman will run a profitable business. Perks Outlet is for those who get business. The better the grade, the better the opportunity, as they say."

"So, Perks Outlet is the better opportunity?"

Mr. Perkins popped open the driver's side door and swung his feet over the side.

"Come inside and see for yourself."

He jumped off the seat and disappeared out of sight, grunting as he landed on the street below. A moment later, Buck's passenger door opened, and Mr. Perkins offered him his cane to help him down.

Once Buck finally reached the sidewalk, Mr. Perkins was already working on the chain blocking the door.

The chain was hooked up to opposing sets of iron bars covering the windows on either side of the entrance and coiled around the door handle in several bulky concentric circles. Mr. Perkins looked over and smiled at Buck as he unspooled one chain layer after another from the door handle. The padlock was already in his hand.

"Even those who are curious can't be bothered to break through this chain," he said. "So, mine's the only business in the area that hasn't been burgled."

Three minutes later, the chain fell to the ground, leaving the door enough room to finally open.

"Need me to help you inside?" Mr. Perkins held out his cane for Buck to take.

Buck declined. "Just pick me up if I fall."

Mr. Perkins nodded. He stepped aside as he gestured for Buck to enter.

"Welcome to Perks Outlet," he said with a friendly smile.

Buck's jaw dropped as he approached the crack in the door. The sales floor inside was glowing neon and gold. It beamed so brightly that the slick colors spilled onto the sidewalk.

"Let me show you around."

Navigating the shop floor was thankfully easier than Buck had anticipated, as each shelf was fitted with a smooth hand railing at waist height. This made it much easier to stop and marvel at the items he found sitting on those shelves, items like air fresheners encased in glass with timers and mechanical hatches attached to the filters, or cuckoo clocks that spat out past and present political candidates touting their greatest achievements on the hour.

But Mr. Perkins gestured for him to keep walking, because there was so much more to see than above-average novelties and conversation starters. Even though the sales floor was a marvel, something like a modern dance floor at the center of a golden luxury cruise ship, he assured Buck that the best part lay below, down in what Mr. Perkins referred to as the "Dungeon of Discovery."

"It's not nearly as ominous as it sounds," he assured him. "More like a reminder to self not to let the wrong people down there."

"Am I the right people?" Buck asked.

"Given your situation, I'm willing to take that chance."

Mr. Perkins pointed at the back of the room where a wooden stairway split off in two directions, one leading to a second-floor balcony, the other leading down into a basement area. He helped Buck down the stairs into the basement.

The pain engulfing Buck's left side made the journey slow, but he got down without falling. Mr. Perkins, who used a cane to walk himself, wasn't much quicker down the steps. Buck was glad the old man didn't rush him.

Once they reached the bottom, Buck found himself in a less impressive concrete corridor lined with somewhat impressive, fuchsia-colored doors. Each door had a wooden sign over it indicating a specialty. Mr. Perkins walked Buck through the door marked "Potions."

"Obviously, I wouldn't take furniture salesmen into this room," he said. "But since you're in the business of serving liquids to the public, I figure you might benefit from it."

Buck had to steady himself against the nearest table when he entered. Although it was a small room and naturally dark like a cavern, the space was filled from top to bottom with wooden shelves stocked with glowing liquids in ornate flasks made of glass, each one shimmering with phosphorescence. It resembled a fancy bar at a ritzy nightclub, but without the bar, or the thirty-something bartender.

"Are these legal?" Buck asked as he picked up the nearest potion and studied it. Before Mr. Perkins could answer, Buck dropped the bottle, saving it just in time as he guided it to the edge of the shelf and slid it back into place. The glass was so hot it had nearly burned him.

"I wouldn't alert the FDA to their existence. But they won't kill anyone, as far as I know." Mr. Perkins chuckled at his grim joke. "They're safe to use, don't worry. Here, let me show you the potion I'm most proud of."

Buck followed Mr. Perkins to a spot in the back corner of the room. About halfway up the wall was a shelf full of golden yellow liquids that glowed so bright they seemed to bear the brunt of the room's lighting. Mr. Perkins pulled a bottle off the shelf.

"Come, I want you to sample this."

Buck stopped his journey mid-step. He was still several paces away.

"I don't know about…"

Mr. Perkins gestured to him to move toward a small table in the back where stacks of dishes, napkins, and test tubes were sitting. He dashed a drop of the yellow liquid into a test tube, then offered the tube to Buck, who was still hobbling towards the table to meet with Mr. Perkins and his product showcase.

"Trust me, you'll thank me."

Not exactly a selling point, Buck thought. But the old man had yet to steer him wrong.

Buck took the tube from Mr. Perkins's hand once he was close enough. Although he didn't love the idea of consuming a glowing liquid in a dark room at the dungeon level of a mysterious shop in a dodgy neighborhood, he didn't have much reason to distrust the old man. After all, if he had been up to no good, his previous customers would've had the city shut him down and Mr. Perkins shuttled off to some asylum somewhere. No one would've allowed him to get away with poison, assuming they'd survived.

So, Buck took the sample.

He blinked. Twice.

And then a hot tingling unlike anything he'd felt before trickled up from his stomach and into his heart, and then through the rest of his body. Almost instantly, his skeptical mood transformed to optimism, and the pain from his previous injuries subsided. In less than a minute, he could move at his regular speed.

"What the—"

"I call it Liquid Sunshine," Mr. Perkins said. "Good for a thousand drops. You drop a dash into your customer's black coffee, no sugar, cream, or anything else, and you'll give him the best day of his life. You'll be able to charge him luxury prices, and he'll still come back the next day for more. Better than a shot of tequila after a hard day's work, and worth more."

"This is amazing…"

Buck tried jumping and was amazed to discover the landing didn't hurt one bit.

"It cured me."

Mr. Perkins shook his head. "It numbed the pain. Your injuries are still there, and you'll feel them again tonight once it wears off, maybe even worse, so don't overdo it. But yes, it is amazing."

"And you're giving this to me?"

"Yes…for a hundred dollars. After a thousand uses, it will have paid for itself in spades. Guaranteed. As I said, you use this, and your security problems won't go away, but they will become more affordable. And it won't shoot bullets at ten-year-old kids."

Buck reached for his wallet. He had never been happier to spend a hundred dollars in his life.

* * *

BUCK AND MR. PERKINS returned to the Chamber of Commerce a few minutes after five o'clock. Because Buck was feeling much better, he didn't need help in getting out of the truck. He just hopped out and raced for the reception area to show Lila what he'd bought. Fortunately, her car was still in the parking lot, probably waiting to fulfill her promise to take him and his damaged bike home.

But when he got inside, she wasn't at her desk, so he took a seat and waited on the sofa for her to return. While he waited, he rotated the bottle in his hand, staring into the golden liquid, mesmerized by its beauty and power. He must've spent several minutes entranced by it because he didn't notice the time pass.

"Whatcha got there?" Ernest Bee said from his office doorway.

"None of your business," Mr. Perkins said as he entered from the back door. "Let the boy enjoy his prize."

Ernest Bee grunted. "Fine, well, he can admire it elsewhere. Time to lock up the place."

"I'm just waiting for Lila," Buck said. "She's taking me home."

"Lila?" Ernest Bee said. "She's left already. Almost an hour ago."

Buck and Mr. Perkins exchanged glances. Both confirmed what the other already knew. But Buck said it out loud for Ernest's benefit.

"But her car's still in the parking lot."

Ernest Bee peeked out the front door. "Hmm, so it is. Maybe she went for a walk."

Mr. Perkins checked his watch. "This time of day? Out here?"

"Yeah? So?"

"Where's she supposed to walk? There are no sidewalks."

Ernest Bee shrugged. "Well, you know what they say about young women. Always wandering off into the woods alone. Maybe she's out picking wild berries."

Buck and Mr. Perkins both stared at him.

"Well, what do I know about women?" Ernest said. "I come to work every day in a bee costume."

Mr. Perkins shook his head. "Given what she's been through this week, we should go looking for her. Right now. Make sure she's not doing something crazy or unsafe."

Buck agreed. Fortunately, his body was no longer in pain, so he could tag along with the search party.

"Where do we begin?" he asked.

"That's a good question," Mr. Perkins said. "I don't know. She's been more unpredictable than usual lately."

Episode 49

The Search for Lila

BUCK, MR. PERKINS, AND Ernest Bee hovered near Lila's desk, each one taking turns monitoring the front entrance but no one addressing the obvious dilemma if she didn't walk in. At some point, they would have to look for her. But now? Later? She was a grown woman capable of taking care of herself. She didn't owe an explanation why she'd left without her car.

But why would she do that in the middle of nowhere? Was it a voluntary decision? Did the car fail to start? Did she think it was better to hike through the woods than ask either Mr. Perkins or Ernest Bee for help in getting it started? Did she think it was better than calling a tow truck?

None of this seemed like her.

This discrepancy in her usual behavior drove other questions into Buck's mind: What if Lila needed to get away? After all, she'd had a rough time with her boyfriend lately, and probably with life in general. Would she want them looking for her? No one was saying it, but it was obvious they were all thinking it. Even Ernest Bee, who was a nitwit, had those questions written on his face. If she was out for a walk, as Ernest believed, was she doing it to clear her head? Would their intrusion clutter it again? If they were to leave her alone, would she come back to her car once she'd found some peace?

The woods were therapeutic, but still…what didn't they know…?

It was Mr. Perkins who finally asked the critical question out loud.

"How long do you suppose she'd want us to wait before assuming something happened to her?"

Ernest Bee tugged at his fake antennae. "Hard to say. She avoids talking to me whenever possible. Even when I say hi, she just looks at me and grimaces. Doesn't realize I notice."

"I see. I see. Buck? You haven't known her long. But since you are of similar age, I figure you know her best. How long would you wait before looking for her?"

Buck had been thinking about that question since the start. Unfortunately, being of similar age wasn't enough for him to get fully into her head. When she'd gone out of reach following her mess with Damon, he couldn't find her, nor did he know where to look. The same was true now.

He glanced at the clock on the wall. It was now 5:15.

"Five more minutes?" he asked. It was a safe number. If she was just clearing her head, then the extra minutes would've given her more time to enjoy it. But if she was in real trouble, then, well, five minutes was already too long and any more could've been tragic.

Each man exchanged glances and nodded—Buck and his temporarily fixed head, thanks to the Liquid Sunshine; Mr. Perkins and his elvish beard; and Ernest Bee and his ridiculous costume antennae. So, they would wait five minutes.

They kept watching the front entrance.

"Did she actually say she was leaving?" Mr. Perkins asked.

"Well, no," Ernest said. "I called out to her just after four o'clock, but she didn't answer. Ten minutes later, I called again. She still didn't answer. I figured she'd left for the day."

"I see. I see. Well, I can confirm she didn't go out back. I didn't see her when I parked the truck. And she wasn't in my tent."

Another thought entered Buck's mind, but he didn't say it out loud, maybe because he didn't want to accidentally manifest it into truth.

"You sure she wouldn't go walking in the woods?" Ernest asked. "I mean, I don't know women very well, but I'm pretty sure Little Red Riding Hood went off into the woods. To see her grandmother?"

"I don't think Lila has a grandmother who lives in these woods," Mr. Perkins said, this time with a bit more edge than usual.

"I mean, we test every theory, right?"

"We test every credible theory. If we assume she has a grandmother in the woods, then we can just as easily assume that the Big Bad Wolf found her and carried her away."

The thought in Buck's head got louder, to the point where he couldn't ignore it. Mr. Perkins's statement had turned up its dial.

"What if the Big Bad Wolf *had* carried her away?" Buck said.

"I don't think—"

"I don't mean literally. Come on, we're all thinking it. She's not the kind of woman who just goes off into the woods alone. Right? Not without her car."

The three of them exchanged glances. But it was Mr. Perkins who checked his watch.

"You're right. Five minutes have passed. Let's go."

Buck glanced at the clock on the wall. It was 5:17.

* * *

THEY'D SCOURED THE WOODS for thirty minutes, each one calling out Lila's name, but they got no answer. On either side of the road, they traveled as deep into the woods as was safe, listening for her reply. Each time, they got an echo, but no response. For every few meters they descended the hill, they yelled louder, harsher, with more urgency. But none of their efforts was of any use. By the time they'd reached the bottom of the hill, they concluded she wasn't out there. If she'd gone walking, then she was down past the neighborhood and near the parks by now, much too far for them to keep chasing a question. They had to head back now.

"What are the odds she had car trouble?" Mr. Perkins asked as they climbed up the highway back to home base. "I've got jumper cables in the truck."

"I'm sure she would've called a tow truck if you weren't around," Buck said. His mind continued picking at the Big Bad Wolf theory. Maybe it was instinctual, some kind of clash between his desire to protect her and the prophet of doom that had attacked her personal life, a clash that probably didn't need taking seriously. But it didn't stop him from dwelling on it.

"Well, either way, I suppose it's time we took to the streets. Buck, once we lock up, I'll take you home. Ernest and I will keep looking."

"I don't want to go home until we find her."

"We don't know where she is. It could take all night."

"I have all night."

Buck was resolute in his decision. Mr. Perkins must've seen it in his face because he nodded and smiled.

"Then let's get down to business."

By 6:30, Mr. Perkins's truck roared down the wooded road and into the neighborhood. Buck rode shotgun while Ernest Bee was in the back, keeping Buck's bicycle from flying over the side. Mr. Perkins had suggested Ernest take his own car so they could cover more ground faster, but Ernest insisted his search would've been wasted since he didn't know Lila's preferred hotspots and wouldn't know where to look. Mr. Perkins admitted not knowing them either, but they still had to try finding her.

Fortunately, Buck had some ideas, so he led Mr. Perkins around town, beginning with the beach and moving inland. Of course, they each kept an eye on the sidewalks in case she turned up along the way.

Once they got to Tealeaf Central, Buck peeked inside to check the clientele. He was nervous about entering because French Girl was waiting tables tonight, and he wasn't clear on where they stood with each other. Asking her if she'd seen Lila would inevitably lead to other questions that he wasn't comfortable answering. But when he didn't see Lila among the customers, he bit his lip and confronted French Girl, letting her know why he was concerned.

"That don't sound like Lila," she said. "I call her. Wait here."

Buck sat at a table and waited. In the meantime, Mr. Perkins and Ernest Bee entered and took spots around the table.

"Nice place," Ernest said. "I smell honey."

Buck and Mr. Perkins both shook their heads.

"What?"

French Girl returned with a frown. "Lila not answer. When she leave work?"

"Just after four," Buck said.

French Girl checked her watch.

"Three hours enough time to get home on foot. She upset?"

"If she was, she hid it well."

At that moment, French Girl noticed something about Buck that she'd missed earlier. She reached out and touched his cheek.

"What happen to face?"

Buck brushed her hand away. "It's nothing. Just a bike accident."

"Some hooligan ran him off the road," Ernest Bee said. "Tried to kill him and everything."

Buck shook his head. "I don't think the driver was trying to—"

"Who try to kill you?" French Girl asked.

"No one. It was just—"

"Someone in a beige car," Ernest Bee said. "Lila said she'd seen it in the parking lot, right after our friend here would've been hit."

"They not see him?"

"I'm sure it was just—"

"It was attempted murder," Ernest said. "Plain and simple." He pounded the table. "Justice must be served."

French Girl took Buck's chin in her hand and turned him toward her.

"Who want to kill you?"

"Again, this isn't about—"

"Who you know drive beige car?"

"No one, just…"

This time, no one had to interrupt him. Like that magical moment when all the answers hit just moments before the teacher calls an end to the test, Buck saw the entire picture painted before his eyes. In fact, he did know someone who drove a beige car. An ugly old beige Datsun, in fact.

"I know who the Big Bad Wolf is," he said almost automatically.

Whether it was appropriate, Buck didn't care. He reached up and grabbed French Girl by both cheeks, leaned in close, and…stopped himself from making a mistake. Last week, she'd spoken about some kid named Johnny who worked with her, and if he kept to his trajectory, then this would get awkward really fast, especially if Johnny was watching. He reached down and shook her hand instead. They could work out their relational troubles later, if there was anything left to work out.

Right now, his concern was with saving Lila. Given the placid expression on French Girl's face, she likely agreed.

* * *

Buck had been to Pigeon Polluck's house three times in his life, once in ninth grade and twice last year.

Minutes before his first visit, Buck was walking home from school when Chet's car skidded to a stop in front of him. Pigeon jumped out of the backseat and tackled Buck to the grass. Next thing he knew, Buck had a blindfold over his face. At that point, a car door opened, and two sets of hands shoved him onto a warm leather seat, likely the one Pigeon had sat on. A few minutes later, they came to a stop, cut off the engine, and dragged him out of the car. After they tossed him in the dirt, Pigeon yanked off the blindfold to reveal the neglected front yard of an equally neglected house.

Buck would figure out later that this was Pigeon's house.

They pulled him to a standing position and marched him past a rusted station wagon on cinder blocks to the only healthy-looking thing in the entire yard, a large oak tree in the corner. Pigeon had wanted to tie him to that tree, pull his pants down for all the neighbors to see, and throw rocks at him, but Chet stepped in. The point, Chet explained, was to intimidate Buck, to show him they could find him wherever he was, that leaving school was no safety net. Not to physically assault him. Once Chet made that point, he and Pigeon threw him in the car, pulled the blindfold over his face, and hauled him off to the spot where they'd kidnapped him, dumping him right onto the sidewalk and driving off.

The second time Buck had gone to Pigeon's house, under the same conditions as the first, Chet and Pigeon thought it would be funny to throw him into the front yard and make him walk home. As soon as he heard the front door close behind him, he removed the blindfold, tossed it in the dirt, and headed off. That trip had taught him that Pigeon lived on the south side, in a lower middle-class neighborhood near the outskirts of town. It took Buck less than an hour to get home.

The third time Buck had been to Pigeon's house, he'd gone voluntarily, intending to terrorize his tormentor. He had sneaked out through his bedroom window in the middle of the night and walked the distance to Pigeon's neighborhood and even got as far as his driveway before he chickened out and returned home. Pigeon's brother Dodo had been creeping around outside, trying to find a way back in—apparently, Pigeon had locked him out that night—and if Buck had gotten any closer, Dodo would've seen him.

He didn't want to call attention to himself. But as he walked away, he realized he also had a weak plan. In his mind, he'd pictured himself throwing stones at Pigeon's bedroom window. He had no backup if Pigeon decided he wasn't scared.

Tonight would be Buck's fourth visit, and this time he was bringing backup.

"This the place?" Mr. Perkins asked as he slowed the truck to a near stop.

Buck couldn't believe he was looking at Pigeon Polluck's house yet again. Never mind how much he hated this neighborhood and its eyesore after eyesore. His heart pounded at the prospect of confronting his enemy on his home turf. A part of him wanted Mr. Perkins to turn the truck around and take him home. But if Lila were here…

"Yeah."

Mr. Perkins threw the clutch, and the truck lurched to a complete stop. Ernest Bee, who was still riding in the back, had hopped over the side before Buck could even get his door open.

"Let's beat this guy's ass," Ernest said. He surveyed the front yard as he headed for the driveway. His face was visibly pained when he turned back toward Buck. "I should also fine him for being an environmental hazard."

"One thing at a time, cowboy," Buck said.

"Is he even home?" Mr. Perkins was the last to get out of the truck, but the first to state the obvious. Pigeon's car wasn't in the driveway.

"We can ask his brother if he's seen him," Buck said. "As far as I know, the kid's always home alone."

Ernest Bee wasted no time following through on Buck's suggestion. He marched up to the front door and banged on it with his gloved hand. It had barely made a sound. Again, he looked flustered by his lack of knocking power.

"Let me try," Mr. Perkins said.

He rapped on the door with the head of his cane. This time, the sound was loud enough to carry. They waited.

And waited.

"Let's check the windows," Ernest said. "If Lila's here, we'll see her."

Buck checked over his shoulder for potential observers. It wasn't yet late at night, but it was, perhaps, too late for pedestrians in a neighborhood like this one.

"Probably be best if we each take a side and be quick about it."

So, it was agreed. Ernest Bee and Mr. Perkins took the right side; Buck took the left. They started by peeking into the living room windows and heading around their respective sides to check the rest. In each window Buck peered into, the room was dark or empty or both. By the time he reached the backyard, he wondered if he'd wasted his time coming here.

But Mr. Perkins and Ernest Bee hadn't been as quick to reach the back as he had, which made him wonder if they'd had better luck on their side of the house. Nevertheless, he checked the remaining windows looking into the kitchen, dining room, and bathroom, when he noticed a light on in the corner window.

Through the glass, he discovered a bedroom and Dodo cowering on his bed with a sheet up to his chin. His eyes reflected terror as they stared at the adjacent window across the room, and his body was shaking. In the adjacent window, which was partway open, an older man with an elvish beard and a thirty-something-year-old man in a bee costume were looking in.

"We just want to talk," Ernest Bee said in a soothing voice. "About fun things. You like to have fun, right? It's perfectly safe. Come talk to us, little boy. You can trust us."

"I've got candy out in the truck," Mr. Perkins added. "You like candy, don't you?"

Buck banged on his window. "No, no, no! Dodo, ignore them. Look over here. Talk to me."

It didn't help. Dodo pulled the sheet over his head.

"Little boy…" Ernest sang. "Come out and play. Wanna play a game? We want to play."

Buck dashed to the side of the house.

"Will you stop? You aren't helping!"

Both Ernest and Mr. Perkins looked wounded.

"But we're here to help," Mr. Perkins said. "How will we ever find Lila if the boy doesn't speak to us?"

"You can't talk to him like that. You ever hear of 'stranger danger'? Sheesh." He returned to the adjacent back window. "Dodo, listen to me. I can see you're scared of us. You don't need to be. We're just here to ask about your brother. Where is he?"

Dodo peeked over the sheet. "I ain't telling!" And then he hid again.

"When's he coming home?"

"I ain't telling!"

"Dodo, come on. Tell us. You won't get in trouble. Promise." Buck winced at the sound of his own words. "I mean, your brother won't find out."

Buck shook his head as his words left his mouth. None of this was going very well.

"I don't know where he is. Go away!"

Maybe he was too busy focusing on the problem at hand to really notice anything more, but now as he stood there pleading with a ten-year-old to help him solve a mystery, he could finally see it. It wasn't just the yard that was a mess, with the scattered junk threatening to trip prowlers and destroy lawn mowers. Dodo's bedroom had two beds, with trash on the floor, and an ominous pile of metal near the bed he assumed had belonged to Pigeon.

But that wasn't all. The wall behind Dodo's head was full of holes, each one roughly the width of a knife blade. The side of Dodo's bed had similar gashes in its side.

At that moment, Buck understood what Dodo was actually afraid of.

"Hey, okay, you don't have to talk to us," Buck said. "If you really don't want to, we'll leave."

"Good. Go away!"

"But before I go, I just wanted to say that I'm sorry."

Dodo peeked out from under his sheet again, but he said nothing, just stared at Buck through the window.

"Boys will be boys. I mean, you shouldn't be trying to blow up other people's property. That's not cool. But you're learning."

Dodo said nothing.

"What happened on the Fourth of July happened, and you can't take it back. Maybe you don't want to. But I can pretend it didn't happen if you promise not to do it again."

Dodo said nothing.

"So, no hard feelings. And…I'm sorry what happened this last time. You'll never see that man or his gun again. I fired him."

Dodo said nothing, but his shaking stopped.

"So, if you promise not to bring firecrackers with you, I'll give you a donut or something the next time you visit."

Dodo rubbed his eye with his thumb.

"And we'll give you candy," Mr. Perkins said.

Buck felt the bile tickling his throat. "Please stop helping."

Dodo held Buck's gaze a moment longer. Then, like a heavy tide snagging a pile of trash off the beach and rolling it back to sea, Dodo's voice removed the tension from the room.

"I don't know when Pigeon will come home," he finally said. "He just sneaks in through that window. But he's probably at his scary friend's house."

"Which one?"

"The blond one."

Buck nodded. He'd suspected as much.

"Has he been home yet tonight?"

Dodo nodded. "For just a minute. He came to get something."

"Did he happen to have a girl with him?"

Dodo shook his head.

"Didn't see one."

Buck glanced at the adjacent window where Ernest Bee and Mr. Perkins were looking on. Like Buck's window, it was partway open.

"Did he come home through the window or the front door?"

"The window."

"Is that also how he left?"

"Yeah."

Buck thanked him for the information.

"Sorry to scare you," he said.

"I ain't scared of you."

Buck smiled at him and gave him the thumbs up. Of course, Dodo had said that while still hiding under his bed sheet.

* * *

CHET'S HOUSE WAS A dud. Mr. Perkins rolled up to his driveway right as it turned eight o'clock, which meant Chet and Tommy would've been closing up the Liquid Shack about now. He wouldn't actually be home for another half an hour.

But the bigger evidence of a wasted trip was that Pigeon also wasn't here. There were cars in the driveway, but no ugly beige Datsuns. Just two Corvettes and a Lincoln Town Car, likely belonging to Chet's parents.

"I don't think she's here," Buck said as he stared down the long driveway to the big house at the end.

"We could still look," Mr. Perkins said.

Buck shook his head. Chet's parents wouldn't have gotten themselves involved in Chet's affairs, and they certainly wouldn't have asked about Pigeon's. And given the size of the house, even if Chet and Pigeon had smuggled a young woman inside, it was unlikely the parents would ever know about it.

"Maybe we should just run by Lila's house," Buck said. "Maybe we're skipping the obvious."

Mr. Perkins nodded. "Perhaps. But I don't believe she's living at her house at the moment. I'm pretty sure she's been sleeping at a motel or a bus station. She won't confirm, but she's dropped hints."

Buck grumbled under his breath.

"Dang it, Lila. Why won't you talk to us?"

Mr. Perkins said nothing.

"Can we check the Chamber one more time? Maybe she came back while we were gone."

Mr. Perkins offered Buck a kind smile. "I suppose that would be a good idea."

But when they returned to the Chamber of Commerce later that hour, the El Camino was still in the parking lot and Lila was still missing.

Frustrated, Buck released an exasperated breath. "Let's check every street in Hybrid City to see if she's walking along any of them."

"We could do that," Mr. Perkins said. "But I don't think it'll make a difference."

"Of course it will. She's out there. She needs us to find her."

Mr. Perkins closed his eyes and smiled.

"Buck, I have something to tell you that you may not want to hear."

"If you won't drive, I'll take my bike and ride." He remembered his bent back wheel. "Or I'll walk. Or hitchhike. We need to find her. There's no telling what Pigeon might do if—"

"Lila's disappeared before," Mr. Perkins said.

Buck was ready to finish his thought, but he stopped himself. For some reason, Mr. Perkins's words didn't surprise him.

"Go on."

"When she gets in a certain mood, she just goes. Yes, she normally takes her car, so this time is unusual. And concerning. But it isn't unprecedented. I do not know if this Pigeon character is responsible. Maybe he is, maybe he isn't. But what I do know is that Lila always comes back, even if she's a day or two late. She usually just has to clear her head first."

Buck listened to Mr. Perkins's words, but he wasn't convinced. Regardless of what Lila had done in the past, this wasn't the past.

Meanwhile, Ernest Bee had climbed out of the truck and was now heading around back, likely to get into his own car. It seemed he was on Mr. Perkins's wavelength about the matter.

Whatever Buck wanted, he wasn't likely to get their help anymore, at least not tonight. Nevertheless, he had to be sure.

"What if you're wrong? What if this time is different?"

Mr. Perkins held his gaze. "What if it isn't?"

Buck was ready to challenge Mr. Perkins, but the kind smile on the old man's gentle face was disarming. It was like looking into the eyes of a woodland elf after he'd baked three dozen chocolate chip cookies, one who happened to drive a monster truck. Who could challenge that?

"Okay," Buck said. "If we're overreacting, then she'll show up to work tomorrow. Right?"

"And if she doesn't," Mr. Perkins said, "we'll start again."

Buck leaned back in his seat and sighed. There was no way he was getting a good night's sleep tonight.

* * *

Mr. Perkins dropped Buck off at his house by 9:30. He also offered to get the bike fixed if Buck left it in the truck. Buck didn't have any reason to keep it if he couldn't ride it, so he agreed to Mr. Perkins's offer. Mr. Perkins promised to have it delivered with a new wheel by midmorning.

He also said he'd give the police a heads-up that a young woman might be missing. Mr. Perkins explained they wouldn't treat her disappearance with any sense of urgency until twenty-four hours had passed, but they could at least keep a lookout for her in case she was out walking. The suggestion was satisfying enough to convince Buck to go in and get some sleep.

Buck thanked Mr. Perkins for helping him search and for the Liquid Sunshine, especially now that the euphoria it caused him was fading and his spine was aching again. Odds were good that the pain would return full force by the time he fell into bed.

The next morning, Buck awoke in immense pain, so he consumed more of the glowing drink. But even as his body relaxed from the effects of the potion, his mind was consumed with thoughts of Lila. Because he had no transportation, he could not resume his search for her, at least not until Mr. Perkins returned his bike. He also had no means of calling her, since she hadn't been home to pick up her phone.

Just before eleven o'clock, a foul beast of an engine roared into Buck's driveway. As promised, Mr. Perkins returned the bike to him with a working back tire. He also updated Buck on Lila's status. She still hadn't turned up, so the police were gearing up to increase their own search.

"It's best we leave it in their hands now," Mr. Perkins said. "We should get back to our normal daily routine."

Buck didn't agree, but he understood Mr. Perkins's viewpoint. What could they do that the police couldn't do better? At best, Buck and Mr. Perkins would've increased the search net. But that assumed they knew where the police would even look.

"I guess you're right," Buck said.

* * *

HE WAS NEARLY LATE, but Buck got the Coffee Pavilion open right at noon. Ronnie and Tiffany were already there helping with marketing, which was good considering how distracted he was. To his surprise, Jennifer had also stopped by to help entice customers into buying coffee. She said she was off from Melty's that day and thought they could use her help.

If not for the dark thoughts swimming in Buck's mind, he would've thought this was a good day at the park.

But he couldn't focus on work. By one o'clock, he asked Ronnie to take over sales and Jennifer service. He needed to clear his head.

He rode around town for several hours, looking down every sidewalk and alley he passed. But of all the pedestrians he'd encountered that day, none of them matched Lila's profile. By nine o'clock that night, Buck resigned to the fact that he wouldn't find her. If she went off to be alone, then it was up to her to decide when to reappear.

It seemed that was just how she operated.

* * *

THE NEXT MORNING, BUCK got a phone call from Mr. Perkins. Something in the old man's tone raised the hair on the back of Buck's neck. His voice was the dead opposite of his normal chipper cadence. It was solemn.

"The police found Lila late last night." Mr. Perkins had a bubble in his throat. "She's in the emergency room now. They expect to move her to the ICU this afternoon. Come to Hybrid Regional if you want to see her." He paused. "It doesn't look hopeful."

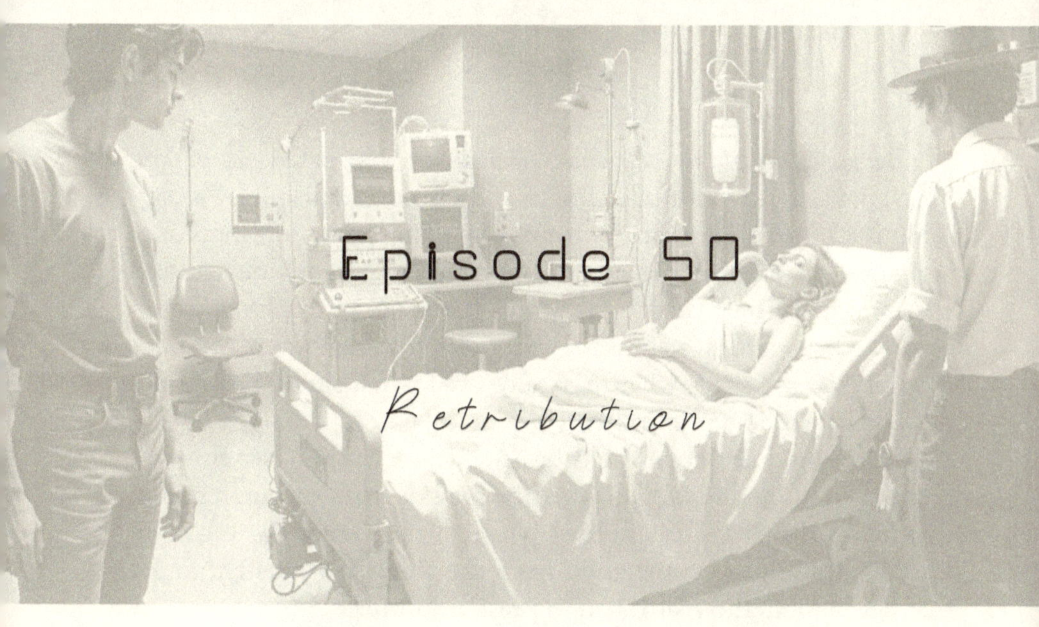

Day 39: Thursday, July 18, 1985

Buck's Savings Account: $120.58

Buck's Wallet: $633.28

Buck's Business Funds: $119.58 (from SDTS Earnings)

Funds-to-Wallet Refund Due: $14.65 + $7.59 + $29.02 + $5.76

(spent on supplies, not including Liquid Sunshine)

Buck's Expenses: $2 a day*

Hours of Operation: pending

Money on Hold: none

HYBRID CITY WAS HOME to thousands of residents and stretched several miles in all directions from its geographical center. But it had just one hospital. If grandma slipped on a puddle, or grandpa banged his thumb with a hammer, they were coming to Hybrid City Regional Hospital for treatment. If Bob's wife Debbie was about to give birth, or if Gary was about to give his war buddy Arnie a spare kidney, they came to Hybrid City Regional Hospital for the specialist's procedure. No matter what the ailment or disease, pet scratch or open knife wound, ankle sprain or broken bone, the patient came to Hybrid City Regional Hospital for help.

For everything else, they visited a private clinic.

Because every known trauma had its designated ward, the hospital was a labyrinth of hallways and directional plaques. Finding Lila's ICU room, therefore, was not easy. The arrows on the floors and signs on the wall helped, but currents of doctors, nurses, and transportation staff had a habit of blocking them. Even when stopping by a nursing station for directions, the nurses were too busy to talk. At least, that's what they said, even when sitting behind the desk doing nothing noticeable.

Of course, the unit would be found eventually. Visitation was made even more difficult, however, by the hospital's visitation policy, which stated that visitors needed permission to enter the Intensive Care Unit, not just an invitation from the family. Fortunately, to get that permission, the visitor had to press a doorbell.

When the door opened for him, Buck entered a small waiting room where he found Ronnie and Tiffany already sitting down. He had called them and told them the news before leaving the house. They had a car. He had a bike.

"They haven't told us much," Tiffany said when Buck entered. Her face was usually a mix of complacency and acceptance with a hint of amusement, a consistent mask to hide whatever secrets she refused to share with anyone, including Ronnie, but today she was serious. Today, she showed the side of her that was rarely seen, a side that emerged from a literary fantasy back into a state of reality. This side of her made Buck nervous. She touched his shoulder when he sat down. "They're still prepping her for visitors."

"So, we don't know what happened?" Buck asked.

"Nobody's told us jack," Ronnie said. "My dad's making some calls as we speak."

Buck said nothing. Lila needed the doctors to do their jobs before the lawyers did theirs.

They sat in the waiting room for almost an hour, waiting for someone to let them in. In that time, Jennifer showed up and offered her sympathies to the group. French Girl also popped in and almost left when she saw Jennifer sitting there. But then her face softened, and she took the closest available seat. She must've remembered that she and Buck weren't together anymore. Mr. Perkins also made an appearance. He couldn't stay because someone had to cover at the

Chamber of Commerce, but he requested Buck let him know Lila's situation the moment he found out.

Shortly after one o'clock, the door cracked open, and a nurse peeked through. She had an awkward smile on her face.

"We've just about got her ready for visitors," she said. "Just a few more minutes."

Everyone said thanks, then returned to their casual conversations with the sadness theme turned on.

"I wish they just fix her." French Girl had her hand over her forehead, and she seemed consciously removed from the world.

"They will," Jennifer said. "This is the best hospital in all of Hybrid City."

French Girl glanced at her and offered a quick nod. Nothing angry in her eyes, nor pleasant. Just neutral.

"I just want to know what happened," Tiffany said, her body language almost identical to French Girl's. "If there's a kidnapper on the loose…"

"It was Pigeon Polluck," Buck said, almost without thinking. He wasn't trying to keep what he knew about her disappearance a secret, but this was the first he'd mentioned the connection. "He's the reason she's here."

Everyone offered him attention.

"You sure?" Ronnie asked.

"Yeah, has to be."

"I thought he was scared of girls. You sure it wasn't her boyfriend or some vagrant that attacked her?"

Buck shook his head. "The person responsible was driving a beige Datsun. Pigeon Polluck drives a beige Datsun. She recently gave him a reason to hate her. It all adds up."

Everyone sat there in silence. Ronnie seemed to connect the dots in his head.

"I guess that makes sense," Ronnie said.

As the words left his mouth, the doorbell rang. A young nurse came out and opened the door to the hallway. She immediately swooned.

"Oh, my…"

A man in his late twenties or early thirties walked in. He was fit, with close-cropped stubble, manicured hair, and was the type of dude who graced the covers of romance magazines for girls. His tailored suit was impeccable, with not a single wrinkle on it. And his shoes were leather, likely fresh off the cow. And his teeth were visible, and straight, and all accounted for.

"I'm here to see Lila Deerborn," the man said.

Buck wrinkled his nose. Even though he had never seen this guy before, something about his voice was familiar. It was somewhere between friendly and aggressive.

"Er…" The nurse had gone dizzy at that moment. She struggled to point to the nearest empty chair. But once she composed herself, she finished her instruction to the man. "We'll be letting visitors in…soon." The nurse couldn't stop herself from giggling as she headed for the door to the recovery area. "Take a seat."

The women in the waiting area, including Jennifer, Tiffany, and French Girl, couldn't help but also steal glances at the man as he found an empty seat between a brunette and a redhead who'd come to the ICU to visit other people. Both women inched their chairs closer to him as he sat down, trying their best not to draw attention to their moves.

As the man crossed his legs and got comfortable, he glanced around the room. His eyes immediately landed on Buck.

"Hey, Buck," the man said. "Any word?"

Buck's mind scrambled for the connection. That voice was so familiar…

"We still got some justice to serve, you and me."

And then the walls of mystery fell before his eyes. That nose…Buck recognized the nose.

"Ernest Bee? That you?"

"'Course it's me. What, you don't recognize me?"

Buck shook his head. "No. Where's your suit?"

"Looks like he's wearing it, Little Camper." Ronnie nudged him in the ribs. "Nice one, too."

"No, where's your bee suit?"

Ernest rolled his eyes.

"Ah, yeah, it's laundry day, so…"

The girls, meanwhile, were too mesmerized by his presence to notice how weird the conversation had just gotten.

"So, what's the word on Lila?"

Buck told him what they knew so far, which wasn't really anything. Ernest scoffed at the hospital's lack of transparency.

"That's how they justify raising the bill," he said.

Buck wasn't interested in small talk with Ernest Bee, and he was already tiring of talking to his friends. So, he crossed his arms over his chest, leaned back, and closed his eyes. He figured he'd pass the time with a nap. He hadn't slept much since Lila had gone missing.

It wasn't long, however, before the nurse returned and interrupted his sleep.

"Lila's ready for visitors," the nurse said. Buck opened his eyes and inched himself forward. "Two at a time, please."

The nurse was looking directly at Ernest, but he didn't seem to notice. He was too busy investigating his shoes for something.

"Buck should go first," Ronnie said. "He's the reason any of us even know she's here."

Buck got out of his chair and headed for the door. Ronnie followed.

"I got your back, Little Camper. In case you cry."

Buck shook his head. "I'm not gonna cry. She's safe now." He glanced at the nurse for approval. "Right?"

The nurse was still staring at Ernest Bee. "She's in a battle right now."

Buck tightened his chest as he went through the door. Even if he didn't know what was coming, he was sure he could handle it. Lila would be fine. Hospitals always overdramatized everything.

The nurse walked him and Ronnie to a unit in the corner of the room. A blue curtain was drawn across the front, and a few metal rollers peeked out from underneath. She pulled the curtain aside to let them in.

Buck and Ronnie both gasped at the sight before them.

Lila was lying unconscious on the bed with a thin sheet up just above her waist. Dozens of tubes ran between parts of her body and pieces of plastic equipment, each with monitors and beeping sounds reporting on her situation. Her arms and face were scratched, beaten, and bruised, almost beyond recognition. Entire chunks of her hair were missing, and wherever her scalp was exposed, her skin was raw or scabbed. Her lips were split in several places, and her cheeks were double in size. Even though the rest of her was clad in a hospital gown, Buck's jaw dropped at the likelihood that the rest of her was in equal trauma.

Neither Buck nor Ronnie had words to say. Ronnie merely gripped the metal handrail along the side of her bed, as if he'd fly away if he let go. His face flushed white.

That was all Buck could take. He turned around without a word and headed for the waiting room. As Jennifer stood and reached out her hand to him, he brushed her aside. His gaze zoomed right to Ernest Bee.

"It's time to dish some justice," he said. "You're driving."

Ernest Bee got to his feet and nodded. Nothing else needed to be said.

* * *

THE GATE TO PARK Center Park rose over the windshield, giving them permission to enter. Ernest Bee was not at all happy about spending the two bucks required to gain entrance, and he vowed to get revenge on the gate guard when all of this was over. Buck reminded him they were there for one person only. Ernest waved him off. He had his own criteria for deciding who needed what justice served.

The car coasted around the shallow curve leading to Park Center Park's first lot, as a predator might sneak up on its prey. With each tree or signpost that drifted by, their opportunity to turn back eroded. Buck's heart pounded as he stroked the head of his golf club, un-knowing whether this prey would go down easily. When he'd dropped off his bike at home and retrieved his weapon from the garage, his head and heart had been so full of rage that he couldn't fathom the truth that made itself all too obvious now: He and Ernest Bee had no plan.

"It's just past that hill." Buck pointed toward their destination. Ernest nodded without a word.

Through the trees, empty fields flickered in the sunlight, with flashes of brightness reflecting off the distant lake. If this were the weekend, those fields would be alive with picnickers or team sports, while the lake might be alive with boaters or skiers. But this was Thursday. If anyone was here at all, they were likely on a hike or just passing through. Whatever was about to go down between Buck and Pigeon, no one was likely to interfere. For the sake of confronting him with the golf club, that would be a blessing. But for the sake of a fight likely to break out between them, a physical match that Buck was unlikely to win one-on-one, it was also a curse. Ernest hadn't come with any weapons of his own, and his contribution to this fight was cosmetic at best. Buck had included him only because he had a car and could get him out of here faster should Pigeon find a thick tree branch to gain the advantage in this fight. The fight was always going to be mano a mano.

The parking lot emerged from behind the hill, revealing three other vehicles, including Pigeon's Datsun and Tommy's truck. The third car was unfamiliar, which meant Chet wasn't at the Liquid Shack today. He must've been at Happy Homewares, where he worked on Thursdays.

"Keep an eye on that red Camaro," Buck said. "I don't recognize it, and we don't want whoever drives it to interfere with our business."

Ernest Bee's gaze went right for the Camaro. He locked on to it as a futuristic cyborg might lock on to a target. Even as Ernest turned into the parking lot, his head pivoted with his motions, maintaining his perfect focus on the car. If anyone was inside, they would not escape his attention.

They parked beside the Camaro. Ernest kept his eyes on it as he got out of the car. Buck shook his head. He was basically alone now.

Across the shallow field, Tommy Slick was sitting cross-legged on a folding chair off to the side of the Liquid Shack's canvas tent. He was reading a newspaper, barely interested in the story before him. His cowboy hat was lowered just below his brow, in the classic fashion befitting a participant in a Western standoff. As Buck marched onto the grass, golf club in hand, he prayed Tommy would stay out of the fight and keep to his reading. In situations like these,

Buck wasn't certain whose side Tommy would take, and he really didn't want him on Pigeon's side.

Tommy must've noticed Buck's approach, however, because he dropped the paper to his lap. His eyes centered on the golf club.

"Please don't cause any trouble this time, Buck," Tommy said, as he folded his paper and placed it on the table. He got up from his chair to emphasize his request.

"I just want to talk to Pigeon," Buck said. "No need to get involved."

Tommy considered Buck's words.

"You know I have to protect the business, right?"

"Not here for the business. I'm here for Pigeon. Where is he?"

"Pigeon is part of the business, like it or not."

Buck checked over his shoulder. Ernest Bee was walking up the hill backwards. His gaze was still on the red Camaro. Buck told him he could stop watching the car now.

Like a lawn sprinkler, Ernest spun around in a single step, now facing the right way. His attention was now on Tommy.

"This the guy?" he asked.

"No, Tommy is a friend," Buck said. "Not involved."

"I'm a friend when I'm not under orders," Tommy emphasized. "As of now, my orders are to protect the business. Make sure I don't have to keep to those orders." He nodded at the golf club.

"Pigeon hurt our friend Lila," Buck said. "Really bad. This one time, Tommy, I need you to look away."

Tommy's eyes drifted toward the parking lot, toward the beige Datsun and his truck. The Datsun was a runt, but Tommy's truck was no slouch of a vehicle. Buck had no idea how many cylinders it packed under the hood, but he imagined it was powerful enough to tow a mountain judging by the size of its body. The blue tarp covering the large bed likely hid a tow chain the size of an anaconda. Tommy seemed like the kind of guy to prepare for any tow job. Buck wondered if he was looking for Pigeon out there, or if he was plotting his excuse to leave for a few minutes to let Buck do his thing in peace.

"What did he do?" Tommy asked.

Buck was just about to answer Tommy's question when Ernest Bee cut him off.

"You ever see what a bear does to a rabbit when it isn't hungry but still wants to torture something?" Ernest said. "Imagine if you swap the bear for a man, and the rabbit for a woman, and then you…"

For the next couple of minutes, Ernest Bee went down into the darkest well of horror that one could imagine, comparing trolls and wolves to maidens and other maidens, simulating the worst fairy tale in the history of fairy tales, using fake voices and animated hand gestures to tell his story. When he finally finished, Tommy was nonplussed.

"So, you're alleging Pigeon is the troll," he said.

"And Lila is the innocent dove broken by the side of the road, yes."

Tommy gave the situation some thought. Then he shook his head.

"Sorry about your friend. But unless I have proof, I still have to protect the business. You two should go now."

"But, Tommy," Buck said, "she's hanging by a—"

"Well, looky who the cat coughed up!"

Up the field, Pigeon was coming out from behind the public restroom building with an ice scoop in hand. His face was a bit smudged with dirt, but he was otherwise bright as day. His eyes focused immediately on the golf club.

"You playing a second round?" Pigeon seemed delighted by his own mockery. "I'm game!"

"That our guy?" Ernest whispered out of the corner of his mouth.

Buck said nothing.

"You need to turn around and come back in five minutes," Tommy shouted at Pigeon.

"And miss out on the opportunity to serve our best customer our best juice?" Pigeon raised his fist and his ice scoop. "That sounds irresponsible. Bet he'd love a good West Coast Punch."

"Pigeon, you need to—"

Tommy jolted backward as Ernest ran forward and snatched the golf club from Buck's hand. Ernest rushed at Pigeon with the club tight in his right fist.

"Ernest, wait!" Buck shouted, his voice also going unheard.

Pigeon's expression, meanwhile, switched to surprise when his eyes fell on the rampaging Ernest Bee.

"Who the f—"

Ernest was fast. Before Pigeon could fully react, the head of the Hybrid City Environmental Council, who was wearing a pressed business suit for laundry day, was upon him. Pigeon ran for the tent.

"Come back here!" Ernest shouted after him. "We have to talk!"

"Ernest, wait!"

"Everyone chill!" Tommy shouted.

But it was useless. Pigeon was also fast. He reached the juice table within seconds, but Ernest was right behind him.

Pigeon's hand slipped down into a pouch hanging from his belt as he tagged the table, but his body spun away as Ernest slashed the golf club down at him. The club head smashed into three paper cups, causing them to explode with ice.

"Guys!"

Tommy's voice went unheard. Pigeon jumped backward as Ernest swiped the club at him and raised the hand that had gone into the pouch. Something shiny appeared between Pigeon's fingers.

"Stop!" Buck's voice also went unheard.

Ernest's eyes darted toward the shiny object as light glinted off its surface. He seemed to recognize it immediately as he couldn't help but curse in response. Pigeon was brandishing a ninja star, and his hand was cocked behind his ear.

Again, Ernest was quicker than he looked. Rather than take that next swipe he was in position to take, he jumped across the table, knocking aside nearly two dozen cups of ice as he slid through them, and tossed the club at Buck's feet. He kept running.

Pigeon threw the star.

The ninja star missed Buck's face by a couple of feet but came within just a few inches of Ernest's shoulder, zipping right past it.

Ernest didn't look back. Just kept running. Right for his car.

Tommy, meanwhile, chased after him.

"Why you causing trouble, Buck?" Pigeon hissed behind his back.

Buck picked the golf club off the ground. As he turned to face Pigeon, another star came sailing at him, this time striking the club shaft and ricocheting sideways, nicking Buck in the left biceps on its way by. This time, it was Buck who cursed.

"Pigeon, stop!"

"I got four more of these. One of them's likely to hit."

Buck backed away from the table as Pigeon reached into his pouch.

"Heard you visited my brother a couple nights ago. What'd you do that for?"

Buck took a few more steps back. Pigeon started circling around to the front of the table. Once again, he was holding a ninja star, but this time he was rolling it between his fingers.

"You attacked Lila," Buck said. "This isn't an unwarranted visit."

"Who?"

Buck stopped moving. His feet wouldn't let him retreat any further. He could feel his heels digging into the grass below, as if he needed to turn direction and charge at this guy, especially now that he was armed again.

"The woman you kidnapped the other night. The woman you…" He couldn't bring himself to finish the thought.

Pigeon didn't seem to hear him. He continued advancing on him, star poised over his shoulder, elbow and wrist cocked and ready.

"You like baseball?" he asked. "Because you have the bat, and I have the ball."

Buck ducked just as Pigeon's forearm pitched forward. The air stirred as the star whooshed right over his head.

"Pigeon!" Tommy was coming back up the field, this time carrying a deer rifle. "That's enough!"

Buck glanced at Pigeon, whose hand was returning to the pouch, then at Tommy, who was marching toward them like a lone stranger preparing to rescue a dusty Western town from a gang leader's iron grip. Past Tommy, down in the parking lot, Ernest's car was already speeding away, heading for the road. Buck cursed under his breath again. Ernest was his ride home.

"We're just having fun," Pigeon said. "Lighten up."

"Get your hand out of your pouch, and then I'll lighten up."

Pigeon smiled. His fingers danced around under the pouch flap. Whatever he was doing, his hand was well-hidden.

"Always threatening to shoot me, but never pulling the trigger," Pigeon said. "Don't make me laugh." He nodded at the mess of broken cups on the serving table. "You should fix up the table while I deal with our nuisance. Maybe put that rifle away."

Tommy didn't put the rifle away. Instead, he raised it.

"Hands out of the pouch first. You know I have to protect the business, even from you."

"Yeah, and what if you don't succeed? Worried I'll become Chet's favorite? You're a laugh a minute. Put the gun away. You're not gonna shoot."

Tommy said nothing. He kept his aim steady. The rifle was pointed at Pigeon's chest.

Buck struggled to take a step backward. He was too close to the line of fire. But he couldn't move. "Tommy, maybe I'll leave. You should lower the gun. Sorry I bothered you."

Pigeon, meanwhile, glanced at Buck. His fingers continued to dance inside the pouch.

"I got three more stars," he said. "You feeling lucky?"

"You should do what Tommy says." Buck remained fixed where he stood. He wanted to run for the parking lot. But he also wanted to run for Pigeon's skull. He couldn't move.

"I could. But he's not going to hurt me, are you, Tommy? He never does. That would be very bad for him if he did. Won't it, Tommy?"

Tommy said nothing.

"We're a family at the Liquid Shack," Pigeon continued. "And around here, we don't hurt family."

Buck tried to bite his tongue, but he wasn't fast or resistant enough. "Is that why Dodo has knife marks all around his bed?"

Pigeon's fingers shot out of the pouch, as if he was about to wreck Buck's world, but they were empty. Buck flinched anyway. Pigeon laughed.

"You are so gullible." He pointed at Buck with his other hand, laughing even harder. "You and Tommy both."

But Buck wasn't watching that hand. He was watching the other, and the other was slipping right back into the pouch.

Tommy must've been watching it, too.

"Pigeon, don't you—"

But it was too late. Pigeon's hand came out again, this time holding a ninja star. But rather than throw it at Buck, who would've been the easier target, he threw it at Tommy as hard as he could, no longer smiling, no longer looking for the support of allies.

"Bite me!"

The star sailed right past Tommy's cheek, barely clearing the brim of his hat. Tommy didn't flinch.

But he did pull the trigger.

Episode 51

The Kid with the Cowboy Hat

BUCK HAD NEVER EXPERIENCED a firecracker exploding close to his ear, but if he had, he'd likely equate its power and fury to the sonic crack from Tommy's rifle. He recoiled the moment the gun went off, then stuck his fingers in his ears once the ringing started.

He fell to his knees. His head was pounding. The sound wave left him trembling.

Just ahead, Pigeon Polluck lay collapsed against the front table, tilting it off its front feet. He was looking down at his hands in disbelief as they covered his upper abdomen. Blood was pooling out from around his fingers. The muzzle must've dropped aim to below his chest just before going off.

Tommy lowered his rifle and marched up to Pigeon. Pigeon glanced up at him and offered him a ridiculous smile. Blood leaked from the corners of his lips.

"Didn't think you'd actually do it," Pigeon whispered. "Ow."

Tommy pushed the muzzle of his rifle against Pigeon's left hand and moved it off his stomach, exposing the wound.

"I told you not to throw your stars."

Pigeon leaned his head back against the table. Ice from the fallen cups was sliding off the table down the other side.

"I was just having some fun." He was now staring at the wound in his upper abdomen. "But this part isn't so fun."

"Sound carries. The park rangers will be here in just a minute to investigate. So, I have to move you out of here." Tommy reached for his newspaper and pressed it against the wound. What was once black and white was now red all over.

Pigeon closed his eyes and gritted his teeth.

"Please don't hurt me anymore."

Tommy glanced at Buck, who was still unable to move.

"I need you to help me."

"To do what?" Buck asked. The ringing in his ears was fading. "I'm not a doctor!"

"Grab his feet."

"Aw, don't let him touch me," Pigeon moaned.

"We've got just a couple of minutes before things get worse." Tommy was serious.

Buck hesitated.

Tommy pried Pigeon off the table by the shoulders, noticed Buck wasn't moving. "Now!"

Buck unfroze, dropped to his knees, picked Pigeon up by the feet.

Tommy pressed his rifle sideways against Pigeon's shoulders, then took it by both ends. He told Pigeon to lean on it.

"Where are you taking me?"

"Out of sight."

Tommy pushed his elbow joints under the rifle and lifted Pigeon under his back with his hands. Pigeon grunted.

"Get me an ambulance. Don't move me. I–I think I'm dying here."

Tommy said nothing.

"Tommy! Tommy?"

"Move to your left," Tommy said to Buck.

Buck obliged. Tommy started walking backwards, carrying Pigeon by the rifle, as if he were on a stretcher. Buck followed forward. With every step, Pigeon's skin grew clammier and his face more intense with pain. And his feet got harder to hold. Pigeon was resisting, trying to pull his legs tighter to his body. Buck struggled to hold him.

"Am I gonna die?" Pigeon asked.

Tommy said nothing.

Pigeon's face drained of color. Fear registered on his face. It was the first time Buck had ever seen it on him. Tears were trickling from his eyes.

"Can you call me an ambulance?" His voice was no longer gruff or angry. He sounded like little more than a young boy asking for a puppy.

"You won't last that long," Tommy said. "So, we're going with Plan B."

Pigeon squeezed his eyes shut. "What's Plan B?"

They were walking toward the restrooms.

"Pretend this never happened."

"I'm bleeding out. How can we pretend…how…you're going to let me die? Over a…prank?"

Tommy said nothing.

They were almost up to the restroom block. Buck wasn't sure whether to drop Pigeon's feet or to keep walking him toward the restrooms. If what he'd read about in health class was true, they could likely save his life by tying something tight around the wound or at least buy him enough time to get the ambulance on the scene. Maybe the park rangers had life-saving equipment on hand to keep his vitals up. They could chalk this one up to a learning experience, one for all of them.

But he remembered Lila lying unconscious in that ICU bed, beaten beyond recognition, on the verge of death herself if things worsened. Buck wasn't so sure he wanted to save Pigeon's life.

What would Mr. Kabuki say about the situation?

Lesson 23, he could hear him saying, *letting enemy die make future partnership impossible.*

No kidding, Buck thought.

Buck dropped his feet. Tommy stared at him. Pigeon pulled his knees closer to his body almost by reaction.

"Let's call it an accident," Buck said. "They come save his life. In return, he stops harassing me and my friends. We put this episode behind us."

Tommy nodded at Pigeon's feet. "Pick him up."

"I just think—"

"Pick him up!"

Buck did as he was told. Once again, he felt resistance as Pigeon struggled to keep his knees close, but he was clearly weakening, fast. They continued toward the restrooms.

Meanwhile, the fear on Pigeon's face faded. The smile returned, but not his usual crazy smile. Just a normal one. A content smile.

"Sorry I…ran you off…the road the other day," Pigeon whispered. His skin was near ashen now.

Buck almost stopped again, but he could feel Tommy pulling hard. He was clearly in a rush to get to the bathroom.

"I survived."

"The irony."

Buck didn't want to have this conversation. It was bound to lead back to Lila.

"Someone's gonna have to…look after…Dodo. He's alone."

"We'll get you home soon," Buck said.

Pigeon rocked his head back and forth.

"No, you won't. It's…over. Tommy's…right. I can feel it…slipping."

Tommy reached the bathroom door and opened it. They maneuvered Pigeon past the inner wall and carried him to the farthest stall.

"I need you to…do me a…favor, Tommy." His breathing was getting so labored now that he was on the verge of incoherence.

Tommy lowered him onto the floor. He placed the rifle across the top of the neighboring stall panels. "What?"

"You know that joke…we used to make, about where…you'd bury me…if I died…before you?"

"Yeah."

Pigeon glanced up at him with what little strength he had left. "I wasn't joking."

Tommy nodded. "Neither was I."

"If I'm…going out, then you burn it all down…in my name."

Tommy lifted him by the shoulders. "That's the plan."

Pigeon's teeth were clenched. But something about his face was suddenly peaceful, as if he were releasing himself from the pain.

His body was going limp.

"And if anyone…asks, Lester Biggins…wasn't my idea."

Tommy pulled him into the farthest stall, where the handicapped rail straddled either side, and leaned him against the wall.

"You still pushed him."

"I never…touched him. I just…scared him. It was a dare."

Tommy washed his hands in the handicapped sink. "He still fell."

More tears leaked out of Pigeon's eyes. Then he took the deepest breath he could manage, which wasn't much.

"Don't let my brother grow up…like me, please?"

This time, he was looking right at Buck. Buck nodded.

"I'll look after him."

Pigeon smiled. Closed his eyes.

"I'm sorry…I bothered you," he said. "I was just…having fun. I won't do it again."

He said nothing more after that.

* * *

THERE WAS NO TIME to process the situation. Tommy was already barking orders at Buck, something to do with the park rangers coming to investigate the uncharacteristically loud pop coming from this part of the park. The short of it was that they had to run through an exact process of actions to cover their asses if they expected to outfox the cops. Buck's brain was too addled to think through anything. But he was clearheaded enough to find it concerning that Tommy already had a plan.

"Grab a wad of toilet paper," Tommy said. "Use it to get his keys out of his pocket."

"I don't—"

"Do it now. Neither of us has the time for questions or explanations. Just do everything I say, and we'll get out of this without a scratch. Get the toilet paper."

Buck swiped off several squares and wadded them into a ball.

"Don't let your skin touch the keys."

Buck pressed the paper against his palm and carefully plunged his hand into Pigeon's pocket, searching for his keys. They were stuffed down at the bottom.

619

"Open his car and search his glove compartment for explosives. He usually keeps a stash of M-80s on hand for whenever he gets the urge to scare something. Find one and bring it to the drink table. Go. Now!"

Tommy ran out of the bathroom ahead of him. Buck was quick to follow. Fortunately, no one had come to investigate the gunshot yet, but Buck could sense curiosity in the air. Someone with a badge would come up the road soon.

They both ran into the parking lot, Tommy to his truck, and Buck to the beige Datsun next to the truck. He was careful not to make skin contact with the keys as he opened the door.

"Remember not to touch anything with your skin," Tommy said. "Actually, here." He reached into his cabin and tossed two rags at Buck. "Use one to interact with the car. Use the other to tie around your head. Don't let your hair fall out."

While Buck tied the rag around his head, Tommy drew back the tarp and retrieved what looked like a picnic blanket.

"Get the firecracker and meet me at the table."

Tommy didn't wait for Buck's questions or a response. He pulled the tarp back in place and raced for the drink tent with the blanket in hand.

Buck put his knee on the driver's seat of the Datsun and was careful about how he leaned across to the glove compartment. Using the spare rag with the toilet paper underneath, he popped the latch, letting the compartment fall open. Several firecrackers fell out onto the floor, along with a spare knife, a screwdriver, and some envelopes stained with cola. He picked up one firecracker, as Tommy had suggested.

He didn't bother to close anything other than the driver's side door, since that wasn't part of the plan. He just ran back to the tent, where Tommy was already hard at work pouring lemonade over parts of the grass where Pigeon's blood had splattered.

"Use the rags to collect his throwing stars," Tommy said.

Buck was watching the road across the parking lot as he jogged to each spot where a star had fallen. His heart pounded at every twitch the trees made from the corner of his eye, or at every squirrel that dashed across the field. At one point he thought he'd seen a jogger in the distance, but it was a trick of the shadows across the lot. No one was out there, and no car was coming up the road.

"Quick, toss them in here." Tommy was angling the open lemonade container toward Buck. Buck dropped the stars into the drink. Tommy closed the lid. "Don't let me forget they're in there."

Tommy stamped out the lemonade-saturated bloodstains with his boot as it all soaked into the earth. Buck marveled at how thorough of a job he'd done. But there was still more.

And now the sound of an approaching car filled the eerie silence.

"I think they're coming," Buck said.

"Yep. Right on schedule. Quick, help me with the blanket."

They each took a corner of the picnic blanket and stretched it across where Tommy had not yet washed the blood into the dirt. Buck noticed it had also covered a shell casing from the rifle. Tommy suggested they place a chair at each corner of the blanket to secure it.

"Give me the firecracker and the rag off of your head."

Buck passed the M-80 over as Tommy sat down on the closest chair. When he took the rag off his head, Tommy reached up, snatched it out of his hand, and shoved it under the blanket.

"We're out of time. Start cleaning the tables as if you work here. Now."

Buck noticed the park ranger's vehicle coming down the road from behind the hill. He fidgeted as he reached for a fallen juice cup, unsure what to do with it. So, he just stood it upright and repeated the action with the next cup and the next, using the extra rag to wipe down the melted ice.

The park ranger's car lit up with flashing lights as it pulled into the parking lot. It seemed to drift across the pavement as it floated toward them. The driver parked the car beside Tommy's truck and got out.

Buck accidentally tipped over the cup that he was trying to stand.

"Stay cool," Tommy whispered out of the side of his lips.

Even as the park ranger dragged his feet up the hill, Buck felt his pulse pounding in his neck. His hands shook as badly as a surgeon having the worst day of his life. He couldn't help but stare at the restroom building where Pigeon and the rifle were stowed away but easy to find. Although he couldn't see it for himself, he was certain his back was soaked with sweat.

If the park ranger had to pee…

"Good afternoon, boys," the park ranger said in slick fashion. Buck and Tommy returned the hello, Tommy matching the ranger's cadence, Buck basically croaking it out like a frog. "Got yourselves a lemonade stand here, I see?"

The park ranger had on a hat befitting the uniform and a pair of sunglasses so dark his eyes were invisible. His emotions were masked, so Buck couldn't read his mood or sense his internal knowledge of the situation.

"We're just employees," Tommy said. "The owner is out for the day."

The park ranger nodded.

"I see. You know there are rules about running a business in a public park around here. Are you aware of them?"

"Yes, sir. We have permission."

The park ranger lowered his sunglasses. His eyes were inquisitive.

"From whom?"

"My uncle."

The park ranger shook his head. "Doesn't tell me anything. Who's your uncle? And what authority does he have to permit you running a lemonade stand in a public park?"

"His name is John Slick, but you may know him by his nickname."

"Which is?"

"The Lease Agent."

Buck spilled another cup, dumping ice onto the table. His hands trembled as he struggled to scoop it back into the cup. That was news to him.

"Your friend there all right?" the ranger asked.

"No. He's new. Just starting today. Already made a mess of things, as you can see."

"Looks that way. This your first job, son?"

Buck stared at the ranger but said nothing.

"Boy looks petrified," the ranger said. "How hard you working him?"

"We don't hire losers around here. New guy always does most of the work until he's comfortable with every role. Then we loosen up a bit."

"Good way to build character."

Tommy nodded. Then he noticed Buck staring. "Hey, give me your rag."

Buck shook his head. "I—"

"Now!"

Buck tossed him the rag. Tommy snapped it at his hip. "Work faster."

Buck knocked over another cup as he tried to pull his bearings together.

"We've had worse than him, if you can believe it," Tommy said. "He's the replacement for another guy we just fired."

"That so?"

"Yeah, the last guy, Pigeon—if you can believe that name—was a disaster. Had to get rid of him in a hurry."

Buck knocked another cup over. If he wasn't careful, he would accidentally tip the entire table over.

"Yeah, what was his deal?"

"Tormented the birds and squirrels. Insulted the customers. Blew off firecrackers to get reactions from everyone. A real menace."

"Firecrackers?"

"Yeah. Actually…" Tommy reached into his pocket and showed the ranger the M-80. "I found a couple of them in our tent box a little while ago. Accidentally set one off when I was moving things around. Loud as hell. About scared me out of my boots."

"Ah, was that what we'd heard?"

Tommy acted surprised.

"You heard it?"

"Yeah. Sounded like a gunshot from our vantage. But that there looks like an M-80. The sound of a firecracker like that can travel long distances. Scare a hella lot of birds."

"Not surprised. Anyway, I'm keeping the extra in my pocket, so I don't accidentally blow it, you know?"

"How do you accidentally blow it?"

"Not sure. Must be why I blew it."

The park ranger paused in thought. His mouth went slack. Must've been confused.

"Well, you wouldn't want it blowing in your pocket. You sure that's the best place for it?"

"I'll probably stash it in my truck once we leave in a few minutes."

The park ranger seemed surprised by that comment.

"Oh, you're packing up already?"

"Yeah, I'm training the new guy to break everything down. Normally we'd do all that at sundown, but he's got a doctor's appointment in an hour, and business is basically dead today, so we're calling it early."

Buck nearly spilled another cup at the mention of the word *dead*.

"I see. That lemonade looks pretty good, if I say so myself. Mind if I have a cup before I head back to the station?"

Tommy glanced over his shoulder at the lemonade pitcher. Buck noticed that the ninja stars were well-hidden in the murk.

"If you want to risk it. It's been in the sun all day, and I'm pretty sure the new guy somehow dropped a glob of dirt in the container."

The park ranger winced.

"Oh, never mind then. Perhaps I'll stop by for a drink next time."

"Yeah, that would be wise. You should do that. Maybe after the new guy is better trained."

The park ranger nodded.

"All right, well, everything here seems to check out. I will have to look into the park's agreement with the Lease Agent just to make sure this here is all appropriate. But for now, you two have yourselves a nice afternoon."

Tommy tipped his hat. "You too, Officer."

The park ranger glanced around the area for another few seconds, then nodded at them. Tommy nodded back.

The ranger hitched up his belt and started for the restrooms.

Buck's heart nearly punched through his chest as he watched the officer's advance. The ranger had barely walked ten steps when Tommy intervened.

"The restroom's out of order," Tommy said, as calm as ever. "That is, if you're thinking about using it."

The ranger stopped.

"Is it?"

"Yeah, it's locked. You may want to use another."

"That's odd. No one reported a broken bathroom."

"Maybe they forgot to tell you. But it's out of order."

"Damn. Looking at all this lemonade makes me have to piss."

Tommy shrugged. "I won't tell anyone if you want to use a bush."

"No. No. I'll use the one at the station. I can hold it a bit longer."

Tommy said nothing. The park ranger, meanwhile, changed direction and headed for his car. He got a few steps past the picnic blanket when he stopped and turned to face Tommy again.

"Oh, one more thing. You say that's your truck over there?"

"Yes, sir."

"I notice you got a tarp pulled over the bed."

"Yeah, keeps my tools dry."

"Your tools?"

"Yeah, I do a few side jobs for extra money. Usually on weekends."

"Like what?"

"Oh, you know. Construction. Landscaping. Painting. Whatever's needed."

"Mind if I have a quick look? Just to clear my conscience?"

Tommy shrugged. "Sure. Here, I'll give you a tour." He glanced at Buck. "Don't slack while I'm gone. Or it's your ass."

He walked the park ranger down to the truck. Buck, meanwhile, breathed a sigh of relief. Tommy was actually getting the guy off their back, at least for now. But it still bothered him that he was so well prepared for it. His hands trembled as he continued straightening the table, but not so blatantly noticeable anymore.

Down in the parking lot, Tommy drew back the tarp and let the ranger examine the bed. Once the ranger seemed satisfied, Tommy showed him the cabin and even pulled the backseat forward so the cop could get a good look. Again, the ranger seemed satisfied with what he'd seen.

A moment later, he was back in his car.

Tommy marched up the field toward Buck, his face serious, but his movements calm.

Once he got within normal speaking range, Tommy gave Buck his next set of instructions.

"We keep up the façade until he leaves. Clean the table as if you're scared of me. As soon as he's out of sight, we'll get Pigeon out of there."

The ranger sat in the parking lot for another five minutes before backing out. For a guy who had to pee, he didn't seem too hurried. Maybe he didn't have to go that badly. Or maybe he was faking it. Either way, Tommy and Buck exhaled in relief the moment his car finally dipped out of sight.

Tommy wasted no time. He tossed his chair to the side and grabbed the corner of the blanket, yanking the whole thing off the grass and tipping the other chairs over. The shell casing hopped as the blanket dragged over it. He noticed it leap and retrieved it, pocketing it with the M-80.

"Follow me."

They raced to the bathroom. Once inside, Tommy instructed Buck to lay the blanket across the floor. It didn't have to be perfect.

Then they moved Pigeon to the blanket and laid him flat on his back, careful not to touch his skin without assistance from a rag. Once Pigeon's body was centered, Tommy reached up the middle stall for the rifle and laid it on Pigeon's torso.

From that point on, everything else was about getting the hell out of there. They wrapped the blanket around Pigeon and carried him out of the bathroom and straight down to the truck, where the tarp was still drawn back. They laid the body beside two shovels and a paint roller. Once the bundle was secured, Tommy pulled the tarp back in place and snapped it to the frame.

Back at the tent, Buck broke down the tables while Tommy filled the other two lemonade canisters with water. He used them to wash out any remaining trace of Pigeon's blood, including any that might've gotten onto the bathroom floor. Once he was finished, he instructed Buck to wash his hands. Tommy also washed his.

At that point, the job returned to business as usual. They broke down the tent, tucked it and the remaining supplies into boxes, and loaded everything onto the truck.

"Now we just got to get his car out of here," Tommy said. "You'll have to drive it, though. Remember to use the rags. I'll follow you to his house."

Buck was nervous about driving the ugly beige Datsun, but he understood why Tommy had suggested it. He'd told the ranger that Pigeon was fired. So, it would've been odd if his car hadn't left when he did.

With one rag over his head, and the other wrapped around the steering wheel, Buck pulled the Datsun out of the parking lot and headed for the park exit, his heart pounding all the way to Pigeon's house.

It was only after he'd passed the gate that he realized they might've left something amiss back at the scene. Something at the back of his mind was certainly nagging at him. But he couldn't quite trace it. As far as he could tell, they'd covered every incriminating detail.

Unfortunately, that feeling they'd overlooked something was growing, and those feelings weren't always the mark of onset paranoia. Sometimes they signaled a real problem. Buck worried that was the situation now. But his scrambled memory couldn't confirm it.

* * *

Tommy told Buck to wait in the truck while he tossed Pigeon's throwing stars around the front and backyard; he'd take him home after he disposed of Pigeon's possessions. Buck asked him to drop him off at the hospital instead.

"What do you want to go there for?" Tommy asked.

"To see if Lila woke up yet. And because my bike is still there."

Tommy said nothing. Just nodded and went off to clear the Datsun of suspicious objects. Once he returned from the backyard, he headed straight for the truck bed and checked under the tarp.

He came back with the rifle in hand.

"Don't want to make this easy to snatch at a stoplight."

Buck said nothing. Tommy set the weapon behind the seat where it would remain out of sight from drivers of taller trucks.

For the next ten minutes, Buck sat in the passenger seat with his heart thumping. In the bed behind him was the body of a kid who had tormented him for years. In the narrow space behind him was the weapon that had ended the torment. Tommy, content with silence, was as calm as a guy dropping off a friend at the hospital.

And there was still that nagging feeling that they had overlooked something at the park.

Conversation was the last thing on Buck's mind, and he kept biting his tongue to keep one from starting, but because he didn't know what was coming tomorrow should anyone figure out Pigeon was missing, he couldn't help but squeak one question out that had bothered him since Pigeon lay on the floor dying.

"What happened to Lester Biggins?" he finally asked.

Tommy didn't answer. Just shook his head.

So, that was the answer. Nothing to talk about. They kept driving.

Past the turn toward the hospital.

Buck pointed at the street, but Tommy ignored him.

"I think you just…"

No response. Tommy kept driving. Past Buck's street. Past Ronnie's house. Outside the borders of Hybrid City. A man on a mission. No time to address the apparent denial of Buck's requested drop-off location. Buck was stuck to the passenger seat, made content to go wherever Tommy wanted—no sense in arguing with a man who'd just offed a kid with a rifle. They were headed for the empty highway out in the countryside, and Buck had no idea why.

Episode 52

The Truth Hurts

Harvey Halloway started his Thursday morning with a deep yawn and a hearty stretch, eager to get the blood flowing. His breakfast had been simple, just a fried egg and some toast, but it was enough to get him going. He'd also stopped by Melty's Coffee and Ice Cream Bar for a wake-me-up, in case the fresh morning breeze wasn't enough to remove the addled haze from his head. Compared to his usual Thursday morning of rushing out the door to submit his latest photos to *The Hybrid City Post* before someone scooped him, this was a nice start.

Today, he was under no pressure to deliver newsworthy images from around town. Today, he had one concern, and that was to photograph as many birds as he could find in the wild.

After paying Park Central Park's two-dollar entrance fee, Harvey parked his red Camaro in the main lot, just around the hill. Fortunately, he was the first one there, so he could photograph his birds without fear of joggers or picnickers corrupting his scenes.

His camera was state-of-the-art, capable of sharp images and quick film reloads. And his film case had room for two dozen rolls, and the seals were tight enough to prevent light leakage should one of the roll containers crack by accident. In theory, he could shoot almost seven hundred pictures today, giving him plenty of opportunities to get one right. If the birdwatching was bountiful, he had a good chance of shooting the full seven hundred.

Harvey lugged his camera and case through the open field, past the restrooms, and out toward the sparkling lake. From there, he headed along the sidewalk, seeking tree clusters likeliest to hide the bird species he'd hoped to encounter today. If luck were on his side, he'd capture a condor, but he would settle for anything rare and captivating. Nature magazines were always on the lookout for the most impressive of species, and Harvey hoped today was the day he'd snap and deliver his masterpiece, earning him far more than what *The Hybrid City Post* paid on average.

For the first hour, he listened for the tweets and squawks that signaled he was headed in the right direction. A few times, his finger got twitchy, and he'd snap a photo of a mockingbird or a seagull. But he kept on through, stalking for the big prize. The condor was out here. And if not, he'd certainly get some birds of prey on film, like the red-tailed hawk or bald eagle.

But by late morning, it was looking likely the birds were sleeping in today, and if the condor was out there, it would come out for food after lunch or dinner. So, Harvey started back to his car.

As he was passing the halfway point, something startled him. A hollow bang echoed through the sky, rolling northward toward the rising hills. It was probably a firecracker, but he wasn't sure. Either way, he watched for birds taking flight, keeping his camera ready to capture entire flocks. Maybe the condor would react and fly right over him.

But the best he got was a flock of mockingbirds he'd already seen today. So, he kept walking.

A few minutes later, Harvey found himself back at the field where he'd started. Only now, there was a shop tent pitched between the restrooms and the parking lot.

The tent had three tables set up, with one of them containing a cash box. The middle table also had a few dozen paper cups filled with ice, with many tipped on their sides, weirdly, and a drink container filled with lemonade.

He didn't know what was going on here, but no one seemed to be around, and he was thirsty after having been out here for several hours without a drink. So, he helped himself to some lemonade.

As he tilted his head back for a proper sampling, he took a step to the side. The grass was slippery under his heel. He looked down to see if he was stepping in mud.

Harvey spat out the lemonade and dropped the cup. Blood had painted the grass under his shoe, and it was still wet enough that he didn't want to touch it. Some of it had splattered away from the tables, but a heavier concentration pooled near the middle table where he'd been standing.

Harvey checked the bottom of his shoe. Sure enough, the heel was now bathed in red, almost like his Camaro. He poured himself another cup of lemonade and used it to wash off his shoe. Whatever blood the lemonade couldn't rinse away, he smeared off in the grass.

As he put his shoe back on, he noticed another odd sight. A throwing star, like what he'd seen in ninja movie commercials, lay near the puddle of blood. A couple more also lay scattered from the first. And right there between them was a rifle shell.

Harvey didn't know what he'd discovered here, but his heart started pounding, and the sweat built up around his neck. Maybe a bear or a wolf had gotten too close to the lemonade stand, or a squirrel had gotten extra aggressive with the picnickers, but he still didn't like this scene.

Fortunately, he had a feeling *The Hybrid City Post* would love to see what he was seeing, in case there was more to this story than a squirrel attack, so he took a few pictures of the blood, the lemonade stand, and the rifle shell. He also took a photo of the ninja stars, even if he couldn't explain their existence.

Not wanting to wait around for the stand owners to return, Harvey gathered his equipment and made a run for his Camaro. He figured he would pack everything properly once he got home, or at least once he got far enough from the scene that he no longer felt the shiver in his spine.

As for his birds, he regretted not having the opportunity to photograph a big one today. Whoever fired the rifle that left the shell on the ground would've scared off all the birds nearby. Something in his gut told him that if he stuck around a little longer, he'd get his money shot, but the money was never guaranteed. He was probably better off letting the thought die.

* * *

THE WORLD OUTSIDE OF Hybrid City was picturesque but slightly alien, rich in wood and agriculture but free of concrete and pop culture. Forest opened to rolling fields of yellow and purple, which dipped into an ever-deepening valley of green grass and jagged rocks, flanking a mountain range so distant that it had gone blue in the horizon. On a quiet early Thursday afternoon, in a region where it hardly ever rained, the clear bright sky should've been as fresh and peaceful as a clothesline-inspired laundry detergent commercial.

But Buck couldn't appreciate the deep blue sky or the rolling hills worthy of a Sunday picnic in a meadow because he was too busy clenching his passenger door's armrest as he squeezed his knees together, wondering what the hell he was even doing out here. Tommy, focused only on the highway ahead, refused to talk to him, not that Buck dared to ask him any questions.

The miles started adding up, and Buck was hyperaware of how hungry he was getting, and how badly he had to pee, and how dry his mouth had gotten, and how much he hated country music, and how uncomfortable he was having a dead body riding in the back of the truck a couple of feet behind him, and how much better off he would've been if he'd just stayed at the hospital with his friends. He would've cursed Pigeon by name if he'd thought it wise to curse the dead.

Tommy was driving north, in the direction Pigeon had taken Lila a couple of nights earlier, if Buck understood the report Mr. Perkins had shared. For all he knew, Tommy could've been taking him to the same spot.

But if that were the case, then that would've meant Tommy was somehow in on it. And if *that* were the case, then—

"Okay, it's time to talk," Tommy said.

He turned off the radio and pulled to the side of the highway, barely off the asphalt and uncomfortably close to an irrigation ditch. He cut off the engine.

"Before I answer *any* of your questions," he said, "I have just one for you."

Tommy reached behind the seat and recovered the rifle. With the barrel hanging over Buck's lap, Tommy checked the lever, then pointed the muzzle within inches of Buck's face, but not exactly at it. Buck's stomach and chest involuntarily tightened as his heart sped up and his neck throbbed. He also felt his back pushing deeper into the backrest.

"Will you and I have a problem about what happened today?"

Buck shook his head. He didn't have time to think about his response. His survival instinct had spoken for him.

"Because you know I can silence you if I suspect this will become a problem."

Buck shook his head again. If Tommy had expected him to talk, he would've been disappointed. Nothing wanted to come out of Buck's throat now.

Tommy returned the rifle to the alcove behind the seat.

"Good. Glad we understand each other. I like you, but I don't have to protect you. Remember that. What do you want to know?"

"I–I don't–I…"

Buck had nothing. Plenty of questions circled his mind, but none wanted to risk landing there. His biggest question had to do with whether he'd ever see the inside of his house again, but he didn't want to verbalize it for fear of finding out the answer the hard way. Everything else was secondary.

Fortunately, Tommy took the initiative and answered one of Buck's earlier questions.

"You asked about Lester Biggins. Here's what I know. Lester fell, but only because Pigeon scared him. I wasn't there to witness it myself, but I'd overheard Chet and Pigeon freaking out about it later that day. I never told anyone because I didn't want to burn my association with Chet."

Buck shook his head again, not because he feared for his life or couldn't speak, but because he couldn't understand what Tommy was telling him.

"Why do you even care?" Buck dared to ask once he found the courage to put words to his thoughts.

"Family business," Tommy said matter-of-factly. "Chet's dad is a big player in town. Pulls a lot of strings, especially with some influential group out east. My uncle, who basically owns the town, has an interest in Chet's dad's moves, as Chet's dad presents a threat to his position. My uncle promised to pay for my college if I infiltrated the Armstrongs' system of power."

Buck stared at him. Tommy had disclosed none of this before. Not once had he ever mentioned an interest in college.

"I'm thinking about becoming an engineer," Tommy continued. "Build the technologies of the future. I often wonder how much water we'll have left by the turn of the century. But that's why I care. I need a college degree."

"I don't…"

Buck gave up on his thoughts. Tommy was the most stable member of Chet's entourage, and now Buck questioned everything he knew about everything.

"I kept Pigeon's secret to keep my place in the group." He looked over his shoulder at the tarp beneath the back window. "But make no mistake. Pigeon deserved what he got today."

"And what about Chet? He knew, right?"

Tommy returned his gaze to Buck. His face was deadly serious. "Chet was partly responsible, though he'd never own up to it. So, I've got his number in my hand. If there's one thing Pigeon and I agreed on, it was that Chet needed a proper fall from grace. I hated Pigeon, but I'll give him credit for one good idea."

"What's that?"

Tommy tipped his hat.

"That, my friend, is another secret. But I intend to fulfill Pigeon's dying wish."

"Which is?"

"That, too, is part of the secret."

Buck looked off through the passenger window, too exhausted over the day's events to invest any more energy into the conversation.

"I'm so confused," he said. "Could you just take me back to Lila now? I really need to see how she's doing."

"Depends. Are we good here?"

"Tommy, I'm tired and angry and hungry. And I really have to pee. Just, take me back now. We're as good as good gets."

Tommy started the engine.

"I guess that'll do. Remember what I told you."

"I'm not causing you trouble. You do what you want and don't tell me another word. And if you don't mind, I'd appreciate if you deal with Pigeon *after* you drop me off at the hospital."

Tommy pulled onto the road and made a U-turn back toward the exit to Hybrid City.

"Already part of the plan," he said.

Once again, country music filled the cabin as they headed south down the empty highway. Buck wanted to close his eyes and sleep off the remaining journey, but he no longer trusted Tommy enough to drop his guard. So, he watched the road as trees, fields, and the rest of Pacific nature skated on by.

But the drive was hardly peaceful. Never mind the claw marks those sad cowboy singing voices had left on his eardrums, or the lingering fear that Pigeon's ghost might be riding along in his lap to ensure the body found a proper resting place. Something about their hasty escape from the park was still bothering him, and now it was intensifying. He just had that feeling that—

And, like the rising of a new sun, Buck realized what was nagging at him.

When he and Tommy had left the parking lot, they were the only two cars there. But when Buck first arrived, there was a third car, a red Camaro.

Somehow, in the time it had taken them to move Pigeon into the bathroom, the Camaro's driver had returned to his car and left the park. Whatever he might've seen, if anything at all, they wouldn't know.

Buck's heart suddenly leapt. What did they not know?

He glanced at Tommy, the man on the mission. Tommy's mind was likely racing all over the place, despite the lack of emotion in his eyes. If he hadn't noticed the missing Camaro on his own, then it was probably better he didn't start thinking about it. Tommy was calm under pressure, apparently, but Buck didn't know his limits. So, he decided he would keep his revelation to himself for now.

* * *

When Buck returned to Hybrid City Regional Hospital, he waited for Tommy to leave, then immediately retrieved his bicycle. As much as he wanted to check on Lila's health status, he wanted a shower even more. After everything that had happened at Park Center Park, Buck wanted to make sure he was clean and untainted before he saw her again.

Once he got home, he threw his clothes into the washing machine and guessed which detergent would do the best job getting bloodstains out. Not that Buck found any stains on his pants, shoes, or shirt, but he understood how loose ends could sink a man's innocence if certain people came along asking certain questions. Unfortunately, his mom had never taught him how to get stains out, only how to wash a sweaty pair of pants, so he wasn't sure how thorough a job he'd do. But he figured he'd wash them twice, just to be sure.

While he showered off the morning's filth, twice, Buck also considered his new legal reality. He could confess to Ronnie's dad about what had happened at the park, and Ronnie's dad could give him professional advice on follow-up actions. But he worried that saying anything would get Tommy to turn on him. At this point, Buck didn't think he could trust him anymore. Maybe Pigeon had the misfortune of attracting Tommy's ire, but Pigeon had also thought Tommy was his friend. Why would Buck expect better treatment from the cowboy kid who'd dunked his head in a toilet on command?

By the time Buck got dressed in a new set of clothes, he still hadn't figured out an answer, so he set the thought aside. After all, if no one claimed Pigeon was missing, then his disappearance wouldn't set off any alarms. As long as Tommy found a good place to bury him, then Buck could go on about his life none the wiser, as innocent today as he was yesterday, even if the memory of watching Pigeon's stomach explode would carve knots out of his own stomach lining. He'd deal with the mental haunting later if and when the time came.

Once he returned to the hospital and entered the ICU waiting room, he took a deep breath and cleared his head. Ronnie and Tiffany were there, but neither was awake. Buck was too exhausted to wake them, so he rang the bell to get the nurse's attention. When she answered the door, she informed Buck that Lila was still unconscious, but her vitals had stabilized. She would eventually recover. But they couldn't yet determine when recovery might start.

"Do you mind if I wait here until she wakes up?" he asked.

"You could, but you might be waiting a while. Hope you brought a few books."

Buck waited until evening. During that time, Ronnie and Tiffany awoke separately, had some meaningless conversation with Buck, then left for dinner. Lila, meanwhile, had remained asleep. By eight o'clock, Buck accepted that tonight wouldn't be the night she'd awaken, so he returned home to check his laundry. When he opened the hatch, he found his clothes were still damp, so he put them in the dryer. And once they finished, he put them back in the washing machine to repeat the process. He had to be sure he was clean and clear.

Then he went to bed.

He didn't sleep.

He spent most of the night crying. Crying while watching the shadows dance on the ceiling.

The next morning, he returned to the hospital, drained and bleary-eyed. Lila was still asleep, but according to the nurse, she had stirred in the night. The nurse estimated she would wake up soon, but how soon was still a mystery.

"You're free to wait if you want," she said. "Hope you brought a few good books."

Buck explained to her that he rarely read, and even if he did, he was too tired to look at words.

"Well, reading makes you smarter, so do with that what you may. I'll let you know if she awakens."

Buck stared at the wall for the next two hours. He was thinking about Lila. But he was also thinking about Pigeon. And Tommy. And Chet. And himself.

Despite all that had happened this week, there was still an active bet in progress, and no one was running the Coffee Pavilion today, at least not for now.

Then again, the odds were good that no one was running the Liquid Shack, either.

* * *

WHEN HARVEY HALLOWAY SHOWED the editor at *The Hybrid City Post* his photos, the editor shrugged.

"How do I know this isn't staged?" he asked. His cigar nearly fell out of his mouth as he spoke.

"I found it this way. It looks like a crime scene, doesn't it?"

The editor plucked the cigar from his mouth, rolled it a quarter turn, then bit on its tip.

"Is it a crime scene?"

"Pretty sure. I mean, if you look here, there's a shotgun shell."

"Looks like a rifle shell."

"Either way, I heard something bang while I was looking for birds. A few minutes later, I found this."

"Have the police said anything?"

"I didn't ask."

The editor took the next few photos into his sweaty mitts and shuffled them as he studied their images.

"I didn't hear anything on the scanners," the editor said, "so I don't know what you actually have here. But if you have the negatives, I could buy them from you in case something emerges. Ten percent the total value up front, the other ninety only if something comes as newsworthy."

Harvey's chest sank. He'd thought for sure these photos would buy him a steak dinner tonight.

"What if I take them to the police? Have them verify it? If they say it's legit, then would you publish them?"

The editor shrugged. "Yeah, whatever." Something behind Harvey caught the editor's attention. He gestured to Harvey to step aside. "Carl, get in here."

A medium-sized man in a dark blue bellhop uniform with a golden button-up shirt and a matching blue bow tie entered the editor's office. The man was a dapper fellow, with a *Magnum P.I.* mustache adding to his classiness.

"You got my review?" the editor asked.

Carl set a single sheet of paper on the editor's desk.

"I'm getting really annoyed with these shops' lack of attention to detail."

The editor scanned the review.

"Does anyone even read it?"

"They better," Carl said. "The good ones seem to double their business after each print. Doubt it's coincidence."

"You value your skills too much. But I hear you." The editor pointed at Harvey with his cigar. "Oh, this is Harvey Hallowbop. One of our photojournalists."

"It's Harvey Hallo*way*."

"No one cares. Harvey, this is Carl, the one we call 'The Coffee Critic.' He's with *Coast Life Weekly*. You might've heard of it. National culture magazine about West Coast living. He reviews shops all around the region for the best dining and coffee experiences. His articles are syndicated throughout the country. He often checks in with us to see if we want his latest scouring. What's the place you just reviewed?"

"Earth Tones Brewery, down in the valley. Awful place."

The editor dropped the review onto the desk. "Again, no one cares. But introductions are in order. No sense in being rude to either of you. So, say hello. Then get out. I'm on a tight deadline. Harvey, get me what I need to know as soon as possible. I'll have your money if you can get a cop to call me and verify the details. Carl, what's next?"

Carl consulted his notepad.

"Some venue in the park. Never heard of it. But it sounds like a dreadful place. Operates right out of a pavilion. Waste of my time, most likely."

"The bad ones are the most entertaining," the editor said. "For your sake, I hope it's good. But for our sake, I hope it sucks."

"You newspaper editors abuse me too much," Carl said.

"All for the art of news and advertising. Way of the future."

"I guess. But yeah, that one's next. Probably tomorrow. I need a palate cleanser today. If you ever wanted to know how close coffee could get to tasting like actual dirt, go visit Earth Tones Brewery. I'm surprised they didn't garnish my coffee with an earthworm."

"No, thank you. I can get that here in the newsroom. Anyway, is this park coffee local?"

"Yeah, I would never make a special trip just for park coffee."

"Great. I'll buy both articles then. My readers love a good dumpster fire. Two's better than one. Now, I mean it. Get out. Both of you. I've got a big slate to sort through today. Purchasing should have your money."

* * *

Buck checked the time. It was almost two o'clock. As much as he wanted to be there when Lila finally awoke, he couldn't leave his business floundering all day. He might've had a strong return to business this week, but he'd already tanked the momentum with everything that had happened since Tuesday. He needed to return to normal today, even if he started late. Thanks to the unpredictability of business, he couldn't ignore the possibility of having a great sales day. Even if his heart wasn't in it, even if the day was half gone. He had to squeeze out as many minutes as he could comfortably allow, just in case he got the one minute that mattered.

And somehow, maybe by miracle, or maybe just coincidence, the nurse popped her head out the door with a smile on her face.

"She's waking up," she said.

Buck jumped out of his chair and nearly toppled the poor nurse over. But he stopped at the door and allowed her to take the lead.

Lila was in the same bed as before. When the nurse peeked behind the curtain to ask if she'd take a visitor, a weak voice responded. The nurse stepped fully behind the curtain and explained to Lila that she was going to pull her sheet up to her neck to make her more presentable. Lila whispered a response.

A few seconds later, the nurse pulled the curtain aside for Buck to slip through. "She's ready to see you."

Buck stepped in close to Lila's bedside. Everything about her was the same horrendous sight as from Buck's last visit, but now she was awake with bloodshot eyes. At least the sheet was covering her bruised arms and everything else.

Lila smiled when she saw him, or at least she attempted a smile. It appeared to cause her pain.

"Funny thing happened…when you left for Mr. Perkins's shop…the other day," she whispered.

"I heard," Buck said, feeling guilty over having her speak at all.

"My ex-boyfriend came to make up with me," she said. "And then he did this…"

Lila closed her eyes and tried to laugh. But it wasn't working.

Buck's mind went blank. Then, other thoughts raced through his head.

"Damon did this?" He didn't want to ask. But he had to make sure he'd heard her correctly. After all, she was just now waking from a long dream.

"That's what I get…for trusting a louse…like him."

"Damon did this?"

Lila rocked her head back and forth.

"Please don't make…me repeat…myself. It hurts…to talk. But…it's so good…to see you. Anyone else…here with you? I dreamt…that goofy kid…with the funny hat…and his way too pretty girlfriend…were here. Are they?"

Buck smiled, but his heart and mind had suddenly gone distant. Ronnie and Tiffany might've been here. Or they might've been at the Coffee Pavilion. Or they could've been anywhere. Anybody could've been anywhere. Jennifer, French Girl, Ernest Bee, anybody, anywhere.

Buck could've been anywhere.

Anywhere but here.

"I'll have to check," he said.

But he didn't move. Was something heckling him from behind, right into his ear? He couldn't tell. Sure felt like it, though. It tasted like acid.

Episode 53

The Coffee Critic Cometh

Buck stayed at the hospital that afternoon. Surrounded by four immediate walls and many additional walls layered out hallway after hallway, he was sitting in a cocoon, insulated from the harsh world of cowboys and hooligans. Maybe there was work to do at the pavilion today, but he wasn't interested. Not anymore. Maybe never again. The hospital was safe. At least here, no one could get hurt.

When Ronnie and Tiffany came to visit half an hour later, they explained they weren't in the frame of mind for coffee, either. Not today. Not while Lila was unconscious.

That was their attitude when they'd arrived, at least. But now that she was awake, they were in a better mood and would return to the pavilion the next day. They probably weren't thinking about the danger or the fatal mistakes they could've made. They were probably just thinking about coffee and money.

"You should come to work, too, Little Camper," Ronnie said. "It'll be good for you. Nothing like a return to normal. That's my dad's motto."

Buck appreciated Ronnie's attempt at inspiring him to "return to normal," but he couldn't grasp it. What was normal? And why was normal considered good? He wasn't buying the propaganda.

"We'll see," Buck said.

Throughout the evening, Jennifer and French Girl each made their appearances, though French Girl had to return to Tealeaf

Central after her break, so she couldn't do more than say hello. Jennifer stayed longer, but she apologized for not being able to stay the whole evening. She, too, had to return to Melty's.

It seemed everyone was set already to return to normal.

Mr. Perkins dropped by toward the end of visiting hours and held a long conversation with Lila. Because visitors were limited to two at a time, Buck had no idea what they talked about. But when he returned to the waiting room, he assured Buck that Lila would be back to normal in no time. He also hinted that he may or may not have smuggled in a vial of Liquid Sunshine to speed up her recovery. Buck smiled for show.

But all was not well in Buck's soul. Life would not go back to normal for him. When he finally returned home that evening, grateful that Lila would recover, but burdened by a new personal trauma, he fell right into bed. Yet, he couldn't sleep. Just like the night before, he could do nothing but scream at the dark images dancing in his head.

The next morning, he rolled out of bed, his mind addled with sleeplessness. At some point during the night, his tears had helped knock him out, but his fitful dreams kept waking him up. By five in the morning, he'd considered getting out of bed and taking a walk through the neighborhood, but he worried the shadows would leap out from behind the trees and haunt him.

Unfortunately, he didn't know what Tommy had done once he'd dropped Buck off the day before. And he'd asked him not to tell him. For all he knew, Pigeon could've been under a tree across the street. Why would Buck ever find out the truth?

He stayed in bed until the alarm went off. Then he threw the clock across the room. It was Saturday, Day 41 of the worst bet he'd ever made, and he was so pissed at himself that he didn't bother recording his latest numbers in his ledger. For all he cared, the ledger could take a hike straight into the fireplace.

Nevertheless, he rolled out of bed. If he were to return to any sense of normality, he'd have to begin by getting out of bed and going to work and maybe filling out the ledger.

On his way to the park, he stopped by the Whipping Shed to see if Mr. Kabuki could offer some roundabout advice for dealing with personal trauma. But as soon as he opened the door, he let it close.

Maybe Mr. Kabuki had sound advice to give, but the last thing he wanted was to encourage him to ask questions, so he moved on.

But he didn't get far. By the time he'd reached the next block, he'd done the same thing at Shop Down the Street, and again at Sapphire's Consignments. He had three mentors on the same street, and not one could give him good advice to get through the moment, not without asking sensitive questions. So, he let his soul burn for another few minutes, or for however long it took him to suppress his feelings and get to the park a little deader inside.

He couldn't complete the trip, however, without feeling a prick in his mind. When it harassed him to the point of madness, he stopped his bike in its tracks.

Buck had made it into Hybrid West. And now he was staring at the front entrance of Pound Cake. Through the door, Irina Swift was icing some cupcakes. He walked in.

"Well, if it isn't my favorite entrepreneur," she said. "Want to try my latest cupcake flavor? I'm testing out a butterscotch cream."

Buck said nothing. He still wasn't sure what to say.

"Everything all right?" Irina asked.

"I–I don't know."

She pointed to the table next to the display case.

"Have a seat. Let's talk."

Within ten minutes, Buck had told Irina everything that had happened to Lila and even got to the edge of spilling the secret about Pigeon, but he stopped himself shy of Tommy getting the rifle out of his truck and sealing everyone's fate.

But Irina was smart. She'd narrowed her eyes at him when he stopped the story at Ernest Bee fleeing in terror.

"I don't think the story ends there," she said. "I don't think you'd be this upset if it did."

Buck pinched the bridge of his nose as he licked the butterscotch icing halfheartedly.

"It doesn't. But I don't know how to finish it."

"Does it end badly?"

Buck hesitated, but he nodded.

"Are you afraid of telling me exactly what happened?"

Buck nodded again.

"Then maybe you shouldn't, because I'm not a licensed counselor, or a lawyer if that's the situation. But you can't keep it inside. If you don't trust me, then find someone you do."

Buck looked up at her. He was still tortured inside, but the knot in his stomach was coming undone.

"Think I should talk to Ronnie's dad?"

"Is he the lawyer?"

Buck nodded.

"Do you need a lawyer?"

"Maybe. But I may also need a counselor. I don't know."

Irina put her hand on the back of Buck's wrist.

"How's Lila now?"

"Awake."

"Will she pull through?"

Buck nodded.

"Then I think you need to take the time now to fix yourself. Whatever is eating at you, don't let it win. I'm glad you came to talk to me. But I think you need to share whatever's bothering you with someone more qualified. If you trust Ronnie's dad, then start with him."

Buck thanked her for the cupcake and left. He wasn't sure if he felt any better, but he understood that she'd told him what he needed to hear. He'd consider bringing up the situation with Ronnie's dad. But he wasn't ready to make that decision today. He still didn't know what to assume about Tommy, or what might happen if Tommy found out Buck was seeking advice about how to deal with the fallout of Thursday's breakdown.

* * *

EVEN WITH IRINA'S ADVICE swimming in his head, Buck was in no mood to work today, so he was grateful to find Ronnie and Tiffany already prepping the pavilion for the day's clientele. But if their sodden faces were of any concern, it seemed they were in no mood to work, either. After yesterday's visit to the hospital, they all had left a little happier thanks to Lila's awakening. So, something else must've happened on the way home.

But Buck didn't want to ask about it. Odds were, their answers would've led to a commiseration that would've led back to his own problems, and he couldn't exactly share his problems, not even with Ronnie.

It didn't mean they wouldn't volunteer their reasons, however.

"Hey, Buck," Ronnie said. "How well did you sleep last night?" He was plugging in the coffeemaker. Behind him, Tiffany was setting up the water bottles. She glanced over her shoulder, but she said nothing.

"Not well," Buck said. "Why?"

"No reason." Ronnie opened the lid for the filter and popped one in. "Any chance you had a strange pickup truck camped out in your driveway last night?"

Buck shook his head. Something inside him kicked at his chest. He didn't like the sound of that question.

"Okay. Because it sure looked like Tommy Slick paid me a late-night visit."

"Tommy Slick? Chet's friend?"

Please don't ask me any more questions about Tommy Slick, Ronnie!

"Yeah. My dad noticed and went out to investigate, but he drove off."

"When did it happen?"

Shut up, Buck! No more questions!

"After midnight." Ronnie poured the requisite two bottles of water into the coffeemaker's reservoir, the amount for making eight cups of coffee per brew. "It was creepy as hell, Little Camper. He just sat there. Didn't he, babe?"

Tiffany groaned at him.

"I'm never spending the night at your house again," she said.

"Yeah, it freaked Tiffany out." Ronnie shook his head. "Why would Tommy Slick sit in *my* driveway at midnight? It doesn't make any sense?"

Buck sat on the nearest bench and exhaled a heavy breath.

"Nothing makes sense anymore, Ronnie. The world grows darker every day."

Ronnie pulled the bag of Store Powder beside the coffeemaker and the bag of Hawaiian beans beside the grinder. Neither coffee type would go into the machine until someone placed the first order. He took a seat on the bench across from Buck afterward.

"I thought life after school would be awesome," Ronnie said. "With the exception of Tiffany, none of this is awesome."

"Thanks for thinking I'm a highlight," Tiffany said. "Right back at ya."

Ronnie leaned in close and whispered, "Is she actually thanking me, or…?"

Buck shrugged. He knew nothing about women's psychology. That was a question for Lila or Irina Swift, neither of whom was there for obvious reasons.

"So, he didn't hang out in your driveway last night?" Ronnie asked.

Buck shook his head. "Maybe we should just change the subject. Back to normal, remember?"

Ronnie nodded and reached across the table to swat Buck on the shoulder.

"Yeah, that's right. Back to normal." Ronnie glanced down at the concrete floor as he trailed off in his thoughts. "Back to normal…"

Buck wanted to share his theories with Ronnie. Ronnie was his best friend, after all. But he couldn't tell him about what had happened at the other park on Thursday, and all his theories pointed at the incident between Tommy and Pigeon.

Theory #1: Tommy was shopping around for a lawyer.

Theory #2: Tommy was checking if Buck was there spilling the beans.

He even had a third theory, but his stomach lurched at the thought. It was too absurd, and gross, to be viable. Besides, Tommy wouldn't have been carrying Pigeon around in the back of his truck for more than 24 hours. That would've been weird. Weirder than sitting in Ronnie's driveway at midnight.

Buck got up from the table and headed down the shallow hill to stand by the lake. The sky was clear this afternoon, and the ducks and the joggers were out in full force today. Business would begin at any moment. He needed his head clear. He needed things to get back to normal. Actually normal.

Up the hill, Tiffany was posting the advertisements on the pavilion's front posts. They were now open for business.

Buck suddenly threw up inches from the lake. There was no way he was ready to serve. He couldn't do this today.

* * *

Business picked up rather quickly, and before he knew it, Buck had served over a dozen coffees and collected about thirty bucks. It wasn't even one o'clock yet.

He should've been happy about the money, but he wasn't. Compared to Lila's situation and Pigeon's, and even Pigeon's brother Dodo's, who was likely home alone and terrified out of his skull in his isolation (not that he'd ever admit to it), money was trivial. With Lila recovering from Damon's attack, which never should've happened, and Buck's growing fear of the repercussions of Pigeon's accident, which never should've happened, and Dodo's increasing odds of becoming a sick little degenerate terrified of his own shadow, which should never be allowed to happen, even the bet with Chet was nonsense.

Why was he still fighting to win this thing?

By 1:20, Buck had had enough of coffee. He was sick of looking at it, sick of smelling it, and sick of serving it. For the last seven weeks, all he'd done was get up early, buy supplies, set up the pavilion, take strangers' hard-earned cash for his low-grade coffee, tear down the pavilion, manage a failing social life, sit at home in the dark, and sleep. This was his summer after high school, his summer before college, his summer to explore the world and enjoy the short window of adulthood where his responsibilities were negligible. And in that time, he'd managed to wrap himself up in three dysfunctional relationships, deal with insurance agents, get on the tracking radar of the town's most powerful man, and get a kid killed. He'd barely seen his mom a dozen times since all of this began. And he'd seen his dad once.

There was no more normal. And there was no amount of money that could earn him a decent summer now. It was all absurd.

At 1:23, Ronnie shook Buck out of his trance.

"We got a VIP under the roof, Buck. Look alive."

An older, mustached man dressed in a ridiculous bellhop-looking uniform strolled past the picnic benches as he approached the counter, absorbing every inch of the place with his eyes and smelling the air with his twitching nose. The sight of him caused Buck to roll his eyes. Absurdity of the highest degree. Why did these lunatics want *his* coffee? All that was missing was the bee suit.

"Interesting place you got here, er?"

Buck shook his head. "I guess." He didn't want to talk to this man.

"I take it you're the owner of this establishment?"

Buck shrugged. "Sure."

The man stretched out his hand for a shake. Buck took hold of the edges of his fingers and rattled them slightly. Hardly a handshake, but good enough. The man casually wiped his fingers off on his velvet blue jacket.

"You have a name?" the man asked.

"Sure."

The man waited for an answer, but Buck gave him none. Buck wasn't interested in chatting with his customers, especially the weirdos. He just wanted the guy to leave. He wanted to go home himself.

"His name is Buck Star," Ronnie said. "And I'm Ronnie Michaels, his assistant. The hot girl over there is Tiffany Hadley, our marketing expert. We are the Coffee Pavilion."

The man nodded and smiled at Ronnie. Ronnie smiled back.

Through clenched teeth, Ronnie demanded that Buck smile, too. Buck did not. What was the point?

"So, I'm here for your best coffee," the man said. "What can you give me that'll knock my socks off?"

"Nothing," Buck said. "It's all tasteless. But if you want the regular—"

Ronnie faked a laugh so hard it was distracting.

"Oh, Buck here is such a comedian," he said. "Of course we have excellent coffee. Right, Tiffany?" Ronnie gestured at the strange visitor with his head, as if to enlist Tiffany for help. She seemed to understand him because she zipped right over. "Babe, tell the man how great our coffee is."

"So great," Tiffany said, in a fake Valley Girl accent. "You can forget Melty's. Their coffee is sewage—no, thin mud compared to our deliciously smooth, hot and creamy, sweet and cinna—"

"Sheesh," Buck hissed. "It's just coffee. Get over yourselves."

Both of his friends looked wounded by his outburst, but he didn't care. He wanted this weirdo out of his pavilion. He wanted everyone out of his pavilion. If he hadn't paid so much for his equipment and supplies, he'd happily unplug the coffeemaker and just let the guy take it home with him. He was so tired of this soul-destroying coffee business. He wanted out. The longer this guy stayed, the longer Buck had to stay. And when Buck stayed in the coffee business, terrible things happened. Why couldn't the guy just take a hint? And a hike?

"Here." Buck poured the Store Powder brand coffee into a polystyrene cup. Rather than dress it up with cream, sugar, cinnamon, or anything with flavor, he dashed in just a drop of Liquid Sunshine. Nothing else. He used a stirrer to mix it, tossed it aside, and handed the cup to the blue bellhop. "Six bucks."

The man raised his eyebrows.

"Six dollars? For plain black coffee?"

"Not plain. It's our luxury brand. You asked for the best. You got the best. It's the Restoration Special, if you care. Six bucks or give it back."

The man frowned at him. But he was obliged. He reached into a pocket on his gaudy golden shirt and handed Buck a ten. Buck, in turn, handed Ronnie the bill, who handed back three singles and change. The man counted it.

"What's the tax here?"

"Four dollars minus whatever you got there," Buck said. "Have a nice day."

The man's eyes were turning acidic as he brought the cup to his lips and blew at the rim.

"Don't mind my friend here," Ronnie said, elbowing Buck out of the way. "We've all had a rough week. Is there anything else we can get you? A cookie? A donut?" Ronnie looked back to glare at Buck.

"On the house." Then he returned his smile and attention to the bellhop to complete the sale. "Just say the word. Your happiness is our reward."

The man raised his hand and shook his head.

"I've just come for the coffee." The man took a sip. His reaction was nonplussed. "I must admit I expected more taste for six bucks plus tax."

"Would you like cream or sugar or—"

"No, no. I think I've experienced enough of this place. Thank you for your time." The man looked past Buck, Ronnie, and Tiffany toward the counter. "Any lids for the cup?"

Buck sighed and walked away. He needed to pee, anyway.

When Buck returned from the bathroom, the bellhop was gone. For a moment, he felt his chest lighten. One less crazy person to deal with.

But his relief lasted seconds. More people would come, and more would demand his service, as if he were some kind of performance monkey.

"Buck, what's your problem, man?" Ronnie met him at the edge of the pavilion. "You know who that guy was?"

Buck shook his head. "I don't care."

"You should. That was the Coffee Critic you insulted."

"Who?"

"The Coffee Critic. The guy who reviews coffee shops for newspapers and magazines all over the country. The guy my dad contacted to check you out. The guy who can make you rich or poor, depending on how well you treat him. *The Coffee Critic.* Dumbass!"

Buck just stared at him. He understood what Ronnie was saying. But he felt nothing. If that guy was the customer he'd been waiting all summer to serve, then he'd picked the worst day to judge Buck's fate, and Buck the worst day to give up the fight.

Now it all really did seem worthless.

"Maybe you and Tiffany should go home," Buck said. "I can see this is upsetting you."

Ronnie poked him in the chest. "No, we're going to finish strong, because if we don't, you're going to become Chet's slave, and that's going to make Friday night hangouts near impossible. I know what happened to Lila was bad. But she's recovering now, so you need to snap out of whatever you're in."

Buck shook his head.

"You don't know what you're talking about," Buck said. "Don't poke me again."

"Sorry. And of course I know. I was there."

Buck gritted his teeth.

"That's not what this is about." Buck waved his hands to his side. "No, this is about nothing. Drop the subject."

"You literally tried chasing off the most important customer you'll ever have. I don't know what's wrong with you, but you need to fix it."

"You want to talk about it, Buck?" Tiffany said, from a few feet behind Ronnie. Buck hadn't noticed her standing there, but there she was. "Is it another girl? Jennifer, maybe?"

Buck marched past Ronnie and sat on the nearest bench.

"It's not about Jennifer. It's not about Lila. Just—it's not about anything. Leave me alone about it. Everything's fine."

Tiffany sat on the table by Buck's arm and rubbed his shoulder.

"I know girls can be complicated. But there's no shame in—"

Buck shook off her touch. "It's not about a girl. What's with you people? Why are you so shallow? Tommy—" He caught himself before he let anything more slip out.

But Ronnie was too sharp. Too attentive. He snatched the subject right out of the air like chopsticks snatching a fly.

"What about Tommy?" Ronnie asked. "Did he–Was he—" He slapped the table by Buck's other arm. "He *did* hang out in your driveway last night, didn't he? Just like ours! That's why you're out of your mind."

"No. Just…let it go."

"Come on, Buck. Say it. He camped in your driveway, too. Right after he left mine. Freaked you the hell out! Now you're delirious from lack of sleep. That's it, right? Say it."

Buck glared at him.

"No. Tommy didn't camp in my driveway. Just *drop it*."

Ronnie was about to respond, but he bit his lip. Thought about what Buck was telling him. After exchanging glances with Tiffany, perhaps seeking support or advice, he dared to speak again.

"What's really eating at you then?"

Buck cradled his forehead in the palms of both hands.

"Guys, please just drop it."

"Is he dunking your head in toilets again? Giving you wedgies? Giving you noogies?"

"I watched him kill a man, dammit! Leave me—" Buck scanned the pavilion as he realized what had come out of his mouth. Fortunately, there were no other customers within hearing distance. "Leave me alone," he whispered.

Ronnie and Tiffany said nothing. Their wide eyes and agape mouths had said enough.

Buck turned his back on them before they found the words to speak again, before they could ask him a follow-up question, before they figured out how this might fit into their insane idea of "back to normal." Fortunately, they seemed to respect his wishes this time.

Episode 54

The Tax Spook Taketh

RONNIE STOOD BESIDE THE serving counter, blinking. Buck could tell he was processing the information that had spilled out of Buck's mouth, and that it wasn't computing. Tiffany, standing just inches behind him, didn't know where to look, so she retreated, lost in whatever thoughts she was spinning. Buck thought about the lake down at the bottom of the hill and wondered if it was safer just to make a run for the shoreline. Ronnie took off his hat and stared at its interior, as if that were the only thing worth his attention anymore.

"Is this the part where I'm supposed to laugh?" Ronnie asked. "Pretend you'd just told me a really outrageous joke?"

"If you want," Buck said.

"Because you sure look serious, and I've never known you to be much of an actor."

Buck said nothing.

Ronnie nodded and placed his hat right back on his dark, mop-like hair, as if this were the normal response.

"You think that might be why he was *camping in my driveway* last night?"

"I don't know why he was there. Everything happened so fast. It was as if—"

"Stop. Say no more. As far as Tiffany and I are concerned, you never said a word to us. Period. Let's just get back to work. Worry about truck-driving psychos living in my front yard later."

Behind him, Tiffany had retreated so far that she was stepping off the concrete and into the grass at the other end of the pavilion. She didn't seem as interested in dropping the subject from her mind as Ronnie was.

"I think we should shut down for the day," Buck said. "I can't get my head in the game, and now I doubt you will, either. Tiffany looks like she wants to go home."

Ronnie started turning his head to look but stopped. No, he wouldn't look. He returned his gaze to Buck.

"Does he think you've told me?"

Buck shrugged. "I don't know what he thinks. Again, it was all so fast."

Ronnie brushed his hands to the side, like a baseball umpire calling a strike.

"No, don't answer any more of my questions. But you should probably talk to my dad. This sounds bad." He shook his head. "Dammit, Buck. Why'd you have to tell me that?"

"You kept prodding me."

Ronnie stepped back into the shade, closer to the coffeemaker, closer to a position that was "back to normal."

"Maybe this doesn't have to be anything," he said to himself. "Maybe I didn't hear anything. I don't even know what you're talking about. Yeah, that's it. What are you even talking about, Buck? I have no idea. If anyone asks, I have no idea what you're talking about. Yeah, that sounds accurate. Who's the victim? No idea." Ronnie stared at Buck. "I have no idea. *No idea.*"

Buck nodded back. If all went well, it would stay that way.

Ronnie changed the filter in the coffeemaker. Poured in some Hawaiian grounds. It was almost two in the afternoon. The procedure required them to prepare for the next batch of customers. Ronnie was prepping for the next batch of customers. That's what he was doing. That's what it looked like. Very normal.

Tiffany, meanwhile, fussed over the promotional materials mounted around the pavilion, checking each sign's tilt and direction, adjusting anything that looked off by a millimeter, muttering something to herself about knowing nothing and hearing nothing. Then she'd check over her shoulders, just in case.

* * *

BUCK WENT TO RONNIE'S house that night, intending to speak with his dad about the events at Park Center Park, but he couldn't bring himself to utter the words. So, he just sat on the couch watching TV with the rest of them, as if they were having a normal Saturday night. A few times Ronnie's dad asked if everything was okay or if they were sure everything was okay, since they each took turns looking out the window through the living room curtains, but each time, Buck, Ronnie, and Tiffany said they were fine. He eventually dropped it.

Whenever Ronnie peeked out the front window, he never registered that there was a problem. And when Buck was ready to head home for the night, Ronnie suggested they were probably okay. Buck's bike ride home seemed to prove it. He had no incidents between Ronnie's house and his own. But his neck was sore from constantly looking over his shoulder.

Sleeping was as difficult as it had been the last two evenings, and his dreams were about as fitful. But he got more of it. And when he awoke the next morning, unsure of whether he should get up or stay in bed, he realized his anxiety had lessened. It wasn't gone, of course. But the day felt a little less fearful. He wasn't sure whether he was using a self-disarming technique to cope with the situation, or if he was self-sabotaging. Either way, he had a bit more energy to face the coming day.

By 8:30, he was ready to leave his house. He'd gotten as far as tying his shoes when the phone rang.

"Have you seen the morning paper yet?" Ronnie asked.

"No, why would I—"

"Go get it. Quick. Turn to the local section, page seven. Call me back."

Buck found the Sunday edition of *The Hybrid City Post* leaning against his garage door. He skimmed each page until he found the story Ronnie must've wanted him to read down at the bottom of 7B.

It was about the Coffee Pavilion:

Fountain of Youth in a Cup of Coffee
By *The Coffee Critic*

Legend has it, in the 1500s, Ponce de Leon searched all over the swamps of Florida for the fabled Fountain of Youth. If he had traveled a few thousand miles west and waited a little over four hundred years, he might've found it hidden under a park pavilion in the back of North Park, at the edge of Hybrid City's downtown district.

The article was brief, hardly more than a blurb, and it was critical of the pavilion owner's attitude toward customers. But it raved about the "healing power" a cup of Restorative Coffee had on the consumer. The Coffee Critic had noted that just seconds after taking his first sip, he noticed a pain in his leg tingling. By the time he'd gotten to his car, the pain was gone. He didn't think it was a coincidence.

The review ended with a statement that raised the hair on the back of Buck's neck:

Despite the expensive price, you'd be foolish to pass up a visit to the Coffee Pavilion or a cup of its Restorative Coffee. It's better than any over-the-counter drug you could buy. What are you waiting for? Get yourself a cup right now.

According to the byline, the Coffee Critic was nationally known, and his column was syndicated throughout hundreds of publications across the country.

Buck's heart hammered. Regardless of his feelings about the week's events, he'd have to get his head in the game now. Reviews like that didn't go unnoticed by everyone. On Day 42 of his bet with Chet, Buck felt in his gut that his fortunes were about to shift exponentially. If there was ever a moment he stood a chance at truly winning this thing, a nationally published rave review would've gotten him there.

Bad week or not, he couldn't throw this opportunity away. The only way to make the week worse was to hand-deliver his freedom directly into Chet's abusive mitts.

He set the paper down, finished tying his shoes, and watched as the fan took each page and flipped it.

And then he almost choked. Just as he tightened the laces on his right sneaker, the newspaper flipped open to a close-up photograph of a rifle shell in the grass just a few feet from a soft-blurred image of the Liquid Shack, and a headline that read: "Squirrel Hunter or Murderer?" Some of the blood on the grass was faint but visible in the background.

The article was speculative, fortunately, and the wording was borderline tabloid material, but it asked too many provocative questions for everyone to ignore.

* * *

As Buck rode into town to prepare for his morning, he had the nagging feeling that he needed to make good on a promise. Maybe the situation with Thursday's events at the park would pass—even though the sight of the rifle shell in the newspaper nearly caused Buck to gag, the article itself was speculative beyond reason, and the writer had spent more time crafting a tale of fiction than predicting what blood at the Liquid Shack actually meant. It looked like he was in the clear, but he wasn't sure whether the story would raise the park rangers' scent or spook Tommy into running or Chet into investigating the scene. The writer laid no claim to responsible parties, as no one was present at the time of photography. In fact, it was framed as if whatever had happened had forced everyone to run, assuming anything other than a squirrel hunt had happened at all. Either way, Buck knew the truth, and he owed Pigeon an apology, and he'd pay him that apology the only way he knew how.

Buck took a detour at the next intersection and headed for Pigeon's street. Once he got to the house, he knocked on the front door. As expected, no one answered, so he moved to the side and tapped on Dodo's window. Dodo was still in bed, clearly in a state of panic.

He was in his pajamas and looked as if he hadn't gotten out of bed in days. His hair was a bird's nest, and his sheets were peeling halfway off the mattress. When he saw who was looking in, he marched across the room and opened the window. Buck could immediately tell he hadn't bathed in a few days.

The kid had lines on his face, and his cheeks were splotched with red marks. He might have been crying, or he might have been sleeping too hard on his pillow, but he was in a rough state. Buck knew why, but he didn't want to let Dodo know he knew.

"Hey, you want a free donut today?" Buck asked.

Dodo shrugged.

"I could use some help at the coffee shop. Wanna come?"

He shook his head. "I wanna go to the arcade."

Buck smirked. The kid was resilient. His parents were on vacation, and his brother hadn't been home in days. Yet, here he was, ready to go to the arcade.

"What's your favorite game?"

"All of them."

"If I take you to the arcade, will you get cleaned up and tag along today?"

Dodo nodded.

"Good, go get a bath and get dressed. Need breakfast? I'll get you a donut. Will five dollars in tokens do for now?"

"Twenty," Dodo said.

"Twenty? That's a lot."

"Pigeon promised me a half hour at the arcade. He hasn't been home in a few days. Don't know when he's coming home. Twenty dollars buys at least half an hour."

Buck didn't want to argue. He was responsible for Dodo's current isolation. No ten-year-old wanted to be home alone for three days straight, no matter how brave they might've pretended to be.

"Twenty dollars it is, then. I'll meet you in the driveway. Take a bath first!"

A few minutes later, Buck and Dodo rode off on their respective bikes for Pound Cake, and then to Blinky's Arcade in the beach district after they each had a donut.

"By the way," Buck said. "Is Dodo your real name?"

"Yeah, what of it?"

"You ever wanted to be called something else?"

Dodo thought about it. "Mikey," he said.

"Then today you're Mikey."

Dodo smiled at that. Today, he would be Mikey.

* * *

As it turned out, twenty dollars added up to almost an hour at the arcade. While Buck didn't want to spend extra money on the machines for himself, he was happy to stand by and watch Dodo, now Mikey, shoot aliens to smithereens, de-segment the body parts of a wild centipede, and gobble up power pellets in time to turn the tables on a quartet of ghosts. With every point that Mikey gained, Buck cheered him on. And he kept it up until the money ran out.

Once they finished, Buck had Mikey ride with him to North Park. Mikey was visibly nervous as they entered the park, and his willingness to continue down the sidewalk diminished the closer they got to the pavilion. But when Buck assured him that everything was safe and no one would attack, he loosened up.

At the pavilion, Buck showed Mikey the coffee equipment and supplies and asked him if he wanted to learn how to make coffee. Mikey seemed disinterested at first, but when Buck told him he could make money making coffee, his attitude changed. By the end of the first hour, Mikey had helped Buck sell five cups of coffee.

Of course, Ronnie and Tiffany had arrived by then, and they helped Buck stem the tide of new arrivals that had come for a cup of "Restorative Coffee." For the next four hours, they had trouble keeping up. In fact, Ronnie had to make a special run to the store during working hours. The Restorative Coffee was a hit.

By five o'clock, Buck was exhausted, Ronnie and Tiffany were about to pass out on the bench, and Mikey was already fast asleep. Mikey had laid his head on Tiffany's lap, and she sat there stroking his hair as he slept, fighting to stay awake herself.

Ronnie got up to help Buck pack the equipment and supplies. As they loaded up the storeroom, Ronnie asked a question Buck hadn't prepared for.

"You plan to tell him about his brother?"

Buck almost dropped the coffeemaker. He managed to get it onto the shelf in time.

"What about his brother?"

"Come on, Buck, do the math. The kid says he's been home alone for three days. Where's his brother? The math says he ain't coming home. Ever."

Buck put his finger to his lips.

"Not so loud."

"Well, you can't exactly let him stay home alone, right? Not with the parents gone for the rest of summer."

"Rest of summer? Where the hell did they go?" Buck put the coffee bags on the shelf.

"Doesn't matter. The kid can't stay alone for another month. You should take him in. He seems to get along with you."

Buck opened his mouth to protest, but he stopped himself. Of course, Ronnie was right. There was nothing Buck could think of to claim he was wrong.

"My mom won't like it," he said.

"When's your mom ever home long enough to find out? Put the kid in the attic. He'll be fine."

Buck considered Ronnie's advice. It probably would've worked, especially since he'd already let Lila spend part of the night in the attic without his mom ever knowing.

"I'll ask him," Buck said.

* * *

THAT EVENING, AFTER BUCK closed shop and counted his earnings for the day, he discovered that the Coffee Critic's review had given him a spike in business. While the customer numbers were about the same as usual, the steady requests for Restorative Coffee had given him one of his best days ever. If positive word got out, the prospect for even better days was great.

He discussed a business plan with Ronnie and Tiffany to see if they could advertise the new product. They agreed that they'd have to pay a visit to the Ad Guy this week, maybe even take out a radio ad if they could afford it.

At the hospital, Buck narrowly avoided running into his mom, who was working on the fourth-floor nursing floor but happened to be down in the cafeteria as he was passing through. He didn't want to explain why he was there, nor did he want to get caught up in conversation or take up her precious free time with his problems, so he slipped behind a row of people who were in line for food and ducked out into the main hall before she could spot him.

Lila was showing signs of improvement, but she was still too weak to hold a conversation, or even to stay awake, so he took turns with Ronnie and Tiffany sitting by her bedside, and once her shift at Tealeaf Central ended, he also took turns with French Girl. Jennifer and Mr. Perkins each stopped by at different times to check in, but neither could stay long. No one else paid her a visit.

After he left the hospital, he helped Dodo, now Mikey, pack a few bags of clothes and toys and mounted them on his handlebars. Then, once he got home, he showed Mikey the attic and gave him the house rules. The main rule was no roaming the house after Buck's mom got home. He had to remain invisible after ten o'clock (even though his mom usually didn't get home until two). Buck hoped the in-house curfew would've encouraged him to get to sleep at a normal hour. The other house rule was to stay off the living room couch. Mikey wasn't allowed to ask why. To keep him from getting too bored up there, Buck also set up an old television and an Atari 2600 he had stashed in the garage. He figured that would keep Mikey busy until his parents got back from vacation.

For the next few days, Buck's routine gradually returned to normal, with Lila's health and Buck's sales days improving. Thanks to the demand for Restorative Coffee and satisfying results, his customers even started tipping again. Mikey remained mostly quiet as he spent his waking hours trying to beat Buck's entire library of Atari games. On Wednesday, Buck almost took out a radio ad but decided the high cost was too big of a gamble at this stage of the bet cycle, so he opted for another two dozen handouts. It was a wimp move, but it was safe. His visitor count rose minimally, perhaps enough to cover his marketing costs, but it was too close to call. On Friday night, he called Jennifer, just because he was thinking about her for some reason. She was on her way out the door and couldn't talk, but she promised to call him back the next day. Buck told her he would be at the pavilion.

A few minutes after they hung up, the phone rang. Buck was ready to ask if she had changed her mind, but someone else answered his greeting. It was his dad on the line. He told him he'd seen the Coffee Critic's review, and that he was both proud of his accomplishment and disappointed that he'd disobeyed his order to shut down. An accolade from the Coffee Critic was a great way to get on the wrong person's radar. Buck thanked him for the reminder, but he kept his real fear to himself. If his dad saw the Coffee Critic review, then that meant others were likely to see it. And if others saw the Coffee Critic review, then they might have also seen the Park Center Park story.

Each morning, Buck worried that someone with a jacket and hat would come knocking on his door with a notepad in hand, preparing to ask him questions about what had happened at Park Central Park on July 18th. But no one did. His door remained quiet all week. And so, his life continued, finding its rhythm, finally, hopefully, entering a sustainable groove that could and would take him across the finish line with Chet's bet.

And then, one morning at the end of July, someone did finally come to Buck's door in a coat and hat.

* * *

DAY 52: WEDNESDAY, JULY 31, 1985

Buck's Savings Account: $2.81

Buck's Wallet: $2,656.89

Buck's Business Funds: none available

Funds-to-Wallet Refund Due: maxed out

Buck's Expenses: $2 a day*

Hours of Operation: 12-5, S-S

Money on Hold: none

BUCK'S SPINE INVOLUNTARILY SHIVERED as he trudged out of his bedroom. Even though it was the end of July, the chill moving through his house got him thinking about his jacket. He turned back toward his closet but stopped himself. It was a crazy reaction to an aggressive air-conditioner. He would be outside most of the day. The jacket could stay in the closet until October.

The kitchen was no warmer. In fact, the chill kept intensifying, through his skin and into his bones. Maybe even into his veins. And his ceiling seemed to darken a little, almost as if a cloud had moved in. Of course, he was inside, barely fifteen feet above sea level. There were no clouds. His eyes were playing tricks on him.

Nevertheless, he couldn't shake the feeling that his house was turning against him, as if the shadows on the wall had grown fingers and were now reaching for his shirt, his chest, or maybe his shirt pocket. He couldn't recall the last time he'd felt that way.

After eating breakfast and brushing his teeth, Buck gathered his wallet and a few backup supplies and headed for the front door. His fingers recoiled as he reached for the knob. It was freezing.

And that's when someone finally knocked.

Buck wrapped the hem of his shirt around the doorknob and turned it. Suddenly, his entire body trembled.

A lone figure in a gray duster and bone-white skin stood at his doorstep wearing a ten-gallon hat and black leather boots. His eyes were pale pink, and a bat perched on his shoulder like a parrot.

Buck's stomach tightened, and he about lost his balance. The ghost of Pigeon Polluck had found him!

"Buck Star?" the figure whispered.

Buck said nothing. He just stood there, wide-eyed, horrified. It didn't look like Pigeon. But the chill in the air—

"Owner of the Coffee Pavilion in North Park?"

That voice, so chalky. Buck's throat turned dry just listening to it.

"I believe you are due to pay your taxes today."

Buck's nerves migrated from his stomach to his chest. All at once, his mind changed. Whatever he was thinking about a moment ago, this was not the ghost of Pigeon Polluck, nor was it anyone involved in his search.

No, this was somebody much worse, someone that no one in town ever dared to speak the name of, though his identity, now that Buck did the math in his head, was unmistakable.

"You–you're—"

The figure grinned slightly out of the left corner of his mouth, but he showed no other emotion or reaction.

"According to my records, you have paid no taxes last quarter, which tells me you're new. Is that true?"

"I–I—"

The figure reached into his duster and removed a notebook and calculator. He also took out a pen and tried to hand it off to Buck. Buck was afraid to take it, so he resisted.

"I need you to write your earnings since your business started. Do not leave off a penny. The consequences are dire for those who try to cheat the system. Write your earnings and *do not lie to me.*" With his last statement, the sinister figure's pale eyes turned fiery. Buck came close to passing out from the sheer power of his dark presence.

Buck's hands shook as he reached for the pen. But his fingers seemingly passed right through it. Or maybe he was so nervous he just missed.

"Can I–can I use my own?"

The gray man shrugged. "Whatever ensures you give me an accurate claim on your income since May the first."

"I–I—" Buck kicked the door closed. He could not look at this man for another second. All he could think about was the warnings he'd gotten from Mr. Kabuki, Mack Green, and others.

Do not speak the name of The Tax Spook, he could hear them saying, *lest he come to your door in the night.* Buck knew that was the man or the being who was standing at his door right now, even though it was now early morning.

Buck's heart was hammering as he escaped to his bedroom and closed the door. Maybe the Tax Spook would leave, or fade away, or do whatever his kind did to make an exit strategy.

But even as he sat on his bed, trying to slow his heart and recover a steady breath, the chill grew worse. Then he leapt and screamed.

The Tax Spook was looking through his bedroom window.

"You cannot escape me," he said through the glass. "So, do not try."

Buck took a deep breath as the Tax Spook floated away from the window, or walked—he seemed to have feet. The ghostly figure was terrifying, but he was here for one thing. If Buck gave him that one thing, he would go away, and Buck could calm down.

Despite his body's resistance to move, Buck reached for his desk drawer and recovered his ledger. Then he forced his feet to bring him to the front door, where the Tax Spook was still waiting. At the door, he showed the Tax Spook the ledger.

"I–I—"

The Tax Spook swiped the ledger from his grip and skimmed its pages at an inhuman speed.

"Your accounting is good," the Tax Spook said. "I'm impressed. Your fine will be less than usual."

"My–my—"

"You have not accounted for earnings before June the tenth, so you shall be fined a small fee for each unaccounted-for day going back to May the first. I assume this is a new business?"

Buck said nothing, even though he tried to say yes. The Tax Spook seemed to understand his silence.

"I see. Well, just because you start in June doesn't mean you've escaped May's taxes. However, the percentage on zero is lighter than if you had earned a dollar or more. The tax office charges only a dollar per day when your business earns nothing in a given period. For every other day, your taxes depend on your earnings. Because you've broken a thousand dollars during the current tax cycle, I will require twenty-five percent for this quarter."

Buck's eyes widened.

"Twenty–twenty-five—"

"Owning a business isn't free, young man. It's time you learned that lesson now. Now, according to my calculations…"

Buck felt like he was melting through the floor. The Tax Spook's fingers flew across his calculator keys, tapping, tapping, and hitting an operator button. Once the Tax Spook figured out what Buck owed, he wrote the figure in his notebook.

"You can pay me in cash or by check, but I must have it before I leave. How would you like to pay?" As he asked the question, his shoulder bat leapt up and fluttered over his head. It landed on the opposite shoulder and fell back to sleep.

It took Buck several minutes to find his feet and his gut, but he managed to recover his earnings from an envelope he kept stashed in his desk drawer.

A piece of him died inside as he passed over 25% of his earnings since June 10th, plus the extra $41 to cover each day since May 1st. In all, he'd handed the Tax Spook $1,457.00 of his total earnings, which he'd needed to win the bet. It left him with just under $1,200 to his name.

"Thank you for your payment," the Tax Spook said, as he tossed the ledger at Buck's feet. "I'll see you again on October 31st."

And with that, Buck's front door closed itself.

Episode 55

Summer Recovery

BUCK WAS TOO DISILLUSIONED by the Tax Spook's home invasion to think about the financial repercussions from "getting taxed." He still had a few errands to run before opening the shop, and if he'd spent too much time dwelling on the hit, he'd lose precious time toward readying the business that gave the Tax Spook such a large Christmas present in July.

However, he didn't get far before finding himself seeking the usual advice for dealing with it. Fortunately, two of his mentors were hanging out in the same place when he picked up another bag of coffee at Store Down the Street. If there was one thing he'd learned this summer about tackling trauma alone, it was that keeping it to himself would've made him angry, and that would've caused him to blow up at the wrong people. He'd nearly sabotaged his chances with the Coffee Critic after the Pigeon Polluck incident. And even though the Tax Spook's mugging failed to press the same emotional weight against him, it was an easier event to discuss without using shadow words to mask the real story. So, he thought it wiser to get it off his mind now than to let it destroy him later.

"We all deal with it our own way," Mack said after Buck told him about the Tax Spook's visit.

Mack was sitting behind his desk with his hands behind his head, while Mr. Kabuki was sipping tea in the visitor's seat across from him. Both had been discussing a similar issue when Buck had walked in, so the conversation was timely. It seemed the Tax Spook had paid everyone the same visit on the same day.

"No shame in admitting dislike for tax man," Kabuki said between sips of tea.

"Does he come every July?" Buck asked. "I was not expecting him this morning."

"In this part of town, yes," Mack said. "According to Sapphire and other business owners in the area, he collects taxes by district. So, everyone on this block will see him today, whereas the owners in Hybrid West may see him at the end of August and those in Hybrid Beach may see him at the end of September. Despite appearances, he's not exactly Santa Claus, or his evil twin Krampus. He's ultimately mortal and can be in only one place at a time. If the rumors are true."

"Up for debate," Kabuki said.

"So, I'm a part of this district?" Buck asked.

"Looks that way," Mack said. "I'd say it's unfortunate, but it all adds up at the end of the year. Whether you see him now or in August, you're getting hit the same."

Buck thought about the math. Mack had neglected one wrinkle in his theory.

"If North Park is part of the downtown district, does that mean Park Center Park is part of the Hybrid West district?"

Mack and Kabuki exchanged glances and nodded at each other.

"Adds up," Mack said.

"So, Chet will also get a visit from the Tax Spook?"

"We all do."

"But his visit will be at the end of August?"

Mack and Kabuki exchanged glances once again. This time, Mack rolled his eyes. He seemed to understand exactly what Buck was getting at.

"Sorry, Buck. But yeah, that's the Hybrid City tax system for you. We all get quarterly visits before the big one in mid-April, but those visits don't always respect our plans or goals."

Buck cursed under his breath. The Tax Spook had very likely just cost him a victory.

* * *

On Day 53, Thursday, August 1st, Buck had to make additional payments to the Chamber of Commerce and the Lease Agent to keep his membership and leasing agreements active. Fortunately, he'd been planning for both fees since he'd signed on with them, so he used the money he'd been squirreling away each day to pay them.

The Lease Agent tried to hit Buck with a surprise clause that stated he had to pay for the month of August in advance, but he'd learned to expect these kinds of side jabs by now, so the Lease Agent's "surprise" did little to catch Buck off guard. He paid his fees dutifully and marched out of the office with his head held high. His relationship to Tommy Slick never came up in the conversation, and Buck wasn't about to ask him about it.

The workday was typical, with the usual customers ordering the usual coffees. And even with Liquid Sunshine rounding out his inventory, Buck's sales had seemed to hit a plateau. Variations on each day depended on the temperature, neighboring public events in the park, and so on, but he found he could count on an average of one-to two-hundred-dollar income days, plus enough money to cover his expenses. Given that the bet's deadline was a week away, he didn't expect any new financial bashes to the head to knock him off course.

The question, then, really came down to how well Chet was performing at the Liquid Shack. He'd sent Tiffany in to spy for him, since Chet didn't really know her or her relationship with Buck, and she'd come back with a report that Chet was working solo. Unfortunately, he was still popular with customers, but working alone had made him so exhausted that he began upsetting them. If the downward trajectory continued, he'd lose money.

Then again, Buck wasn't so convinced this was a good thing. If Chet was working solo, then he was also working with minimal expenses. After all, if neither Pigeon nor Tommy were coming to work, then who was he supposed to pay? Buck wondered if Chet's savings on employee income made up for lost sales from disappointed customers.

To become a better spy, Tiffany had ordered a lemonade from Chet and engaged in a bit of small talk while she drank it. One of her questions was about Chet's operations, namely why he was working alone. He'd told her that his employees had seemed to abandon him. It surprised Buck to hear that Chet was so open with her, but she admitted that she'd used some of her disarming techniques to get him to talk, just as an actual spy would've done. When Buck asked if Ronnie should've been worried, she'd simply responded with a smirk. Ronnie, according to her, shouldn't have felt worried; he should've felt lucky to have her.

On Friday night, Day 54, Buck considered Ronnie's luck with Tiffany. Although Buck would never admit jealousy of his best friend, he felt a sting in his chest that a weirdo who walked around with a top hat could have such a beautiful and cool girlfriend who stuck around and supported him regardless of how well she could charm jocks and businessmen and completely up-class her situation. When Buck ran through the list of women he'd cared for in the last few weeks, never mind the past year, he couldn't understand what he'd been doing wrong. Granted, Tiffany was more guarded than the women Buck had latched onto and would never admit her reasons for sticking around with Ronnie, so whatever Ronnie was doing right, only Tiffany would ever know. Asking her to share her secrets would've been pointless. Regardless of her hidden answer, however, either Tiffany was unusual, or Buck was just unlucky.

Buck had tried to build a relationship with French Girl that was going nowhere. He'd built a friendship with Lila that shouldn't have gone anywhere but was nevertheless strong enough to create genuine worry in him when she'd gone missing and turned up in the hospital. And he'd even allowed Jennifer back into his life after she'd betrayed him with Chet, but after her initial support in relaunching his campaign to win the bet, she'd become more difficult to reach. She hadn't ignored him or his calls, but her busy schedule had increased since the Grand Reopening.

As Buck sat in his bedroom on a Friday night, tired from work but lonely for a night out with a beautiful woman, he attempted to call Jennifer again. For some reason, she was the one most in the forefront of his mind, perhaps because she was the most accessible, which wasn't saying much these days.

To his surprise, she picked up the phone.

* * *

"WOW, WHAT A PLACE!" Jennifer said as she took in the sights and sounds around her. "So much neon."

"Yeah," Buck said, equally intoxicated by the surrounding sights. "Heard lots of great things about it."

In truth, he'd heard nothing about Synthmania, the outdoor poolside lounge bathed in competing blue and purple neon lights located deep within the Hybrid South Entertainment District. But he needed a place to take Jennifer that could simultaneously get his mind off everything swarming at him while also allowing him to focus on her. The contrast of cool colors against a lit pool and dark night had a calming effect on him that he hadn't experienced since before graduation. And the soft ambient tones of synthesizer music coming out of speakers in the brick walls surrounding the pool cast a trance over him.

This was almost as peaceful as the night he'd met her at the beach for his birthday. Only this time, she had no other plans to meet elsewhere. It was just the two of them, sitting on adjacent lounge chairs, sipping fruit-flavored seltzer water through straws shaped like umbrellas, mesmerized by the atmosphere.

"This is the place I've been missing my whole life." She sipped her drink and closed her eyes to savor what had touched her tongue. "I could die here."

"I'm glad you're enjoying it with me."

She glanced over and smiled. Reached out for the back of his wrist.

"Glad you invited me."

Buck sipped his own drink. It was some kind of tangerine-grape concoction with bubbles.

"Maybe we could make a habit of this."

He dared to look her in the eye. She was watching the pool now, which had a few young couples swimming about non-aggressively, but she smiled when she turned her head and saw him looking back.

"And invite all our friends," she added.

Buck held her gaze. His guts nearly burned at her suggestion, but he tamped it out through willful ignorance.

"Or we could just make this our place," he said. "Ours to enjoy ourselves."

Her lips parted, showing her teeth, now awash in blues and purples.

"That sounds nice, too."

Buck turned his hand around and gripped her on the underside of her wrist. Her hand loosened as he stroked her skin with his fingers.

She closed her eyes and reset her position on the lounge chair so that she was fully on it, back pressed flat against the plastic slats. Then she pulled her wrist free and laid it across her belly.

"Let's just enjoy the music," she said. "Keep the moment perfect."

Buck left his hand dangling off the side of his lounge chair. He wasn't sure what she'd meant by "keeping the moment perfect." Wasn't "perfect" what would come of the moment as the tenderness progressed?

"Okay."

In reality, he didn't know enough about perfect moments to decide when they'd reached that level. He'd had too many awful moments to think "perfection" was any greater than just "working out."

Then again, Jennifer was lying in a lounge chair beside him in a place where the sights and sounds punctuated the romantic mood he was hoping for.

In short, this moment was pretty near perfect already.

* * *

THAT NIGHT, BUCK WENT home happy. Nothing more had happened between them by the neon-lit pool, but it ended on a pleasant enough note that the door for future romance was once again open. Hard to believe given how their summer began, but it was true. Before he'd gotten out of her car, she wrapped her arms around his shoulders and hugged him. She'd smelled of peppermint and fruit drink. It was intoxicating.

"We'll definitely do this again soon," she said.

Buck had almost suggested a date and time, like tomorrow night, but he held his tongue. He didn't want to jinx the next date by making it too soon. He had to walk this new line with her carefully.

"For sure," he said.

Once he stepped inside the house, he stood by the curtains covering his living room window, waiting for the headlights to disappear. The moment they vanished, he cheered.

Now satisfied that his life was back in balance, he entered his bedroom and took off his shirt. It had been a long day.

As he was about to remove his pants, however, the doorbell rang. He checked the time. It was almost 12:30 in the morning.

He peeked into the living room to see a pair of headlights through the curtain. Jennifer must've forgotten something. Or maybe she wanted…

Buck ran to the front door and flung it open. Lila was standing on the other side, still in her hospital gown, but also with a pair of jeans on underneath. A taxi was parked in the driveway behind her. Her face was splotchy in the ambient light, signs of her past trauma still visible despite the contrasting darkness. Her hands were empty.

"Mind if I crash here?" she asked, not at all nervous or ashamed about such a late-night visit.

Buck's right foot moved to the side, but the rest of him stayed secure in the doorway. He glanced past the taxi to see if Jennifer's car was still lingering behind it.

"I have to let the cab driver know, or he'll keep the meter running."

Buck hesitated. Although he was glad to see Lila moving around again, he wasn't expecting her to come here, especially not at such a late hour, or so soon after Buck had gotten home from a hot date with another woman. The situation had put him in a combination of gratefulness and awkwardness. He wasn't sure how to respond in a moment like this. He just knew that his cheerful spirit was slowly deflating.

After several seconds passed, Lila stopped waiting for his decision. She turned and hobbled toward the cab. She offered the driver something from her pocket, then turned back for the house as the cab drove off.

"I've got a backup stash of clothes and things at the office," she said as she stepped past Buck and headed for the dining room table. "Think my car's still there, too. I'll see if I can get it tomorrow. Got anything to eat?"

"Vanilla ice cream," Buck said.

"That'll do."

Buck's thoughts didn't matter now, nor did his date with Jennifer. It was time to play the friendly host, so he prepared Lila a bowl of ice cream and put it before her at the table.

"Did they just discharge you?"

"No." She took a bite of her meal. "I snuck out. They kept coming up with reasons to keep me. But I'm fine. Just a few pains in my cheeks and my ribs. Maybe a few other places." She took another bite. "I'm sure I'll live."

Buck said nothing. He just let her eat.

"Sorry it's so late," she said, as she scraped together the last bite. "Just couldn't stand another minute with all those lights in my eyes and machine noises in my ears. For a place designed to heal me, it sure makes me want to kill myself."

"My mom works there."

"My condolences."

"She'll also be home soon. Sorry I don't have much time to set up a place, but obviously I have to keep you out of sight."

"Yeah, why is that?"

"She still thinks I'm a kid. And she doesn't like people she doesn't know in the house, especially after dark."

"I can respect that. Lots of creeps out there."

Buck studied her. "Are you sure you're well enough to be out of the hospital?"

Lila shrugged.

"Guess we'll find out." She reached out and touched the back of his wrist, much the same way Jennifer had a few hours earlier. "Thanks for caring."

"Yeah. You know you have to sleep in the attic, right?"

The idea didn't seem to bother her in the slightest.

"Better than on the street."

"I wish I could give you a spare bedroom, but—"

"Buck, it's cool. I was chancing the idea you'd even open your front door this late at night. You don't have to justify anything. I'm just glad you're home and willing to let me stay."

"Yeah, I think you've been through enough. We both have."

Lila raised her eyebrows at his follow-up remark, but he pretended to ignore it. He didn't want to get into any explanations about Ernest Bee or Pigeon Polluck or anyone right now, especially if it somehow turned back around on her.

"You remember where the attic is, right?" he asked.

Lila laughed at his question, then gripped her side and winced.

"I'm sure I can find it."

Buck put her bowl in the sink. Once he returned to the dining room table, she'd already gotten up the stairs.

So, that was it then. Lila was staying the night.

He went back into his room and finished undressing. Just as he pulled on a pair of sleep shorts, a knock came at his bedroom door. Lila was standing on the other side.

"I have to sleep in here," she said as she pushed past him.

"What? Why?"

She unbuttoned her jeans and slipped them off, leaving just her hospital gown on.

"There's a ten-year-old boy already in the attic," she said. "He's already claimed the couch."

She climbed into Buck's bed and pulled the sheets up to her neck. Within seconds, she was fast asleep.

So, that was it then.

Buck put his shirt back on and headed for the attic. No longer in possession of a bed, he spent the next hour playing Atari with Mikey. He fell asleep on the attic floor.

* * *

THE NEXT MORNING, RONNIE picked up Buck and Lila and took them to the Chamber of Commerce. While on the drive, Buck filled Lila in on everything she'd missed while she was in the hospital,

677

including the Coffee Critic's review, the Tax Spook's visit, and his date with Jennifer. When Lila asked why he'd been so mean to the Coffee Critic, he just chalked it up to a bad mood that day. Ronnie had laughed a nervous laugh at that comment but zipped it up when Buck cast him a glare.

"Well, at least you got the good review," Lila said. "That's all that matters."

"It definitely helped," Buck said. "But the Tax Spook killed the momentum. And now my sales have leveled off. Not sure I can generate enough to win now."

"Sure, you can. You started at zero, didn't you?"

"See, that's what I've been saying," Ronnie said. "You keep the momentum by pushing harder and harder. Never let the sales dry."

"Easy for you to say," Buck said. "Between you and Tiffany, business has never been better. But even you two have your limit. I think we've hit it as of late."

Ronnie was about to respond, but he held his tongue. Lila, meanwhile, shook her head.

"That's nonsense," she said. "The game's never up until the day you stop fighting. You said you had a date with Jennifer?"

"Yeah, last night, just before—"

"Tell me about it. In detail."

Buck told her all he could remember about the date, right down to the hand-holding and the music-listening-to.

"That sounds sweet," she said.

Buck's gaze drifted off toward the urban landscapes racing by.

"You're not impressed, are you?"

"Compared to my dating history, you're doing pretty well. I wish I could have dates like that."

Buck considered her situation. He decided it was better not to stir up additional regret.

"Well, I had fun," he said.

"I'm sure you did. What about her?"

"What about her?"

"Did she have fun?"

Buck nodded. "Sure."

"Are you sure?"

Jennifer had called the night "perfect," even though all they did was sit by the pool listening to music.

"Yes."

"Then I'm glad you had a good time."

Everyone in the car was silent for several minutes. It seemed there was nothing left to say on any topic. Then, as Ronnie turned the corner into the residential area below the hill where the Chamber of Commerce sat, Lila spoke her thoughts.

"I know how to get your sales over the top, by the way."

Buck looked over his shoulder to give her his full attention. "How?"

"You need a blowout," she said. "The sales event to end all sales events."

"Okay, that sounds kinda obvious. But how?"

She thought about it. "Special event. Big prizes. Heavy advertising. The whole nine yards."

Buck's mind was blank.

"We're a small operation. How do you suppose we do that?"

"I think I have an idea," Ronnie said.

Buck turned his attention to him, surprised that Ronnie had such a quick response.

"Know any celebrities?" Ronnie asked.

"Of course not."

Ronnie nodded. "Would you be surprised if I told you that Tiffany does?"

"Yeah, a little. Which celebrity?"

"You know that hot weather girl on Channel 13?"

"Melissa Stone?"

Ronnie winked and gave Buck the finger gun. "Apparently she's the best friend of Tiffany's cousin's girlfriend's sister."

Buck thought about it.

"Not sure she's a big enough draw."

"Have you not seen her?"

"I have. But when I think of celebrities, I'm thinking movie stars or rock stars. Know any of those?"

Ronnie said nothing.

They were now headed up the hill. Buck watched the trees with caution. He also checked the side-view mirror for unwelcome pursuers. The road was empty behind them.

"I know how to get one's attention," Lila said. "Would you like me to get you a celebrity? A real one?"

Buck didn't see the harm in saying yes. As long as he didn't have any expectations, disappointment wouldn't catch him off guard.

"Get me your best," he said. His expectations were about dirt high.

A few minutes later, when they reached the top of the hill, Lila got out and checked her car for damage.

"With Damon, you can't be too sure," she said. "So, I'll come by later with the rest of my stuff?"

"Yeah, about that," Buck said. "I think we need a new plan."

"Such as?"

"You need a place to stay. I get that much."

Lila nodded, as if she already understood where this conversation was going. "But I can't stay with you."

"It's not my decision. If it were mine, you'd stay there for as long as you needed."

"Right. I figured. So…you have something other than your house in mind, or are you just kicking me out, hoping I land on my feet?"

"As a matter of fact…you know that kid sleeping in my attic?"

Lila nodded.

"His parents are out of town until the end of summer. And I'm sure he'd rather stay in his own house than in my attic. But he can't be alone all season, so—"

"Got it. Just give me the address."

And with that, Buck found Lila a new place to live and Mikey a new big sister in one solution, at least one that could last for the next few weeks.

* * *

Buck was glad to have the house to himself again, but now he had the weekend to think about how to turn his situation around. Nothing about the last few weeks had escaped his mind, and with every passing hour, he expected one of several shoes to drop.

Shoe #1: He expected Jennifer to change her mind about being part of his life again.

Or Shoe #2: He expected the ghost of Pigeon Polluck to sneak into his house and haunt him, or the living embodiment of Tommy Slick to drive up and silence him.

Or Shoe #3: He expected the Lease Agent to claim he'd underpaid on his lease and subsequently turn the park rangers against him.

Or Shoe #4: There was the expectation that the Coffee Critic would change his mind and publish a scathing retraction about the Coffee Pavilion and its Liquid Sunshine-powered coffee.

Or Shoe #5: The list was endless.

But all he could think about was whether Lila might come through for him in his time of need, especially after the ways in which he'd come through for her. Could she actually find him a celebrity to help him get over the line? And if so, would that celebrity be good enough to get him there?

He'd spent the rest of Saturday getting an ill stomach over it, but by Sunday, he'd resolved to pull out his own stops because, despite his many expectations, the one thing he actually expected was that no celebrity would show up to help him win this bet. It was just too little, too late, and grossly unrealistic.

Buck thought it was better to throw all his extra money into advertising. It was the only thing he knew that could give him a fair shot. So, Monday morning, on Day 57 of the bet, he visited the Ad Guy and ordered hundreds of flyers and a radio ad. The message, he told him, was straightforward.

COFFEE PARTY BLOWOUT

Wednesday, August 7th from 12-5

Coffee Pavilion at North Park

Win Prizes

*See Celebrities**

Drink Great Coffee

On this 59th Day of a 60-Day Bet,

Come Help Buck Star Win His Freedom

From the Evil that Is Chet Armstrong.

**If they show up.*

"You sure that good message?" the Ad Guy asked as he wrote it all down.

"If it helps me win," Buck said.

"Then Ad Guy make letters big and bold. Death to evil."

Once Buck placed his order, he used the Ad Guy's phone to call Ernest Bee.

"I have a big order of flyers coming," he said, when Ernest picked up. "After what happened at Park Center Park, you owe me a literature pass, regardless of how much litter it makes."

Ernest Bee hesitated with an answer. Then, as if winded by the prospect, merely said, "Fair enough."

So that was it. With Ernest Bee now on Buck's side, he had every remaining ally possible to finish this bet with a grand performance.

All that was left now was for him to buy the supplies and prep the team. He had only two days to do it all. The 59th day was coming in hot, but he was ready. The summer had given him the muscle memory to succeed because he'd already failed enough.

No matter what happened next, Day 59 would present the coffee party blowout of a lifetime. Because it would be the nail in his coffin otherwise.

THE FLYERS WERE READY for posting early Tuesday morning, and Buck wasted no time getting them out to the public. With Ronnie and Tiffany helping him hit every storefront, park bench, and light post they found, they ensured that everyone walking the street today would get the message about tomorrow. Hopefully, they'd get the message in time.

Lila had to work that morning, but she assured Buck that she'd make as many phone calls in his favor as Mr. Perkins and Ernest Bee would allow. Fortunately, Mr. Perkins was sympathetic to Buck's situation and encouraged Lila to put most of her focus on those calls that morning. To his credit, Ernest stayed out of her way.

Mack Green helped the cause by promoting a twenty percent-off coupon to anyone who proved they'd bought a coffee at the Coffee Pavilion during the Day 59 Blowout. When Buck realized he would need to give out receipts to bear this proof, he nearly panicked, but Mack calmed him by promising to send French Girl over to keep accounts for him. As much as she worked at Tealeaf Central, French Girl was still allowed to have days off, and the Day 59 Blowout could be a reason to take one. To piggyback off Mack Green's coupon, Mr. Kabuki offered a free karate lesson to any visitor who appeared on French Girl's list.

Buck wasn't sure if these prizes would be of much interest to visitors, but he was grateful to both Mack and Mr. Kabuki for offering them. They inspired him to ask around for other free or discounted coupons. Even though most of the businesses he visited laughed in his face, he got support from those who knew him, including Irina Swift at Pound Cake, Sapphire at Sapphire's Consignments, Rory Stickmeyer at Wild Trends, Ping Sierra at Water Monkey, John Sully at Corner Grocery, and Bridget Sachs at Tealeaf Central. None of them could offer freebies to those on his visitor list, but they could offer enticing discounts. Buck said he'd take whatever they'd give him. Then Irina Swift changed her mind and told Buck she would give away a free cookie to every one of his customers. He thanked her for bettering the offer.

Once business hours began on Tuesday, Day 58, Buck had to quit his pursuit of great deals and put his focus on the job. He didn't like the idea of putting momentum of any kind on hold, but Ronnie made him an offer that allowed him to ease his worry. It was such a great idea that neither of them could believe they hadn't thought of it before. Ronnie even laughed at his oversight.

"I'll have to ask him, of course," Ronnie said. "But I'm sure my dad would be willing to give each customer free legal advice."

That evening, as Buck wound down from a busy day at the park, Lila appeared at his front door. She assured him she wasn't planning to stay—they'd already arranged for her to stay at the Pollucks' house until the parents returned home—but she did have some news about the celebrity search.

"Didn't go exactly as I'd hoped," she said.

Buck wasn't surprised. He'd already prepared for that avenue to fail.

"But I did find someone," she continued. "C-list actor from the Valley. Appeared in an episode of *Airwolf* last season. Might've also done a local car commercial. Haven't been able to verify that one."

"I guess that's something," Buck said. "Will he attract a crowd?"

"Beats me. I'm hoping he attracts other celebrities. Maybe *that* will attract a crowd."

"What will it cost me?"

Lila rolled her eyes.

"That's the hitch. It won't cost *you* anything."

Buck held her gaze for hardly half a minute when her silent message hit him full force between the eyes.

"No," he said finally. "Absolutely not."

"I'm sure if it'll help you win—"

"No, you've been through enough. Thanks, but it's not worth it."

She reached out and touched his biceps. "Really, it's no big—"

"Lila, stop." He pulled her in for a tight embrace. "Forget it. You really want to help me?"

"You're squeezing me a bit too tight. Ow."

Buck released her.

"Help Mikey not suck as a human being. Be a big sister. That'll help me in ways you'll never know."

"But…the guy from that one episode of *Airwolf*…"

They both thought about what she was saying, and neither one could stop themselves from laughing at the absurdity behind the statement.

"Okay, you win. I'll be a big sister to that adorable little brat."

Buck kissed her on the cheek. "Thank you."

Later that night, Buck sat on the couch in the attic and stared at his television and Atari system, wondering if it was unreasonable to keep so many secrets from his mom, because he was tired of forcing so many good people who gave him purpose out of his house.

* * *

DAY 59: WEDNESDAY, AUGUST 7, 1985

Buck's Savings Account: $2.81

Buck's Wallet: $2,448.74

Buck's Business Funds: none available

Funds-to-Wallet Refund Due: maxed out

Buck's Expenses: $2 a day*

Hours of Operation: 12-5, S-S

Money on Hold: none

SOMETHING IN THE AIR smelled funny the morning of the Coffee Pavilion's Day 59 Blowout. When Buck opened his bedroom curtain to look out the window, his heart sank. A dark cloud hung low and wide in the sky.

He stepped out into his backyard for a closer assessment. No rain had fallen yet, but the cloud was thick with potential. Of all the days for the summer dry spell to end. Today's rainfall would not be the blessing the meteorologists would claim it was.

He went back in and picked up the phone to make a call. Ronnie answered.

"Think Tiffany can still get that weather girl to show?" he asked.

"She already asked. Melissa has to work. I suppose you saw the weather already?"

"Yeah. Hoped it would pass. We still on for today?"

"Hey, a blowout's a blowout. Why waste advertising dollars?"

"I guess our job is to show up. We'll let the people decide if the weather is a problem for them."

"My thoughts, too, Little Camper. See you in an hour."

"See you in an hour."

Buck hung up. For the next few minutes, he stared at his shoes. Tomorrow was the last day of the bet, the day all his earnings would be calculated. There would be no chance of recovery if tomorrow went badly. So, everything rode on his sales today.

He got to his feet and brushed the wrinkles out of his shirt. Then he went into his bedroom and fished around in his closet for his best business attire. Today was a day worthy of his blue silk tie. No matter the weather, today he needed respect more than anything else. Respect and lots and lots of money.

* * *

By 11:30, it was obvious Buck and his friends were in for a rough blowout when the wind came through the pavilion and subsequently blew out the lights. It had lasted only a few seconds, but the flickering of power was an ominous sign. They were standing on fragile ground, and there were no guarantees they wouldn't lose the juice again.

The weather was deteriorating by the minute. The sky had turned from a hazy blue to a deep gray in the brief period he'd been at the park, and now the first drops of rain were hitting the roof. It was a slow drop, indicative of a reserved rainfall. But judging by the thick clouds lingering over the area and the selective discoloration of chunks of horizon, the rain would fall harder and faster soon enough.

Nevertheless, Buck wouldn't let it stop him from making coffee. Rain or shine, the Coffee Pavilion would serve the best.

Tiffany tacked the open sign onto the southeastern post. The wind tore it right out of her hand and blew it down the hill.

"This doesn't look good, Little Camper," Ronnie said. "Not sure why anyone would come during a storm."

Buck plugged in the coffeemakers, both his and the one Ronnie had brought from home. The lights overhead flickered.

"A storm is the perfect condition for drinking coffee," Buck said. "When would you consider a better time?"

Tiffany ran down the hill after the open sign. The chase led to one of her flip-flops slipping right off her foot. Ronnie watched her run.

"When it's not carrying half the shop away?"

Buck tried to ignore him. He didn't have time to be pessimistic today.

"I probably need head back to work," French Girl said.

As Mack had promised, she'd shown up to help with customer follow-up. But her eyes were nervous as she watched the heavy clouds rolling in. Buck had a feeling he was about to lose her again.

"Didn't you call out?" Buck asked.

"Yes. But don't want to get wet."

"Can't you stand where it won't rain?"

French Girl pulled at her long, frizzy hair. She said nothing.

Buck glanced at the sky again. The western horizon resembled night. If French Girl didn't want to get wet, then now was the time to run.

He turned around and hugged her.

"Thanks for wanting to help. We'll be in touch."

She kissed him on the cheek. "Nice boy. Good luck."

She ran for her car. Now it was just Buck, Ronnie, and Tiffany who would man the business on the day engineered to obliterate all sales days.

"We didn't need her, anyway," Ronnie said when French Girl drove off.

"We kinda did," Buck responded.

Ronnie set his attention on the sky. "No, I don't think we did."

The rain remained subdued for the next few minutes when Buck finally got his first visitor. A powder-blue Corvette drove up and parked beside the pavilion. Irina Swift got out carrying several rectangular cardboard boxes stacked on one another. She approached him in a hurry.

"Three boxes of assorted cookies," she said. "There's enough here for a hundred customers to get a freebie. Be sure to tell them where they're from."

Buck set the boxes down by the coffeemakers. As he positioned them for service, however, he wrestled with his optimism. Ronnie was being dark today, but he wasn't entirely wrong.

Before Irina dashed off for her car, Buck dared to ask her the important question. "You've been in the service industry for a while. Based on your experience, what are the odds people will still come for coffee today?"

Irina needed no time to think about it.

"Not great," she said. "But you never know. The important thing is that you're ready to serve if they show."

Buck thanked her for the cookies.

Irina had reached the edge of the pavilion when she stopped cold in her tracks. The sky had finally turned on the faucet at full blast.

"Maybe I'll be your first customer," she said, as she turned around and headed for the tables.

And then the power went out. This time, it stayed out.

* * *

BUCK WAS GETTING BORED sitting at the picnic tables, watching the empty sidewalks by the lake stay empty. Every time he blinked, the downpour seemed to grow in strength, falling harder and faster as the wind blew through. At one point, he had to change tables because the rain had gone horizontal and got his seat wet.

The power flickered on and off throughout the early afternoon, giving him a smattering of hope, but it ultimately crushed it as it never stayed on long enough for Buck to brew even a single pot. By two o'clock, Irina Swift, who had made several attempts to run for her car only to be thwarted by another blast of rain, decided she'd had enough. She wished Buck good luck and tied her shoes tight, readying her mad dash for the exit out of there. Just before she got up, however, Buck made a lame request for her to take him and his coffee equipment with her.

"I'm sure I could set up a table for you by the front door," she said, almost with a smirk. "If you're willing to move in this mess."

Seconds afterward, she raced through the rain. Buck, meanwhile, exchanged glances with Ronnie.

"You don't suppose she means it, do you?" Buck asked.

"Not sure it matters, Little Camper. No one's leaving home in this rain."

Buck agreed.

He reached for a cookie from the box Irina had brought with her. Since no one was here to eat one, he didn't see the harm in eating one himself.

The cookie was moist, full of peanut butter and macadamia nuts. His potential customers were missing out on some great cookies.

Ronnie was right. No one was leaving home in this rain. So, it was stupid of them to stay here in the open where the driving rain might pour in so deep that it would get their equipment and supplies wet. They were better off somewhere dry.

Somewhere like Pound Cake.

"Let's pack up and follow her," Buck said.

* * *

Pound Cake was not much better off for customers, but it had power running through its circuits. Irina helped them set up a table near the front of the shop where they could plug in their coffeemakers and set up their garnishes. Once everything was ready for service—assuming there would be any service required—Buck, Ronnie, and Tiffany took seats around another table and watched the rain fall outside the front window.

Irina resumed her own duties, since she had been closed for almost three hours during the middle of the day, but she was in no hurry cleaning up or moving things around. When Buck had apologized for keeping her away from her shop for so long, she winked at him and assured him she'd lost no business that the weather hadn't already stolen from her. Given that no one came walking through that door the moment she'd unlocked it, or during the twenty minutes it had taken Buck and his friends to set up their own station within Pound Cake, Buck accepted her answer.

Nevertheless, watching the minutes tick by without a single customer entering the shop bothered Buck to his core. He was basically out of time to turn this bet around. Sure, he had one more day to pull out all the stops. But this region was normally dry, and today it was stormy, so he had no guarantees. If there was ever a time he needed sunshine, it was today. And yet, he had none.

So, there were no guarantees.

"My dad sometimes says we have to make our own luck," Ronnie said. "Not sure if that's a lawyer thing or a human thing. He's not sure, either."

"Yeah, I don't know—" Buck's eyes landed on Irina. She was checking the display case under the register, still nursing the cup he'd given her when he finally got the coffeepot to brew. She had to be near the end of it. Or maybe she had secretly refilled it with her own back-office blend. But she was drinking something out of that old cup he'd given her. And whether she enjoyed it made no difference. She was drinking it. Even while working.

Buck couldn't help staring at her and her coffee cup.

"I have an idea," he finally said when staring at her was getting weird. "Ronnie, could you man the station for a little while?"

"Of course."

"Tiffany, I need your help. Has the rain diminished any of your charm?"

"Never," Tiffany said, with a hint of flirtation in her voice.

"Good. Here's what I'm thinking."

* * *

Buck ran through the rain and ducked inside Tailor Made, the shop where he'd bought his silk tie a few weeks earlier. Handsome Ted was leaning against the shop counter, checking over an inventory sheet when Buck approached. One of Buck's Day 59 Blowout flyers was sitting beside his register.

"Oh, welcome, customer, how can I—" His eyes landed on Buck's tie. "Ah, I see we've met before. The tie looks marvelous. Well, I'm sure it did before it got soaked."

"Yes, I love it, even now. Question. Would you like a cup of coffee?" He pointed at the flyer perched on the counter, but Ted didn't notice.

Handsome Ted glanced through his front window. His face seemed to long for something he didn't have.

"That does sound marvelous. Are you taking a survey, or…?"

"No, offering. Come next door to Pound Cake, and I'll pour you a cup. What would you like in it? Cream? Sugar?"

Handsome Ted thought about it.

"Will it cost me anything?"

"Just a couple of bucks, plus a small premium if you get one of my specialty coffees."

"Specialty coffees? Such as?"

Buck gave him a quick rundown of his options.

"That healthy coffee sounds nice, if not a little pricey."

"It's an expensive ingredient that makes it healthy."

"I see." Ted glanced through the window again. He seemed to dream of something far beyond his reach. "Tell you what. I'll give you an extra two dollars if you bring it to me."

"Deal," Buck said.

A few minutes later, Buck caught up with Tiffany at the Office Place and told her about their new business model. She told him she was way ahead of him and had already collected the delivery tip.

Episode 57

The Final Tally

Buck, Ronnie, and Tiffany were exhausted by the time they'd finished serving customers out of Pound Cake's tiny dining room. Even though Buck and Tiffany had been the ones venturing into the rain, searching for customers across several blocks and many shops, Ronnie had been the one fulfilling the orders, making the deliveries, and taking the money. So, they'd all gotten their exercise on that wet Wednesday afternoon, and their bodies showed signs of exhaustion each time they collapsed onto their chairs.

On top of that, Irina Swift had suggested they stay beyond their normal closing time of five o'clock to maximize their sales. She even offered they keep taking orders until her own closing time at nine o'clock. Because Buck hadn't experimented with coffee sales at such a late hour, he thought it was worth a try.

The experiment proved fruitful, but only up to a point. Customers followed them to Pound Cake from the neighboring shops and ordered their cups of coffee (along with pastries from Irina) during the dinner hour and into the dessert hour. Sales plummeted by seven, however, especially once customers knew they couldn't get decaffeinated coffee, but those extra two hours had made up for the time Buck had lost at the pavilion earlier that day.

Once Buck, Ronnie, and Tiffany had collected all their things and put them away in Tupperware boxes, Irina suggested they leave the supplies at the shop.

"Tomorrow's the final day, right?" she said. "May as well go out with a bang."

Buck couldn't thank her enough. Even if he hadn't gotten the massive spike in customer sales he had hoped the big Day 59 Blowout would've given him, he certainly saw a difference in the attitude and quality of customers who came in for coffee at a pastry shop versus those after running around a lake at a public park. These people seemed more grateful and willing to return.

Some of them had even said they'd come back for more.

But Buck, Ronnie, and Tiffany wouldn't stay until nine o'clock at Pound Cake. Once sales dried up, they called it a night. Ronnie dropped Buck off at his house by 8:30 and congratulated him on turning their dark afternoon around. Buck wanted to go out and celebrate their successful turnaround, but Ronnie and Tiffany were tired and just wanted to go home. So, Buck called Jennifer to see if she wanted to celebrate with him. She didn't answer her phone.

He decided he would celebrate alone. With his tie still on, he hopped on his bike and headed into town. On his way to the Hybrid South Entertainment District, Buck considered stopping by the Pollucks' house to see if Lila wanted to get out and celebrate with him. Just before turning down their street, however, he thought about Mikey and his perpetual abandonment and thought better of it. Lila's job right now was to play the big sister role, and that meant giving her an incentive to stay home. So, he rode on.

The Hybrid South Entertainment District gave him plenty of options for celebrating a victory. His choices included restaurants, movie theaters, bars, nightclubs, and late-night recreational facilities, including bowling alleys and pool halls. But he wasn't interested in visiting any of those places. For one, he didn't want to spend the money he needed to win the bet. But he also had a place he preferred.

Buck rode up to the brick façade outside of Synthmania and locked up his bike on the public bike rack. Once inside, he found an empty lounge chair by the pool and took a seat. The electric synth music was already working its way through his veins when he put his feet up.

He had just gotten interested in the game of chicken fight happening in the pool when the waitress appeared to take his order.

He ordered the same fruit drink he'd had on Friday night with Jennifer. Even though she wasn't here now, he wanted to remember and relive the experience as much as possible. It was the best way he could think of to celebrate a victorious turnaround.

The waitress left. Buck replayed his date with Jennifer in his mind, retracing every step they had taken to these lounge chairs, and rethinking every word of their conversations. And then, as if by magic, Jennifer was there.

He pitched forward, rubbing his eyes with his knuckles. Surely he hadn't seen her walking in. But there was no mistaking it. She was there in the doorway, in her pink skirt and yellow top, absorbing the surrounding neon like a sponge. Her hair was pinned back, and a rose nestling on her right ear accented her face. She was as lovely as ever.

But she also wasn't alone.

A guy with a cowboy hat trailed in behind her with his hand on her lower back. At first, he was hidden. But as the guy floated out from behind her and took his own shape, his identity became clear.

Jennifer and Tommy both made eye contact with Buck at the same time. Jennifer's face lit up when she recognized him, and she waved at him and pulled Tommy in his direction when it had gotten a second too late for Buck to pretend he hadn't also recognized her.

"What a surprise," she said, bouncing on her toes as she got within speaking range. "Mind if we sit with you?"

Buck offered her an awkward smile. He couldn't help but glance at Tommy watching him from behind her. She pulled a plastic chair over from the brick wall and slid it beside Buck's lounge chair.

"What are you doing here?" she asked.

"Celebrating," he said. His eyes were still on Tommy. Tommy hadn't taken a seat yet. He was just standing there, hands in pockets, watching Buck from under his hat.

Jennifer noticed him staring and acknowledged Tommy's existence.

"Oh, so I guess I hadn't told you yet. Tommy asked me out on a date Saturday night, and, well, we kinda hit it off. We'd been friends before, you know, so we'd never really considered it. But he took a chance, and I didn't see a reason to say no. And, well, it was fun, so we're giving it another go." The energy in her demeanor suddenly dropped. "And now I can see how this might be awkward."

Buck set his feet on the ground and got out of the chair. Tommy was right there beside her, which put Buck nearly chest-to-chest with him. Tommy's face was like stone when Buck reached him at eye level.

"No," Buck said. "Not awkward at all."

"I'm glad you think that," Jennifer said. "I suppose after my time with Chet, you'd be worried about me. But you shouldn't. Tommy's a really good guy."

"The best," Buck said. He faked a smile, teeth and all. "No one better. Tommy, why don't you take my chair? It's really comfortable. Only the best for the best."

Tommy tipped his hat to him.

"You don't have to do that," Jennifer said. "We don't want to crowd your space. We just—"

"No, no," Buck said. "I insist. Tommy, take the chair. It's no problem at all. I really must be going, anyway. Tomorrow's such a big day, with the bet coming to an end and all. I should really get my sleep."

Buck stepped away from the lounge chair and gestured at it for Tommy's sake.

"Take the chair, Tommy."

Tommy didn't move.

He did speak, however. As Buck walked closer to the pool and away from them, angling for the exit, Tommy called out after him.

"Floor's a bit slippery over there, Buck," Tommy said. Buck turned to face him. Tommy lowered the brim of his hat a fraction. "So, you better watch your step. Wouldn't want you to get hurt or anything."

Buck nodded at him. Then he dipped his hands in the pool and washed them together for Tommy's benefit. Just before leaving, Buck flashed him both of his palms. His hands were clean.

* * *

Buck didn't go straight home. He needed to clear his head first.

The weather was still damp, and the clouds still hung low that evening, but the rain had subsided, so he rode around town until his legs were tired. He stopped first at Tealeaf Central and looked through the glass. French Girl had taken the night off, mainly to help him, which she basically didn't, so she wasn't there. Even if he wanted to go in and talk to her, he couldn't. So, he rode on. This time, he stopped at the beach.

Storms had an effect on the ocean that made them dangerous. While the Pacific was named after its general calm, tonight it was restless. Anyone who went out there without a surfboard was unlikely to come back. Buck parked his bike in the sand and marched down to the shoreline for a closer view. Wherever the clouds briefly parted, the ferocious whitecaps glowed under the half moon's emerging light.

He watched the waves ebb and flow for several minutes, working the summer's narrative through his head. He'd lost two girlfriends already, one of them twice, and now he was a day away from finding out if he'd also lost his freedom. Walking out into the ocean was tempting.

But the wind blew powerfully against him. Even if he had wanted to tempt fate tonight, the weather held him back. At this point, he just had to ride out the rest of the storm.

So, he hopped on his bike and headed for home.

Or almost for home. Before making the final push for his neighborhood, Buck turned down the Pollucks' street to peek in on Lila and Mikey. He didn't want to knock on the door or anything—he hadn't intended to drop by for a visit. He just wanted to see if he'd made at least one good call this summer.

To his relief, Lila and Mikey were sitting on the living room couch playing a video game. Mikey tossed his Atari joystick in the air and jabbed his finger in Lila's direction, as if to taunt her. She laughed and threw popcorn at his face. He brushed his nose and laughed back at her. Then he picked up his joystick, and they resumed their game.

Buck couldn't help but also notice that the living room was clean. In fact, as Buck moved around the perimeter, checking inside each window, he couldn't help but notice the entire house was clean. Pigeon's pile of metal was long gone.

That night, Buck slept soundly.

* * *

Day 60: Thursday, August 8, 1985

Buck's Savings Account: $2.81

Buck's Wallet: $2,756.58

Buck's Business Funds: none available

Funds-to-Wallet Refund Due: maxed out

Buck's Expenses: $2 a day*

Hours of Operation: 12-5, S-S

Money on Hold: none

Buck's alarm clock blasted in his ear. He knocked it onto the floor.

This was it. The final day. What he earned today would lock him forever to his fate. He had to give the job his all. Pull no punches. Have no mercy. Waste no extra money. Forget everything that happened to him this summer, including last night.

Ronnie and Tiffany were already in his driveway when he emerged from his house. Like yesterday, he would leave the bike at home. Like yesterday, they would serve their customers from Pound Cake's dining room, going nowhere near North Park or the Coffee Pavilion. But unlike yesterday, the rain was gone. Nothing but sunshine today, at least for now.

"We still have to do a supply check," Ronnie said when Buck opened the passenger door. "But I think we're set to get started."

Buck checked his watch. It was 9:36.

"Irina said we could start as soon as we get there," Buck said. "She's already open."

"Then there's no reason to waste any time. Babe, you feel like replenishing stock as we need it?"

"I'm in it to win it," Tiffany said. "Kicking jocks' asses is my specialty."

"And that's why you kick mine," Ronnie said. He leaned in to her for a kiss.

"Make out with each other after we win," Buck said. "We're already wasting time."

"You got it, Little Camper."

Normally, Buck bought replacement supplies in the mornings before opening the shop. But because they were running on a different schedule today, he kept a notebook handy to track his low inventory. As usual, cream was on the short list, and sugar was nowhere near running out. But given that Pound Cake was close to Shop Down the Street and Corner Grocery, Buck's main coffee and garnish suppliers, he didn't stress over falling short. If Tiffany were willing to make that mid-shift run to the store as needed, then they could keep the sales momentum hot today.

So, once they arrived at Pound Cake, they set up the tables and plugged in the coffeemakers. Irina already had visitors in the dining area waiting for donuts. When they saw what Buck was doing, her customers offered to buy large coffees to go with their donuts. By 10:15, Buck had made four sales. Day 60, the final day, was already ahead of the average for him.

Of course, starting the day so early also had its downside. By noon, when Buck and his friends were normally getting started, they were now getting tired. Working from inside a pastry shop instead of a remote park pavilion meant more relevant exposure to potential customers, but that also meant more popularity for the product, and Buck, Ronnie, and Tiffany were having trouble keeping up. Irina offered to help with some of the load, given that they were working out of her shop. But the help was minimal. She still had to keep tabs on her own products.

So, when 1:30 came around and business slowed to near abandonment, Buck and Tiffany were reluctant to make the neighborhood rounds as they had the day before. But, because today was the make-it-or-break-it day, they went out anyway. Exhaustion was an obstacle but not a barrier. Buck visited Handsome Ted first.

"That healthy coffee was magnificent," Ted said. "I'll take another. You'll bring it to me, right?"

"It's two extra dollars," Buck said.

"Take four."

Dr. Regular at Health Matters, the neighborhood health food store and fruit and vegetable supplier located at Pound Cake's west side, had the same response.

"Not sure what you're putting in it," he said, "but I want to stock it."

In fact, all the neighborhood shop owners and their customer base were happy to take a delivery. The only shop Buck and Tiffany didn't visit was that ominous one at the back end of the alley behind Health Matters, the one with the sign that said, "The Un-Shop." Buck's guts burned at the thought of entering its crooked doors or passing under its yellow tape. So, entering its space offered him no temptation.

By four o'clock, Buck, Ronnie, and Tiffany sat alongside the coffee serving table, collapsed on their chairs. They needed a break.

"How much longer we gonna do this?" Ronnie asked.

"Till we drop dead," Buck said.

"I think we've already burned through most of our potential clientele," Tiffany said. "There's no one else in the neighborhood to visit unless we want to take a chance on that Un-Shop place."

Buck and Ronnie simultaneously shook their heads.

"Not serving coffee to a potential crime scene," Buck said. "Probably just rats there, anyway."

"Or one really big one," Irina said from behind the counter. Everyone glanced at her. She shrugged. "You work in this neighborhood long enough, and you begin to hear rumors. I don't think any of you should go in there, just for the record. None of us do."

Ronnie winked and pointed at Tiffany.

"Wisdom has spoken yet again," he said.

The four o'clock hour was a slow one, enough for them to catch their breaths. By five o'clock, they each had replenished enough energy to go for one more massive push into the neighborhood.

They decided to stand outside and pull customers in as they walked by. Because the sky was clear again, this was much easier to do than it was yesterday. They must've brought in over twenty people for "dessert coffee" that hour.

* * *

As the evening wound down, Buck reviewed the contract he had signed at the beginning of the bet. Ronnie's dad still had the original, but he'd made Buck a copy to remind him of the terms. Although it wasn't clear what time the bet officially ended, the wording suggested he had until the close of the business day to finalize his accounts. Because the Liquid Shack usually closed at eight o'clock, Buck assumed he'd have to finish his sales by the same time. So, when Ronnie asked him when he should call his dad, Buck told him 7:30.

Ronnie's dad arrived at Pound Cake at 7:52. By that point, customers had stopped coming into the shop, so Buck, Ronnie, and Tiffany had already begun packing the equipment and supplies. They left one coffeepot half full of Hawaiian blend in case they got a last-minute arrival. As it turned out, Mr. Michaels was that last-minute arrival.

"Give me a hot coffee with caramel, cream, and sugar," he said. "And what the heck, throw in some whipped cream and cinnamon. What is that? The Works? Give me that."

Mr. Michaels handed over a five-dollar bill and collected a few coins for change. Once he took a sip, he offered Buck a thumbs up.

"Perfect," he said.

And with that, Buck earned his last dollar toward the bet. He put the money in the cash bag and sealed it. He wouldn't open it again until he met with Chet to finalize their tallies.

* * *

Buck thanked Irina for her hospitality as he carted his supplies to Pound Cake's front door. She told him, "Anytime," and wished him luck. Then he shook Ronnie's hand and offered Tiffany a hug. They were welcome to keep working at the Coffee Pavilion after today, if all went well at the Liquid Shack. But whether the Coffee Pavilion existed tomorrow depended on how he fared at the Liquid Shack. They wished him luck, too.

Once the boxes were in Ronnie's car, Buck got into Mr. Michaels's car, and Mr. Michaels drove him to Park Center Park, where Chet would be waiting. Dark clouds once again appeared on the horizon, as they had the day before.

Twilight settled over Park Center Park when they passed through the entrance gate. The streetlights were already coming on when they drifted up to the parking lot. Buck's stomach turned queasy as the memories of his last visit assaulted him. He tried to block them from his mind, but he couldn't shake them. Every inch of the road reminded him of his drive with Ernest Bee. And the sight of the parking lot reminded him of his time with Tommy Slick.

"Looks like he's packing up," Mr. Michaels said. "Is he alone?"

Buck scanned the area. He didn't see any other cars on the lot. Certainly no trucks or ugly beige Datsuns.

"Looks that way."

They pulled into a spot beside Chet's black Porsche. Through the windshield, Chet noticed their car and abruptly stopped what he was doing, which had been making a lame attempt to collapse his tent. Three of the four tent stakes were out of the ground, but he was wrestling with the leg opposite the one that was still staked into the ground when they came to a stop.

Mr. Michaels waved at him as he got out of the car.

"Need some help?" he asked.

Chet glanced around his work area and relented of any idea he'd had about finishing the work himself. He waved them over and pointed at the tent legs.

"I mainly need help getting this thing down," he said.

Mr. Michaels grabbed a leg and folded it over, pulling the corner of the tent down. Buck, meanwhile, was reluctant to step in. Mr. Michaels noticed and gestured for him to take the opposite leg. Buck followed Mr. Michaels's lead.

"You all alone here?" Mr. Michaels asked.

"Yeah. Girlfriend is working late hours as usual, so it's just me this week."

"Don't you have employees?"

Chet shrugged. "Yeah, I thought I did. Until they stopped coming to work. Can't get either one to pick up their phones, and neither one ever seems to be at home even though Pigeon's car is always there."

Buck's stomach lurched, and for a moment he had trouble breathing. Fortunately, no one noticed.

"Has that affected your business?" Mr. Michaels asked.

"Hasn't made it easy, that's for sure."

"What about your other job?" Buck asked.

Chet was pulling out the last stake when he froze and glared at him.

"Had to take a pause, as no one seems to be running this job if I'm not here anymore."

Mr. Michaels glanced at Buck and shook his head. Buck understood the gesture. The bet was over. Time for civility.

"Sorry if that's been hard on you," Buck said without really meaning it.

Chet uprooted the tent stake and lowered the leg. This brought the rest of the tent down to the ground.

"Well, I suppose you know why we're here," Mr. Michaels said.

"Yeah, I know."

"Are you ready to count your final sales tally?"

Chet cast a glance at Buck and nodded at him. "Are you?"

Buck nodded back.

Mr. Michaels put his fists on his hips and raised his chin to the sky. His tie flapped around a bit.

"It's still a bit windy out," he said. "And the weather looks like it wants to take another piss on us before the night ends. Let's say we relocate somewhere indoors."

"Gladly," Chet said.

Once Chet packed up his car with all the Liquid Shack's equipment and supplies—a super tight fit for a Porsche, probably never an issue before when Tommy and his truck had come to work on a regular basis—he led them out of the park and into the Hybrid Beach district. They found a small club on the north side of the district, before the road ventured out onto the seaside highway.

"My girlfriend's workplace," he said, when they met in the parking lot. "She'll let us into the back room where we can count the money."

The club was dark yet intimate. The clientele was comprised of men in suits, each one sitting alone at a circular table, nursing some drink that glowed in the dark. A familiar dark-haired woman dressed in a hot pink bikini met the three of them by the bar and kissed Chet on the cheek. She led them to a meeting room at the end of a smoky hallway.

In the meeting room was a conference table, and sufficient lighting kept the place office-bright. A television displaying the events of the main room was mounted on the wall, but it had no sound. On screen, nothing interesting was happening.

"Get you guys a drink, babe?" the woman asked Chet.

"Three Scotches," he said.

"You got it." Chet's girlfriend winked at him and left.

"We're underage," Buck said.

"That doesn't matter here," Chet responded. "Okay, I'm ready."

Mr. Michaels removed the original contract from inside his jacket and placed it on the table. He reminded them both that they had signed their names and agreed to the terms of the bet.

"So," Mr. Michaels said, "it's understood that each of you has kept an accurate record of your earnings from June tenth to today, August eighth. Every penny you have today counts toward your final earnings. Every penny you've spent does not. Considering the values of your accounting ledgers, as well as the money you have in your possession today, whomever of you has the higher count will win the bet. The loser, then, must abide by the terms of the victor, as written in this contract. Do we agree?"

Buck and Chet said yes simultaneously.

"Good, then you will sign below your previous signatures, confirming the end of the bet and your agreement to abide by its terms."

They both signed and dated the contract. As Chet looped the "g" in his last name, his girlfriend entered the room with a tray supporting three glasses with ice cubes and dark liquid. She passed a glass to each person at the table.

"Enjoy." She kissed Chet on the cheek. "And good luck, babe."

She left them alone.

"Okay," Mr. Michaels said, his drink now raised to them. "Let's begin the tallies."

* * *

BUCK'S HEART POUNDED AS he reviewed his ledger from over the last 60 days. Even though he hadn't yet recorded today's income, he couldn't help but marvel at the drastic turns the summer had taken him through. There was the slow but promising start of his first week and the growing momentum of his second and third weeks. But then there was the disastrous turn during the fourth week following the Fourth of July incident and the subsequent bush-beating he'd endured from the Lease Agent's insurance adjuster. His heart lifted a little as he recounted the days following the Grand Reopening, but none of them ever really gave him peace, especially once he reached the sharp drop he'd suffered after the Tax Spook's visit. As he took sips of his scotch and felt it burning his throat, all he could do was cross his fingers and hope for the best. And as he swallowed, he noticed Chet across the table basically doing the same thing.

When it came time to count today's income, both he and Chet were visibly sweating. Every dollar and every coin carried a weight with it that spelled either relief or misery. But they counted on, never letting a single cent get past their attention. With every bill and every coin to pass under their fingertips, the ledger got a new mark, and another one.

And then, as ten o'clock approached, they both got to the end of their counts. Once they both folded their hands over their stomachs and leaned back in their chairs, Mr. Michaels gathered their books and checked their final sales scores.

His eyes scanned across both books. Then he passed them back for each to see.

"Do you both assert that these values are correct?" he asked.

Buck nodded. So did Chet.

"Okay, pass them back. Let's see how we did."

Mr. Michaels collected their books, then went to the dry-erase board in the corner of the room and wrote each of their names across the top. Under Buck's name, he wrote the words FINAL TALLY and Buck's closing score underneath:

$$\$3,345.43$$

And under Chet's name, he wrote FINAL TALLY and Chet's closing score:

$$\$3,363.26$$

They both took a breath, let the numbers sink in, and then…

Chet deflated for what must've been a split second. Then he punched his fist in the air and cheered.

Buck's heart, meanwhile, fell into his stomach. He couldn't help but stare at his drink. Then he dumped the whole thing down his throat.

So, that was it. He'd lost.

Chet got up from his chair and spun a small circle where he stood, then fell back onto his chair and let out a sigh of relief.

"Nightmare over," he said. He took a sip of his own drink.

Buck shook his head. "I can't believe it."

Chet stared at him and gave the faintest smile. Victory was his, and his alone. The glint in his eyes was enough to drive a rage into Buck's soul. Buck tried to suppress it. After all the hell Chet had put him through, the last thing he needed was to give him extra ammunition to humiliate him. But his rage was so strong, and his defeat so personal. Buck's guts boiled from having thrown so much into the last two months, and losing so much innocence, just to come up short.

Short by less than twenty freaking bucks!

He couldn't contain himself any longer. Buck leapt from his chair and pointed his finger at him. He wouldn't let Chet abuse him over this.

"All right. Here's the deal. I've had a hellish summer, and I will not take any crap from you! Got it? I will respect the bet. But you better respect me. You treat me fairly, or I will ruin you." Buck gave Chet a wicked smile. "You want to know why your guys dumped you?

They crossed me. That's why." Buck laid his hands on the table and leaned in close enough for Chet to feel him breathing. Chet's eyes were wide at his invasion. "You cross me, you end up like them. Got it? High school's over. Treat me like a damn adult now. Or you will pay!"

Chet reached for Buck's forehead and pushed him back into his own chair.

"Dude, chill," he said. "I took a beating this week. Working alone is the worst. I'm not going to make your life hell. I just need an employee, one who will show up and do a good job."

"What about the Coffee Pavilion?"

Chet shook his head. "What about it? I don't care. Run it on the weekends if you want. Or let your friends run it. I don't care. I need help. According to the terms, you agree to help me. End of story."

Buck exchanged glances with Mr. Michaels. Mr. Michaels nodded at him. Buck's anger simmered down a little.

"You mean it?"

Chet let out a deep sigh.

"I'm a business owner, and I'm drowning."

Buck was skeptical. He would never trust Chet Armstrong. Four years of high school torture could never be erased overnight, not even over scotch in the back room of a smoky gentlemen's club. But after running the Coffee Pavilion for two months, he understood the message. The bully he knew was a man of desperation now.

"Okay then. I'll report to work tomorrow."

"Thank you," Chet said, the relief on his face genuine. "Make it Monday. Take the weekend off. Sounds like the bet wrecked both of us good."

"Fine, but I swear, if you—"

"Buck, stop." Chet's face was serious now. "Our war is over." He extended his hand. "Welcome to the Liquid Shack."

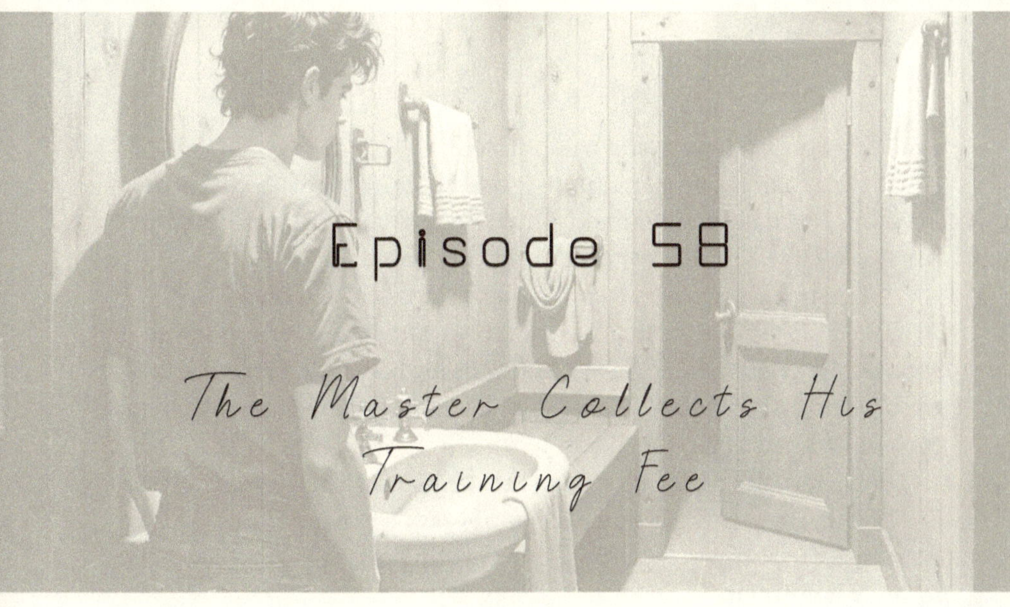

Epilogue

BUCK SLEPT IN ON Friday morning, the day after his bet with Chet had come to an end. He still couldn't believe how close he'd come to winning, losing by barely twenty dollars. There were so many points along the journey when he could've pulled ahead. Yet, he still lost.

He guessed that in business, it didn't matter how much money he'd lost by. It was still a loss. So, despite Chet's assurance that the war was over, Buck wasn't sure he'd felt it yet. There would be plenty of time for Chet to resurrect it, now that he'd become Buck's boss. It was just a question of what might prompt him to initiate a new strike.

But hopefully, Chet would honor his new position and treat Buck fairly. Time would tell the truth.

When he finally got out of bed, Buck called Ronnie and told him the result. Ronnie said he'd already heard about it from his dad.

"He came home with a look on his face that said it all," Ronnie said. "How much you lose by?"

"Seventeen dollars and eighty-three cents."

"Man. Now I feel bad about taking a paycheck from you."

Buck chuckled under his breath. "You mean like you would if you worked for me?"

Ronnie was quiet for a moment.

"So, what are you going to do now?"

"Well, I figure we got a pretty good thing going with the Coffee Pavilion. I was hoping you and Tiffany could keep it running during the week while I play second fiddle at the Liquid Shack."

"Aren't you supposed to give Chet the keys to the business?"

Buck shook his head. "He doesn't want it. At least not yet. I suppose he could take it from me whenever he wants, since that was the agreement. For now, I'd say keep it running in my name. If I can find an escape clause, I'll take it."

"You should. That guy's gonna make your life hell until you do."

"Yeah, maybe. But I don't know. He says we're good now. I'll see how far I can throw that. We still got dirt on him, though, if we need to put a light on it."

"What dirt?"

"You know…Lester Biggins."

"How would we prove that? We'd need Pigeon for that, and well, he's fallen out of the coop if I recall."

"Not sure. I'm still not sure how to broach the topic with Lester's mom, either. Or your dad for that matter."

Ronnie was quiet again.

"I suppose we'll deal with that if and when it becomes necessary," Buck said.

"I guess so."

The conversation changed gears after that to more banal topics like the latest movie to hit the cinema and whether Tiffany had a friend Buck could date. Now that the bet was over, he could slow down and appreciate real life again, or at least do something other than just work.

* * *

LATER THAT AFTERNOON, BUCK entered the Whipping Shed and found Mr. Kabuki on the dojo floor sweeping up some dirt. When Kabuki saw him standing in the doorway, he gestured for him to enter.

"What bring boy by?"

Buck took off his shoes and approached the master. He bowed.

"I came by to thank you for your help this summer. Now that the bet's over, I wanted to pay you for your services."

Kabuki stopped sweeping and leaned on his broom handle.

"What boy offer for payment?"

"Well, it occurred to me that we never discussed a fee, so I thought we should do that now, especially now that my money is no longer tied up. How much is fair?"

Mr. Kabuki thought about the question.

"How much boy make?"

"Just over thirty-three hundred dollars."

Mr. Kabuki grunted under his breath. He stroked the broom handle as he considered the sum.

"What boy think is fair?"

"I don't know. Twenty percent of earnings? So, six hundred and change?"

Mr. Kabuki began sweeping again. Started humming.

"So, is that good then?" Buck asked. "Six hundred enough?"

"Depend," Kabuki said. "Did boy defeat enemy?"

"Well, that's complicated. You see—"

"Not complicated. Boy win or lose?"

"Well, technically I lost, but—"

Kabuki dropped the broom to the floor. It clattered as it hit the mat.

"Then training not over."

"Okay, well, I'm not really in need of—"

"Follow Kabuki."

Mr. Kabuki marched across the dojo floor toward the hallway. He instructed Buck to pick up his shoes on the way out.

"Lesson fifty-two, learn to wash hands."

Buck hopped along behind him as he tried putting his shoes back on.

"We're at lesson twenty-four," he said.

"Number don't matter. Lesson important."

Kabuki led him down the hall past the break room. This was now only the second time he'd brought Buck so far from the main lobby.

"Okay, but I already know how to wash my hands."

Kabuki shook his head.

"Not way Kabuki teach. Come, almost there."

Buck followed him to the end of the hall, to the room where Kabuki sometimes went when he wanted to be alone. In the past, he'd forbidden Buck to enter. But now it seemed he was ready to invite him in.

Kabuki unlocked the door and opened it. He led Buck inside.

Buck wasn't sure what he'd expected of the room Kabuki had forbidden visitors to see, but now that he was looking at it, he was underwhelmed. It was a small cubic room, with wooden panels and a bench. Along one wall were a sink and a towel rack. On the opposite side of the door was another door, likely a utility room for Kabuki's broom, or maybe a shower since this was a training center. Kabuki instructed Buck to wash his hands.

"Feel the water over fingers and palms," Kabuki said as he turned the faucet on for Buck. "Feel it getting hotter. Let the water relax hands."

The water heated, but not aggressively, and not to where it burned. It was hot, but just right. Buck felt his blood tingling a little.

"Kabuki spent summer teaching boy art of business. But it seem Kabuki's lessons not good enough if boy lose. What rule one?"

Buck thought back to Kabuki's list of rules. The details were getting fuzzy, and he wasn't sure how well he could recall the specific wording, but he still remembered the basics.

"Lesson one," Buck said. "Never give in to enemy."

Kabuki bowed. "*Hai*. Most important rule." He turned off the water. "Dry hands."

Buck pivoted from the sink and reached for the nearest towel. Kabuki caught his hands as they touched the towel, and he wrapped it around his wrists. With the pressure of both of his palms pushing against him, Kabuki pressed the towel down hard on the back of Buck's knuckles and rubbed them dry.

"No more lesson in art of business," Kabuki said. "Now boy must learn *martial art* of business."

"Martial art of business?"

Kabuki pulled the towel from Buck's hands and whipped the utility door with it.

"Go. Behind door is new training ground. Enter."

Buck hesitated to move away from the sink. All summer he had been learning how to make coffee and take money. Such a simple process had led him into a series of complicated events, including a few that had shattered his heart and soul. What more could he learn from the back room of a training center that he couldn't learn in the real world?

Kabuki snapped the towel at the door again.

"Enter."

Buck raised his hands and nodded. He approached the wooden door and turned the handle. It creaked open to reveal a stairway down to the basement. The only light on the stairs was the one shining in from the washroom.

"This lead to a private dojo?" Buck asked.

"*Hai*. Take stairs. Kabuki follow."

Curious, Buck stepped onto the stairs and took the first couple of steps down.

"Kinda dark down there, isn't it? There a light switch near—"

The door behind him closed. Buck, now in pitch darkness, swung around for the handle, but it was locked from the outside. He jiggled it as hard as he could, but it refused to move. He pounded on the door.

"Mr. Kabuki! I can't see!"

"Light switch beside you," Kabuki shouted through the door. "Feel wall."

Buck scraped his fingers along one wall and then the other. When he couldn't feel it, he dared to take another step down.

"I can't find it!"

"Keep looking. Never give in to enemy!"

Buck took another few steps down, feeling his way along both walls with every inch.

"It's not here!"

No answer. Buck kept feeling around.

"Mr. Kabuki!"

No answer. Just silence behind him now.

"There's no light switch!"

No answer. He was alone. Alone reaching out to where he couldn't see.

So that was it, then. Buck was on his own in the darkness. His heart started pounding, but he wasn't about to freak out. The last place he wanted to be was on a stairway in pitch-dark conditions, but he was sure there was a bottom step. He descended the stairs one careful step at a time until he found it.

It was on the last step that he found the light switch.

A series of fluorescent lights buzzed to life seconds after he flipped the switch. Like rolling thunder, they took turns coming on until the entire space beneath them was lit.

They revealed what looked like a concrete bunker with a boxing ring in the middle. In the center of the ring was a piece of furniture with a canvas blanket covering it. The blanket was old and stained with different-colored liquids. Dust motes floated up and around it.

A series of tables surrounded the boxing ring, each with different objects on top. The table closest to him had a dozen bottled waters standing in a row like dominoes. Another one had a stack of towels folded on top of each other. A table at the far end had a series of weapons spread across it, including swords, knives, and nunchucks to name a few. Another table had a dead electronic scoreboard leaning against it.

Something that sounded like a speaker crackled in the corner of the room. A buzzing that reminded Buck of his old homeroom announcements followed.

"Can boy hear me?" Kabuki's voice came out of the speaker.

"Yes. What's going on?" Buck wasn't sure if Kabuki could hear him.

A pause. Then Kabuki's tinny voice continued.

"*Hai*, Kabuki hear boy. Good. Now boy can begin training."

"What training? You've locked me in here!"

"Boy leave any time. But first boy must learn how defeat enemy."

Buck glanced around the room, but he wasn't sure what Kabuki had expected him to do down here. There were no coffee machines or notepads or anything for him to use. Other than the bottles of water, he had no idea how any of this stuff would help him as a business owner or new employee at Chet's Liquid Shack.

"How?"

"Good question. Go to table with weapons."

Buck approached the table with the weapons. His hand drifted right for the katana, though the blade itself didn't seem particularly sharp.

"Select weapon boy like most."

"I have a sword."

"Good. Now go to boxing ring in center of room. Climb inside."

Buck was more confused than ever before, but he did as instructed. He wanted out of this basement. Nothing about it felt right.

"Okay," he said, when he slipped under the bottom rope. Something old and pungent assaulted his nose, but he tried to ignore it. Probably the blanket. "I'm in the ring."

"Boy should see target in middle."

"Maybe. I just see a blanket covering some furniture."

"*Hai*, that target. Boy must use katana to whack enemy dummy. Strike hard."

"Okay, I don't understand how this helps in business. But you'll let me out once I swing this sword?"

"*Hai*. First lesson in martial art of business. Swing first. Teach enemy fear. Make enemy respect."

Buck shrugged. Mr. Kabuki had taught him two dozen valuable lessons up to this point. If this was lesson number twenty-five, then he would trust it, and trust Kabuki's process whether Buck understood it or not.

"Do I take the blanket off first, or…?"

"No. Strike first. Expose dummy later. Teach dummy respect."

Buck gripped the katana's handle with both palms. He'd never swung a sword like this at an object before, so he wasn't sure what to expect from the impact or the vibrations it would send through his wrists. He didn't want to grip it so hard that he'd hurt himself, but he didn't want to keep it so loose that it flew out of his hand on contact. Maybe the blade was dull, but it would still hurt like hell if it bounced back at him.

He set one foot forward and the other one back and raised the sword over his head like a baseball bat. Again, the stance didn't necessarily feel correct, but Buck didn't know the proper way to hold a katana. Kabuki had literally sent him down here blind and gave him no additional instructions he deemed useful.

"Boy hit dummy yet?"

"No, I'm trying to do this without hurting myself."

"Boy don't have time to think. Boy must act on muscle memory. Just strike enemy. Evaluate strategy later."

Buck exhaled through his mouth. "Okay."

He swung the sword at a spot shoulder high, with just enough power to make him grunt. The blade impacted the blanket and the dummy underneath hard enough to jostle it. It didn't slice the blanket open or anything, but it did cause the dummy underneath to groan.

That was weird, Buck thought, as he lowered his weapon.

Buck knew little about the martial arts, but he knew martial artists like Mr. Kabuki liked to practice on wooden poles with varying points of contact, objects they sometimes referred to as "training dummies." Sometimes these dummies rotated as the martial artist danced around them. But they never groaned.

So, he pulled the blanket away from the dummy. What he expected to find was a wooden pole with contact points on a four-legged foundation. But what he actually found was a blindfolded and gagged man in a pair of shorts and a white tank top, perched on and tied to a wooden chair, sweating through his clothes and whimpering through his gag.

Buck dropped the katana onto the mat and ran to the other end of the boxing ring.

"Mr. Kabuki!" he cried. "There's a man here! I just—I just hit him with the sword! I—"

In his panic, Buck hadn't looked the man over very well. But now that he was staring at the whimpering mess, he realized the man wasn't bleeding. The katana hadn't broken any skin.

"*Hai*," Mr. Kabuki said. "That Kwan, man who try take Kabuki's lady. Man who regret try taking Kabuki's lady. Man who Kabuki defeat to get back lady. Man who never forget defeat, who never go after Kabuki lady again."

Buck's knees shook. He dared to approach the man who was tied to the chair. "I'm sorry," he whispered.

"Never be afraid to hit enemy with sword," Kabuki said through the speaker. "Especially if man try take lady from boy."

Buck was just about to pull the man's blindfold off his head when the lights went out again.

Another light came on over the stairs. This time, it was the light from the washroom bleeding down into the basement.

"Come upstairs," Kabuki said through the speaker. "First lesson always hardest. Kabuki make boy a cup of coffee to ease pain."

Buck retracted his hand. He didn't know who this Kwan was or why Mr. Kabuki was keeping him tied to a chair. He just knew that this was Mr. Kabuki's enemy and that they had been at war over a woman. He also knew that Mr. Kabuki was giving Buck permission to leave the basement, now that he'd completed his first exercise.

"Boy have thirty seconds before door close again."

Kwan was saying something, pleading about something through the gag, but Buck didn't understand. His muffled words came with more harsh groans and whimpers.

"I don't—"

"Twenty-five seconds," came Mr. Kabuki's voice through the speaker.

Buck didn't know how to help Kwan, but he knew how to help himself.

Lesson #24: Learn to wash hands.

With no time to waste, he wished Kwan well, then started up the stairs, on his way back to freedom, or at least back to one phase of it.

"Fifteen seconds."

Once Buck got to the top of the stairs, he returned to the sink. Mr. Kabuki was there waiting for him, slow clapping. He handed him a towel. It was then that Buck noticed there was no mirror in there. He washed his hands anyway.

Buck followed Kabuki into the break room, to the place within the Whipping Shed he was most familiar with. The message was hazy but not impossible to decipher. To get the rest of his freedom, Buck would have to take out his enemy completely. Maybe Chet was the enemy. Or maybe his true enemy was just emerging. Either way, it looked like Kabuki was ready to teach him how.

And if Buck knew what was best for him, he'd take the time to learn. Thanks to Tommy, the Lease Agent, and several others he'd encountered this summer, his list of enemies was growing.

But first, he needed that cup of coffee. He needed the hot liquid to clear his head and calm his soul. If Kabuki's warnings were any indicator, time would not wait for him.

Buck was likely in for a busy and messy autumn ahead.

And Now a Quick Message from the Author

Thanks again for reading *The Hybrid City Entrepreneur*. If you enjoyed your time in Hybrid City, please be sure to sign up for my email newsletter to receive information about any upcoming sequels I have in store for Buck and his friends, as well as news about the game it's based on, plus news about other coming-of-age novels and thrillers I have in the works. I'd love to hear your feedback about which stories you'd like to see continued and which ones you hope remain one-and-done.

Signing up will also give you access to exclusive current and future short stories and novellas, including *Read My Shorts: Volume 1*, a trilogy of short corporate satires, and *The McCray Parables: The Elf and the Shoe* (arriving, hopefully, in time for the release of *The McCray Parables: Snow in Miami* in November 2025), the story of a Christmas elf who gets stranded on a deserted island thanks to a sleigh mishap on Christmas Eve and must find his way back to civilization so he can deliver the left shoe a woman in Ohio was supposed to get on Christmas to complete the pair.

Sign up at my website: https://swiy.co/jb-signup-hybrid-city-entrepreneur-1

Acknowledgments

The Hybrid City Entrepreneur is a novel that I had dreamed about for years, ever since I started fleshing out the story for *Entrepreneur: The Beginning*, the business adventure computer game it's based on, in my mind. Although the appeal of making coffee and serving it to digital customers for profit is a staple mechanic for a "tycoon" style game where supply and demand are constantly at war, turning that same mechanic into a plot thread for a novel is a harder sell, so for it to work, it must have a compelling story arc with likeable characters as its engine.

Of course, I think this is true of the game, as well. Buying ingredients at various shops and turning those ingredients into coffee that people want at a park pavilion can get tedious quickly if there's no good reason to do any of it. So, forcing the player to race against the clock to outsell his rival adds to the tension.

But what of his friends? Or lovers? What about the people who sell him the ingredients? Do they have stories worth telling?

Although I want to add plot threads to the game that include many of the characters featured in the novel, the outcome will always be dependent on the player's interaction. The game would never tell the definitive story, so I decided to write the novel in 2021, when a certain popular retailer announced it was starting a serial fiction site, to give it a definitive story.

Even though the novel took two years to write, and the serial fiction site never quite got the readers it wanted and eventually shut down, the experience was worth it. At the end of that journey came a novel that tells the story that the original game would never quite do.

So, for those reasons, I would like to thank the creators of the failed serial fiction site for inspiring me to get the story out of my head and onto the page. But I would also like to thank the

OHRRPGCE gaming community for hosting so many contests over the years, including the inevitable 1980s-inspired 8-bit contest I'd entered in May 2009, that I would eventually force myself to make my dream business adventure game and call it *Entrepreneur: The Beginning,* just to see if I had a worthy idea.

Out of about 15 entries, my game ranked 4th that year, for the record.

Now, I would be remiss to thank the gaming community for inspiring me to make my dream game without also thanking the engine's developers, James Paige and Ralph Versteegen, for the ways they've bent the engine's capabilities to make my vision for *Entrepreneur: The Beginning* possible. It would also be remiss of me if I didn't also thank them for playing early, terrible versions of the game and providing valuable feedback to help me think of ways to improve it over the years. These suggestions helped shape the game that would eventually shape the way I'd think about the story.

And, well, there would be no novel without the story.

For the novel itself, I would like to thank Michelle Gomez for previewing an early copy to ensure I haven't left behind too many plot holes or created too many stupid characters. With a book this large, a few holes might find their way in. I would also like to thank any future readers who spot additional mistakes and report them to me before a random BookTok star discovers it and launches it to extraterrestrial heights, where *everyone* might find those same mistakes.

Remember, just because it's published, it doesn't mean it's too late to fix it.

I would also like to thank the filmmakers of the 1980s who gave us some of the best teen movies of all time. This book would not exist without the inspiration I've taken from great minds like John Hughes, Cameron Crowe, Savage Steve Holland, and others. I hope their legacies live on for decades to come.

And, finally, I would like to thank you, the reader, for getting to the end. The problem with releasing a serial fiction story on a failing serial fiction platform is that no one is likely to discover it, so the likelihood of anyone providing the feedback needed to improve it is low. So, if you've read to the end, then that tells me I've done my job, and that makes the time devoted to this project worth it.

Other Books

Want to discover what else I've written? Then visit my website and explore my library of titles to see what other books catch your eyes. You'll find them divided by genre and size, and you may even discover some freebies and discontinued books. It's the best way to discover my entire body of works, for better and for worse.

https://swiy.co/jb-books-hybrid-city-entrepreneur-1

The Golden Paperweight

He gave them an apple. They gave him a job.
All parties may soon come to regret it.

Lewis Urlong is a treasure hunter by trade. Relying on his years of skill, he can locate and liberate most relics in quick time. Once his handler arranges a buyer, Lewis gets into action, scouring whatever jungle, desert, or urban wasteland he must, to recover the client's most desired object. All that's left, then, is to deliver the prize, collect the payment, and move on to the next mission.

His latest assignment in the jungles of Guatemala breaks that routine. His job is to recover the Fruit of Huracan, or "the golden apple" as outsiders call it, a forbidden treasure from the ancient Maya Empire that hunters avoid, but the buyer goes MIA before Lewis can return it.

Now desperate to find a new buyer, Lewis offers the golden apple to the CEO of a fledgling investment company in Dallas who believes the apple will bring him luck. To ensure trouble doesn't come calling after the new owner, Lewis takes a job at the company to watch his back. "Trouble," of course, is Rory "The Jack" Sampson, the man responsible for the buyer's MIA status, a man on a mad mission to take the apple at any cost, a man neither Lewis nor the apple's new owner has yet met. And trouble is coming.

The Golden Paperweight is the upcoming comedic thriller from Jeremy Bursey that asks the question: What if Indiana Jones joined *The Office*?

Jeremy Bursey is the author of many short stories, novels, and other things he no longer remembers writing, each covering topics and genres that differ from what he had written previously because why not? He holds a bachelor's degree in English from the University of Central Florida, which he's been paying for since the '90s, and currently works as a writing tutor, so he, like that organ grinder who severs his business relationship with his pet monkey, will pay for it indefinitely. He appreciates feedback for anything he posts, and he hopes you'll read it—any of it—now, preferably.

You can follow him on Facebook, YouTube, Twitter, Goodreads, and Bookbub, as well as at his official author site, jeremybursey.com. Or visit his smartpage biolink (QR Code below) to access all relevant links and recommendations from one convenient location.